SINISTER TIDE
AND
THE STONE LEOPARD

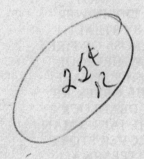

25¢
12

Colin Forbes writes a novel every year. For the past twenty-seven years he has earned his living solely as a full-time writer.

He visits all the locations which will appear in a new novel. Forbes says, 'It is essential for me to see for myself where the book will take place. Only in this way can I conjure up the unique atmosphere of the chosen locales.'

He has explored most of Western Europe, the East and West coasts of America, and has made excursions to Africa and Asia. Each new book appears on all major bestseller lists. He is translated into thirty languages.

Surveys have shown his readership is divided equally between women and men.

COLIN FORBES

SINISTER TIDE
AND
THE STONE
LEOPARD

PAN BOOKS

Sinister Tide first published 1999 by Macmillan.
First published by Pan Books 2000.
The Stone Leopard first published 1975 by William Collins Sons & Co. Ltd.
First published by Pan Books 1977.

This omnibus edition published 2003 by Pan Books
an imprint of Pan Macmillan Ltd
Pan Macmillan, 20 New Wharf Road, London N1 9RR
Basingstoke and Oxford
Associated companies throughout the world
www.panmacmillan.com

ISBN 0 330 43669 4

1 3 5 7 9 8 6 4 2

A CIP catalogue record for this book is available from
the British Library.

Printed and bound in Great Britain by
Mackays of Chatham plc, Chatham, Kent

SINISTER TIDE

For my Editor,
SUZANNE

Author's Note

All the characters portrayed are creatures of the author's imagination and bear no relationship to any living person.

The same principle of pure invention applies to all residences whether located in Britain or Europe. And equally, certain small villages in Britain are imagined and non-existent.

Prologue

The dark wave, a motionless fisherman on its crest, rolled across the estuary north of Dartmoor towards them in the chill night. A new moon cast a pallid light on the sea-sodden body.

'That man is dead,' Paula Grey said, her tone sombre. 'Look for yourself.'

She handed the night-vision binoculars to Tweed, standing beside her. They were leaning against the stone sea wall at Appledore, an old town located where the rivers Torridge and Taw met to form the wide estuary. On the opposite shore small houses, their walls white-washed, glowed in the moonlight. Instow.

'Yes, he is dead,' Tweed agreed. 'With the tide still coming in he'll soon be washed up on the beach below us.'

'Must have fallen overboard from a fishing smack out at sea,' commented Superintendent Roy Buchanan from Scotland Yard. 'I'm still wondering why you summoned me here so urgently.'

'I told you, Roy,' Tweed snapped. 'Because of the message that came into SIS headquarters in London. From that evil genius, Dr Goslar.'

'Probably a hoax . . .'

Buchanan, tall, lean, in his forties, stood speaking as Bob Newman, international foreign correspondent, came running up the steps from the beach. He addressed Tweed, the Deputy Director of SIS and a man he had worked with for years.

'Something very weird going on. Shoals of dead fish are floating in. They're spread all over the beach. Rock salmon, sea bass and mackerel if I'm not mistaken. Poisoned by the sea is my best guess.'

'You must be wrong,' Buchanan told him. He glued his own pair of binoculars to his eyes, scanned the beach below. 'Damned peculiar,' he went on. 'You're right. Whole beach is covered with them.'

'And there's an odd-looking chap nearer the sea using a video camera to record what's happening,' Newman added. 'Can't imagine why.'

'What's odd about him?' Inspector Crake enquired.

A short stocky man in a shabby overcoat, Crake stood next to Buchanan. Like Tweed, he was quiet and stood with both hands in his pockets.

'The way he's dressed,' Newman replied. 'He's sporting a deerstalker hat and a long check jacket. Quite tall and thin with a bony face. Jumps about a lot.'

'That will be our local reporter, Sam Sneed,' Crake informed them. 'Very ambitious to get a big story in the national press. He's mad keen to get out of here into the big wide world.'

'You're local?' Tweed enquired. 'You are. Any idea where this Sneed lives?'

'Yes. At 4 Pendel's Walk. Situated in the maze of cobbled streets behind us in Appledore.'

'Now there's a dead seal coming in,' Paula burst out, binoculars back in her hands, pressed against her eyes. 'I'm sure it's a seal. Where on earth could that come from?'

'There are seals on Lundy Island,' Crake informed her. 'You know, Miss Grey, I think you're right. That thing just cresting a wave does look like a seal. I don't understand any of this.'

'It's horrible,' Paula replied. 'Look now at the beach. It is *littered* with dead fish, as Bob said.'

'Something very deadly is happening,' Tweed said grimly. 'I sense the presence of Dr Goslar. We need samples of that sea water.'

Buchanan turned to a tall wooden-faced man behind him, his assistant, Sergeant Warden. His instructions were terse, brisk.

'Warden, we have airtight canisters in the car. Get them and take samples of the sea water. Wear rubber gloves. I'll come with you to the car, see if I can get paramedics here. That fisherman's body is about to reach the beach. He might just still be alive . . .'

'We need specimens of the dead fish,' Tweed called out. 'The seal should be collected too.'

'It's a sea of death,' Paula whispered.

'That's my impression,' Tweed agreed. 'And a few minutes ago I thought I heard the engine of a large powerboat vanishing out to sea.'

'I heard it too,' Paula confirmed.

There was a brief silence, heavy and disturbing, the only sound the breaking of the waves on the shore. Tweed glanced to his left where he could just make out the open sea. Not all that rough, so how could a fisherman fall overboard, then make no attempt to swim for the shore?

The fisherman's body slid up the beach. Shortly afterwards the seal flopped ashore a few yards away. Neither victim moved. A minute later a lean agile man ran up the steps Newman had mounted earlier. He clutched a large bulky object to his chest, ran over the promenade without a glance in their direction, vanished into Appledore.

'Sam Sneed, in one hell of a hurry,' Newman commented. 'Why the rush to get away?'

'As soon as we can, I think we'll visit Pendel's Walk,'

3

Tweed decided. 'Any idea how we get there?' he asked Crake.

'This should help you.'

Crake pulled out from a pocket a folded sheet of paper. He handed it to Tweed, after marking it with a pen.

'A crude map of Appledore. Get one at any newsagent's. You'll see I've marked with a cross where Sneed lives. An old house. Lives there with his sister, Agnes.'

'Thank you.'

'And now we have reinforcements,' Crake commented, 'I'll have this section of the promenade taped off. Scene of the crime, and all that.'

'You think there has been a crime?' Paula pressed.

'No idea. There's been a mystery. Lights are coming on in the houses behind us. I don't want the front crowded with ghouls. I'll go and instruct them now . . .'

A police car had arrived from their right. Four uniformed men got out fast. Within minutes police tape had been erected at either end of a section of the promenade, across the area behind them. Newman had volunteered to help Warden collect samples. Tweed had warned him to use the rubber gloves the correspondent always carried. Both men were now down on the beach. Warden was scooping up samples of the sea into large canisters. He had brought large transparent envelopes and Newman was using a scoop Warden had given him to collect dead fish. Buchanan returned from his car, where he had used his mobile phone.

'I got lucky,' he told Tweed. 'A couple of ambulances with paramedics had been summoned earlier. Turned out to be a hoax call at a place on the edge of Appledore. They'll be here any moment.'

'Hoax call?' Tweed said sharply. 'Get any details of who made it?'

'No. Some reference to a bad connection, the caller's voice distorted.'

'It would be,' Tweed said, offering no explanation for his remark.

'A big car's approaching from our left,' Paula reported.

They all looked in that direction. A Daimler with tinted windows cruised slowly along the front. It didn't stop when it reached the tape. Simply drove on, breaking the tape. Buchanan rushed after it as it broke through the second tape. They saw him hammering on the windows. It stopped, the engine still running. Buchanan was talking to the driver. Then the car drove on, disappeared as Buchanan returned, a livid expression on his face.

'What do you think about that?' he asked Tweed.

'Why did you let it get away?'

'It had diplomatic plates. The chauffeur said her passenger had to return for an urgent conference. You can't force the passenger in a diplomatic car to get out.'

'You saw the passenger?'

'Yes and no. I had the impression he was Middle Eastern. But the tinted glass separating passenger from chauffeur was shut. I only got a blurred view of him. Then the chauffeur said her passenger had an urgent appointment. I had to let them go.'

Buchanan's frustration registered in his voice. It irked him that there were so many people moving around he couldn't touch – all with diplomatic immunity.

'Her?' Tweed repeated. 'The chauffeur was a woman?'

'Yes. Quite a looker, from the little I could see of her. Which wasn't much. She wore dark wrap-round glasses. She had jet-black hair, I'd say.'

'A chauffeuse?' Tweed's tone was sharp. 'Are you sure?'

'Pretty much so. She wore a large peaked cap and I think she'd tucked most of her hair under the cap. But some of it projected at the back – saw it by the glow of a street lamp. What makes her important?'

'How old?'

'Late thirties, early forties would be my guess.'

'Interesting. Dr Goslar worked with a young woman assistant back in the old days.'

'Oh, come. You're not suggesting Goslar was the passenger? So what does he look like?'

'We never had any idea. Not a clue. I see two ambulances have arrived. Paramedics are on the beach. They'll take away the fisherman's body – if he's dead. I also want them to transport that seal in the second ambulance.'

'You must be joking,' Buchanan protested. 'Seals are heavy – and slippery.'

'The police may have a piece of canvas they could wrap it up in. There are enough of them to carry the seal . . .' He paused as a paramedic ran up the steps from the beach, reported that the fisherman was dead. 'Everything must be transported straight to Charles Saafeld,' Tweed went on. 'As you know, he's the cleverest pathologist in the country, probably in the world. He's also a brilliant biophysicist and a professor of bacteriology. The man's a walking brainbox.'

'There's a large roll of canvas in the police car,' Crake interjected. 'Perfectly clean. Never been used so far. It will be tricky but we can shift the seal into an ambulance.'

'Please do it, then,' Tweed requested. 'The canisters with water samples must also go to Saafeld.'

Paula nudged Tweed. 'The tide has turned, has

started to go out again. The waves aren't coming so high up the beach.'

'Then we need more samples of the sea,' Tweed decided.

'What for?' demanded Buchanan.

'Because there's something strange and sinister about this whole business.'

'We can manage that,' said Warden, who had just returned with Newman after depositing samples in the ambulance nearest to them. 'There were plenty of spare canisters. I'll go and organize that.'

'Don't bother to consult me,' Buchanan said ironically. 'After all, I'm only your superior. Now, go and do it.' He looked at Tweed. 'I haven't a clue what you're after.'

'Neither have I. The key to all this is what Saafeld finds. If anything.'

Buchanan raised his eyebrows, then strolled off with Crake to help supervise the operation. Tweed was left alone with Paula and Newman, who had removed his rubber gloves carefully and slipped them inside a samples bag. For a few minutes they stood in silence.

It was late March. The night air was chilly. Paula glanced to her right where the two rivers were surging into the estuary. There had been a lot of rain recently. Looking behind her she saw houses of dark grey stone huddled together, a small hotel. A bleak prospect in the dark. It was more cheerful to look across the estuary to tiny Instow. The distant group of modest houses was far more cheerful – due to their whitewashed walls, standing like a toy village in the moonlight.

'What next?' asked Paula, zipping up her windcheater to the collar.

A cold breeze had started to blow in. She looked to her left and caught a glimpse of the sea. It had a swell on as the water surged out of the estuary. Newman had run back to the beach to make sure the new specimens of sea water Tweed wanted were collected. He returned at that moment, reporting the men down there were doing a good job.

'Then I think we'll go and have a word with Mr Sam Sneed, ambitious reporter, at 4 Pendel's Walk. If we can ever find the place.'

Before leaving, Tweed had asked Inspector Crake whether they could drive there. He had advised them to walk, pointing to a side street leading off the front. Tweed soon realized that Crake had been right. The side street was narrow. Emerging at the other end they entered a maze of even narrower ancient cobbled streets. By the light of a street lamp he studied the map Crake had provided.

'We turn left here,' he said to Paula and Newman, 'then the first on the right for starters.'

'This is creepy,' Paula said.

The labyrinth of streets, little more than wide alleys, was another world. She felt completely cut off from the front they had left. The streets were lined with ancient terraced houses built ages ago of granite, Dartmoor granite. There were no lights in any of the thin, blocklike houses. No sign of a human being. The only sounds were their footfalls on the cobbles.

Paula kept glancing back over her shoulder. Inside her shoulder bag her hand gripped the hidden Browning. It was a secret world with some streets running into the distance, then vanishing behind a corner. Hampton Court Maze has nothing on this, she thought. Leading the way, Tweed turned again, into a street curving uphill. A wall lamp suspended from a bracket faintly illuminated a name. *Pendel's Walk*.

No. 4 was, of course, more than halfway up the hill. Here there were lights behind shabby black curtains closed over the narrow windows. Tweed gestured and Paula and Newman stood on either side of the door. A motorcycle was perched against the wall. Newman felt the engine. It was warm. Tweed pressed the bell, had to wait a couple of minutes before a lock turned, the door opened on a chain. A plump middle-aged woman in a print dress peered at him.

'Mrs Sneed?'

'Miss, if you please. Who are you?'

She had been drinking. The alcoholic fumes came out to meet him. Tweed had the Special Branch identity in his hand, forged by boffins back at Park Crescent. As good as the real article.

'Sorry to call on you so late. My name is Tweed. You must be Agnes. I need to have a word with Mr Sneed.'

'He's busy.'

'Miss Sneed, I have authority to ask him to help me. It will only take a few minutes.'

'Better let him in, Agnes. Special Branch can get in anywhere.'

A gnomelike face had appeared at Agnes's shoulder. He was still wearing the deerstalker hat, the heavy check jacket. He gave Tweed a smirk. His expression changed when Paula and Newman followed Tweed inside.

'Hey! How many of you are there?'

'My assistants, Miss Grey and Mr Newman,' Tweed introduced.

They had walked straight into a cramped sitting room. Arranged at random were sofas and armchairs, covered with well-worn chintz. Sneed, still looking disturbed, ushered them to sit down. Agnes had rushed ahead, shoved a gin bottle behind some cushions, sat down with her back to them.

9

'I'm just finishing some work,' Sneed said nasally. 'Give me a minute and I'll be with you.'

He disappeared through a half-open door, closed it. Tweed sat carefully in an armchair, feeling broken springs under him. He smiled at Agnes to put her at her ease.

'Your brother is a reporter, I understand. So I suppose he works all hours,' Tweed suggested.

'No. He's on the daytime roster. Another rep works nights.'

'I sympathize – he's on a local paper so he can't make a lot of money.'

'He's doing all right just now. Sometimes you get lucky—'

Agnes broke off. Her face was flushed as though she realized she had said too much. Her right hand reached out for the half-full glass on a small table, then she withdrew it into her lap. Without the glass.

'You've lived here for long?' Tweed went on genially.

'All my born days. When Mother died my brother and I decided it seemed sensible for us to stay on here.'

'Familiar surroundings,' Tweed chattered on. 'Your brother is busy in his workroom tonight . . .'

'Making copies of the the video—'

Again she broke off. Again her expression suggested she had said too much. She kept clasping and unclasping her plump hands. She glanced down at her watch. Tweed turned in his chair as though to make himself more comfortable. He stared briefly at Newman, who got the message.

'Excuse me,' Newman said.

He stood up swiftly, went across to the workroom door, opened it before Agnes could protest. He walked into a dark room with tables piled with photographic equipment. A dim red light was the only illumination. No sign of Sneed. He went over to a door in the side

10

wall, opened it, found himself in an alley. He heard Agnes calling out.

'You can't go in there . . .'

Newman ran the few paces down the alley, found himself back in Pendel's Walk. At the bottom of the hill he heard a motorbike starting up, saw a thin figure wearing a crash helmet astride the saddle. The machine disappeared round a corner. Newman pressed the bell of No. 4 three times and Tweed opened it.

'Sneed's motorbike has gone – with Sneed on it,' Newman reported to Tweed. 'There's another exit from that room he disappeared into.'

'I thought he was there a long time.'

Tweed had stepped into the street. Paula stood behind him in the entrance. She suddenly felt a plump hand push her into the street. She nearly stumbled on the cobbles but Newman grabbed her by the arm. Agnes shouted behind them.

'Now you can all shove off.'

She slammed the door and they heard a key turn in the lock. Paula shrugged and smiled.

'For a plump lady she's got some strength.'

'I'm popping back up the alley to take another look at Mr Sneed's workroom,' Newman decided.

He began running and his companions followed. As Newman re-entered the alley they heard a door slam shut. They reached it just in time to hear bolts being thrust home. Paula shrugged again as they looked at the closed wooden door.

'We're not welcome,' Paula commented. 'Not wanted on the voyage. And dear Agnes can really move when she wants to. So it was a waste of time.'

'We'll get back to our car on the promenade,' Tweed announced. 'And it wasn't a waste of time. We did learn quite a bit . . .'

When they eventually found their way back they

were just in time to see the two ambulances driving away. The policeman on duty lifted the tape so they could walk to where Buchanan stood with Crake.

'Any joy?' enquired Crake.

'Not really,' Tweed told him. 'So the ambulances are on their way to Saafeld?' he continued, addressing Buchanan. 'The drivers know his place in town?'

'Of course,' Buchanan replied tersely. 'And I phoned Saafeld to warn him what was coming – that it was at your suggestion. That one of the specimens on the way to him was a dead seal. I was relieved to get him on the phone at this late hour.'

'Saafeld is an owl. He likes working through the night. How did he react to the news of the seal?'

'As though it was a normal delivery. Thanked me for warning him. Said he'd now be able to contact someone else. It was a very brief conversation. He's remarkable. I made another phone call.'

'That's right. Keep me in suspense.'

'I got that Daimler's registration number, of course. While you've been away, seeing Sneed, I checked the number. Wait for it. The Daimler belongs to an Arab embassy in London. An Arab state on the Gulf which is hostile, the one which discovered it was sitting on vast oil reserves six months ago. We're talking billions and billions of dollars.'

'Didn't the girl who was driving give you any reason why they were in this part of the world?'

'Yes. She quickly volunteered the information that her important passenger was looking for a large house he could buy in the West Country.'

'You believed that?'

'No. I hadn't asked her what they were doing. Any idea what is happening here?'

'Too early to say. It could be something sinister, dangerous, even catastrophic.'

1

They were driving away from Appledore. Newman was behind the wheel of his Mercedes SL with Tweed beside him. Paula sat behind them. She thought Tweed's mind was miles away when he suddenly gave an order to Newman.

'Drive slowly. Put your headlights on full beam.'

'Will do. Mind telling me why?'

'So I can see the road surface more clearly. I noticed that where Buchanan had stopped the Daimler there was a small patch on the promenade. The Daimler has a slow leak when it stops.'

'That tells us exactly what you mean,' Paula said ironically.

Tweed didn't reply. He was leaning forward against his seat belt, peering through the windscreen. After a short time they left Appledore behind, were driving through hedge-lined open countryside. Tweed sat still as a Buddha, motionless as he continued his vigil of staring through the windscreen.

'Stop!' he said suddenly.

Newman glanced again at his rear-view mirror, steered the car on to a grass verge, put on his hazard lights. Tweed was out of the car before anyone could say a word. Paula followed him. Tweed was examining something on the road with the aid of the left headlight. He was stooping when Paula reached him.

'What is it?'

'Another oil patch. The Daimler stopped here for a short time.'

'Why?'

'To take a delivery.'

'Delivery? What kind? Who from?'

'How long do you reckon it would be between the time we saw Sam Sneed rushing up the steps from the beach and our arriving at 4 Pendel's Walk?'

'I'd say at least an hour, probably longer. I happened to look at my watch when Sneed appeared at the top of the steps and it was 10.30 p.m. It's now 12.30 a.m.'

'The timing is right, then.'

'What timing? Don't go cryptic on me,' she said in exasperation.

'Time for Sneed to get back to his house, make copies of the video, then deliver the original to the mysterious passenger in that Daimler. He'd use his motorbike to get here, make his delivery, then get back to his house before we arrived. And don't forget his sister, Agnes, let slip he had made copies of the video.'

'So what is going on?' Paula demanded as they walked back to the car.

'We witnessed a demonstration. I know, to my cost long ago, that Dr Goslar is a brilliant planner. Back to Gidleigh Park Hotel on Dartmoor,' he instructed Newman as they climbed back into the car. 'You can drive as fast as you like now, safety permitting. I think we might get a drink at the hotel, even considering the late hour. We are guests.'

Eventually Newman drove slowly through Chagford, an ancient Dartmoor village of grey stone houses and closed shops. The final approach to the magnificent-looking old hotel led up a narrow drive over a mile long where only one car could hold the road. The hotel was a blaze of lights as Newman parked the car close to the entrance. The moment they walked into the comfortable and luxurious hall a waiter greeted them.

'Any chance of the odd drink?' Tweed enquired. 'I know it's late – or should I say early?'

'Certainly, sir,' replied the waiter with a smile. 'I'm only temporary staff, but the manager has gone to bed. So I won't ask him. What would you like?'

'Double Scotch for me,' Newman said promptly. 'No water.'

Tweed and Paula each ordered a glass of Chardonnay, then they all went into a large empty lounge. After taking off their coats and piling them them neatly on a chair, Tweed and Paula sank into a comfortable sofa while Newman hauled an armchair close to them.

'I like this place,' said Paula. 'And don't they keep it warm?'

'Everything is perfect,' Tweed agreed. 'The food is excellent, the service impeccable. I've a mind to come here for a break one day.'

'You're always saying that,' Paula chaffed him. 'But you never actually do it.'

A chambermaid, on her way to bed, paused at the entrance to study the new guests. Paula, five feet six tall, was slim and very attractive. In her thirties, she had glossy dark hair falling to her shoulders. She had good bone structure with a well-shaped nose, a firm mouth with lips which hinted at concealed affections and a determined chin.

Tweed, a couple of inches taller, was well built, of uncertain age, clean-shaven, with penetrating eyes behind his horn-rimmed glasses. He was the sort of man you pass in the street without seeing him, a characteristic he had found invaluable on certain occasions as Deputy Director of the SIS.

The chambermaid thought they looked nice people, but her gaze lingered on foreign correspondent Bob Newman. Five foot ten in height, he was well built without a sign of fatness. He too was clean-shaven and had fairish hair. In his forties, he was a man many women looked at twice. They liked his buoyant smile.

'We are being observed,' Tweed whispered. 'It's all right, she has gone now. And here are the drinks.'

Tweed looked hard at the young waiter as he served their drinks. He decided he was intelligent and probably a trainee. He spoke to him just before the waiter was leaving.

'Are you by any chance local?'

'Yes, sir. Born in Chagford and I love this part of the world. Between us, I've turned down offers from London. I love the peace of Dartmoor.'

'Has anyone new moved into a large house recently anywhere near here? Someone mentioned this had happened.'

'You're probably thinking of Mr Charterhouse. He leased Gargoyle Towers about three months ago. They gossip about him down in Chagford.'

'Sounds interesting. Why the gossip?'

'They call him the Mystery Man. No one has ever seen him. He arrives late at night in a chauffeur-driven limousine. He has dark curtains closed over the windows and you never even get a glimpse of him. A poacher on his land at night had the closest look.'

'So you can describe him?'

'I'm afraid not. The poacher saw the limo draw up at the entrance and the passenger get out on the far side. The main door was open for him but there were no lights in the hall, which the poacher thought was strange. Jim, that's the poacher, gives the place a wide berth now. If you get close at night searchlights come on and you're blinded. I shouldn't really be talking about him, I suppose.'

'Mr Charterhouse.' Tweed reflected. 'Sounds like an old friend of mine. Is this Gargoyle Towers far away?'

'No, sir. It's almost next door to us, in a Dartmoor manner of speaking.'

'How do you get there?'

'It's a very long and devious drive by car. But in daylight you can walk there. You start by going through the Water Gardens you pass driving up on your left just before you reach the hotel.'

'We're all fresh. After we've had our drinks we might feel like paying him a visit. I know he stays up half the night. How would we get there after leaving the Water Gardens?'

'There is a forest. I could show you on this map I have in my pocket. A lot of our visitors like to walk. But I'd advise you to borrow a pair of gumboots – there are plenty for visitors by the front door.'

'I should be all right in my boots,' Paula suggested.

'Perfect footwear for climbing, madam,' the waiter assured her. 'I will be at your service if anything more is required. Is the map clear, sir?' he asked after Tweed had scanned it.

'If will be an excellent guide, I'm sure. Thank you.'

Paula waited until they were alone before she spoke.

'Now, what is all this about?' Paula asked, turning to Tweed at her side. 'I'm confused. First we have a dead fisherman washed ashore. Then the beach is littered with dead fish. And, on top of that, a dead seal is beached. While all this is going on Sam Sneed, local reporter—'

'Ambitious reporter,' Tweed reminded her.

'All right, ambitious local reporter, uses his video camera to record the whole scene. Then he rushes off to

17

his little house. Meantime, a mysterious limo with tinted glass appears, breaks through the police tapes, is stopped by Buchanan, who can't do anything as the limo has diplomatic plates. The chauffeur is a dark-haired girl. We visit Sneed's place, Bob detects Sneed has just come back from somewhere – his motorcycle engine is warm. Agnes, his sister, lets slip her brother has made copies of the video. Sneed sneaks out of a back door, rides off somewhere on his motorcycle.' She paused. 'Funny, we didn't hear him start up his engine.'

'That's simple,' Newman broke in. 'He slipped out, wheeled his machine far enough away before he starts the engine so we won't hear him.'

'Later,' Paula continued, 'Tweed spots an oil patch outside Appledore. Then, when we get back, we hear about the invisible man, Mr Charterhouse. I'm confused,' she repeated.

'Cheers!' Tweed lifted his glass of wine. 'Paula, you have just given an excellent summary of events so far. The pieces of a jigsaw which don't link up. We need more pieces to begin to see the whole picture. And don't forget Buchanan found out whoever was in that limo belongs to a hostile Arab state sitting on a newly discovered treasure of oil. Billions and billions of dollars, Roy said.'

'I'm more confused than ever,' said Paula. 'Tweed, aren't you going to give us a reaction?'

'I'm very worried – almost frightened. I fear we are facing a danger the world has never before experienced. Truly global. Remember it all started with this strange communication from Dr Goslar – the message inside an envelope pushed through the letter box at Park Crescent early this morning. You'd both better look at it again, refresh your memory.'

He extracted an envelope from his breast pocket, took out the folded sheet inside, handed it first to Paula.

My dear Tweed, is it not time we crossed swords again? Years ago you were a formidable opponent – but I eluded you. Tonight, say about ten o'clock, be on the front at Appledore, north of Dartmoor. That is where the inevitable fate of this planet will start. Do not expect to win. H. Goslar.

'It's weird handwriting,' Paula commented. 'Almost old-fashioned copperplate. But the writing jerks up and down like the lines you see on a seismograph. I suppose it isn't a joke?'

'What we saw at Appledore wasn't a joke,' Newman commented.

'No,' Tweed told her, 'it isn't a joke. It's Goslar. I have a short specimen of his handwriting I obtained years ago. To me it looked genuine. I took the precaution of showing it to Pete Nield. Among his other talents he's an expert graphologist. He confirmed without a doubt it is Goslar.'

'When did you last encounter this Goslar?' Paula asked.

'Over ten years ago – before you joined us. He was very active during the Cold War, before the Berlin Wall came down. He cooperated with the Soviets and sold them data on American secret weapons. Formulae for producing certain poison gases. But he also cooperated with Washington, selling them data on Soviet secret weapons for large sums of money.'

'Can you describe him?'

'I have no idea what he – or she – looks like. We didn't even know whether it was a man or a woman. I have one picture of him – or her.'

Tweed took out his wallet, gave her a small photograph. It was dog-eared, as though it had been examined many times before being secreted in his wallet. The photo had been taken at night, and showed a tiny figure – its back – in the distance. The odd factor which struck Paula was both arms were held out at the side, away from the blurred body, dangling awkwardly. It wore some kind of headgear. She handed the picture to Newman.

'I think I might recognize that figure if I ever saw it standing with its back to me,' she reflected.

'Then you're cleverer than I am,' Newman told her.

'When was it taken?' she asked.

'Bob took it,' Tweed explained. 'That was the night we nearly caught him. It was taken at the very edge of the Iron Curtain. East of Lübeck on the Baltic coast. But by the time we got there Goslar had crossed over, threading his way through the minefield of the Iron Curtain. He obviously knew the safe path.'

'Maybe if it was enlarged,' she suggested.

'Paula,' said Tweed, 'we have blown it up, examined it under a high-powered microscope. The image gets worse, more blurred.'

'What is it wearing on its head?'

'Some kind of woolly cap. It was very cold that night.'

'Surely,' Paula protested, 'if he did business with the Americans someone in the States could describe him?'

'No go,' said Newman. 'I flew over there to see Cord Dillon, just appointed Deputy Director of the CIA. After the Berlin Wall came down Goslar moved to America. They welcomed him with open arms when he told them he could create a new gas which would destroy any enemy before they knew what had hit them. He bought a chemical plant, kept his word. They paid him ten million dollars – but he had expected twenty million. One morning, when all the workers were present, a huge bomb destroyed the entire plant. Over a hundred workers were killed. Goslar then disappeared. Maybe down to Mexico, or across the border into Canada. No one knew how.'

'But I don't understand why they have no description.'

'He always communicated by phone – from a street call box. The voice was recorded, of course, but it was just a screech although every word was audible. My theory is he feels he was tricked over the amount of money paid, so now he hates America.'

'But the Russians must have known who he was, could have described him,' Paula persisted.

'They never did,' Tweed replied. 'Goslar used the same technique. Always phoning his top contact in the Kremlin. Demanded once more that a certain huge sum be deposited in a Swiss bank account. Once he knew it had arrived, he told them where to find the formula – in some remote place outside Leningrad, as it was then, or Kiev, or wherever.'

'I'm surprised both the Americans and the Russians went along and dealt with the invisible Goslar.'

'They did it because what he supplied was pure gold. Moscow thought Goslar was a woman, Washington thought he was a man. Take your choice.'

'Goslar sounds ruthless. That bomb which killed all those workers at the plant in the States.'

'Goslar, man or woman, is the most evil person I've ever encountered. But I gradually built up a dossier on some of his habits and methods. They were so successful the same techniques will be used again. That just might give Goslar to me. Eventually.'

*

21

Paula asked to see the photograph taken at the edge of the Iron Curtain years before again. She sighed, then shuddered.

'What kind of methods?' she asked.

'He always has a secret base fairly close to his theatre of operations. He delights in leaving false clues. Bob and I followed up a number of them – they all led to dead ends. Except for the last one, which was when we almost caught him near Lübeck.'

'What was the clue?'

'Bob caught a glimpse of a red-headed woman entering a building in Lübeck. We'd found out he worked with a red-head. We waited for her to come out. We could see the entrance and the fire escape. What we didn't realize was there was a second fire escape. We heard a motor-cycle start up. We pursued it in a car. The figure crouched over the machine reached the Iron Curtain just ahead of us. It escaped, as I've explained.'

'What did the red-head look like, Bob?'

'I only caught a glimpse of her. In her late twenties, I'd say.'

'Over ten years ago,' Paula mused. 'So now she'd be in her late thirties – if she's still alive.'

'We went back to the building afterwards, broke in-to it. Place was empty. In a room at the back where the second fire escape led down we found a wig – red-haired, a woman's.'

'So Goslar is probably a man?' Paula speculated.

'Unless it was another false clue,' Tweed warned. 'I said earlier that Goslar always had a base not too far from an operation. So now you know why I asked the waiter if anyone new had moved into the area . . .'

'And he told us about this mysterious Mr Charter-house,' Paula interjected. 'Described him as someone no one in Chagford had ever seen. That he is driven in a limo with tinted glass to Gargoyle Towers.'

'Exactly,' Tweed agreed. 'It does sound like the behaviour pattern of Goslar. He leased the place three months ago. He would need that sort of time span to organize what we witnessed up at Appledore.'

'So we'd better check out Gargoyle Towers as soon as it's daylight,' she suggested.

'That might be too late. Goslar keeps on the move. It's a pity we didn't bring Harry Butler and Pete Nield with us – to say nothing of Marler. But I think we have to check out the place now, even though there are only three of us. At least both of you are carrying weapons. And we all have flashlights. We'll need them, I'm sure.' He looked at Paula. 'Unless you're tired. In that case we'll wait until morning.'

'Fresh as the proverbial daisy,' she assured him. 'Let's get on with it now.'

Tweed led the way out of the front door. Like Newman, he had equipped himself with gumboots. They walked back down the drive, aided by the light of the moon. Tweed found the entrance to the Water Gardens, just before the bridge which crossed the rushing stream. He switched on his torch, hurried along a tricky path hemmed in by shrubs and trees.

Paula followed Newman, who walked with a torch in his left hand, his Smith & Wesson in his right. It was an eerie experience, the only sound the surging torrent, the moon blotted out, threading their way along the uneven path, isolated from the outside world. They passed a house on the far side of the stream which had lights on in several windows. Then Tweed was climbing a flight of stone steps. Some distance beyond, he opened a small gate and they could no longer hear the water. The gate creaked as he opened it and started along a pathway. He paused to call over his shoulder.

'I think we've left behind the property belonging to Gidleigh Park. Here is the forest that waiter mentioned.'

He used his flashlight to check the map. They began to climb rapidly through a dense forest of evergreens which towered above them. They came to a narrow path which led steeply upwards. Tweed decided there should be a more negotiable path and continued past it.

'I'm going up this way,' Paula called out. 'Bet I beat you both to the top.'

'Stay with us,' Newman called back.

When he looked back she had disappeared. He shrugged and went on after Tweed. Within minutes Tweed found a gap in the forest and beyond it a wide drive climbing steeply. Switching off his torch, he mounted the drive, his legs moving like pistons. Newman, who had doused his own torch, saw him pause. When he caught up with him Tweed pointed.

'Gargoyle Towers. What a horror.'

The mansion's ancient and immense bulk loomed above them at the end of the drive. It was built of Dartmoor granite, three storeys high, with numerous turrets, clearly visible in the moonlight. Leering down from each turret was a grim gargoyle, as though watching them approach. No lights in any window.

'This is just the sort of place Goslar would choose as a base,' Tweed commented. 'I almost sense his presence. Let's hurry – and where's Paula?'

'She insisted on making her own way up along a path through the forest. Said she'd get there first.'

'So she's probably coming up by a devious route before she gets out of the forest.'

Tweed had started walking again, soon reached the entrance at the side of the grim bulk. A heavy studded wooden door stood partly open. Newman pushed ahead of Tweed, eased the door wider. It creaked ominously. Newman reached inside, felt round the wall, found a battery of switches, pressed them. Lights came on everywhere. He stood quite still, his revolver gripped in both hands, staring. Tweed came alongside him, blinked.

The vast hall was empty. Doors leading off the hall were wide open with lights on inside the rooms. Tweed had the impression the place was empty. His impression was confirmed when they began exploring. Not a stick of furniture anywhere. No carpets on the woodblock floors. What struck Tweed as they moved from one large room to another was the clinical cleanliness. Not a speck of dust. As though the mansion had never been occupied.

On a window ledge he found a pair of leather gloves. Picking them up, he slipped them into his coat pocket. They found the same clinical emptiness on the first and second floors. They were returning quietly down the massive staircase leading to the hall when Tweed turned to Newman.

'Where is Paula? She should have got here long before now.'

'I told you. She went off on her own up—'

'I remember what you said.' Tweed came as close to sounding agitated as Newman had ever known him. 'Show me the damned path. And don't hang about. We go back the way we came . . .'

Newman walked ahead of him, back down the drive, into the forest again. Using his torch, he eventually found the path. Tweed pushed past him, moved slowly up the path. He walked with his head down, shining his torch. Here and there he could trace where her footsteps had trodden down bracken. Continuing his slow search, his head was bowed. Suddenly he bent down and picked up something. He swung round to Newman.

'I heard the distant sound of a helicopter taking off.'

'So did I . . .'

'Look at this.'

He opened his hand. He was holding a silver ring. His expression was a mixture of fury and anxiety. He held the ring out to Newman.

'This is Paula's. She always wore it. Her father gave it to her on her twenty-first birthday. She slid it off her finger to warn us when she was attacked. They've got her. Goslar has.'

'So what next?'

'Back to Gidleigh Park. I want to use a phone. My God, she's in Goslar's hands.'

2

The pathway Paula had taken between the fir trees was narrow and steeply twisting. Last year's bracken, dead and brown, brushed her feet on either side. It was eerily quiet. The night darkness made the heavy silence even more unsettling. Once she thought she'd heard faint heavy footsteps coming up behind her.

She paused, turned, listened. Nothing. Imagination. She plodded on up the incline. She would have liked to use her torch, but Tweed's orders had been explicit. *No lights.* Here and there moss-covered boulders leaned over the path, but her eyes were now accustomed to the intense blackness. She eased her way past them.

She was relieved she was wearing boots. The ground was damp and slippery. The fronds of a fir brushed her face. Like ghostly hands touching her face. She nearly jumped, then she realized what it was. The gradient of the path was increasing. She took careful longer strides. She wanted to get out of this clinging wood.

Hearing no sound, seeing no sign, of her companions, she guessed they had found another path up to the summit. Then she saw a gap in the trees ahead. Beyond, a strange house perched on a ridge. She paused to study it. Built of granite, it was a mansion with turrets at each corner silhouetted against the starlit night sky. No lights in the windows, it had an abandoned look. Vaguely she made out a wide terrace running its full length, a wide flight of steps leading up to it. A twig cracked behind her. She began to spin round.

A large hand clasped her mouth. She had managed to spin half way round, to catch a glimpse of her attacker. A *huge* man, over six feet tall, heavily built. An apelike figure, the impression emphasized by hair trimmed very short over the massive skull. A small moustache. His other hand and arm pinioned her arms to her body in a vicelike grip. Another smaller figure came beside her, grasped her right arm, pulled up the sleeve of her windcheater. The moonlight penetrating from the gap in the wood showed her he held a hypodermic.

She lifted her right leg, felt a leg of the ape, ground her boot down the shin. No reaction. It was like scraping down the side of a tree trunk. The needle plunged into her exposed arm. She used the fingers of her right hand to push the ring off her finger. Her head was swimming. She gritted her teeth, tried to fight the drug they'd injected into her. The world went hazy. She lost consciousness.

Paula had brief bouts of coming awake. She was lying on a stretcher, flat on her back. A rug or a blanket covered her. The sound of jet engines vibrated in her ears. A sensation of climbing fast. She was aboard a plane. Oh, God – where was she being transported?

Under cover of the blanket she flexed her hands,

27

realized her wrists were tied to the stretcher. Same thing with her ankles. She opened her eyes slowly, ready to close them quickly. Near, and in front of her, she saw the back of a huge man standing up. One large hand, covered with hair, grasped the back of a seat. The Ape. Her vision blurred, cleared again. A small man dressed in whites, like a hospital attendant, was coming down the aisle towards the Ape. She closed her eyes.

Again she gritted her teeth, struggling to stay conscious. The plane went on climbing as she heard voices.

'Time to give her another shot? Don't want her waking during the flight – not till we get her off and delivered.'

A growly voice. The Ape would have that kind of voice. The voice which answered was different, lighter in tone, more educated. Had to be the hospital attendant.

'We could wait a little longer.'

'Any risk in doing her again?' Growly voice.

'Not with the amount I'd give her, but still . . .'

'Then do her.'

As in a dream Paula felt the blanket lifted. A careful hand rolled up the sleeve of her windcheater. She braced herself, felt another prick in her arm. Her head was swimming again. She was aware the plane was flying level now. It would be a more moderate dose of the drug. Inwardly, motionless, she swore, then started counting. Anything to stay conscious. She loathed the feeling of helplessness. A wave rolled over her – reminded her of the wave carrying in the body of the dead fisherman at . . . What was the name of the place? She sank deep into the wave, deeper, deeeper, deeper. Everything went. She was again completely unconscious.

*

The world stood still. No longer the sound of jet engines. No longer the gentle swaying motion of an aircraft in flight. She surfaced suddenly, quickly. She had a pounding headache. She felt muzzy. Apart from these discomforts she felt the situation was better. Or was it far worse?

Paula was still on her back, still tied to the stretcher. The blanket, or rug, whatever the damned thing was, still covered her. She was careful not to stir noticeably until she had found out what was going on.

The palms of her hands were wet. Slowly she slid them under the cover, drying them off. She had a strong bladder but now she desperately wanted the loo. She became aware her leggings had been pulled well down below her thighs, that her backside was perched on some kind of rubber-like receptacle. They had given her the facilities to relieve herself. She heard a heavy footstep some distance away. She performed very carefully so they would not hear her. Afterwards she felt better, but would have given a fortune for a shower. Then she heard lighter, more deliberate footsteps. Someone had entered the room.

The man, who called himself Dr Goslar, stood, profile sideways to their captive. When he spoke to the other man his voice was light, unpleasant. A small man, thin, he had a high forehead, was clean-shaven, his face long and pale. He wore an expensive blue two-piece suit, white shirt and black polka-dot bow tie, and rimless glasses, which gave him a sinister look, were perched on the bridge of his long nose. He spoke to the other man.

Paula saw all this as she risked half-opening her eyes. The man he spoke to was the Ape, clad in a thick grey pullover which clasped his bull-like neck tightly. She now saw that the cropped hair was brown, like stubble.

'It's time the drug wore off,' the thin man said in precise English. 'You know what you have to do with her, the questions to ask. We are in a hurry.'

'What's the rush?' demanded the Ape throatily. 'We're OK here.'

'You think so? I have a feeling this building is no longer secure.'

'Don't get nervous, Goslar . . .'

'Don't talk to me like that. You're being paid a lot of money for your services,' the thin man hissed.

Paula noticed he spoke with a slight lisp. While they argued she concentrated on strengthening her body. Slowly she eased her ankles up from the ropes as far as she could. She gently revolved her legs. She kept stretching her fingers. The circulation was present. She clenched her hands, unclenched them, repeated the process.

'Get on with it,' the thin man ordered. 'At least you've opened the window.'

Paula froze at this latest item of information. What the hell were the bastards going to do to her now? She had her eyes shut when the Ape swung round, came over to the bed where she lay. He began slapping her roughly across each side of her face. She let her head jerk but kept her eyes closed. He began slapping her very roughly and she let out a low moan. Opening her eyes she blinked in the overhead light, closed them again.

'Come on, you whore,' the Ape snarled. 'We haven't got all night. Time for you to take your exercise. Next thing you get is a bucket of ice-cold water. It isn't all that warm outside.'

You bloody swine. Give me just one chance and I'll kill you, she said to herself.

She opened her eyes, glared at him with hate. He had small eyes under bushy brows. The eyes were like marbles, entirely without feeling. He hauled the cover off her, removed the receptacle by lifting her with one meaty arm. Shoving it under the bed, he padded to the end, removed the ropes binding her ankles, then bound them up again, leaving a strand of rope between them so she could hobble. He performed the same action with the ropes round her wrists, hauled up her leggings.

'You remember the sequence of the questions, Abel? The sequence is important.'

The thin man stood with his back to her. Again Paula noticed the lisp when he had spoken.

'I know what I'm doing, Dr Goslar,' the Ape growled irritably.

'Then hurry. We must leave soon. This building is no longer secure.' The thin man repeated what he had said earlier.

The Ape suddenly jerked her upright. She had a brief moment to check her surroundings. A large bleak room with the only furniture the bed she had been laid on. One door on an inner wall, closed. A large window, wide open. Which accounted for the chilly atmosphere she now experienced. She was suddenly lifted over his massive shoulder, upside down, her face and chest against his back, her thighs and legs hanging in front of him. He began ambling towards the open window. She used her pinioned hands to hammer his back, hoping to hit his kidneys. It was like hammering a punchbag.

He ambled towards the open window and she was really frightened now. He spoke as he paused by the window, his tone grim.

'Just one shriek. Only one – and I drop you. Got it?'

'You'll pay for this, you animal.'

'Lady, I've already been paid. Out you go . . .'

He swung round, grasped her legs in both hands, lowered her out of the window. She forced herself not to scream as the nightmare developed. She was

31

suspended outside the window and for the first time realized how high up she was. Below at least thirty storeys of the building's wall plunged down. It was night. Street lamps cast an eerie glow over the empty street so far below. No sign of anyone. Facing her was another modern building soaring vertically above her. God knew how many storeys high these buildings were. She was in New York.

'This is the first question,' the Ape called out. 'Who is your boss?'

'Jackson.'

It was the first name which jumped into her head. When the Ape had lowered her over the edge of the window his coarse hands had thrust up her leggings, grasping her round the knees. Now she felt his hands sliding back, her legs easing through his hands. This is it, she told herself, gazing down into the abyss.

'One more chance, then you drop.'

'Tweed,' she called out urgently.

The hands reached her just above the ankles, tightened their grip. She twisted her neck, looked up briefly. The Ape had his head turned, presumably giving her answer to the thin man inside the room. She was poised next to the top of a window in the floor below. No light inside. Clenching both hands into fists she beat them against the glass, which broke. She didn't think he could see what she was doing. A small round section of the broken window perched on top of the glass still in place. Careful not to cut herself, she grasped it with her right hand, concealed it inside her closed fist.

'Why did Tweed go to Dartmoor – to Appledore?'

'He had a message to go there.'

'From who? Answer more quickly . . .'

'From Dr Goslar.'

Her head began swimming again. Was it the remains of the drug or vertigo? It seemed such a helluva a long way down. She'd end up squashed to mush. *Stop thinking like that*.

'What did Tweed think of what happened at Appledore? What did he see?'

'Dead fisherman floating in on a wave. Dead fish on the beach.'

'Damn you! What did he think about it?'

'That there must be poison in the water. He didn't know what to think . . .'

Hanging upside down had one advantage. The blood rushed to her head. She was thinking more clearly. She put her hands together, moved the small piece of round glass more comfortably inside her right fist, closed it again.

'Did he think Dr Goslar had something to do with what he saw?'

'He did once. Only once. He was puzzled. We couldn't grasp what was happening. It was dark . . .'

She stopped speaking. Way below her she saw the first sign of life. A car driving slowly round a corner, blue light flashing on its roof. For a second she thought of screaming, dismissed the idea at once. He'd drop her. She heard his voice calling out louder, speaking to the thin man somewhere inside the room.

'Police car's arrived . . .'

She didn't hear the thin man's reaction but felt the grip on her ankles tighten. The Ape was hauling her up fast. Her windcheater protected her against contact with the wall but her legs were being grazed. She took a deep breath as he heaved her inside the window, threw her over his shoulder. She had a brief glimpse of Goslar turned three-quarters away from her, saw he held an

33

automatic in his right hand. No chance of cutting the beast's throat. She might manage that but Goslar would shoot her to ribbons.

'What do we do with her?' rasped the Ape.

'Throw her back on the bed.'

'I could shoot her—'

'You've got a silencer?'

'No . . .'

'The police will hear the shot. Do as I said – throw her on the bed. We've got to get out of here fast.'

She was thrown down on her back onto the bed. The Ape ran back to the window. He peered down, swung round, moving swiftly for such large man. Turning back, his thick lips opened, then closed. The thin man, standing by the internal door now open, hissed at him.

'What is it now?'

'The police car was just cruising. It's disappeared round the corner of another building.'

'We're going now. It may come back. The police play tricks like that. They may have seen her when you were hauling her up again. *Move!*'

During the brief moment when she was slung back over the Ape's shoulder Paula had seen through the open door. Had seen a wide empty space, dimly lit – and a bank of elevators on the opposite wall. Goslar left swiftly, his footfalls quiet. He hadn't had time to glance at Paula. She lay still, her eyes almost closed as the Ape ambled after Goslar, his huge shoulders lifting and falling, as though walking on the deck of a boat in a swell. Apelike in every movement. She watched him from behind her lashes, to conceal her hatred.

She remained motionless for a few seconds. Her acute hearing caught a whirring noise, the gentle click of elevator doors opening, closing. Then she got to work with the piece of rounded glass.

She had plenty of illumination from the fluorescent

tube attached to the ceiling. She used her right hand to quickly saw through the section of rope between her wrists. Once it was cut she eased each hand out of the rope round her wrists. She was sitting up now, leaning against the wall behind her.

She leaned forward, cut herself free from the ropes binding her ankles. She stood up carefully, not sure how strong her legs might be. Finding she could walk easily, without much hope she peered under the bed, saw both her boots lying beside the revolting bedpan.

Hauling them on quickly she walked quietly over to a cupboard in the wall. She opened it, without much hope again. Her shoulder bag lay on the floor. Opening it she realized they had not even examined it. Everything was in place. She took out her Browning .32 automatic, checked it, was both surprised and relieved to find it had not been tampered with. Very quietly she slid back the magazine into the butt. Gripping the weapon in both hands, she tiptoed to the open door, listened. A heavy silence, broken only by the whine of the descending elevator.

She stepped out into a large empty hall, luxuriously furnished with blue tiles. It had an atmosphere she had come to associate with an empty building, closed down for the night. She ran across to the elevator, which was still going down. It had reached the fourth floor. She waited.

It arrived at the ground floor. She still waited. If she tried to use one of the other elevators too soon Goslar and Abel, presumably outside the elevator, would see the light showing it was descending. A minute or two later through the open window in the room she had left she heard the sound of a car starting up. Moving to another elevator, she pressed the button, waited again as it came up.

The waiting was getting on her nerves. There is

something eerie about being trapped inside a large building you hope is empty. The elevator seemed to take for ever to reach her. When it stopped and the doors slid back she stood braced, her automatic aimed in case someone was inside. It was empty.

Diving inside, she pressed the button for the third floor. She had noticed beyond the elevator bank a flight of stairs leading down. If they were waiting for her downstairs she needed to surprise them. *Hurry! Hurry!* Watching the numbers above the closed doors she realized now she had been on the thirty-second floor. She shuddered at the memory of the drop from the open window.

The moment the doors opened she pressed the button for the thirty-eighth floor, darted out just before the doors closed and the elevator began its ascent. If they were waiting on the ground floor that would give the bastards something to think about.

Her rubber-soled boots made no sound as she ran down the first flight, pausing to peer round the corner. Reaching the ground floor she ran into a dim-lit vast hall. She whipped to left, to right, to left again, Browning held chest high, her finger on the trigger. No one. Ahead of her on the far side was the exit door. Crouching low, she ran, zigzagging. Next to the door, on the right, a box was attached to the wall. It had a series of digits. Oh God! She didn't know the combination. Then she saw the door was partly open. Goslar and Abel had left in such a hurry they hadn't bothered to close it.

She peered out into the moonlit night. A vast smooth space where the police car had appeared. Opposite, the building she had seen from the window soared up. No lights. To her left she saw what appeared to be a small park with trees and public seats. She walked along the side of the building she had just left, in the narrow shadow it cast on the smooth area.

Without seeing a soul she reached the park, looked round, then sank onto a seat facing the way she had come. By the light of a nearby lamp, perched on a post, she checked her bag thoroughly.

Again she was surprised to find it had never been opened. A woman knows when her bag has been searched by a man. However carefully he replaces its contents he never manages to put everything back exactly as it had been. Her passport was in the special zip-up pocket. Inside a similar pocket she found all the money in several currencies Tweed insisted everyone carried. Wads of Deutschmarks, French francs, Swiss francs, English money. A woman appeared from nowhere. Paula froze.

An old woman, poorly dressed in black, walking with a stoop, her head down. She never even saw her. Paula watched her walk to the end of the park, then suddenly vanish, as though walking down steps. Looking round again, listening, Paula got up and followed her.

Once she looked up at the colossi which loomed above her – a whole series of modern monoliths towering above her. The sight gave her a feeling of vertigo. She looked down and reached the entrance to a wide flight of steps leading down. She stopped briefly to stare in disbelief at a large illuminated sign above the steps.

Métro.

She wasn't in New York. She was in Paris.

3

Newman drove Tweed back to London through the late night. They reached Park Crescent well after daylight. George, the ex-army sergeant who acted as doorman and guard, let them in. Tweed ran upstairs to his first-floor office overlooking Regent's Park. He found Monica, his faithful assistant, a woman of a certain age, her grey hair tied in a bun, seated at her desk. She jumped up the moment he entered.

'Am I glad to see you back! I called Gidleigh Park but they said you had left.'

'Why? Has there been a development?'

'We've had a weird phone call. Came through at 4 a.m. Luckily, I recorded it.'

'Switch it on, then, please.'

Newman had followed him into the office. Tweed took off his coat, carefully placed it on a hanger and hooked it over the coat stand. His normal iron self-control had asserted itself. He sat down in the swivel chair behind his desk to listen.

'The voice is very strange,' Monica warned.

'Let us hear it, then.'

My dear Tweed, you should really look after your staff more carefully. It is becoming a real hazard to work for you. Perhaps you ought to find a replacement for the lovely young lady. As ever, H. Goslar.

The voice sounded robotic. It spaced out each word and had a low twangy screech. To Newman it sounded like a voice from hell.

'That's it,' Monica said as she switched off the recorder. 'It scared the wits out of me when I first heard it.'

'He's used a voice-changer to make it impossible to hear his real voice,' Tweed said quietly. 'Monica, would you say that is man or a woman speaking?'

'It could be either sex. Very creepy. What does it mean?'

'Brace yourself. Paula has disappeared, kidnapped on Dartmoor.'

'Oh, no!' She was going to burst into tears, but managed to subdue it to snuffles. She blew her nose. 'That horrible man!'

'We need reinforcements. Contact Marler. Then Harry Butler and Pete Nield. I want them here fast.'

The door opened and Marler walked in as soon as Tweed finished speaking. A slim man, five feet seven tall, he was smartly dressed in a Prince of Wales check suit, and a crisp white shirt with a blue Chanel tie. His feet were clad in handmade shoes with rubber soles. He spoke with a drawl.

'Mornin' all.'

'Play it back again,' Tweed requested Monica. 'I want Marler to hear it.'

They listened again. It sounded no less sinister. Marler took up his usual position, standing against a wall. He extracted a king-size, but didn't light it as he listened, his clean-shaven face expressionless.

'Don't like that last bit about finding a replacement,' he said. 'Is it Paula?'

'Yes, it is,' Tweed told him. 'My fault, my responsibility. She was kidnapped on Dartmoor when she was with Newman and me, checking out a mansion called Gargoyle Towers. Early in the morning. She took a different route through a forest. Probably took her away in a helicopter.'

'That could be tracked,' Marler observed.

'I've done more than that. When we got back to the hotel I phoned the air controller at Exeter airfield. Not knowing me, he refused to give me any information. I called Jim Corcoran at Heathrow to contact Exeter. Unfortumately Jim wasn't there. Driving back, we stopped at a phone box near here and I got Jim. He'll be calling back.'

'Surely there's more we can do to find her,' Marler insisted.

'Before we left Gidleigh Park,' Tweed went on in full flood, 'I managed to phone the local police inspector at Appledore, chap called Crake. I asked him to get a search warrant for Gargoyle Towers. Told him why, that the place was empty. I want his men to check for fingerprints.'

'Gargoyle Towers? Funny name,' Marler queried.

'So now for your benefit and Monica's I'll brief you on exactly what happened at Appledore.'

Tersely he started with the message from Goslar. He paused and asked Monica to play it again on the recorder. Then he went on, explaining their whole experience at Appledore, and later at Gargoyle Towers. Normally he would have sat behind his desk but as he spoke he was pacing round the office. Monica realized it was a sign of the acute anxiety he was feeling for Paula. He completed his explanation, sat down again behind his desk. The phone rang, Monica answered, looked at Tweed.

'It's Jim Corcoran . . .'

'Any news, Jim?' Tweed asked the Security chief.

'Quite a lot. Don't know what to make of it. I contacted my opposite number at Exeter. He told me a big private jet, a Grumman Gulfstream, so a long-range job, was parked at Exeter. In the middle of the night an ambulance arrived, drove up to the jet. Paramedics

40

hauled out a stretcher with someone on it, took it aboard the machine . . .'

'Could anyone see who was on the stretcher?'

'No. The patient was well muffled against the cold. A medic said the patient had a broken leg, compound fracture, was being flown to a private clinic in London.'

'They named the clinic?' Tweed demanded.

'No. Let me finish. There's more. The pilot had already filed a flight plan for Heathrow. It all happened very quickly, I gather. The Grummann took off—'

'You intercepted it?'

'Tweed, if you'll just hold your horses until I finish. You keep firing at me like a machine-gun. No, we didn't intercept the Grumman. The reason is the pilot changed his flight plan soon after leaving Exeter. He's permitted to do that just so long as he gives sufficient notice of the change.'

'What change of plan?'

'I *was* going to tell you. He changed his destination. Instead of Heathrow he was proceeding to Rome . . .'

'Rome!'

'That's what I said.

'Can I check on the Grumman's progress?'

'You could try – by calling Paris Air Traffic Control. Although just how long it would take you to make the contact is anyone's guess. The pressure on flights and air space is growing.'

'Thank you, Jim. Thank you very much.'

'Tweed, is something wrong? I've never heard you so tense.'

'Nothing to worry about.'

Tweed placed the phone back gently. He looked round the office, told the others what he had heard. They stared at him. Marler was the first to react.

'Why would they be taking her to Rome, of all places?'

'I have absolutely no idea. Monica, get me René Lasalle in Paris on the line. Urgently.'

'Why call him?' Marler enquired. 'The head of the DST, French counterespionage?'

'Because he's a friend, as you know. And he co-operates. He'll be able to contact the French air traffic controllers.'

As he spoke Monica was obtaining the number. She was signalling to Tweed that she had Lasalle on the line when George knocked on the door, entered. He carried a batch of newspapers under his arm which he laid on Tweed's desk.

'Sorry about the delay. It's a late edition. They held the presses, apparently, to change the main story.'

'Thank you, George ... René, I need your help urgently – very urgently. A private Grumman jet took off from Exeter early this morning. The pilot filed a flight plan for Heathrow. Then in midair he gives a different flight plan, says he's headed for Rome instead of Heathrow. Did you get that? I'll repeat it.'

'Not necessary,' Lasalle said quietly.

'I want you to contact your Air Traffic Control, to find out where that machine is now. I need the answer in five minutes.'

'May be difficult,' Lasalle continued in perfect English, his tone still cool, almost distant. 'We have a crisis here. I'll deal with your request as soon as I have the time.'

'But this is terribly urgent!'

'I heard you the first time. I must go now.'

Tweed stared at the phone. Lasalle had broken the connection. He replaced the phone. He looked at the others.

'What *is* going on? He's usually so very cooperative.'

He told them the gist of his conversation. Then he

unfolded a copy of the *Daily Nation*, London's leading newspaper. He gazed at the screaming headline.

POISON SEA NORTH OF DARTMOOR
Special report by Sam Sneed

The text below was long and detailed. Tweed scanned it swiftly. Then he handed a copy of the newspaper to each member of his staff. Monica watched him, saw Tweed settle back in his chair, relaxed now, a look of extreme concentration on his face. His normal icy self-control had returned. Newman reacted first after reading his copy.

'What the hell's going on? This is a report by Sneed of exactly what happened at Appledore. He even hints that Whitehall is concerned about the invention of a new secret weapon. "Far deadlier than the hydrogen bomb", he reports an unnamed government source as saying.'

'He made up that last bit,' Tweed told him. 'To give his story an extra edge. My guess is that by now copies of his report will have been wired to Washington, Paris, Berlin and Heaven knows where else. It's created an international crisis. On the instructions of Goslar, of course.'

'Goslar?' Newman queried.

'Well, you see the splashy pictures of what we witnessed happening on the beach. The dead fisherman, dead fish, dead seal. I think on his first trip on that motorcycle – after making copies – Sneed delivered the original of his video to a prearranged rendezvous outside Appledore – to whoever was inside that Daimler with the tinted windows. You remember the oil patch we found in the road. Then – I'm guessing – a second helicopter picked him up with the copies, delivered him

eter airfield where another chopper was waiting to
him to Battersea Heliport. From there he was driven
the *Daily Nation*, where he typed his story. It would
all fit in with our past experience of Goslar. I told you
he was a brilliant planner. He hasn't lost his touch.'

'But who will believe this?'

'The people we didn't want to hear about it. Washington, Paris, etc., probably contacted the police in Appledore. Crake would give them a "no comment". That response would convince everyone the story was true.'

'What is Goslar up to?'

'He's creating panic, advertising a weapon "far deadlier than the hydrogen bomb", to quote Sneed – who undoubtedly has been well paid to meet Goslar's wishes.'

'How does the disappearance of Paula fit in?'

'Goslar is manipulating me, trying to throw me off balance. I suppose that's a backhanded compliment. But that is my great worry – Paula's safety.'

'This Sneed report will set the world alight,' said Marler.

'One thing I forgot to include, Marler, when I explained the events at Appledore. The trigger was this note from Goslar. Newman and Monica have seen it.'

He handed Marler the weird note which had arrived through their letterbox during the night. While Marler read it he gazed at the phone.

'I wish Lasalle would call me back. I can't think of any other sound way of locating that aircraft. Paula must have been alive when they carried her on to it on a stretcher.'

'You don't think they'd . . .' Newman began sombrely.

'Don't say it,' snapped Tweed.

He had just spoken when the door was pushed open.

Paula, clothes crumpled but hair freshly brushed, walked into the office with a spring in her step.

4

Tweed jumped up, rushed forward and hugged Paula. She rested her head on his shoulder, squeezed him with both arms. She whispered in his ear, 'God, it's wonderful to be back.'

'We've been going nearly out of our minds with worry,' he told her.

'I'd like to sit at my desk again.'

She hugged them all, then settled herself behind her desk. Monica made the suggestion, 'How about a cup of tea, well sweetened?'

'A cup of tea would be great, but no sugar.' She grinned. 'I'm sweet enough as I am. And I had breakfast on the plane back from Paris.'

'*Paris?*' Tweed exclaimed. 'Not Rome?'

'No.' She looked puzzled. 'Paris. I've had an adventure. But I'm so sorry I caused you all anxiety. I did think of phoning, but when I grabbed a taxi from Madeleine and arrived at Charles de Gaulle airport there was a flight for London just about to leave. To reach Madeleine I'd caught the Métro from La Défense.'

'La Défense?' echoed Tweed. 'That's the amazing French business centre well west of the Arc de Triomphe. Incredibly tall buildings.'

'Which is why, for a while, I thought I was in New York. You're an angel,' she told Monica, who had brought her a cup of tea. She took a sip. 'And I can describe the mysterious Dr Goslar. Oh, I'm not telling this well. I'm going to slow down and start from the beginning.' She looked at Newman. 'I was an idiot. You

45

did warn me not to go up that path through the forest on Dartmoor on my own. I'll start from there . . .'

'Do you want to go home and have a rest first?' Tweed suggested.

'Not yet. Later I'd like to go back to my flat and have a shower. But first you should have the information I can provide. Now, I'll go back to where I stupidly left Bob and went up that path . . .'

She recalled concisely every single event, this time in sequence. Nobody spoke, giving her their full attention. Tweed sat leaning forward, hands clasped on his desk, his eyes never leaving hers. His mouth twisted grimly as she described being held out of the window, thirty or so storeys above the ground. Newman muttered under his breath.

'The bloody swine . . .'

'So,' she eventually concluded, 'I said I could describe Goslar – and, incidentally, Abel the Ape. Is Richard, the artist, here?'

'Yes, he is. But—'

'I insist on having a session with him now. While my memory of what those two men look like is fresh. I know where his office is upstairs. I'm on my way.'

She was out of the office before Tweed could protest, suggesting again she went to her flat first to get some rest. He looked at everyone.

'Well, what do you think of that? Typical of Paula to refer to it as an adventure.'

'I tell you what I think,' growled Newman. 'Sooner or later I'll meet the Ape. I'll break both his arms. Then I'll do his legs. And that will only be for starters.'

'Paula has pulled off a coup,' drawled Marler. 'We've identified Dr Goslar.'

'Maybe,' replied Tweed. 'And don't tell Paula I said that. I'm just so relieved she's back in one piece.'

He stopped speaking as the phone rang. He let Monica deal with it. Quickly she called across, 'Lasalle's back on the line . . .'

'Good of you to call back, René. Any news?'

'Tweed, I'm not in my office. I'm calling from an outside phone. Is your end secure?'

'Yes. What is the problem, René?'

'First, you asked me to check on that plane. I found out that a Grumman Gulfstream jet landed at Charles de Gaulle early this morning – in the middle of the night, actually. An ambulance was waiting. Two paramedics carried someone off on a stretcher, drove away. Later the ambulance – stolen – was found abandoned in a side street. After that I drew a blank.'

Once again Tweed marvelled at Lasalle's command of English. He also detected Lasalle was under pressure, in a state of tension. Normally he was one of the coolest men Tweed had ever met.

'René, I can tell you now Paula was the so-called patient. She had been kidnapped from Dartmoor—'

'Did you say Dartmoor?'

'Yes. Why?'

'Doesn't matter. Do go on.'

'She was transported to a building in La Défense. She had been drugged during the flight. When she woke she was subjected to a terrifying experience while two men questioned her. She was suspended by her feet out of a window over thirty storeys up.'

'Oh, my God! Poor Paula. That's fiendish . . .'

'They eventually hauled her back again into the room. Briefly, they left her when a patrol car appeared below the building. She escaped and she's now back here with me. Do you know what happened to that Grumman jet?'

'Yes, it took off for Geneva. That's all I know.'

'Is it? Ever heard the name Goslar?' Tweed enquired.

'Did you say *Goslar*?' A brief pause. 'I can't help you with that.'

'Which means the name does mean something to you. We've known each other a long time. This is the first occasion you've felt it necessary to use an outside phone to call me. What is going on, René?'

'You'll keep the fact that I phoned you within your closed circle?'

'Only if you tell me why,' Tweed replied grimly.

'Tweed, the Élysée is on my back. Signing off now . . .'

Tweed put down the phone, then told the others the gist of his conversation. There was silence for a short time. Then Marler spoke.

'That's not the René we used to know. Why?'

'The last thing he said. The President of France has involved himself. Goslar is spreading a vast net. As I remarked earlier, this thing is global.'

While he had been speaking the phone had rung. Monica, looking furious, gazed at Tweed.

'Trouble. Two men from Special Branch tried to storm their way past George and up here. He's holding them at bay with his revolver.'

'Tell George to escort the gentlemen up here.' He looked at Newman. 'It is starting. Why do my thoughts run to the Prince, otherwise known as Aubrey Courtney Harrington, newly apppointed Minister of General Security, member of the Cabinet?'

Two unusual men entered. One was over six feet tall, upright as a Douglas fir, in his late fifties, his rugged face wearing an aggressive expression, his hair grey, his clean-shaven face pink, his ice-blue eyes swivelling to everyone in the room. His manner exuded domineering self-confidence. He wore an expensive camelhair coat and he was removing expensive pigskin gloves, exposing large hands with thick fingers.

'I'm Jarvis Bate, Acting Head of Special Branch. Too many people in here. Need to see you alone, Tweed.'

'First I'd like to see some identification.'

'Identification?' He rumbled the word. 'Damnit, I've shown that to the cowboy you have on the door. I suppose he has a permit for that revolver. I've a good mind to report that.'

'I'm waiting.'

Bate extracted an ID card from his wallet. He dropped it on Tweed's desk. Then he gestured to the small man who had come in with him.

'This is Mervyn Leek, my assistant. Show the man your ID, Merv. He has a bureaucratic mind.'

Newman stared at the small man. No more than five feet six tall, he was dwarfed by his superior. If anything, Newman disliked the look of Leek even more than he did of Bate. He had shifty grey eyes and a perpetual smile, which was more a smirk. He had a pale face, his eyes hooded frequently, his manner was deferential to the point of creeping. His voice was public school and quiet, in contrast to Bate's grating delivery.

'I'm sure you will wish to see my ID also,' he said, placing it carefully on the desk. 'It really is a pleasure to meet you, Mr Tweed. I have heard of your great accomplishments in the field. It is an honour.'

'Sit down and shut up, Merv,' ordered Bate.

He had already seated himself, sitting erect in an armchair. Leaning forward, he grabbed hold of the ID card Tweed had examined, then exploded.

'I did say there were too many people here.'

'I heard you the first time,' Tweed replied mildly. 'No one is leaving. They are part of the core of my organization.'

49

'Then be it on your own head. We're taking over here. Dartmoor. Know what I mean? We'll need an office where Mervyn can work on the premises. Everything about Dartmoor passes through his hands. You're out of that neck in the woods. Got it?'

'For one thing we don't have any office space available.'

'I don't think you understand the situation. I have a document here from the Minister of General Security. Be pleased to read it,' he said, handing over a large sheet of paper folded once.

'The Prince,' Newman said half aloud.

'What?' Bate swung round to gaze at Newman. 'For your information the Minister intensely dislikes that insulting nickname coined by the press.'

'Poor old thing,' Newman remarked, staring straight at Bate.

'This document has no meaning to me,' Tweed said, handing it back.

'It gives full authorization for Special Branch to take over all general security matters,' Bate said furiously.

'But it doesn't make any mention of the SIS . . .'

'That can be remedied,' Bate almost shouted.

'Are you sure about that?'

For once Bate looked uncertain. He made a great performance of refolding the document before returning it to his pocket. Then he took a deep breath.

'You can rest assured that I shall be back.'

'Perhaps,' Leek began, looking more sneaky than ever, 'I could be permitted to wait here while Mr Bate regularizes the situation. I have no doubt you could park me in a cubbyhole.'

'When Bate leaves, you leave. And I've run out of the amount of time I can devote to both of you. I would appreciate it if you left now.' Tweed stood up. 'We are rather busy.'

Paula came in. She stopped with the door still half open. Two heads swung round to stare at her.

'Who is this?' demanded Bate.

'The tea lady,' Monica called out.

Paula withdrew, closing the door quietly. Bate obviously felt compelled to stand up. Leek, like a marionette, followed suit. Everyone could see Bate was having trouble controlling his temper. He looked even less pleased when Tweed asked him his question.

'On the odd occasion previously when I've communicated with Special Branch I've always dealt with the head of your outfit, Caspar Pardoe. Where is he?'

'I've taken over from him for the time being. Pardoe is overseas, taking a rest.'

'Whereabouts overseas?'

'I really have not the slightest idea. Nor have I any interest in the wanderings of Pardoe. I am in charge now.'

'Don't have a breakdown,' Tweed said with the ghost of a smile.

'I really can't imagine why you have a newspaper correspondent sitting in on a conference like this,' Bate exclaimed, glaring at Newman. 'Sloppy security, in my book.'

'Then get another book,' Tweed suggested amiably. 'Newman was vetted years ago and, as I'm sure you do know, works closely with me on difficult cases.'

'The sooner Merv is installed here the better, I'd say.'

'I had the impression you were on your way out, Bate.'

'Oh, I'm going. I shall give the Minister a full report of the state of affairs I found here. He won't be best pleased.'

'Poor old thing,' Newman repeated.

'If you ever want to see me again,' Tweed said,

51

'please be so good as to phone and make an appointment.'

Bate transferred his glare from Newman to Tweed. Opening his mouth, he thought better of what he'd been going to say, closed it again and left. Leek turned at the door, smirked all round, bobbed his head, followed his lord and master.

Paula returned almost at once, hurrying into the room. She let out her breath.

'I hope you don't mind, Tweed, but I was listening outside the door. What a ghastly couple. The tall and the short. Almost more than Bate, I detested Leek – a real creep.' She went back to her desk, sat down. 'Well, we won't have to worry about them any more.'

'You could be wrong there,' Tweed warned.

'Why do you say that?'

'The arrival of the present top man from Special Branch shows how seriously the government is taking the Appledore incident. I'm sure Harrington discussed this with the Cabinet before he sent in his two lapdogs to us. On top of that the French are taking an interest.'

He told them about his strange conversation with Lasalle, the unique change in attitude on the part of his old friend. He was repeating the story for the sake of Paula, who had been absent earlier. Under her arm she carried a large blue folder of the type used by Richard, the artist, expert at creating Identikits.

'Get me the PM on the phone, please, Monica,' Tweed went on. 'I want an appointment with him later today.'

Sam Sneed walked quickly along Fleet Street, his deer-stalker hat perched at a jaunty angle. He had left the headquarters of the *Daily Nation* half an hour earlier. En route he had called in at his bank, had paid in £2,000 in cash into his account. This was the money he had been handed in an envelope by the chauffeur of the Daimler when he'd handed over the original video outside Appledore.

His gnomelike head was bent forward and he felt like dancing. He was on his way to his favourite London pub to celebrate. At this hour in the late morning it would have just opened, so he was counting on it being quiet. He could sit by himself with a beer in front of him, dwelling on his victory. At long last he was on the escalator, moving up.

He had a copy of the newspaper tucked firmly under his arm. Sneed couldn't read his long article again too many times. On the front page – with his byline. The editor had been pleased, had even hinted he was thinking of taking Sneed on the permanent staff.

'Mr Sneed? Mr Sam Sneed?'

He was being accosted and it annoyed him. He wanted to revel on his own. The voice was cultured. He looked up, studied the man who had stopped in front of him. Late thirties, early forties? Good-looking cove. Yellowish hair, a smile on his clean-shaven face. He was clad in a smart military-style trench coat with wide lapels, and he held a carrier. *Aquascutum* was printed on the carrier.

'What do you want?' Sneed demanded. 'I'm in a hurry.'

'His Lordship – the boss – was pleased with the way you handled your first assignment. A couple of grand for that, which we gave you. How would you like to earn double that amount?'

Double £2,000. Another £4,000? Out of the blue?

'What would I have to do for that?' Sneed asked, his manner more friendly.

'It's a bit public – the two of us standing here in the street. And you're a public figure now. That paper under your arm has a small photograph of you. You'll get people asking for your autograph.'

'Do you think so?'

'Don't forget,' the man in the trench coat grinned, 'charge them a fiver. Now, we need somewhere quiet where I can give you the details. My club is very close. Let's repair to it.'

'I was on my way to my favourite pub.'

'The club will be safer. I have to show you a plan. This way.'

They walked a short distance and then Trenchcoat stopped. Leading off Fleet Street was a narrow alley which turned a corner a short distance inside. Trenchcoat gestured with his gloved hand down the alley.

'After you, sir. The entrance is the door on the left just beyond the corner.'

The adrenalin was pumping inside Sneed as he made his way down the deserted alley. After all these years of living with his unpleasant sister – who paid the rent on the house – he was in the money. He'd buy himself a good car, sell the motorbike, and some good clothes. He turned the corner, looking for a door on his left.

Behind him, Trenchcoat glanced back. No one about. Rounding the corner, he took out a long black wire with wooden pegs at either end. He swung the arc of wire over Sneed's hat down to his throat. Gripping a peg in each hand, he twisted the wire at the back once, tightening it with all his strength. The wire bit deep into Sneed's throat. He gurgled, hands reaching up. Trenchcoat continued tightening the wire, even though Sneed, already dead, had sagged to his knees.

5

Three hours later Tweed returned from Downing Street. He found everyone present who had been in his office earlier. Removing his coat, he looked at Paula.

'You're supposed to be home at your flat in Fulham, resting.'

'I've been there,' she told him with a smile. 'Bob insisted on driving me there as bodyguard. He waited in my sitting room while I had the most glorious hot, then cold, shower. Felt so much better. The Ape had his hands over me – I felt grubby and soiled. Then I had a complete change of clothes and Bob drove me back here. We stopped on the way for a snack. I'm ready for anything now. How did your meeting with the PM go?'

'Very well. He was annoyed when I quoted him the wording of the document Bate shoved at me. Said Courtney Harrington had no authority over the SIS. Situation remains as before – I report only to the PM. And, of course, he knows Harrington is after his job.'

'Any reaction about Appledore?' Newman enquired.

'Yes, he's very worried about the whole business. Strictly between these walls, I think everyone is jumping the gun.'

'Which means?' queried Marler.

'We don't know yet that the sea was poisoned. I used a phone box on the way back to call Professor Saafeld. He has performed the autopsy on the dead fisherman but wouldn't tell me his conclusions. Wants to see me at his place in Holland Park this evening at nine o'clock. He's also called in an expert on fish to dissect the seal – and the fish. You know him, Paula, so you can come with me if you want to.'

'Of course I do. Any chance of my showing you the Identikits of Dr Goslar and Abel the Ape? Richard and I work quickly together.'

'Now would be a good moment. Gather round my desk, everybody.'

'This is Dr Goslar,' said Paula.

They all stared at the charcoal sketch. It showed a small thin man, clean-shaven and with a high forehead. His face was long and he wore rimless glasses. Unpleasant, shrewd eyes gazed out from behind the glasses.

'It's pretty accurate,' Paula told them, 'thanks mostly to the skill of Richard.'

'And your powers of observation,' Newman added. 'I wonder if he always wears a bow tie?'

'Possibly,' said Tweed.

'What was his voice like?' Marler wanted to know.

'Precise,' she replied. 'He speaks perfect English, but with a slight lisp.'

'Does he smoke?' Monica broke in.

'Good question,' Paula responded. 'No, at least not during the short time I saw him. And there were no ash trays in the room, nor any smoke fumes.'

'Everybody got him?' Tweed asked.

Heads nodded and Tweed knew they had all memorized the essentials. Had imagined what he'd look like without glasses or a bow tie, and wearing quite different clothes. Paula removed the sketch and replaced it with another.

'Abel the Ape,' she announced.

'What a horrible menacing creature,' Monica exclaimed. 'He is huge, almost looks like a gorilla.'

'If I met that on a dark night,' Marler commented, 'I'd kick him in the crotch, stick a gun in his thick-lipped mouth -- and then ask questions.'

'Voice?' Tweed queried.

'Growly,' Paula replied. 'Growly, aggressive, hostile. Sure that he can cope physically with almost any man on earth. At least that was my impression.'

'And you heard him called Abel. What about a surname?'

'Nothing. Just Abel.'

'And you heard this Abel call the other man Dr Goslar how many times?'

'At least twice. Quite clearly. In a loud voice.'

'You've done well. Very well, Paula.'

'Now, I think,' she said, gathering up the sketches, 'I'd better get copies made of these for everyone.'

'Including Harry Butler and Pete Nield. Yes, please.'

Tweed waited until she had gone. Then he looked at the others and lowered his voice.

'So, there we are. What do you think?'

'It's a huge step forward,' Newman commented, 'since we now have for the first time a clear idea of what Goslar looks like.'

'Have we? We don't pass on to Paula this part of our conversation. She has tried so hard, endured so much. And, Bob, your memory isn't too good.'

'What do you mean by that?'

'One of Goslar's many tricks, years ago when you and I were tracking him during the Cold War, was to get someone to impersonate him, to use the name Goslar. When whoever it was completed his mission, he usually ended up dead. And on occasion it was a woman who impersonated Goslar. He believes in shooting the messenger.'

Tweed broke off as the phone rang. Monica told him Superintendent Buchanan was on the phone.

'Roy, Tweed here. Anything happening?'

'You could say that. Sam Sneed has just been murdered. It was a brutal job. His body was found in an alley off Fleet Street. Killer used a wire round his neck.

He had been decapitated. The head was missing. Found later inside an Aquascutum carrier along with the wire which did the job. Together with a trench coat spotted with blood. We'll do a DNA test – but my bet is it will turn out to be Sneed's blood.'

'Any clues as to the assassin?'

'None. No witness. Nothing. A very professional job. Imagine what the press will do with this tomorrow – maybe earlier if the *Evening Standard* picks up on it. Must go.'

'Thanks for informing me . . .'

'One more thing. That Inspector Crake at Appledore phoned me. A team has gone over Gargoyle Towers for fingerprints. Not even one print. The place was cleaned out.'

'Which is what I expected. More of Goslar's technique. Bye . . .'

He had just replaced the phone when Paula returned. She sat at her desk, saw his expression, asked if something had happened. He told her about Buchanan's call.

'That's horrible,' she said. She shuddered. 'I feel even more lucky to be alive.'

'As you described it those two men were in a heck of a rush to get away. Lucky, as you said.'

Tweed didn't think he wanted to explain to her the real reason. That she had been left to return to London with her description of the alleged Dr Goslar. There had been no need for Abel to use his name in front of her – unless deliberately.

'Why would they murder Sneed?' she asked.

'I was reminding Bob that Goslar always shoots the messenger when he – or she – has done their job. That way no one can be interrogated and reveal what instructions they were given – even by an invisible Goslar over the phone. Incidentally, I've sent the recording of his phone call down to the boffins in the basement, on the off chance they can recover the real voice.'

'You think they'll manage that?'

'No, I don't. Goslar will have used the most sophisticated voice-changer in the world. But we have to try.'

'So what next?'

'As soon as we can we're going to Paris.'

'We are?'

'So everyone should have their bags packed for the trip. I'll be taking a heavy delegation. Everyone here except Monica, of course, who will hold the fort. Contact Butler and Nield, who will be coming too. Monica, book seats for us on a flight late tomorrow afternoon. Make separate bookings, so it's not obvious we're together, and don't use our real names. Paula and I can travel together.'

'And,' Newman said firmly, 'I want the seat behind you. Also we'll come with you when you visit Professor Saefeld this evening.'

'That's going over the top. It's only Holland Park.'

'It was only Fleet Street where Sneed lost his head.'

Marler had left Park Crescent to visit the East End. He was going to contact some dubious characters he knew to see if anyone had heard a whisper about the murder of Sam Sneed.

'I'll probably have more luck in Paris,' he said when he was going. 'I have a real underground network there . . .'

Earlier Tweed had remarked they needed reinforcements. He'd asked Marler to locate Alf, the Cockney cab-driver with a number of other chums, also cab-drivers. He wanted them to keep cruising past Park Crescent to see if anyone was watching the building.

Paula had been disturbed by his request, to the

extent she had stood up to peer through the heavy net curtains over the windows. She voiced her concern when she sat down again.

'I've never heard you take that precaution before. Are you worried about Dr Goslar? You think we could be under surveillance?'

'I'm not worried, Paula. I'm just not underestimating my ancient adversary. He always operates with a vast organization. He has the resources – all the money he obtained from the Americans and the Russians during the Cold War. Plus the ten million he grabbed from selling his plant in New Jersey. Before he blew it to kingdom come, together with everyone inside.'

'He sounds so incredibly brutal and evil.'

'What we have to remember is he is so very *thorough.*'

The phone rang. Monica looked puzzled when she'd answered it. She asked the caller to repeat the name, then put her hand over the mouthpiece.

'There's a strange woman on the phone. Gave the name Serena Cavendish. No, she won't talk to you, sounds in a rush. She wants you to meet her at Brown's Hotel in the tea room. She said you should be able to pick out her table. She has very dark hair. She also said it was about Appledore . . .'

Tweed travelled in a taxi. Paula had insisted on accompanying him. He'd agreed, provided she kept in the background. Newman had said he would follow them in his car. Tweed decided he hadn't the time to argue with him. On the stairs Newman had encountered Harry Butler and Pete Nield. He had told them to come with him.

Arriving at Brown's, Tweed paid off his taxi and cautiously entered the hotel. The tea room was on his right, shielded from the hall by a thigh-high panelled wall. Above it were windows of thick glass, enabling him to scan the people taking tea. A large number of fashionable women chatted to each other as they consumed the famous and excellent meal.

Paula had picked up a magazine, moving away from Tweed so she stood near the dining room entrance as though waiting for someone. Tweed quickly spotted the striking woman with very black hair. She was sitting by herself facing him, long shapely legs crossed at a table for two. Then he saw something odd.

By himself, with his back to Tweed, sat a man with yellowish hair. In his late thirties, Tweed estimated. Very smartly attired in a blue bird's-eye suit. He sat reading a newspaper, the paper above his eye level. A smart business type entered, looked around, went over to the elegant lady with black hair. He bent down to ask her something. She smiled up at him, shook her head, and he walked on into the second room where they were serving tea.

While this was happening, Yellow Hair lowered his paper slowly to a level where he could gaze across at the glamorous lady during her brief exchange with the business type. Then he slowly elevated the paper to its original position. The head waiter had come out into the lobby. His face lit up in a pleased smile.

'Mr Tweed. How are you, sir? It's a while since we've seen you here.'

'I want you to do me a favour. Discreetly. You see the lady with the black hair? The one sitting by herself.'

'Yes, sir. I don't think she's been here before.'

'This is for you,' Tweed continued, handing over a banknote. 'I want you to be very discreet, as I said a moment ago. Go to her and whisper that I'm waiting here and want her to come out to me. *Whisper*. Get her bill quickly.'

61

'She's already paid, sir.'

'Good. I don't want anyone else in the room to hear you.'

'I'll deal with it now, sir . . .'

Tweed moved swiftly. First he beckoned to the head porter, who had just appeared.

'John, I need a taxi urgently. Now, in fact. If anyone asks where I've gone you don't know.'

'I wouldn't tell them anyway, sir. I'll get on it now . . .'

Tweed looked across at Paula who had heard every word. He shook his head, indicating he didn't want her to come with him. The dark-haired woman wrapped a fur coat round herself, then quickly walked into the lobby. He took her arm gently.

'You are Serena?' he said in a low voice.

'Yes. Serena Cavendish. You're Tweed . . .'

'Excuse the hustle. We're getting out of here quickly. Have tea elsewhere. Get in the cab.'

He saw Newman behind the wheel of his Merc, parked near the cab. Glancing back, he saw no one beyond John, the porter. He dashed to Newman, who had lowered the window.

'Yellow hair, smartly dressed . . .'

Darting back to his own taxi he sat next to Cavendish, who was already inside. He gave the destination to the driver.

'Fortnum's. We're in a hurry.'

'Who isn't these days?' the cabbie responded with a grin.

He moved off immediately. Glancing back through the rear window, Tweed saw Nield jump out of the back seat of the Merc. Paula slipped in to occupy it, next to Butler. What was going on? Then he saw Yellow Hair emerge with brisk steps, his hand up to flag a cab.

At the entrance to Brown's Pete Nield, slim, with a trim moustache and snappily dressed, also had his hand up. He handed John two one-pound coins as the cab pulled in to the kerb.

'I was first. This is my cab,' Yellow Hair snapped in an uppercrust voice.

'Sorry, old man,' Nield responded, his hand on the door's handle, 'but I was just before you.'

'Damned well weren't!'

'Plenty more cabs coming,' Nield said amiably, jumping in and slamming the door.

'Where to, sir?' asked the driver.

'Follow that Merc, please,' Nield whispered. 'There's a fiver in it for you.'

Newman had already driven off after Tweed's taxi. Butler showed Paula the very small camera he had dropped in his lap. She raised an eyebrow.

'Got a pic of Yellow Hair,' Butler told her. 'At least I hope so. I was just snapping him when he looked my way. Camera may have wobbled. Hope for the best.'

Paula reflected again on the contrast between the two men who so often worked together as a team. Harry Butler had no interest in clothes. In his early forties, five feet eight tall, heavily built, he wore a shabby anorak and equally shabby corduroy slacks and his shoes hadn't seen polish in ages. He had thick dark hair in need of a comb and his large face had a stubborn nose and a formidable jaw.

On the other hand Pete Nield took almost as much care of his clothes as Marler. He had a handsome face, rather longish, but like his partner his eyes were quick-moving and missed nothing. As a team they worked together brilliantly and ruthlessly when the occasion demanded it.

'I wonder what all that was about,' mused Newman.

'Incidentally, Yellow Hair got a cab but three cars and a van are now between him and us. Anyone hear where Tweed is going with his femme fatale?'

'Fortnum's,' Paula said promptly.

'Drop you off there, then I'll cruise round the block. No place to park, of course . . .'

Fortnum's restaurant on the top floor was crowded but Tweed managed to obtain a table at the far end. He sat with his back against the wall. It would give him a perfect view of anyone else entering the place.

'Now, why did you want to see me so urgently?' Tweed asked when they had ordered tea.

'Let me just compose myself first. I suppose you're not going to tell me what happened at Brown's?' his guest enquired.

'Had you a bodyguard with you?' Tweed suggested, adjusting his napkin.

'I most certainly had not.'

Tweed swivelled in his chair to give her his full attention. He had noticed when they came in several men had gazed at her with longing. No wonder, he thought. About five feet seven tall, she had a well-rounded figure in a green dress with a slim gold belt. At her throat she wore a Hermès scarf and above it her calm face had a superb bone structure. It was her eyes which held his. Greenish, they exuded intelligence. Her glory was her hair, cut so it hung in a carefully arranged disarray, ending above the collar of her dress. She used her left hand to pull her fur coat more securely on the back of the chair.

'You'll see there's hope for you yet,' she said with a smile.

'Pardon?'

'You were looking at the third finger of my left hand. No ring.'

'I think you ought to tell me, Miss Cavendish—'

'Serena, please.'

'I think you ought to tell me now, Serena,' he said firmly, 'what you wanted to see me about.'

'You'd better look at this.'

From her Gucci handbag she took a neatly folded copy of the *Evening Standard*. He waited patiently while she unfolded it and placed it before him. The huge headline jumped at him.

'POISON SEA' REPORTER MURDERED

He scanned the text quickly. It reported the discovery of the headless body of Sam Sneed, discovered in an alley off Fleet Street. No mention of the fact that the head had been found. Tweed felt sure Buchanan was holding that back in the hope of locating the killer, then tripping him up – using information that had not been published. He handed the paper back to her.

'Very strange,' he commented.

Tea had been served and Serena was eating a sandwich. Tweed sipped from his cup, then looked at her. He gestured towards the newspaper in her lap.

'Could you tell me something?' he asked with a smile. 'How did you get my phone number?'

She shook her head. Using her napkin she wiped her lips delicately. She drank some more tea. He had hoped to catch her off guard but it hadn't worked.

'That's a secret,' she said with a ravishing smile.

'We don't seem to be getting anywhere,' he remarked abruptly.

'Patience, Tweed.' She touched his arm. 'I don't think you've realized it but I'm scared stiff.'

'Why?'

'Because I was involved in the Appledore business.'

'In what way?'

'A Mr Charterhouse asked me to go to Appledore two weeks ago. I had to photograph the whole front, then the sea front further out beyond the estuary – where it flows into the sea. He phoned me at my flat here in London, gave me instructions, said there would be a fee of £3,000. He also said if I'd go to my front door I'd find an envelope with half the fee inside. The balance would be paid as soon as he had the photographs. I went to the front door when his call ended and found thirty £50 notes in an envelope.'

'Posted from where?'

'No postmark. It had obviously been hand delivered while I was on the phone. I'm short of cash, so I drove to Appledore and did the job for him. When I got back another blank envelope – with £1,500 inside it – was lying on the doormat.'

'Mr Charterhouse, did you say? Have you met him?'

'Never. His only communication was the weird phone call.'

'Weird in what way?'

'It didn't sound like a human being at all. More like one of those talking robots you see on TV.'

'And why would he choose you for this assignment, I wonder?'

'You're interrogating me. I can't blame you. I turn up out of nowhere. I can only assume he chose me because I'm a professional photographer. Not all that well known. But I have had lucrative assignments for society weddings, for magazine features. I have a reputation for reliability.'

'And when you'd taken these photos at Appledore how did you deliver them to the elusive Mr Charterhouse?'

'That was weird. I did what he'd told me to do over the phone. Two days later, after I'd developed and printed the pics, I put them in a large plain envelope. Then at exactly 10 p.m. I left the envelope in a phone box in Curzon Street, got back into my car, drove away.'

'Did you see anyone in Curzon Street?'

'Only a man in the phone box as I drove towards it. Later I decided he'd held the box until I arrived. He came out before I reached it, got into a car and drove away.'

'Can you describe him? And the car? Did you note its registration number?'

'Heavens, Tweed, which question first?' She smiled at him invitingly. 'The man who'd occupied the phone box was medium height, wore a dark overcoat and a Borsalino hat. I never saw his face. No one else was about. I did what I was told, dropped the envelope inside the box, got back into my car and drove straight off. I'm a good girl.' She was gazing round the restaurant, which was still busy. 'If you'll excuse me I'm going to the ladies'.'

'One brief question while I remember. Why are you scared stiff? I think that was the phrase you used.'

'Well, wouldn't you be? I did a job in Appledore. Then this Sam Sneed does another job in the same place – and ends up headless.'

Grabbing her coat, she threaded her way through the crowd to the cloakroom. The door was opposite to their table in the far wall. Tweed paid the bill, then sat thinking about her. On their way in, as she had walked in front of him, he had observed not only her elegant movements, but that she walked with a steely tread. Not a woman to scare easily.

After waiting ten minutes he began to worry that she was feeling ill in the cloakroom. He had watched the cloakroom exit but there had been a lot of to-ing and fro-ing. A waitress came up to him.

'Excuse me, sir. A lady asked me to give you this message.'

He took the sealed envelope, sniffed at it. He caught a trace of the perfume she'd been wearing. He opened the envelope, unfolded the sheet of good quality paper. No address at the top. Just the message, written in an educated hand which had character.

Tweed, thank you for the tea. Sorry to leave you.
But I saw someone in the restaurant. Love, Serena.

Now he knew why she had taken her fur coat with her. Standing up, he looked round, then walked at his usual deliberate pace, gazing round all the time. No sign of Yellow Hair. In the open room beyond the elevators he saw Paula, pretending to examine an antique. He went up to her.

'Where is your stunning companion?' she asked.

'She gave me the slip. We'll go down and find Newman and his Merc.'

'What's next?'

'Our appointment with Professor Saafeld in Holland Park this evening. We should know then whether what we saw at Appledore is a storm in a teacup, the result of an oil slick, or something extremely dangerous.'

6

The large house in Holland Park – a small mansion, in fact – was situated back from the road, three storeys high. Tweed and Paula had reached it by opening a tall wrought-iron gate and walking up a very short drive. On either side were rhododendron shrubs which gave Saafeld's house even more privacy. They mounted steps leading up to a massive front door, flanked by ancient lanterns which gave illumination.

'It's very quiet here,' Paula commented. 'I remember thinking that when we were last here.'

Tweed was pressing digits in a box attached to the wall. Then he waited. Paula commented on the amount of security. Floodlights, operated by sensors, had come on, blazing down on them. Normally she would have been facing the small garden, checking their safety. But she knew Pete Nield, who had followed them in, was hiding somewhere in the shrubs. Newman was in the road, standing behind his Merc. She had no idea where Butler had disappeared to.

A Judas flap in the door slid aside briefly, then closed. They next heard someone turning keys in the single Chubb and two Banham locks. The door swung inwards and a large man told them to enter. Once inside, in a small hall paved with a woodblock floor, the door was closed, the locks turned.

Charles Saafeld was an imposing figure. Taller than Tweed, he was wearing a white smock buttoned to the neck. His build suggested a bon vivant, fond of his food and wine, which Tweed knew to be the case. In his sixties, his round, plump face had a pinkish complexion and he exuded an air of authority. He looked at Paula over his half-moon glasses.

'How are you? You look fit. I recall you're not squeamish. Welcome to the Chamber of Horrors. Let's get on with it.' He looked at Tweed. 'Something very odd here.'

He spoke in staccato bursts. His manner was courteous but he didn't like wasting time. His movements were quick and he led them briskly to a slablike door at the rear of the hall. His right hand started tapping digits in a box similar to the one outside the front door.

'You have a lot of extra security since I was last here,' Paula remarked. 'And why "Chamber of Horrors"?'

'Phrase used once by a tabloid paper. Cranks had the idea I was experimenting on corpses. Too many idle people with crackpot notions. Down we go. Mind the steps. Hold on to the rail.'

The slab had opened. Saafeld led the way, followed by Paula and Tweed, down into the large basement, a very large room, temperature-controlled. At first glance it looked like a laboratory. A system of perspex pipes ran across the ceiling, illuminated by fluorescent tubes. From the pipes ran more of the same, attached to chemical retorts and other equipment on white plastic tables. On the far wall Paula saw large metal drawers built into the walls, the containers for bodies.

A small man with beady eyes, agile, with a nut-cracker jaw and also wearing a white smock, looked at the newcomers as though they might be potential specimens.

'This,' said Saafeld, 'is Dr Fischer, expert on all forms of life inhabiting the seas and rivers. No pun on his name.'

'The number of times idiots have made that pun,' Fischer said, lips pursed.

'We'll start with the dead fisherman,' Saafeld continued. 'A chap called Gravely, so Roy Buchanan tells me. Again, no pun. I've completed the autopsy. Gather he fell overboard from a fishing vessel. He was dead before he reached the water – or the moment he did so.'

'Heart attack?' Tweed queried.

'Definitely not. He stopped breathing. Lack of oxygen.'

'I assumed he'd drowned,' Paula ventured.

'Definitely not. No water in the lungs. The only conclusion I've come to is he was asphyxiated – suffocated, if you like. No oxygen.'

'Strangled?' Tweed suggested.

'Definitely not. No such marks on the neck.'

'I don't understand,' said Tweed.

'Join the club. We don't either. Won't show you the corpse. Might spoil your dinner. I've removed several organs for fresh examination. Don't expect to find anything more. Listen to Fischer. You still won't understand.'

They moved further into the basement. Fischer was standing by another table. It held tanks of fish swimming around and canisters of transparent liquid. Paula thought she recognized them as the canisters used at Appledore to take samples of the sea.

'If you don't grasp something I've said, tell me,' Fischer began, addressing his remarks to Paula. 'I'll rephrase what I've said. It's complicated, but I'll try and keep it simple. You know how fish breathe?'

'Through their gills.'

'Correct. A fish has no lungs. It breathes through what we call gills, a complex system for filtering oxygen out of the water. There's only a small amount of oxygen in the sea – far less than on land. That's all they need to survive. Put a fish on the beach and it expires – even though it's surrounded by huge amounts of oxygen. The gills can't cope, don't work. So the fish dies.'

'Buchanan,' Saafeld interjected, 'told me they've found tons of dead fish at Appledore. So many they've used giant mechanical scoops to clear the beach.'

'Did you understand me so far?' demanded Fischer, obviously annoyed at being interrupted.

'Yes,' said Tweed and Paula together.

'In other words,' Fischer went on in his lecturer's

manner, 'the fish were asphyxiated. No oxygen at all in the sea.'

'Like the fisherman,' Tweed suggested.

'Yes and no. As I've explained, the breathing systems of men and fish are very different. Now we come to the seal, which makes everything even more mysterious. I've carried out an autopsy, let us say . . .' Fischer's eyes kept staring at Paula's, then at Tweed's. As though he was checking their concentration to make sure they understood. 'It was quite a job but I've done it.'

'You know how the seal died?' asked Tweed.

'I know *why* it died, which is a different matter. First, you'd better know how seals function, how they breathe. Unlike fish, seals have lungs. Also, again unlike fish, they are covered with fur and have a system circulating warm blood. Their lungs give them the ability to store oxygen which they can use over a period of time. A kind of reserve supply, if you like. Which is why they can exist on land. Saafeld, could you tell our visitors the incident Superintendent Buchanan related?'

'There was a witness,' Saafeld began brusquely. 'An inhabitant of Instow, a hamlet on the river shore opposite Appledore. He saw the seal surface, start to climb a rock, then immediately collapse back into the river. That must have been before you and Paula saw it drift ashore,' he explained, turning to Tweed.

'What is the significance of that?' Paula enquired.

'Significant is the word,' Fischer agreed. 'There was not only no oxygen in the water – hence the thousands of dead fish – but there was also no oxygen in the air above the water. That is why the seal died instantly – it came up to replenish its oxygen supply in its lungs and there wasn't any.'

'Which I find disturbing,' Saafeld interjected. 'I think it's time to show them your experiment, Fischer.'

'It's fortunate,' Fischer said, 'that someone thought

of taking water specimens as the dead specimens came ashore – and then a bit later when the tide turned. You see what is on this table.'

'Tanks of fish – a lot I don't recognize, and herring. Then two canisters which look like the ones used at Appledore to collect water,' Paula said.

'Correct.' Fischer picked up a transparent scoop with a long handle and a mesh cap which he opened by pressing a trigger. 'Your two canisters,' he went on, moving down the bench.

'Labelled, for some reason,' Paula noted.

'For a good reason,' Fischer told her. 'This one contains water taken after the tide turned. Now watch.'

He used the scoop to dip in the large tank and capture a herring. He quickly held the scoop over the canister, used the trigger to lift the mesh lid, dropped the contents into the canister. The fish began swimming rapidly inside the canister, touching the transparent walls, swimming on.

'Seems quite happy,' Paula commented.

'It's normal environment. Sea water. Now watch what happens when we perform the same experiment with the other canister – which contains water collected as the dead fish were still coming ashore.'

Paula clutched the strap of her shoulder bag more tightly. An atmosphere of tension had suddenly gripped the laboratory. With the same care Fischer used another scoop to capture a herring from the large tank. He removed a lid from the second canister, dropped the fish inside quickly, clamped the lid shut. The fish hit the water, struggled for a second, turned over, slowly sank to the bottom.

'Dead as the dodo,' said Fischer. 'The gills tried to take in air – oxygen, dissolved in the sea – and there wasn't any. Almost instantaneous death.'

'That's horrible,' exclaimed Paula.

'I think,' Saafeld said decisively, 'you've had enough of the unfamiliar atmosphere of a laboratory. We'll repair back up to the hall. I'll be back, Fischer . . .'

'I don't like what you showed us,' Tweed said when Saafeld had closed the slab door and they stood in the hall.

'You're going to like it even less. There's something else.'

Reaching inside his pocket, he brought out a transparent sample envelope of the type used by the police. He opened his hand and inside the envelope Paula saw a tiny transparent perspex cylinder. She estimated it was no more than a quarter of an inch in diameter, hardly more than half an inch in height. She had never seen such a small container.

'This was discovered, obviously washed ashore, among a mess of dead fish by some policeman at Appledore. Crake, I think his name was. Buchanan had it flown to him in London, then loaned it to me – knowing you were coming.'

'You think the poison was emptied out of that container?' suggested Paula.

'Don't use the word poison. Agent is the word,' Saafeld told her.

'We heard a powerboat disappearing out to sea,' Tweed recalled. 'Someone aboard could have emptied the contents of that tiny phial into the sea. Possible?'

'I'm a scientist,' Saafeld said abruptly. 'I never speculate.'

'If enough of this agent filled one of those canisters down in the lab,' Tweed mused, 'then it was introduced into the water supply of a country, what would be the effect?'

'Millions and millions would die, I suppose,' Saafeld replied. 'There you go, catching me on the wrong foot – speculating.'

'Any chance of identifying the agent which caused the havoc?'

'I would have you know – ' Saafeld gazed at Tweed grimly – 'we have analysed for hours and hours. Using every known test to identify the agent. The result? Nothing.'

'Goslar has invented the ultimate weapon of war,' Tweed said half to himself. He looked at Saafeld. 'If you do identify the agent I'm sure you'll phone me. If I'm away speak to Monica. Use just one word. *Breakthrough.*'

'Don't hold your breath for that call.'

7

The next development in the growing crisis hit Tweed the moment he walked into his office, followed by Paula, Newman, Butler and Nield.

'You'll be pleased,' Monica greeted him as he took off his coat.

'Please me, then.'

'While you were out this evening Cord Dillon phoned. To tell you he'll be aboard a flight from the US of A tomorrow. He expects to arrive here before lunch. He also emphasized it was a private visit, and he'd appreciate it if you kept it that way.'

'I see,' Tweed replied, looking anything but pleased as he relaxed in his chair.

'You don't look very happy,' Paula commented. 'The Deputy Director of the CIA is an old pal of yours. Again, I'm confused. What is happening?'

'What is happening,' Tweed said grimly, 'is Goslar is orchestrating his master plan step by step. I've said before, he really is a brilliant planner.'

'Explanation, please,' Paula pressed.

'First – if she was telling the truth at Fortnum's – he organizes Serena Cavendish to go down and photograph the whole scene of his future action from the shore. Because he knows he'll only see it from the sea when he arrives in his powerboat. That is a guess.'

'Why lure you there?'

'Two reasons. One, he knows I'll bring in some heavy talent from the police. Buchanan will swiftly inform the Home Secretary who, in his turn, will inform the Cabinet. A menacing cat among the pigeons. Two, he's confident he'll beat me again, as he did all those years ago. That should ruin my career. It's personal. That's just the beginning of the orchestration.'

'I'm all ears – that's why I look so funny,' she said, deliberately trying to reduce the teasion building up in the office. 'Now, go on.'

'His next move – a key one – is to hire Sam Sneed to video what happened. The original is handed to an emissary from a powerful and hostile state which is now controlled by fundamentalist Muslims. He'll also have had a copy of the *Daily Nation* sent to the head of that state by a fast international carrier.'

'Why?' asked Newman.

'I'll come to that later. Next he shoots the messenger, his normal technique. In this case Sam Sneed, who ends up decapitated. He knows this will hit the press. The *Evening Standard*, as you've now all seen, has splashed the story. Naturally – it's sensational news. The momentum of Goslar's orchestration balloons.'

'But, as Bob asked, why?' enquired Paula.

'All in good time. René Lasalle phones me from an outside call box, warns me the Élysée is interested. The President of France, no less. My bet is one of Sneed's copies of that video was sent to the Élysée. He'll have seen the *Daily Nation* too.'

'I won't say "why" again,' Paula promised.

'Don't. Now we hear Cord Dillon is en route to see me. With a request that his visit be kept quiet. Echoes of Lasalle asking me not to report his phone call. So I'm sure another video was sent by fast international carrier to the Oval Office. For the President of the United States. For all I know another one went to Berlin and to Tokyo. No, not to Tokyo – they haven't got the money.'

'The money?' Newman queried.

'Yes, the money. Goslar is going to make a killing – no pun intended, as Saafeld would say. The money to buy this ultimate weapon which makes the hydrogen bomb passé.'

There was a heavy silence in the room as they absorbed what Tweed had said. He asked Monica to be kind enough to fetch him something to eat and drink from the nearby all-night delicatessen. Tweed took off his hornrims, extracted a clean folded handkerchief from his pocket, polished them, replaced them on the bridge of his nose. Then he leaned forward, hands clasped on his desk.

'Whichever country buys that hideous weapon is automatically the leading power on the planet. It can threaten larger states, bend them to its will. In short, rule the world. We do have rather a lot on our plate.'

'What's the next move?' Newman wanted to know.

'I have no idea. Yet . . .'

As he spoke the door opened and Marler walked in. Paula blinked. For a moment she didn't recognize him. On the bridge of his nose was perched a strange pair of glasses, with large squarish lenses and thin rims. They were pushed back close to his eyes, gave him an aggressive look, menacing. He was clad in a foreign-looking anorak, zipped up to the neck, foreign-looking slacks and shoes.

'What on earth have you been up to?' Paula asked.

'Been to Paris and back, haven't I? Caught a flight out by the skin of my teeth. Same thing coming back. Hired a car at Charles de Gaulle. Drove French drivers mad as I cut them off, missed others by inches. Their cry, *Merde!*, *Merde!* must have been heard in Marseilles.'

'The object of this exercise?' Tweed demanded.

'To visit my top contact in Paris. A jewel in the underworld. You have to meet him very soon. You're almost as fluent in French as I am. These damned glasses.' He took them off, sighed with relief, looked at Paula. 'The latest thing – made of Flexon, very flexible metal frames. This pair is Calvin Klein. I got them to put plain glass in quickly. Do that a lot, I gather. Frenchmen find they make girls swoon into their arms.'

'This contact you met,' Tweed said impatiently. 'He gave you information?'

'Yes and no. He insists on meeting the top man. Which is why you have to go and see him.'

'We're going to Paris – after I've met Cord Dillon, who is flying over to see me tomorrow. Unofficially. So officially he never came to London. Now, this contact. What is his name? What does he do? Where will I meet him?'

'That's wicked of you,' Marler said with mock severity. 'You do know I keep their identities secret – all my contacts, I mean.'

'But if I'm meeting him I'll know who he is, where he is.'

'True.' Marler paused, then walked over to the wall close to Paula, turned, leaned against it. 'You remember the Île de la Cité, of course?'

'Of course. We could have a meal at that marvellous Restaurant Paul on the Place Dauphine. Superb food. Go on.'

'You'll also remember the footbridge linking Cité to another island in the Seine – the Isle St-Louis.'

'Yes. Do get on with it.'

'My contact's bookshop is in a side street off the Rue St-Louis en Île.'

'Name of contact?'

'You're interrogating me.'

'He's in that mood,' Paula commented.

'Vallade. Étienne Vallade. He deals in very rare books. That gives him entreé to some pretty high-up people in the security services – and the government. But I emphasize he'll only talk to you.'

'Did you mention the name Goslar?'

'I did. That's when he closed down. He looked frightened. He then said – I quote him, "I'll only discuss this with your chief, Tweed." '

'That's interesting. He knows my name.'

'I told you he was a jewel.'

'Now, Marler,' Tweed said, his tone serious, 'I'd better brief you on everything that's happened so far. The others will have to put up with hearing it twice – but it may hammer it into their heads. The sequence is important. But first I'll jump forward and tell you about our meeting with Professor Saafeld . . .'

Marler lit a king-size as he continued leaning against the wall. His manner suggested he was hardly listening but Tweed knew he was memorizing every word.

'So,' Tweed eventually concluded, 'you've heard about Saafeld and Fischer, and my analysis of the brilliant way Goslar has orchestrated this business. One more thing – ' he became very emphatic, his eyes moving from one member of his team to another – 'this is going to be the most dangerous assignment we have ever undertaken. We are up against Goslar and his vast organization, but on top of that I'm sure Bate and his

Special Branch, a rough lot, will appear on the scene as rivals sooner or later. And, as though that isn't enough, the French security services, their police and Lord knows who else over there are the enemy.'

'And all of them after the Holy Grail,' Marler remarked. '"The Holy Grail" – not really a good description of the most devilish weapon ever devised.'

'We need more people,' Paula said quietly. 'I think that has already been said.'

As though on cue, the door opened and the Director, Howard, sailed into the room. A plump-faced man, over six feet tall, he had a build which suggested he liked gourmet food and wine – and didn't hesitate to indulge in what he liked. He had a lordly manner and an upper-crust voice.

'Great news for you, Tweed,' he announced as he occupied an armchair and placed his right leg over the arm. 'I have reinforcements. Two chaps – both out of the top drawer. I'm sure someone will have heard of the first one. Captain Alan Burgoyne, ex-military intelligence. Gulf War and all that.'

'I've heard of him,' said Newman. 'What he found out in Iraq changed the whole Allied strategy.'

'Ah!' Howard swung round the face Newman. 'The filthy rich, world-famous international correspondent. Expect a wallah like you to get the message.'

'A wallah like me reported the Gulf War,' Newman retorted with an expression of distaste as he gazed back at the Director.

Howard, in his sixties, had greying hair, was clean-shaven and, as always, impeccably – expensively – dressed. He wore a blue Chester Barrie pin-striped suit from Harrods, a cream shirt, blue Chanel tie and gleaming black shoes.

'Burgoyne has got fed up with the army, retired recently of his own volition.'

'Probably,' drawled Marler, 'got fed up with taking crackpot instructions from superior officers with plummy voices. The type that always sports the old school tie.'

Howard frowned, stared hard at Marler, as though he didn't like the description. Marler transferred his king-size to his left hand, gave Howard a mock salute with his right, grinned.

'Despite his record,' Tweed broke in quickly, 'I can't take him on until he's been thoroughly vetted.'

'Already done, old chap,' Howard assured him. 'By myself. And I really put him through the hoops. Then checked independently. Isn't that the way you'd have proceeded?'

'Something like that.'

'Come on, boys and girls,' Howard protested. 'Show us a bit of enthusiasm. I've pulled off a coup . . .'

'I'm not a girl any more,' Paula said icily. 'I'm thirtysomething, in case you'd forgotten.'

'Oh, my dear,' Howard faced her, 'I wasn't referring to you. Just a mode of expression. I know you went through hell in Paris. You do have all my sympathy.'

'Ancient history,' she said.

'And who is the other candidate?' Tweed asked.

'Candidate?' Howard was indignant. 'I've taken him on.'

'I haven't. Not yet. Who is he?'

'Evan Tarnwalk. From Special Branch. He resigned.'

'This sounds very tricky,' Tweed warned. 'Why did he resign?'

'Because he couldn't stand Bate any longer. No one can stand Bate. Swaggering around like a company sergeant-major, bullying his way to the top, stabbing subordinates in the back if they look like rivals.'

'I think you're going to say he had to be vetted to join Special Branch. That won't do for me. We'll have to do our own vetting.'

'Already done. Again by myself personally. You don't think I'd just accept the chap at face value, do you?'

'I'll have to talk to him.'

'He's a wizard at disguises,' Howard snapped.

'Then maybe we won't recognize him at a vital moment,' Newman suggested with a straight face.

'*God in Heaven!*' Howard exploded. 'Is that supposed to be funny?' He glanced at Paula. 'Do excuse me, my dear.'

And I wish you'd shut up callling me 'my dear', Paula thought.

'What other qualifications does this Tarnwalk possess?' Tweed enquired.

'He's a wonderful tracker. Can follow a target for hours without being spotted. Hence his flair for disguises.'

Howard turned to look at Newman, ready for another comment. Newman, studying a file, didn't look up. Tweed pursed his lips, then stretched his arms. He could take only so much of Howard.

'Where are these two candidates?'

'Alan Burgoyne is coming to see me in about an hour. Shall I send him down to you?'

'Phone me first. I may be up to my eyes in something.'

'Some people don't get any thanks for what they do,' Howard said resentfully and left the room.

'There,' said Monica, 'you've spoilt his surprise. Now he's disgruntled.'

'I'll thank him when I've seen them. Ever met this Burgoyne, Bob?'

'He was always elusive. Probably part of the secret of his success. Because successes he certainly had. And no, we've never met.'

Tweed looked at Butler and Nield. Ever since they

had sat down neither had said a word. Butler had listened to Howard without showing any reaction. Several times Nield had raised his eyes to the ceiling, as though to ask how much longer they had to stand Howard prattling on.

'What do both of you think of what Howard told us?' Tweed asked.

'I'll reserve judgement until I've seen them. Takes a long time to get a new addition to merge into the team.'

'Me too,' said the reserved Butler.

Tweed knew they had hit the nail on the head. Everyone in the room knew how the others would react in a dangerous situation. There were times when their swift reaction would save the lives of the other members – or even their own lives. Familiarity and trust were the key words.

'Tweed,' Paula said suddenly, 'I haven't had the chance till now. But I can tell you something about the mysterious Serena.'

'You can?' Tweed concealed his surprise. 'I'm very interested in any light you can cast on her background.'

'I'm going back to my teens, when I was a wild young thing. Only up to a point,' she emphasized. 'Lots of parties, in London and out in the country at mansions owned by aristocrats and dubious self-made men. There were coteries, groups of girls who went around together.'

'Did these coteries mingle with each other?'

'Not on your life. Sounds cliquey but that's the way it was. The Cavendish sisters were leading lights, but not in my crowd.'

'Sisters? Where is the other one now?' Tweed enquired, relaxing in his chair.

'No longer with us, I'm afraid. Serena and Davina were very much alike in appearance. Not twins, but one could pass for the other. They were devils. They used to wear each other's clothes, makeup, then one would go out with the other's boyfriend. The boyfriend rarely caught on he was taking out the sister. They were careful – no intimacy. Just for laughs.'

'Tell me about Davina.'

'She's dead, I'm afraid. She was the clever one. A brilliant mind. Had come down from university with a double first. In science and biology. It was a tragedy when she died.'

'How did it happen?'

'She was driving a sports car by herself in the country. In the middle of the night. She liked to ram her foot down. On a lonely bend she collided with a heavy truck. Her face was badly smashed up. She died instantly. Serena, who had gone to meet her, saw it happen.' Paula paused, shivered. 'Must have been terrible for Serena – and no one else was about. They never did find the driver of the truck. She's buried at Steeple Hampton in Hampshire. Serena was so upset she left the country, disappeared for years.'

'How long ago would this be?' Tweed asked quietly.

'Oh, quite a few years ago. I'm not sure how many.'

'And her parents?'

'Both died when the girls were in their early teens. Ironic. The parents also died in a car smash.'

'Anything more about Serena?'

'Somewhere abroad she took up photography, became good at it. I don't want you to get the impression Serena was dim. She wasn't. It was just that Davina was so brilliant. Her tutor once said she was well on her way to becoming one of the world's really great scientists.'

'You knew either of them – or both?'

'No, we never met. They were in a different set. Higher up the social ladder than mine.'

'Did the parents leave them money?'

'Not a penny. The father was an inveterate gambler. Left huge debts. A lawyer friend sorted out the estate, found a way to clear the debts. But that left them penniless. A wealthy boy friend of Davina's gave her the money for them to buy a small cottage at Steeple Hampton. That's about all I can tell you.'

'When did Serena surface in this country again?'

'I think it must have been about two years ago. She quickly established herself as a society photographer. Also she has a sparkling personality, which helps. Not a second David Bailey, but very good.'

'You must have seen her while we were having tea in Fortnum's. What was your impression of her?'

'You were quite a distance away, but she seemed animated and full of self-confidence. Very attractive. Wouldn't you agree?'

'Yes.' Tweed looked thoughtful. 'She has most unusual eyes. Several times I had the feeling she was looking straight through me. Slightly disturbing.'

'She was getting to you,' Paula said with a warm smile.

'And I think,' Tweed decided, 'it's time you went home. But not by yourself. Newman can drive you.'

'I don't think that's necessary.'

'Have you forgotten Sam Sneed so quickly?' Tweed asked ominously.

'It would mean leaving my car here,' she protested.

'I'll drive that back behind Newman,' Butler said. 'Just give me a tick to collect my kit. Never travel without it if I can help it.'

'His kit?' Paula queried when Butler left the room.

'He is an explosives expert,' Newman reminded her.

Butler parked her car behind Newman's Merc when they arrived at her flat, the upper storey of a small

85

house in a mews off Fulham Road. Paula jumped out, with Newman and Butler close at her heels. She held the door key in her hand as she mounted the outside staircase which led to her flat.

'Don't insert that key,' Butler said roughly. 'Both of you go back to the car while I check this place out.'

'I'm not going back,' said Paula. 'I'm dying to get inside.'

Butler pushed in front of her. He looked at the front door, which had a Banham lock. Then he ran delicate fingers round the top and sides of the door. His expression became grim.

'Go back to the car, both of you. Don't argue. Stay there until I fetch you. I may be a while.'

From the car they watched Butler in the distance. Then they saw him disappear round the side. They sat chatting for over half an hour. Newman lit a cigarette. Butler had not reappeared. The next thing they knew was a heavy metal van pulling up beside them and two men in protective apparel running out to the house.

'That's the bomb squad from Park Crescent,' Paula said. 'I can't make out what's going on. The two men who have arrived are carrying a heavy metal box . . .'

'Just leave it to Harry. He knows what he's doing,' Newman assured her.

A few minutes later the front door opened, the two men came out carrying the metal box between them. Reaching the van, they took it to the rear doors, slid the box inside, locked the doors and drove off. Butler appeared, carrying his kit, walked to the car as Newman lowered the window.

'What on earth is happening?' Paula demanded.

'I'll tell you.' Butler bent closer to her. 'I think you said you were dying to get inside. That's what would have happened – you'd have died. The moment you turned your key a huge bomb planted behind the door would have detonated. It would have wrecked the house – and bits of what was left of you would probably have ended up on the far side of the street. I'm staying to double-check. Then I'll drive back to Park Crescent.'

'We'd better go now,' Newman said. 'Tweed will want to know about this.'

8

'What's happening to my bomb?' Paula asked, smiling ruefully as she gazed at Tweed.

'Your bomb,' Tweed informed her from behind his desk, 'will now be clear of London. The A3 will be quiet at this hour. They are taking it to the training mansion in Surrey.'

'I imagine they'll dismantle it there.'

'Harry phoned me while Bob was driving you back here. They will photograph the mechanism thoroughly, but no attempt will be made to dismantle it. It's an entirely new and sophisticated device. Trust Goslar to come up with an advanced variety. After it's been photographed it will be detonated in the quarry. Probably bring down half the rock face, according to Harry.'

'You'll tell Buchanan, I imagine.'

'Only after the thing's been detonated. Roy will be furious, but at least I'll send him copies of the photos – for his own Bomb Squad people to browse over.' He looked up as the door opened. 'Enter Marler and Pete Nield . . .'

Tweed quickly told them about what had happened at Paula's flat. Marler gave a slow whistle, went to Paula, squeezed her arm affectionately.

'You lead a charmed life.'

'It's my virtuous habits,' she said with another smile.

'Now, Nield,' Tweed began, 'have there been any watchers outside our building today?'

'There have,' Nield told him. 'Marler can tell you.'

'We've just come in from having a chat with Alf of the East End mob,' Marler reported. 'Alf and his buddies in their cabs have been patrolling the area at intervals. They caught some fish.'

'Tell me.'

'Early this afternoon Alf spotted a watcher. English chap, well dressed, hanging around and pretending to read a newspaper. The second time round, half an hour later, the watcher was still there. Alf pulled up, told him there'd been a lot of burglaries round here, that he'd had time to read his paper three times over, so he was informing the police. Chap swore at him foully, walked off.'

'Then there was another of them,' Nield said. 'After dark in early evening. Same technique – the watcher leaning against a wall, also pretending to read a paper. English, again smartly dressed. Bill, one of Alf's pals, saw him off.'

'And now?'

'Nobody. Marler and I have just toured round. Coast is clear.'

'Interesting,' Tweed mused, 'that he uses smartly turned out Englishmen. Typical of Goslar not to employ scruffs. I wonder where he gets them from? Private detective agencies? I think not.'

'Alf's guess,' Marler explained, 'is the watchers are men on drugs. Cocaine, probably. His chap was jittery, as though in need of his next fix.'

'Sounds likely. That type needs a constant supply of money – and Goslar was always generous with cash for services rendered. Until he had them eliminated.'

'I've been wondering about that,' Paula said. 'That business of Goslar always shooting the messenger.

Maybe I was a messenger of a sort. I brought back the description of Goslar.'

'Paula, you brought back the description of a man who called himself Goslar – or rather Abel did. If you'd been wiped out by that bomb I might have thought your description was accurate. Or that you'd been killed so you couldn't describe him. But he knows me – would assume you'd come straight here to describe him.'

'Are you saying that man in rimless glasses wasn't Goslar?'

'I'm sure it wasn't.'

'What a diabolical mind he has.'

'Well, we are dealing with the Devil himself. Oh, Monica, re-book us all on the latest flight to Paris tomorrow. Late so I can see Cord Dillon first.'

'And I'll be watching over you,' Newman said firmly.

'Then,' Tweed continued, 'book us rooms at the Ritz in Paris – in our real names. I don't want it to appear we're together when we arrive at the hotel.'

'Then,' Paula suggested, 'I'd better take turns with Monica. She books in some of us, I book in the rest.'

'Clever idea,' Tweed agreed.

'Could you tell us why we're going to Paris?' she enquired. 'I know—'

'Three things,' Tweed interjected. 'First, I want us when we arrive to go by hired car straight to La Défense. You will be able to identify the building where those thugs held you?'

'Absolutely!'

'Second, we visit Marler's contact, Vallade, rare-book dealer on the Île St-Louis.'

'Take Paula in with you,' Marler advised. 'I'll be there. Vallade may not be as young as he once was – he is still susceptible to attractive women.'

'Thank you. Third, I want a brief word with Lasalle about something.'

'Lasalle!' Paula exclaimed. 'From what you said, at present he won't give you the time of day.'

'René and I go back a long time. I think I can persuade him to tell me what I'm after. So we'll be busy in that beautiful city.'

The phone rang. Monica listened briefly, then looked at Tweed. She was grinning.

'You've got a treat. Howard says he has Captain Alan Burgoyne with him, that he could see you now.'

'Wheel him in, I suppose.'

Paula stared at the man who entered the room, her interest aroused at once. Burgoyne was of medium height, and muscular – which showed in his face and hands. In his forties, she guessed. Athletic, with a spring in his tread, and a strong face with a hint of humour in his expression. The moment he entered his clever blue eyes had scanned everyone in the room. Paula decided he already had a mental picture of everyone present.

He wore a camouflage jacket and his beige slacks had a razor-edged crease. His well-polished brown shoes had thick rubber soles. He would move as silently as a cat, she thought. Burgoyne looked at Paula, slapped his jacket twice with a tanned hand.

'Excuse this. Makes me look a bit like a thug, which I suppose I am. But there are a lot of them about these days.' He smiled at her as he spoke. 'Helps me to merge with the crowd. Which is the general idea, said he hopefully.'

'Do please sit down,' said Tweed, his tone neutral.

'Thank you. I guess you are Tweed.'

'Yes. What do we call you? Here we're on first-name terms.'

'Not Alan, please,' Burgoyne said. 'Never liked the name. Why not call me Chance – my nickname in the army.'

'Why Chance?' asked Paula.

'They all used to call me that.' He swivelled round to look again at Paula. 'Because I took chances a lot. Now please don't get the wrong impression. By chance I mean taking a coldly calculated risk – after weighing up the odds.'

'From your track record you weighed them up well,' Tweed remarked.

'I know a general who wouldn't agree. A stuffed shirt back at HQ. Never seen a bullet fired in anger. If you do decide to take me on, there'll be a document to sign, I imagine.'

'You've signed the Official Secrets Act at some time?'

'I have.' Burgoyne looked at Newman, grinned. 'I can recite the Official Secrets Act backwards – and it makes more sense that way.'

'You could be right.' Newman smiled back. 'We don't go in for a load of bumf here.'

Paula was watching Burgoyne closely. She liked his remark, 'If you do decide to take me on.' She detected plenty of self-confidence – but not a trace of arrogance. Burgoyne looked round at everybody again, meeting their gaze eye to eye. Behind his back Monica held up a piece of paper. On it she had scrawled, 'Paris?'

Tweed nodded. Then he stared at Burgoyne, his expression very serious. He spoke quietly.

'Chance, is there someone at the MoD I can talk to about you?'

'Colonel Bernard Gerrard. Don't expect him to be too complimentary about me.'

'I know him. I'll give him a call. Pack a small bag. And be ready here in the morning for a possible departure tomorrow. Now I suggest you return to Howard . . .'

'What do you think?' he asked everyone after Burgoyne had left. 'You're the ones who'd have to work with him.'

'I like him,' Paula said promptly.

'Looks pretty tough to me,' Newman commented.

'We could at least try him out,' Marler suggested.

'I'm not sure,' Butler told Tweed. 'He could be a loose cannon,' he added. Nield agreed.

Tweed asked Monica to see if she could get Colonel Gerrard on the phone. After a few minutes she waved her phone at him and nodded.

'Bernard, Tweed here.'

'Long time no see. I'm sure you want something from me.'

'I was thinking of using Captain Alan Burgoyne sometime. What do you think?'

'He's a wild card.' There was a pause. 'Haven't seen sight or sound of him since he retired over a year ago. Half a mo. I'm forgetting something. Seven months ago he visited Kuwait off his own bat. He went to see what Saddam was up to. Sent me a report by courier. It said Saddam was in the market for the ultimate weapon, whatever that meant. I just filed it.'

'And after that?'

'Heard he'd retired to some village on Dartmoor called Rydford. Which fitted in with his character. His pension is sent to a bank in London.'

'That's all?'

'Tweed, I haven't been very positive. Burgoyne pulled off some amazing coups. The type of thing no one else would have dared attempt. He was particularly daring – and effective – in the Gulf War. Gave us information about Saddam's Presidential Guard which changed our strategy. Can't give you any details.'

'You've heard from him since?'

'Not a dicky bird. Which is what I'd expect. He's a

loner. All right, I'll go overboard – he was a brilliant intelligence officer. Come to think of it, you're the sort of chap he would take orders from – something about your personality. Let's have a drink together one day.'

'We'll do that.'

Tweed sat back in his chair, told the others everything Gerrard had said, word for word. Newman ran a hand through his fair hair.

'I'm impressed. Those MoD types rarely say anything so positive about one of their own.'

'We need extra manpower,' Paula insisted. 'He's dynamic and, I think, very clever.'

'I agree,' Tweed told her. 'I wonder where on earth Rydford is?'

'I've found it,' said Paula. She had an Ordnance Survey map open on her desk. 'It appears to be a very small place off the main road from Moretonhampstead to Princeton. It's located just under Hangman's Tor.'

'Very encouraging,' said Butler.

The phone rang. Tweed looked at the ceiling. Monica answered, then looked at Tweed.

'You'll never guess who's on the phone wanting to talk to you urgently.'

'I'm not even going to guess.'

'Serena Cavendish. Long distance . . .'

'I'll have a word with her . . . Serena? You walked out on me,' he said, his voice cold.

'Didn't you get my note? I gave it to a waitress, with a big tip.'

'I got it. You could have come back to the table and told me.'

'I was so frightened by a man I saw watching me from another table, I panicked.'

'You didn't think I'd be sufficient protection for you, then?'

'I told you. I panicked . . .'

'Describe the man.'

'Not now. I'm in one hell of a rush. But I have information about Appledore. Could you pop over to Paris tomorrow? We can arrange a rendezvous.'

'Tomorrow is impossible. Maybe the day after. Or the day after that. How would I contact you – if I can make it.'

'Take down this number ... Got it? Good. A man will answer. It's a small café opposite where I'm staying. Say you're Maurice and want to speak to Yvonne. That's me. He'll dart across the road and fetch me. You shouldn't have to wait more than a couple of minutes. Try to call that number between 9 a.m. and noon, local time. You'll be glad you did.'

'Where are you speaking from now?'

'Brussels. You sound so unfriendly. You'll be glad you came when you hear what I have to tell you. Must dash. Greetings ...'

Tweed put down the phone. He waited a moment, then picked it up again and asked for the international operator.

'Operator, I've just been speaking to someone who called me from the Continent. She gave me her number in Brussels. Unfortunately the call was broken in mid-sentence. Can you help me? The line wasn't all that clear and I must call her back.'

'Did you say Brussels, sir?'

'I think that's what she said. But there was a lot of crackle.'

'There must have been. I handled that call myself. It was from Paris.'

'It *was* a bad line. Thank you so much ...'

Tweed looked at the others. He reported the whole gist of the phone call. He asked them what they thought.

'Serena is devious,' Paula reflected. 'Odd that she

should be in Paris, where I had my little experience. What are you going to do?'

'It's what *we* are going to do. If I recall correctly, you said the Cavendish sisters had a cottage in Steeple Hampton. That's in Hampshire. I recall seeing a turning off to the village on the A303 just beyond the Barton Stacey area.'

'You're right.' Paula had glanced at the map still open on her desk. 'You've been there?'

'No. I noticed the signpost when I was driving to the West Country over a year ago.'

'You do have a remarkable memory.'

'I need it. I rely on my memory – and my observation for detail. Did you notice Burgoyne has just a slight limp? Right leg?'

'No, I didn't.'

'Probably result of a war wound. I must phone Gerrard at the MoD tomorrow and ask him if Burgoyne was injured. Slipped my mind.'

'Is he coming with us to Paris?' Paula asked.

'I haven't decided. I want to think it over.' He looked at Monica. 'We can always cancel his air and hotel bookings if I decide against. Now, Paula, I want you to come with me to Steeple Hampton early tomorrow. A woman notices things a man misses.'

'I'll be glad to join you. Why are we going there?'

'I want to get all the background I can on Serena. There may be people in the village who knew the sisters.'

'You have to be back for when Cord Dillon arrives,' she warned.

'I know. If we start early we can do it easily. Not all that long to get there.'

'With you driving like the clappers it won't be long.'

'So, I think,' said Tweed, 'you ought to go home, get

to bed in good time. I'll call for you at seven. Not too early? Good.'

'I'll drive Paula home,' Newman decided. 'We can get a bite to eat on the way. I could stand guard over her during the night – considering what has happened.'

'I'd be grateful for that, Bob,' Paula agreed. 'And you could sleep on the couch in the living room.'

'Then let's get cracking,' said Newman, standing up. 'Tweed, I think I should come with the two of you tomorrow.'

'Won't be necessary. Enjoy your meal . . .'

He waited until they had gone, followed by Marler, Butler and Pete Nield. Then he asked Monica to scribble the MoD number on a bit of paper. She did so and handed it to him.

'I'll phone Bernard Gerrard from my flat before I leave in the morning. He's an early-bird-catches-the-worm type. Always in his office from 6 a.m. onwards.'

'He ought to work for us,' Monica commented with a wicked smile.

'What glorious countryside,' Paula enthused the following morning as Tweed drove along the A303. 'It's good to get away from town.'

The sky was overcast with grey clouds scudding east but there was a fresh breeze. Tweed, behind the wheel, had his window open. On either side of them fields stretched away into the distance. Many had been ploughed and brown clods of earth were covered with frost. When a shaft of sunlight broke through it gave the fields a crystaline appearance. Paula glanced at Tweed.

'I could have sworn you're carrying a gun in a hip holster.'

'I am.'

'That's very rare for you. And we are in England.'

'Sam Sneed was beheaded in England. Also, we are being followed,' he said with mock seriousness.

'I know.' She glanced again in the wing mirror. 'By Newman in his Merc. Against your orders.'

'I think he'll keep well away from us in Steeple Hampton. And we're very close to the turn-off. Yes, here it is.'

He slowed down, swung off the highway down a narrow lane after passing a signpost. *Steeple Hampton*. The lane twisted and turned. Tweed had slowed to a crawl. Paula expressed approval.

'Well,' he explained, 'you never know what's round the next bend. Maybe a whacking great farm tractor which assumes it has the right of way. I suppose it does – it belongs here, we don't.'

'Do you think we may be too early? I imagine you'll want to talk to some locals.'

'Too early?' Tweed chuckled. 'In these isolated villages they live as they did long ago. Early to bed, early to rise. Farm workers want to make use of all the daylight. And here we are – what there is of it.'

Steeple Hampton was one street of old cottages. Near the end a church spire like a spike bisected the sky which was now blue and cloudless. Small gardens, neatly kept behind gated walls, fronted the cottages. There was a pub, the Black Bull. Outside, a white-haired man was sweeping a paved area.

'That's the chap we need,' Tweed said, pulling up and getting out.

'What a lovely morning,' Tweed said cheerfully.

'If it lasts.'

'Nice-looking pub.'

'We're not open till twelve – if it was a pint you wanted.'

He had gnarled hands gripping the bristle broom. His skin was weatherbeaten, his shoulders stooped, his voice had a tinge of some local accent. He managed a smile at Paula, who had alighted with Tweed.

'Come the wrong way, 'ave we? Lots of folk do, specially in summer. Where you 'eading for?'

'We're where we wanted to come to,' Paula replied with a warm smile. 'Steeple Hampton. I had two girl friends who lived here years ago. The Cavendish sisters . . .'

'Ah! Davina and Serena. Nice ladies. Always 'ad a word for me when they came into village.' He paused. 'Suppose you know? The tragedy? Davina's gone.'

'Yes, I do know. Died in a car crash.'

'Shockin' business. Drivin' back to the cottage at three in the mornin' and hit by a truck. Musta been the size of Exeter Cathedral. I've only been here forty years. Comes from West Country, I does. Truck driver was an 'it-and-run. Police never did find 'im. The cottage is still 'ere.'

'It's years since I knew them,' Paula went on. 'Someone told me Serena still lives in the cottage. I'd like to see it.'

'See the church? The cottage is just beyond it, on its own. Hedgerow, it's called.' He was warming up. 'Serena still owns it. Hardly ever see her, though. Mrs Grew looks after it for her. Her husband tends the garden. A cheque comes regular for them. But it's ages since we've seen 'er.' He gestured with his free hand to the open countryside beyond the pub. 'See all that land? Once belonged to their father, Sir Osvald Cavendish. He gambled it all away on the 'orses. The big 'ouse, the land – all went to pay off his debts. Suppose that's why those sisters bought the cottage. Near where they was brought up.'

'Did you say Sir Osvald?' Tweed enquired.

'I did. Father was German.' He looked at an old fob watch he took from his pocket. 'If you goes up to cottage now you'll probably find Mrs Grew there. She could tell you more. The sisters were so alike. Clever too. But the really clever one was Davina. Became a scientist. Who knows what she might 'ave discovered if she'd lived? Make you a cup of tea and a sandwich when you come back – if you're peckish.'

'That's very kind of you,' said Tweed. 'Let's see how we feel later . . .'

They got back into the car and drove slowly through the village. An old woman was on her knees in front of the doorstep of a cottage. She was scrubbing the doorstep Persil white.

'They do work,' Paula commented.

'That was how England used to be. There have been great changes – some very much for the better, others very much for the worse.'

While they had talked to the innkeeper Newman had crawled past them in his Merc. He hadn't given them a glance. Now he had his car backed into a track alongside the church – so he could drive whichever way we leave, Tweed surmised. Newman had the bonnet up, was apparently attending to some mechanical defect. Tweed drove slowly past him.

'This is Hedgerow,' Paula said, pointing to a cottage standing away from the village. 'Maybe that woman weeding the garden is Mrs Grew.'

'Only one way to find out,' Tweed replied, stopping the car and getting out. 'Being a woman, you may have better luck with her,' he said quietly to Paula.

'Good morning,' Paula said cheerfully. 'Are you Mrs Grew?'

'I might be.'

The late middle-aged woman with grey hair, wearing gardening clothes, stood up from her kneeling mat. She dropped her gloves. Both hands were placed on her back as though it ached.

'I'm Paula. Years ago I knew Serena and Davina Cavendish. We met at parties in London. Days of youth. I thought I'd just call in as we were passing. Have a natter about old times.'

'Davina's gone. Her grave's in the yard behind the church.'

'I do know. It was Serena I thought I might meet. Oh, she isn't here. I gather Hedgerow still belongs to her. Does she come down often?'

'Never. At least not that I sees her. I think she does come. But always in the middle of the night. I cleans the cottage, so I knows where everything is. You can put things back thinking that's where you found them. But even a woman can get it wrong.' Her sharp eyes gleamed. 'Maybe she brings a feller. So they'd get here after dark and get away very early. Once I couldn't sleep. It was a warm night so I got dressed, came out for a short walk. All the lights were on behind the curtains in the cottage. And further up the road a car was parked on the verge. Facing the other way, which I thought was odd. Looked as though they'd come that way, then turned the car round. You can get back to the A303 that way, but it's a roundabout route. Much quicker the way you two came. I guessed they didn't want anyone to hear the car driving through the village.'

'How long ago would that incident have been?' Tweed asked.

'This is my boss,' Paula introduced. 'I work for him in London. He kindly offered to drive me down here.'

'Your boss.' Mrs Grew's eyes gleamed again. 'I see.'

Paula smiled to herself. Mrs Grew had already tagged her as Tweed's mistress. But funny things go on in villages.

'You asked how long ago,' Mrs Grew said, addressing Tweed. 'I'd say it must have been six months ago. They've been back since. I found a kitchen towel which was still damp from use. Those two sisters were as alike as two peas in a pod,' she continued. 'Davina was the clever one. Got a scholarship to Oxford to study science and biochemistry.'

'I think you mean biology,' Tweed interjected.

'When I say biochemistry I mean biochemistry.' She glared at him. 'I'd like to have had the chance to go to university. I read a lot. Every month I cycle to a second-hand bookshop in Andover. Science, travel, biography. Now I must get on.' She bent down to pick up her gloves but Tweed was quicker and handed them to her. 'Thank you.' She lowered herself back on to the kneeling mat, looked up. 'While you're here you might as well see Davina's grave. I look after it and the headstone.'

'Thank you,' said Paula. 'We've enjoyed talking to you.'

They walked back to the church. Fifty yards away Newman was still having 'trouble' with his car. He treated them as though they didn't exist.

Paula pushed open the shaky wooden gate into the churchyard. Tweed followed her as she made her way round the ivy-clad walls.

A weed-strewn path behind the church led to the graveyard. She found what they were looking for at the very back. The grave, unlike most of the others, was well tended. The headstone had been so carefully looked after it almost appeared new. They stood side by side, reading the modest wording.

DAVINA
Never to be forgotten
SERENA

9

They were driving back to London. The sun shone out of a duck-egg-blue sky. Passing the ploughed fields Paula noticed the frost had gone, exposing clearly the clods of brown earth. A flight of birds swooped above them. She looked at Tweed, who had a preoccupied expression.

'What did you think of Davina's grave?' she asked.

'Something unusual about it,' Tweed replied. 'Only a few words. No dates of her birth and death. Strange.'

'I thought so too. Was the trip worthwhile – from what the innkeeper and Mrs Grew told us?'

'Their father was German. Must at some time have changed his last name to Cavendish. Who visits Serena's cottage in the dead of night? I can't see her taking all that trouble just over a boy friend to keep the visits secret from the village. Not these days. Why should she care tuppence about what the villagers think? Then you told me Davina had studied science and biology. Mrs Grew was very emphatic it was biochemistry.'

Paula looked again at Tweed. She had the impression that he wasn't so much answering her question as thinking aloud, assembling facts, trying to put them in some sort of order. His jigsaw puzzle.

'Professor Saafeld,' he went on, 'is not only a top pathologist, the man Buchanan goes to for autopsies in difficult cases. He is also a biochemist, a biophysicist, a clinical microbiologist and a professor of bacteriology. He has no less than fourteen honorary degrees from various universities on the Continent and in the States.'

'How does he do it?'

'He has an extraordinary brain. And he never stops

working. His wife once told me she has adapted her lifestyle to his routine. She's good at embroidery and patchwork. She also reads a lot, like Mrs Grew. She listens to the BBC's World Service and keeps her husband in touch with what's going on in the world. The interesting thing about Saafeld is he has the same expertise as Dr Goslar.'

'How on earth do you know that?'

'From snippets I've picked up here and there – particularly from America. Remember Goslar, staying in the background, produced in his New Jersey plant an advanced weapon of war – a gas, or so Dillon said.'

'Then Saafeld is the ideal man to crack Goslar's secret agent.'

'You mean the agent – or ingredient – which caused havoc in the sea at Appledore. Unfortunately it's one thing to invent such a deadly agent, but quite another to detect it. I checked up again on Burgoyne early this morning. Got in touch with Gerrard at the MoD.'

'So are you going to tell me what the result was? And whether Burgoyne comes with us to Paris?'

'First question. I wanted to hear how Gerrard reacted after I had slept on our earlier conversation. I asked him to describe Burgoyne. He only met him once briefly – quite a long time ago. But he said my description fitted, especially his manner. Very buoyant and direct.'

'So that's it?'

'I'm making one more check. I phoned Marler. He'll be well on his way to Rydford on Dartmoor, the village Burgoyne was retiring to. See if he can pick up anything there.'

'Then Marler will never get back in time to catch our flight to Paris this evening,' she objected.

'Oh, yes he will. Marler can go thirty-six hours without any sleep. He drove off in the middle of the night. He could be in Rydford now. He'll be back in

103

good time for Paris – and that reminds me. I was intrigued by what we heard and saw in Steeple Hampton. So I'll be keeping an appointment with Serena. But not as early as she suggested. I'm not having her thinking I'm eager. I'm building up a picture of what is happening. The trouble is it's a misty picture. I need more data to clarify it. I just hope to Heaven that I'm wrong. If I'm not, the world faces a horrendous disaster.'

Marler drove along the deserted road across Dartmoor from Moretonhampstead towards Princeton. A mist hung over the countryside but here and there he saw the peak of a tor peering out above it. Well west of Moretonhampstead he saw a signpost to his right. *Rydford.*

He turned off the main road on to a narrow lane which began to climb. He drove slowly now. Turning a corner he saw ahead of him the village. He was about to back his car up a track with a lot of shrubbery round it – ready to leave quickly if that proved to be necessary. Then he saw in his rear-view mirrow a sports car stopping behind him. The driver, by herself, was an attractive girl with her dark hair cut short. He got out, walked back slowly, stopped a couple of yards away to avoid frightening her.

'Sorry, I was just going to back up that track, ready to leave later. You wouldn't happen to know Rydford?'

'Yes and no. Who have you come to see?'

As she spoke he realized she was assessing him. When she gave him a smile he knew he had passed muster. She had a perky nose, warm eyes – without a come-hither look, and a pointed chin which suggested determination. In her thirties, he guessed.

'I'm looking for a Captain Alan Burgoyne. I understand he lives here.'

'He does. I'm a friend of his. Coral Langley.' She extended a hand for him to clasp and he knew the confidence-inspiring exercise was over. He clasped the hand quickly, careful not to hold on too long. 'I can show you where he lives,' she suggested. 'Park your car and I'll take you there. It's a short way. It's a short village.'

'I'm David Miller. If I could just back my car . . .'

He stopped speaking. She was already reversing. He backed into the track, hauled out his golf bag, locked his car, sat next to her, nursing the bag between his knees.

'Hope you don't mind my carting this with me. Good irons cost a fortune these days. I don't want someone breaking in and walking off with them.'

'Very wise – even out here. Salesmen travel around, trying to sell household equipment. You've known Alan long? I refuse to use his nickname, "Chance". Don't like it. He's given in.'

'Known him? Off and on.'

'Same with me.'

She had a soft appealing voice. Marler now saw she was right in her description of Rydford. The cobbled street was short and steep. On either side small terrace houses, two storeys high, were built of granite. He saw a poster advertising a fair.

'Seems very quiet,' he remarked. 'Can't see a soul. Is it always like this?'

'No. I expect they've all gone off to the fair. We're nearly there.'

They had left the village behind and Marler saw the menacing bulk of Hangman's Tor looming above Rydford. No mist at its summit. Great crags protruded alarmingly from it and Marler thought it looked unstable. Coral Langley seemed to read his mind.

'Don't like that tor behind Alan's place. It will come down one day. I tell Alan that and he just shrugs. Here we are . . .'

Marler prepared to hoist his golf bag over his shoulder. It contained his Armalite rifle. Dartmoor was a lonely place and he recalled Paula's grim experience near Gargoyle Towers. Burgoyne's cottage was a replica of the village houses, but larger because it was detached. Close to the lane, the front garden was a riot of gorse in golden bloom. Coral froze by her car, staring at the cottage.

'The front door's half open. That's funny. Alan always keeps it shut even when he's inside. Very security-minded.'

'When did you last see him?'

'About two months ago. He roams about a lot. A legacy of his military career, I suspect.'

'I suggest you wait here while I check the place out.'

'Would you? It's very odd . . .'

Marler glanced up at the tor. Out of the corner of his eye he had caught movement. He paused to take a better look. A precipitous path wound its way up towards the summit. No sign of anyone now. He put his right hand under his anorak, gripped the butt of the small Beretta 6.35mm automatic tucked inside the top of his slacks. He walked up to the door, shoved it open with his foot, listened. No sound. No giveaway creak of a foot on the plank floor. He used his foot to push the door flat against the wall. No one waiting behind it.

He walked into a large living room, modestly furnished with a wooden table and chairs arranged round it. Two chintz-covered armchairs on either side of the inglenook fireplace. A wall-to-ceiling bookcase. Beyond, a door opened into the kitchen.

A narrow curved wooden staircase led upwards out of sight. He peered into the kitchen. Empty. The back door was half open. He strolled across, first looked out of a window. The back garden petered out into the moor. He walked out, looked up at the tor. No sign of the intruder.

He had explored upstairs, checked two bedrooms, a shower and a toilet, was walking down the stairs when he saw Coral standing at the open front door. She had a club in one hand, presumably kept in her car.

'Are you all right, Miller?'

'I'm afraid there's been a break-in. Someone picked the lock on the front door. Scratches round it. Come in. Is anything missing?'

Coral surveyed the living room, opened a few drawers. He was watching her, wishing she wasn't attached to Burgoyne. He'd have waited his moment, asked her out to dinner in London. She went into the kitchen. He had closed the back door, using his elbow. He had long ago been trained not to leave fingerprints in suspect situations. He heard her exclamation.

'Damn him! He's taken Alan's photo.'

'Where was it?' he asked as he followed her into the kitchen.

'On that shelf. In a silver frame. Alan, like a lot of people, including myself, didn't like his picture being taken. I took one, bought a silver frame. He put it on that shelf. Used to say it gave him something nice to look at when he was preparing a meal.'

'That's a shame.'

'And the old copy of the *Daily Nation* which had his picture in it has gone. Used to wrap up the silver frame, I suppose.'

'Petty thieves will take anything.'

'With no thought of other people's sentiments. I used to spend time with him here.'

107

And probably nights – lucky Alan, Marler thought.

'Want to check upstairs?'

'Nothing up there.' She was opening another drawer. 'He also whipped Alan's old army paybook. The things they take.'

'Probably a market for army paybooks. Forgers use them. This is bad luck for you, Coral.'

'Never mind. The photos are gone. I'll take another of him when I can.'

'How did you two first meet?' Marler asked.

'At a dance in London. We took to each other right away. He may have been a soldier but he was such a gentle man. I'll call him again at his London flat. I did so before I came up here. No reply. That often happens.'

Marler would like to have asked for the number. He desisted – it would seem strange to her that he didn't know it. She said she needed some fresh air. She moved quickly. Before he could stop her she had opened the back door, walking into the garden. He was following her when he heard the shot.

From the back door he saw her collapse. He unzipped the pocket in the golf bag hiding the Armalite, ran out, looking up at the tor. A man stood on the crag projecting high up. He held a rifle. When he saw Marler he raised the rifle. Marler aimed his Armalite, caught him in the cross-hairs, pressed the trigger, firing an explosive bullet of great power.

The man was perched near the edge of the crag. Marler fired again. The explosive bullet hit the crag where it joined the mass of the tor. He saw the man start to topple, screaming as he cartwheeled down the long drop. Then the whole crag gave way, parting from the tor as tons of rock plunged down. Then there was a heavy silence.

Marler ran to Coral. She had fallen on her back. He

only needed one look to know she was dead. Half her face had been blown away. He didn't even check her pulse.

'*Bastard!*' he said aloud. 'Used a dumdum bullet.'

He ran to the base of the tor. He half-expected to find he was looking down at Yellow Hair, the man Tweed had seen at Brown's Hotel through the window. If there was any trace visible of the killer.

There was. He stopped running when he reached the edge of the rock fall. Only the killer's head was visible, dead eyes staring at the sky. The rest of his body was hidden beneath a massive boulder which, Marler thought with satisfaction, must have crushed every bone in his body. The hair was thick, black. Again he didn't bother to check the neck pulse. He had to get away quickly . . .

He ran round the end of the cottage, peered down the street.

Still empty. No one about anywhere. He slid the Armalite back inside the special pocket, walked rapidly back to his car. As he drove out and reached the highway he thought how lucky it was that the fair had cleared the village out. Then it struck him the killer might never have broken into Burgoyne's cottage if there had been people about.

He felt rotten about leaving Coral Langley lying there in the garden. But Tweed had always emphasized to his team they must never get mixed up with the police – especially during an operation.

Well on his way from Dartmoor, Marler stopped at an isolated phone box. He asked Directory Enquiries for the number of the Exeter police and called it.

'I'm reporting the murder of a girl. You'll find her body behind a cottage near the tor in Rydford on Dartmoor. I said Rydford, spelt . . .'

He put down the phone when the man who answered asked for his name. Then he drove – just inside the speed limits – back to London.

10

Only Tweed and Paula were in the office when Marler arrived back after dark. He sat down in an armchair, lit a king-size. Paula brought him an ashtray, perched it on the arm of his chair.

'Nothing ever turns out the way you think it will . . .' Marler began in a distant voice.

He then proceeded to report every detail of his trip to Rydford. Tweed listened without interrupting him, absorbing every word, imagining the scenes Marler was describing graphically. He had just recalled the death of Coral Langley when he stopped his account.

'Any hope of a drink?'

'Brandy and soda?' Tweed suggested.

Marler nodded and Tweed leaned down, opened his deep bottom drawer. He produced a glass, a bottle of good brandy and a soda siphon. Planting them close to Marler he let him fix his own drink. Marler fixed a stiff one, drank half, placed the glass within reach. Paula squeezed his shoulder. He looked up at her, winked.

'That's better. I just had a flash of what Coral's face looked like after the bullet hit her. Now, to continue . . .'

He ended by recalling his phone message to the police. Gazing at Tweed, he raised an eyebrow.

'I felt I couldn't just leave her there. She might not have been found until tomorrow morning.'

'I think,' Tweed said, 'you acted correctly and very sympathetically. And you were right. If you'd got caught up in a police investigation they might have forbidden you to leave the country, even treated you as a suspect. And you've given me a big piece to help me build up the picture I'm forming. I am grateful.'

'Is Burgoyne coming with us to Paris?' Paula asked.

'I told you in the car this morning that I had made a second call to Gerrard at the MoD.' As he spoke he was staring at the ceiling, which struck Paula as curious. 'I also told you that he'd given Burgoyne a very positive assessment.' He looked down at both of them. 'Since he's new, I will be the only one to give him orders when we are on the move. Marler, you might pass that bit of information on to all the others before we go.'

'Will do.'

'Now we have something to tell you – about our visit to Steeple Hampton . . .'

Tersely he described every detail of their experience. Marler sat very still, watching him. Tweed ended with a flourish of his hands.

'Paula,' he went on, 'thinks there's something strange about what we heard – and saw. Any comment?'

'I find the wording on that headstone on Davina's grave quite bizarre. And I gather Serena's hardly ever there – apart from those secret visits to the cottage at night. So where does she go to, what does she really do?'

'Our own reactions. She called me from abroad, wants me to meet her when we're in Paris. I shall meet her. I shall want to know a lot more about her. Where she goes to. Where the money comes from – her clothes are very expensive.'

'Her fur was sable,' Paula remarked. 'But some of the questions you're going to put to her are pretty personal.'

'She approached me. She must expect searching questions.'

'I sense there's something you haven't said,' Paula told him.

'She has jet-black hair. She admits being in Appledore, albeit at an earlier date – when she carried out her commission to photograph the area. Buchanan reported that the chauffeuse, who drove a Middle Eastern diplomat on the night we were in Appledore had jet-black hair tucked under her peaked cap . . .'

He looked up as Monica, red-faced, hurried into the office. She settled herself behind her desk and spoke apologetically.

'Hope you haven't had a lot of calls. I rushed out to get a quick meal. Couldn't face the deli.'

'No calls at all,' Tweed assured her. 'And I wish you'd go out for a meal more often. You need to keep up your strength, the way I work you.'

'I've just remembered something else about my trip,' Marler reported. 'I was driving back along a deserted stretch of the A303 when a motorcyclist came tearing up behind me, then slowed down. I thought that was odd. Those chaps usually overtake with a roar. I drove with one hand, had my Beretta in the other. Thought he might have a present for me – like lobbing a grenade through the open window. Then a police car appeared in the distance, coming towards us. Motorcyclist roars straight past me, never to be seen again.'

'He could have been working in cahoots with the man on Hangman's Tor,' Tweed mused. 'Went back to Rydford to pick him up after delivering him there. Saw you leaving.'

'Then I was lucky he didn't arrive when I was inside the phone box calling the police.'

'From what you told us, he'd have to find his villainous chum. That probably took a while. I said Goslar has a huge organization.'

'Have I got time to dart back to my flat?' Marler asked, standing up.

'Bags of time,' Monica told him.

Marler had just left when the phone rang. Monica answered, then called across to Tweed.

'Our transatlantic visitor has arrived. Cord Dillon is downstairs.'

'Tell him to come up now. I'm intrigued by this visit. Why do I have the strong feeling that what he is bringing us is bad news?'

The door opened and Cord Dillon strode in. The Deputy Director of the CIA wore a duffel coat, fastened up to the neck, a pair of blue denim slacks and loafers. His large craggy head always reminded Tweed of one of the Presidential heads carved out of rock at Mount Rushmore. Clean-shaven, his thick hair was turning white. In his fifties, he moved like a man twenty years younger.

'Hi, Monica,' he greeted her as she took his coat. 'Paula, you look younger than ever. Can't say the same about you, Tweed,' he said with a weary grin.

'Welcome, Cord. What have you been up to? We expected you earlier.'

'At Dulles Airport I spotted a tail. Lost him and booked on a flight to Canada, then flew on here.'

He was sitting upright in one of the armchairs. He refused the offer of a drink from Monica. Earlier Tweed had put away the brandy bottle and siphon. Paula had taken away the glass Marler had used.

'You did that?' Tweed remarked. 'I hope you're not in bad odour in Washington again.'

'Far from it. I'm running Langley myself for weeks

on end. My chief keeps getting recurring bouts of flu. It was another lot I was keeping away from.'

'I sense that what you're going to tell me is secret. Do you mind if Paula stays?'

'Hell, no.' He looked across at her. 'Last time I was here she saved my life. That business in Albemarle Street. As for Monica . . .' He swivelled to grin at her. 'She's been with you for more than a few years. If Bob Newman turns up he can also listen in. But no one else, if you don't mind.'

'So what is the secret?'

'You're not going to like this. I don't think you're going to like it one little bit. And you're going to have to watch your back over this Goslar thing.'

'Tell me, Cord. I'll try not to tremble.'

'That will be the day, when you tremble.' The American paused as though gathering his thoughts. 'I'm talking about Unit Four. A body of highly professional agents who answer only to the President's right-hand man, Vance Karnow. A tough guy if ever there was one – like his subordinates. Here's a pic of Karnow.'

He handed Tweed a photo he'd extracted from an inner pocket. The photo was protected by a slim plastic folder. Tweed handed it back to him without comment. Dillon passed it to Paula, his long arm just reaching her desk.

'Like your reaction, Paula. You're good at weighing men up.'

She studied the pic, taking longer over it than Tweed had. She pursed her lips.

'Photos can be so misleading.'

'I think you formed an impression,' Dillon insisted.

'A strange face. You can see the European origins. Probably from a few generations back. Prominent cheek-bones. A long face, long nose, thin lips, pointed jaw. A lot of smartly brushed dark hair. Eyes like bullets. Hard,

114

ruthless, amoral. I'm guessing,' she concluded, handing back the photo.

'On the button,' Dillon said approvingly.

'What is the function of Unit Four?' Tweed enquired.

'The dirty work they'd sooner not hand to the CIA – because we have such a large organization. Also, Unit Four prides itself on doing its job underground. They dress in suits, like respectable businessmen. Often pose as just that – businessmen.'

'Do they work on direct orders from the President?'

'Not on your life. Officially he isn't aware they exist. The orders always come from Karnow. But my guess is the President makes an off-the-cuff remark to Karnow about someone who is worrying him. Result, Karnow and his men see that the someone is not walking the earth much longer.'

'Why are you telling us about Unit Four?' Tweed wondered.

'Because an informant – very reliable – told me they were coming over here.'

'With what purpose?'

'To grab off you – if you get it – the ultimate weapon of war invented by Dr Goslar. My informant told me the President sees it as ensuring America remains the top world power.'

'Cord . . .' Tweed leaned forward over his desk. 'You and I know about the mysterious Dr Goslar – but how come the President also knows about him? If he does?'

'He does. Recently – very – the Oval Office received a video showing what happened at Appledore. Also he received a recorded phone call from Goslar. I gather in that weird screechy robot-like howl he speaks in. He said he might consider selling the formula and a specimen to the States for three hundred million dollars. The President would go berserk at the idea of paying that sort of money – even for world supremacy. Hence his using Unit Four. A copy of that article by Sneed in the *Daily Nation* also reached the Oval Office. Unit Four could already be here – which is what I came to warn you about.'

'That would be quick.'

'There is Concorde. What is it? A three-and-a-half-hour trip from Washington to London. Unit Four is a squad of élite killers. Karnow himself could be in London now.'

'Cord, I really appreciate your coming all this way to warn us.'

'One huge favour deserves another. You hid me away down in the Romney Marsh when a gang of thugs were after my hide. But you must understand these people in Unit Four are not thugs scooped up out of the underworld. They are educated, clever and sophisticated. Far more dangerous. Maybe a dozen of them. Maybe more. I just don't know.'

'Have you time for a drink at a nearby bar?'

'No.' Dillon checked his watch. 'I have to catch a flight back to Washington. I know the pilot of the plane. I'll leave it at Dulles dressed like an officer of the crew.'

'Have you any information on Goslar, no matter how vague?'

'Well . . .' Dillon settled back again in his chair. 'I started to read a file on Goslar before I came over. There's a second file on him I have to trace when I get back. I'll contact you when I've located and read it.'

'What about the first file you were reading?' Tweed pressed.

'That had a weird report in it. All based on rumours – so I can't vouch for its authenticity.'

'I'd still like to hear it.'

'It's about the Galapagos Islands – way out in the

116

Pacific off the coast of Ecuador. They belong to Ecuador. It sounded like a fairy story to me, Tweed.'

'I like fairy stories.'

'I'm sure you know that in the sea around the Galapagos there are huge turtles. Occasionally wealthy tourists go there to see these strange creatures.' He looked at Paula. 'You're probably wondering where I'm going.'

'Then let's go there, Cord,' she encouraged.

'They're a kind of protected species – because they're unique in the whole world. A fisherman from Ecuador was in the area. He saw a giant seaplane moored offshore. Later, apparently, he heard it belonged to a Dr Goslar.' Dillon waved a dismissive hand. 'I stress this is all nothing but rumour. I didn't believe a word of it myself.'

'Let's see if I believe it,' Tweed suggested. 'Do give us all the details you have.'

'And you were talking about a fisherman from Ecuador,' Paula reminded the American.

'This fisherman – if he ever existed – had a pair of high-powered glasses. He used them to check on what was going on. There were very big dinghies drawn up on the beach. The fisherman saw a landing party capturing two turtles, lifting them into tanks of water. Then the crates were transported to the dinghies, presumably on their way to the seaplane. The sail of the fisherman's boat was very distinctive. That is important later. A red sail with a white half-moon on it.'

'How long ago was this?' asked Tweed.

'Date's obscure. Within the last year. The fisherman returns to Guayaquil, Ecuador's port. Tells his story in a waterfront bar crowded with people. Tells it to a freelance agent of ours – who sends off this report. A copy goes to our main agent in Quito, capital of

Ecuador. He decides to check, goes down to Guayaquil. Finds the fisherman and our freelancer have both been murdered. That's it, for what it's worth. I must catch my flight now.'

Tweed had gone over to the windows. He pulled aside a gap in the closed curtains, peered out into the night. Below a taxi waited. He came back to shake hands with Dillon.

'No watchers that I can see out there. Safe flight back. Oh, how were those two men murdered?'

'Beheaded. Tough place, that port. Be in touch. If you ever get hold of that nightmare weapon of Goslar's, destroy it. Destroy him too . . .'

'That is encouraging,' Paula commenced.

'Unit Four arriving on our doorstep? Isn't it,' Tweed agreed.

The door opened and Newman walked in, carrying a bag. Dumping it against a wall, he sat down. He looked first at Paula, then at Tweed.

'You two look as though a bomb had dropped on you.'

'It has,' said Tweed. 'Where are Butler and Nield?'

'Downstairs in the waiting room with their bags. They're playing poker.'

'Monica, get them up here right away.' He looked at Newman. 'Any idea where Burgoyne is?'

'Having a good old chinwag with Howard in his office.'

'We'll leave him there. Howard is very good at getting people into the atmosphere of how we work.'

He waited until Butler and Nield appeared, each carrying a bag. They dropped them alongside Newman's, sat down. Nield studied Tweed before he made his remark.

'You look godawful serious.'

'Pretty much what I've just observed,' agreed Newman.

'Pay attention, everyone,' Tweed said. 'Cord Dillon has been in to see us. Flew over for that express purpose. Now he's flying straight back to Washington. He brought interesting news . . .'

Concisely, his manner grave, he gave a résumé of what the American had told him. They sat very still as they listened. Marler had arrived just before Tweed began explaining. He took up his normal stance, leaning against a wall. Tweed concluded his résumé. Nield was the first one to react.

'We're going to have fun. First we'll be up against the invisible Dr Goslar. Then we'll have to keep a sharp lookout for Bate and his Special Branch thugs, who don't play by the Queensberry Rules. The French security services, and maybe the police, will be hostile. Now, on top of all of them, we have Unit Four Yanks on the prowl. Yes, it should be fun.'

'If you like to describe it that way,' Tweed remarked.

'One important point,' Marler spoke up. 'We can't take weapons on the plane, which is why I've been back to my flat so I could be on my own. I contacted a friend in Paris who sells every type of gun – for a price. I told him I'd see him tonight, and he'll wait for me. I'll hare off to him in one of the cars hired by Monica over the phone and waiting for us at Charles de Gaulle. But everyone should be armed quickly, so where can we meet?'

'On Madeleine,' Paula suggested. 'You know the Restaurant Valais? Marvellous Swiss food. There's a bar next to it. On the right as you face Valais. It's not well lit and stays open all hours. We'll probably get a table at the back.'

'All right, Marler?' Tweed checked.

'Perfect rendezvous. Close to where I'll be coming from.'

'Then we go on to La Défense, to look at that building where you had that appalling ordeal, Paula.'

'We'll be there in no time,' Paula said. 'Go by Métro.'

'Everyone has plenty of foreign currency?' asked Tweed. 'Good.'

He unlocked a drawer, took out a long fat white envelope. He handed it to Marler.

'Underground gunsmiths come expensive.'

Marler opened the flap, glanced inside. The envelope was crammed with five-hundred-franc notes. He grinned.

'Enough to buy an artillery piece.'

'Which we may need, considering what we'll be up against,' Nield said with a smile.

'What's that bulging canvas bag you've got as well as your case?' Paula asked Marler.

'Crammed with newspapers and magazines. An empty bag might look suspicious to Customs at one end or the other. I'll dump them on my friend in exchange for the weaponry.'

'You'd better get moving to catch that flight,' Monica warned.

'Then ask Burgoyne to come down here *tout de suite.*'

11

The flight to Paris was three-quarters empty. Tweed sat next to Paula. Newman occupied a seat behind them. Further back Butler sat with Nield and, at Tweed's suggestion, Burgoyne occupied a seat on his own several rows behind them. Marler, however, had taken a front seat, nearest the exit. He wanted to be first off the plane so he could grab his hired car and drive swiftly to his gunsmith.

'I don't like night flights,' Paula remarked. 'All you look out at is blackness.'

'Luckily it's a short flight,' Tweed replied. 'I'm going back to have a word with Chance Burgoyne . . .'

'Because you were with Howard I didn't get the time to brief you,' Tweed began as he sat next to the retired officer. 'We drive from the airport to Madeleine. Marler is acquiring an armoury of weapons and will meet us there. What is your choice of weapon?'

'Sounds as though we're going to fight a duel,' Burgoyne said and grinned. 'I'd like a .38 Smith & Wesson, hip holster if possible, and plenty of spare ammo.'

'I'll tell Marler. From Madeleine – after we've met Marler – you, Paula, Newman and Butler, plus myself, will take the Métro to La Défense. You know it?'

'I know Paris but I've never had reason to visit La Défense. It's the business district, isn't it? Whacking great American-style skyscrapers. You can see them in the distance from certain parts of Paris.'

'That's the place. We want to visit the building where Paula had a bad experience . . .' Tweed briefly described what had happened to her. 'I told you about Dr Goslar when we had a few minutes on our own at Park Crescent.'

'A right swine, if there ever was one,' Burgoyne commented. 'I liked the look of Paula. Summed her up as tough. After what you've told me I underestimated her. She must be as tough as old hickory. I really admire her.'

Tweed glanced at Burgoyne. Having discarded his

camouflage jacket, he was now wearing a military-style trenchcoat. The change of apparel made him look much more like a soldier.

'It will be late at night when we get to La Défense,' Burgoyne observed, looking out of the window.

'That's the idea. We arrive at about the time Paula was there. Now, if you'll excuse me, I'll go and tell Marler the type of gun you prefer.'

Earlier that afternoon a huge man, clad in a grey overcoat with a fur collar, stood watching a phone box on the Île de la Cité. His brown cropped hair was protected with a beret. He needed the garb – a bitter wind was blowing down the River Seine.

A man was using the phone inside the box, had been talking for over fifteen minutes. The man in the grey overcoat checked his watch, pursed his thick lips. The phone box was not far from the HQ of Police Judiciaire, which amused him. For the third time he checked his watch. It was coming up to the hour.

He strode forward after extracting a banknote from his wallet. Opening the door of the box, he placed a large hand on the shoulder of the man inside, hauled him straight out. The victim swung round, blazing. Then he saw the size of the intruder.

'I need this phone,' the huge man said, handing a hundred-franc note to the much smaller man.

Grumbling, the small Frenchman walked away. He stared at the banknote greedily, shrugged, walked faster.

Inside the box the giant picked up the dangling receiver. He rammed it back on the cradle and waited. Once again he checked his watch. On the hour. The phone began ringing.

'Yes. Who is this?' he asked in English.

'Identify yourself,' a cool voice, speaking the same language, requested.

'Abel. I repeat Abel.'

'Hold on for a moment and then listen . . .'

Abel looked all round the outside while he waited. Two uniformed policemen walked out of the Police Judiciaire headquarters. They gave him not so much as a glance. Hunched up against the cold, they walked away, disappeared round a corner. The weird screeching voice began speaking.

'I expect Tweed, if I read his mind correctly, to visit the deserted building in La Défense. As I suggested, go there and prepare a suitable greeting for him. Go *now*.'

Abel replaced the receiver. He knew he had heard a recording, played by the man who had answered him when he first spoke. For a large man he moved swiftly after leaving the box. The equipment would be waiting for him inside the building. As he walked he repeated to himself the correct sequence of digits he must press on the combination device on the outer door of the La Défense building.

They had the Métro coach to themselves as the train rushed through the tunnel. Tweed sat with Burgoyne on one side and Paula on the other. Facing them were Newman and Butler, who carried his kit inside an airline bag. Butler had had to open the bag at Security, and had explained he was a plumber. The tools had the outward appearance of what a plumber would use.

Paula slipped her hand inside her shoulder bag, into the special pocket. She felt confident as her hand gripped the butt of her Browning .32. They had met Marler at the bar on Madeleine and he had distributed his purchases.

Newman and Burgoyne had their hip holsters, each

with a .38 Smith & Wesson. Butler and Nield had been provided with 7.65mm Walther automatics. Everyone, except Tweed and Paula, had an additional armoury of stun and smoke grenades. Marler was equipped with an Armalite rifle and a .455 Colt automatic pistol. Only Tweed carried no weapons.

After leaving the bar at Madeleine, Nield had driven the hired estate car to the Ritz. Marler had followed him in a Renault. It was the estate car which had transported Tweed and those who accompanied him from the airport to the bar. As the Métro train sped endlessly through a long tunnel – next stop La Défense – Paula was aware of nervousness and the pumping of adrenalin. She became calm and cold as they alighted and, with Burgoyne on one side, Butler on the other, she mounted the steps she had run down when escaping so recently.

Emerging into the night near the small park, she saw the seat she had sat on for a short time. She checked her watch. It was 10.30 p.m. – just about the time when she had endured her ordeal.

'Which building?' Burgoyne asked, his tone commanding and crisp.

'I'll lead you to it – but first let's make sure there's no one about . . .' Paula responded.

They waited in the shelter of the park. Paula stared up at the blue, glass monsters shearing up above them. The wide forecourt spaced out between the buildings was eerily quiet and apparently deserted. Tweed, hands in his coat pockets, glanced at her to see how she was reacting. He was impressed by her calm, purposeful look.

'I can see the building,' she said suddenly. 'Let's get on with it.'

Under her windcheater she wore an extra jumper, remembering the cold. She was also clad in leggings and rubber-soled boots, which made no sound. Burgoyne marched alongside her with Butler escorting her on her other side. Behind them Newman followed, his Smith & Wesson in his hand, concealed under a trenchcoat he wore not unlike Burgoyne's. Paula began to walk forward as she reached the entrance to the door leading into the vast hall beyond.

'The door's open a bit,' she said. 'It was when I left.'

'*Get back!*' ordered Burgoyne.

Butler repeated the same instruction almost simultaneously. He grabbed one of her arms as Burgoyne grabbed the other. Acting in unison, they turned her round, pushed her away, told her to return to the park.

'Something wrong?' Tweed's quiet voice enquired.

'Plenty,' said Butler. 'You all go back to the park. You, too, Newman. That's an order.' He had pushed Burgoyne aside and was reaching up to the top of the door, his sensitive fingers tracing the course of the wire, painted blue to merge with the building.

'I saw it, too. Remember?' grated Burgoyne. 'I've seen rather a lot of boobytraps – just in time.'

'Doesn't take two of us to do this job,' Butler snapped. 'In fact two fiddling with this apparatus could end up with us both being blown to kingdom come. For Pete's sake, let me concentrate.'

'It's all yours,' Burgoyne replied calmly. 'I'll just stay and watch. You want me to give a hand, just ask.'

'I'll do that thing.'

From a distance, standing between Tweed and Newman, Paula had a strange sensation of déjà vu. She recalled how, sitting in Newman's car outside her flat, she was waiting while Butler did what he was doing now. But this wasn't Fulham Road – this was a hell of skyscrapers and she'd been dangled from that floor halfway to heaven. No, heaven was hardly an appropriate word.

'I have to get inside some other way,' said Butler. Picking up his kit case, he left the door, walked to a nearby ground-floor window. Standing with a small torch clenched between his teeth he peered inside, saw only a vast hall stretching into infinity. He took out a special cutting tool after checking round the window. He used the tool to trace out a large oblong area near the lower ledge. His other hand held a powerful sucker at the tip of a wooden handle. He had the sucker pressed against the middle of the loose sheet of glass. Very slowly he withdrew the sheet, laid it on the ground, releasing the sucker.

'I'll go in first,' Burgoyne snapped.

'I don't think so. Just keep well away from that damned door.'

Butler crouched down, stepped slowly inside, Walther gripped in his right hand. He waited in a crouched position until his eyes were accustomed to the darkness of the interior. While he did this he listened. He might have been inside a tomb. No sound. No movement anywhere.

Walking slowly towards the door, he held his torch so it scanned the floor. He found what he'd expected behind the partly open door, in a position so that as the door was opened wide enough for someone to enter it would detonate. Same device as they'd used in Paula's flat back in London.

Down in Surrey, when the bomb squad had taken the previous device, they had done more than photograph it. After examining the photographs an expert had carefully studied what they had. He had taken a chance, pressed a switch. It had turned off the bomb mechanism.

'The green switch, not the red one, as you might imagine,' they had reported to Butler over the phone.

'Know what you're doing?' a soft voice asked behind him.

'You would follow me in,' Butler told Burgoyne. 'Now you can just hope I know what I'm doing. Where are the others?'

'Well clear. Back at the park.'

'Hold your breath, Burgoyne.'

Butler bent down, his torch illuminating the device's innards as he raised the lid. He shrugged, pressed down the green switch. Small illuminated bulbs inside the metal casing went out. He had done the right thing.

Butler severed the wire running along the top of the door, down the hinged side, connecting up with the bomb. He then lifted the metal casing containing the bomb, put it down against the wall well away from the door. He didn't want Paula to see it. Going outside, he waved to the others to tell them the coast was clear.

'Chance,' Paula said when she arrived, 'you saved our lives. Thank you.'

'Harry spotted the wire a split second after I did, called out a warning.'

'So thank you both.'

They were talking in whispers. Burgoyne followed suit.

'Can't understand what's going on. I'd swear this whole building is empty. No sign of a guard behind that counter with a phone.'

'Phone's dead as a doornail,' Butler told them after picking it up.

'Goslar's normal procedure,' Tweed explained to Burgoyne. 'He leases a base for longer than he thinks he'll need it. Just as he did at Gargoyle Towers, his temporary base on Dartmoor. He has vast sums at his disposal.'

'I'd like to go up to that room where they held me,' Paula suggested. 'They might just have left something. The thirty-second floor.'

'In that case,' Burgoyne said, 'Harry and I will go up to the thirty-third floor in another elevator. We'll check it out quickly, then come down those stairs I see to join you. Just in case. Agreed, Tweed?'

'Yes, do that.'

Newman asked his question while he was travelling up in their elevator with Tweed and Paula. He noticed she looked tense again as the elevator ascended.

'Maybe, Tweed, we'll find another pair of gloves. What did you do with the pair we found at Gargoyle Towers? He slipped up there – Goslar. A boffin back at Park Crescent could measure those gloves, come up with some idea of the wearer's weight and height.'

'I threw them into my wastepaper basket. You're forgetting, Bob. Goslar likes to leave false clues, hoping we'll waste so many hours coming up with useless ideas. I'll go into the room with you, Paula. Bob can watch our backs . . .'

Like Newman, Paula had her gun in her hand as she stepped out of the elevator. She walked slowly to the room where the door was still open, as she had left it. Tweed glanced round the spacious hall, his hands still in his coat pockets.

'This place must have cost him a packet,' he remarked. 'That wouldn't worry him for a second . . .'

Paula paused at the open door. The lights were still on. She gripped her Browning with both hands, peered inside, sweeping the interior with her automatic. Then she walked inside with a firm step.

'It's just as I left it. That's the bed they threw me on – and the window they dangled me from is still open. No one has been here.'

'Someone has,' Tweed corrected her. 'At least on the ground floor. To fix up the boobytrap bomb.'

He walked over to the open window, peered down at the moonlit area thirty-plus floors below. His mouth tightened. He turned and looked at Paula.

'What an appalling experience you endured.'

'I'd just as soon not have to repeat the performance,' she replied with a wan smile.

'I've found something,' reported Newman, who had been searching under the bed. 'An unsmoked cigarette. Does Goslar smoke?'

'He did. Menthols. St Moritz brand.'

'Well, I've found one which must have rolled under the bed.' He was dropping it inside a transparent specimen bag. 'We can, in due course, have it checked for fingerprints.'

'Then that man with rimless glasses I described could have been Dr Goslar,' Paula said.

'Sorry to disappoint you,' Tweed told her, 'and don't waste your time, Bob. Just another false clue. I'm sure Rimless Glasses, using latex gloves, placed it there while the Ape was suspending Paula from that infernal window. The idea was she might find it when the two men had gone.'

'Then why did they go to all that trouble of scaring the wits out of me and asking useless questions?'

'I'm sure they meant to let you go all the time. It was another of Goslar's elaborate plots to lure me back here so I would be blown to pieces.'

'Goslar is incredibly subtle and devious.'

'Something we must not forget. But one day he'll accidentally leave a real clue. Then I can track him and find the fiendish weapon he tried out at Appledore. Also he's repeating some of the tricks he used over ten years ago. Remember, Bob? That may lead to his eventual destruction . . .'

He became silent. Newman had crouched just inside the open door, his Smith & Wesson aimed at the foot of the staircase leading down from the floor above. He had heard a faint footstep.

'Don't shoot the postman. He's doing his best,' Butler called out as he appeared at the bottom of the staircase.

'Nothing up there,' Burgoyne called out as they walked to the room. 'Place is as clean as a new pin. No furniture, not anything. Just as though the building was never occupied for weeks.'

'Dr Goslar's trademark,' Tweed said, looking at Burgoyne. 'He is the most careful man I've ever encountered. Yet there are times when he takes risks. *Toujours l'audacité.* One of his favourite maxims. He used it twice when he called to taunt me in his – or her – disguised voice. I'm talking about years ago. He repeated it at the end of the second call. *Toujours l'audacité.*'

'Interesting.' Burgoyne frowned briefly, a crease appearing in his tall forehead. 'Napoleon, isn't it? Napoleon said it first.'

'He did,' Tweed replied. ' "Always audacity." Either he or – more likely – one of his thugs was, I'm sure, in the building opposite this one. When I looked out of the window the moonlight was shining on it. I saw a shadow behind an unlit window.'

'Then let's get over there,' said Newman.

'Pointless. It's a huge building. The door is certain to be locked. The shadow figure will have gone by now. We'll take the Métro, make our way to the Ritz.'

'I'll put in an anonymous call to the police about that bomb,' Newman decided as they walked out of the building.

He was the first to go outside, followed by Tweed and Paula, with Butler and Burgoyne bringing up the rear. Tweed looked to his left, saw a uniformed guard with a peaked cap strolling out of the next building. The guard, obviously emerging for a spot of fresh air, stretched his arms. Tweed walked swiftly towards him with Paula by his side. He spoke in French.

'Excuse me. I came here to meet someone but the building is empty. Do you know when they left?'

'About a week ago. A convoy of big vans turned up well after dark. I watched from a window. A large crew spent half the night carrying out small containers and loading them into the vans. I could see a number of the containers were marked "fragile". I was curious so I approached them when a lot of them were loading. Only one man spoke French, so he told me. Said he'd been hired because he was also fluent in Serbo-Croat.'

'So the rest of the crew were Croats?'

'Yes. So were all the staff in that building. They were escorted everywhere, only got out for the occasional meal. The Frenchman told me he didn't fancy moving to Annecy – he was Parisian – but the pay was good. Then the big man came out and all hell broke loose.'

'The big man?'

'Big as a giant. When he walked he padded like an animal. His shoulders – they were huge – dipped up and down when he moved. Had cropped brown hair.'

'Sounds like an ape,' Paula interjected in French.

'You've got it!' The guard clapped his gloved hands together. 'I wondered what he reminded me of.'

'You said all hell broke loose,' Tweed reminded him.

'The giant was furious because the Frenchman had been talking to me. Practically dragged him away. Heard him swearing foully. I know enough English to recognize swear words.' He grinned. 'Particularly the foul sort. I heard the Frenchman protesting that all they'd been talking about was the weather. Then there was something else . . .'

'Annecy,' Burgoyne's voice said behind them. 'Could that be significant?'

Tweed waved at him to keep quiet. He returned his attention to the guard.

'You said there was something else?'

'A whacking great limo arrives. A woman dressed like a man comes out. She hurries into the back, slams the door shut, the limo takes off.'

'How can you be sure it was a woman?' Tweed pressed.

'Wears trousers, men's shoes, long man's overcoat, a Borsalino hat, brim pulled well down.'

'Sounds as though it could have been a man,' Tweed insisted.

'I'm French.' The guard laughed. 'A Frenchman can always detect a woman. Body language.'

'Of course.' Tweed chuckled. 'Any idea who owns the building?'

'That was strange too. Leased by a company in Luxembourg City. But when they left the lease had another three months to run. I'd better get back to my post. Hope you find your friend who worked there . . .'

'Annecy,' Burgoyne said again as the guard disappeared. 'Might that not be significant?'

'Maybe. Let's leave this weird place. We'll take the Métro, make our way back to the Ritz.'

Again they had an empty coach to themselves as they travelled back from La Défense. Paula sat next to Tweed and Butler faced them two seats further back. Further along the coach Newman sat with Burgoyne, engaged in conversation as the two men got to know each other.

'Chance was very quick,' Paula recalled. 'I mean spotting the wire along the top of the door.'

'He was,' Tweed agreed. 'He is most promising material.'

Paula glanced at him. What he had said was the highest praise he could bestow on a new addition to the team.

'Howard's other reinforcement, Evan Tarnwalk, never appeared,' she remarked.

'Ex-Special Branch. We can do without him. You realize that we were followed from Heathrow?'

'No!' She was startled. 'What makes you say that?'

'There were two people on our flight. One, a woman by herself in a seat well behind us. Several seats behind her, across on the other side of the aisle, was a man, also by himself. They rushed into the final departure lounge at Heathrow – separately – waving their tickets when we'd started boarding. When we left Marler and Nield at Madeleine to drive the cars to the Ritz, I saw the woman hail a cab and follow Marler. Then, when we got into the Métro coach for La Défense I saw the man dive into the last coach. He skipped out again at La Défense just before the doors closed.'

'This is very serious. Alarming. It has to mean that Goslar knows where we are.'

'Which suits me to the ground. I know now we're in the right place – on his track. That puts pressure on Goslar. People under pressure sooner or later make a mistake. I'm waiting for him to do just that.'

'You're as manipulative as he is,' she commented.

'More so, I hope. The interesting thing is the couple following us made their actions obvious. No attempt to conceal the fact they were following us.'

'Why would they do that?'

At that moment Burgoyne turned round. He waved buoyantly at Tweed and grinned. Tweed beckoned for him to join them. Burgoyne sat on the facing seat, looked at Paula.

'I reckon a good night's sleep will do you no harm at all when we get to the Ritz.'

'Sounds like a good idea,' she agreed. 'You look as though you could go on for hours. How do you manage it?'

'Clean living.' He grinned again. 'At least that's my story and I'm sticking to it. You need stamina prowling around in the desert.'

'Chance,' Tweed said, leaning forward, 'tomorrow I have to go and see someone. I want you to stay inside the hotel with Nield as backup. Stay there all day. They have more than one restaurant.'

'What do we do – Nield and me?'

'You're on the lookout for any odd characters – men or women. I need to know if anyone starts making enquiries about me. Paula and I will give Pete Nield keys to our rooms.'

'Why?'

'So you can both check them at regular intervals. I don't want to open a cupboard door when I get back and get blown to pieces all over the room.'

12

After breakfast the following morning Tweed called Lasalle. He used a public phone box on rue St-Honoré. Outside, at intervals on both sides of the street, Paula, Newman, Butler and Marler waited – and watched.

Rush-hour traffic had evaporated, and the street was quiet. It was too early for the wealthy ladies to be strolling, looking in expensive shop windows. Spasmodically the pavements were wet where shopkeepers had hosed them. The sun shone out of a clear blue sky but there was a chill wind. It was still almost the end of March. A few optimistic shopkeepers had lowered striped blinds but there were no tables outside.

'Tweed here, René. In Paris.'

'Go back to London.'

'I appreciate the warm welcome. I have to see you urgently – we may be working on the same thing. An exchange of information might help us both. You owe me.'

'I knew you would say that.' A pause, a sigh. 'What you said is true. Where are you?'

'In the rue St-Honoré.'

'In thirty minutes I'll meet you. Facing Madeleine there's a brasserie, a bar. Le Colibri. Just the two of us. Don't come with your team, which I'm sure you have with you. Thirty minutes from now.'

The connection was broken. Lasalle had not even bothered to say goodbye. A man under great pressure, Tweed said to himself. There was tension in Paris in certain quarters. When he emerged Paula and Newman strolled across the street, joined him, one on either side.

'Marler and Butler are providing backup,' Paula said.

'I suppose it's necessary,' Tweed grumbled.

'It's not necessary,' Newman said grimly. 'It's essential. Or have you forgotten Sam Sneed, Coral Langley, who had her face blown away when Marler visited Rydford, the bomb waiting for Paula in the Fulham Road, the bomb waiting for you at La Défense?'

'You have a point,' Tweed conceded.

He was walking slowly, glancing in shop windows. Once he looked back quickly, but there was no sign of Marler or Butler. They would be there, he knew, but both were experts – not only at tracking but also at remaining invisible to whoever they were following. Tweed told Paula and Newman the gist of his conversation with Lasalle.

'Doesn't sound like him,' Paula commented.

'Goslar is brilliant at creating an atmosphere of uncertainty – and tension. He's succeeding.'

'Why?' asked Newman.

'To push up the bidding sky-high.'

'The bidding?'

'Yes, for the ultimate weapon he's invented. Sooner or later he'll get large offers from America and France. I'm convinced he's determined to sell it to the Arab Fundamentalists. They now have vast resources. He – Goslar – will use the bids from other countries to squeeze far more from the Arabs.'

'Will Britain make an offer?'

'Not if I have anything to do with it. Why should we play his hideous game? As I said before, we have to find him, to destroy this maniac and all his works.'

As Tweed entered, Le Colibri had the usual curving bar on his left. To the right and deep inside were round glass-topped tables with wicker chairs. No sign of Lasalle. Tweed checked his watch as he made his way to the back, where the tables were empty. Nearer the front, groups of workmen and the odd couple chattered non-stop over drinks or coffee and croissants.

Tweed was early and had come in by himself. When the apron-clad waiter arrived he ordered a Pernod. A moment later Paula came in, chose a table at the front with its back to the wall. Tweed pursed his lips. At least the others had dispersed somewhere in the vicinity outside.

The waiter brought his Pernod. Tweed sipped at it for the sake of appearances. Paula had not even glanced in his direction. She appeared to be reading a copy of *Le Monde*. She ordered something from a waiter, which he guessed would be coffee. Tweed took off his horn-rims, cleaned the lenses on a new handkerchief, put them on again.

A small man with a trim moustache entered. For a moment Tweed didn't recognize him. Lasalle wore a shabby anorak, buttoned to the neck, equally shabby denims and shoes. A stained hat with the brim pulled down covered his head.

His normal brisk step was absent. He slouched between the tables, his head moving from side to side. Checking on everyone in the place, Tweed knew. He chose a chair close to Tweed with its back to the wall. The waiter appeared.

'I will have one of those,' he said in French, pointing at the Pernod in front of Tweed.

'Thank you for coming,' Tweed said in a quiet voice.

'I took a chance. Remember that,' the Frenchman said, speaking English. 'And why is Paula sitting at that table?'

'She has a mind of her own. I told her to stay outside.'

'She looks after you. That is good. You first. Thank you,' he said to the waiter who had just returned. 'How much? I'm paying for both drinks . . .'

'I'd like to know where the Grumman aircraft that I spoke to you about from London is now.'

'That private jet intrigued me, so I made enquiries. First, as you know, it flew from Exeter to Charles de Gaulle – where an ambulance was waiting to take away a patient on a stretcher.'

'The so-called patient was Paula – who was kidnapped on Dartmoor, drugged, transported to Exeter Airport and then flown here. She had a bad experience. At the hands of Dr Goslar's thugs.'

'Then thank God she looks her normal fit self. To continue, the pilot filed a flight plan for Geneva, then changed it at the last moment. The private jet flew straight back to Heathrow.'

'That's strange.'

'I thought so. Maybe to pick up a passenger – to deliver one to London. Who knows?' Lasalle drank half his Pernod. 'From Heathrow it then flies straight to Geneva. I contacted Swiss friends. They tell me the aircraft is parked in an area reserved for private aircraft at Cointrin, Geneva's airport.'

'You said a private jet. Any idea who owns it?'

'A company called Poulenc et Cie, registered with a company in Liechtenstein at Vaduz. You know it is impossible to penetrate that place. So the trail ends there.'

'Meantime the jet is sitting on the tarmac at Geneva.'

'Yes.' Lasalle removed his hat, placed it on a chair. His dark hair was lank and greasy. The Frenchman saw Tweed's glance. 'I used plenty of oil on it – to merge with the background.'

'You're wearing your undercover work gear?'

'Yes. Awful, isn't it?'

'Changing the subject,' Tweed began, 'I suspect you have heard the name Goslar. Is that so?'

'Ah!' Lasalle shrugged, paused. 'I think we now come to what you call the nitty-gritty. You mentioned that name earlier.'

'And you didn't react. Which told me you'd heard of him.'

'I know you are a master interrogator. Slipped up there, didn't I? What I am going to tell you is so confidential I would lose my job if anyone came to hear of my talking to you. We are both referring to a strange incident at Appledore. Have I pronounced that correctly?'

'Yes. Please go on.'

'The Élysée received a video of that affair. You understand me?'

'Perfectly.'

By 'Élysée' Lasalle meant the President of France. He was being as frank as he dared. Lasalle took out a coloured handkerchief, mopped his forehead before he went on.

'The Élysée also received a recording made by someone with the most doctored voice. The message said the sender would consider sending his device – then he said *selling* his device – to France for eight thousand million francs.'

'That's roughly eight hundred million pounds. Didn't want much, did he?'

'There was an explosion of fury inside the Élysée at the amount. The security services were immediately ordered to track down the speaker, to get hold of the device with extreme urgency. So . . .' Lasalle looked embarrassed, 'I fear that we are rivals, fighting each other.'

'At least we can be civilized about this.'

'You must be careful. We believe the enemy has employed a very dangerous assassin. The Yellow Man. So called because he is believed to have yellow hair.'

Nothing in Tweed's expression betrayed the fact that he was startled by this information. He nodded to encourage Lasalle to keep talking.

'A few months ago a very rich man, a friend of a Cabinet Minister, was murdered horribly by, we believe, the Yellow Man. The victim was found decapitated in his apartment.'

'I think it made the English papers.'

'This assassin is so reliable the underworld believes that he was paid a million francs for that job.'

'Which is roughly a hundred thousand pounds.

Thanks for the warning. So on this Goslar business we're on opposite sides.'

'I'm afraid so, my friend. Expect no help from France. Take care.'

Tweed watched Lasalle putting on his old hat, pulling down the brim. Then he slouched away, head down. As he passed Paula's table he took no notice of her. She didn't look up, was apparently reading her newspaper.

There was a phone on the bar. Tweed stood up, went over to it. He called the number Serena had given him. A rough voice demanded in French who the hell it was.

'Maurice, a friend of Yvonne's,' Tweed replied, using the same language. 'I believe you can contact her. I can wait while you—'

'Not available!'

The phone was slammed down. Tweed walked slowly out of the brasserie. A few yards along the street he gazed round as though not sure where to go next. As Paula joined him a minute later Marler appeared out of nowhere.

'We'll go now and visit your rare-bookseller friend,' Tweed told Marler. 'Where are the others?' He had just spoken when Butler and Newman walked up to them. 'No point in going back for the cars,' he decided. 'We'll take a taxi.'

He hailed one. The driver pulled in to the kerb with a screech of brakes. He looked ahead, conveying the impression that passengers were a nuisance.

'Please take us to the Île de la Cité. We're in a hurry.'

'You always are,' the driver responded rudely. 'Traffic today is terrible. We get there when we arrive . . .'

'I think we're being followed,' Paula said after looking back.

'We'd better get used to it,' Tweed replied calmly. 'Is it,' he whispered, 'someone in another cab?'

'Yes.'

'Get a look at the passenger?'

'I'm afraid I didn't. But back at Madeleine I saw, out of the corner of my eye, someone flag down another cab as we got into this one. The same cab keeps following the route that we are taking.'

'Try and see who is inside if it stops when we do . . .'

Despite what the driver had said, once they had left Madeleine the traffic was light. Following Tweed's instructions the driver crossed a bridge over the Seine onto the Île de la Cité, then stopped outside the Palais de Justice. Paula got out quickly, looked back. She saw the cab which had tailed them pulling up. Then a huge truck stopped in front of it, blocking her view.

'Here you are,' said Tweed, handing the fare over plus the tip a Frenchman would have given him. The driver held out his hand with the money in his palm. He glared at Tweed.

'Is this all?'

'Fare with normal tip,' Tweed told him.

'Tip? Is this all? You are a miser.'

'Drop dead!' Paula snapped in French.

The driver stared at her as though unable to believe a woman had answered him back. He shrugged, drove off.

'Couldn't see who got out of the cab which followed us,' Paula said. 'A truck got in the way.'

'It doesn't matter. We'll walk past Notre-Dame.'

As they approached Notre-Dame Tweed stared up. Each time he saw it it always seemed larger, more massive. There were hardly any tourists about – it was the time of year and the weather. At the end of Cité they saw the Île St-Louis, the smaller island with the Seine swirling round it.

They came to the narrow bridge linking Cité with St-Louis. It was just wide enough for a car to cross but a barrier prevented wheeled traffic. As they walked round past the end of the barrier Marler caught up with Tweed.

'When we're the other side of the bridge take the right turn – along the quai d'Orleans. Vallade is in one of the narrow streets off to the left.'

'And I'm sure we're being followed,' said Paula.

'You warned us of that earlier,' Marler recalled, 'but neither Newman or Butler – or I for that matter – have spotted anyone. If Paula is right it must be someone very clever.'

'Paula is right,' Paula said obstinately. 'I can sense it. I just hope it isn't the Yellow Man.'

Earlier, while walking across the Cité, Tweed had told them about what Lasalle had said concerning the now notorious assassin. He felt he was not breaking his word on this subject. On the other hand he repeated not a word Lasalle had told him about the Élysée.

'We'll stroll along the embankment,' Marler suggested. 'I will tell you which is Vallade's street but it might be better if we continued on past it. That will give Newman and Butler an opportunity to check our rear. Paula's shadow has to cross the bridge to keep after us.'

'Except,' said Paula, after glancing back, 'a tour party has appeared. It is about to cross the bridge. An assassin could easily mingle with them . . .'

They continued along the *quai*. To their right the Seine flowed swiftly, a dark green current. A stone wall, roughly three feet high, separated them from the river below. On their left were ancient buildings five storeys high, also built of stone and with an appearance of having wealthy occupants.

As they strolled on Tweed was aware of an atmosphere of tension building up. They had been convinced by Paula's assertion that they were being followed. They all resisted the temptation to look back – which would have given the game away. It was up to Newman and Butler, somewhere behind them. They arrived at the first street leading straight down on their left. Tweed peered at it.

'Not that one,' snapped Marler.

'If there is a watcher,' Tweed pointed out, 'and I look down each street we come to, it will tell him nothing.'

'Hadn't thought of that.'

They kept walking and the wind was growing stronger. When they came to a certain side street Tweed peered down it. Marler spoke quickly.

'That's the one.'

Like all the streets on St-Louis the street was narrow, dark. On the ground floor there were shops, and above, Tweed assumed, would be apartments. They walked a short distance further and the *quai* curved round a sharp corner. There was a large gap in the embankment wall where a wide stone ramp led down to the water's edge. Tweed stopped.

'What is it?' Paula asked.

'There's a very modern powerboat moored to a bollard down at the bottom of the ramp. No one about. Interesting.'

'Why?'

'We'd better get on with it, Marler. Time to visit Vallade and see what he can tell us.'

'I hope he's still alive,' Paula said.

13

In his suite at the Hôtel Crillon in Paris Vance Karnow, aide to the President of the United States, sat in a carver chair and stared at his guests with hard eyes. Tall and thin, with a long face which had prominent bone structure, his mouth was wide with twisted lips. Below the mouth his jaw was pointed.

'Everyone present and here on time,' he said in his harsh voice. 'You know I demand punctuality on the rare occasions when I call a full meeting.'

Including Karnow, there were eleven people in the luxurious room. All were members of Unit Four. Ten men and one woman. They sat spread round the room, seated in armchairs or on sofas. The woman sat in her own carver chair close to Karnow.

'We now know,' Karnow continued, 'that Tweed is in Paris, staying at the Ritz. Thanks to Trudy.' He turned to her. 'Show them the photo of Tweed.'

Trudy Warnowski was an attractive woman in her late thirties. Her blaze of soft red hair was perfectly coiffeured and she wore just enough makeup on her cheerful face. She had a good figure, and was clad in a fashionable and expensive black suit.

From a folder she produced a photograph. Walking elegantly to one of the men she gave him the photo.

'Hand it round, Brad,' she told him. 'After you've memorized Tweed. That's important.'

Karnow gave her a verbal pat on the back when she had returned to her chair.

'You should all know that Trudy followed Tweed to Paris on his late flight last night. She then drove after him from Charles de Gaulle in her hired car. During the flight she saw Tweed speak to another man sitting by himself further down the aircraft. At Madeleine she had to take a quick decision. She saw the man Tweed had spoken to getting into another car. She decided to follow him, thinking he'd lead her to where they were staying. She had parked her car by a meter. She hailed a cab, wanting a different vehicle so she wouldn't be spotted. She was smart. She waited inside the reception area and later Tweed himself arrived, booked in.'

'Nothing to it,' Trudy said in her soft voice.

By this time the photograph had passed round the room. A short, heavily built, fat man with a large round face ambled over to Trudy, handed back the photo. She knew he had been gazing at her legs as he approached her.

'You did a good job,' he said in his hoarse voice.

'I've just spent time telling everyone that,' Karnow said coldly. 'Weren't you listening, Bancroft?'

The fat man was the only member of Unit Four Karnow always addressed by his surname. He knew Bancroft was the only man present who wasn't frightened of him.

'So I paid her my own compliment,' Bancroft retorted, staring at Karnow. 'Anything wrong with that? And where's Milt? Not here.'

'Milt,' Karnow replied through lips which had almost vanished, 'is following Tweed Inc. at this moment.'

'Waiting for an opportunity to use his knife?'

'Anybody ever tell you that you talk too much?'

'Lots of people. I do it all the time. Milt's going to carve up Tweed if he can?'

Bancroft was referring to the fact that Milt Friedman always used a knife to persuade men – or women – to talk. He had once used an axe to kill a target.

145

'Milt will use his own discretion. Subject closed. Although if any of you get Tweed on his own he is *very, very* embarrassing.'

Translation: kill him. Karnow used a number of careful phrases to explain what was needed. *Very embarrassing* meant beat up the named subject. *Lose him* meant cripple the subject, man or woman.

Bancroft grinned at Trudy, gave her a mock salute, ambled back to his sofa.

Trudy recalled that, despite his fatness, Bancroft was a winner with women. She knew he'd had a number of successes – often with classy ladies. Something about his personality. Then she recalled the strong thin piece of rope he had once carried. It was attached by one end to his belt while the length dangled down inside his left trouser leg. He had strangled two women with that piece of rope. She took out a lacy handkerchief and dried her moist palms.

'Your task is simple,' Karnow began again. 'All members of Tweed's team – when we have identified them – are *very, very* embarrassing. You circulate round the Ritz, inside it. First you identify his team – I suspect there are a number of them.'

And they could do that, he thought as he paused. Because they were all well dressed in good suits. They were all educated – even Bancroft. He had recruited Unit Four with great care. No thugs from the back streets of Chicago.

Several had been trained as lawyers. They had then found it would take years to earn big money. Some were from Harvard and thought the world was their oyster. They'd had a shock when they discovered the lowly jobs, the low pay, the endless hours they'd be expected to work for years.

Karnow had looked for frustrated men. Those who

would never get anywhere – and knew it when they started exploring the jungle of the real world. Karnow had looked for those with a streak of amorality, brutality. He had offered them regular money they'd have taken years to get near in any profession. Generous money. Paid in cash – so they could forget about forking out tax. He looked at Brad Braun, a good-looking man in his late twenties.

'Brad, you book yourself a suite at the Ritz. Keep an eye on Tweed and see who he mixes with. Circulate descriptions to the rest of the unit.'

'A suite at the Ritz will be expensive,' Brad observed as he stroked his thick black and well-groomed hair.

'You all have a load of dollars. Brad, when you pay you just tell the desk you've lost your credit card. They're French,' he said with a note of contempt, 'they'll grab your dollars. Oh, there was a woman travelling on the plane with Tweed.'

'Great!' Bancroft grinned. 'Do I get a description?'

'Only a vague one,' Trudy informed him. 'Thick black glossy hair. A looker. Slim, in her thirties would be my best guess. About five feet six tall. That's it.'

'That's enough,' Bancroft said with another suggestive grin.

'Move,' Karnow said. 'All of you – except Trudy.'

'Have a cosy get-together,' Bancroft said as he was leaving the room with the others.

Karnow caught his eye, the fact that he was still grinning. His expression would have scared the daylights out of any other member of the unit. Bancroft just went on grinning until he shut the door and disappeared.

'He's a character,' Trudy said, lighting a cigarette.

'Do you have to smoke?' Karnow asked.

'We're not in America now. Thank God. I like

147

Europe. I knew a Frenchman who told me over here they think political correctness is treating a woman friend generously.'

'Do you think they got my message – the unit?'

'Hardly fail to – the extremely diplomatic way you put it across to them.'

'Nobody talks back to me the way you do,' he commented with a grudging note of admiration. 'But I meant it – when I said you'd done a good job tracking Tweed.'

'Oh, I think there was another man with him. A military type. I couldn't be sure. It would have meant turning my head round and staring.'

'You rescued your parked car?'

'Took a cab back to pick it up after Tweed arrived. A piece of cake.' She went silent for a short time, then glanced at Karnow. 'I thought the object of this exercise was to locate Goslar, to grab this new weapon.'

'It is.'

'Then I think it was a mistake to order them to eliminate Tweed. You got someone to ask Cord Dillon about Tweed. Dillon said he was the most formidable security officer in Europe.'

'So?'

'Keep him alive. Follow him. I think eventually he'll lead us to Goslar. This is his back yard.'

'You could be right.' Karnow pondered briefly. 'I think you are right. I'll put that order on hold.' He picked up the phone, called a room number. 'Brad, I imagine none of our associates have left the hotel yet? Good. Get them all back up here in ten minutes from now . . .'

He clasped his cruel, long-fingered hands, looked at the woman sitting next to him with what passed for a smile.

'How about having dinner with me tonight?'

'Vance, I made it quite clear when you hired me the

relationship must remain strictly professional. You agreed. The agreement still stands. I must go now.'

'Anything you say,' he responded as she was leaving the room.

He sat ruminating. His first meeting with Trudy had been at a Washington party. She was English, which, added to her appearance, he knew would make most American men a pushover for her. He had been looking for the right woman to add to Unit Four and she fitted the bill. He had just finished talking to Bancroft when he had encountered her.

She had told him she was a widow. He had told her he was the right-hand man to the President. It hadn't seemed to impress her. He had arranged several lunches with her – while he instructed a detective agency, through an intermediary, to check on her. Vance Karnow was a careful operator.

The agency had confirmed what she'd told him during the lunches. She was employed by a top security outfit, handling difficult assignments brilliantly. She'd had a two-year stint in New York. She lived alone in an apartment in Washington after her transfer. The one item the agency couldn't come up with was the identity of her late husband. He had casually asked her about him over lunch.

'We lived in a very different part of the States,' she told him. Gazing straight at him, she went on. 'It's a painful subject and I don't want to talk about it. Don't ask me again . . .'

He'd glossed over that. His next move was to offer her a highly paid position with 'a confidential organization not so different from the one you're working for now'. He had emphasized that the difference was the work was absolutely top secret.

'If you think by now that I can't keep my mouth shut, forget it,' she had told him.

He had hired her for three times the salary the security agency had been paying her. She had accepted, but had refused point-blank to sign any kind of contract. He had reluctantly agreed to the condition, so impressed was he by her personality.

Taking his time, he had gradually revealed to her the function of Unit Four: that it was to protect state secrets. He had not told her that it was in any way involved with the Oval Office – which, in a way, put her on a level with the President.

When Karnow had come up with the idea he had no more than hinted about how Unit Four would operate. He had been vague when he had talked to the President. First, he had laid the groundwork.

'Neither of us are very happy about the leaks which filter out of the FBI and the CIA,' he had suggested. 'I've been thinking that we need a small, tough group of élite men to handle sensitive situations . . .'

'You mean "I" not "we",' the President had corrected him.

'Yes, I do,' Karnow had agreed. 'A slip of the tongue.'

'Very unusual for you, Vance. I have so much to do I must leave decisions like that to your discretion.'

The President had winked at him.

Karnow was recalling that wink when Brad Braun walked into the suite, followed by Bancroft and the others. The nine men sat in the same places they had occupied earlier.

'Trudy,' said Bancroft, 'isn't coming. Said she wasn't needed for this conference.'

'She has something to attend to,' Karnow improvised.

Mentally he gave her top marks. She had thought it tactful to stay away, to give him the floor.

'I have been thinking about what I said to you earlier

concerning Tweed,' he began. 'We let him walk the face of this planet. It has struck me . . .'

Long ago Karnow had learned to take the credit for other people's ideas. It comfirmed his own cleverness.

14

Tweed and Paula managed to walk side by side down the meagre width of the pavement. Marler walked alongside them in the narrow street. The area was deserted and Paula had a claustrophobic sensation as the old buildings on either side seemed to close in on them. It was too quiet and there was no wind.

'There's the shop,' Marler said.

'I've seen it,' replied Tweed. 'Looks pretty rundown.'

He could just make out the name in crumbling gold paint on the fascia above the grimy windows. The name, *Vallade*, hadn't been repainted for ages. Quite a narrow frontage with a warped wooden door which had pebble glass windows in the upper half. Tweed paused by the first window. He could see ancient volumes in worn leather bindings.

'He speaks English,' Marler said. 'You two go in to get the feel of the place. I'll come in when I've checked the street.'

The door creaked when Tweed turned the old-fashioned handle and he had to lift and push to get it open. With Paula he walked inside and immediately met a musty smell. The shop was narrow and long, went back further than he'd expected. On a counter was a huge glass dome housing a large stuffed owl. Paula stared at the left-hand wall facing the counter. From floor to ceiling were glass-fronted bookcases crammed with old books side by side.

Tweed was walking further down the counter. Behind it stood a small plump man. Everything about him was plump. His plump face was a surprisingly healthy pink colour and his grey hair was brushed neatly back from his forehead. He wore a shabby velvet jacket with gold buttons and a pair of corduroy trousers which had seen better days. Perched on his short nose were half-moon glasses. He peered at his visitors over the top of them.

'Have you a copy of Hogarth's *Characters in My Times*?' asked Tweed.

'No, sir. And no one has. Such a title does not exist.'

'Just checking,' Tweed said with a smile.

'I do know books, sir,' Vallade replied with a smile which included Paula.

'It's like *The Old Curiosity Shop*,' Paula whispered to Tweed.

'Charles Dickens,' Vallade called out.

Paula then realized the Frenchman had exceptional hearing. When he smiled his chubby red cheeks seemed even plumper. At that moment Marler entered.

'Ah!' Vallade commented. 'When Tweed appears Marler is not far behind.'

'How do you know my name?' Tweed enquired.

'I presume you have come for any information I can provide. So I know a few things about this jungle of a world we live in – including the existence of Mr Tweed.'

'What is that ferocious-looking thing hanging from the wall near the door?' Paula asked.

She was looking at a long curved oriental sword. The handle was large and decorated with strange designs. There were more weird symbols on the blade.

'That is a Japanese . . .' Vallade paused – he had been going to say 'execution sword' but because she was a lady he changed it – 'ceremonial sword. The Japanese pay a lot of money for such articles. We don't see Japanese much these days – now their economy has collapsed.' He looked at Tweed. 'I said the world was a jungle. Now the Americans drop 2,000 pound bombs from a height of 15,000 feet on Serbia – killing many women and children. This is mass murder. I fear your government trots along behind Washington. Excuse me, I digress. How can I help you?'

'I am hoping you can tell me something about a man called Dr Goslar.'

'He is a client of mine. Not in person. He phoned me with a screeching voice and wanted me to find a copy of a book on the Galapagos Islands in the Pacific, the home of giant turtles. It is a rare medical book on these strange creatures.'

He paused and came through a gap in the counter. He had noticed Paula peering into the glass bookcases against the opposite wall. Producing a bunch of keys he opened a bookcase, took out a small black cardboard case, handed it to her.

'You may find this interesting . . .'

Tweed intervened quickly, realizing he had not introduced her to the bookseller. Vallade shook her hand, smiled again.

'Inside the case is a first edition, illustrated, of J. M. Barrie's *Peter Pan*. I think you will like it.'

He shuffled back behind his counter. His visitors saw he wore a pair of slippers. He gazed at Tweed.

'Excuse the interruption. I told this Goslar I had one copy but it was expensive. He asked how much and told me to keep it for him.'

'He came to collect it himself?' enquired Tweed.

'No, as arranged on the phone, he sent someone to pick it up. A good-looking red-haired lady.'

'She gave a name?' Tweed asked casually.

'No. She said she had come to collect the book Dr Goslar had called me about, paid me, took the book away.'

'Could you describe her?'

'About as tall as Miss Grey. Another beautiful lady. Her eyes were grey-blue. She wore a scarf round her head. I only saw the lovely red hair because when she opened the door to leave the wind blew the scarf off her neck. The hair was long.'

'How long ago was it since she collected this book?'

'My memory is not good these days for time lapses. I would say about ten days ago. Maybe a little longer.'

'One other point, Étienne,' interjected Marler, 'do you know anything about the Yellow Man?'

'Oh dear.' For the first time Vallade's expression became grave. 'That terrible assassin. He has killed three important men so far. One in Germany, another in Switzerland – and a wealthy man here who lived in a big house just along the *quai*. They say he receives a million francs for an assassination. He is so efficient but no one ever sees him. Certain top informants I know in the underworld tell me it is rumoured he has yellow hair. Which is why he is called the Yellow Man.'

'Any clue as to his whereabouts?' Marler suggested.

'None at all. Another rumour is that he is English. But he is invisible. Please do not tell anyone what I have told you.'

'We wouldn't dream of ever mentioning your name,' Tweed assured him. 'And you really have been most helpful.'

Tweed was hesitantly reaching for his wallet when Marler nudged him. Tweed withdrew his hand. Vallade did not expect any payment. The plump little man shuffled through the gap in the counter to Paula, who had been admiring the *Peter Pan* book.

'This is quite beautiful,' she said, handing it to him after carefully placing it back in the case.

'It is for you, Miss Grey.'

'But this is a first edition. I couldn't possibly . . .'

'It is a present.' He squeezed her hand. 'You cannot refuse a present from Vallade.' He turned to Tweed, shook his hand.

'Always be on the lookout for a man with yellow hair. Take great care.'

'Thank you so much for the magnificent present,' Paula said. 'Your English is perfect. Where did you learn it?'

'Thank you.' Vallade beamed at her. 'As a young man I studied my profession with a rare-book dealer in a street off Piccadilly. I go back to London when I can to listen to how they speak English today. Languages change. You also take great care. You are a nice lady . . .'

He closed the door behind them gently as they stepped onto the pavement. Marler glanced to his right.

'We're nearly at the end of this street. We could go into the main thoroughfare, the rue St Louis en l'Île.'

'No,' Tweed decided, 'we'll go back the way we came. I'm hungry and that is the direct route to the Restaurant Paul on Cité. We'll get an excellent meal there.'

Newman appeared. He walked slowly alongside Tweed as they proceeded to the *quai*. He had his hand over his mouth as he took his time lighting a cigarette.

'Coast appears clear. Neither Butler nor I have seen anyone following us. Hard to be sure. Several individuals have wandered down here while you were inside.'

'They went past the shop?'

'Some did. Others disappeared into houses. I'll walk ahead. Harry is bringing up the rear . . .'

They had reached the end of the street, and were

about to turn right on to the *quai*, when Tweed looked back, stopped, hesitated, then walked on slowly. He had his head down, hands inside the pockets of his grey overcoat. Paula kept quiet. She guessed he was turning over in his mind what Vallade had told them.

When they reached the bridge he paused again. He was staring at the River Seine, which was less choppy. Paula wished he'd get moving. She was starving. After a minute or two he looked at her.

'We're going back to Vallade's shop. At the top of his street I thought I caught a glimpse – out of the corner of my eye – of someone walking into one of the buildings near the bottom of the street. It could have been Vallade's bookshop.'

'Something up?' asked Newman who had walked back to them.

'Tweed thinks he saw someone going into Vallade's place,' Paula told him.

'We'll go back now,' Tweed decided. 'Peripheral vision can be deceptive, but I thought I caught a glimpse of yellow hair.' He began stepping it out. 'Move, everyone.'

They were halfway down the street when Tweed paused. He looked back, listened. There was the distant sound of an engine starting up.

'Sounds like that powerboat we saw,' he said. 'I don't like this . . .'

Butler had moved ahead of them. His right hand was tucked inside his anorak, gripping his Walther. He arrived at the bookseller's shop. Paula, close behind him with Tweed, was about to enter when Butler grasped her by the arm, pulled her back.

'You stay outside while I check the place.'

He entered, opening the door slowly. Tweed was at

156

his heels. Newman remained on the pavement, restraining Paula, who snapped at him. He tightened his grip on her arm, glancing up and down the street.

'Our job is to keep an eye open for watchers.'

Butler, Walther in his hand, had gone into the shop in front of Tweed. He stopped suddenly. Turning round, he gazed at Tweed.

'Better prepare yourself,' he whispered.

'What is it?'

'Stay where you are while I search the back.'

Tweed waited where he stood. He was not able to see much inside. Butler ran to the back, crouched down. He tried a door at the end, found it was locked. His expression was grim when he walked back. Tweed walked further in, stopped. For a few seconds he was in a state of shock.

The large stuffed owl was no longer inside the glass dome. It lay on the floor on his side of the counter. In its place he found himself staring at the head of Étienne Vallade, perched upright inside the dome. The eyes were open and he had the odd sensation that the bookseller was staring at him. Lying on the counter was the Japanese sword, its blade smeared with blood. More blood coated the rim of the dome inside. The bookseller's half-moon glasses were perched on the nose, a hideous insult.

'No one here,' Butler reported. 'The rest of the body is lying on the floor behind the counter. Whoever did it must have come in, seen the sword, snatched it off the wall and beheaded Vallade with one savage sweeping blow. Then he lifted the glass dome, threw out the owl, replaced it with Vallade's head. Some nice people in this world . . .'

He had just spoken when Paula broke free from Newman's grip and rushed inside. She stopped suddenly. Tweed tried to shield her gaze from the thing inside the dome, but he was too late. She stood very still, all her colour vanished from her face, in a state of deep shock, Tweed assumed.

'Get out of here,' Butler ordererd. 'All of us. If the French police catch us we'll be interrogated for days.'

Tweed turned to leave, pulling at Paula, but she wouldn't move. Butler also took hold of her. Between them they pushed her back to the doorway. Her reaction astounded Tweed. She stopped in the open doorway, had snatched her Browning from her shoulder bag. She hissed the words as the others stared at her.

'If I meet whoever did this I'll empty all nine bullets into them. Vallade was such a lovable character,' she gulped.

'Put the damned gun away,' Butler growled at her. 'If anyone in the street sees you like that—'

She slid the Browning back inside its pocket, walked like a robot into the street. Tweed called out to Newman quietly that Vallade was dead. Newman put his arm round Paula while Butler joined them. Tweed still had his wits about him. He took out a handkerchief, wiped fingerprints off both sides of the handle to the door, then closed it, his hand wrapped in the handkerchief.

'We go left, back to the *quai*,' he said calmly, decisively. 'At the end of the street we turn left. I want a second look at the ramp where that powerboat was moored. Don't hurry. Walk at a normal pace. Stay with Paula, Bob. Let's spread out a bit.'

Paula was breathing heavily but refused the offer of Newman's arm. She walked stiff-legged, one foot in front of the other. At the end of the street she took a deep breath of air off the Seine. Tweed, after glancing left and right, walked quickly to the left. Paula and Newman had to hurry to keep up. Behind them, a number of yards away, Butler brought up the rear.

Reaching the gap in the embankment wall where the ramp ran down to the river, Tweed looked down. No sign of the powerboat. It might never have been there. He looked round for witnesses but there was no one. Normally, he recalled from a previous visit, men with rods had fished from this ramp. They were either away at lunch or – more likely – had not fished this morning because of the bitter wind.

'We'll go to lunch at the Restaurant Paul,' he decided. 'I'm anxious we get off St Louis and onto the Île de la Cité.'

'It was the Yellow Man,' Paula said quietly.

'I think so. Then he darted to the end of the street, along the rue St Louis en l'Île, turned down another side street to the ramp where he had that powerboat waiting. He'll always have his escape route planned.'

'The Yellow Man,' Paula repeated, almost to herself.

15

The Restaurant Paul on the Île de la Cité is curiously situated. It stretches from the triangular *place* Dauphine, invisible from the Seine, like a wide corridor to a street overlooking the river embankment. It was very crowded but the manager found a table for the five of them at the river end. Marler had appeared from nowhere as they'd crossed the bridge linking the two islands.

'I don't want anything to eat,' Paula said, putting the menu aside.

'Then I'll order something for you,' said Tweed. 'You must keep up your strength.'

'Then I won't eat it . . .'

When their orders came they all started except Paula. They said nothing important because they were surrounded with other diners. Suddenly Paula picked up her knife and fork and attacked the fish on her plate, devouring it. Tweed looked across at Newman, who smiled and surreptitiously gave a thumbs-up signal.

'We'll get back to the hotel,' Tweed said as he paid the bill. 'Maybe someone will have something to report.'

He was referring to Burgoyne and Nield, who had been left behind to check on the other guests. During the taxi ride back Newman diverted the cab driver into a side street. He had spotted an isolated phone box. With his back to the taxi he took out a silk handkerchief, held it over his mouth to blur his voice as he called police headquarters. He reported a murder at Vallade's bookshop, slammed down the phone when asked for his name.

He whispered to Tweed what he had done as the cab continued to the Ritz. Tweed merely nodded his approval. Newman then passed the same message to Paula. She looked relieved. The thought of Vallade's remains staying in the shop had revolted her.

The first people they saw when they entered the hotel were Nield and Burgoyne, seated in the lobby apart from each other. Tweed collected his key and, with a little wave of his hand, indicated they should both join him. Marler took off his coat, folded it over his arm, began strolling round the ground floor.

'I suppose nothing has happened,' Tweed began the moment they were inside his suite.

'It has,' said Nield.

Paula glanced at Burgoyne, who smiled, nodded agreement with what Nield had said. Newman sat in an armchair, lit a cigarette. Butler had gone straight to his room.

'The Americans have arrived,' Burgoyne announced. 'In force. Here in the hotel. Pete told me about Unit

Four. We do have distinguished company. Pete, I'll leave you to tell them.'

'The early indication I had that they were on their way here was not conclusive,' Nield began. 'A well-dressed American – expensive suit – arrived, booked a suite. Chap by the name of Brad Braun.'

'How did you find that out?' asked Tweed.

'Heard his American accent when he spoke to the doorman as he walked in. He goes up to reservation so I join the queue, standing next to him. Saw his name when he registered. He goes up to his suite. Soon he comes down, has a late breakfast. I go into the dining room, get a table close to him, order a second breakfast of coffee and croissants. Braun is joined by another American, a short fat character with wide shoulders and large hands. Smiles and laughs a lot, though his eyes never smile. While talking he's scanning the other guests in the place. I hear his name when Braun calls him Bancroft. Very tough, this Bancroft, I'd say.'

'Chance,' Tweed said, addressing Burgoyne, 'you referred to distinguished company. Who was that?'

'Hold on to your hat. None other than Vance Karnow, chief aide to the President. I saw a picture of him in the paper once. A striking-looking man.'

'Sell his own mother if the price was high enough,' Nield added.

'I wonder who is running the Oval Office in his absence,' Tweed mused. 'From what I've heard Karnow handles all the tricky situations. Advises the President how to react – or how not to react.'

'The Oval Office must be taking what happened north of Dartmoor pretty seriously,' Burgoyne commented.

'Yes,' Tweed agreed, 'sending a big gun like that over here.'

Before leaving Park Crescent he had privately briefed Burgoyne on aspects of what he had called the Appledore 'trigger'. He sat back, drummed the fingers of his right hand on the arm of his chair.

'I have to find a way of getting the French and the Americans off our backs. I believe I now know where Goslar's main base is. Something Lasalle said to me.'

'So where is it?' asked Burgoyne.

'I could be wrong. I need more confirmation. Where are our transatlantic friends now?'

'In the bar, last time we saw them,' Burgoyne told him. 'I think I should check the streets near here – see if they have any reinforcements waiting in cars or whatever.'

'Good idea. Nield, you check inside the hotel again.'

Burgoyne was sitting relaxed in an armchair. Paula had been watching him with interest. Catching her gaze he gave her a wink and she smiled back. When they had left the room, Burgoyne following Nield, there was a knock on the door. Newman went to unlock the door. Marler stood outside, came in, then stood against the wall.

'You've probably heard the Yanks are here.'

'We have,' Tweed said.

The phone rang. Paula answered it. She frowned, covered the mouthpiece with her hand.

'We have company. Lasalle is on the phone, calling from downstairs. Wants to see you urgently. *Now*, he said.'

'Ask him to come up.'

'I think,' Marler decided, 'I'll hide myself in your bathroom. Otherwise with all of us here Lasalle is going to feel outgunned.'

'Good idea . . .'

Newman again attended to the door. Paula's eyes

162

narrowed as Lasalle walked in with another man. Lapin, his assistant. A small thin man, he had a face like a monkey. He wore a neutral-coloured raincoat, denims and shoes with thick rubber soles. Newman frowned. He had seen this man recently.

'Sit down. Make yourself at home, René,' Tweed greeted their visitors.

'This is an official visit,' Lasalle said stiffly,

'Sit down, stand up – whichever you prefer.'

They perched together on the edge of a sofa. Lapin's ferret-like eyes switched from one occupant to the other. He had a sallow complexion and always looked as though he'd come to work after having a row with his wife. Tweed said nothing more, waited.

'Were you on the Île de la Cité earlier this morning?' Lasalle demanded.

'As a matter of fact, we were. Why?'

'And then on the Île St-Louis?'

'What is this all about?' Tweed asked mildly. 'I suppose your associate, Lapin, followed us for some reason?'

'Do you know a seller of rare books called Vallade?'

'How do you spell that name?'

'Is Vallade a friend of yours? Someone you have known for quite a while?'

'No,' said Tweed, answering the second question.

'Why were you on the Île de la Cité this morning? Please don't say you were taking the air.'

'We wanted to see if we would be followed, wherever we went to. Obviously we were. By Lapin.'

The monkey-faced assistant had the grace to stare at the floor. He moved his feet uncomfortably.

'So you have no information to give me.' Lasalle had stood up, obviously annoyed. 'In that case we will leave.' Newman had unlocked the door, opened it. Lapin walked into the corridor as Tweed spoke.

'René, I do have some information which is confidential.'

Lasalle shut the door, leaving Lapin outside in the corridor. His previously stiff demeanour changed and he became more like his normal self. He walked over to Tweed but did not sit down again.

'I'm listening,' he said.

'You might like to know this place – this hotel – is crawling with Americans. I'm sure they're on the same mission you and I are. From what I've heard they're a team of sophisticated thugs – well dressed, well spoken. And this is the clincher – their leader is a certain Vance Karnow, who is probably still downstairs in the bar.'

'Karnow?' Lasalle was startled. 'The American who runs the White House? Probably the second most influential man in the whole world? Here in Paris?'

'I just told you – he was downstairs in the bar. With some of his very tough and sleek-looking associates. One of them, a Brad Braun, has actually taken a suite here. The Americans have a lot of money. Neither of us wants them to reach Goslar first.'

'True. The source I spoke of earlier when we met – the one where the video and message was sent to – will be enraged.'

Tweed knew he was referring to the President of France. He made his suggestion in an off-hand manner.

'Would it be in the interests of France if you harried these Americans? Threw them off balance, so to speak. You might even be able to charge them with some offence.'

'You know me. I'll think of something. I'd better get moving. And thank you for the information . . .'

'What is the plan?' Paula asked as Marler came out of the bathroom.

'Up to the moment of Lasalle coming to see us,' Tweed began, 'we were fighting too many outfits. Goslar's vast organization. On top of that the French security services. And on top of that the American contingent. With just a few words to René I've simplified the situation. The French security services will be paying attention to hassling the Americans. I'm sure that when the President in the Élysée hears what Lasalle tells him he'll order all firepower to be turned on America. That gets Karnow and his men out of our way. It also concentrates the focus of the French security services away from us. That leaves us free to concentrate *our* efforts on what matters. Locating and destroying Goslar.'

'That was a clever gambit,' Newman commented.

'Just a thought on the spur of the moment. A tactical move.'

'That is a real plan,' Paula agreed. 'Top marks. I thought it strange that Lasalle didn't tell us what had happened to poor Vallade. He didn't even tell us he is dead.'

'He's trying to keep the story out of the press as long as he can. Imagine the panic in Paris when it comes out. Vallade was not a famous and powerful politician. In the eyes of the public he'll be an ordinary person – so everyone will feel at risk. I wonder if the Yellow Man really has yellow hair? I was inches away from him in Brown's Hotel in London. It struck me he had very thick hair. Could it be a toupee?'

'I hope not. In that case we'll never recognize him. Why do you think Goslar had Vallade killed?' Paula wondered.

'I think because he used his name, Goslar, when he phoned Vallade about the book on Galapagos turtles. He used to do that on rare occasions in the old days of the Cold War. Remember, Bob? It's a form of bravado.

Then he regrets having done it. So he shoots the messenger, so to speak.'

'Why would he want a book on Galapagos turtles?'

'I've no idea,' Tweed admitted. 'But remember the so-called fairy tale Dillon told us in London? A fisherman with a distinctive red sail and a half-moon. Therefore easy to track him down after he'd landed in Ecuador. He was killed – together with the freelance agent he spoke to. Both beheaded. Shades of the Yellow Man?'

'Weird,' Paula ruminated aloud. 'So what's next?'

'You and I, with Bob, go down to the bar to see if the Americans are still there. Marler, trail us down there, then stay outside the bar. Just in case of trouble.'

They were still in the bar. Vance Karnow sat upright with his back to a wall. Next to him sat an attractive red-head. On his other side sat a good-looking man Tweed thought could be Brad Braun, the American with the suite. The fourth member of the party was short and wide-shouldered, and was grinning. Fatso, Paula thought – probably Bancroft.

Tweed chose a table not too close to them, which gave him a sideways view. As he walked towards it he saw out of the corner of his eye Karnow staring straight at him. He sat down as Karnow nudged the red-head, who glanced up at Tweed.

They had ordered their drinks when Braun gazed at them. Soon afterwards Bancroft took his time observing them. Taking a sip from his glass of wine, Tweed looked at the Americans, making no attempt to conceal his action. Karnow, his eyes hard, stared at him again. Tweed looked back at Karnow point-blank. It was the American who turned away first.

'They know who I am,' Tweed remarked. 'And look who's in the corner to the left of us.'

Paula looked over the rim of her glass as she also sipped wine. Sitting by himself, pretending to read *Figaro*, was Lapin. As she watched a much larger Frenchman came in, went to Lapin's table, shook hands with him and sat down. As soon as the newcomer had ordered his drink the two men engaged in a close conversation.

'Lasalle doesn't waste much time,' Paula observed.

'He doesn't,' Tweed agreed. 'And my guess is that by now he's got men covering every exit, including the one onto the side street. Men equipped with motorcycles in case any American leaves by car or taxi. Now Lapin has produced a mobile phone, is talking into it. Giving a description of every man – and the woman – at that table.'

'I like the look of her,' Newman commented, after drinking more of his double Scotch. 'How old would you say she is?'

'Late thirties, early forties,' Paula told him.

'I think there's someone else she's interested in,' Newman replied.

While Karnow was deep in conversation with Braun, the woman was gazing straight at Tweed. He looked back at her and she held her gaze. He had the impression she was weighing him up. As he watched her she glanced at Karnow, saw he was looking the other way, then gazed back at Tweed and gave him a half-smile.

'You've struck lucky,' Paula teased Tweed. 'Why would a nice-looking woman like that be mixed up with a mob of Americans who look as though they'd snatch a dollar out of a beggar's hand?'

'Maybe I'll get the chance to find out,' Tweed joked back.

'You'd better keep your mind on why we're here,' she teased him again.

'That's why I said what I did.'

'Is it really a good idea to be here?' Paula wondered. 'It gives them an opportunity to recognize us.'

'That works in the opposite direction,' said Tweed. 'Know your enemy. And now, if everyone's ready, I think we ought to go . . .'

He signed the bill, added his suite number, and they left the bar. No one at the Americans' table gave them a glance. They met Marler outside, perched on a chair, a magazine in his lap. He joined them.

'I want to try and contact Cord Dillon,' Tweed decided.

'I peered in through the door,' Marler reported. 'Got a good look at them. Nice people.'

'Fatso looks rather jolly,' Paula remarked. 'A nice smile.'

'Bancroft,' said Newman. 'They all probably thought he looked rather jolly – with a nice smile. I'm talking about his previous victims. They thought that, and then it was too late. He is the most dangerous. Think I'll patrol round the hotel.'

'I'll do that thing also,' Marler remarked. 'See if we've missed anything. Anyone . . .'

Tweed and Paula had just sat down in his suite when the phone rang. Nearest to it, Tweed picked it up.

'Yes?'

'Mr Tweed?' a soft feminine voice enquired.

'Speaking.'

'This is Trudy Warner. We looked at each other long enough in the bar. Could we meet and have a talk? I do know your suite number.'

'Then why not come up now? You'll be on your own?'

'I promise. And will you be on your own? I really do want to talk to you alone.'

'There is no one else in this room as we speak.'

Tweed was telling the truth. Paula had slipped into the loo in his bathroom. The door was closed.

'Could I come up now, then? I don't often get the opportunity to do this.'

'Yes, come now . . .'

Paula came out of the bathroom. He told her quickly what the phone call had been about. He added that Trudy Warner was very anxious to see him on his own. Paula looked worried, spoke rapidly.

'I don't like that at all. Look what's happened. Sam Sneed murdered in London, my experience at La Défense, the murder of Coral Langley when Marler visited Chance's place Rydford – and Vallade. I could hide in the bathroom. No, she might want to use it.' She walked to a tall cupboard, opened both doors. 'If you don't mind, I could hide in here. Plenty of space next to your clothes.'

'Get in quickly, then. She'll be here any moment.'

She took out the key and, with her shoulder bag over her arm, she stepped into the closet. She shut the doors from the inside, peered through the keyhole. She could clearly see Tweed seated on the sofa. She opened the door again.

'Get her to sit next to you. Then I can see both of you.'

Less than half a minute later there was a light tapping on the main door. Tweed jumped up agilely. He positioned himself to the hinged side of the door, reached across, unlocked the door, leaving it on the chain. He didn't think it a sound idea to be standing in front of the door if bullets came flying through it.

'Who is it?'

'Me. Trudy.'

Silently, he walked past the door, unlocked it with the chain in place. She stood outside, alone. She looked nervous. While he removed the chain she had glanced up and down the corridor. She came in quickly and he relocked the door, replaced the chain.

'Come and sit with me,' he said. 'Tell me what this is about.'

Following Paula's suggestion, he occupied the same seat on the sofa and she sat beside him. Seen close up she was very attractive. Her long red hair, just touching her shoulders, framed a face with a good complexion, pencilled eyebrows above grey-blue eyes which stared straight into his, as they had done in the bar. He sensed that she was unsure what to say first. He waited.

'I know about you, Mr Tweed,' she said.

'You do? How?'

He was still wary. On previous missions he had encountered several murderesses. The breed seemed to be growing.

'I listened in – on an extension – to a call Vance Karnow made to Cord Dillon, Deputy Director of the CIA. Karnow wanted to know who was the toughest man among the security services in London. Dillon was very abrupt in his reply. I can quote his exact words. "A man called Tweed. The most formidable of them all. And, Karnow, he's as honest as the day is long – a very long day. So you won't be able to practise your tricks on him." Dillon then slammed down the phone and I replaced my receiver at the same moment – so Karnow wouldn't hear the click.'

'May I ask why Karnow is over here? Why are you with him?'

'Let me tell the story in my own way, please. I've spent five years in the States . . .'

'You're English, aren't you?'

'Yes. I married an American called Walt Jules Baron. Jules is pronounced Jewels over there. He was an accountant, told me he worked for a security outfit in Washington. It was a good marriage and I knew it would have lasted. We'd been married eighteen months when one night Walt drank a lot, which was unusual. He said he was worried about the outfit he worked for. He told me its name. He had realized he was being used to launder huge sums of money to finance the outfit. He was thinking of contacting the FBI.'

'Did he do that?'

'Wait, please.' Her hands were folding the top of her handbag, her knuckles white. 'The following evening ... The following evening, after dark, a car pulled up outside. We lived in a house outside a small town in Virginia. The only other property near was a house next door. Walt peered through the net curtains, then ordered me to stay out of sight. I went into the kitchen. It had an oval window which was open to the living room, masked by a heavy net curtain. The visitor was a fat man I'd never seen before. He told Walt to sit down. Walt did so. The fat man didn't say much.'

'Can you remember what he did say?'

'Every word,' Trudy said tensely. ' "Walt, you've been checking bank statements which are confidential. Open your mouth – you have a cyanide capsule on your tongue." Walt looked astounded, said that was the most ridiculous thing he'd ever heard. At that moment the fat man shoved the muzzle of a gun into his mouth and pulled the trigger. I went into shock.'

'Would you like something to drink? Coffee? Water?'

'Water, please.'

She drank the glass Tweed had poured from a carafe, thanked him, continued talking.

'The fat man wore gloves. He took hold of Walt's

171

dropped hand, pressed it on the gun, let it fall. I was in a trance but I knew I had to leave – so I could identify the killer later. I went out the back way, closed the door quietly, rushed to the house next door. The couple who lived there were away and the wife had given me a key. I went inside, locked the door, and didn't put any lights on. A few minutes later I heard the fat man rattling the handle of the locked front door. It was a nightmare. Then I heard him drive away.'

'Can you describe the fat man?' Tweed enquired gently.

'Wait.' She checked her watch. 'I'll have to tell you the rest later. I told Karnow – he's the head of the outfit I'm working for – I was going to the Hôtel Crillon, where they're staying, to get a shower. I must be back when he returns. Could I come and see you again between seven and eight tonight? They'll be having dinner at the Crillon.'

'Yes, I think that would be all right.'

'Must go.' She stood up and Tweed accompanied her to the door. She put a hand on his to stop him unlocking it. 'They're after you – they were going to kill you. Now Karnow has decided not to. Yet. The name of the man who murdered my husband is Bancroft. I'm going to kill him at the first opportunity. Now, could you let me out, please . . .'

16

'What do you think of her?' asked Tweed when Paula had emerged from her closet.

'At first I was suspicious. I thought Karnow was trying to put a plant inside our team. Then I changed my mind. What about you?'

'Same reaction to begin with. What convinced me she might well be genuine was that last remark, just before she left. The fact that she named Bancroft.'

'She sounded very bitter, very determined, from the way she expressed herself.'

'I think the same. You didn't see the expression in her eyes as she said that. Her eyes narrowed and were full of pure hate.'

'So we assume she is the genuine article?'

'Not yet,' Tweed warned. 'Let's hear what else she has to say, when she comes back this evening.'

'I was going to have dinner with Chance Burgoyne. He invited me out while we were downstairs. I agreed.'

'Then I insist you keep your dinner engagement. It will give you the opportunity to get to know him better, to help him merge in with us. One proviso. I'm going to ask Nield also to have dinner wherever you're having it. Being on his own he will be more alert – when you two are involved in conversation. Dinner here?'

'No. Chance suggested Maxim's.'

'Better still. I'll get Nield to book himself a table. He'll be difficult to recognize.'

'We're not sure about Trudy. Shouldn't I stay here, hide again in the closet?'

'Newman will take your place.'

The Yellow Man sat in a swivel chair inside his attic flat at the top of an old building overlooking the Bastille. He liked the hideaway. The Bastille was not in the most upmarket arrondissement in Paris. The message from Goslar had come through over the phone earlier.

'Is that Mr Danton?' a cultured voice had asked in English.

'No,' the Yellow Man had replied, 'this is Marat.'

'Then kindly be so good as to listen carefully.'

He'd had to wait while the unknown caller put on the recording. It was the usual screeching voice.

Your next assignment is to eliminate Tweed's assistant, Paula Grey. Lure her to a quiet place. This will devastate Tweed, make his mind go round in circles. Timing is your choice. I have deposited half the usual fee in your Swiss bank. You can confirm that. The balance paid on results.

'Tweed must be getting too close,' the Yellow Man said after hearing the recording once more. He spent so much time on his own he often talked to himself. 'This little device should do the job. All women like jewels,' he commented later.

After receiving the message he had bought a string of pearls from a jeweller in the Rue St-Honoré. Returning to the attic flat, he had detached the pearls from the rope which had held them, then fed the pearls carefully onto a long length of razor-sharp wire.

The wire was spring-loaded. Holding it up to a desk light in the gloomy attic, he admired the way they hung close together. Then he gripped both ends of the large clasp he had attached. His fingers had a firm hold on the clasp ends as he pulled hard. Substantial lengths of the wire were exposed. Enough for him to pull it tight round a neck – tighter and tighter. Until a head rolled onto the street.

He looked up at himself in a mirror perched on the desk and smiled unpleasantly. The dark wig he wore completely covered his own hair. At about midday he wore black tie and a dinner suit. He stood up to look at himself critically in a cheval glass. The effect was of a smart man about town out for an evening's entertainment.

He slipped the pearls into a pocket of his dinner

jacket. Now all he had to do was to watch and wait. He tried on a woollen scarf, which hid his black tie, then a black overcoat. Now he could almost have been wearing day-time clothes. All he had to do when the time came was to lose the woollen scarf. He was confident that Tweed and Paula would dine outside the Ritz in the evening.

Leaving his attic room, he walked along a short corridor, opened a door to an ancient fire escape, walked down the metal steps carefully and into the Bastille. He hailed an empty cab, rare in this district, but the Yellow Man was always lucky. He told the driver to drop him in the rue de Rivoli, close to the Ritz.

After telling Paula that Newman would replace her in the cupboard when Trudy arrived for her second visit, Tweed stood up and stretched. He checked his watch.

'I think that was a good idea of Burgoyne's to check up on what is going on outside,' he said to Paula. 'I feel the need of a bit of fresh air myself. Let's go out and see for ourselves.'

In the foyer they met Newman, wearing his overcoat and just back from a swift surveillance. He spoke quietly when he saw they were both dressed for going out.

'What do you think you're up to?'

'Taking a spot of fresh air.'

'Then I'll come with you. Don't argue. Paula can walk between us.'

'I'm beginning to feel overprotected,' she joked.

'For a very good reason,' Newman said grimly. 'I haven't detected any watchers, any Americans.'

They spent some time walking.

Tweed moved slowly. He kept stopping, gazing round, looking up at buildings like a tourist. He saw no one — and nothing — suspicious. For a while they encountered men and women hurrying, obviously office workers making the most of their lunch hour. Then the streets became quiet, hardly anyone about.

They completed a wide circuit along the streets round the Ritz. Back at the entrance to the hotel, Tweed stood for a few minutes. He seemed to be in a dream, Paula thought.

'It has to be somewhere close,' he said half to himself. 'We will now walk up to the Opéra.'

'What has to be close?' Paula enquired.

But Tweed was off again, heading for the street leading up to the Opéra. Paula felt frustrated. What was the bee Tweed had in his bonnet? They began walking up the street to the Opéra. Tweed stopped again.

'There is the fox on the trail.'

'What?' asked Newman.

'Ahead of us. Walking towards us. Chance Burgoyne.'

Paula and Newman then saw him. Burgoyne was wearing a shabby raincoat, had his hands in his pockets as he strolled. He was looking to left and right as he came nearer. Tweed had again stopped when he reached them. He was staring down a side street. Burgoyne withdrew both hands, spread them in a gesture of resignation.

'I'm puzzled,' he said. 'No sign of the enemy. No sentries on guard. No skirmishers.'

Paula thought it was typical that he had reverted to employing military terms. Burgoyne noticed Tweed's fixed gaze, looking down the side street. He looked in the same direction.

'Chance,' Tweed said urgently. 'See that small furniture van? The two men have just carried out a modern swivel chair, put it inside. Try and find out where that furniture van is off to. Who employed them. Quick, they're leaving . . .'

Burgoyne took off like a rocket. His legs loped like a tiger who has sighted prey. They began to follow him, saw him arrive just too late. The van – no name on it – was driving off. Chance turned round, again spread his hands in a gesture of resignation. When they arrived at the building, which needed a coat of paint, a woman had emerged from the open front door, had hung from a railing a crude notice painted on a sheet of cardboard. *À Louer.*

'Good morning,' Tweed said in French, smiling.

'It's afternoon,' she spat at him.

She was plump, wearing a dress which had a washed-out look. Her eyes were greedy, her thin mouth tight. She glared at Tweed from the top of the steps.

'So it is. Afternoon. You're right,' he said, smiling again.

'People are crazy,' she snapped. 'They pay to rent a room for a month and in twenty-four hours they're gone. You want a room?'

'I'm police,' Tweed told her. He took out his forged Special Branch identity, flashed it in her face, put it away. He hoped she wouldn't ask to examine it more closely. She didn't. 'We need to look at the room which has just been vacated. You saw the tenant?'

'Only once. Then I didn't really see him – or her.'

'Why do you say that?' Tweed asked as he mounted the steps.

'Very early this morning the tenant is walking up the stairs to the room – on the third floor. I was in the hall. I only saw it from behind. It wore black trousers, a black cape and a Spanishlike hat. Big brim, well pulled down. I called up and it hissed "thank you" back at me without turning round. Then it was gone.'

'I need to see the room,' Tweed repeated. 'That furniture van which just left took away an office swivel chair. What else?'

'Nothing. The chair was delivered late last night. Why I can't imagine. The room is let furnished. The door's still open. I'm not climbing all those stairs again. Here's the key. Lock it when you've had your look-see.'

'Anyone else up there?' Tweed asked.

'I told you. The tenant has gone.'

'I didn't mean in his flat. I meant the others. Or aren't they occupied?'

'Gone to work. People have to work to live. Or didn't you know that? With the cushy job you've got.'

Tweed shrugged. Burgoyne went up first, with Newman on his heels. As soon as they turned a corner, out of sight of the irate old woman, both men had their revolvers in their hands. Tweed went next, holding Paula back so she brought up the rear.

The staircase was narrow, with a moth-eaten strip of carpet laid in the middle of each tread. The landings were equally narrow. When they reached the second floor the strip of carpet vanished. They mounted the last flight and one door stood wide open. Very slowly, Burgoyne, gun held at chest level, peered inside, then entered.

'Nothing much here that I can see,' said Newman. 'A few sticks of furniture only good for firewood.'

Paula thought it an apt description. She stroked her gloved finger along a section of a chest of drawers against one wall. It was covered with dust. The room was a small oblong. Standing by a wall below a grubby window was a wooden table with a wicker chair shoved under it.

'Where does that door lead to?' Paula asked.

'Let's see,' said Burgoyne.

He opened it cautiously and an unpleasant latrine smell drifted into the cell-like room. Burgoyne peered in, then took two paces forward and was inside. He came out, wrinkling his nose.

'Toilet and a rusty shower. Hardly able to close the

door when you're inside. What a shower – and I'm not referring to the one inside.'

'I think this is a bed let into the wall,' Newman said. He took hold of the apparatus at the top to haul it out.

'Careful,' Burgoyne warned. 'Might be a body inside.'

Paula tensed but kept her expression neutral. Holding the mattress firmly in position, Newman lowered it. The bed stretched the full width of the apartment, squeezed at the end against the opposite wall. Whatever bedlinen was laid on it was covered by a stained duvet.

'No one has slept in that,' Tweed observed.

'What are you doing now?' Paula asked him.

Tweed had pulled out the wicker chair, was sitting on it with the table in front of him. He wriggled as the chair wobbled. One leg was shorter than the other three. He pulled a face as he rocked on the chair.

'Damnit!' he said quietly.

'I'll fix it,' Paula said. 'Get up for a moment.'

Taking a notebook from her shoulder bag, she tore out a number of sheets of blank paper. Folding them, she bent down, tucked her improvised wedge under the short leg. Tweed sat down again and the chair was firm.

'Thank you,' he said.

He then began performing a strange pantomime while Paula, fascinated, watched him. He cupped his right hand to his mouth as though speaking into a trumpet. His left hand reached out to poise over a section of the table and he pretended to be turning a dial.

'What on earth are you doing?' Burgoyne enquired.

'Demonstrating why Goslar needed this room, how he used it. My right hand is holding a very advanced form of voice-changer. My left is adjusting a recording machine. There's an oblong outline in the dust where the recording machine was placed. "It,"' he said in

French, mimicking the landlady, 'used this out-of-the-way apartment to record – in a screeching voice – either one message or several. He then took everything away, including the cassette – or cassettes. They would be hidden in a prearranged hideyhole, maybe a loose brick with a space behind it, for an accomplice to collect later ready for playing it back over the phone.'

'So Goslar is still in Paris?' Burgoyne suggested.

'I wouldn't bank on that now. He moves around a lot.'

'Look at this – on the floor near the toilet door,' Burgoyne said suddenly.

'Don't touch it!' Tweed warned. 'Bob, use tweezers to pick it up and pop it in a sample envelope.'

Newman bent down, used tweezers he'd extracted from a small case he carried, carefully picked up what Burgoyne had pointed out. Straightening up he held them to the pallid light penetrating the room from the window.

'It's strands of hair,' Newman reported. 'Yellow hair.'

'The Yellow Man,' Paula said quietly.

'Goslar tripped up this time,' Newman remarked. He looked at Tweed. 'You said he would, sooner or later.'

Tweed stood up. Paula collected her home-made wedge, stowed it away in her shoulder bag. Never leave anything behind to show you've been somewhere outlandish was one of Tweed's instructions, delivered long ago.

'That explains the expensive-looking swivel chair,' he explained. 'Goslar came prepared. He needed a firm stance to produce his recordings. Nothing more here. Let's get back downstairs. The aroma is beginning to get me down. Plenty of places like this back in London. And I want another word with Mrs Cheerybye.'

The landlady stood at the bottom of the stairs, her arms akimbo, her expression sneering as she watched them descending the last flight.

'Finished messing up my place?' she demanded.

'Just a few more questions before we go,' Tweed said, smiling at her. 'What is your name?'

'Antoinette Markov, if you must know. My grandparents escaped from Russia when the Revolution came.'

'Good for them. Good for you, too. This mysterious tenant. How did it pay you a month's rent in advance?'

'Phoned up first, didn't it? Funny voice. Then sent a month's rent by cash in a blank envelope. And, before you ask, the money was delivered by courier on a motorcycle. Don't know which outfit.'

'Surely you can give it a better description since you saw it walk upstairs,' Tweed persisted.

'Told you before all I saw.'

'And was that really the only occasion when you observed it?'

Tweed was standing close to Markov and gin fumes assailed his nostrils. Rather early in the day to start on the bottle. She was probably sozzled by midafternoon. So her reply in no way surprised him.

'I've already told you it was. How many times do I have to repeat myself before it sinks in?'

'Thank you, Madame Markov. We'll leave you in peace now.'

They had reached the street when she shouted down at Tweed, in a voice which was part wheedling, part sarcastic.

'Don't you want the flat, then? It's a two-minute walk from here to the Ritz.'

'If you're an Olympic sprinter,' Newman said *sotto voce*.

'I don't understand it,' Paula whispered to Tweed as

181

Burgoyne walked ahead of them, with Newman behind. 'You said Goslar used the apartment but Chance spotted those yellow hairs. He was quick. How does that link up with the Yellow Man?'

'I've no idea. I'll phone Lasalle when we get back to my suite. I'm sending him those yellow hairs Burgoyne spotted on the floor of that flat – for analysis. Butler can take them to the rue des Saussaies.'

'Are you building up your jigsaw?'

'I need more pieces. I may have them after my talk with Trudy Warner this evening at seven. I'll also try again to contact the elusive Serena Cavendish. She fits in somewhere.'

As they entered the street leading in the opposite direction to the Opéra, Newman and Burgoyne followed them. Newman suddenly looked back, stopped. His right hand slipped inside his raincoat to grip his Smith & Wesson. The action was not lost on Burgoyne, who also stopped and gazed back.

Two hundred yards behind them a giant in a dark coat padded towards them. His huge head was cropped with a fuzz of brown hair. He fitted perfectly Paula's detailed description of the Ape, who had kidnapped her on Dartmoor. The Ape stopped, hailed a cab moving towards the Opéra, climbed inside. The cab moved away.

'Who was that mountain of flesh?' Burgoyne asked.

'Tell you later. Let's keep up with Tweed and Paula . . .'

They were close to the entrance to the Ritz when a man walked to the end of the rue Castiglione, which gave a good view of the entrance across the rue St-Honoré and the *place* beyond. He wore a dark overcoat, had a woollen scarf wrapped round his neck and his hair was thick and black. He stood on the kerb, rocking back and forth, as though waiting for traffic to clear. Hands in his pockets, he watched Paula as, with Tweed, she came close to the entrance.

'Well, at least we've seen no one menacing,' Paula remarked.

'Maybe we just didn't see them.'

17

Vance Karnow sat at one side of a long table in his suite at the Hôtel Crillon. The only other person in the room sat facing him. Bancroft, as usual, was grinning. His fat hands were clasped on the table top.

'What's up? Got a job for me, Chief?'

'Yes. Tweed is sitting back in the Ritz. Waiting for something to happen, would be my guess. I don't think this Goslar is in Paris. I want to get Tweed, Inc. moving so we can follow them.'

'So how do we make that go down?'

'I want you to scare the living daylights out of Paula Grey. I think that might do the trick. The only problem is she could so easily recognize you – she saw you in the bar at the Ritz.'

'Can I use your bathroom for a minute?' asked Bancroft.

'Hurry it up, then.'

Karnow's expression was bleak, his mouth no more than a thin line. At the American Embassy he'd answered a call from the White House. The aide he'd left temporarily in his place had told him the President wanted a progress report. Yesterday would do. Karnow had told the aide he was expecting developments very shortly – anything to keep the Oval Office off his back.

He was thinking sourly about that phone call when Bancroft, who had gone off carrying a large shopping carrier, emerged from the bathroom. Karnow stared.

Bancroft now wore a dark blue French raincoat, a beret and large horn-rimmed glasses with plain glass lenses. When he sat opposite Karnow again he had a cigar clamped in the centre of his mouth. His thick lips gripped the cigar so tightly his normally plump cheeks had sunk.

'Not bad. Not bad at all,' Karnow commented. Always sparing with praise.

The fact was that, without this preview, he would not have recognized Bancroft had he seen him in the street. He sat erect in his, chair, gazing at his deputy.

'Follow her,' he said eventually. 'Wait your opportunity, then frighten the hell out of her. Mess her up a bit.'

'You mean – ' Bancroft leaned forward with an eager look – 'I go all the way with her?'

'Godamnit, no!' Karnow exploded. 'And don't put her in hospital. You do that and I'll never get Tweed off my back. He'd never give up until he'd smashed us.'

'Tweed worries you?' Bancroft enquired softly, grinning.

'Of course not. And take that smirk off your ugly face.'

The truth was Tweed did worry Karnow. First of all, Dillon had told him Tweed was formidable. But second, Karnow, good at assessing men, had been impressed and uneasy when he'd studied Tweed in the bar at the Ritz. Beneath the apparent placid manner he had detected an aura of power, of immense stamina. He would never have admitted it to anyone, but Karnow had no intention of tangling face to face with Tweed.

'Be careful,' he warned. 'Just frighten her.' He leaned close to his deputy. 'Bancroft, do you understand me?'

'Perfectly. It's a soft job – but I have to make her want to leave Paris, hoping Tweed will agree. Then we follow them.'

'Then get to hell out of my suite . . .'

Tweed stopped after walking a few paces into the lobby of the hotel. He looked up at the tall man with the aggressive manner who had appeared. Jarvis Bate, Acting Head of Special Branch in London.

'Oh, no. Not you,' Paula said under her breath.

'Tweed, my dear chap. What a pleasure to meet you again.'

Bate held out a paw to shake hands. Tweed ignored it and stood staring at this unexpected arrival, who was smiling wolfishly. It was probably the only way he could smile.

'Follow me,' said Tweed. 'There's a quiet lounge where we could talk. Paula, please join us.'

Paula saw Bate frown at the suggestion. She had the impression Bate regarded women as an inferior species. He had not even had the courtesy to acknowledge her presence. She followed Tweed and Bate was compelled to stride after them. Tweed mounted several steps and there was no one else in the small lounge. He sat down on a sofa, patted the seat behind him for Paula to occupy. Bate picked up a carver chair, carried it over to face the sofa so he looked down on them.

'How did you know we were here?' Tweed demanded.

'Pure coincidence.'

'Coincidence my foot. Was it the man or the woman aboard our flight from Heathrow? I think it was the woman. She hailed a cab at Madeleine, followed one of my people here.'

'Do we have to discuss this in front of a junior

185

member of your staff? Discretion, Tweed. These are policy matters which go right to the top.'

'She happens to be one of the most senior members of my staff. She stays. Or our conversation ends now.'

'I just thought that as you are almost the top SIS man—'

'That's right. Shout it from the rooftops.'

Paula knew that he was referring to Bate's mention of the SIS. Bate swallowed, adjusted the points of the silk handkerchief in his top pocket.

'Sorry,' he said more quietly. 'Perhaps I was a bit out of order.'

'Why are you here?' Tweed repeated.

'Well . . .' Bate leaned forward, lowered his voice. 'I assume you were at Appledore in north Devon.'

'I was there six or seven years ago.' Tweed waved his arm in a wide circle. 'Roaming round on holiday. I thought the place was rather boring so I moved on after an hour or so.'

'I'm referring to the story which appeared in the *Daily Nation*. Written by a certain Sam Sneed, if I recall correctly. Harrington, the Minister of External Security, is very concerned with what took place there – when the dead fisherman, and shoals of dead fish came ashore.'

'I don't work for Harrington. You do. I have no further comment, Bate.'

'Actually,' Bater responded, smiling again, 'it's Jarvis Bate. Jarvis. Surely we can converse on first-name terms.'

'We have nothing to converse about,' Tweed said, standing up.

'You can't just walk out on me like that,' Bate rumbled.

'I have things to attend to. Where are you staying?'

'At a small hotel in rue St-Honoré.' His mouth curled in a sneer. 'We don't have the funds you have at—'

He stopped suddenly. Followed by Paula, Tweed descended the steps into the lobby, walked along it so they could collect their keys. At the bottom of the steps a small sneaky-looking man sat in a chair on the other side of the lobby. He kept his eyes hooded, staring at the carpet, careful not to look at them.

'Did you notice that little man sitting in a chair?' whispered Paula. 'Bate's sidekick, the little wretch he brought with him when he visited us in London. Mervyn Leek. Straining his ears to try and catch a snatch of our conversation, I expect.'

'Yes, I did see him.' They collected their keys. 'Now let's go up to my suite. Plenty to think about . . .'

'So now we have more rivals to watch out for,' Tweed said. He drank some of the coffee Paula had ordered from room service, put down his cup, counted them off on his fingers. 'First the Americans, who may – or may not – have been neutralized by Lasalle. Then we have the French security services who may – or may not – have turned their full attention to the Yanks. Now, on top of that, we have Bate and his Special Branch gang. I'm sure Bate will have brought over a team with him. Far more than just Mervyn Leek.'

'And we want to concentrate our full attention on Goslar,' she said.

'Which we will do. But warn everyone when you can of Mr Jarvis Bate's arrival on the scene. Now I must contact Lasalle and ask him to analyse the yellow hairs from Mme Markov's flat. Newman slipped the sample envelope into my pocket as soon as we'd left. Could you find Harry Butler so he's here for me to give him the envelope . . .'

He phoned Lasalle. As soon as he mentioned the Yellow Man the Frenchman agreed to cooperate. Paula came back with Butler and handed him the envelope. Paula had already told him about the situation. Butler left at once with the sample envelope . . .

He had only just gone when the phone rang. Tweed had perched himself on the edge of the king-size bed. He knew that getting out of a chair would help him to think. Paula answered the phone, put her hand over it, called out to Tweed.

'It's *him*.'

Tweed picked up the bedside extension while Paula listened in. He just caught the closing words of the cultured English voice.

'. . . a message for you which is important. Please hold on just a moment.'

While whoever had spoken switched on the recording, Tweed thought. The next thing he heard was Goslar's screeching voice.

Not getting very far with your mission, Tweed, I gather. You are walking round in circles. I thought you might appreciate a tip. Aniseed. I repeat, Aniseed. Good luck.

Tweed put down the phone. The recording had ended. He swivelled round to look at Paula.

'Well?'

'Aniseed. Sounds very much like Annecy. The place the guard at La Défense told us one of the furniture remover crew had said they were going to. Or could it be a trap?'

'We'll walk into it – after taking certain precautions. I need to discuss this with Marler. You're having dinner with Burgoyne tonight. Tomorrow we'll leave Paris and head south.'

He stopped speaking as there was a knock on the

door. Paula opened it cautiously, then wide. Burgoyne walked in, raincoat over his arm, smiled.

'Hope this isn't an inconvenient moment? I've been on my feet trawling the area and could do with a sit-down. There isn't a drink, I suppose?'

'Yes, there is,' said Paula, taking his raincoat, settling him in an armchair.

Tweed watched with amusement. These two were getting on like a house on fire. Paula produced a bottle of vodka, a glass and ice. Burgoyne relaxed in his chair, grinned at her.

'Just the job. You've got a secret bar?'

'No. The waiter who brought coffee also brought this. I think it was for someone else but I hung on to it. Just in case.'

'Make it a stiff one, please.' He raised the glass she had filled. 'Cheers! And damnation to our enemies.'

While they sat chatting Tweed used the phone to call Monica. She answered immediately.

'Tweed, it's great to hear from you . . .'

'I'm calling from my suite at the Ritz,' he warned.

'Understood. Saafeld hasn't phoned, so no break-through. Also the boffins working on that strange conversation have not broken it. Sorry, that's all the news I have. And none of it good.'

'Not to worry. Monica, we may be leaving Paris during the next few days. I'll contact you wherever we end up. Nice to hear your voice . . .'

'Anything happened?' Paula asked.

'Two negatives. Which is what I expected. No news from Saafeld. No success by the boffins in trying to extract Goslar's real voice from the machine he uses.'

There was a knock on the door. When Paula opened it Newman entered, looking as fresh as though he was starting a new day. The stamina of the man, Tweed thought.

'We kept out of the way,' Newman said, nodding towards Burgoyne as he flopped in a chair. 'I thought you'd sooner tackle that hyena on his own – on *your* own, I mean, with Paula.'

'That was very sensible of you.'

'Well, I don't think Goslar will ever return to Mme Markov's flat,' Newman ruminated. 'So no point in my going out and watching it. After all—'

'Mme Markov!' Tweed had jumped up, was grabbing his coat. 'I should have thought of her. My God! I hope we're not too late. We're going back there now.'

Once outside, Tweed was walking so fast he was half-running. He was near the turning into the side street when Paula caught up with him.

'What's the matter?'

'I just hope to Heaven I haven't killed someone else . . .'

18

Burgoyne overtook them as they hurried down the side street, again loping like a tiger. He paused at the foot of the steps leading up to the Markov apartment to let the others catch him up. Tweed paused as he reached him. Paula was by his side and Newman, who had protected their rear, stood behind them.

'That front door's half open,' Tweed observed. 'I'm sure Mme Markov always keeps it locked. We must be careful. The Yellow Man might be inside.'

Burgoyne leapt up the steps, his revolver concealed under his poloneck sweater. Tweed was the only one who had grabbed a coat before leaving. Newman followed Burgoyne, his Smith & Wesson in his hand. Burgoyne paused at the half-open door, pushed it quietly back against the wall. Newman knew why he'd taken that precaution – in case someone had been hiding behind it. The ex-intelligence officer knew his way around.

The hall was empty. While Burgoyne, with Newman following, crept up the winding staircase, Tweed slowly turned the handle of the only other door in the hall. Mme Markov's living room, he felt sure. Paula stood with her Browning in her hand as he turned the handle until it stopped, then pushed gently.

'The door's locked,' he said. 'She'd do that before she went upstairs to check the flat we'd been inside. We'll go up now.'

'I'll go first . . .'

'No, you won't.'

'Then take my Browning.'

To please her Tweed took the gun, automatically checked it, began to mount the stairs. On the third floor the door to the flat was still open. Paula pushed past him, entered the room. Then she stopped.

'Oh, no!'

Newman swung round, gripped her by the forearms, gently guided her back onto the landing. But she'd had time to glimpse what was inside. The wall bed had been pulled down. Stretched along it was the prone body of Mme Markov, on her back, a pillow over her head and neck. Newman released her by Tweed's side, but he still blocked the entrance to the flat.

'She's been smothered,' she said in a choking voice. 'But why all the blood on the pillow? It's stained red.'

'Stay with her,' Tweed ordered Newman.

He walked inside. Apart from the bed and what lay on it everything looked as they had left it. Burgoyne's expression was grim. He took Tweed by the arm, led him to the far side of the table Tweed had used to conduct his pantomime.

'It's in the metal wastepaper basket,' Burgoyne told him.

Tweed walked round the far side of the table, stopped. Inside the metal bin was Mme Markov's head, her eyes open. Her hair was dishevelled. The killer had lifted the head by the hair to carry it to the bin. Blood everywhere. Tweed swivelled round. Now he saw spots of blood leading from the bed to the bin.

'Don't touch anything,' he warned. 'We don't want to see what's under the pillow. We know. Let's get out of here fast.'

On the landing Newman offered to help Paula down the staircase, suggesting she took his arm.

'I don't need any bloody help,' she flared. 'I'm not feeble yet. And don't warn me about leaving finger-prints. I'm wearing gloves.'

Newman didn't reply as she moved steadily down the steps, one hand holding the banister. When she reached the hall she walked straight out into the street. Tweed followed, looking to left and right. The street was deserted.

'Back to the hotel,' he said.

Paula didn't answer him but walked alongside him. Newman came behind them while Burgoyne moved ahead. As he walked, Burgoyne glanced at all the windows they were passing. Tweed realized he was check-ing to make sure they weren't being observed by a nosy neighbour.

'I'm all right now,' Paula said as they left the side street.

Burgoyne dropped back to speak to Tweed. He was not smiling.

'I'm staying out here for a little while, keeping an

eye open. There's a little shop near the Opéra where I can get a newspaper. Good cover. Be back soon.'

'We'll see you then,' Tweed replied in a strange voice.

Paula glanced at him as Burgoyne left them. Tweed's expression was like that of a man walking in a trance. His complexion was ashen. She put her arm through his, squeezed it.

'Are you all right?'

'Of course I am.'

Newman had heard the exchange of words. He came alongside them, peered at Tweed, then looked away. He said nothing until they were about to enter the hotel.

'I'm going to my room to freshen up. Maybe take a shower. I'll come along to see you later.'

'I'll get the keys,' Paula said when they were inside the lobby.

As she returned with the keys an expression of fury crossed her face. Tweed had been stopped by a tall man with a wolfish smile. Bate. She heard the brief exchange of words.

'Tweed, my dear fellow. I have some questions for you which I simply must put to you. We are on official business, if I may remind you. They'll serve us a snack, and a drink, in the bar.'

'To hell with you, Bate,' Tweed snapped. 'And to hell with your silly questions!'

'You saw the hyena off,' Paula said with a smile as they entered Tweed's suite and she locked the door.

'Bate is someone I can do without any time. Particularly now.'

'You're shaken by what happened to Mme Markov,' Paula observed. 'You could never have prevented it.'

'I could, if I'd had my wits about me. Asked Lasalle to send her a guard . . .'

'Which she probably wouldn't have accepted inside her property.'

'A plainclothes man could have been stationed outside.'

'Tweed, stop it. Feeling guilty. When we left the hotel you said you hoped you hadn't killed someone else. You haven't killed anyone.'

'There's Vallade. Poor devil.'

'He'd have been killed anyway – even if we hadn't visited his shop. You said yourself Goslar was shooting the messenger again – all because he used his own name when ordering that book on turtles . . .'

'There's someone else I should have thought of,' Tweed exclaimed. 'Pray God I'm not too late.'

Again he had perched on the edge of the bed. He grabbed the phone and from memory called Roy Buchanan's number at the Yard. Paula watched him anxiously.

'Roy? Thank heavens. Tweed here, speaking from the Ritz in Paris. I think Miss Sneed, Sam Sneed's sister, out in Appledore, could be in grave danger of being murdered. Take my word for it. Could you contact that Inspector – Crake wasn't it? – and ask him to check immediately that she's safe? Then get him to move her miles away at once. She may have relatives or friends in the West Country. She must not stay in that house a minute longer than is necessary. Can you call me back when you know the situation? My suite number and phone number are . . .'

'Deal with it immediately. Then come back to you.'

Buchanan was gone before Tweed replaced the receiver. Paula had had something on her mind for a while. She decided to come out with it to give Tweed something else to think about.

194

'You may think I'm crazy but I've been pondering something and I think I ought to bring it up.' She paused. 'How much do you know about the background and previous life of Bate?'

'Not much. What I do know Howard told me. Bate has only been with Special Branch for two years. He rose very rapidly to his present position. By climbing over other people's backs. Someone else gave me that titbit. Prior to then he'd been with some international security organization. I suppose that's what gave him clout in getting the job with Pardoe, the head of the outfit, who is away on holiday. Bate's earlier experience was mostly in the States, I heard. He's away from Special Branch's HQ, travels a lot. That's it.'

'Not a lot, is it,' Paula commented. 'Bate,' she said. 'Bate,' she repeated.

A few minutes later Cord Dillon was on the line, speaking from the States.

'I'm talking from a hotel,' Tweed warned quickly. 'Good to hear from you. How did you reach me?'

'Called Howard. I'm talking about the subject you're most interested in now.' Tweed knew he meant Goslar. 'I decided to go through some old files. You might like to know the subject spent a couple of years or so in Britain.'

'I see. Doing what, do you know?'

'I do. He controlled a very profitable security organization in Germany. No description, of course. Of the subject, I mean. I guess it was some kind of tax dodge – owning a company abroad and living in Britain.'

'Which two years was this?'

'No information on that.'

'Switching to another subject, ever heard of a Jarvis Bate?'

'That tough. Met him once. His technique was to impress people out of their crazy minds. "What wonderful people you Americans are. You deserve to rule the world. Such dynamism. Such know-how, can-do. Love that phrase." And so on – and on and on. It went down a storm. He had key people, hard people, in the palm of his hands.'

'Where was he based?'

'In New Jersey. Except he was hardly ever there. Flitted about like a goddamn mosquito. Disappeared off the face of the earth for long periods. I thought he was a phoney.'

'Thank you. I find what you've said intriguing.'

'Any time. That's it?'

'It is.'

In typical American fashion Dillon ended the call abruptly. Tweed looked at Paula, who had just put her phone down.

'I hope you don't mind,' she said. 'I listened in.'

'I'm glad you did.'

'You look tired. How much sleep did you get last night?'

'Not a lot. I was up, pacing round while I recalled everything that's happened, trying to link up factors, but they didn't fit together. I could do with a drink.'

'Vodka any good?'

'Sounds tempting. Make it weak.'

He got off the bed and the phone rang again. They both picked up their phones at the same moment.

'Yes?' Tweed answered.

'Roy here. All's well. We got lucky. Crake just phoned, said a patrol car was near Miss Sneed's house. She's all right. She agreed to go to stay with an aunt elsewhere. Crake said she was packing. He'll have an unmarked car, no uniforms, to collect her. One of his men is inside the house while she packs.'

'I'm very relieved. Can't thank you enough.'

'Then don't try . . .'

Tweed again got up off the bed. He walked over to an armchair, sank into it. Paula was mixing his drink. She spoke as she handed it to him.

'There. You don't have to worry about Miss Sneed. And, by the way, Chance told me he couldn't get a decent table at Maxim's. Full house almost. So he's taking me to Sandolini's. The new in-place, he said. Then he chuckled. At least for the last couple of years, I heard.'

'Where is it?' Tweed asked after sipping his drink.

'In a street leading off this side of the rue St-Honoré. We get there at 8.30 p.m., leave here in a taxi at 8.15.'

'I think it's a good idea that you get away from it all for an evening out. Enjoy yourself.'

'I think I will. Chance is fun. When you've finished your drink I suggest you get some sleep.'

'I have Trudy Warner coming back to see me.'

'That's not until seven o'clock. Don't forget to get Newman to hide in the closet. Do you believe Trudy's story?'

'I'll tell you when I've heard Chapter Two. Then I must phone that number Serena Cavendish gave me again. I might fit her in before it's time for Trudy.'

'Just so long as you get some sleep first. You've finished your drink. To bed before I go and have a shower, then try to decide which of two dresses I'll wear. That will take hours.'

Tweed got up, walked slowly to the side of the bed with the phone. He couldn't be bothered to take off more than his jacket and his shoes. Paula took his jacket, hung it inside the closet. Tweed sat up in bed under the duvet. He didn't want to fall asleep yet.

'You might call Newman – if he's in his room, will he pop over for a moment.'

'On his way,' she said after using the phone. 'Sleep well – you have bags of time. Make the most of it. You don't look comfortable.' She walked over, adjusted his pillow. 'I'll just wait to let Newman in.'

Newman arrived quickly. Paula frowned, signalled with her eyes that Tweed was washed out, then left. Newman, freshly showered and shaved – his first effort had been a rush job early in the morning – played it softly.

'What can I do for sir?'

'Sir? Didn't know I'd appeared in the New Year's Honours List.'

'Would you take it, if they offered you a K?'

'No. Not my style. Bob, has Paula told you Trudy Warner will be back here at seven this evening for a second session with me?'

'Yes. I don't like it – or her sob story. She's Karnow's girl.'

'Maybe. Paula hid in that closet while Trudy was here last time. Would you do the same thing? Paula insisted on it.'

'Good for Paula.' Newman walked across to the closet, opened it, pushed some clothes aside, shut the door. 'I'm bigger than Paula. I can't hide in there. The bathroom's the answer.'

'Supposing she asks to use it?'

'Tell her it's out of order. Management is sending up someone to see to it. She can use the one downstairs.'

'All right. I agree, then. I'll know if she's genuine when I've heard what more she tells me this evening. Before you go, could you call Nield, ask him to come here now? And I haven't seen Harry Butler for hours.'

'Because he's cruising the whole area on a motorbike. He told me he'd peered into the bar while we were there. He saw Vance Karnow glaring at you. I later told him who he was. A few minutes ago Harry popped in here, told me Karnow is staying at the Crillon.'

'Harry has covered a pretty big area. Oh, have you seen Bate anywhere? I suspect he has more than Mervyn Leek with him. A team of six or seven, would be my guess.'

'Saw two of them downstairs. Easy to spot them. Amateurs.'

'How did you recognize them?'

'They always wear grey suits, well-polished black shoes. And they can't hang around like normal visitors. They're too obvious.'

'I have heard they can be rough.'

'We can be rougher. I'll call Nield. Mind if I leave him with you? I'm keeping an eye on Bate's gnomes.'

'You get off when Nield arrives . . .'

Newman put a finger to his lips as he ushered Nield in, warning him not to linger any longer than he needed. Nield nodded. When Newman had left he walked to Tweed's bedside, held out his hands in a what-can-I-do? gesture.

'Pete, there's been a change of plan. Chance Burgoyne couldn't get a good table at Maxim's, so instead he's taking Paula for dinner to Sandolini's. It's somewhere off—'

'I know where it is. I'll be there to back up Burgoyne, to look after Paula. Same time? 8.30 p.m.? Piece of cake. I'll book a table from my room.'

'Might be awkward, being on your own,' Tweed ruminated.

'I won't be on my own. I'll find a nice lady as my dining companion. Not off the street, of course.' He used his index finger to stroke his moustache. 'It will be easy. I'm off now. But what about the door?'

'Lock it from the outside, take the key with you. I have a spare in the bedside table. Look after Paula.'

'Nothing will happen . . .'

Tweed thought his last words had an ominous sound as he pushed down the pillow. He went into a deep sleep the moment his head rested on the pillow.

19

'We're going to war,' Bate announced in his dominating voice.

He sat in a tall, hard-backed chair in his room at the hotel on the rue St-Honoré which was his temporary base. He was addressing four members of his team who sat on sofas the Ritz wouldn't have accepted for its staff.

'What does that mean?' asked a slim man in his late thirties. He spoke in an upper-crust voice.

'Clive.' Bate paused, his ice-blue eyes glaring. 'If you will kindly listen without interrupting you may learn something.'

Clive Marsh, almost as tall as Bate, was the maverick in the team. He adjusted his tie, stared back at his boss, raised his eyebrows. Bate might be his superior but Clive would interrupt him whenever he felt like doing so.

'We're going to make our presence felt to Tweed,' Bate went on. 'Put the pressure on him. At the moment Leek and Prendergast are stationed inside the Ritz, both armed with mobile phones so they can report the moment they see Tweed & Co. are on the move.'

'And then?' Clive enquired.

'We have six cars, so you all have transport,' Bate thundered on as though he hadn't heard the question. 'I have worked out that Tweed will move either east into Germany or south into Provence – and maybe beyond.

You take it in turns to overtake him. In that way he will not realize he is being followed. Get me?'

'Quite clear,' answered Wilbur Jansen, a small, plump man with a toothbrush moustache. 'Quite clear,' he repeated unctuously.

'You are all armed by Leek, who obtained your weapons here in Paris from some source I don't wish to know about. But on no account are you to engage in a shooting match unless it becomes inevitable.'

'When does it become inevitable?' Clive enquired, suppressing a yawn.

'My God! Sometimes I think you are thick. If – or when – they start shooting at us first.'

'It helps if we do know when,' Clive commented. 'And has this authority behind us back home? Shooting, I mean.'

'One more interruption from you,' Bate snarled, almost with a screech of rage, 'and I'll send you back home.'

He knew he would never do that. Unfortunately, Clive Marsh was his most efficient and reliable operative. He glowered at the offender before continuing. Clive again adjusted his tie. All the men present wore grey suits and gleaming black shoes.

'I am leaving on my own in a few minutes,' Bate informed them. 'In my absence Mervyn Leek is in command. You take your orders from him. He, in turn, will be in close touch with me. You may not hear from me for some time but, I repeat, in my absence Leek is running the show. Also, none of you leaves this hotel without an instruction to do so from Leek. You eat here, sleep here, stay put. Understood?'

'Quite clear,' said plump little Wilbur Jansen. 'Understood.'

'Go back to your rooms, then,' Bate ordered, standing up and donning his camel-hair coat.

On his own, Bate took from a cupboard his packed bag. Going down to the desk, he wrote out a cheque backed by a bank card, handed it to the desk clerk.

'That will cover everything. If expenses go beyond that then my associate, Mervyn Leek, will deal with any extras. Now, if the concierge will bring round my Renault, wherever he has hidden it, to the front . . .'

When Paula, after tapping on the door, unlocked it and walked into Tweed's suite, she stared in surprise. Tweed was fully dressed, his eyes and movements the peak of alertness. She'd seen this transformation once before. No longer exhausted, he was a dynamo of energy.

'Newman will be here in a moment,' he said briskly.

There was a tap on the door. When she opened it Newman walked in. Tweed stood, hands clasped behind his back.

'Those two snoops, Bate's underlings – are they still here?'

'Yes, sitting in the lobby where they can watch the exit and the elevator.'

'I want them out of here. Is Pete Nield about? Good. Both of you find seats opposite them, as close to them as you can. Sit there and stare at them. Keep on staring. Make them feel nervous. It is a tactic we've used before.'

'On my way.'

'Before you go, is Bate still patrolling down there?'

'No. He seems to have disappeared. Some time ago. No sign that he's coming back.'

'Interesting. Start the staring match. Is Burgoyne about? Good. Ask him to come here ASAP.'

Paula smiled after Newman had left. She perched herself in a carver chair, quickly adjusted her skirt, which she preferred to her leggings.

'You've meditated,' she said. 'Now suddenly it's all go.'

'Can't hang around here for ever. Goslar could be miles away by now. Probably is.'

Paula jumped up as there was another tap on the door. Burgoyne strode into the room, grinned at Paula, looked at Tweed.

'You've come alive. Haven't seen you like this since we flew in from Heathrow.'

'Chance, I think we should move to Annecy. I've spoken to Marler and he's geared up for a swift departure. In the middle of the night.'

'Could I make a suggestion?' Burgoyne enquired, folding his arms.

'Make it.'

'I think I should go on ahead of you . . .'

He stopped speaking as the phone rang. Tweed, who was pacing restlessly, answered it.

'Yes?'

'It's Serena. You're going to want to shoot me. I'm awfully sorry but I can't come and see you this afternoon. Something has cropped up which I must see to. Could I come at four o'clock tomorrow afternoon instead? I do need to see you. What I have to tell you is important. But not over the phone. Can you make it then?'

'Yes. But be sure you do.'

He put down the phone. Picking up a carver chair he placed it close to Burgoyne, who had sat on a sofa.

'You were saying?'

'I think I should drive down ahead of you after Paula and I have had dinner this evening. I want to make a recce along the route you'll take.'

'Why?'

'To forestall your being ambushed. I'll check out the locales where Goslar's thugs could set up an ambush.'

Behind Burgoyne Paula nodded. Then she mouthed 'yes.'

'It might be wise,' Tweed agreed after thinking for a moment.

'Which route will you follow?'

'From here we'll drive first to Geneva. Then on from there to Annecy across the border. You know the area?'

'I do. Not so long ago I did an extra job for the MoD. Drove to Aix en Provence, a walled city. I was looking for an Arab agent. Found him.'

'An Arab?' Paula queried in surprise.

'Job's done, so no harm in telling you. In Aix there is a scribe, an Arab. He occupies a hut in a small square for his business. There are – or were – a lot of Arab refugees from North Africa. They only spoke Arabic and they'd want to send a letter to their relatives back in Algiers, Constantine, or wherever. Couldn't pen a word. They'd tell the scribe what they wanted to say in a letter and he'd write it for them. It wasn't the scribe I was after.'

'Annecy is further north,' Tweed commented.

'I know the place. What do you think?'

'You'll be driving through the night. Less traffic. I agree. How do we communicate with you?'

'Via my mobile.'

Burgoyne took out a pad, scribbled a number on it, handed it to Tweed.

'You can reach me at any hour of the day or night. If I find anything suspicious, I'll contact you. Marler thinks it a good idea. I have his mobile number. Now, I'd better pack – ready for a swift departure late tonight. After I've delivered Paula safely back here, of course . . .'

Tweed resumed his pacing when Burgoyne had left. His head was bowed in thought.

'It is a good idea,' he said eventually. 'Paula, why were you so approving?'

'Chance is used to operating on his own. Prowling through the desert. He's a good precaution . . .'

She went to the door as someone tapped. Marler strolled in, leaned against a wall.

'Burgoyne wants to drive off ahead of us tonight. I thought it a sound move.'

'Except,' Tweed told him, 'we're not leaving until tomorrow night.' He looked at Paula. 'That phone call was from Serena. Can't get here until four in the afternoon tomorrow. It delays us but I want to hear what she has to tell me. She did have arm's length contact with Goslar when he hired her to photograph the Appledore area two weeks before the night the sea was poisoned.'

'If it was arm's length contact,' Paula commented.

'You suspect everyone.'

'You trained me to do just that. Hadn't you better tell Marler about the route to Annecy?'

'Just about to do so. Marler, we'll be going via Geneva, then across the border to Annecy.'

'Why Geneva?' Marler enquired.

'To check something. You don't sound very happy.'

'Just thinking. From Geneva we'll pass through a Swiss checkpoint. That should be all right. Then comes a French checkpoint. We'll have to be careful with the armoury we're carrying. I'll manage it somehow. I've hired a third car.'

'Why?'

'We'll be travelling in convoy to Annecy. I'd worried about an ambush before Burgoyne raised the possibility. If there is an ambush the enemy will expect you to be travelling in the middle car. You won't be. You'll travel in the last car.'

'If you insist.' Tweed checked his watch. 'I'm expecting a visitor. I want to see them alone.'

'And I want to check that third car thoroughly . . .'

At about the time Marler left Tweed it was dark outside. In a side street, leading off the rue St-Honoré down to the rue de Rivoli, a very large man pressed the button on an entryphone. Alongside the button a card gave the occupant's name. *Serena Cavendish.*

When no one answered he looked up and down the street. People were hurrying past. No one took any notice of him. The French, released from their boring jobs, were on their way home. He was on the verge of pressing the button again when he saw a curtain on the ground floor pulled aside, then closed. He waited.

The front door was unlocked, opened. The concierge, a tall thin woman in her sixties with bright pink hair, stood looking at him. She wouldn't have opened the door but it was rush hour. Plenty of people about.

'What you want?' she demanded in English.

She could see this big brute was English from the style of his clothes. A long dark overcoat, pigskin gloves over his huge hands.

'I have come to see my friend, Serena Cavendish. She doesn't answer the entryphone.'

'Then she's not in.'

'She's expecting me. Which room?'

'Flat Two, first floor. Come later . . .'

'I said she's expecting me. Probably taking a bath.'

He pushed into the lobby, pressing her aside. Then he mounted the staircase as the concierge called after him in French. He turned, dropped a banknote over the banister. She picked it up. A hundred-franc note. She looked up but he was gone. Shrugging, she tucked the note into the purse concealed under her apron.

The big man walked along a narrow corridor on the first floor. He saw the figure '2' attached to a door. The next door further along had a '3' screwed to it. Taking out a square of metal with one serrated edge, he eased it between lock and the wooden frame. He twisted hard, damaged the frame but opened the lock. He walked inside.

He had checked the living room, the small kitchen, the bathroom, had found the flat was empty when he heard someone behind him. The concierge was glaring at him, one bony hand tapping the damaged frame. She was staring hard at him, memorizing his appearance. She would have no difficulty describing him.

'You pay damage,' she snapped. 'It cost lot of money. New lock. New everything. Who are you?'

He walked to the window of the living room he had entered direct from the corridor. A surge of people below, hustling along the pavement. The gridlocked traffic began moving again. No sign of a police car. He looked at her, staying where he was.

'Who are you?' she repeated. 'I call police.'

He took out a wallet. From it he extracted three five-hundred-franc notes. He held them in his gloved hand. Irresolute, she licked her lips, walked towards him, towards the banknotes. A third of that amount would repair the damage.

'Of course I pay,' he said, his voice hoarse. 'I push the door too hard. Don't know my own strength.'

He held out the banknotes. As she extended her hand he dropped one. He apologized and she bent down to retrieve it. As she straightened up one large hand grasped her by the throat, the other gripped the back of her neck. His movement was a swift jerk. Her neck was broken. To make sure he grasped her throat in both hands, squeezed in a vicelike grip. She sagged and he let her go.

He stooped, picked up the banknote he had dropped, then extricated the two notes still clutched between her dead fingers. He looked out of the window again, moved towards the door and looked back once.

'I am Abel. You shouldn't have opened the door to me.'

Newman was inside the suite's bathroom, the door almost shut, his foot against the bottom when Tweed ushered Trudy Warner in. At his suggestion she occupied a sofa while he sat in an armchair, facing her. She had taken off her fur coat, laid it across the back of the sofa.

'Can I get you something to drink?' Tweed asked quietly.

'No, thank you.'

Second impressions of a person are sometimes more powerful than the first. Trudy was a very striking woman, Tweed was reflecting. Her glorious red hair rested on her shoulders, but it was her nose which caught his attention. It was strong, but not so prominent that it spoilt the perfect symmetry of her features. Trudy was a beautiful woman and he was sure she had turned the heads of many men. Behind this façade he detected an inner strength.

'I'll go on from where I left off,' she began. 'The brutal murder of my accountant husband, Walt – by Bancroft, when he shoved his gun into Walt's mouth and pulled the trigger. Bancroft left when he'd tried to get into the house next door where I was hiding. I knew I also had to leave immediately. That Bancroft would come back. After packing the things I liked most I drove – my car had been locked in the garage – to New York. Leaving Virginia behind for ever. To cut a long story short, I got a job with a big security outfit in New York. Being English helped.'

'What sort of work?'

'Tracing – following – men and women who had embezzled quite large sums from their firms and then done a bunk. I was so adept at the work I was promoted to run their Surveillance Division. Then I was posted to Washington – which was just what I wanted.'

'Why?'

'Because I knew Karnow and his secret outfit, Unit Four, was based there. I'm sure that's why they murdered Walt. He knew so much about how Unit Four was financed, and was thinking of contacting the FBI. Once settled in Washington I went to a lot of parties – I was hoping to bump into Vance Karnow. I'd almost given up hope, then one evening Karnow was at a party I attended. I even saw him first talking to Bancroft. I was stunned. Later Karnow came over to me, said he'd heard of the efficient Trudy Warnowski. He ended up offering me a job. I played hard to get, told him I was a widow and only accepted when he asked me at the third lunch. I was on the inside of Unit Four.'

'What about your name? He must have known your husband had a wife.'

'It isn't my real name. As soon as I got to New York I visited a man Walt had told me about, an expert in creating a new identity. I had enough money to buy a driving licence in the new name I'd invented, social security number, passport and all the other papers. I did this before I applied for the job I got.'

'May I ask what was your real name, your married name?'

'Petula Baron. My husband was Walter Baron. My friends back in England called me Pet – rather like the singer's name.'

'But surely – ' Tweed's tone was sceptical – 'the Unit Four people must have seen you while your husband was their accountant.'

'Never. Walt was suspicious early on about what he'd walked into. He told them I suffered from a mild case of agoraphobia, that I'd break down among a crowd, so I was never asked to Washington. And none of them ever saw me. Walt thought it would be safer if he kept me hidden away in the little town in Virginia. He was right.' She swallowed. 'It was awful. I didn't even dare attend his funeral, which I still regret terribly. But it wouldn't have been safe.'

'And your maiden name is?'

'Petula Pennington. The girls at school in Surrey used to call me Pippy. The two "P's" – the ones who didn't like me. You can check that. I was at Ramstead.'

'And why did you join Unit Four?' Tweed asked casually.

'I told you.' Her voice was quiet, steady, but there was a glitter in her grey-blue eyes. 'I'm going to kill Bancroft when I get him on his own. I loved Walt very much,' she said calmly.

'Bancroft – I've seen him – is very tough.'

'I'm tougher. What happened made me that way. You want to know what Karnow plans for you?'

'It would be interesting.'

'First, he was going to have you killed. Then he changed his mind. He wants you alive – so you can lead him to Dr Goslar.'

'Dr Goslar?'

'You know who he is.' She leaned forward and Tweed caught a whiff of expensive perfume. 'He's the Invisible Man who's invented a world-beating weapon. The Americans will do anything to get their filthy hands on it. No one seems to know even what he looks like.'

'So Karnow intends to follow me?' Tweed remarked, still playing it coolly.

'He has men in this hotel waiting for you to move. One, Milt Friedman, has a suite here. He's tall, clean-shaven, in his late thirties with weird eyes. Then they have another one here, also in a suite. A Brad Braun – German spelling. He has thick black hair, takes a lot of trouble over his appearance, has a long nose which twitches when he's nervous. Yes, he intends to have you followed. He's convinced that you'll leave Paris, that Goslar isn't in the city.'

'Why are you telling me all this?'

'Because of what I overheard Cord Dillon saying about you – I told you about that when I was here before. I'm confident you will destroy Unit Four. I want to help you – so I can reach Bancroft.'

'If I did leave Paris how would we keep in touch?'

'Could you give me your mobile phone number?'

'I'd sooner you gave me yours.'

'Here it is.' She had it already written on a card she handed him. The numbers were written in a refined script. 'If, when you call me, I'm with people I'll say "wrong number". It will then be up to you to try again later. When I'm on my own I can tell you where we are.'

'I fear you're putting yourself in great danger,' Tweed warned.

'I don't give a damn. I can cope. I've had the training. Can I rely on you? Do check me out at my old school, Ramstead.'

'Can I, discreetly, check you out at the security agency you worked for in New York?' he suggested, watching her closely.

'National Intelligence and Security, Inc. Known as NISI. Don't forget I worked there as Trudy Warnowski.'

'I'll be careful. Incidentally, when you escaped from Virginia didn't you leave photographs behind?'

'I did not. I grabbed every photo of myself, of myself and Walt, and shoved them in my case. Then I called on my neighbour who had come back that evening. We got on well together. I told her what had happened, said Walt had found out he was working for the Mafia, that he'd been killed. I would be next, so I was flying back to England.'

'Anyone else in the States Unit Four might have contacted?'

'Yes.' She smiled grimly. 'I phoned my widowed sister living in San Francisco, told her the situation, that she might be contacted. She said she'd tell them I had visited her and then flown on to Seattle. If they asked for my description she'd tell them to go to hell and slam down the phone.'

'They might have asked your neighbour for a description.'

'I covered that. If they did she was going to describe a friend of hers, a Mrs Cadwallader who lives in Richmond.' She paused. 'I hated leaving Walt behind in that room – but I knew he'd have told me to run for it.'

Tweed stared at her and she tilted her nose cheekily. He was full of admiration for how she had handled a situation most would never have coped with. She checked her watch.

'I'd better get back to the Crillon. Karnow has a habit of checking up on where his people are. I'll use my mobile to take messages from you. If possible – if I'm alone – I'll reciprocate by keeping you informed of Unit Four's movements. I really must go.'

'Isn't there a risk you might be spotted by Milt Friedman or Brad Braun, since they're both staying here? On your way out, I mean.'

'Watch me.' She stood up, took a cap she'd hidden

under her coat. Using a mirror on the wall, she adjusted the hat, tucked her hair under it, dropped a black lacy veil over the upper half of her face. She slipped on her fur. 'Imitation,' she told Tweed. 'What do you think?'

'I wouldn't have recognized you,' Tweed said, standing up to let her out. 'Now you take great care. No risks. You're dealing with killers.'

She threw a kiss at him and then was gone.

20

'Well, what did you think of Trudy Warner?' Tweed asked as Newman emerged from the bathroom.

'My money's on her.' Newman was grinning. 'What a looker – saw her through the keyhole.' His expression became serious. 'What hell she's been through – seeing her husband shot in the mouth by that bastard, Bancroft. Good job you briefed me earlier. I was able to follow every word. And the way she covered her tracks. We could use her on the team – we really could.'

'Well, maybe she is on the team. But I want her checked out. I would like you to contact her New York employer, National Intelligence and Security. You could say she's been recommended to you for security work and ask their opinion.'

'I'll go back to my room. I'd like a quiet few minutes to work out how I'll handle it.'

He opened the door and Paula was standing in the corridor. She whispered, 'Coast clear?'

'Yes, I'm just leaving.'

'Musical chairs. One out, one in.'

'I forgot to tell Tweed something.' Newman went back into the suite with her. 'We've shifted those two Bate snoops,' he told Tweed.

'Good. How did you manage that?'

'Pete and I just sat on the other side of the lobby and stared straight at them nonstop. They didn't like it. Then Butler arrived back – he'd had the sense to take off his motorbike gear and leave it behind. Underneath he was wearing a business suit. He caught on immediately to what we were up to. So he plonks himself down in a chair next to me and stares at Mervyn Leek. I think he did the trick – when Harry stares at someone they get very uncomfortable.'

'They've left the hotel?'

'They have. It was comical. Watching them try to get up casually as though they'd just been resting. Made a real mess of it. I don't think Special Branch training comes within a mile of ours.'

'Good work.'

'Now I'm on my way back to my room to do that check on Trudy.'

'What check?' Paula asked when he had left. 'I'm back early because I decided quickly what I'm wearing tonight for my evening out with Chance. I'm wearing my black number. I rejected the frilly job – a bit too exotic. Now, what check on Trudy?'

Tweed told her about his second meeting. From memory he recalled every word that had been said. Paula, serious-faced, leaned forward, tucking away in her mind every detail.

'Newman thinks she passes muster,' Tweed concluded, 'but I asked him to check with the New York security agency she says she worked for. He's doing that now. You've heard of Ramstead, the school she says she attended in Surrey?'

'That's like asking if I've heard of Roedean.'

'I want you to phone Ramstead, try to get through to the headmistress, check her out as best you can. Might be difficult.'

'No, it won't be. I've just had a baby, a little girl, want to get her a place at Ramstead when she's old enough. A friend of mine, Petula Pennington, recommended it to me. I'll see if the name strikes a chord. I won't ask what the fees are. If you have to do that you can't afford Ramstead. I'll do it now.'

While Paula was getting the number, then started talking to the headmistress, Tweed had taken a pad of blank paper from his briefcase. He began writing names, trying to link them up with loops. Bate, Karnow, Mervyn Leek, Milt Friedman, Brad Braun, Lasalle, Bancroft, Goslar, the Yellow Man . . .

He easily looped up the Yellow Man with Goslar. He had more people looped up with a query when Paula finished her conversation, came over to sit with him, a Ritz notepad in her hand.

'I got lucky. Spoke to the headmistress, who is retiring soon. She was working late. She remembers Petula Pennington well. We got chatting. She said Petula got on well with most other girls, then chuckled. Said the ones who didn't like her called her Pippy.'

'Sounds as though she checks out.'

Paula went to the door, let in Newman, who was nodding. Tweed asked him what the nodding donkey act meant.

'I was quick,' Newman reported. 'Got straight through to the agency, found the man who employed Trudy Warnowski. It's early afternoon in New York. He said she was very good, that I'd be wise to grab her.'

'Checks out on both fronts, then,' Paula commented. 'I'm off now to change.'

'You've had a bad time,' Tweed told her. 'Have a relaxing and fun evening. You should enjoy it. Peace for a few hours.'

*

A well-built man with thick dark hair walked into Sandolini's. He handed his black overcoat to the hat check girl as the manager greeted him.

'Pierre Martin. You have a table reserved for two.'

'I cannot find the booking,' the manager said after checking his register.

'Then I'll take that table in the corner at the back.'

The manager was about to say it was taken when he was discreetly handed a banknote. I can shift the tables about, the manager said to himself. He led the guest to the table. As he sat down the dark-haired man looked at him.

'I'll start my meal now. She's always late, my companion . . .'

When he ordered a lock of hair fell across the side of his face. He left it there. Feeling in a pocket of his jacket his hand touched the string of pearls with the razor-edged wire. He took from another pocket a copy of Marcel Proust, began reading. Occasionally he glanced across the restaurant where Paula chatted with Burgoyne.

In the bar, Pete Nield sat on a stool next to an attractive woman with a sophisticated appearance. Reaching for a menu, he knocked over her drink.

'A thousand apologies, madame. You must let me order another,' he said with a smile as the barman mopped the counter. 'I'm on my own. Business in Paris. I'm sure I'm not lucky enough for you to be on your own.'

'Actually I am,' she said, after a good look at him. 'I found my boy friend in a compromising situation. I've just ended the relationship. I came out to be among people.'

'You are. You're with me. I think dinner here would cheer you up . . .'

At their table Paula was finding Burgoyne animated,

amusing. He told her jokes which, at times, had her almost in hysterics. She asked him about his experiences in the desert and then sipped at her champagne.

'Had to disguise myself as a baby camel once,' he said seriously. 'Very difficult, getting the arms and legs moving like a camel.' His fingers did an imitation on the tablecloth. 'Arabs stared at me then looked away. It was hard work – moving on all fours for hours.'

'You are an idiot,' she chaffed him, enjoying herself.

'Then I had coffee with Saddam.'

'Saddam Hussein? How did you manage that?'

'Saddam Ali, a bazaar contact,' he told her. 'Very fat.' His arms described a huge circle. Burgoyne moved constantly on the banquette. He blew his cheeks out, mimicking the fat man. 'He told me where secret missiles were hidden.'

'And did you find them?'

'When I arrived at the location, disguised as an Arab, they were already moving them on transporters. A load of medieval cannons. That was all the armoury he had,' he said solemnly. 'Which is why we won the Gulf War. All he fired at our troops was cannon balls.'

'I don't believe a word of it.' She chuckled. 'You really are a fool, you know.'

'I know,' he agreed amiably. 'When I was in Kuwait . . .' he began.

Sitting at a table in a niche, Nield could just keep an eye on Paula and Burgoyne. She was so absorbed, so relieved to have an enjoyable evening, she hadn't seen Nield with his temporary woman friend.

The dark-haired man watched their progress with the meal carefully. As they finished their coffee he paid his bill, walked slowly out.

'Care for a short walk before we ritz back to the Ritz?' suggested Burgoyne.

'I could do with some fresh air. I saw some interesting shops in a side street opposite. The windows are illuminated.'

'Closed, I hope. Diamonds cost a fortune . . .'

The street was narrow, the lighting dim except for the shops with glares of light in their windows, protected with grilles. Paula had walked a distance when an American, lost, asked Burgoyne how to get to Concorde. Burgoyne had to explain his directions three times. Paula reached a corner, turned into a small square in a direction she felt confident would lead them to the Ritz. Dimly lit, it had a number of alleys leading off it. In an alcove the dark-haired man waited.

She paused in front of an illuminated window so Burgoyne could catch her up. The round end of the barrel of a gun was rammed into her back. Behind her a short plump-faced man wearing a beret spoke with an American accent.

'Don't move or I'll blast you to hell.'

She felt him take hold of a handful of her hair. He began pulling her hair backwards. Bancroft was grinning. This was just the kind of sport he revelled in. Then he felt a gun rammed into his back.

'Take your hand off her hair,' Nield ordered. 'Or I'll blow your spine to bits.'

'Stand-off,' Bancroft snarled, not turning his head. 'Do that and by reflex action I'll shoot her.'

'Then the only thing to do,' Nield said calmly, 'is for both of us to drop our guns on the pavement. On the count of three.'

Bancroft backed a short distance away from Paula. His gun was still aimed point-blank at her. As he backed, Nield also retreated, his Walther still pressed into Bancroft's back.

'Here we go,' he said in the same calm voice. 'One . . . two . . . three.'

Bancroft let go of his gun and it hit the cobbles a millisecond before Nield dropped his own weapon. The American swung round, lowered his shoulders, charged to head-butt Nield in the face. Nield darted to one side. Bancroft ran, disappeared round a corner just before Burgoyne appeared.

The shadow of the dark-haired man slipped out of the alcove. Burgoyne raised his Smith & Wesson, fired. The bullet chipped stone from a corner of the alcove. Burgoyne fired again, chipped more stone off the corner of an alley the dark-haired man had vanished down. Burgoyne ran like a greyhound, stopped at the entrance to the alley, walked back.

'He'd gone. The alley went round a corner. He could have been waiting for me. Paula, are you all right?'

'I suggest we escort her straight back to the rue St-Honoré,' Nield said firmly. 'Grab the first taxi and go back to the Ritz.'

'Have a nice evening?' Tweed asked as he let Paula into his suite.

'Super. Until two thugs tried to do me in.'

Her tone was brittle. Tweed sat her down when she'd thrown her coat onto a sofa. Someone tapped on the door. When Tweed opened it Burgoyne stood outside.

'Paula will tell you what happened. I've got to drive like hell down the route you'll be following tomorrow night. Geneva first, then on to Annecy. I'll keep in touch – when I can . . .'

'You look shaken,' Tweed said when Burgoyne had gone. 'Room service can bring up some tea and plenty of sugar.'

'Don't want tea.'

Tweed was already ordering it. Paula sat very still and erect, so Tweed said nothing until the waiter arrived. He poured a cup of tea, added a lot of sugar. She lifted the cup and saucer and her hand shook. She swore, tried again, holding the cup in both hands. When she had emptied it he was going to pour a second cup but she shook her head. She began talking calmly, describing what had happened in detail. Tweed's expression was grim as he listened.

'So,' she concluded, 'Nield grabbed us a taxi and we all came back here.'

'Then it was Bancroft who put a gun in your back before Pete sorted him out. I expect the thug in the alcove was the Yellow Man. Pity Burgoyne missed shooting him.'

'He did try. It all happened so quickly.'

'How are you feeling now?'

'Very tired. The tea was a good idea. Settled me. You look livid.'

'I've had an idea to eliminate the Americans. You go to your room, get some sleep. We're not leaving until midnight tomorrow. You can sleep all day.'

'Lovely idea . . .'

She bent down, kissed him on the cheek. She had just gone when the phone rang. Tweed answered. It was Trudy.

'The whole unit has left the Crillon for another posh hotel nearby. I don't know why. I'm in my bathroom with the shower running. Here are the details, including Karnow's suite where they all dine in the evening at nine o'clock . . .'

'Do you dine with them?' Tweed asked after he'd noted her data.

'No. It's a men only thing. I eat by myself in the dining room.'

'On no account dine with them tomorrow night.'

'I won't. Must go now. Bancroft keeps bothering me,

trying to get into my room. I always open the door on the chain, keep him out.'

'Don't ever let him in. He's a very savage piece of work – but you know that . . .'

Tweed summoned Newman and Marler to his suite as soon as he'd ended Trudy's call. They listened as he gave them the data Trudy had provided. He then outlined a plan, to which Marler added a few touches. Tweed asked him if he could get the equipment for the operation.

'Easily,' Marler replied. 'I have a contact who stole a load of police equipment. I think we should bring Nield and Butler in on this little shindig.'

'Agreed,' Tweed responded. 'And when Paula eventually appears I will get her to type out the documents. Hit them hard. Have you heard what Paula went through this evening?'

'Pete told us a few minutes ago,' Newman said. 'We will hit them very hard. It will be a pleasure. Haul down the Stars and Stripes.'

The following afternoon, when Paula arrived in Tweed's suite, he told her that all the members of his team were packed, ready for departure.

'I'm packed too. I slept nonstop. Now I'm ready for anything.'

'Then could you type out something for me on blank paper?'

'The Ritz can supply anything. I'll get them to send up a word-processor. What do I type?'

'Head the first page *Direction de la Surveillance du Territoire*. Put in brackets D.S.T.' He asked if he was going too quickly as she scribbled on a pad. She shook her head. 'Next line should read Director, René Lasalle.

Then, Assistant, Lapin. In brackets First Name Unknown. Next line, Function of Organization – Counterespionage. Then, Address – rue des Saussaies . . .'

Tweed continued dictating. When he had finished he smiled without humour.

'When Lasalle finds that he'll go berserk. He'll arrest the Americans, probably get an order for instant deportation once he's consulted the Élysée. The French President will blow his top. When you have it ready put it inside a blank file. Scrawl on the front *Vance Karnow. Top Secret*. Then give it to Newman.'

'You're hatching plots. I'll get the word-processor sent up now. This won't take me long.'

'It's a new kind of bomb,' Tweed told her.

At 8.55 p.m., Marler knocked on the door of Vance Karnow's suite in the hotel he had moved to. He wore a white jacket, taken off a waiter who was now unconscious in a service elevator. Brad Braun, the tall, dark-haired American, unlocked the door, opened it.

'Room service,' Marler announced.

'It's already been delivered—' Braun began.

He never finished the sentence. Marler had kneed him in the crotch. As Braun groaned, bent over, Marler stood aside. Three men, wearing gas masks and carrying tear gas pistols, burst into the suite. Eight members of Unit Four sat eating dinner at a long table. The three attackers fired their bulky-nosed pistols. The suite became a fog of tear gas as Marler, now also wearing a gas mask, entered. The Americans were choking, couldn't see, some collapsing with their heads in their plates. The four intruders moved swiftly. They circulated the suite, hammering each American unconscious with a blow from their pistol muzzles. Marler had shut

the door to stop fumes leaking into the corridor. Newman produced Paula's file, looked round, hid it under a
leather blotter on a desk. All four men left the room,
closing the door behind them. Butler and Nield ran to
the service elevator they had ascended in. As soon as
Newman was inside Marler pressed the button, and the
elevator descended to the ground floor. Newman
stooped, inserted a five-hundred-franc note between the
fingers of the unconscious elevator operator lying in a
corner.

Before the door opened they had replaced their gas
masks and pistols inside strong carrier bags from a well-
known London store. They had only a short distance to
walk in the open air. Then they dived inside the waiting
car they had parked earlier. On their way back to the
Ritz, they stopped once in a side street. Newman ran
inside a public phone box, rang Lasalle on his private
number. He made no attempt to disguise his voice.

'Lasalle, better get over to this hotel with a strong
team. A lot of mayhem. The Americans in suite . . .'

'He sounded alarmed and almost on his way before
I broke the connection,' he told Nield, who was driving.

21

At five minutes to midnight three cars left the Ritz. The
front vehicle was driven by Marler with Butler hunched
by his side. The second vehicle was driven by Pete
Nield, travelling by himself. In the third car Newman
was behind the wheel, with Tweed and Paula seated in
the back.

There was so little traffic that after leaving Paris
behind the cars spread out, but not so far away from

each other that they could not see the car ahead of them. It was a cold, brilliantly starlit night with the moon casting a glow over the countryside to left and right.

'Sorry it was a last-minute pickup,' Newman said, 'but we were checking the cars thoroughly.'

'An excellent precaution,' replied Tweed.

'I wonder if we'll find Goslar?' Paula mused.

'Eventually, yes,' Tweed assured her. 'He's started making mistakes. Leaving his signature behind.'

'His signature?'

'Yes. Repeating himself. At Gargoyle Towers, way back on Dartmoor, he leased the place for three months, then moved on after two or three weeks. Then at La Défense he leased the whole building for a long period and cleared out after a month or whatever it was. We know he leased Mme Markov's flat for a month. He's out of the place in twenty-four hours.'

'Why did he get the Yellow Man to kill poor Mme Markov?'

'Because she saw him climbing the stairs to the flat. The cloaked figure. Doesn't take any risks, our Dr Goslar. Lasalle called me while you were asleep, about the yellow hairs Burgoyne spotted on the floor inside the flat. Told me his analyst said they were definitely a woman's hair.'

'That's strange,' Paula commented.

'Another phoney clue. Like the gloves he left behind at Gargoyle Towers, then another pair at La Défense. He was always doing that even in the Cold War days. To confuse us.'

'Unless the figure on the stairs wearing that cloak Mme Markov saw was a woman.'

Paula opened her holdall, which was divided into sections. It held a variety of grenades. Marler had come to her room at the Ritz just before they left. From a deep canvas bag he had produced more grenades.

'Take these. They're firebombs.'

'I've already got shrapnel and stun grenades,' she'd protested.

'And now you've got fire-bombs,' he'd replied.

'What about a machine-pistol?' she'd joked. 'I shall be protecting Tweed.'

'Here you are,' he'd said, handing her the deep bag.

Inside it she'd found a machine-pistol with plenty of spare ammo. It was now lying on the floor at her feet. As Marler was leaving she'd joked again.

'You must be expecting the grandmother of all battles.'

'I am,' Marler had replied, not smiling.

Her brain was working overtime now as the convoy of three cars sped along the autoroute through the night. Moving at just inside the speed limit. She nudged Tweed.

'Serena Cavendish never turned up. She was coming to see you.'

'She did, while you were asleep. She wanted to tell me she'd seen the messenger who delivered the second payment to her flat. You remember? She was paid to photograph Appledore and its surroundings two weeks before Goslar poisoned the sea. She was paid half before she did the job, the balance after she'd left the photographs in a phone box in Curzon Street.'

'So what did the messenger look like?'

'She happened to look through her net curtains when the delivery was made. It was after dark but she got a good look at him by the light of a street lamp. A very big man with hair like stubble in a wheatfield. She's flying ahead of us so we can pick her up when we reach Geneva.'

'You can phone her to warn her where we are? Maybe now?'

225

'Yes. I have her mobile phone number. But not yet. From what you told me,' he went on, addressing Newman, 'you cleaned up the Americans at their new hotel.'

'I loved that,' said Paula, almost hugging herself. 'So they at least are out of the picture.'

'Not quite.' Newman paused, knowing the news would not be welcome. 'Trudy wasn't there, thank Heaven. But neither were Vance Karnow – or Bancroft.'

'Then Bancroft is still roaming around,' Paula commented quietly.

'He is. Somewhere.'

Paula felt a frisson of apprehension. To take her mind off it she gazed out of the window. France, by moonlight and at night, was a dream landscape. Across a peaceful field she saw, stepped down a distant hillside, a grid of vineyards. Next summer's wine was coming. There was very little traffic on the autoroute, most being huge juggernauts lumbering south, which they overtook, and others heading north, for distant Paris.

'You tried to make two calls,' she said to Tweed.

'Yes, to Burgoyne. No answer. You know I mistrust wretched mobiles. They don't always work.'

'Probably he hasn't found any ambush sites. Could be good news. Actually, he was going to call us. So he's found nothing so far. I imagine he's passed through Geneva now, is on his way to Annecy. You know something, that description Serena gave you of the messenger who delivered the balance of her money sounds to me like the Ape.'

'I think you should know,' Newman called back to them, 'that we are being followed. From the moment we left the Ritz. I expected that. I wonder who our friends are? We were driving round a long curve a while ago and I'm sure I saw not one, but two cars, tagging along on our tail. They've dropped back quite a bit but I'm sure they'll still be there. I wonder which lot it is?'

Had there been a pilot flying a plane above the autoroute he'd have seen the traffic far below. In front, well spaced out, was Tweed's convoy of three cars, appearing to move slowly even as they raced along the autoroute. Some distance behind he'd have seen another car.

Behind the wheel sat Abel, the Ape, his eyes glued to the distant red lights of Tweed's car. He was alone. Back in Paris he had waited in an all-night café, drinking coffee, his car parked outside. From his window seat he had a view of the exit from the Ritz. He had seen Tweed leave with Paula and Newman. What he hadn't recognized the significance of was Marler and Butler strolling out first to their car parked in the street leading to the Opéra. Nor had he taken any notice when Nield had followed them to pick up his own car.

Earlier, in another message from Goslar in his screeching voice, Abel had been given the mobile number of a certain Gustav Charles. He had been told to report Tweed's progress to Charles at regular intervals. Goslar had given him no idea of the location of the mysterious Charles. When he called him, Charles confirmed his name, listened, then gave only one answer.

'Merci.'

The Ape, often operating on his own, had a habit of talking to himself. He was doing so now.

'The end of the line for you, Tweed. Somewhere ahead a gang of storm troopers is waiting to blast you to hell.'

Abel was looking forward to this. His only anxiety was that he was sure *he* was being followed.

*

Inside the car which worried Abel were two men. The driver was Mervyn Leek. Beside him, a map open on his lap, sat Bate.

The warning that Tweed was leaving had come from one of Bate's men planted inside the Ritz. They had driven into the *place* outside the Ritz just as Tweed's car was leaving.

'There should be more of us,' Leek said nervously.

'Just keep your eye on the road,' Bate had snapped. He opened the glove compartment, took out a gun. 'When they eventually lead us to Goslar we'll use his girl friend, Grey, as a hostage while we take Goslar. Too many of us could have been noticed, I decided.'

'If you say so.'

'Damnit, Leek, I just did say so.'

Inside the last car a pilot would have seen, sat Vance Karnow. By his side Bancroft gripped the wheel. Karnow also had a road map open on his lap. He was an excellent navigator and knew exactly where they were.

Bancroft, wearing a beret and an anorak, had waited inside the same all-night café the Ape had used. Bancroft had taken no notice of the huge man. The café was full of French people, catching up on their drinking, smoking Gauloises.

Bancroft had been cleverer than the Ape. He had recognized Marler from the brief glimpse into the bar at the Ritz when Marler had glanced in. That had been on the occasion when Tweed, with Paula and Newman, had watched Karnow and his henchmen drinking with Trudy. Bancroft had immediately left the café, had seen the first car. Walking back, slouching with a bottle in his hand, he had then seen Nield get into the second car. On his mobile phone he had called Karnow as

Tweed had emerged with Paula and Newman to get into their car.

Karnow had been sitting earlier in a nearby night-club. Bored stiff, he had watched the scantily dressed French girls performing. He'd thought they did it much better in Vegas. In fact they did everything much better in the States, in his opinion. He had joined Bancroft as soon as his call had come through, thankful to get out of the nightclub.

Earlier, from outside, he had called his suite at ten o'clock to tell them he'd be late for dinner. A waiter had answered.

'There's been an attack on that suite. Everyone arrested . . .'

Another voice suddenly took over the conversation.

'Who is this?' Lasalle, furious with the waiter, had enquired. 'Please identify yourself!'

Karnow had broken the connection, had told Bancroft they would eat in a small restaurant near the Ritz. Later, Bancroft had moved by himself to the all-night café while Karnow wandered into the nightclub, after paying an extortionate entrance fee.

As they continued along the autoroute Karnow checked his map yet again. Bancroft was hunched over the wheel as he followed the red lights of the car ahead.

'Two more cars behind the first three,' he reported again.

'They'll be more backup,' Karnow said coldly. 'Shouldn't cause us much trouble when the time comes, when Tweed contacts Goslar.'

'We'll blast them all off the planet,' Bancroft growled.

'You mean you will,' Karnow told him.

'We – I – have a load of firepower,' Bancroft said with eager anticipation.

He was right. An executive case perched on the floor held an incredible variety of handguns. Plus the three machine-pistols stashed away in the boot. He had once gunned down fifteen men.

Dr Goslar wore whites, similar to those worn by Professor Saafeld when Tweed had visited him in his Holland Park mansion in London. The whites skirted a table as Goslar walked to a Norman-style window and peered out into the night.

There was deep snow on the steep slope running down from the old castle to the lake below. The moonlight reflected off ice rimming the lake's edges. No sign of lights in the distant village on the far side of the lake. Goslar returned to work in the room at the top of the castle.

The laboratory was nothing like a scene from a science fiction film. It was also totally different from a scene in a Frankenstein movie. Despite the intense cold in the mountains outside, the room was warm. In the centre stood an ancient stone chimney-like structure, thigh-high above the floor, about six feet in diameter at its open top. A blazing fire burned thirty feet down, well below floor level. The fire was so strong it warmed the room.

It had a dual purpose. It not only heated the stone-walled room, it was a useful place to throw in unwanted material. The ferocity of the fire was such that it immediately consumed whatever might be tipped into it. The heat was so intense that the large section above floor level was hot. Goslar's hand held the whites close to avoid them touching the chimney.

Overhead was a series of transparent glass tubes leading from one large globelike container to another. As liquid left one globe on its way through tubes to another, it passed through a filter. This process continued until, finally, the treated liquid dripped into a large canister placed on one of the laboratory tables. The canister was barely a quarter full. It would take some time before the canister was full.

On another table stood two canisters already filled with the liquid. The canisters were made of the very strong perspex used to create the pilot's cabin in a helicopter. Almost unbreakable. Each of the two filled canisters was sealed with a screw-top cap. There was enough liquid in them to kill at least fifty million people instantly if it was introduced into the water supply of a largely populated country – or dropped as a spray from a missile.

In essence, the laboratory was a large distillery, distilling the liquid into its final deadly state. The figure in whites checked a watch on its wrist. Time to leave. Goslar checked a door in the wall which led to an outside fire escape. It was locked. Goslar took one last look round. On another table lay a dead turtle, at least four feet long. At an early stage it had been injected with a hypodermic, dying instantly. The shell had been carefully cut open, exposing its inside. Goslar had extracted a rare ingredient, the key element in producing the weapon.

Satisfied that the third canister would take plenty of time to fill up, Goslar left the laboratory, stepping carefully down a circular stone staircase to the next level. This room was comfortably furnished. Goslar spent time in the bathroom, then emerged in warm outdoor clothes.

Descending another staircase, the doctor opened the door to a garage housing a car with snow tyres. Now for the tricky drive to the city. All the lights had been left on so the villagers in the distant hamlet would assume the castle was still occupied.

The moonlight glittered on the heavy fall of snow covering a small mountain above the castle. A few hundred yards below the summit towered a monstrous crag, projecting like a huge platform. There was hardly any snow in the cave underneath it.

22

The motorcyclist, crash helmet pulled well down, visor closed, masking the face, roared down the autoroute. It overtook the car with Bate and Leek inside, raced on. It sped past the Ape's car, reduced speed as it approached the next car. Tweed, seated on the right, lowered his window. Paula gripped her Browning, aimed it out of the window.

'Don't react,' Tweed warned. 'Not unless it makes a hostile move.'

He looked out as the rider drew alongside. There was now no glove on the rider's left hand. He caught sight of a varnished thumb gesturing back, then three fingers raised, then the cyclist sped ahead. Paula frowned as Tweed closed the window, keeping out the icy night air.

'Did he make a rude gesture?' she asked. 'Or was it a she?'

'You were right,' Tweed called out to Newman, 'there are three cars following us still.'

'How do you know that now?' Newman enquired.

'Just trust me,' Tweed replied.

Ahead of them the motorcyclist roared past Nield's car, drove on towards the first car. Butler saw the motorcyclist coming in his wing mirror. Agilely, he climbed into the back seat, grabbed a machine-pistol off the floor, lowered the left-hand window, perched the barrel on the window's edge.

The motorcyclist saw the muzzle protruding in the moonlight. Slowing down, the rider saw a petrol station ahead. Slowing even more, the rider turned into the station, stopped, then wheeled the machine round the back. When the rider appeared again it walked into the ladies'.

Trudy had thrown her crash helmet into the ditch where she had dumped her machine. In no time at all she brushed her hair, applied lipstick, went outside. It had been a long and tiring trip from Paris. Standing in a shadow she counted Nield's car flashing past, then Tweed's. The Ape raced past next and a minute later Bate's vehicle drove by. Trudy then walked out and stood where she could easily be seen, clad in her leather motorcycle gear. She had gloves on both hands now.

Bancroft reduced speed, then stopped on Karnow's order. Trudy opened the back door, stepped inside, closed the door. As the car began moving again she revelled in the pure pleasure of its warmth. She let out her breath in a sigh of relief.

'What have you got to report?' Karnow demanded.

'Tweed is in car number five ahead of us,' she lied.

'So, when the time comes, that's the one we blast,' Bancroft said enthusiastically.

'You've done well,' Karnow said in a burst of rare praise.

Yes, I have, Trudy thought. Car number five looked by far the most dangerous. Two men inside, one armed with a machine-pistol. Walk into it, Bancroft. Walk into it.

'Trudy did well in the States,' Karnow recalled. 'She put three men we were after in a compromising position.'

'She went all the way,' Bancroft said, licking his lips as he leered.

In her rear seat Trudy managed to keep the fury out of her expression at Bancroft's filthy remark. She started removing her boots, replacing them with fur-lined shoes.

'Actually,' Karnow corrected Bancroft, 'she did no such thing. The mere fact that she was alone with each man in a hotel room was all we needed to put pressure on them. All were married.'

'So she says,' Bancroft sneered.

'Bancroft.' Karnow's tone was savage as he looked at the driver. 'Are you questioning what I just said? We had a video in each hotel room. She did not go anything like all the way at all. You underestimate her cleverness, you stupid schmuck.'

'Sorry, Chief,' Bancroft mumbled.

Some time later, following Nield, with Marler ahead of him, they had turned off the autoroute, had passed through Belfort, and were travelling along a country road lined with trees. They had passed through several small French villages without lights and drove more slowly.

This was one of the very attractive areas of France, with cultivated fields beyond the trees on both sides. The villages consisted of old houses built long ago, their walls covered with plaster and colour-washed in different pastel tones. They had intriguing names like Ranspach Bas and Chavannes sur l'Étang.

In places the road became a series of switchbacks. In others there were long ruler-straight stretches. Newman was whistling to himself, enjoying the change from the endless autoroute.

'We're now on Route D419, heading straight into Geneva,' he called out.

He had just spoken when Tweed's mobile started buzzing. He answered cautiously.

'Yes?'

'This is Serena. Lovely to hear your voice. I'm in a motel on the edge of Geneva. I've hired a car. Where are you now?'

'Approaching the suburbs of Geneva. We should be in the city in twenty minutes. Half an hour at the most. No traffic. Meet you at the main station.'

'Then I'll drive to the station now. I can wait in the buffet. I should warn you there's been an exceptionally heavy fall of snow here. From what I can see the mountains behind Geneva are thick with it. Of course the Swiss are saying it's most unusual at this time of the year.'

'You had a good flight?' Tweed asked.

'Smooth as silk. I got a shock when the plane was coming in. It flew over the mountains and then I saw the snow. Specks of it glittered like diamonds in the moonlight. I'd better get moving now. See you . . .'

'That was Serena,' Tweed told them. 'She'll be waiting for us at the main station in the buffet.'

'And I thought it was Burgoyne,' Paula said with disappointment.

'No call from him, no ambush,' Newman said cheerfully. 'Yet.'

'Did you talk about anything else when Serena visited you at the Ritz?' Paula asked. 'Besides identifying the Ape?'

'We had quite a long chat. She talked for a while about biochemistry. That led on from our recalling Appledore. She's really pretty bright – at least from what I could gather with my limited knowledge of the subject,' Tweed mused.

'But I thought her sister, Davina, was the scientist.'

'Sisters pick up things from each other. She was very relaxed, had several glasses of wine. She was speculating on what the key ingredient could be in whatever poisoned the sea. Couldn't come up with an answer. Some of it was too technical for me.'

'Sounds more like Davina who, I gathered, was brilliant in her subject,' Paula observed.

'As I said a moment ago, sisters – especially when they're lookalikes – talk to each other a lot. I found Serena much brighter than I'd realized.' Tweed looked out of the window as they passed through another village, then glanced at his map. 'I meant to ask you, did you really have a good evening with Burgoyne before it all turned hideous?'

'Wonderful. He kept telling me jokey stories. I'll give you an example . . .' When she had finished she pursed her lips. 'You may not think it all that funny from the way I told it – but he has this flair for acting out what he's describing. That's what makes it hysterical. He's a natural born actor.'

'We'll probably hear from him soon.'

'Incidentally,' Newman broke in, 'we are still being followed – the car behind us had to close up nearer on this road. It will be interesting to see what they do when we reach the main station. Nowhere for them to hide in the middle of Geneva. And I'm calling Nield and Marler to warn them to head for the main station.'

Earlier, while still on the autoroute, Paula had more than once detected the sound of a helicopter. She had mentioned it to Tweed, wondering if it was checking traffic speeds.

'More likely to be checking a juggernaut they suspect

236

of collecting drugs across the Spanish border. Small boats come into isolated coves, deliver the drugs, collect their money, then return to their mother ship well offshore – which sails back to Colombia.'

In fact, aboard the chopper a well-built man with thick dark hair sat in the pilot's cabin. He had a pair of night-vision glasses screwed to his eyes, focused on Tweed's vehicle. He kept warning the pilot to keep his distance.

He watched Tweed's car all the way to Geneva and then to the main station. Only then did he lower his binoculars.

'Land me at the airport quickly,' he ordered. 'In addition to the agreed fee there's a bonus if you land within three minutes.'

Close to the main station, they drove a short distance along the promenade with the wide River Rhône on their right. Paula gazed at the furious surge of lime-coloured water.

'It's an odd colour,' she remarked.

'As you know,' Tweed replied, 'the Rhône starts miles and miles away to the east at the glacier near Andermatt. Maybe the temperature has risen in that area, melting snow. That would account for the exceptional height of the river. The colour comes from melted snow . . .'

They arrived at the main railway station, Cornavin, just in time to see Serena, muffled up against the bitter cold, hurrying inside. In front of the station there was a wide open area surrounded by buildings. They passed the entrance to a large underground garage.

'I see Marler, Butler and Nield are parked in their cars,' remarked Tweed. 'We'll go into the buffet and pick up Serena.'

'I'm going to stay outside,' Newman decided. 'I want to see what happens if our camp-followers arrive. They won't know what to do.'

'I think I'll stay with you,' Tweed replied. 'Paula, could you go in and find the buffet. You'll be able to spot Serena easily – with her jet-black hair. You saw her at Brown's Hotel, then at Fortnum's when I had tea with her. Tell her who you are, keep her company. I'll join you in a few minutes.'

Tweed, who had listened to weather forecasts for the Continent in his suite at the Ritz, had warned everyone to wear plenty of clothes. Newman, clad in fur-lined boots, two pullovers and his overcoat, was thankful he had listened. As he waited, he slapped his arms round his body.

A car appeared. Shadows made it impossible to see who was inside. The driver reacted quickly – probably after seeing who was standing outside the station. He drove straight for the entrance to the underground car park. Newman caught a glimpse of the make and the colour of the vehicle as it vanished down a sloping ramp.

'That was one of them,' Newman commented. 'A very distinctive green Citroën, I saw it way back on the autoroute as we came round a long curve. Don't ask me which one it was.'

'That underground car park is vast,' Tweed told him. 'I used it once. It covers almost the whole area under the square.'

'Here comes Number Two. A Renault, again of an unusual colour.'

This car paused in the shadows.

'No way of seeing who – or how many – were inside . . .'

As he spoke the car suddenly shot forward, headed

for the ramp, slowed, then vanished like its predecessor. Tweed turned his gaze in a different direction.

'I'm watching the pedestrian exit. No one has appeared yet.'

They waited a few more minutes in the bitter cold. No one else was visible. Behind them the station was dead. The Swiss, Tweed thought, were sensibly keeping indoors. He checked his watch. It was nearly eleven o'clock. Geneva had gone to sleep.

A third car, an Audi, then drove into the square. The driver of this new arrival was decisive. He must have just had time to see the two men standing outside the station before he increased speed, flashed out of sight down the ramp into the garage. Again Newman couldn't see how many people were inside.

'That's Number Three,' he said. 'I do remember seeing an Audi among the three cars following us – when we were on that narrow country road passing through French villages. But don't ask me the sequence. I was absorbed on driving.'

Newman was concentrating so hard on watching that entrance to the square where the vehicles appeared he completely missed something. A hired Renault, which had been waiting at the airport, had driven into the square from another direction. Behind the wheel sat a man with thick dark hair. He drove into a side street, parked his car, got out, fed a meter with coins.

The Yellow Man then strolled back into the square, walked into a hotel and asked for a room overlooking the station. He paid for the room in advance, using cash. He didn't like credit cards – they could leave a trail which might be followed.

'A lot of snow seems to have fallen,' he remarked amiably to the night receptionist.

'It's terrible. Never happened before like this. Tons

of it have come down on the mountains. If the temperature suddenly rises there will be avalanches . . .'

'Strange,' Newman commented, outside the station. 'You'd expect at least some of the people inside those cars to either walk out by the pedestrian exit or drive out again.'

'I've got an idea,' Tweed said. 'I'm going to that phone box to call Arthur Beck.'

'But he's in Berne!'

Newman shrugged. Tweed was already inside the box. Marler and Nield got out of their parked cars and wandered over to him.

'Just what is going on?' Marler asked.

'No idea. Did either of you recognize anyone inside those three cars?'

'No,' they both replied in unison.

'They're in a huge underground garage – vast,' Tweed said. 'Can't imagine what's happening down there.'

'Sounds to me like an ideal place to take out the lot,' Marler suggested.

'We do nothing until Tweed gets back. He's phoning Beck in Berne. Can't imagine why . . .'

Several minutes later Tweed came striding briskly back from the phone box. He had his hands inside his coat pockets.

'We're in luck. Beck is away – at some security conference held in Chicago. Expected back any moment. I got hold of his chief assistant, a woman who knows me. She gave me the number of Captain Charpentier, based at police headquarters here in an odd building with walls which look like plastic. Just on the other side of the Rhône. I know Charpentier well, explained the situation we have here. He's heard of Dr Goslar. Everyone has now. This is Goslar's doing – publicizing what he has for sale to the highest bidder.'

'So what is Charpentier doing?' Newman asked impatiently.

'Sending across the river to here a whole fleet of patrol cars. I warned him not to let them arrive with screaming sirens and flashing lights. He's got plain-clothes men coming too – so they can walk down into the garage and check out what's going on.'

'Then what happens?'

'We'll know soon enough now.'

The atmosphere seemed full of menace. The silence in the square was disturbing. Then patrol cars began to pour into the square from every direction. Several stopped, took up a position in front of the entrance ramp. Others circled the exit ramp. A man in a business suit climbed out, walked down the entrance ramp. Charpentier told Tweed later what happened next.

The man in the suit, a Sergeant Davril, stood at the base of the ramp, looked at the cars parked everywhere. Charpentier explained that there were no tourists at this time of the year, in this weather. The parked cars belonged to Swiss businessmen, some sleeping in their nearby apartments while others, often bankers, were there to visit their mistresses.

Davril walked further in. Without warning a machine-pistol began to chatter. One bullet chipped his arm, a second one passed straight through his left shoulder. He sagged between two cars, hauled out his automatic, fired back several times where he thought he saw a figure. Then all hell broke loose.

Guns were being fired all over the garage. At least two machine-pistols rattled away. Handguns opened up. A bullet struck the petrol tank of one parked car. It exploded with a roar, ignited the car next to it, which also detonated. Then other cars blew up. Flames soared to the ceiling. Smoke began to obscure what was happening, blossoming in great clouds. Uniformed, armed police rushed down both ramps. The whole garage was beginning to explode. The fire brigade arrived, unreeled great snakelike hoses, flooded the whole interior. Chaos and confusion everywhere. Many cars had become burnt-out wrecks. It was Dante's Inferno.

23

Tweed, realizing he could do nothing, had told Marler and Nield to go back to their heated cars, to wait and report later. With Newman he went into the station, found the buffet. The only two occupants were Paula and Serena.

Paula was chatting animatedly to Serena, in fact telling her nothing, when Tweed and Newman arrived. The sole waitress was asking them if they would like more coffee.

'I think we're swimming in it, thank you.' Paula smiled at the waitress. 'Thank you also for letting us stay so late.' She looked at Tweed and Newman.

'This kind lady has stayed open just for us. I think it's because we're English.'

'You're welcome,' the waitress replied with a warm smile.

'Hello, Serena,' Tweed said quickly. 'Sorry to rush you both but we're staying at the Hôtel Richemond for the night. We can talk later. Oh, this is Bob Newman, my staunch protector. Bob, meet Serena Cavendish. I think we'd better go now.'

Paula gave the waitress a generous tip, thanked her

again, then they were outside. Paula stopped. All the police cars. From below the rumble of gunfire. She stared at Tweed.

'What is happening? Sounds like the end of the world.'

It will be for some people, Newman said to himself. Charpentier, a tall, handsome man in his forties, was introduced briefly. He nodded, shook hands, turned to Tweed.

'This is sensible of you to go to the Richemond. I will come over later to have a word with you.'

Paula and Serena occupied the back of Newman's car while Tweed sat in the front next to Newman, who drove the short distance to the Richemond. The night manager was waiting for them as they walked into the luxurious surroundings. He gave them the good news as they registered.

'Captain Charpentier phoned to say you would be coming. The chef has agreed to stay on to provide you with a meal. After you have settled in your rooms please come down at your convenience. You can choose whatever you want from the menu . . .'

Tweed was about to join the others on their way to their rooms when he heard a noise. He turned round and saw, almost hidden behind a corner, Trudy.

'I'll follow you up,' he told the others. When they had gone he turned to Trudy.

Her hair was dishevelled, quite unlike her normal coiffeured appearance. Her clothes were rumpled. She carried a shoulder bag over one arm.

'What are you doing here? You look as though you've been in a war.'

'I have. Come into the bar. I'll tell you . . .'

'Nice of you to stay open,' Tweed said to the barman when he brought their drinks.

'We knew you were coming, sir,' the barman replied with a smile and left them.

243

'*I* was in that underground garage,' Trudy began. 'Hence my appearance.'

'You look OK to me. Your makeup's perfect.'

'I rushed into the bathroom as soon as I'd walked here, then dashed down so I could catch you. I'm lucky to be alive.'

'Take it slowly. Start from the beginning.'

'You understood my hand message when I signalled to you back on the autoroute? I was the motorcyclist. All the way from Paris.'

'You must be exhausted. Are you sure you want to talk now?'

'I won't sleep if I don't. Vance Karnow suggested I travel that way. He wanted to know how many of you there were in different cars. I agreed. Anything rather than travel with Bancroft as the driver. There were just the three of us. Something happened to the other lousy Americans back at the hotel in Paris. When I'd checked up on you I dumped my machine behind a petrol station and I was picked up by the car. Then the world blew up in that underground garage.'

'Want to tell me what did happen?'

'Karnow couldn't make up his bloody mind what to do next. So we sat in the garage. Then a man in a business suit walked down the ramp and inside. Bancroft thought it was Newman – the man did look a bit like him. He went berserk, grabbed a machine-pistol, got out of the car and opened fire, shooting all over the place. That's what started the holocaust, if I can use that expression. Shooting everywhere, bullets flying all over the shop. Cars exploding. I got out, ran for it, crouching down . . .'

'What happened to Karnow? To Bancroft?'

'Karnow was still in the car when it caught fire. There was a lot of smoke. I saw in a blur a figure climbing a ladder by the wall. I ran to it. I heard in a brief pause in the mayhem the sound of something metallic. It was just an ordinary aluminium ladder. I think it was lowered by pulling a lever on the wall. I shinned up it – whoever had gone up first had vanished. At the top I realized it was a ventilation shaft. The cone protruding above the ground had been knocked off. I scrambled out, saw you talking to another tall, good-looking man. He had raised his voice to be heard above the noises below ground. I heard him say something about going to the Hôtel Richemond. I know Geneva, so I walked here, avoiding the station. I still can't believe I got away.'

'But you did.' Tweed squeezed her round the waist and she nearly burst into tears, but stopped herself. 'Have another drink,' he said, summoning the waiter.

'I'll be drunk.'

'Doesn't matter.'

Normally he would have suggested sweetened tea, but he could tell she was not in a state of shock. Relating to him what had taken place had calmed her down. He asked the question when the second drink had been served.

'Was Bancroft in the car when you fled from it?'

'No. I don't know where he was. He started it all, by opening fire with his machine-pistol on the man he thought was Newman. When I scrambled out of the car he'd disappeared in the smoke.'

'You could catch a flight back to London from here in the morning.'

'Can't I stay with you? You're still after Goslar, aren't you? I would like to see where it all ends – remember, I was the motorcyclist who tried to warn you. Did you understand my signal? I asked you earlier and you didn't answer.'

'Sorry, I should have done. Yes, I did understand. You indicated there were three cars behind me. Thank you for—'

'I also lied to Karnow – told him you were in the first of the three cars. I'd seen two men in that one and the barrel of a gun protruding from a window. Bancroft was going to blast the front car when the time came, as he put it. I thought when he did carry out his threat two men would be more than a match – even for Bancroft. I'm determined to see this through, Tweed.'

He thought about it, looked at her, looked away. She was intense but, despite her ordeal, now quite calm. He sipped at his drink before he spoke.

'Let's both sleep on it after a good dinner. I don't imagine you are carrying a weapon?'

She glanced round. The barman had his back to them, was polishing glasses. Slipping her hand inside her jacket, she produced a 6.35 mm automatic from her hip holster.

'I can use it. When I was in New York I took shooting lessons in my spare time. I shouldn't say it, but I was a crack shot. I was keeping it in case I ever encountered Bancroft. When I did, I never got the opportunity to use it.'

'Hide it now. My team will be coming down for dinner. Everyone will be ravenous – including yourself, I'm sure. I'll introduce you to them as Trudy Warner, if that's all right by you.'

'I'd like you to go on calling me Trudy.' She smiled. 'You have always known me as Trudy during our brief acquaintance. And I do want to come with you wherever you're going.'

'Tell you my decision in the morning. Now we'll go into the dining room. I have a Captain Charpentier of the Swiss police coming to see me later. I want food first before he arrives.'

After a sumptuous dinner they all realized they were very alert and didn't feel like going to bed yet. Tweed invited them to his suite to drink their coffee. He had taken one sip from his cup when the phone rang. It was Captain Charpentier downstairs. Tweed asked him to come up to the suite.

Charpentier frowned when he entered and surveyed the gathering – his gaze fixed on Paula and Trudy. They were seated together on a sofa. During the dinner they had got on very well with each other. Tweed invited the Swiss police officer to sit down, to have coffee. Charpentier remained standing.

'Something wrong?' Tweed enquired.

'I was going to describe what we have found in the garage,' their visitor said in impeccable English. 'Some of it is grisly.'

'You're thinking of the ladies.' Tweed introduced Trudy. 'I can tell you both have seen some pretty grisly things. Like the rest of us they will want to hear this.'

'If you say so.'

Charpentier took off his outdoor coat and sat down. He accepted a cup of coffee, drank it greedily.

'Then I won't pull any punches. We found several corpses, burnt to a shrivel almost. Behind the wheel of a Citroën was a big man. Very big. An odd thing had happened. His body was badly burnt but the upper part of his head was intact. We think while he was on fire foam was flooded over him by the fire brigade, then later he was hosed down. He had very close-cropped brown hair. Like stubble. The fire hadn't reached it. He must have had it cut that way.'

'The Ape,' Paula said to herself, but still aloud.

'You knew him?' Charpentier asked.

'Yes. Briefly and unpleasantly. One monstrous thug.'

'Could you give me his name?'

'Abel. I'm sure that was his Christian name. No idea of what his surname might have been.'

Paula felt no regrets at the news. After her experience of being suspended by him from a window up thirty floors she experienced only relief that he was no longer walking the planet. Tweed had been watching Trudy closely. She had shown no signs of distress at the description. Instead, she was leaning forward, watching the Swiss closely.

'I'll go on,' Charpentier continued. 'Inside a Renault, well away from the Citroën, we found what must have been a tall man in the front passenger seat. He was a black stick. His door was open and we think he tried to escape. On the concrete floor of the garage near the open door we found his passport.' He consulted a notebook. 'Jarvis Bate. Officer, Special Branch.'

'Was there anyone else in that car?' Paula enquired.

'Yes. A much smaller man behind the wheel. Burnt almost down to a skeleton.'

'Mervyn Leek,' Tweed said. 'Also an officer of Special Branch, for your records.'

'Thank you, sir.' Charpentier made a note in his little book. 'Lastly there was a corpse in a third car, again well away from the other two vehicles. An Audi . . .'

My car, thought Trudy, leaning forward further. What's coming now?

'With this one,' Charpentier went on, 'I'm glad my chief, Arthur Beck, arrived in Geneva an hour ago on a much-delayed flight from America. It has delicate international implications. The body in the front was charred to the waist. Again, the brigade had pumped in foam, which saved the top half of the corpse. And it was later hosed down. Features singed but clear. A fireman emptied his breast pocket, gave me the contents. They included a passport. The dead owner was Vance Karnow, top man in Washington.'

'Was there any other body in the car?' Trudy asked.

'No.' Charpentier looked surprised at the question after what he had just told them. 'Why?'

'I just wouldn't expect a man like that to travel alone. You did say the body was in the front of the car,' she continued. 'What about a driver?'

'No sign of one. But two people escaped.'

Trudy concentrated on straightening a crease in the slacks of her trouser suit. When she looked at Tweed her eyes were like stones. They'd both had the same thought.

Bancroft.

'Escaped?' Tweed asked. 'How did they do that?'

'Climbed up inside one of the ventilator shafts, knocked the top off, vanished. I saw them running.'

Tweed and Trudy again exchanged glances. He knew what she was thinking. He wasn't far off. She recalled the figure she'd seen disappearing above her. Had she known she could have shot Bancroft in the back with her Beretta.

'Any evidence of anyone else shooting?' Tweed enquired to divert the attention of the Swiss from the ventilator shaft. 'I mean, any sign of weapons?'

'Yes. Inside the Renault,' he said, 'Bate had an automatic clenched in what was left of his right hand. 'In the first Citroën – the one with the man you called the Ape – there was a machine-pistol on the floor. Both weapons had been fired.'

'So it was a shoot-out,' Tweed commented. 'Made far worse when bullets hit petrol tanks, which promptly exploded.'

'That sums it up.' Charpentier was standing. 'I think

that is enough for tonight. We'll know more after the autopsies – I don't envy the pathologists their job. Beck will be coming to see you at eight o'clock in the morning, Mr Tweed. I'd better get back. I suggest you all try to get a good night's sleep . . .'

Tweed looked again at Trudy. When he saw the steely look in her eyes he had no doubt she would be coming with them to Annecy.

24

From his front-seat view the Yellow Man had watched it all with interest. Careful not to turn on any lights in his bedroom, he had carried a chair, placed it behind the thick net curtains across a window, had sat with night-vision glasses.

He had seen Tweed and Newman standing in front of the station, the arrival of a horde of patrol cars which had formed a cordon round entrances and exits. Soon he had heard the muffled sound of gunfire from inside the underground car park. It hadn't meant a thing to him.

Later he had focused his glasses as another woman and Paula had joined Tweed and Newman. With his free hand he had felt the string of pearls with the razor-edged wire, had imagined placing them round Paula's neck from behind her.

Later still he had gone to bed, setting his alarm clock for an early start. After using room service to have a 6 a.m. breakfast he had left the hotel, walked to his car through deserted streets. Patrol cars were still parked barring entrances and exits to the car park.

Getting inside his vehicle parked in the side street, he had taken off his suit, then donned a dark blue uniform. He took off the black wig, which he was fed up with. Quickly he rammed a peaked cap over his hair. He then drove into the square and parked where he could see the entrance to the Richemond. He had, before leaving his own accommodation, phoned several hotels asking for Tweed before a temporary receptionist informed him Tweed was at the Richemond. He had broken the connection before the receptionist could say any more.

Dissatisfied with his viewpoint, he drove closer to the hotel, parked. Slumped in his seat, pretending to read an old newspaper, he looked like a chauffeur waiting for his employer to arrive.

As arranged the night before, Paula arrived at Tweed's suite in time to have breakfast with him. She thought Tweed looked amazingly alert. He thought she looked tired. They were just finishing their meal when Beck arrived.

The Chief of Federal Police hugged Paula when he entered the room. They had always liked each other. Beck, in his late forties, was of medium height, slim, had greying hair and a neat trim moustache. He had a paper under his arm and he handed it to Tweed.

'*Le Monde*. Flown in by express from Paris this morning. The headline is interesting.'

AMERICANS DEPORTED
ACCUSED OF ESPIONAGE

Tweed scanned the text underneath. The gist was that incriminating documents had been discovered in the suite of a top-class hotel where an American delegation was staying. Vance Karnow was involved, but had gone missing.

'Interesting, as you say,' Tweed agreed, handing the newspaper to Paula.

'And where was your last port of call?' enquired Beck, settling himself in an armchair. 'That is, before you arrived here.'

'Paris.'

'So you wouldn't know anything about René Lasalle and his team finding the Americans tear-gassed and recovering consciousness?'

'I wasn't there.'

'As always, a devious answer,' Beck commented, his expression quizzical.

'You've heard about a Dr Goslar?' Tweed responded, changing the subject.

'Heard about him! All the security services in Western Europe – and the States – are talking about nothing else.'

'That will be Goslar's network – spreading the news as a prelude to raising the bidding sky-high for his fiendish new weapon. Anything in the press about what is really going on?'

'Not a peep so far. The security people, who do know, are so scared they have kept their mouths shut outside their own circles. This has caused them to create a miracle for the moment – keeping it out of the press. Of course here we have something else to think about which will make the headlines in tomorrow's papers.'

'The devastation in the underground garage?'

'Yes.' Beck paused. 'You wouldn't have been involved in that in some way, I suppose?'

'Indirectly, we were. Three cars followed us from Paris. Newman, standing outside the station, watched as at intervals all three cars entered that garage.'

'Why is it, Tweed, that when you arrive somewhere the whole city blows up?'

'Obviously I'm mixing with the wrong people.'

'You do that all the time. To be fair it's your profession, rather like my own job. Washington is already screaming about what has happened to Vance Karnow.'

'Let them scream. Arthur . . .' It was Tweed's turn to pause. 'Can I ask you a favour?'

'I knew that would be coming. Just when I'm up to my eyes in my own problems. Tell me the worst. What is it?'

'Goslar has a habit of leaving what I call his signature when he moves on. It's his great mistake. He needs a base, wherever he happens to have alighted. So he leases a large property on a long-term agreement. Then, when he's ready, he leaves while the lease still has weeks – or months – to run. He has tons of money to operate in this way. It means he can dart on elsewhere the moment he wants to. Do I make myself clear?'

'Yes. But what do you want me to do?'

'With your authority, could you approach the two top estate agents in Geneva? I want to know if an expensive property has been leased recently – within, say, the last three months.'

'Oh, that's easy,' Beck said sarcastically. 'This is Switzerland.'

'I hadn't finished. The property will be fairly large – but not a Blenheim Palace. Essentially it will be in a remote location, but within one hour's driving distance from Geneva. I emphasize it will be remote. And on its own. No neighbours. It could have been leased in the name Charterhouse, but I very much doubt that. Also within driving distance of Geneva's airport.'

'Could be anywhere. You think Goslar is here?'

'I haven't a clue. It's a long shot. While I think of it, could Charpentier contact the airport, ask them if a private jet registered in Liechtenstein – under the company name of Poulenc et Cie – is still waiting there. A Grumman Gulfstream jet.'

'That's the easy one. I may phone you before you leave. When are you going – and where? If it isn't a state secret, which it probably is.'

'As soon as possible we leave for Annecy. This morning definitely.' Tweed reached for a hotel notepad. Tearing off a sheet he placed it on the cardboard back, scribbled, handed the sheet to Beck. 'There's my mobile phone number. I want us to keep closely in touch.'

'Thought you didn't like mobiles.'

'I don't. Mistrust them. They can be intercepted. But it's the only way we can contact each other this time. All my team have them.'

'What do you expect to find in Annecy?' Beck asked.

'Maybe Goslar.'

'Isn't he wonderful?' Beck said, turning to Paula. 'He asks me to contact estate agents here, then says Goslar could be hiding in Annecy.'

'In addition,' Tweed went on, 'we don't even know whether Goslar is a man or a woman. There are indications both ways.'

'He's looking for a phantom,' Beck commented, standing up. 'I'll check with the estate agents myself. This afternoon I'm flying back to Belp, the airport for Berne. Then I'll be locked up in my HQ. You have the number?'

'In my head. Always.'

'Have a nice quiet trip to Annecy. The weather will be better down there. I must go.'

'I expect that trip to be anything but quiet. Take care, Arthur.'

'You two are the ones who should take care. Goslar, I suspect, is one of the most dangerous men in the world . . .'

*

Marler arrived with a canvas holdall soon after Beck had departed. He walked over to Paula.

'One Browning for my collection, please. We'll pass through one of the French checkpoints. Thank you,' he said as Paula reluctantly handed over her gun, holster and spare ammo. 'I had trouble with Trudy Warner, getting an automatic off her. Had to promise to give it back once we're over the border. See you.

'Hello, Bob,' he said as he opened the door and Newman walked in. 'Feel naked without your Smith & Wesson? Thought so. I'm off . . .'

Paula got up, picked up her fleece from a chair. She explained when she'd put the garment on, 'Poor Trudy. All her clothes were in a case inside the trunk of the Audi, which is a wreck. We're going shopping to get her something to wear. I loaned her a nightdress after we'd left this suite last night, plus a few other things. Serena is coming with us.'

'Don't be too long,' Tweed warned.

'Why do men always say that when women go shopping?'

'What do you think of Serena?' Tweed suddenly asked.

'Mystery woman,' was Paula's reaction.

Newman threw his coat on a chair, dumped his bag beside it. Then he settled himself in an armchair, lit a cigarette.

'What is the situation now?' he enquired. 'After last night.'

'Simplified,' Tweed assorted. 'Up to a point. Don't think me callous, but Goslar is the target. Now Bate is out of the way, no longer following us, that's one less enemy to think about. The same applies to the late Ape. All we have to worry about is Goslar – and his huge organization. There is one other highly lethal danger.

Bancroft. When I saw him at the bar in the Ritz back in Paris he struck me as a thug, but a very dangerous thug with brains.'

'He may have caught a flight back to the States.'

'No. He'll still be around,' Tweed said grimly.

'Still no word from Burgoyne?' Newman asked. 'That worries me.'

'It shouldn't. Burgoyne is used to operating on his own. And he is not a man to waste time just keeping in touch. When he finds something we'll hear from him.'

'Let's just hope it's in time. When do we leave?'

'As soon as the ladies get back. I hope Marler has hidden all the armoury properly.'

'He has. I helped him tape weapons under the chassis of his car. He wants to lead the pack again – says when the French checkpoint people see three cars they're liable to let the first one through without much bother.'

'Let's hope he's right.'

Newman had spent some time explaining Marler's plan of manoeuvre – if they ran into an ambush – when the door opened. Into the suite trooped Paula, Serena and Trudy, with carrier bags.

'I see,' said Tweed, 'you've bought up half Geneva.'

'Why do men always say that when women go shopping?' asked Paula, repeating her earlier remark.

'And from the names on the carriers you've spent a fortune,' Tweed continued.

'Same reply as the one I've just made,' Paula responded. 'Trudy is fixed up now. As you see, we managed to find her a fleece. And a nice fur cap. Don't take it off yet, Trudy. Circle, let them admire you.'

'I'd say,' Newman commented with enthusiasm as

Trudy swivelled round, 'that you look rather more than terrific.'

'Thank you, kind sir,' Trudy replied, curtsying.

'Serena also has a few new things – including a really warm coat,' Paula pointed out.

'And fashionable new boots,' Newman observed. 'She also makes me wish we were staying in Geneva. Then I could take the three of you out on the town.'

'You can forget that,' Tweed said severely. 'We have a job to do.'

He had just spoken when the phone rang. He grabbed hold of it, sat back.

'Yes?'

'I have the answers,' Beck's voice told him. 'First the private jet at Cointrin. Charpentier has two men out there at the airport permanently – to check on who is arriving. The news is the Grumman is kept fully fuelled, regularly maintained, ready for instant departure. Furthermore, there are eight-hour shifts on round the clock, three teams of air crews, who take it in turns to occupy the cockpit. That jet could take off for distant points at any moment. Most unusual. Most expensive.'

'Then I could be right about the Geneva area.'

'You could. I've also contacted the two top estate agents. They are checking on leases on the type of property you described, going back three months. Charpentier will get their reports later. I gave him your mobile number. Hope you don't mind.'

'I agree. And thank you for taking action so quickly. I believe we're now facing a race against time.'

'You've had that in the past. You coped. Must go now to catch my flight to Belp. Again, take great care . . .'

Everyone in the suite was seated. They had all kept quiet during the conversation, something Tweed appreciated. These were women with heads on their shoulders.

'A race against time?' Paula enquired.

'Yes. I've paid the hotel bill. I can give you five minutes to get yourselves organized. Then we leave.'

'You look very grim,' Newman remarked when they were alone.

'I feel very grim.'

'Your old adversary from all those years ago. He managed to get away then. We don't want a repeat performance.'

'My old adversary,' Tweed repeated.

Much earlier, the Yellow Man had been slumped behind the wheel of his hired Mercedes when the door to the hotel he was parked outside opened. A small business-man, wearing an astrakhan coat, walked briskly down the steps.

The assassin straightened up, adjusted his peaked cap. The businessman spoke as the 'chauffeur' lowered a window.

'You're my car for Stuttgart? I am early, I know.'

'*Yes sir!*' The Yellow Man was out of the car, opening the rear door with a flourish. He bowed his head as the businessman handed him his case, then stepped into the rear. He closed the door. Then he opened the boot, deposited the large case inside, shut the lid.

Returning to his place behind the wheel, he caught the eye of the man in the back. The businessman wore rimless glasses, exuded an air of wealth and success. He spoke English with an accent.

'I know I'm three hours ahead of schedule. I phoned your firm this morning but no one answered.'

'Staff comes on duty later, sir,' the Yellow Man replied.

'My meeting in Stuttgart has been brought forward. I'd like to stop somewhere for breakfast later. Just a quick one.'

'That can easily be arranged, sir.'

The Yellow Man was scanning the street. It was totally deserted at that hour. He started the engine, cruised forward slowly a short distance, then stopped. He scanned the street in his rear-view mirror, in his wing mirror, ahead of him. His hand reached under a newspaper spread out on the seat beside him. He turned round.

'I don't think the lid is locked. I must protect your—'

As he was speaking he aimed the gun with the silencer he had in his hand. He shot the passenger once. A red patch like a flower blooming appeared on the businessman's chest as he slumped down. The Yellow Man jumped out of the car, unlocked the boot, took out the heavy case. Then he opened the rear door, placed the case next to the dead man. He wrapped the white silk scarf the corpse was wearing in such a way that it concealed the bullet hole.

He then swiftly lifted the body so it was upright against the seat. The corpse looked as though it was sleeping, head resting against the back. He wedged in the case to prevent the body slipping sideways. Satisfied with his exertions, he sat again behind the wheel. Then he steered the car forward until it was close to, but not opposite, the Richemond.

He waited.

When, eventually, Newman drove a car to the hotel entrance, the Yellow Man started his engine. Again he waited. He watched as Tweed, with three women, emerged and entered the car. Two women squeezed into the back with Tweed. The third woman – he recognized her as Paula Grey – sat next to Newman.

As Newman drove off the assassin drove after him.

In his rear-view mirror he saw a limousine pull up in front of the hotel the dead businessman had come out of. The Yellow Man smiled callously. He was leaving the area just in time.

25

As they left Geneva behind, heading for the French border, Tweed sat with Trudy on his right and Serena on his left. The original plan had been for Serena to travel in Nield's car, seated beside him. Serena had not liked the idea at all.

'I want to travel with you,' she had told Tweed firmly. 'I'm going to feel much safer that way.'

'Why shouldn't you be just as safe with Nield?' he'd asked.

'After what happened last night in that underground garage I will feel safer with you,' she had repeated.

'Then I'll sit in the front next to Newman,' Paula had decided.

She had been watching Serena, had seen the upward tilt of her nose and the determined expression on her face. She was puzzled as to why Serena was so insistent. During the previous evening Paula had again watched Serena when they were all assembled in Tweed's suite.

Paula had observed that Serena had shown no signs of fear – or distress – when Charpentier had described in gory detail the condition of the corpses found inside the garage. She had almost seemed to take it as all in the day's work.

Reaching her hand back over her seat she now called out to Tweed.

'Could I have that map you've been studying? Sitting where I am makes me in an ideal position to act as navigator.'

'You're quite right,' Tweed agreed, handing her the map. 'In any case, I have the route in my head now.' He looked to his left. 'Are you comfortable, Serena? We have just enough room, I think.'

'I'm very comfortable,' Serena assured him with a warm smile. 'I hope Nield didn't think I was avoiding him.'

'No, he wouldn't. In fact, I'll tell you now – he prefers to be on his own. If trouble comes he won't have to worry about you.'

'Are we expecting trouble, then?' she asked casually.

'Hard to say. Depends on whether Goslar knows where we are.'

'How could he know that?'

'I've no idea,' Tweed lied.

He was thinking of the weird phone call from Goslar when he had given a 'clue'. *Aniseed*. Which Paula had interpreted as Annecy.

He felt fairly sure they were heading into a trap – an ambush. But Marler had outlined a reaction to such an eventuality which he had approved with Newman. Which is why it was important that on a straight stretch of road he could see Marler's car leading the way. Followed by Nield's vehicle, then his own. So far it was their only possibility of contacting Goslar's men – of capturing one of them. If they were successful Harry Butler would persuade a captive to talk – and he could do that without resorting to the brutal methods of torture used so widely these days.

'We are going to Annecy, aren't we?' Serena asked. 'Paula told me she thought we might be going there but she wasn't sure that it might not be somewhere else.'

Good for Paula, Tweed thought. A very discreet

response. But Paula trusted no one except the members of the team.

'What is your working method when grappling with a man like Goslar?' Serena enquired.

'Well, when the Duke of Wellington was fighting the Peninsular War, in Portugal and Spain, he said that his method was like tying knots in a length of rope. He meant he reacted as the situation developed. My method is similar. Of course he was a long way from becoming Duke of Wellington at that time.'

'Sounds to me as though you haven't got a plan,' she suggested with a hint of humour.

Tweed was saved from answering as Newman glanced once again in his rear-view mirror. Then he called out to Tweed.

'I've been wondering whether we were being followed by a limo with a chauffeur behind the wheel. Seemed unlikely. He had a passenger in the back. And there was always one car between us and them. Now he's disappeared. Won't be long before we're at the border.'

The Yellow Man's quicksilver mind had moved at its normal speed when he had shot the businessman in the back of his car. He had been worried that after the devastating events at the garage there would be patrol cars swarming round the area the following morning.

A lone chauffeur driving a Mercedes might have been stopped for questioning. He would present a much more normal image with a passenger in the back. He had been right.

As he had followed Tweed's car through the city numerous patrol cars had appeared. None of them had given him more than a fleeting glance when they saw the 'sleeping' passenger in the back. But now he had a serious problem. He knew the French checkpoint was coming up at the frontier. He couldn't risk arriving with a corpse in the back.

Knowing the route he was taking, he kept glancing in his rear-view mirror, saw nothing behind him. Suddenly he swung off the road along a track strewn with small rocks. He drove slowly, passed a big sign with the word 'DANGER' in large red letters.

He was out of sight of the road when he stopped the car near the edge of an abandoned quarry. Moving swiftly, he jumped out of the car, leaving the engine running. Opening the rear door, he was strong enough to have no difficulty lifting out the dead businessman. He carried the body close to the brink of the quarry, hurled his burden over. It slithered halfway down the quarry face, came to rest on a ledge. He then collected the suitcase, carrying it with gloves on his hands, hurled it down. His last task was to throw the gun and silencer he had used into the quarry.

The loss of the weapon didn't worry him. He had two more handguns taped under the dashboard. Getting back behind the wheel, he managed to turn the car in a circle and return to the road. He was confident he would soon catch up with Tweed's car.

Paula worried about Marler as she saw his car stop in the distance at the border post. She knew he spoke fluent French – what she did not know was that before they left the hotel he had dashed out and bought himself a French suit and a pair of shoes.

As the French guard approached him he switched off his engine. He had his window lowered as the guard peered in, checked the empty rear.

'Where are you going to?' the guard demanded.

'To Annecy. I hope the weather is better there than it was back in Geneva,' he replied in his perfect French.

'On business or pleasure?'

'Officially on business.' Marler looked straight at the guard. 'Of course, if a little pleasure is offered by an attractive lady who am I to refuse it?'

The guard smirked. He waved him on and prepared for the next car, which had Nield inside it on his own.

From a distance Paula watched as first Marler, then Nield were waved through. She heaved a sigh of relief. Taped to the chassis under Marler's car was an armoury large enough to start a war. Tweed had lowered his window as they stopped. As he anticipated, the guard peered in at the rear.

'A short holiday,' Tweed explained in English. 'Switzerland is so stuffy. In your country it is so much more relaxing. If the weather is better then we shall have a most relaxing time.'

'The weather is much better,' the guard told him. 'None of that snow the Swiss seem to love so much, although they deny it. So,' he smirked at Trudy and Serena, 'enjoy your holiday.'

He waved them on with a flamboyant flourish of his hand. He was still smirking.

'Unpleasant type,' snapped Serena.

'He has a boring job,' Tweed said placidly, 'therefore he varies it with his idea of a joke.'

'I thought it was strange the way we passed through the Swiss checkpoint,' Paula commented, 'only a hundred yards back. The barrier was raised, no officials came out.'

'There's a difference. We were *leaving* Switzerland so why should they worry about us. Entering a country is a different matter.'

'Well, thank Heaven Marler got through all right.

And that saucy guard was right. The weather is much better, even though it must have been raining earlier.'

She was referring to two things: the sun was shining down on them out of a clear blue sky, and the road was damp from recent rain. They were out in the country now with rolling hills stretching away into the distance like a huge green sea. Here and there trees had a sprinkling of leaves on them. Spring was arriving.

They were driving along a rare straight stretch with hill slopes rising on either side when Tweed saw Marler's car stop. Nield drove closer to him, then he also stopped. Newman had glanced in his rear-view mirror again.

'Nothing coming. That chauffeur-driven limo must have turned off somewhere. I know why Marler has stopped. He's going to distribute his armoury. Think I'll go and give him a hand.'

'I'd like to stretch my legs,' said Paula. She turned round and gave Tweed a certain look. 'Care to accompany me?'

'Good idea. We'll climb this slope. I don't think it goes up very far.'

As they began the climb they heard Trudy and Serena start chattering to each other. The grass beneath their feet was short and firm. Arriving at the top of the ridge they had a panoramic view. Distant villages huddled inside deep valleys. It was a scene of perfect peace.

'You know,' Paula began as they admired the view, 'I've been thinking. In the past you've chivvied members of the team for never noticing the absence of something. Well, I've noticed something like that which I find odd.'

'Tell me.'

'You've said Goslar always shoots the messenger, as you put it. He eliminates anyone he's had a connection with, however remote. He had that reporter from

Appledore, Sam Sneed, murdered in an alley off Fleet Street. Seems ages ago now. Then poor Vallade, the rare-book seller on the Île St-Louis was also decapitated. Finally, Mme Markov's head ended up in a waste basket in the flat near the Opéra. A pretty hideous roll call of murder.'

'What's your point?'

'That there's been no attempt to kill Serena Cavendish. Yet she took photographs of Appledore for him. She saw the Ape deliver the balance of her fee through her letter box.'

'I had noticed that fact myself . . .'

'It's that helicopter again,' she interjected. She swung round. 'There it is. It's a distance away and flying at about five hundred feet.'

Tweed had turned round with her. The machine was flying parallel to the ridge on the far side of the road. Too far away see what markings were on its fuselage.

'I don't like it,' Paula went on. 'When we were leaving the Richemond I heard a chopper circling – as though it was above the square with the underground garage underneath.'

'I heard it too. That one was probably from a TV station, shooting the scene they'll feature on their next news programme. The one over there could be a different job. Quite a lot of businessmen use helicopters these days to get fast from A to B.'

'Then there was the helicopter we heard while we were driving down the autoroute from Paris to Geneva,' she persisted.

'Don't worry.' He looked down the slope. 'I think Newman wants us. Time to get back to the car.'

Newman met them halfway down the slope. Keeping his back to the car parked below, he handed Paula her Browning and spare ammo. She quickly hid them inside her shoulder bag.

'Funny we still haven't heard from Burgoyne,' Newman remarked as they came close to the road.

'He'll call us when he has something to report,' Tweed replied.

He was within thirty feet of the car when his mobile started buzzing. He looked at Newman as much as to say, I told you so.

'Hello?' he said, stopping.

'Monica here. Thank God I've reached you. I've had another of Goslar's weird screechy messages. Quite short. He said, I quote, "If you wish us to meet, Tweed, try the Château de l'Air." That was all. Do you know where it is?'

'No idea. It's possible you've told me just in time. All is well. Do not hesitate to contact me again. Take care.'

'*You* take care . . .'

Staying on the slope, Tweed beckoned to Marler and Nield to join him. When they were gathered round him he told them about Monica's message. He reminded Marler to tell Butler who had stayed with their car.

'I've handed back the armoury to everyone,' Marler said. 'Here is Trudy's automatic and spare ammo. She'll raise Cain if she doesn't get those back.'

'I think we should proceed,' Tweed ordered.

'You've seen that helicopter, I'm sure,' Marler remarked.

'Yes, we have. Paula pointed it out to me. It seems to be heading south now. Off we go. Warily.'

Marler passed Paula a canvas holdall. He opened it so she could see inside. He pointed out the three compartments it was divided into.

'Stun grenades in there, firebombs here and shrapnel grenades in this one.' He looked at Tweed. 'Warily is

267

the watchword. Since we left Geneva it's been rather too quiet for my liking.'

Inside the helicopter, flying south towards Annecy, Bancroft sat next to the pilot. The previous night he'd had no idea, as he climbed the ventilator shaft to escape the inferno in the underground garage, that someone was coming up behind him.

After prising off the louvred cone at the top he had emerged into the night. He had crouched low, keeping in shadows, as he left the square after spotting Tweed and Newman standing outside the railway station. Darting into a side street he had waited by the corner where he could see the two men.

Bancroft had caught a glimpse of a blurred figure climbing out of the shaft he'd used. Since Trudy was dressed in a trouser suit he couldn't make out whether it was a man or a woman. Then the vague figure, also keeping in the shadows, had disappeared.

He was still standing by his corner when he saw Tweed, Newman, Paula and another woman get into a car. He thought he had lost them as, boldly, he had hurried after the car. He had arrived just in time to see them disappear inside the Richemond.

Bancroft had then walked into a nearby hotel and reserved a room for the night. In a money belt wrapped round his waist under his coat he was carrying hundreds of dollars. The only similarity between Vance Karnow and Tweed was they both provided members of their teams with plenty of money. The hotel – typically Swiss – had provided him with a shaving kit, toothbrush and a pair of pyjamas.

He had risen early the following morning and a department store had opened its doors as he was passing. Inside he had purchased a leather coat, heavy motoring gloves and a fur hat, Russian style. Leaving the store, he had hailed a cab, asked the driver to take him to the airport. There he had found a company which hired out helicopters with pilots.

Bancroft had flashed in front of the pilot a card which had proved effective before. In large letters were printed the words *State Security*.

'I'm cooperating with the Swiss Federal Police,' he had told the pilot. 'We're on the track of terrorists who blew up the garage last night.'

What turned the trick was the sheaf of dollars Bancroft agreed to pay. The pilot followed his instructions, circling for some time high above the underground garage. Bancroft's eyes had almost popped out of his head when, using binoculars he had bought, he saw Trudy Warner leaving the Richemond with Tweed and Paula.

So now I have three targets, he decided. The traitor, Trudy, Paula Grey and Tweed.

Also in the forefront of his ambitious mind was the memory of seeing Karnow's dead body, hit by two bullets in the shooting, in the front of the car. Bancroft saw the opportunity to let Tweed lead him to Goslar – to seize the secret weapon for Washington.

He would be the new chief of Unit Four.

Now he was gazing through the binoculars at Tweed and Paula, perched on the top of a hill. He couldn't see anything that was down on the road.

As Newman drove his car behind the two spaced out in front, Tweed was recalling Monica's message. Where was the Château de l'Air? He sensed a trap, but sooner or later Goslar had to commit a major error. When he did that would be the moment to pounce – with ferocity. No holds barred.

Seated beside Newman, Paula was studying her map. She glanced up as the road suddenly started to wind, to go steeply downhill. Then she stared. At the bottom of the hill, where she knew the road curved round a sharp bend, a curtain of white mist was rising. Due, she guessed, to the brilliant sun shining on the damp road surface. It was more like a fog.

Tweed's mobile buzzed. He grabbed it, pressed it to his ear.

'Hello?'

'Marler here. Prepare to go into the planned manoeuvre. Nield has been warned.'

Marler was obviously bothered by, even suspicious of, the heavy mist. Tweed passed on the message to Newman.

His phone buzzed again as they came close to the fog.

'Hello?'

'Tweed?'

'Speaking.'

'Burgoyne here. Potential ambush point at bottom of road near Choisy. Ambush warning . . .'

'Ambush!' Tweed said urgently into his mobile, first contacting Marler, then Nield. Newman had heard him anyway.

It all happened so quickly it was like a fast-forwarded film. Marler swung off the road up a track, turned his car to face the way he had come. Nield reversed, backing towards them, then turned his vehicle sideways on, lowered his window. Newman backed, drove into the entrance to farmland, smashing a gate. He left the front part of the car exposed, lowered his window at the same moment as Paula lowered hers, grabbing the canvas holdall.

Paula sucked in her breath as she saw what was coming out of the mist curtain. Tweed put an arm round both Trudy and Serena, pushing them down as he shouted, 'Keep your damned heads down as far as you can!'

Through the mist curtain a small army of strange men was advancing. Their faces and bare arms were tanned a dark brown. Round their heads they wore green cloths. Each man carried a machine-pistol aimed at two cars – Nield's and Tweed's. They hadn't noticed Marler parked in his niche. Tweed's voice was grim.

'Arab Fundamentalists . . .'

One group came walking rapidly along the side of the bank to the right. They ignored Nield's apparently empty car. A rattle of bullets hit the road in front of Newman's car, became a hail of gunfire. Four men were suddenly very close. Paula hurled one of her firebombs. It burst at the feet of the attackers. A sheet of flame enveloped them. They screamed, running in all directions, their clothes on fire, flaming torches rolling on the ground, running up the bank before they collapsed.

A much larger body of men burst through the curtain. Marler's machine pistol opened up, catching them in the rear. They fell like ninepins. Paula threw a second firebomb, further this time. Its flames consumed mist, exposed a pick-up truck with its back towards them. In the open back a man stood holding a bazooka, aimed at Newman's car. Nield sat up, fired three times. The Arab with the bazooka staggered, jerked his weapon upwards, fired it by reflex. The shell soared high into the air, exploded harmlessly.

Marler was firing his machine pistol at random into what remained of the mist, traversing it as he pressed the trigger. There were shrieks, then silence. A few moments later an enormous Arab appeared, armed with a machine-pistol. He advanced towards Newman's car. Newman fired at him once. Hit him. The Arab continued to advance. Newman threw open his door, jumped out, emptied his Smith & Wesson at point-blank range. The Arab looked surprised, tottered briefly, then fell forward on the weapon he had never fired.

A heavy silence descended as Newman swiftly reloaded. The mist evaporated, particles of it glowing like diamonds in the sun.

Parked by the bend which could now be seen, were several trucks, the vehicles which had brought the killers to this point. Marler jumped out of his car, held his machine-pistol ready as he walked slowly forward, checking each truck. All empty. Weapons scattered on their floors. He walked back, called out, his voice cool as a cucumber, 'All clear!'

'That was something,' Paula said quietly. 'Burgoyne warned us just in time.'

'Except Marler smelt danger first,' Tweed reminded her.

'Are you all right?' he asked the women on either side of him.

'I'm OK,' said Serena, sitting up and adjusting a crease in her trousers.

'Nothing wrong with me,' replied Trudy, slipping the automatic she had been holding back under her coat.

Marler appeared at the open rear window. He looked quickly at everyone. They looked back at him as he gave a snappy salute.

'Time we got moving. Don't drive over anything in the road.'

'Does this often happen?' Serena enquired very quietly.

'Nield has just said this must be the first of them.'

'Hurrah for Pete!' Paula said ironically. 'I really do love an optimist.'

26

They were driving along another stretch of country road, the carnage of dead Arabs well behind them. There had been no difficulty passing along one side of the pick-up truck where the Arab with his bazooka had stood. Paula sensed that the atmosphere of tension inside the car was gone. The scenery beyond hedges on both sides of the road was beautiful and the sun was a warm glow.

'I wonder where Burgoyne is now?' Paula mused aloud.

Probably locating the site of the next ambush, Newman thought, but he kept the idea to himself. Time enough to worry about that when it happened.

'Probably somewhere ahead of us – could be any distance away,' said Tweed, answering Paula's question. 'We'll hear from him when he's ready.'

'We must keep a lookout for this Château de l'Air,' Newman reminded them.

'I have been looking for it ever since we received Monica's phone call,' Paula retorted.

'Pardon me for speaking.'

'Do you expect to find Dr Goslar at this Château de l'Air? Sounds in English like "lair".'

'Very apt,' Tweed commented. 'As for finding him there, maybe.'

They were travelling along an unusually straight stretch in their same formation – Marler leading in the distance with Nield behind him – when Newman peered in his rear-view mirror. A car was coming up behind them at great speed. As it came closer he thought it was the Mercedes they had seen earlier with a chauffeur behind the wheel.

'This one is ramming his foot down,' he remarked.

The car, moving like a rocket, overtook them, sped on. Newman caught only a blur of the driver, but enough to see it was not the chauffeur. Instead of a peaked cap he thought the driver wore a beret. At the same speed he overtook Nield and raced on to roar past Marler.

Earlier, the Yellow Man had started driving over a hilltop, then stopped when he saw what lay well below. With nothing in sight behind him he had backed swiftly. He had caught a glimpse of heavy mist rising at the bottom of the hill, of Tweed's scattered convoy, of figures advancing out of the mist. He had heard the first sounds of gunfire.

Parking his car on the grass verge, he had waited a long time. He had eventually walked cautiously to the top of the hill, peering down. Everything had gone. The mist. Tweed's cars. Only bodies strewn along the sides of the road remained. He had then driven on, hoping he had not lost Tweed.

At the bottom of the hill he had hardly given the bodies a glance. He had, however, been careful not to drive over one. Not from any compunction – such emotions were alien to the Yellow Man – but he did not want any remnants attached to his tyres which might catch the eye of the police.

Before starting up again, he had taken off the chauffeur's cap, had hurled it way into the undergrowth. He had then replaced it with the beret he had worn in the dark square in Paris when he had come so close to killing Paula. Having got rid of the cap he now wanted to get rid of the car.

It was a relief when he saw, ahead of him, Tweed's cars driving along a straight stretch. He pressed his foot down, hunched over the wheel. Marler's car had disappeared in his mirror when he reached the turn-off to

Choisy. At this point a magnificent old bridge, still intact, crossed a deep gorge. It was no longer part of the highway – a new stretch had been built over a new bridge. But the road swung in a sharp curve.

It was as he approached this point that he saw a car parked by the roadside. It was pointed in the direction of Geneva and beside it stood an erect man, hands on his hips. He had the impression the man was staring hard to see who was behind the wheel of his car. He increased speed. It was almost his downfall.

Pressing his foot down even further to avoid the man's gaze, he began to swing round the sharp curve. He felt his machine skidding. He kept his nerve, went with the skid, straightened up, continued along the road to distant Annecy.

He drove at speed for about fifteen minutes. There was no other traffic on the road when he pulled up, parked his car on the edge of what he knew was a steep slope. Getting out, he lifted the bonnet, pretending to fiddle as if the engine had broken down.

A large truck and several cars passed him. He was hoping for a car with only the driver inside. Then he saw a Peugeot coming towards him at thirty miles an hour. Behind the wheel was a white-haired man, smartly dressed. He stood up, waved both hands in a gesture of despair. The driver stopped, spoke through his window.

'Do you speak English?'

'I am English,' the Yellow Man said with a broad smile, thankful that he had left his beret under a newspaper in the car. 'And I am no mechanic.'

'Let me have a look,' the man said, getting out. 'I used to run an agency for selling Rovers before we retired to Annecy.'

The assassin stood back as the Englishman bent over to peer inside. Glancing up and down the empty road, he whipped out a knife from a curved sheath concealed under his coat. The blow was so strong and savage that it completed the job instantly. He lifted the severed head by the hair and hid it behind a clump of shrubs.

He was wearing leather gloves and had no trouble lifting the dead body into position behind the wheel of the Mercedes having had the foresight to leave the door open. His coat was covered with blood but this didn't worry him. He quickly searched his victim's pockets, took out a wallet from one pocket, some letters from another. He stuffed the letters inside the wallet. Checking the road in both directions again, he walked to the edge of the steep slope, hurled the wallet, watched it sail through the air and land in a tangle of wild shrubbery.

He next checked to make sure, as he'd observed, that the elderly driver had left his keys in the Peugeot's ignition. Returning to the Mercedes, he adjusted the gears so it would roll freely. He then slammed the door shut and pushed. The car began to roll backwards. He took off his blood-soaked gloves, used the one which was least affected to clean his knife. He returned it to his sheath.

The car was still rolling slowly backwards as he took off his leather coat – which was too warm for this climate anyway. Stuffing it inside a large carrier bag, he added the gloves, keeping his hands away from streaks of blood. He then picked up several small rocks and dropped them inside to give weight. He looked up, stared.

The Mercedes had reached the edge of the slope and stopped there, a rear wheel wedged against a small rock. He looked up and down the road once more. He put the fingers of his left hand in his mouth and frowned. It was one of the few times in his life when he had felt nervous.

Pulling his fingers out of his mouth he rushed forward. He used his right foot to kick at the offending rock which was spoiling the whole scenario. The rock dislodged. The Mercedes started rolling backwards at speed down the shale slope. It charged inside a forest and was lost from view amid dense shrubbery.

'Do better next time,' he said aloud as he climbed behind the wheel of the Peugeot.

He had remembered to throw the head into the forest.

27

They had driven further towards Annecy when Paula saw Marler's and Nield's cars parked close together. They had got out of their vehicles and were talking to a man who stood very erect, hands on his hips. He wore tropical kit – beige trousers, a jacket and shirt of the same colour. His shirt was open at the neck.

'It's Burgoyne!' She almost shouted, she was so pleased to see him again.

Butler, who had travelled with Marler, sat on the verge. By his side, half-hidden in grass, was a machine-pistol. Butler never let down his guard.

'You survived the ambush, I gather,' he said, grinning at Paula.

'You warned us just in time.'

'I was beginning to give up hope,' he said to Tweed. 'I'd tried to call you several times. No response.'

'Mobile phones,' Tweed replied with an expression of disgust. 'I never trust them. As you see, we brought two attractive ladies along for the ride.' He introduced Trudy and Serena to Burgoyne, who shook hands and eyed both of them appreciatively. 'Welcome to the party,' Tweed concluded.

'"Along for the ride,"' snorted Serena. '"Welcome to the party." Some ride, some party. A delightful delegation of Arabs came to meet us.'

'Arabs?' queried Burgoyne.

Tweed explained tersely details of their encounter in the misty hollow. He left out some gory details since he didn't think either Trudy or Serena would appreciate too vivid a description.

'I drove all the way to Annecy and back,' Burgoyne told them. 'I didn't see this gang of cut-throats. My guess is they must have assembled at Choisy, only a few miles up that side road.' He pointed to a road leading off the main highway. 'They must have emerged soon after I'd driven past it. I can guess where they came from.'

'And where would that be?' asked Paula.

'A number of Arab Fundamentalists are regularly smuggled across the Med from Algeria into France. They come in by night aboard small fishing boats, are landed at remote coves near Marseilles. They have transport waiting to get them away from the coast. Goslar has worldwide connections, I've heard. He'd pay them well and they are used to killing. Heaven knows they've done enough of that back in Algeria.'

'I find that interesting,' said Tweed.

'I find *that* interesting,' Trudy remarked.

She was gazing behind Burgoyne at the ancient bridge which spanned a gorge. Paula also was gazing at it. A stone-paved approach led to a curved arch. On either side of the arch enormous old stone pillars, at least three feet in diameter, reared up a great height.

Cables, anchored to the ground near them, sloped up and disappeared inside huge cavities near the tops of the towers. The tops were castellated and gave the impression that they guarded the approach to a great castle. They looked as though they had stood there since the beginning of time.

'That is the Pont de la Caille,' Burgoyne explained. 'It's a suspension bridge which once carried the highway across the valley – hence the huge cables.'

Trudy walked rapidly along the paved area and when she stepped on to the bridge she felt a faint tremor. She walked on, staring down into the incredibly deep gorge with a small river running along it – in a cutting which seemed miles below her as she paused and gazed over.

'What interests me is *that*,' Tweed said emphatically.

'What is that?' Paula enquired.

'That old noticeboard across the road by the entrance to a track with old rusty gates wide open beyond.'

'*Château de l'Air*,' she said half to herself. 'Is it possible Goslar is still inside? Look up there, where the hill rises beyond the trees.'

They were standing less than a hundred yards from where the track on the far side of the road began winding its way upwards, through the open rusty gates, then disappearing round a bend. Tweed walked forward, stood in the middle of the road. He appeared to be looking at the mildewed board, perched on a post, where the name of the château could just be made out. Actually he was staring at an estate agent's board which had toppled, face up, into the grass.

À Vendre. For sale. Below the words were the estate agent's name. C. Periot, Annecy. Then a telephone number. The sun almost burned the back of his neck. Paula joined him, began to walk further to explore the track.

Her arm was grabbed, she was hauled back and when she looked round she saw it was Burgoyne who had taken hold of her.

'Go back and join the others by the bridge. Don't argue. Tweed, go with her. *Now!*'

'Got a bee in his bonnet,' Paula grumbled.

'Better do as he suggested,' said Tweed.

They joined Marler, Newman and Nield, who stood chatting to Serena. Trudy was a long way off, halfway across the bridge. She was leaning over the railing, gazing down into eternity. On the grass verge Butler still sat hunched up, seemed to be asleep, but his eyes were everywhere. A car was driving slowly towards them from the direction of Annecy. It stopped near the far end of the suspension bridge.

'It's like a fairytale,' Paula remarked, calm again. She was gazing at the beautiful old bridge, which was now redundant. 'Pity they couldn't have left it as part of the highway. I love it.'

'What is Burgoyne doing?' Newman asked.

Paula swung round to look in the direction in which they were all staring. Burgoyne had walked to the edge of the track leading up to the château. He moved slowly, with deliberation, walking a few yards up the side of the track, treading down grass. Bending down, he picked up a small limestone rock, then came back along the path he had just walked over. He turned his head, shouted.

'Everyone stay where you are! Don't come an inch closer!'

They stood very still, watched as Burgoyne crossed the road, then crouched down, still holding the rock in his right hand. He swung his arm backwards and forwards, then lobbed the rock in an arc. As he did so he dropped flat. The rock landed on the track. An explosive *thump!* echoed. Huge quantities of soil and grass soared into the air above the point where the rock had landed. A lot of it showered down into the road, a mix of splintered rock and earth.

Burgoyne stood up, strolled to where the others gazed at him, then he smiled.

'Anti-personnel landmine. I saw the sun glint off it. The rain must have uncovered a section of it. Not the place for a morning's walk, wouldn't you agree?'

'And I was going to go up that track,' Paula said after swallowing hard. 'All I can say, Chance, is thank you for saving my life.'

'I've seen them like that in the desert,' Burgoyne explained casually. 'The wind blows sand off them and that same sun reflects off them . . .'

He stopped talking suddenly. Butler had rushed past them like a greyhound, racing across the bridge. Paula turned and gasped with horror. A small thickset man, who must have emerged from the car from Annecy, had grasped Trudy round the waist, was lifting her so her waist was now level with the railing between her and the immense drop behind her. She looked down at his brown face, his open mouth, exposing teeth, savage determination. Her right hand pulled out her automatic, pressed the trigger. The bullet entered the assassin's thigh. He grimaced, but was still hoisting her higher. Butler's hands closed round his neck, hauled him backwards. Trudy slid back, her feet on the floor of the bridge. Butler rammed the assassin's head down hard on the rail. Then he elevated the Arab in a business suit. He toppled him over the brink as Paula rushed forward, Browning in her hand. She stopped, watched as the Arab cartwheeled down and down, arms and feet flailing. It seemed to take a long time before he hit the bottom and Paula couldn't hear any sound as the body, tiny, lay still under a huge limestone crag on the Annecy side.

'He never even screamed,' Trudy said. 'I don't understand it.'

'Being an Arab, a Muslim,' explained Burgoyne who now stood beside Trudy, 'he had no doubt that he was on his way to the Arab version of heaven. Which is why he didn't utter a sound.'

'How far is it down there to the bottom?' asked Paula, who now stood on the bridge, with the others.

'It's two hundred metres deep. Or two hundred yards. Or six hundred feet.'

'You do hammer it home,' commented Serena. 'I can't see him.'

'He's down there somewhere,' Tweed said quickly. He could see the minute shape, but felt it better not to point it out. 'Now, I feel like a little walk before we move on to Annecy. Bob, Paula – like to accompany me?'

As they walked back along the bridge it swayed very slightly, an unsettling feeling. Looking back, Tweed saw that Burgoyne had taken Trudy's arm. So she would have someone to talk to after her horrendous ordeal.

'There's that château,' Paula said as they left the bridge. 'Do you think we should check it out?'

'No.' Tweed lifted the binoculars he had borrowed earlier from Marler. 'All the shutters are closed. I'm sure the place is empty. But if we forced a door or a window it could blow up in our faces. Remember what was waiting for us at the front door of Goslar's building at La Défense. How do you summarize the situation now?' he asked as they strolled along the road.

'Looking for Dr Goslar.'

'More to it than that. We have to check out Annecy to make sure Goslar wasn't practising a double bluff. But the main thing is I know he hasn't yet manufactured enough of that hideous poison – enough to wipe out fifty million, a hundred million, two hundred million people. Who knows how much?'

'How do you know he hasn't done that yet?' she asked.

'Because if he had, he'd never have bothered to organize such a ferocious attack on me when the Arabs came through the mist. I still bother him because I'm alive.'

'Then we have time,' Newman said.

'No, we haven't. He might complete his work at any moment. It is even more a race against time. Let's start out for Annecy now.'

At Tweed's suggestion they altered the sequence of cars. Newman's car remained at the rear of the convoy. Paula again sat next to Newman while Trudy and Tweed sat in the back.

Nield drove ahead of Newman. Alone for so long, he now had Serena for company by his side.

Marler again drove in front of Nield. And again he had Butler in the seat next to him.

Burgoyne took the lead at the head of everyone else, He drove his own hired car. Resting on the seat by his side was the machine-pistol Marler had handed him.

'I can't think of that bridge as fairyland any more,' Paula called back. 'I don't imagine you do either, Trudy.'

'Well, at least I put a bullet into the bastard,' Trudy responded grimly. 'It was him or me. I'm glad it was him.'

'All this started back in England on Dartmoor,' Tweed recalled.

'I know. I knew before I left the States,' Trudy said. 'I read about it in a Washington newspaper. It became a lead story when someone leaked the reaction of the White House. Sorry, I think I interrupted you.'

'That's all right. I was going on to say that when we reach Annecy I first want to contact an estate agent called Periot. He's the one who has the sale of that château in his hands. I want to see if Goslar is using the same technique he's used several times before, taking a long lease and then evacuating a property early.'

'Shouldn't be difficult to find,' Newman commented. 'All we need is a phone book in a telephone box.'

'There are two more factors we must not forget,' Tweed continued. 'Somewhere the Yellow Man is still on the loose . . .'

He explained to Trudy who the Yellow Man was. He turned to face her and went into detail about how the assassin operated. She listened with a serious expression but showed no sign of fear or revulsion at what he told her. She really is tough, he thought.

'And the other factor?' Paula prodded.

'The missing Mr Bancroft. I studied him in the bar at the Ritz. He's not only vicious and ruthless – he's also shrewd and has, I believe, plenty of stamina.'

'He was the worst of the lot,' said Trudy. 'I haven't forgotten seeing him shove a gun inside Walt, my husband's, mouth and then pull the trigger. I've got an automatic full of bullets for him,' she went on savagely. 'I'll only be able to forget that terrible scene in my house – when I felt so helpless – when he's dead.'

'I think you'll like Annecy – at least the old town,' Paula said to switch her mind to something else. 'I only spent a short time there but it's unique. Strange ancient buildings with waterways everywhere. I think they eventually empty into the lake.'

'It does sound interesting,' Trudy agreed. 'Is it like a rabbit warren?'

'Yes, except I doubt if rabbits could find their way round the place.'

Trudy chuckled, smiled at Tweed. He was smiling

back when his mobile buzzed. He assumed it had to be Monica – or Beck.

'Hello?'

'Wait just a moment, sir,' a cultured English voice said, 'someone wishes to speak to you.' Tweed gripped the phone tightly. 'Here we go,' the English voice, said. 'Please listen carefully. The words will only be spoken once . . .'

The screechy voice began. Tweed pressed the phone close to his ear, trying to decide whether it was the voice of a man or a woman.

'*Mr Tweed, welcome to Annecy. May I suggest you cross the Pont Perrière into the old town. On a railing to your right at the start of the bridge you will see a sign for a three-star hotel. Hôtel du Palais de l'Isle. Across the bridge you will see a restaurant – Les Corbières. Go in there and you will find a message waiting for you. Do take greater care. H. Goslar.*'

Tweed waited but the connection was broken. He repeated word for word to the others what he had heard. There was silence for a short time, broken by Newman.

'Where the hell is Dr Goslar?' he rasped in exasperation.

'That helicopter has reappeared,' Paula said.

28

When Tweed had described Bancroft as shrewd he was not far off the mark. Seated beside the pilot in the helicopter, Bancroft was thinking hard. He was an unusual combination of talents. Before Karnow had recruited him as a member of Unit Four he had been a semi-successful lawyer.

He had acted as defence counsel in a number of trials. He had often managed to bring in a verdict of 'not guilty' for his clients, whether they were innocent or guilty. He had studied the history of law deeply, concentrating on legal precedents. So it was not infrequent for him to challenge successfully a direction by a judge, quoting an old legal precedent the judge had never realized existed.

This had gradually made him the *bête noire* of judges in general. So they had hit back by giving him a hard time at every possible opportunity. Often a judge had overruled a Bancroft objection when it was a borderline instance. Bancroft's track record of obtaining 'not guilty' verdicts began to wither.

So when Karnow offered him the job of joining Unit Four, Bancroft, disgusted with the law, accepted. The size of the salary offered was also a factor.

Seated in the helicoper, he was now using his acute brain to assess what was happening, how he should proceed next. Also, brought up in the back streets Brooklyn, not the most salubrious district in New York, he had maimed three thugs who had attacked him on different occasions. Training with Unit Four had honed his natural flair as a fighter – as a thug.

Tweed and his team are now on their way to Annecy, he said to himself. *So Dr Goslar has not yet been found – otherwise they wouldn't be driving along the highway to Annecy, a nowhere place he had never heard of before. First, I have to arrive ahead of them. Second, I'll need transport to tail them . . .*

He stopped talking to himself inside his head and checked the map open on his lap. He had bought it from a shop in Geneva after stocking himself with fresh clothes. What had given him the idea of hiring a helicopter was his recollection of the chopper which had appeared to follow them along the autoroute from Paris.

286

'How long before we reach Annecy?' he asked the pilot.

'Five minutes. Maybe less. I can slow down a bit.'

'Wait a minute.' Bancroft raised his binoculars to his eyes, scanned the four cars proceeding along the highway, looking like toys from his altitude. 'Is there somewhere close to Annecy where you could land me?'

'The old town or the more modern area?'

'The old town,' Bancroft replied, relying on instinct.

'Then that will be easy. There's a large park at the edge of the lake. It's very close to the old town. I could land there.'

'Also I'll need to hire a car ... to follow those terrorists,' he added quickly to keep up the fiction.

'There's a car-hire place only a short walk from where I'll land you. I'll point it out to you. Will you need me later to fly you back to Geneva?' the pilot enquired.

'Quite possibly,' Bancroft replied, having no idea whether he would require the pilot's services again. 'That will mean you waiting around, so here is a bonus.'

He had already paid the pilot a large sum but he hauled a sheaf of hundred-dollar bills out of the money clip in his pocket. He was careful to keep his money belt concealed. He handed the pilot a folded sheaf of five bills. Another five hundred dollars. He had always found that money bought loyalty and reliability.

'I'll wait for you,' the pilot said. 'Our chopper still has plenty of fuel. Do I slow down?'

'No. Keep going.'

Inside the car Paula focused the bincoculars she had just borrowed from Newman. She pressed an elbow on the edge of the open window to give herself more stability. She was trying to identify who was aboard the

287

helicopter. Like Bancroft, who had focused on the four cars, she found the distance was too great. All she could make out was a blur. She gave the binoculars back to Newman, carefully looping them round his neck.

'Any luck?' he asked.

'Can't see who is inside it. It worries me – the way it keeps flying on a parallel course to us.'

'Forget it.' Tweed called out, 'When we get to Annecy I need a local map to locate this estate agent, Periot.'

'Burgoyne may already have one,' Newman suggested. 'I think we are getting very close to Annecy. I could overtake Burgoyne and ask him if he has got a map.'

'Let's do that,' Tweed agreed.

'That helicopter is flying well ahead of us now,' Paula observed. 'I suppose it's not landing somewhere close to Annecy. It's losing height now.'

Bancroft left the helicopter which had landed in a large parklike area at the northern edge of the Old Town. He walked rapidly over the grass, glancing back at the machine. The pilot had his back to him and was starting to consume his packed lunch. Bancroft was heading for the car-hire establishment the pilot had pointed out.

He felt the sun on the back of his thick neck and realized he felt hungry. Scattered across the park were various structures for children to play on. A roundabout. A short ladder leading up to a slide. Children were yelling with delight as one of their friends swooped down the slide, landing on a huge rubber cushion at the bottom. Bancroft pulled a face.

Children screaming and rushing about reminded him of his early days in Brooklyn. But there the children had been different, growing up quickly, wielding knives at an early age. These were far more civilized young-sters, but their screams recalled to him the number of times he'd made sure his back was to a wall as two or three of them came at him. How he'd held them back with a long club, then had beaten them to a pulp. It had been the survival of the quickest.

There had been times when he had wondered whether it would be best to settle in Europe. An idea he had always quickly rejected. The really big money was in the States. Away from anyone, he paused to check which of two passports to use. The one he chose did not show his name as Bancroft. He had it in his hand as he crossed the road, entered the car-hire establishment.

He had a warm smile on his face as he approached the attractive brunette behind the counter. He handed her the passport. When she saw it she looked at him with interest.

'We don't get many Americans in this part of the world. Maybe a few during the season, but only a few. What can I do for you, sir?'

'I need to hire a car for a few days,' Bancroft began. 'I've just flown in here.'

'I saw your chopper land. Have you come far?'

'From Paris.'

His mind moved fast. He decided it would be unwise for him to be associated with Geneva. Not after what had happened in that underground garage.

'That's quite a flight.' She opened the passport, made notes on a form, talking as she did so. 'Mr Conroy. I see your first name is August – the same as the month you were born in.'

'Which is why I was christened that,' he lied. 'I'd like a Peugeot, if that is possible. I'd prefer a grey colour.'

'There are two Peugeots available. One is grey, one is red.'

'Definitely the grey job, please.'

Bancroft thought grey was a less noticeable colour. He paid the deposit in dollar bills. It was impossible to trace someone if they used cash. He'd made up his mind not to use a credit card while in Europe. When the formalities had been completed she led him through a back door into a small garage, showed him the car. He said it would do nicely, took the keys from her, then paused.

'You do speak good English.'

'I spent two years with a big car-hire firm in London. Thank you for the compliment.'

'I made a mistake in Paris,' he said, lingering. 'In a bar I met another American I didn't like at all. Wanted to borrow money off me. I let slip I was coming to Annecy. He said he might be coming down here. I guess he'd need to hire a car. If someone asks if there's an American in Annecy maybe you'd say you haven't met one.'

'Tried to borrow money! That's shocking.' She smiled warmly. 'I will keep quiet. You can rely on me.'

Bancroft didn't think he would be followed. But, as in the States, he always covered his tracks. She waited while he got behind the wheel when he appeared to remember something.

'I do hope to meet a friend who is driving down here today from Geneva. Is there some place I could intercept him?' He looked at his watch. 'He should be arriving soon.'

She produced a local map from a leather pouch hanging from her waist. Using the bonnet as a table, she drew a route, starting from where they were. Then she bent down, showed him the map and explained.

'Your best bet is to follow this route. It's not far. It will take you to where the highway from Geneva reaches the outskirts of Annecy. Your friend has to pass this point.'

'That's very good of you. You should have a sign in that window at the front. Service with a smile.'

'Thank you, sir.'

He thought she blushed just before he drove off. He looked at the park and saw the lake beyond, glittering in the sun. In the distance he could see mountains covered with snow. Above them hovered menacing dark clouds. The weather further south was looking very different from the atmosphere at Annecy.

The route he had to follow was easy. He had just left behind the outskirts of Annecy when he saw the highway leading to Geneva – a signpost confirmed the fact. He also saw a wide farm track leading off to the left. He didn't hesitate – he left the highway, drove onto the track, reversed the Peugeot, stopped, got out.

He lifted the bonnet of the car, stooped over it as though there was something wrong he had to attend to. Then he waited. He was well versed in waiting. He reckoned Tweed's convoy had to pass this point.

Earlier, the Yellow Man, reaching Annecy, had driven past the sign *Vieille Ville* – Old Town – and had continued on until, very shortly, he saw a public phone box. He was relieved. He must make a phone call quickly. There were specific hours. Parking his car, he opened his notebook and called the number, as instructed. He had no idea where he was phoning to but recognized the code as Switzerland.

'Good afternoon. Who is calling?' the cultured English voice enquired.

'Hobart. Oscar Hobart.'

'And where are you calling from, Mr Hobart?'

'Hell!' the Yellow Man exploded. 'What the devil does it matter where I'm calling from?'

'It does matter, Mr Hobart,' the voice explained

politely. 'I can only play the recording if you are in a certain place.'

'Bullshit! All right? I'm in Annecy. That's in France, in case you didn't know.'

'I do know, Mr Hobart. Please hold on a moment. I have a message for you . . .'

The Yellow Man sighed audibly. He waited for the screeching voice to start speaking. He didn't have to wait long. He held the phone hard against his ear, not wishing to miss a word.

'*You are in Annecy. Proceed at once to the Old Town. You go to the Pont Perrière, a bridge leading into the Old Town. Across the bridge is a restaurant – Les Corbières. I will spell that out for you . . . Tweed will be visiting this restaurant. Get there first. Ask for the proprietor. Tell him you are Francis. He will give you a long sealed box with the label "machine tools". It contains a sniperscope rifle with ammunition. Kill Paula Grey. H. Goslar.*'

29

Newman waved Burgoyne down after overtaking him. He parked his car on the verge. He got out with Tweed and Paula as Burgoyne slowed down, stopped. Nearby, a man wearing a panama hat stooped over the engine of his grey Peugeot. He had driven the car off the highway a short distance up a track. He wore large wraparound dark glasses and was peering into the interior with the bonnet up.

'French cars are always breaking down,' Newman commented. 'It is nothing to do with their quality – it's the fault of the way the French drive.'

'I need a local map of Annecy,' Tweed told him.

'Have you got one? I need to find that estate agent, Periot.'

'Easy,' Burgoyne said with a grin. 'I remembered afterwards seeing the name when I reached Annecy earlier. He's near the Old Town. Just follow me. I'll wait till you're back in your car . . .'

Because of the heat they walked back slowly. Tweed had his head bowed, an expression of concentration on his face. Paula nudged him.

'You're brooding on something.'

'Yes, I am. I have the feeling we're moving in the wrong direction. At the moment we can only follow the trail – the obstacle course – I'm sure Goslar has laid out for us. Sooner or later I hope to get a phone call which will pinpoint where we should be.'

'You're being mysterious again,' Paula chided him.

When they reached their car Trudy was swigging water out of a bottle she'd obtained from the kitchen at the Richemond before they left Geneva. She looked up as Paula stopped by her open window, wiped the top carefully with a clean handkerchief.

'Not very ladylike,' Trudy said with a smile. She offered the bottle to Paula. 'But in this heat you can get dehydrated.'

'Nice to have a good Samaritan as a companion.' Paula upended the bottle, took several swallows. 'That's much better.'

'Maybe Tweed and Newman could do with a drink,' Trudy suggested. 'I have two more bottles in my canvas bag here. I'm only charging one hundred francs a drink,' she went on as Tweed handed the bottle to Newman after helping himself.

'Cheap at the price,' Newman replied. 'Give you an IOU.'

When they were settled back in the car, Burgoyne

drove slowly past. Newman put his hand out of his window, waved for Marler and Nield to precede him. Marler saluted as he overtook them. Butler was peering out of his window as Nield started to follow Marler.

'Don't too much like the look of Panama Hat,' he growled as they passed the stranded Peugeot parked on the track.

'You see killers everywhere,' Nield joked.

'Well, I got his registration number,' Butler said obstinately.

They began to pass houses set back from the road. Then they were inside the town. Burgoyne slowed even more as he passed a sign pointing to *Vieille Ville*. He parked, not caring whether it was legal or not. Newman waited with Trudy while Tweed and Paula got out, crossed the road.

Periot et Cie had a modern plate-glass window. It was covered with coloured pictures of a variety of properties. Tweed scanned the photos, saw nothing which looked like the old pile he had seen, perched on a ridge, from the ancient bridge, where Trudy had been almost hurled into the valley. They went inside.

'I am looking for M. Periot,' Tweed said in French as a tall good-looking man in his thirties came forward to greet them.

'You have found him, sir. It is I.'

'I might be interested in an old mansion near Choisy. You can see it from the Pont de la Caille. Perched on the top of a ridge. It had a "For Sale" board at the entrance.'

'I see.' Periot frowned, then smiled quickly. 'There is a problem, sir. At the moment it is rented for a year. But the tenant has left suddenly. I cannot get in touch with him. Frankly, I am not sure what the position is. Will the Englishman, Mr Masterson, be coming back? I went to inspect it recently. The property had been leased unfurnished. There was nothing in the place when I arrived. Even the window ledges had been carefully washed. None of his personal possessions are in the mansion. He appears to have left for good – with seven months' rental time still left. He paid everything in advance.'

'Mr Charterhouse, Gargoyle Towers, now Mr Masterson, Château de l'Air,' Tweed mumbled to himself, but Paula caught the words.

'Pardon, sir?' Periot enquired.

'Sorry, I dropped my voice. May I ask when this Mr Masterson first leased the place?'

'Five months ago. None of us ever saw him. And – I shouldn't say this – but the whole year's lease was paid in five-hundred franc notes. Delivered in an executive case, which I had to sign for.'

'Yet you have a "For Sale" board up.'

'True.' Periot looked embarrassed. 'A form of insurance. Just in case we never hear from him again.'

'I understand.' Tweed smiled. 'But under the circumstances I had better get in touch with you later. In the meantime you may have solved a puzzle.'

'I am most sorry, sir . . .'

Tweed waited until they were outside. Periot had accompanied them and closed the door, repeating his apologies.

'It was Goslar,' Tweed said grimly. 'Same technique as at Gargoyle Towers, the building in La Défense, the flat where Mme Markov was murdered. He can afford to throw money about like confetti. He rents a place for longer than he needs it, so he can leave in the night, so to speak, with no one the wiser. I'm guessing, but I suspect he perfected his fiendish weapon at the Château de l'Air, then moved all the way to Gargoyle Towers on Dartmoor. That was his base from where he could "go public". Demonstrate openly the power of what he had invented. We'd better go to the Old Town now, cautiously.'

'Cautiously? What is worrying you now?' asked Paula.

'I'm convinced that strange phone call from Goslar, inviting me to collect another message from that restaurant, can only be a trap.'

Panama Hat (as Butler had nicknamed him), who was Bancroft, decided he had been clever, and had then made a bad mistake. He had bought the hat from a stall near the estate agent, Periot. Other people had been buying similar hats to ward off the heat, so Bancroft felt he merged with the locals.

The mistake had been to park where he had. Expecting Tweed's convoy to drive on, he had anticipated the four cars would be easy to follow. Now they were all parked a few hundred yards up the road from where he pretended to tinker with his engine. Worse still, Newman's car was backing up the entrance to a house, prior to coming back. Earlier he had seen Paula point to the notice leading to the Old Town. He must move quickly.

Slamming down the bonnet, he climbed behind the wheel, started his engine, drove back down the highway and turned off towards the Old Town. When he got there he saw it was forbidden to drive over the Pont Perrière. Pausing, he looked round, saw an area nearby next to an ancient stone wall where two cars were parked. They were also in the shade. He drove his car the short distance and parked near the other two vehicles.

Getting out, he hurried across the bridge over the river to enter a small restaurant, Les Corbières. A moment before he reached the entrance a tall, stocky man wearing a beret emerged. He was carrying a long cardboard box with the words 'machine tools' written on the outside. Bancroft walked in, sat down, ordered a drink and a glass of water. This seemed a likely vantage point if Tweed and his team were heading for the Old Town.

A short time earlier, the Yellow Man, beret rammed well down, had entered Les Corbières and asked to see the manager. A very young Frenchman with a napkin over his arm had appeared.

'You want a table, sir? Just for one?'

'My name is Francis. *Francis.* A messenger has left a box for me to collect from you.'

The Yellow Man held a hundred-franc note between his fingers. The manager glanced at the note, became voluble.

'How pleasant to meet an Englishman. I spent time in Bournemouth, training there. A delightful town. The residents were very high class. Of course tourists were a different breed, at least some of them. I had one couple coming in to the restaurant at lunchtime asking if they could just have a cup of tea. Can you believe it? The restaurant was full of people taking lunch, most of them à la carte. I just looked at them—'

'The box you have for me,' the assassin interjected, forcing himself to sound polite.

'Of course, sir. I kept it behind the counter out of sight. It says on the outside "machine tools". It is really rather heavy to contain flowers . . .'

'Thank you,' said the Yellow Man, grasping the box when it had been brought. 'Here is something for your trouble.'

He walked out just before a man wearing a panama hat came in to the restaurant. He immediately turned left along the rue Perrière. He hoped it was not going to be difficult – searching for a firing point overlooking the bridge. He soon realized there was no such convenient site and walked on, continuing his search.

Burgoyne drove into the Old Town, followed by the other three cars. On his earlier visit he had found it was forbidden to drive over the bridge. He parked alongside three other cars in the shadow of a stone wall.

As Newman parked in the same area and got out, followed by Tweed, Paula and Trudy, they saw Burgoyne standing at the entrance to the bridge, hands on his hips. He was gazing round quickly. As Tweed paused with Paula, Butler came up, lowered his voice.

'We may be walking into trouble. Panama Hat's car is parked near to ours.'

'Panama Hat?' Tweed queried.

'Just before we reached that estate agent, Periot, there was a car parked off the road. A man in a panama hat had the bonnet up, was fiddling with the engine. I told Nield I didn't like the look of him. Now his car is parked where ours are by that wall. I took the registration number earlier.'

'Could be a local,' Tweed said, only half-listening.

'So why did he suddenly get the engine working, then drive down here ahead of us?'

'Which one could it have been?' mused Paula.

'Which one?' queried Butler.

'Yes. The Yellow Man or Bancroft? Both of them are still at large.' She shrugged. 'One could have been in the helicopter, the other one may have been in that car which flashed by us at breakneck speed on the highway.'

Tweed's eyes had been staring everywhere across the river. Nowhere could he see anything that looked in

298

the least suspicious. Burgoyne had already walked across the bridge at a fast clip. As Tweed began to follow him Newman appeared on one side, Nield on the other.

'That bridge is pretty exposed,' Nield warned.

'It may be,' Tweed retorted, 'but I'm not running across it.'

Newman and Nield still guarded him on both sides as Tweed strolled across the bridge. Paula was behind them. She was gazing round in wonderment at the bizarre beauty of Annecy. To the right of the bridge a weird triangular-shaped building reared up where the river divided into two sections, flowing on either side of it. The building had a castlelike appearance and looked as though it had stood there since the beginning of time – as did other three and four-storeyed edifices.

'This is like something you see in medieval paintings,' she commented.

Tweed was more concerned about entering Les Corbières. The restaurant had a polished wooden bar and a few tables. Some were occupied but several were empty. He asked for the proprietor.

A young Frenchman appeared, napkin over his arm. He glanced at the members of Tweed's team crowding in behind him. Raising his eyebrows he asked what they required.

Bancroft, sitting by himself at a table at the back, froze as he saw Tweed at the far side of the bridge, then saw him advancing towards the restaurant. He removed his hat, tucked it under his chair. Some of them must have seen the panama earlier as he had pretended to fix the engine of his car.

He was thankful that he had made another purchase at the stall where he had bought the hat. He now wore a large pair of dark wraparound glasses which concealed the upper half of his face. Before entering the restaurant he had seen his image, reflected in the polished glass of the window. He had also quickly adjusted the cravat under his bull-like jaw. He had hardly recognized the image which had stared back at him. Now he picked up a copy of a French newspaper someone had left behind on a chair. Opening it, he placed it beside his plate. If they were going to eat here he had the problem of leaving unseen.

'My name is Tweed,' he said to the manager. 'I believe someone left you an envelope to give me.'

'Heavens,' the manager burst out. 'We're not the Post Office.'

'I'm sorry,' Tweed replied. 'Why do you say that?'

'Not ten minutes ago someone else called for a box which has been left here for me to deliver to him.'

'A box?' Newman realized Tweed's omission. He held a fifty-franc note, which he played with between his fingers. 'Can you describe that person? Was it a man?'

'Supposing someone came in here after you have gone and asked me to describe you. Would you like it if I did describe you?' He handed Tweed an envelope. 'For you, sir.'

'I don't suppose I would,' replied Newman.

His hand holding the banknote was extended. The manager acted like a conjurer. His hand moved in a blur and the banknote vanished. Practice makes perfect, Newman thought.

'How long would you say this box was?' Marler spoke up. 'And your display handkerchief isn't quite right.' He slightly adjusted the handkerchief in the top pocket of the manager's jacket, tucking a fifty-franc note down behind it.

'About so long,' the Manager said promptly.

He held his hands wide apart. Then extended them a little further.

'Marksman's rifle?' Marler whispered in Tweed's ear. 'Could even be an Armalite, like mine.'

'Welcome to my restaurant,' the manager said smiling broadly. 'I am only a temporary manager for a month. I go when the real manager returns from holiday. May I offer you some lunch?'

'Yes, we'd like that,' said Tweed.

He sat down at a table for four and was joined by Burgoyne, Paula and Trudy. Newman hosted a larger table for Serena, Nield, Butler and Marler. They all ordered a light lunch with water instead of wine.

Bancroft was relieved when Trudy sat with her back to him. He couldn't recall the number of meetings when Trudy had sat opposite him. In a hip holster he had a Walther. He briefly considered shooting eight of them – the number of rounds in his automatic – with no bullet left for Serena. He rejected the idea quickly. He'd never make it to the helicopter – people from the restaurant might follow, shouting to the pilot. Attempting to drive off in the Peugeot carried the same risk. Now he wanted a distraction, so he could quietly leave without being noticed.

'I've been wondering about something, Chance,' Paula said to Burgoyne when they had ordered. 'Those Arabs who attacked us,' she began, keeping her voice down. 'They had business suits but they all wore a green headband. Why?'

'Because they were Muslims and in their religion martyrs who die for the cause of Islam go straight to heaven.'

'Makes them formidable,' Tweed commented.

At his table Bancroft, from behind his dark glasses, saw Serena gazing straight at him. She turned away, began talking to Newman.

They had finished their meal, had paid the bill, when Butler got up, said he would be back in a minute. He had to fetch something from his car. They were leaving the restaurant when Tweed handed Paula the envelope he had opened earlier. She took out the folded sheet inside and read the brief letter. It was written in copperplate, slanting slightly to the right.

My dear Tweed, I apologize for not meeting you in Annecy. I was delayed. May I suggest instead we meet at Talloires, further down the lake. H. Goslar.

The manager, who had been well tipped for the meals, accompanied them to the door. He gave another of his broad smiles.

'I hope everything was to your satisfaction, sir.'

'An excellent meal,' Tweed replied. 'Do you know anything about a place further down the lake? Talloires?'

'You reach it by driving down the far side – the eastern side – of the lake. I can't recommend it. The resort is still out of season. Everything will be closed. A few locals ski there. But nearly everyone goes instead to Grenoble or Chamonix. It will be dead now.'

'Thank you.' Tweed went outside and Butler had arrived back. He was carrying an outsize tennis racquet container. 'What is it you have there?'

'Machine-pistol,' Marler whispered. 'Harry is obviously expecting trouble.'

'I think we'll explore Annecy a bit before we go. Let's walk to the left along the river front.'

Bancroft waited until they had disappeared from view. He then got up and left the restaurant in a hurry.

The Yellow Man had found his vantage point. He just hoped Tweed and his team would walk along the rue Perrière. Perched high above a road, which he trusted was an extension of the rue Perrière, he gripped an Armalite rifle.

A wooden staircase, enclosed with a wooden partition, but open to the sky, ran up the side of an ancient stone tower, topped by a sloping roof. At the end of the staircase where he crouched, it was rather like being in a pulpit. He had a clear view down into the narrow street below. He waited.

30

'This street is the rue Perrière,' Paula commented. She was feeling fresh after her meal. 'This really is the most beautiful place. Like Paradise.'

'It's a maze of waterways and alleys, with small bridges over the water,' Burgoyne called out behind her. 'It just goes on and on with a new delight every corner you turn round.'

'And I love the ancient lanterns hanging from the walls,' enthused Paula. 'At night it must be mysterious – and marvellous. I really should have brought a camera.'

'This is not a pleasure trip,' Tweed warned, walking slowly.

'Don't be grumpy,' Paula chaffed him.

Burgoyne had dropped back. He was now

accompanying Serena, who was also enchanted. She pointed out various features which attracted her, her chin tilted up. Burgoyne took her hand and she showed no signs of objecting.

Butler, carrying his 'tennis' case, had joined Paula and Tweed. She noticed he had opened the zip. Right-handed, he was now carrying it in his left hand. His shoulders were hunched forward, his eyes looking always upward.

'Don't look so serious, Harry,' Paula teased him. She looked back at Newman, walking with Trudy. 'Isn't all this wonderful. I'd love to explore it at night.'

'Without a map you'd soon get lost,' Burgoyne called out. 'And some of the alleys are very dark.'

'When were you last here, then?' she asked over her shoulder.

'A century ago. When I was on my way to Aix-en-Provence. I told you about that trip earlier.'

'Yes, you did. That weird Arab scribe.'

'That ingenious Arab scribe.'

There was no traffic. At the point they had reached the only sound was the running water of the river. It created a soothing, hypnotic atmosphere. In the river white ducks, soaking up the sun, paddled leisurely along the surface.

'There's nothing modern,' Paula observed. 'It's all as old as the hills. There can't be many places like this left.'

She had seen the ducks when they first crossed the bridge to the restaurant. Now she paused by the railing, dropped pieces of bread into the water. Half a dozen ducks rushed towards the floating pieces of bread she had brought from Les Corbières and bumped against each other in their determination to be first to reach the prize.

'I don't think I've ever felt so serene,' Paula said.

'Funny I should say that – considering we have someone called Serena with us.'

'Under the surface she may not be as serene as you think,' Tweed replied.

'Don't you like her, then?'

'On this expedition it's not a question of liking or disliking anyone.'

'Yet another conundrum. I won't ask you what you mean – I know you won't tell me.'

They resumed their walk along the rue Perrière. They were the only people walking. Paula assumed the heat was keeping people indoors. It must be cool inside all these stone buildings.

'Why do you think Goslar keeps leaving these messages?' she asked.

'To keep us away from somewhere else.'

'And where might that be?'

'I'll know if I get that phone call I've been waiting for. I hope it happens soon. We are losing vital time and can do not a thing about it. Those green headbands Burgoyne explained are significant.'

They had come to a corner where the street turned sharply to the left. They went round the corner and Paula felt a tiny stone inside her shoe. She looked up and saw a great tower with a sloping roof looming over the next stretch of road.

The Yellow Man had her head in his cross-hairs. His rifle was perched on the edge of the pulpit for maximum stability. His finger was curled round the trigger. Her head was motionless as she paused, dead centre in the cross-hairs. He pulled the trigger.

Paula stooped to extract the stone from her shoe. The bullet passed over her head, splashed in the water beyond the railing. Butler dropped the tennis case, whipped up the muzzle of his machine-pistol, fired a hail of bullets which shattered the pulpit. Shards of wood tumbled down the side of the stone wall into the street.

Butler took off. He ran up a twisting steep pathway. Through an arch in the wall and on beyond. He reached the foot of the staircase leading up to where the pulpit had existed less than a minute before, looked up it, machine-pistol aimed. No sign of a body. He swore.

He searched swiftly round the base of the tower. Alleys led off in all directions. He listened for the sound of running feet. Nothing. Only a heavy silence. Sighing, he returned the way he had come.

Tweed had hauled Paula back round the corner, out of sight of the tower. He looked a question at Butler.

'Marksman got away. Must be nippy on his feet. God, that was close.'

'I'm perfectly OK,' said Paula quietly. 'Thank you. I'll buy you a present.'

'Don't want a present. What do we do now?'

'Drive on to Talloires,' Tweed decided. 'Let's explore, see what Talloires has to offer us. Back to the cars. It's a bit of a drive, from what I remember from the map.'

31

The blazing row built up soon after they had left Annecy. Again, Burgoyne, in his car, led the pack. Behind him Marler drove with Butler by his side. Just before leaving, Serena had asked Tweed in her most polite manner if she could travel with him. Trudy had immediately volunteered to give up her place to her, saying she would ride with Nield. So now Newman, behind the wheel of his car, had Paula beside him and in the back Serena sat next to Tweed.

They drove past a park where there was equipment for children to play on, and a stationary helicopter. At that point they were at the head of the lake. Checking his map, Tweed estimated the lake was about ten miles long as it swept south. It was rather like a snake fully extended, curving here and there as the coils moved forward. It was mid-afternoon as they set off for Talloires.

A few yachts cruised the upper part of the lake unenthusiastically. Their sails were limp because there was no wind. Then the water was deserted as they moved further south. The landscape also was almost deserted. Steep hills climbed on their left and only here and there stood an isolated house. Paula had a feeling they were moving into no man's land.

'I told Burgoyne,' Tweed said, 'that we'd better hurry. It will start getting dark soon and we may want to race back to Geneva to get there before dark, if we can. He agreed, saying it was a treacherous route.'

'I think we're wasting our time,' Serena suddenly burst out. 'I can't see that our visit there produced anything.'

'Except I was a target,' Paula called back quietly.

'Well, the bullet missed you by a mile.'

'It came rather closer than that,' Paula responded, still quietly.

'I thought we were looking for Goslar,' Serena snapped. 'Who is Goslar? Where is he? We're no nearer finding anything out than we were back in Geneva. I feel I'm wasting *my* time.'

'In that case,' Tweed enquired, 'why did you come with us?'

'I thought you knew that. For protection. Everyone

else who had anything to do with that fiend has been killed.'

'Is that really the only reason you did come with us?' Tweed asked.

'Why should there be any other bloody reason?' she demanded, raising her voice.

Tweed looked at her. She kept her profile towards him. He detected a dominant streak in her nature she had carefully concealed up to then. She looked beautiful, but her Roman nose was tilted and her lips were pressed close together. Turning her head towards him for a moment, she glared, then turned away.

'Because,' he explained, 'I sense there is another reason.'

'Tweed's famous sixth sense,' she hooted, then laughed gratingly.

'Serena – ' Paula had twisted round in her seat to stare at her – 'I think it's time you cooled it. Your belly-aching could distract our driver.'

'Belly-aching! How vulgar. All right. There was another reason. Goslar – if you'd ever caught him – would be world famous. I'm a photographer. If I'd had pictures of him I could have syndicated them all over the world for a fortune. And I damned well need the money.'

'So where is your camera?' Tweed wanted to know.

'Are you calling me a liar? My camera is in my suitcase, which I brought from Nield's boot and put in ours.' Her voice began to drip sarcasm. 'If you like to stop the car, I'll get it out and show you. It's a Nikon. Newman, stop the car.'

'I take my instructions from Tweed,' Newman replied mildly.

Paula was still twisted round, watching Serena. She was getting the impression Serena was putting on a big act. Why?

'That does it, then,' Serena said, her voice cold. 'When we get back to Annecy I'm hiring my own car. I'll drive myself back to Geneva.'

Tweed again looked at her. Serena turned her head, looked back at him. She was no longer glaring. Her pallid eyes had a weird expression, as though she had withdrawn into herself, into another world.

'The temperature has dropped a lot suddenly,' said Paula. 'And the weather is changing. Oh Lord, look what's ahead of us.'

Tweed had noticed a few minutes earlier. The sun had gone. A low heavy overcast of threatening grey clouds had sealed it from view. In front of them, on their side of the lake, mountains sheered up steeply, mountains covered with deep snow. They were moving into a new climate zone.

'Tweed,' Paula called back, 'could you hand me my fleece? It is folded up in the seat next to you.'

'Here it is.'

Paula wriggled into her fleece, being careful not to jog Newman's arm. She pulled a pair of fur-lined gloves out of the pockets, put them on. She settled back, opened the glove compartment, brought out Newman's binoculars. For some time the road had been curving round the edge of the lake, twenty feet or so below them. She raised the binoculars, altered the focus, stared through the lenses for about a minute before lowering them.

'I think we're approaching Talloires. Gloomy-looking little town. No sign of life anywhere.'

'How far off?' Serena asked in a normal voice.

'About a mile, maybe a bit more. Burgoyne has slowed down quite a bit.'

'Tweed,' Paula commented, 'you did say back in

Annecy we would find what Talloires has in store for us. Something like that. Soon we'll know the answer.'

'Welcome to the lively resort of Talloires,' Newman began, singsong fashion. 'The jewel of France. Bunting hanging across the Avenue de Joie, people dancing in the streets, girls at windows with flowers they throw at passers-by. Oh, what a cheerful, lively town is Talloires.'

'Burgoyne is pulling up,' said Paula. 'I suggest you do the same behind Nield. And shut up!'

'The lady doesn't appreciate my musical talents,' Newman replied.

'Well, look at the place.'

They looked. Reluctantly they got out of the car and joined the others. Burgoyne, who seemed impervious to weather, stood in his jacket and slacks, his arms folded. Tweed was scanning their surroundings as he issued the warning.

'Spread out, everyone. We make a mass target here.'

'Isn't it incredibly bleak?' commented Paula, standing with Tweed and Burgoyne.

There was snow in the road. Heavy falls of snow on the slopes of the mountains which rose straight up from close to the road. There was a scattering of houses with steep roofs, some with plaster walls on the ground floor and first floors of dark wood. All their shutters were closed, downstairs, upstairs. Two small hotels had a notice on a board hanging from entrance doors. *Fermé*. Closed.

'I'd say the whole place is *fermé*,' Paula snorted and wandered off to join Serena, hoping she was in a better mood.

Tweed stood alone with Burgoyne under a huge fir tree. There was no sound. A heavy silence. An eerie sensation that no one lived here, that all the inhabitants had fled to the Bahamas. Tweed thought he had never experienced a place where *stillness* was the main element in the oppressive atmosphere. He felt that night would fall at any moment.

'What are you going to do when this is all over?' he asked.

'That's a good question.' Burgoyne's weathered face broke into a rueful smile. 'I suppose I'll go back to my cottage at Rydford, see if my girl friend, Coral Langley, is still interested. She's probably gone off with someone else by now.'

Tweed thought this wasn't the moment to tell Burgoyne that Coral no longer walked the planet.

'Rydford is a small place?' he asked.

'Small?' Burgoyne cupped his hand. 'I could hold it there. The place where nothing ever happens.'

'I can imagine you climbing the tors.'

'Rough Tor is only quite a short drive away. I think I've got too accustomed to roaming the earth. To seeing all the strange sights in this bizarre world of ours.'

He lifted his arms high, began to rotate, wiggling his hips, his stomach. He was nifty on his feet as he slowly swivelled round, gazing at Tweed with his dark eyes, pouching his lips invitingly. It was a professional performance and Tweed heard Paula chuckling as she watched from a distance. Burgoyne stopped, resumed his Stonehengelike stance, arms folded.

'Belly dance in Istanbul,' he explained, although Tweed had understood. 'A bit coarse, I suppose,' he said, eyeing Paula. 'But the world is full of coarseness these days. The whole structure is collapsing before our very eyes. No more honour, no more a man keeping his word once he's shaken your hand. All gone with the wind, as that lady novelist said who wrote about the American Civil War.'

'You've been to America?'

'Me?' Burgoyne threw out both arms, danced in a brief circle. 'I have been everywhere. Always on my own. Which is why I chose to join army intelligence. Then became a spy. Couldn't stand taking stupid orders from stupid buffoons who didn't know the time of day.'

'You'll miss that,' Tweed ruminated.

'Will I? Who says I'm going to settle down, grow old gracefully? I prefer to grow old disgracefully.' He grinned at Paula, who watched him, fascinated. 'Don't ever get mixed up with me, lady. I'd lead you one hell of a dance.'

Ever restless, Burgoyne did a little dance, stopped by the massive trunk of the fir spreading its branches above them. Tweed heard a sound, caught movement out of the corner of his eye. To their right the road turned a corner. An old man appeared.

He was hobbling. Had a stick in his left hand to help support him. His right hand was behind his back. Wrapped round his head was a large white bandage covering the top of his head and part of his forehead. His face was covered with white cream, presumably medicinal.

'Looks as though he's been in the wars,' Burgoyne remarked. 'Maybe it was a car crash. But I can ask him when he reaches us if he has seen anyone else at all in this benighted place.'

The old man kept coming, stick prodding into the road for balance. What happened next was a blur of movement. The stick was dropped. The hand behind the back appeared, holding a machine-pistol. His other hand took a firm hold on it. He was aiming it at where Paula stood with Serena.

A shot rang out, echoing across the mountains. Followed so fast by a second shot only a keen ear could tell two shots had been fired. The man with the bandaged head stood stock-still for a moment, then he sprawled forward full length, hitting the road with a heavy thud. The bandage slipped off his head.

Tweed ran forward, bent down, checked his pulse. He stood up and shook his head. Paula lowered the Browning she had fired twice, came forward. Tweed looked up at her as the others ran to join her.

'That was one of the quickest reactions I've ever seen. What was it that made you suspicious?'

'Look at what he's got wrapped round his head, for Heaven's sake.'

Underneath the white bandage which had slipped off the dead man in the road was a green headband. Paula looked at Burgoyne.

'Remember what you told us about fanatical Muslims wearing green headbands when they went into battle – as they did coming out of the mist on the road from Geneva. That they welcomed being martyrs to the cause. Well, I saw a thin strip of green below the bandage, so I was alerted, had my hand on my Browning when he whipped out the machine-pistol concealed behind his back.'

'You've got even better vision than I have,' Marler commented.

'I could have used you in the Gulf War,' Burgoyne said quietly.

'I want that body removed out of the road, and the weapon,' Tweed ordered.

Burgoyne said he'd oblige. As though it were an everyday job, he picked up the white bandage, stuffed it inside the assassin's jacket. He pulled off the green headband and added it to where he had hidden the bandage. Without its disguise, when Newman twisted it round, the face of the dead man was no longer old. It was the face of a man no older than thirty.

Burgoyne, using both hands, expertly picked up the body and the weapon. Standing upright, it struck Paula that Burgoyne, so recently the comedian, was now every inch the soldier. Carrying his burden in both arms he walked to the edge of the road, looked down, saw there was a sheer drop to the lake. He heaved body and weapon over. There was a brief splash and then the grim silence descended once more.

'Oh, my Lord,' said Serena, one hand clutching her throat, 'it's no wonder you work with Tweed. I hardly saw what happened until after it *had* happened.'

Paula was withdrawing the magazine still in her Browning. She tossed it into the lake, replaced it with a fresh magazine, then slid the gun back inside her shoulder bag.

'I should have been quicker,' Butler said to himself.

'So now sing "Welcome to Tailloires",' Paula chaffed Newman.

'There are times – ' Newman rubbed fingers down the side of his jaw – 'when I wish I'd kept my big mouth shut.'

'Someone else is coming round that corner,' warned Paula, her hand back inside her shoulder bag, gripping her Browning.

The last type of person in the world Tweed expected to see in this wilderness was strolling towards them. Tall and slim, he wore a Savile Row suit, a Hermès tie over a crisp white shirt and handmade shoes. The epitome of the Englishman you might expect to see in the City, he was swinging from his right hand a tightly rolled umbrella.

His other arm was swinging back and forth.

'Caw! I don't believe this,' said Butler.

'Don't,' warned Tweed.

The new arrival halted a few yards from them. He was about Newman's height and stood in the road with the end of his umbrella near his shoe while his arm held the handle at an extended angle. He was clean-shaven, had dark hair so trim it gave the impression he had just visited the hairdresser.

'Good afternoon, everyone,' he called out in a highly cultured voice. 'I must say it is rather a pleasure to meet someone from back home, don't you know? Bit like the outback of Orstralia round here.'

'Posh voice, don't you know,' Paula whispered to Tweed.

'Reminds me very much of the voice which introduces the recordings of Goslar,' Tweed whispered back. 'Very much indeed.'

'I have been asked to pass on a message to a Mr Tweed. Sorry, I really should have introduced myself. I am Peregrine Arbuthnot.'

'May I ask how you got here, Mr Arbuthnot?' asked Tweed. 'And I am Tweed.'

'How very pleasant to make your acquaintance, sir. How did I get here? Drove along the road down the other side of the lake, didn't I. Parked the Jag a bit further back, decided I'd take a bit of a walk the rest of the way. So here I am.'

'The message,' Newman said in a rough voice, walking closer and accompanied by Butler. 'Stop fooling around and give me the message.'

'I would appreciate a little courtesy, sir. Actually, the message is for Mr Tweed who, I gather, is standing over there.'

'So you're not armed, then,' Newman snapped, very close now.

'Armed? I say, you do harbour some rather quaint notions. And I must insist on—'

He never finished his sentence. Butler had slipped round behind him, had rammed the muzzle of a Walther into his back. As Arbuthnot began to splutter protests Newman slipped his hand inside the jacket where it bulged, spoiling the otherwise immaculate outfit. From a shoulder holster he withdrew a Beretta 6.35mm automatic. He held it in the palm of his hand. Closer up, Arbuthnot was more heavily built than he had realized.

'Call this a quaint notion?' Newman enquired pleasantly.

'We're rather in the wilds out here. One does need a modicum of protection.'

'And one lied in one's teeth when I asked whether one was armed,' Newman said savagely.

'Does Tweed want the bloody message or not?' Arbuthnot snapped, his upper-crust accent slipping. 'And he doesn't get it unless the thug behind him takes his gun away.'

'Just give me the message,' said Tweed, who had joined them.

'I'd do as he says,' Marler warned, arriving so silently no one had noticed his approach. 'Mr Tweed has the most frightful temper when people try to play games with him.'

'I have attempted to deliver this message in a civilized fashion. That being so, I would appreciate some sign of respect.'

'The message,' Tweed repeated grimly.

'If you would kindly ask these morons to keep their distance – the message is for your ears only.'

'Let me take him behind that tree,' Newman pressed. 'I doubt if it would take me long to extract his perishing message.'

'Go ahead,' Tweed agreed, throwing up his hands in disgust.

Newman grasped Arbuthnot by his tie, dragging him behind the tree Tweed had stood under with Burgoyne. His captive used one hand to try and wrench Newman's grip away but his efforts were futile. With the other hand he kept pointing at his mouth. For a moment Newman eased his grip, realizing Arbuthnot was desperate to speak.

'Tweed! Tweed!' he gasped.

'I'm here,' said Tweed.

'Give you the message . . .'

'Let him talk,' Tweed ordered. 'If it's rubbish give him hell.'

'A moment, please . . . A moment.' Arbuthnot put up a hand to rub his bruised throat gently. 'Give you the message now . . .'

Tweed held out his hand, expecting an envelope with another scrawl inside it. Arbuthnot shook his head. Newman was just about to grab hold of him again when Arbuthnot spoke slowly, painfully.

'Message is verbal. Need my umbrella to show you . . .'

Butler, who had been close to Newman all the time, went back, fetched the umbrella which had been lying in the road. He first examined it carefully – to make sure there was no hidden weapon, that it was not a swordstick. Then he passed it to Arbuthnot.

'Up the mountain.' Arbuthnot walked a few careful paces to where he could see across the road. 'That cabin up there.' He pointed with the umbrella. 'See it?'

Tweed had earlier noticed a very large wooden cabin perched about two hundred yards up the steep snow-covered slope. Along the front, overlooking the lake, ran a long veranda. The shutters over the windows were all closed. No sign of life in the place.

'I see it,' Tweed acknowledged. 'What about it?'

'Dr Goslar is waiting there. To have a meeting with you. Just you. But the members of your team can escort you to the door at the left-hand side.'

'How were you given this message?' Tweed demanded.

'I had to call a number from a phone box in Annecy. He said, "Tell Tweed I will meet him at the cabin on the mountain at Talloires. It has a veranda at the front. We can settle this problem with a quiet talk." That was the message. He ended by telling me not to call the number again, that it was in a rented house. He would not be going back to it. That is all.'

'So how much did he pay you for this service?'

'Twenty thousand Swiss francs.'

'About ten thousand pounds,' Tweed calculated. 'Expensive message. Where did you collect the money?'

'From behind the phone box I was using. Inside a waterproof envelope.'

'Show me.'

'It is *my* money.'

Arbuthnot extracted from his breast pocket a fat white envelope and handed it to Tweed. Glancing inside Tweed saw there was a wad of about twenty thousand-franc notes. Swiss banknotes. £10,000. Goslar was throwing his money about. He handed back the envelope.

'What does Dr Goslar look like?'

'Look like?' Arbuthnot sounded astounded. 'I have never seen him. No one ever sees him . . .'

'It is a him? Or a her?'

'How the devil do I know? I've listened to the screeching voice on the tapes I have to play back. I can't tell whether it's a man or a woman.'

Tweed believed him. He turned again to stare at the isolated cabin. Single storey. Snow piled on its roof. He looked at Newman.

'This is where I take over,' Newman said firmly. He took off his camel-hair coat, stared hard at Arbuthnot. 'Put this on. Don't argue. Do it. You are going to walk up to that cabin to make sure Dr Goslar is waiting inside. Make with the feet.'

'There's snow on the slope,' Arbuthnot protested indignantly. 'I'm not dressed for it.'

'You're not dressed for anywhere within a hundred miles of here. I give you ten seconds to start climbing.'

'Otherwise,' Marler interjected, 'say goodbye to this paradise.'

Lifting his Armalite, Marler shoved the muzzle underneath Arbuthnot's chin. His target retreated, bumped into Newman, who held him still.

'You couldn't shoot down a man in cold blood,' stuttered Arbuthnot.

'Unfortunately,' Marler told him, without a smile, 'I'm the hot-blooded type. Now get moving. And while you're climbing remember I'll have your back in my cross-hairs.'

32

Arbuthnot had begun his climb up the slope through the snow. His feet sank into it up to his ankles, soaking the bottoms of his trousers. At one point he paused, looked back, waved his umbrella to express his rage. Marler raised the barrel of his rifle. Shaking a fist, Arbuthnot continued his climb, still some distance from the cabin.

'I don't like this,' Burgoyne said. 'There could be another bunch of Arabs inside the place. We're very exposed here. They could burst out suddenly and mow us down. I think we ought to hurry up the slope to that big copse of firs.'

'I agree,' said Tweed. 'Take everyone with you. I'll wait here with Paula and Newman. In an emergency we can hide behind the massive trunk of this fir. I'd go now . . .'

Burgoyne gathered the others together. They began climbing, heading for the copse which stood about the same height as the cabin and a hundred yards or so away from it to the right. Burgoyne led the way, holding Serena's arm to help her keep moving. Trudy went up behind them on her own, striding briskly. Behind her Nield and Butler brought up the rear.

Serena glanced back, saw Trudy by herself, tore her arm away from Burgoyne, said something to him, continued up under her own steam. Although they'd started later, they gained height more rapidly than Arbuthnot, who was trudging resentfully at a slower pace. Again he stopped, looked down. Marler again raised the muzzle of his Armalite and Arbuthnot started climbing once more.

'Do you really think Goslar is waiting inside that cabin?' Paula asked.

'No idea,' Tweed replied. 'Goslar is full of tricks. He could be close to us, he could be miles away.'

'I can't feel sorry for Arbuthnot,' she said, watching the solitary figure plodding upward. 'You seemed sure it was his voice which introduced Goslar's screeching recordings. Arbuthnot must have realized some of them would end in murder.'

'He probably closed his mind to that aspect – for the sake of the money.'

Paula switched her gaze to the five people who were disappearing into the copse. She started, grabbed Tweed's arm. He looked at her.

'What is it?'

'That photo you always carry, the one of Goslar disappearing behind the Iron Curtain east of Lübeck all those years ago. The blurred image – the way it swung its arms well clear of its body. I just saw that.'

'Are you sure?'

'Oh!' She let out her breath. 'I was wrong. It was Trudy in her trouser suit. She just reappeared for a moment.'

'Bet Arbuthnot finds that cabin empty,' Newman speculated. 'And another message from bloody Goslar.'

'Could be,' Tweed mused.

'On the other hand,' Pauia suggested, 'Chance could be right. He is a soldier with a lot of experience. If there are Arabs waiting inside that cabin I think we'd better take shelter behind that fir trunk.'

They moved behind the massive trunk, peering round it to watch the solitary figure with its absurd umbrella getting close to the door in the left-hand side. Marler used a convenient short thick branch to perch his rifle on.

Paula was again aware of the haunting silence of the place. Not a sound. No movement – except for the plodding figure approaching the side of the cabin. It was beginning to get on her nerves, to emphasize their isolation from the rest of the world. Clenching her fingers tightly inside her gloves she took in a deep breath, had a presentiment of great danger.

She tried to locate the source of what was bothering her so much. Burgoyne's group had become invisible, hidden deep inside the copse. Then her gaze became fixated on Arbuthnot's movements as he slowed down. He had just passed the end of the long veranda, had stopped close to something at the side of the cabin. The door, she assumed.

The nerve-racking silence was broken by the sound of his distant voice. He was calling out something, but she couldn't catch the words. She guessed he was asking Dr Goslar if he was inside, maybe telling him Tweed had come to meet him. Arbuthnot still paused for a short time. Then he began to move, hand extended, presumably to take hold of the door handle. He began to move inside, to disappear from view. The world blew up.

A booming roar smashed the silence. It coincided with a brilliant flash. The deafening explosion elevated the entire cabin. It broke into pieces in midair, casting beams of wood across the slope, sending shards towards the sky like shrapnel, everything bursting into flames. Tweed pulled Paula behind the tree as debris clattered on to the road. As the clatter ceased she peered round the trunk. A column of black smoke mushroomed above where the cabin had stood, was rapidly dispersed by an icy breeze which sprang up suddenly. The heavy silence again descended on Talloires.

Butler, holding his machine-pistol, was the first to emerge from inside the copse. He cautiously approached what was no more than a pile of ash. Paula realized he was wary of a second explosion. Then he moved close, used the muzzle of his weapon to stir the ash.

Paula ran up the slope, accompanied by Newman. Tweed followed at a more leisurely pace. Trudy appeared out of the copse with Nield on one side, Burgoyne on the other. The last figure to arrive was Serena. Butler looked up as Paula and Newman reached him.

'Nothing left of Arbuthnot. Can't find a trace of him.'

'I'm not surprised,' said Burgoyne. 'We felt the shockwave inside that copse. That was quite a load of explosive.'

'Triggered off when Arbuthnot opened the door,' Paula suggested.

'I guess so,' Burgoyne agreed.

'It would have wiped out the lot of us,' Tweed

commented calmly, 'if Bob hadn't had the sense to send Arbuthnot up first. Another typical Goslar trap.'

'I suppose Arbuthnot was an employee of Goslar's,' Serena remarked. She lit a cigarette. 'I don't think we need waste time mourning him.'

Paula glanced at her. Serena's tone of voice had been cold, verging on the indifferent. You, my girl, she thought, are one tough cookie. Far more so than you pretend to be. Tweed thrust his hands into his coat pocket. His tone was decisive.

'I think now we'll drive on to the end of the lake and back along the road on the other side to Annecy. I need to have an urgent word with that estate agent, Periot. So let's try and get back before he goes home.'

'What about?' Paula whispered as they started to descend the slope.

'The Chateau de l'Air. I may just have missed something.'

33

Marler was waiting for them by the roadside. Tweed guessed he had sensibly stayed there in case more trouble arrived while they were exposed on the slope. Within minutes they were travelling along the lakeside road. Paula took one last glance at the place where the cabin had stood. The ashes were still smouldering but she thought that soon it would snow again, burying for ever Arbuthnot's funeral pyre. She heaved a sign of relief as they left Talloires behind.

They passed a number of old houses set back from the road. In all of them the shutters were closed, both downstairs and upstairs. It was like a small town the inhabitants had abandoned, fleeing from the plague.

The dark trees clustered close to the road did nothing to lighten the atmosphere.

Before leaving, at Serena's suggestion, they had changed places in the cars. Now, in the rear car, driven by Newman, Paula still sat next to him. But instead of Serena, Tweed had Trudy seated next to him. He was puzzled by Serena's request – she was now seated next to Nield in the car in the middle of the convoy. Ahead of Nield, Marler drove with Butler and Burgoyne was again in the lead.

'I expect you found that a pretty frightening experience,' Tweed remarked to Trudy.

'A brief shock – the sound of the bomb exploding – but nothing more. After living with Unit Four it takes a lot to upset me.'

'I can understand that. Especially after the death of your husband. What was his name, by the way?'

'Er . . .' Trudy hesitated. Tweed glanced at her. 'It was Walter Baron,' she then said. Another hesitation. 'Third-generation American. We lived for each other. No, that sounds rather like something from a poetic sonnet. How can I put it? We were a good match.'

Paula had heard the hesitations. She twisted round in her seat, looked at Tweed.

'Why do you think Goslar is still trying to kill us? There's something relentless, even desperate about his attempts.'

'Desperate is the word,' Tweed replied. 'I'm convinced he is almost ready to deliver his horrific weapon to the highest bidder. He's getting nearly frantic that in some way I'll thwart him at the last moment.'

'So you think there isn't much time left to stop him?'

'That is my great anxiety. There could be only hours left.'

The conversation ended. They were now moving along the far side of the lake on their way back to

Annecy. Paula was pondering the situation. She sensed in Tweed a grim determination to reach Goslar in time. Then something else occurred to her.

'We haven't seen sight or heard sound of either the Yellow Man or Bancroft. I wonder where they are now?'

'I have no idea, but I can hear a helicopter approaching.'

'And now we're getting close to Annecy I can see a speedboat on the lake.'

After his botched attempt to kill Paula, the Yellow Man had escaped Butler's attempt to kill him by dodging a devious path along the network of alleys inside Annecy. He had then returned to the rue Perrière – in time to see Tweed's cars leaving. Running to his parked car, he had followed them a short distance until he had realized they were heading for the far end of the lake.

Parking his Peugeot near the car-hire firm, he had hurried across the park to a small marina. As he had hoped, he found a jetty where speedboats were for hire. He'd had to wait a while for one to be returned. In the meantime he had used field glasses to follow the progress of the convoy along the lakeside road until it disappeared from view.

'How much longer am I going to have to wait?' he had demanded.

'Until the previous hirer returns. Do not ask me how long that will be,' the owner had replied unhelpfully. 'He said he only needed it for an hour – and that was an hour ago.'

'Can't you call him on a mobile phone?'

'You tell me how. I have one, but he hasn't. Just a moment. I do believe he's coming back now . . .'

In a fever of impatience, which he fought to control, the Yellow Man had watched enviously as an agile man ran towards a helicopter resting in the park. He could have hired that machine to follow Tweed. Then he had an idea.

'I'll be back in a minute,' he said to the speedboat hirer. 'And you will promise to keep that boat coming in for me?'

'How long do you want it for?' the hirer asked off-handedly. 'The charge is one hundred francs an hour.'

'Take this.'

The Yellow Man pulled out of his pocket a wad of French francs. He peeled off six fifty-franc notes, shoved them into the hirer's hand. Confident that such an amount would hold the speedboat for him, he dashed back to his parked car. When he returned he carried a canvas holdall. Inside it were four grenades.

The speedboat was now waiting for him, moored to the wharf. The hirer, with three hundred francs in his pocket, was now most helpful. He handed down the Yellow Man into the craft, offered to show him how the controls worked.

'I've often used powerboats,' the Yellow Man replied and started the engine.

Before he took off he rammed his beret more tightly over his hair. He then headed at a modest speed along the western shore – the shore opposite to the one Tweed's convoy had proceeded down along the road. In this way he would be less likely to be noticed.

Earlier, when Tweed and his team had left the restaurant in Annecy, Les Corbières, Bancroft had also left a short time afterwards. He had decided he could wear his panama hat again and walked into a nearby bar. Tweed and his men had to return for their cars sooner or later.

Impatient by nature, Bancroft had swilled down only half his drink when he decided he had made another mistake. When Tweed and his team returned to pick up their cars, he'd have to wait until they had gone before he dared to walk out of the bar. He was convinced their arrival in Annecy was only a stopover, that as soon as they'd come back from their walk they would drive to the highway leading to Geneva.

He left the bar quickly, went to his car, backed it away from the wall and headed for the highway. He needed somewhere he could park until he saw the convoy leaving the area. Turning onto the highway, he drove a short distance in the Geneva direction, parked his car on a grass verge. He took off his panama hat but kept on his large wraparound glasses. This time he made no attempt to pretend he was fiddling with the engine. He slumped in his seat like a man asleep. Then he waited.

Stirring restlessly in his seat, he went on waiting – and waiting – and waiting. Eventually he could stand the inaction no longer. He drove back to the Old Town. The moment he saw the parking area he was appalled. All the cars belonging to Tweed's team had gone. He parked again by the wall, jumped out of his car and ran across the park to where the helicopter stood, the pilot in his seat, gazing round.

'I've lost track of the terrorists,' he snapped as he climbed up beside the pilot. 'They're in a convoy of four cars . . .'

He described the cars while the pilot listened. The pilot scratched his forehead, nodded.

'Well, have you seen them, for God's sake?' Bancroft rasped.

'Yes. They went east along that road over there. They continued along the road by the lake, heading south towards Talloires.'

'Then let's find them. I'm paying you good money . . .'

The pilot switched on the engine, the two rotors began to whirl – the small one at the rear which stabilized the machine and the large brute which lifted the chopper. The pilot flew out over the lake, climbing all the time. He didn't want any complaints from the locals about the noise it made. He'd experienced that before. The few yachts crawling over the water became like toys and then the pilot headed his machine south.

'Fly closer to the western shore,' Bancroft ordered. 'Then they're less likely to hear us coming.'

He had the communication kit strapped over his head. Headphones were clamped to his ears. At his mouth was a small microphone he could use to speak to the pilot, who had his own communication equipment.

'Why don't you just arrest these terrorists?' the pilot asked.

'We can't – without evidence.' Bancroft's legal mind improvised as a reflex action. 'We need to locate them when they are collecting weapons from one of their arms dumps. I can summon the CRS on my mobile.'

'CRS? They're a tough lot. Just what you need to cope with terrorists.'

'Where does that lakeside road they drove along lead to?'

'Only to Talloires, then it curves round the end of the lake and returns on this side to Annecy. You can't lose them . . .'

The pilot was flying at a moderate speed. Bancroft would have liked to tell him to hurry up, but decided not to put any more pressure on him. He looped the powerful binoculars he always carried round his neck, used them to sweep the road along the eastern shore, saw nothing. He stopped looking.

A short time later he heard a faint distant *boom!* He saw smoke rising a good way off on the eastern shore. When they got closer he raised his binoculars again, made out four cars parked below a snow-covered mountain. People were getting into them and the cars started moving.

'I think that's them,' he told the pilot. 'The cars have started to move off, still heading south.'

'In that case they'll soon be moving up the road by this side of the lake.'

'Then we'd better keep this height and cross the lake – so we'll be flying well away from them. I'd change direction now, if I were you,'

'There's a powerboat ahead of us, hugging this shore. Powerboats don't often get this far south at this time of the year. It will be cold down there . . .'

The Yellow Man, not wishing to get too close to Tweed while he had a large team with him, was staying close to the western side of the lake. He had to launch a surprise attack. He stopped the engine, looked above him. The trouble was that a cliff, about twenty feet up, leaned over the water. He looked at the holdall which contained the four grenades. It was going to be difficult at this point to lob grenades at the cars as they passed him on the road.

He had watched Tweed's team through binoculars at the moment when Arbuthnot was nearing the wooden cabin. He had arrived too late to see Newman drop the Arab's corpse into the lake. Now trees masked his view of what was happening on the snow-bound slope. His first clue that something had happened was when he heard the explosion.

He saw debris soaring into the air, dropping back again. He was mystified, therefore bothered. Later he saw the four cars driving off down the lakeside road. When he had escaped from Butler, after attempting to kill Paula, he had bought a map of the area. He was studying it now, noting that the road led round the base of the lake and returned towards Annecy above him.

He started the engine, glanced up at a helicopter crossing to the far side of the lake, turned the boat round, began chugging back along the smooth surface. He was still close to the shore while looking for a place where the road was exposed to view. Again, he switched off the engine briefly. He could hear the cars coming.

He was bitterly cold and wrapped a cloth round the lower half of his face. Starting up the engine, he moved out towards the middle of the lake, looking ahead for a suitable location to use his grenades. He was now moving at speed, spray bursting over the prow, splashing on his half-covered face.

When he looked back to the shore he saw the four cars racing along and realized it would be almost impossible to throw a grenade and hit the lead car. It was partly this realization – and partly the icy cold – which made him take a fresh decision. He would overtake the cars and reach Annecy ahead of them. He opened the throttle.

The prow lifted itself out of the water. A surging wake tumbled the lake behind him. He looked back at the road. The cars were now some distance behind him. He would be waiting for them when they reached Annecy.

So great was his concentration on Tweed's convoy that he missed seeing another development. The helicopter had also changed course. It also was now heading at great speed for Annecy.

34

It was still daylight and very warm again when they reached Annecy. Their cars pulled up outside the estate agent, and there were lights inside. Tweed jumped out, followed by Paula, and as they walked inside Periot came forward to greet them.

'A surprise to see you again, sir. We were just closing but you are most welcome. Both of you.' He bowed to Paula. 'What can I do for you?'

'I've decided I'm interested in the Château de l'Air,' Tweed explained. 'Would it be possible to borrow the keys? We shall be driving past it.'

'Certainly you may have the keys.' Periot smiled. 'It will be dark when you get there but the electricity is still on. Excuse me for a moment.'

He returned quickly with a bunch of keys. As he handed them over he showed them which was for the front door, the back entrance and the main drawing room. He also gave Tweed a thick addressed envelope.

'To save a long journey you could post them back.'

'Thank you.' Tweed turned to go, then swung round. 'I believe you said you had inspected the place recently. How long ago would that be?'

'Let me see. At least a couple of months. Could be longer. If you are interested in buying we could try to come to some arrangement with Mr Masterson.'

'Oh, you can get in touch with him, then?'

'Yes. Via a poste restante address in Grenoble. A curious method of communication, I thought. But, as I told you, we never saw Mr Masterson. Rather an eccentric character I would imagine.'

'Thank you.'

Burgoyne was waiting for them outside. He lowered his voice so the others across the road could not hear him.

'I think it might be a wise precaution if I drove on ahead by myself. To check the road again. We can't assume Goslar has given up on his murderous attempts to wipe you out.'

'Good idea,' Tweed agreed.

'I'll check the route all the way to Geneva. If I spot anything I don't like the look of I'll call you on my mobile. No news from me is good news.'

'Where can we make contact again, then?'

'At the Richemond, I suggest. It's a very good hotel. See you . . .'

'The tough soldier plays his part,' observed Tweed as they watched Burgoyne drive off.

'I'd like to take another look at Annecy,' Paula said. 'Despite the bullet episode I think the place is enchanting.'

'Give us the excuse to have a drink,' remarked Newman who had joined them. 'Don't you think so, Marler?'

'If you say so.'

Tweed stared at him. He thought he'd detected a note of doubt in the way he had replied. At that moment Serena crossed the road to join them. Her pallid eyes gazed at Tweed.

'Did I hear you say you were going to spend a little time in Annecy?'

'Just a short while. It's such a beautiful town.'

'Then I'll come with you to that old bridge. When we drove off to Talloires I noticed a car-hire place. I'm going to hire a car and drive by myself to Geneva now.'

'Why?'

'Do I damned well have to give a reason? It looks as

though I have to. I don't think you're ever going to find Goslar. And I do have another photographic commission in Geneva. Quite a lucrative one – a fashion thing. By getting there this evening I can contact the director and he'll start setting things up for me. You can always get me at the Richemond.'

'It's up to you,' said Tweed. He looked at Nield who had crossed the road. 'Maybe you could drive Serena to this car-hire place.'

'Not necessary,' Serena said in her most commanding voice. 'If you drop me by the bridge it's only a short walk across that park.'

'As you wish.'

They got into their cars. Nield, on his own, was now following Marler, also on his own. It took no time at all to reach the Pont Perrière, to park their cars by the wall. Serena got out quickly, waved a hand, walked briskly away. Tweed followed her, watched her hurry across the park, saw there were lights in the car-hire establishment. He also noticed the helicopter had landed, that the pilot was seated in his cabin. He walked back as Paula began to cross the bridge.

Butler rushed forward, Walther in his hand. He pushed in front of Paula, raised his automatic, fired a shot at a shadowy figure at the entrance to an alley. The shadow vanished. Customers seated under umbrellas outside Les Corbières with drinks gazed in astonishment.

'What is it?' Tweed asked urgently.

'Man with gun just about to shoot Paula,' Butler said quickly. 'I saw him for a second by a street lamp, his yellow hair. It's the Yellow Man. I'm going after him.'

'Wait,' Tweed ordered.

'Time we cleaned this place out,' said Newman.

'I said wait.' Tweed had a map of Annecy in his hands. Swiftly he drew a cross, dividing Annecy into four quarters. 'Butler, this is your zone – where you saw the gunman. Newman, Marler, this is your section. Nield—'

'I'll go with Nield,' Trudy rapped out.

'Then this is your quarter. Paula will take this quarter with me. Scour the place. Hunt him down. I don't want him leaving Annecy alive. Watch the dark alleys. Go to it.'

Paula thought she had never known Tweed look so grim. Butler had disappeared inside the alley where he had seen the shadow. Trudy and Nield had gone, hurrying along the nearer bank of the river. Paula noticed Trudy had her right hand inside her fleece. She knew she was gripping her automatic. Newman palmed a Walther and ammo inside Tweed's jacket pocket, then moved off with Marler. Tweed and Paula crossed the bridge together. The temporary manager of Les Corbières came out to meet them, addressing Tweed.

'May I ask what the devil is going on?'

'You just did. It's a game we play with schoolboy cap pistols – and the winner makes a lot of money.'

'This is the oddest day I have experienced since I came to Annecy.'

'Livens the place up a bit. One of your customers inside wants his bill . . .'

They began walking along the rue Perrière, the same route they had taken when Paula missed death by inches. As they approached the same corner Tweed held Paula back. With the Walther in one hand and a torch he had brought from the car in the other, he peered round the corner. He turned on the torch. A powerful beam illuminated the wrecked 'pulpit' by the side of the strange tower. No sign of anyone. He nodded for Paula to join him.

'I thought Serena acted very weirdly,' Paula began. 'Her sudden rush to reach Geneva. I can't imagine the director of any fashion house being available by the time she gets there.'

'She did seem in a bit of a hurry.'

'I find her weird altogether. Her eyes.'

'Don't underestimate her extraordinary intelligence. Now, keep *your* eyes open – for any unexpected movement . . .'

The helicopter transporting Bancroft was flying slowly over the northern end of the lake, close to the children's park, when Bancroft gave the pilot a fresh order.

'Keep to your present height. Circle round a bit. I can see the four cars which have stopped outside the Old Town.'

He had the binoculars pressed to his eyes when he saw Tweed and Paula walk out of Periot's office. His tactic now was to check whether they were going to return to Annecy or proceed north towards Geneva. He wasn't going to be caught out again. The moment he saw three of the cars turning along the road to the Old Town he rapped out another instruction.

'Land in that park – where you did before. As fast as you can . . .'

The machine bumped down on the grass. Bancroft threw open his door, dropped to the ground. He waited impatiently for the engine to stop so he could be heard.

'Wait for me again. I may be some time.'

He hurried across the park at a diagonal, crossed the road, looked towards the bridge. He had chosen just the right place. He slipped into the shadow thrown by a closed shop, raised his binoculars. What he witnessed puzzled him. A burly man, close to Paula and Tweed, about to cross the bridge, produced a handgun, fired a single shot. The rest seemed to be confusion, then Tweed and his team departed in different directions.

He lowered his glasses. He didn't want to make another mistake. He decided quickly. Walking quickly along the road to the Old Town, he passed the wall where they had parked their cars. Then he went into the same bar he had visited earlier for a short time. Sitting down at a table by himself he ordered a drink.

I've got it right this time, he said to himself. They have to come back here to pick up their cars. Then I can go back to the chopper, follow them from the air.

Paula and Tweed walked slowly along the narrow street, which they had to themselves. Dusk was beginning to fall. The Old Town was illuminated by ancient lanterns, some projecting in iron brackets from the old walls, some perched on top of posts. The glass in the lanterns was amber-coloured and now they were lit they cast an eerie glow at intervals between the shadowed areas.

'This town is Heaven,' she said. She glanced at Tweed. 'You look angry.'

'Anger? No. Anger – like grief – upsets a man's judgement.'

'What are you trying to do here then?'

'Use the same strategy I have adopted ever since we left England. Eliminate all the enemies who might get in the way of our locating Goslar. In Paris I used Lasalle to get rid of the Americans – by getting Newman to plant false documents in Karnow's suite. In Geneva I used the Swiss police chief, Charpentier, to get rid of our pursuers. I certainly didn't intend it to end so brutally in that underground garage. My original idea had been to have Karnow himself – and Bate of the Special Branch, as it turned out – arrested and deported.'

'But you did eliminate them.'

'Yes, I fear I did. Now, here in Annecy, I am sure we

have both Bancroft and the Yellow Man. I need to eliminate both – without too much compunction considering what they are – so we can concentrate finally on Dr Goslar.'

'I think you've been very clever.'

'If you say so . . .'

They turned down another narrow street of amber glow. It led them to a wide stone walk alongside a river. The silence of the previous street had gone. Now Paula listened with delight to the sound of water gushing over a small weir. She pointed with her left hand to flowers draped over an iron bar above the weir. They were a riot of yellows, greens and whites, a massed fantasy of colour.

'That's beautiful. Early flowers out in full bloom. It must be the sun and the warmth they get here in the spring. This place is a galaxy of dreams. Look at those walls opposite, caught in the lamplight.'

She was gazing at ancient houses where their walls fell straight down to the river's edge. Their plaster hadn't been painted for a long time so they were a mosaic of ochre and brown. All the shutters were flung wide open. From inside one of them drifted the strains of violin music.

'I could stay here for ever,' she enthused.

'Just so long as you don't forget why we are here,' he warned.

Tweed's eyes had been everywhere, scanning the street in both directions. He even kept glancing up at the open windows. When he looked at Paula he saw her right hand was inside her shoulder bag and realized he had underestimated her. The hand, gripping her Browning, could appear in a flash.

'We'll next check this way,' he said.

Further along the street, deeper into Annecy, tables were laid outside a bar. As they drew nearer he saw locals sitting outside, enjoying drinks and snacks. The joyful chatter of their voices – people enjoying themselves – was a relief. Paula then spoke, showed her mind was still alert.

'That was the Yellow Man Butler fired at across the bridge, was it?'

'Harry said so and therefore it was him. He also said he'd caught a glimpse of his hair.'

'I don't know how we're ever going to find him in this maze.'

'By trawling it street by street – until we do.'

Trudy and Nield walked side by side as they explored their own district. She found her companion's presence comfortable. He made no attempt to talk just for the sake of talking. It was almost as though they had known each other for years and didn't need to keep up an endless stream of meaningless chatter. They were walking along a paved pedestrian area with a stone wall separating them from a fast-moving stream, part of the network of waterways which sprawls everywhere through old Annecy.

Ahead of them was a footbridge with a tumbling weir just beyond. No one else was about in this part of the town and the light was the haunting mixture of light and dark when dusk falls. They came to the bridge and paused. Nield looked at her.

'Let's cross over.' He checked the map divided into quarters Tweed had handed to him, because it was a complex district. 'We will still be in our area.'

Halfway across the bridge Trudy stopped, leaned on the rail to stare at the weir. It had a hypnotic effect on her. Brushing back her blaze of red hair, she watched the rushing water, the whirlpools which formed beneath it. Nield stood beside her, also leaning on the rail. He kept glancing along both banks of the stream, content to let her drink in her pleasure. She stood up straight.

'I suppose we'd better get on. Sorry to hold you up.'

'After what you've seen today a few minutes' restful contemplation is good for you. On the other side of the bridge where we're going is a dark narrow alley. I'll go ahead with my torch.'

They left the narrow bridge. On the far side, before venturing inside the alley, Nield paused. He wanted to give Trudy a last opportunity to look at the stream which had so caught her fancy. They stood together in the street which ran parallel to the stream along its other bank. Trudy took one last look at the weir.

It happened so quickly they were both taken by surprise. At one moment they were the only people in sight. The Yellow Man, running, appeared on the other side of the footbridge. Trudy was startled by how tall he was. He rushed over the bridge straight at them. Nield was lifting his Walther when the Yellow Man head-butted him in the chest. Nield fell back, knowing there was a hard stone wall behind him. As he fell he jerked his head forward to prevent his skull smashing into the wall. Trudy aimed her automatic but the assassin was gone, running inside the dark alley.

Butler appeared, moving at great speed. He charged over the footbridge like a rampaging bull. He stopped briefly at the entrance to the alley, Walther gripped in both hands. As the assassin passed under a wall lamp he fired. The bullet grazed the Yellow Man's right leg. He stumbled, recovered his balance, ran on as Butler followed.

Nield was at Butler's heels with Trudy just behind him. Yellow Man was zigzagging from one alley to another. Trudy lost all sense of direction, heard running feet behind her. Risking a look back she saw Newman and Marler racing along the same route.

Butler, pounding along, zigzagged, refusing to lose sight of his target. Suddenly Tweed and Paula appeared out of a side alley, joined the marathon pursuit.

Bancroft's impatience had given way. He walked out of the bar, headed across the park to the helicopter. He'd decided to get a better view of where all Tweed's team was from the air. He reached the chopper.

'What happens next?' asked the pilot, after throwing open the passenger door.

'We take off. We fly as low as you dare. Over the Old Town. I want to locate those terrorists fast.'

'There's a regulation as to how low I can fly over a built-up area,' the pilot warned.

Bancroft put on his headset as the pilot did the same. Now they'd be able to communicate above the roar of the engine and Bancroft was in no mood to argue. He pulled out another sheaf of hundred-franc notes, thrust it into the pilot's hands.

'Goddamnit!' he snarled into the mike. 'I want to see down inside every street, every alley. How much more do I have to pay to get you to do what I tell you?'

The pilot started the engine. The rotor blades began to swivel – tail rotor, main rotor. They had their backs to the Old Town so neither of them saw what was happening, what had happened.

The Yellow Man emerged from the Old Town into the children's park. Butler was about two hundred yards behind him. About the same distance behind Butler the others had appeared, running across the park.

Seeing the helicopter, the assassin knew he had found his way to escape his pursuers. He was short of breath now but his powerful legs kept running. He'd threaten the pilot with his Smith & Wesson, force the pilot to take him aboard.

His one fear was Butler. The bastard had clung to him like a leech through the labyrinth of alleys. He looked back to see how close Butler was, kept running at high speed across the soft grass. It was when he looked back that Butler hurled the grenade he'd grabbed out of his pocket. The missile soared through the air, landed close behind its target.

The Yellow Man couldn't stop looking back. For once in his murderous life he was scared stiff. When the grenade detonated it would probably be close enough to reach him. The grenade lay on the ground, didn't detonate. The Yellow Man couldn't believe his luck.

He turned to face the front and opened his mouth to scream. The main rotor blade struck him just below the jaw, sliced off his head. It flew through the air like a melon, a leaking red melon. The Yellow Man's trunk fell forward, brushing against the side of the chopper's fuselage as the machine took off.

35

They were driving north along the N201 in the direction of Geneva. Only three cars made up the convoy this time. The lead vehicle was Marler's, who was driving with Butler. Behind him came Nield, driving alone. In the third and last car Newman was behind the wheel with Paula alongside him. His passengers in the rear seats were Tweed and Trudy.

'No message yet from Chance,' Paula called out.

'Not yet,' Tweed agreed. 'But he'll still be some-where on the road between here and the city.'

After the 'execution' of the Yellow Man, as Newman

had referred to the event, Tweed had ordered everyone to move straight back to the parked cars. He had urged them to walk without appearing to be in a hurry to get away from the park. There had been no one else about to witness what happened and it was Paula who had made the observation.

'Thank Heaven there were no children left in the park,' she had said.

'All gone home for supper, fortunately,' Tweed had remarked.

They had been driving away from the Old Town when Newman had made a suggestion just before Tweed voiced the idea himself. Newman had parked by a public phone box, looked up the number of the local police station, and spoken through a silk handkerchief when he called it – to report that he had seen a body in the park. He had ended the call when asked for his name. He had also taken the precaution of speaking in French.

It was quite dark now and Paula found herself gazing along the headlight beams as they drove within the speed limit. After a while she turned to look at Trudy, to see how she was feeling. Trudy seemed to read her mind.

'I'm OK,' she responded with a smile. 'How many people had that awful man beheaded? You told me about him when you came to see me in my room at the Richemond.'

'One in London, a reporter called Sam Sneed. Two in Paris – one was a bookseller, the other an innocent landlady. The bookseller was equally innocent. But there were others. He was known as the most professional assassin in Europe.'

'Then how ironic,' Trudy commented, 'that he ended up being beheaded himself in an accident.'

'Which shows that there is some justice in the world,' Newman said.

'Will we ever know who he was?' Trudy wondered.

'We know now,' Tweed told her. He extracted a British passport from his pocket. 'Don't worry – Butler slipped it out of his jacket before anything had tainted it.' He meant blood. 'Have a look.'

'Darcy Stapleton,' she read out aloud. 'Born in Manchester. Aged forty-two. He'd been to the States. There's a Non-Immigrant visa stamped in it by the embassy in London.' She handed it back. 'His photograph is authentic. I caught a good look at him when he rushed over that footbridge and headbutted poor Pete Nield.'

'We can trace where he lived when we get back,' Tweed said. 'I have a friend who is high up in Scotland Yard. That is if the passport is genuine, which I doubt.'

'So that only leaves Bancroft,' Trudy said quietly. 'Apart from Dr Goslar, of course.'

'No news still from Beck?' Paula asked.

'Not a whisper,' Tweed replied. 'And I do need that call by the time we reach Geneva. But first we must explore the Château de l'Air.'

'Expect to find anything there?' enquired Newman sceptically.

'We have to try. Leave no stone unturned, to coin a cliché. At some point Goslar must slip up.'

'He didn't ten years ago,' Newman reminded Tweed.

'Most important, while I remember. When we do get there we won't risk driving up the main entrance – not after that anti-personnel mine Burgoyne spotted. But I did notice another track leading up to the crest near the mansion when we were there this morning. So we must look out for an earlier entrance of some sort. Bob, better

343

warn Marler about that now. The best way is to risk using your mobile . . .'

'At least there's no sign of Bancroft following us,' Paula commented. 'And no more helicopters, thank goodness. Haven't heard one since we left Annecy.'

In this assumption Paula could not have been more wrong.

When their helicopter took off from the children's park neither the pilot nor Bancroft was aware of the violence their machine had committed. They were staring towards the eastern shore of the lake as they gained height. When the chopper changed direction, on Bancroft's orders, he used binoculars and was just in time to see the three cars leaving Annecy.

'The terrorists are heading back towards Geneva,' he reported. 'It will be easy to track them by their headlights. I want you to gain much more height, then move away from the highway so they can't hear our engine.'

'They might see the port and starboard lights. Obligatory when flying at night. I'm not risking losing my licence.'

'Goddamnit! That's why I told you to gain plenty of height. They are not likely to see us from any of the cars. Just do as I tell you. I'm paying you enough. And any minute now it will be dark.'

'There will be a moon.'

'I do not like people who argue with me. Just do as I've told you.'

It was soon dark. The pilot gained height as instructed. He also changed course, flying well away from the highway. Bancroft proved to be right. Through his binoculars he was able to track Tweed's convoy by their headlights. He settled down, assuming his quarry was returning to Geneva. But he still kept the three cars under observation.

'I expect everyone is hungry,' Tweed remarked at one point. 'We will be able to refuel palatially when we reach the Richemond.'

'I can go for hours without food,' Trudy assured him. 'Just so long as I've had a big breakfast, which I did. It's an American habit I brought back with me. I'm going to cure myself of it.'

'Why do that?' Paula asked.

'Because I hate anything American. The US is a land of barbarians.'

They then travelled a long distance in silence. Tweed had relaxed, his back firmly against the seat. He might have been asleep but when Trudy looked at him his eyes were wide open. She kept quiet, sensing that he was sunk deeply in thought. Paula peered out of her side window, stared.

'I can see a winking light high up and a long way off to our right. It couldn't be that helicopter, could it?'

'You're thinking of Bancroft,' Newman told her.

'So am I,' said Trudy. 'I never stop thinking about Bancroft.'

Her tone was grim. Paula decided it would be best not to enter into conversation with her on that subject. They drove further on. The moon had risen, casting a luminous glow over the countryside they were passing through. She lowered her window and an icy blast blew in. She hastily shut it again.

'I thought it was getting much colder,' she remarked.

'That's the Bise wind blowing off Mont Blanc,' Newman explained. 'At times it freezes this part of France. I remember it from long ago. I was down here visiting a girl friend. A shade from the past.'

'And that's what we are pursuing,' Tweed said, his voice very alert. 'A very dark shade from the past. Dr Goslar. The most evil man I have ever fought at arm's length.'

'Let's hope we confront the swine face to face this time,' Newman responded.

'If he hasn't already disappeared again to the East. This time to a different East – the Middle East . . .'

He had just spoken when Newman leaned forward, staring at something ahead of them. As he did so he reduced speed a lot. Paula peered through the windscreen, realized what he had seen. A dense white mist was swirling across the highway. She recalled the encounter with the Arab fanatics on their way from Geneva in the morning.

'At least we've had no warning from Burgoyne of an ambush,' she remarked.

'Unless he ran into them and is no longer in a state to warn us,' Trudy said quietly.

'I don't think Burgoyne is a man who would run into anything,' Tweed said flatly. 'Why have we stopped, Bob?'

'Because Marler has stopped. Nield has stopped. And both of them are here on foot.'

'We'll get out and see what's happening.'

'Tweed,' Paula asked, 'could you hand me my fleece? I bet it's like Siberia outside.'

The mist swirled around them as they alighted. To Paula, for a moment, she thought ghosts were materializing out of the mist. Then she saw they were Marler and Nield. Marler spoke first in his normal way – calm, terse, cooler than the mist floating everywhere.

'I thought we were close to that old suspension bridge. I spotted an old farm gate with a crumbling tarmacadam track behind it. I'm sure this is the back way to the château. Don't be startled – you will hear a grinding engine starting up. Butler found behind the gate a huge excavator with one of those big scoops in front. The machine was padlocked but he said he'd get that open in a tick – and the fuel gauge shows a full tank. There, hear it?'

The question was superfluous. They all heard the grinding noise of heavy machinery starting up. At first it started, stopped, started again. Then it got into its stride and was a steady humming sound, broken at regular intervals by heavy metal thumping the ground.

'May I ask what is happening?' Tweed enquired. 'It's making enough racket to wake the dead. If there is anyone inside the château it will be like a cavalry charge announcing our arrival.'

'Do you really expect to find anyone inside?' Marler asked.

'Well, no. Goslar has gone somewhere else. Always moving on.'

'It was Butler's idea,' Marler explained. 'Have you fogotten that landmine Burgoyne spotted, just in time, at the main entrance? Harry, in his youth, worked for a quarry firm. Used to operate a similar machine. He's testing the ground ahead of us while we drive behind him. Actually, it was an anti-personnel mine Burgoyne detonated. If the scoop he keeps hammering down hits one it will warn us.'

'I don't like that,' Paula said vehemently. 'It could kill Harry.'

'Harry says it wouldn't. It might mess up the scoop but he's sitting well back in the control cab. I suggest we get cracking. I'll drive behind the machine, Nield will drive his own car behind me, then Bob can bring up the rear with Tweed, Paula and Trudy as passengers. All systems go . . .'

Paula peered through the windscreen as they moved past the broken-down gate and started bumping over the potholed road. The mist cleared suddenly. She saw the side road curving and climbing up a steep hill with grassy fields on either side. The moon was casting a strong light and now she could see the château, perched by itself on the top of the ridge.

It was a large oblong four-storey building of no great beauty. It had a mansard roof peppered with tiny oval dormer windows, which looked in danger of sliding off at any moment. Paula observed that all the windows had their shutters closed, some of them tilted at an angle. It was an old hulk no one had bothered to preserve for many years. Stone steps led up to a terrace running the full length of the front of the château.

'Not a masterpiece,' she commented.

'I don't think Goslar is interested in fine architecture,' Tweed replied. 'Gargoyle Towers on Dartmoor was an ugly brute. He simply needs space and isolation to perfect his weapon. Now what is Harry doing?'

Butler had driven the machine more than halfway up the drive to the château. He had suddenly turned off the bumpy road, had steered the machine onto the grass. Getting out of the cab, he ran back to Nield's car, which stopped to let him climb into the front passenger seat.

'Harry,' Newman said, 'has decided – correctly, I'm sure – that they didn't lay any mines on this side of the drive. Soon, Tweed, you'll be opening the front door. What's the betting we find nothing inside?'

'I repeat, Goslar has to make a mistake sometime. So we make the most thorough search of this property.'

'I wonder where that helicopter went to,' Paula mused.

*

Leaning forward in the copilot's seat, Bancroft had observed everything from a distance. He was puzzled when he saw the convoy stop as it reached the bank of mist. Then he assumed they were being cautious. When the mist cleared he was even more puzzled – watching the large machine with the scoop rising and falling as it made its way up a drive leading to a château. He decided quickly when he saw the cars following it.

'That machine must be making one hell of a row. It will cover the sound of your engine. See that plateau halfway down the steep slope running from the side of the château? You could land me there, wait for me to come back.'

'Anything you say,' the pilot agreed wearily.

Still some distance from the château, he lost altitude, flying now about a hundred feet above the ground. Smoothly, he settled the chopper on the plateau, switched off his engine.

'Wait a minute,' he warned. 'Don't get out until I tell you. The rotor blades are dangerous.'

Given the word, Bancroft opened the door, dropped to the plateau. Before beginning his steep climb up the rest of the slope he took out his Smith & Wesson from its holster. He was armed with the .22 automatic model, which had a magazine capacity of ten rounds. More than enough to kill all of them.

I'll try and get Tweed last, he said to himself. Ram the muzzle inside his mouth and ask him where Goslar is before I pull the trigger. If Goslar himself is inside this place I'll use the same technique to make him tell me where the weapon is. This is where I win the battle. Then return to Washington. Karnow's dead. I'll be the next chief of Unit Four.

With these triumphant thoughts in his mind Bancroft increased the pace of his difficult climb up the slope. A short while later he reached the top. The side of the château lay before him.

36

By the time the three cars had parked under the terrace and turned off their engines, the pilot of the invisible helicopter below them had also switched off. A weird stillness descended, a silence broken only by their footsteps as they mounted to the terrace.

Something about the atmosphere disturbed Paula. She looked up at the closed shutters, which did not invite entrance. Tweed was holding the bunch of keys Periot had given him, the largest one projecting, the key to the tall, wide double front doors. He pursed his lips, looked sideways, caught Butler's gaze.

'I don't think so,' he said.

'I can't see any giveaway wiring round them,' Butler replied, the beam of the torch in his left hand sweeping round the entrance's top, sides and bottom. 'But I still don't think this is the place to enter.'

'What do you suggest, then?'

'A window at the side,' Butler said firmly, pointing to his right.

'I see you've brought your tool kit.'

'Won't take me a moment to find a way in. Let's get on with it – if you agree.'

'I agree.'

'So do I,' Paula whispered to Tweed as Butler left them. 'Without my fleece I'd be a statue of ice. Lord, it's cold up here.'

'The mist is coming up behind us. What was that wind you mentioned, Bob?' Tweed asked.

'The Bise. Straight off Mont Blanc.'

'Oh, do stop reminding us,' Paula chided him as they followed Butler, who had disappeared round the side of the mansion. 'Are you warm enough, Trudy?'

'I'm OK,' Trudy assured her with a smile. 'In New York the temperature can drop out of sight in January. In February and March, too. This coat is fur-lined – and so are my boots. And can you tell me what Butler is doing?'

They had walked round the corner at the end of the mansion. A stone ramp led down from the terrace to ground level. Further along Butler was crouched down with Nield helping him. They had the shutters of a window open, pushed back against the wall. Butler was working a long steel bar, bevelled at one end, inserting it under a security lock.

'What is that tool?' Trudy asked.

'I think he calls it a jemmy,' Newman told her. 'It levers a lock open, often without leaving a trace.'

As he spoke Butler took hold of the lower sash, heaved it up until it was wide open. Between his teeth he held a pencil torch. Leaning forward, he peered inside, nodded to himself.

'He was checking for a trip-wire,' Newman explained. 'Or any other extra security device. Looks all clear.'

Butler had wriggled his burly body through the opening, vanished. Holding a Walther, the slimmer Nield followed him with ease. They waited a short time, then the lights came on inside the room. It was as per Tweed's earlier instruction given on the terrace.

'Switch on the lights in every room in the house, one by one.'

Trudy peered inside. She saw Butler, gun in hand, standing to one side of the door inside the large room while Nield stood on the other. They looked out, then Butler disappeared. Nield followed him after thirty seconds. It was an operation which had been practised over and over again at the training mansion in Surrey.

'I'm going in now,' said Trudy.

Paula went in after her, followed by Newman who had been going to enter first. Tweed stood alone for a moment, listening. The mist had now reached the mansion, was swirling everywhere. He had cold droplets on his face. He climbed in, found Paula waiting for him.

'Look at it,' she exclaimed. 'Clean as a whistle. Even the wide window ledges have been washed down.'

'Goslar's trademark,' Tweed said and grunted.

'And this room was . . .' Paula began.

'The dining room, probably. With French windows at the back giving, I suspect, a panoramic view in daylight. You've noticed in that opposite wall one of those old-fashioned serving hatches?'

'Yes, so the kitchen must be behind that wall.'

Tweed turned back to the open window. Leaning out he took hold of a shutter, pulled it to. As soon as he let go it swung open again. He pulled a face.

'So we can't do anything about that.'

'They've switched on more lights. Let's explore.'

She swung round, aiming her Browning as she heard a noise outside the open window. Marler appeared, holding his Armalite in his right hand, his left raised in a salute. He grinned.

'Don't shoot. I'm just delivering the milk. Actually, I was checking all round the house. Quite a walk. All shutters firmly closed. Back door locked.'

'You gave me a shock,' Paula chided him. 'Don't do that again.'

'I don't like leaving that window open, but there's nothing we can do about it,' said Tweed. 'Let's see what the others are up to.'

Marler had already disappeared after Butler and Nield. Gazing cautiously round the open door, as she

352

had been trained to do, Paula saw Butler pressed against a wall, peering upwards. She walked into what she realized was a vast hall with the double entrance doors leading from the terrace in the middle of the far wall. Nield was crouched a few yards beyond Butler, also staring up. She caught up with Trudy, who was gazing up over Butler, who had now dropped into a crouch.

She was looking up a grand curving staircase which split into two at a landing halfway up. No carpets anywhere. Not a single stick of furniture. Not even a film of dust. She whispered to Tweed, 'It's eerie. It's so incredibly clean. No dust even. Like a haunted house.'

'Goslar's trademark,' he repeated. 'I'm willing to bet there's not one single fingerprint in the whole place. As to dust, it's high up, so far from any traffic on the road miles below.'

'And our footsteps don't make the slightest sound. I find that eerie too.'

She was referring to the fact that everyone had rubber soles on their footwear. Even Trudy's boots were rubber-soled. Newman opened a door, reached in, switched on the light. As Paula had guessed, it was the kitchen, a large room without any equipment. Tweed pointed to dents in the wooden floor.

'Things like the fridge and freezer and cooker stood there – and were taken away. Goslar leaves nothing which might give us a clue.'

Tweed walked round, looking down, looking up. Newman shrugged in exasperation.

'Just so long as we don't find another bloody pair of useless gloves.'

They explored a huge drawing room leading off the hall which had a polished woodblock floor. Here there were wall lights – ancient lanterns which threw a soft glow over the room. While they explored more rooms

Marler had taken up station at the bottom of the wide staircase, his eyes never leaving the curving landing high up.

'Ah!' said Tweed as they opened another door, turned on lights. 'I would say this was the library. Obvious remark.'

He was referring to bookcases which lined the walls from ceiling to floor. They had glass-fronted doors and Tweed quickly walked along, peering into all of them with Paula behind him. She sighed audibly.

'They've even carefully washed the shelves behind the bookcase doors. You were hoping for something here, weren't you?'

'Yes – and no. Where have you been, Newman?'

'Enjoying myself – checking the toilets. Old-fashioned but very clean. We'd better look at the upstairs, although it will be a waste of time.'

'Wait in the hall while Pete and I take a shufti,' ordered Butler, using the odd Arabic word.

Trudy, standing with the others in the hall, was fascinated at what happened next. Nield went up first, slowly, his left hand on the banister. Several treads behind him Butler followed, keeping to the wall side, staring up all the time, like Nield. Both men had guns in their hands.

They reached the landing, which had stone pillars at intervals, opened several doors, switched on lights. Then they gestured for the others to follow. Trudy skipped up the many treads like a young fawn. Paula was impressed by her agility, followed her and went inside a huge bedroom. Trudy came out, passing her.

'Not a damned thing. The door in the wall leads to the bathroom. In case you feel like a bath.'

Left to herself, Paula walked slowly, looking at the floor, at the wide window ledges, at the chandelier light which was suspended from the ceiling. She opened the side door, saw the point of Trudy's joke. There was a toilet and an enormous old-fashioned bath with claw legs. She went back into the bedroom, started walking along the edges of the room. Her foot caught something.

Bending down, she saw the floor had dropped slightly from the skirting board, leaving a gap. Slightly protruding, something glittered, the something which her shoe had brushed against. She eased it out, stood up as Tweed entered. She looked at him.

'I've found something. Goslar's first mistake, maybe.'

'What is it?'

'Looks like a large piece of tortoiseshell. Here you are.'

Tweed took it from her, sat down on a window ledge. Placing what she had given him in his lap, he took off his horn-rims, polished them on a clean handkerchief, put the horn-rims back on the bridge of his nose. Then he picked up her discovery, studied it, held it up to the light.

'It doesn't look like normal tortoiseshell. Remember what Cord Dillon told me? Some rumour about Goslar visiting the Galapagos Islands, stealing several giant turtles. This is a very unusual piece. Turtles,' he repeated. 'Then the fisherman with the distinctive sail on his boat who saw them. Later he was found murdered in Guayaquil, the port in Ecuador on the South American mainland.'

'Just rumours I thought Cord Dillon told you.'

Tweed held up the specimen Paula had discovered.

'This isn't a rumour.'

When Bancroft reached the top of the slope he saw, almost opposite him, the open window with the shutters thrown back. He listened carefully before easing his way into the lighted room. His right hand held the Smith & Wesson. He stood still, listened again. He heard creaking boards above him.

Goddamnit! he thought. If they're all upstairs – scattered in different rooms – they're the perfect target . . .

He peered into the vast hall. Empty. Quietly he checked all rooms downstairs. Empty. For the second time he looked up the great staircase leading to the landing. Empty. He began walking up the long curving staircase slowly, his gun by his side. He was two-thirds of the way up when he took the precaution of looking up at the landing again. Trudy appeared from behind a pillar near the top of the staircase, automatic in her hand.

She stared down at Bancroft, her face a frozen mask. Bancroft stared back at her. Normally he'd have raised his weapon at once, but he was in shock. His voice was hoarse and quiet when he spoke.

'Trudy! What the hell are you doing here with these people?'

'Do you remember Walter Jewels Baron?' she asked in a whisper.

'Who?'

'You drove to a small town in Virginia. To two houses on their own just outside the town. On a mission. To kill Walt Baron, accountant to Unit Four. You greeted him amiably. Then you rammed the muzzle of your gun inside his mouth, blew off the back of his head. I was his wife. I am his widow . . .'

Bancroft started to elevate his gun. She fired her first shot. It hit him in his right shoulder. He dropped his own weapon. It clattered down the stairs. His left hand grabbed the banister. She fired again. The bullet entered his stomach. He doubled over in agony, groaning. She fired six more times in rapid succession, emptied the

356

magazine. Both his arms jerked up. Already dead, he toppled backwards down the stairs, slithering down the last few treads. The others had just rushed out on to the landing when his corpse reached the hall floor.

37

Newman drove along the bumpy road from the château, stopped close to the broken-down gate leading to the highway. Paula, who had had a word with Marler before leaving the terrace, sat next to him. In the rear seats Tweed had Trudy beside him. Now they waited for the other two cars to join them.

'What happened to it?' Trudy asked.

'It,' said Tweed quietly, 'is being put in a place where no one will find it for ages. Probably ever.'

By 'it', Paula knew Trudy was referring to Bancroft's body. Marler had told her they had discovered the ideal place – a septic tank in the back garden, the lid half-covered with grass. Butler had prised the lid off and, with Nield's aid, they were dropping the corpse inside the tank before replacing the lid. Paula thought it was a suitable resting place for Bancroft.

'You will never hear a word about him again,' Tweed assured his redheaded companion.

Trudy's hands were shaking. She clasped them together. Her face was ashen. Reaching down between his feet, Tweed unzipped a small canvas bag, produced a flask, a spoon, a carton of sugar. Taking the top off, he carefully poured tea into it, relieved to see it was steaming. The flask had been wrapped in cloths to keep the contents hot – and the weather in Annecy had helped.

He used the spoon to add sugar from a carton to the tea. He stirred it, then turned to Trudy.

'Drink some of this. Sweetened tea is the best thing when you are in shock.'

She grasped the plastic cup with both hands. It wobbled. Tweed placed a hand underneath it to help her from spilling it. At first she sipped, then she began to drink mouthfuls. She emptied the cup and handed it back.

'Thank you so much. That really is much better.'

'You've kept that a secret,' Paula accused him, twisting round in her seat. 'Where did that come from?'

'Just before we left the Richemond I visited the chef in his kitchen. He was most obliging. Even supplied the canvas bag. I kept it for an emergency.'

'I think I rank as an emergency,' Trudy said, turning to him with a hint of a smile. 'Any more for the fake invalid?'

He gave her another cup. This time she was able to cope with it by herself. Paula saw colour beginning to return to her face. Trudy winked at Paula, who was surprised at how swiftly Trudy was returning to her normal self.

'My hair's a mess,' Trudy decided.

She began to ferret in her bag. Paula gave her a comb and a pocket mirror. Trudy looked sideways at Tweed before she started work.

'Do excuse me. I wouldn't normally do this in public.'

'But we're not public,' Tweed replied. 'We're your friends.'

'I do know that – and I do appreciate it . . .'

She used her hand and the comb to bring order back to her blazing red mane. Handing back comb and mirror to Paula, she sighed deeply.

'Thanks. Now I feel half-civilized. And the mist is returning.'

A white fog shrouded the car. A few minutes later they heard the cars from the château crawling down behind them, stopping. Marler jumped out and Tweed lowered his window. Glancing at Trudy, Marler turned away from her so only Tweed could see his movement. He gave the thumbs-up sign. They had disposed of the body. He leaned in.

'So what next?'

At that moment Tweed's mobile started to buzz. He was taking it from his pocket when Newman spoke urgently.

'Burgoyne?'

'Hello,' Tweed said.

'Arthur here,' a familiar voice answered. Beck. 'I am a trifle nervous, knowing the instrument you are using. I'm speaking from a public phone box. How long before you get back here?'

'At a rough guess, one hour.'

'Well, you'll find Harrington, Minister of General Security, waiting for you at the Richemond. He knows you're staying there. I heard him saying at reception that his friend, Tweed, was staying here, and asking for his room number. The trainee receptionist told him. I complained to the manager. No sign of that receptionist now. He's been given his marching orders. The Richemond prides itself on its discretion.'

' "Friend"!' Tweed snorted. 'When did the bastard arrive?'

'On a late-morning flight from London. I shouldn't say it, but I do not like him.'

'He's the man they invented the word *arrogant* for. Thanks for the warning. Anything else?'

'Yes. I should have put this first. I have three different prospects for properties you're interested in. Won't give you them over the phone. Any luck down there?'

'One or two interesting events. Tell you later. Where can I meet you?'

'I'll stay in the lobby at the Richemond until you arrive. Take care.'

Tweed put his phone back in his pocket. Newman turned round to face him.

'Who is the bastard?'

'The Right Honourable Aubrey Courtney Harrington, who has arrived in Geneva and is waiting to see me. That I could do without at this vital stage. I could do without it at any time.'

'I wonder how he knew you were in Geneva?' Paula speculated.

'My guess is that Bate, in that underground garage and before he was killed, phoned His Lordship to report where he was – where I was. My first task when we get back is to get Harrington out of Geneva. To anywhere. Singapore would be a good idea.'

'Anything else?' asked Newman.

'Yes. The important thing. Beck has located three properties, any of which might be occupied by Goslar.'

'So how do you decide which is the right one?'

'Frankly, I have no idea.'

Marler had remained by the open window, listening to every word. He started stamping his feet, clapping his gloved hands together. Then he spoke.

'I don't trust the route back to Geneva. I know we haven't heard from Burgoyne, but he may have walked into something he couldn't handle. So I suggest the same driving sequence. I go in front – with Butler at my side – and in the car behind me Nield drives. You bring up the rear. It's worked so far.'

'Agreed,' said Tweed, 'if that's all right with you, Bob.'

'Marler is right,' Newman agreed. 'They can just ease their cars past me and still stay on the drive. Let's get the show on the road.'

'You don't think we're going to run into trouble again?' Paula queried.

'No guarantees. And Marler's instinct for danger has

so often proved to be right in the past. We're not out of the wood yet.'

When the two cars had driven past on to the highway Newman followed. They had to crawl. The mist was now very dense and their foglamp beams penetrated only a few yards. Paula glanced back. Trudy had fallen fast asleep, her head resting on Tweed's shoulder. Tweed looked back at her, smiled briefly, raised his eyebrows. As much as to say, *what other choice do I have?*

38

They crawled on. Almost at once they reached the old suspension bridge and the mist thinned. Paula stared at the ancient structure, which looked unreal – with coils of mist curling round the cables. She glanced back. Trudy had opened her eyes, had seen where they were. At the place where a solitary Arab had come close to heaving her down into the bottomless valley. Paula could have sworn Trudy gave a little shrug with her elegant shoulders, shut her eyes, fell asleep again. Nerves of steel, Paula said to herself.

Within minutes the mist vanished. The moon shone down, illuminating the deserted highway ahead clearly. The three cars increased speed, drove on and on. All Newman had to do was to follow the red rear lights of Nield's car. He straightened up. His driving was becoming too automatic.

They had travelled some distance, but were still quite a way from Geneva, when it happened.

In Marler's lead car Butler had started to study a map, trying to locate where they were. He took out a glasses case, extracted a pair of horn-rims, perched them on his nose. Marler stared at him, then decided to comment.

'I didn't know you needed glasses.'

'Just for the small print,' replied Butler, embarrassed. 'I got them recently before we left London. I can easily read a novel without them, a newspaper. But it's the small print in the index of a map I find difficult.'

'You were wise to get them then.'

'Didn't like going to the ruddy optician. They make such a song and dance about it. To justify their fat fees, I imagine. The woman who saw me said map indexes are in four-point print. Very small. She told me novels are in ten- or twelve-point print. A bloody big difference.'

'Where are we, then?'

'No idea. That village we passed through didn't seem to have a name.'

'No villages round here. No sign of anyone. You'd think a meteor had wiped everyone off the surface of the planet.'

Marler's remark was apt. They were driving up a gentle hill. On their left hedges lined the highway and beyond them fields stretched away for ever. On their right a steep hill slope climbed. A few feet from the highway black stands of fir trees mounted the hill as though about to sweep down and overwhelm them. The moon illuminated the highway clearly – and the cars moving along it. Marler was driving at a moderate speed, remembering there were sudden sharp bends.

He arrived at one and slowed down further. He was rounding it when some kind of large animal scuttered across in front of him. He slowed almost to a stop. The animal vanished under the hedge to their left. The bullet hit his bonnet, ricocheted off at an angle. If Marler hadn't slowed for the animal Butler would have been killed.

Marler switched off engine and headlights, grabbed his Armalite, was out of the car as Butler left on his own side. Marler called out his order quickly.

'Sniper. In the trees. I'm going straight in from the road.'

'I'll make a wide circuit, try and get up behind him.'

A second bullet whipped past Marler's shoulder just before he had plunged up the hill, into the trees. Behind them Nield realized what was happening, pulled up, switched off his own engine and headlights.

Newman had also stopped, had taken the same precautions. Behind him Trudy woke up, totally alert. She already had her automatic in her hand. Tweed stared at her.

'I heard a bullet hit something metallic, probably Marler's car,' she said. 'I'll give them a hand.'

'You will please stay exactly where you are,' Tweed told her in a kindly tone. 'They can deal with it.'

He was startled for the second time by Trudy's quicksilver reaction. The first time had been when he stood on the landing at the château. Bancroft's body had already hit the hall floor, was tumbled in an untidy heap. Obviously as dead as dead can be. *Trudy, at the top of the staircase, had extracted the empty magazine, inserted a fresh one.* Most professional.

'They were heading up the bank on the right side,' Newman warned. 'We'll get out of the car and shelter behind it, crouched down. Tweed, Paula, don't get out on your side. Wriggle your way over to the left and join us.'

Marler, who had caught a glimpse of a flash from the forest when the first bullet arrived, was slowly advancing up between the tree trunks. He held his Armalite at the high port, ready for a moment when he could shoot very fast. Butler had vanished some way over to his right.

Butler was circling as he climbed. Shafts of moonlight shone on the ground between the trees. He was avoiding stepping on last year's dried leaves – crumbling them could announce his presence. Instead, he trod on cushions of moss, silent as a phantom. He heard the sound of running water to his right, moved towards it.

A narrow stream gushed down, tumbling over rocks, some of them flat, acting as stepping stones. He crossed over to the far side, then continued climbing, following the course of the stream. Its sound would muffle his steady upward approach. He was aiming to reach the top of the hill, his Walther held in his hand.

The nearer he came to the top the more moonlight flooded through. He began to move faster, his head swivelling to his left. He was worried about Marler, who had to be moving up towards a head-on collision with the sniper. It was cold inside the dank forest, but he welcomed the cold – it gave an extra edge to his alertness. He was thankful when the stream's course moved to his left, closer to where the sniper had to be hiding.

He reached the summit unexpectedly. Beyond the forest a great panorama of the French countryside spread away for miles. Still crouching, he began to make his way along the top of the ridge, then he stopped. His eye had caught movement lower down, below him.

Stationed behind a tall tree was a squat shadowy figure. It was holding a rifle loosely, muzzle pointing upwards. Butler now moved very slowly, downwards, treading always on moss. He was close to the squat figure when he became alarmed. Marler was climbing slowly up towards it, obviously couldn't see the squat sniper. Butler did not panic. He kept moving downwards, watching where he placed his feet. The sniper suddenly came alive, raised his rifle to his shoulder, held it steady. Butler guessed he had Marler in the cross-hairs of his weapon.

He aimed the muzzle of his Walther within a foot of the back of the sniper's head, pressed the trigger. The squat man fell forward, half his head blown away, a cloth dangling from what was left of the head. Butler bent down, took hold of an end of the cloth untainted with blood, pulled it free. It was a green headband.

'Why they're so keen on green I wouldn't know,' Butler remarked.

'You saved me there,' Marler told him. 'I couldn't see him. Now where are you going?'

Butler, still holding the end of the headband, walked across to the stream, dropped it in. He watched it caught up in a swirl of water, washed down way out of sight. Then he straightened up, looked at Marler.

'All in a day's work. Do we have to move the body?'

'No point.' Marler paused. 'You realize he thought he was shooting Tweed when that first bullet hit the bonnet?'

'Why would he think that?'

'He'd have been given a vague description. You sat beside me wearing those horn-rims – so like Tweed's.'

'I'll have to change the frames,' Butler ruminated. 'I just took the nearest ones to get out of the place.'

Newman, by himself, met them as they emerged from the forest. He had a grim expression. He listened while Marler explained in a few words what had taken place.

'I don't think I'll mention to anyone it was an Arab,' he decided. 'Trudy is holding up amazingly well but she's gone through enough already for one day. We'll just say "a sniper", and leave it at that.'

'I think you underestimate her,' said Tweed, who

365

had appeared behind Newman. 'Now I think we'd better get on back to Geneva. I'll need a stiff drink before I manipulate Harrington.'

'What happened?' asked Trudy as Newman got behind the wheel while Tweed settled in beside her.

'A sniper,' Tweed said. 'Just one. Goslar is artful. This morning we had a massed attack. Didn't work. So this time he uses a solitary sniper. Marler and Butler dealt with him.'

'Was it another Arab, then?' she pressed.

Newman turned round to look at her. Tweed suppressed a smile before answering.

'Yes, it was.'

'It looks to me as though Goslar has already decided that he can get the biggest price for his weapon from that Arab state where the fundamentalists have taken over,' she remarked. 'Hence the ease with which he can get hold of Arabs to attack us.'

'You could be right.'

Inwardly Tweed was admiring the way she had hit the nail on the head. Her supposition exactly fitted in with his own private reading of the situation. Newman had already started driving again, keeping up with Nield, who was pressing his foot down.

'We didn't get any warning from Burgoyne,' Trudy went on.

'Not surprising,' Tweed explained. 'The sniper would have been informed we were in three cars. I think he was after me, probably. You've seen the way Burgoyne drives. The sniper would see one car only coming at speed – I doubt if the mist was about then. Therefore Burgoyne wouldn't have been the sniper's target – assuming in any case that he'd have a cat's chance in hell of hitting him.'

'And I imagine by now Serena will have arrived at the Richemond,' Trudy continued. 'I suppose she and

Burgoyne will get there about the same time in their separate cars.'

She does cover the waterfront, thought Paula, approvingly. I'd expect her to be exhausted after what happened inside the château.

'I think Serena will arrive ahead of Burgoyne,' Tweed commented. 'I sensed that when she drives she goes like the wind. In any case, she wouldn't be checking ambush points – which in places would slow Burgoyne down.'

'Would it be a good idea to phone her? I think she wasn't in the best of moods when she left us.'

'Good idea,' agreed Tweed.

He had to dial three times before he got through to the Richemond. Paula glanced back. Trudy had fallen asleep again, her head on Tweed's shoulder. The best medicine for her, Paula thought.

'Am I speaking to reception at the Richemond? Good, I'm staying with you. Tweed speaking. Can you tell me whether another guest, Serena Cavendish, has arrived yet?' He cleared his throat. 'She has. Can I speak to her? What was that? Did you say she has reserved her suite for seven weeks? She has. And now she's left the hotel? Thank you.'

'That,' said Paula slowly, 'that arrangement has strange echoes for me. She can't possibly need that amount of time for taking pics of some fashion do. Yes, it definitely has echoes.'

39

Inside the circular laboratory with its conical roof Dr Goslar wore whites. The third canister, which for many hours had slowly filled with drips from the glass tube suspended above it, was now full. A hand carefully placed an airtight lid over the top.

There was enough of the deadly liquid inside the three canisters to destroy seventy-five million people. Maybe far more. Two hands, wearing surgical gloves, grasped the latest canister, lifted it, placed it alongside two more filled canisters resting on a tiled table top. They were now a distance away from the ancient chimney-like structure elevated thigh-high above the floor. It was necessary for the contents of the third canister to cool a little before being transported. The cooling process would take a while.

The figure's feet were clad in close-fitting slippers made of polystyrene, this material protected with a hygenic covering composed of the same cloth as the surgical gloves. Slippered feet shuffled back to where the third canister had stood, a hand closed a tap at the end of the glass tube where liquid had dripped from it.

The feet then shuffled over to where the Norman-style window in the large turret was let into the stonework. Goslar stared out into the moonlit night. More snow was falling. Beyond and below the flakes the moon illuminated the steep slope running down to the distant lake. Ice rimming the shore had now spread further out and the lake's surface, at this point, looked like mottled glass.

Goslar walked slowly away from the window, approached the elevated mouth of the chimney which heated the room. Heat rose from the crackling flames burning thirty feet down. Removing the surgical gloves, Goslar bent down to where three small logs perched against the chimney. The logs were lifted, one by one and dropped down inside the opening, which was six feet in diameter. The fire flared up.

Tucking the gloves, which had been held under an armpit, into the pockets of the gown, Goslar left the room, opening a heavy door, stepping carefully down the stone steps of the circular staircase – after closing the heavy door – and reached the living room at the next level down.

Goslar sank back onto a sofa, legs crossed, gazing at the luminous screen of a TV set which was turned on permanently. Soon there would be a weather forecast. The figure checked its watch. The timetable had to be adhered to. One important factor had been built into it. The time taken to drive to the airport with the canisters, carefully packed inside special containers.

40

Tweed and his team arrived back in Geneva without encountering any further hostile action. The street lamps' reflections were glowing in the still waters of the Rhône. The city was quiet, with very little traffic. They arrived outside the Richemond.

'All peace ceases now,' Tweed warned.

He was right. As he walked into the large lobby with Paula and Newman, a slim man, over six feet tall, impeccably dressed in the most expensive suit, stood up from a sofa and strode forward with a smaller man a step behind him. That's right, Tweed thought, keep one step behind your master.

The Rt. Hon. Aubrey Courtney Harrington towered over Tweed, looked down his long nose at him. His grey hair was perfectly coiffeured, his nails were perfectly manicured, his lean hungry face was perfectly shaved. Paula smelt powder on his pugnacious jaw. His long, lean face had a bleak expression.

'In here, Tweed.' He gestured as he might towards a child. 'I have reserved a private room. Only Adrian Diplock, my assistant, will also attend.'

He gestured towards the smaller man behind him, who had ferret eyes. Harrington had totally ignored Paula and Newman. Very erect, he went towards a closed door. Tweed went in another direction, on his way upstairs. Diplock ran, caught him up.

'The Minister wishes to see you *now*.'

'Get lost,' said Newman.

'Where the hell do you think you are going?' demanded Harrington, catching up with them.

'I am going up to my suite,' Tweed began quietly, still walking. 'I am going to have a shower, a drink and a snack before I come down again. It has been quite a day.'

'I have been waiting *hours* while you have been off gallivanting God knows where,' Harrington snapped.

'I don't think you'd have enjoyed what you termed our gallivanting,' Tweed informed him. 'My guess is you'd have been scared witless.'

'The Minister expects you to confer with him at once,' Diplock explained in his soft upper-crust voice. He laid a hand on Tweed's arm. 'I would comply with his wishes if I were you.'

Newman jerked the hand roughly away from Tweed's arm. He was very angry.

'Touch him again and I'll break your arm,' he growled.

Diplock took a step back. He was frightened and couldn't think how to handle the situation. And Harrington had seen the fiasco.

'In about an hour,' said Tweed. 'Now, I'm off.'

Beck appeared from nowhere as Tweed was entering his suite. Tweed ushered him inside, indicated to Paula and Newman that they should join him. After consulting everyone he called room service.

'We want scrambled eggs for three people. One double Scotch, two brandies and soda. If you could get the drinks and the food up fairly quickly I would much appreciate it.' He put down the phone. 'Do sit down, Arthur. I'm sorry we have been so long. And thank your lucky stars you have hardly any government in Switzerland.'

'I've already encountered – yes, that's the word – your Minister,' Beck explained from the comfort of a sofa. 'But first things first.' He got up as Paula was about to sit down, hugged her, kissed her on both cheeks. 'Welcome to Geneva.'

'Thank you, Arthur. It's always good to see you.'

Those two always get on well together, thought Tweed. From the moment they first met, which is nice. He looked at Paula.

'How is Trudy? I didn't have time to have a word with her when that bear advanced on me.'

'I did. She's very tired. She said she might just flop into bed. I told her she should. She's in good spirits.'

'I'm relieved.' Tweed looked at Beck. 'Arthur, you have the floor.'

Beck, slimly built, about Newman's height, had grey hair and a trim moustache. His eyes were alert, as always, his manner courteous. He had a high forehead and his personality exuded dynamic energy. The Chief of Federal Police was a man they all felt comfortable with.

'The first thing,' he began in his fluent English, 'will be a shock. There's a strong rumour – which I think is reliable – that Ali, the head of the coup which took over an important Arab state, is paying Goslar three hundred billion pounds for the weapon.'

'Billion?' echoed Paula. 'Sure you don't mean million?'

'*Billion*,' Beck repeated. 'And pounds – not dollars. The price of oil may have dropped but he has oil gushing out of his ears. He can easily afford such a gargantuan sum.'

'So the weapon,' Tweed remarked, 'must be ready for delivery – or almost ready.'

'I think you are right. Time has run out. There's more. I know through confidential sources that one hundred billion has already been deposited in the Zürcher Kredit Bank – to be made available the moment the weapon reaches Ali.'

'Time is running out, then.'

'I'd say time *has* run out.'

'Is that Grumman jet still at Cointrin?' As Tweed asked the question Paula detected a note of anxiety in his voice. 'I mean is it still waiting on the tarmac?'

'It is. Still being attended to with nonstop maintenance. And a twenty-four-hour roster of crew ready to take off at any time.'

'Can't you stop it? Fake some regulation?' Tweed pressed.

'Sorry, but, as you know, Switzerland is a neutral country. There is no reason I can think of to have the machine impounded. Heaven knows I've tried.'

'I understand, Arthur. Can we turn to another subject? You told me on the phone you had traced three likely properties Goslar may be occupying.'

'I had to twist the arms of certain estate agents, but I twisted hard.' Beck picked up an executive case he had brought into the suite. He took out three folders, handed one to Tweed. 'There's a brochure of the property inside. It's a big old mansion just outside Montreux. Rented for a year by an American, a Mrs Jefferson.'

'How long has she been there?'

'Eleven months. Her husband is a millionaire banker in New York. I checked that. There is a banker called Jefferson in New York.'

'This doesn't seem at all likely. Montreux is too far from the airport here. And I don't detect Goslar's pattern of behaviour.'

'This one,' Beck said, producing another folder, 'is a palatial villa in Vevey, not too far this side of Montreux, as I'm sure you know. Rented by a Professor Gastermann. Supposedly a successful owner of hypermarkets in the Far East. Couldn't trace much data on him.'

'Rented for how long?'

'Two years. He's been living there for eighteen months.'

'Very doubtful,' said Tweed, scanning the brochure. 'Again, too far from the airport. Again, not Goslar's behaviour pattern. He rents for a long period, then disappears overnight – long before the lease is up.'

'Last one, then. The Château Rance. Built ages ago by an eccentric Swiss banker. A weird place,' he went on, handing the brochure to Tweed, 'looks like a castle – not your idea of one. It's up in the mountains behind Geneva. Rented for two years by a Mr Arnold Aspinall. Lease started two months ago. Very isolated. Behind a village called Le Brassus – at one end of the Lac de Joux.'

'Charterhouse, Gargoyle Towers, Masterson, Château de l'Air, now Aspinall,' Tweed said half to himself.

'Pardon?' queried Beck.

'Just talking to myself. How long to drive from Château Rance to the airport?'

'Roughly three-quarters of an hour. Might be a bit longer just at the moment. There's been yet another heavy fall of snow.'

'I like the look of this, Arthur.' Tweed was examining the brochure carefully. 'Weird-looking, as you say. Has a big turret at one corner. Bizarre architecture. Anyone ever seen our Mr Aspinall?'

'I phoned a friend I have in Le Brassus. He said no one had ever laid eyes on the occupant. But after dark all the lights are on. They are tonight.'

'It's him! I can smell him,' Tweed said with the nearest to excitement Paula had ever witnessed. 'What do you think, Bob?'

'Sounds like our man to me,' Newman agreed. 'Isolated. Chap never seen. Within driving distance of the airport.'

The food and drinks arrived at that moment. The waiter, at Tweed's request, gave each of them separate tables. Tweed gave the waiter a generous tip. They began eating immediately. Within five minutes their plates had been scooped clean.

'What's the drill now?' Newman asked.

'Get rid of Harrington first. Then we'll drive up to Le Brassus. I suppose you couldn't guide us to the area, Arthur?'

'My pleasure. I'll go down and get my car brought round. I'll be waiting when you're ready. Take your time. One thing I haven't mentioned. I've posted a man outside all three properties. At any sign someone is leaving I'll hear on my mobile. So take it easy . . .'

'I'm going to have the quickest shower of my life,' Tweed decided. As he spoke he was gathering new clothes from his case. 'Give me seven minutes.'

'I'm doing the same,' said Paula as Tweed vanished into the bathroom.

'Me too,' said Newman, leaving the room.

Paula was about to follow when the phone rang.

As she picked up the phone she could hear Tweed's shower running behind the closed door. She hoped she'd be able to take a message.

'Hello,' she said.

'Urgent call from the United States,' the operator told her. 'From a Mr Cord Dillon.'

'Put him on ... Hello there, Cord. Paula speaking. Tweed is in the shower. Can I pass on a message?'

'Sounds like you,' the familiar gruff voice said. 'Where were we when you saved my life in London?'

'Albemarle Street. I'd just come out of Brown's ...'

'OK. Sorry to be so wary. Tweed asked me to vet Trudy Warner. I have done so. Her history equates exactly with what he told me. She was married to a Walter Jewels Baron. Accountant to Unit you-know-what. Her husband was murdered in their house. Out in the sticks in Virginia. Killer never found. She left overnight for New York, got a job with a big security agency. OK so far?'

'It equates.'

'Spoke to the boss of the security outfit. With them two years. The boss praised her ability to the moon. She meets Vance Karnow at a party. He's impressed, hires her as a member of the Unit. She's a big asset there. Oh, going back a bit, to Virginia. She has a sister in San Francisco. I spoke to her. Sister had a plea from Trudy – if anyone enquires about me, say I was there but then went to Seattle. To me she sounds to be quite something. Oh, she's British. Only in the States because she met the guy who became her husband. OK so far?'

'It still equates.'

'Karnow is dead now. Some business about being caught up in an explosion in Geneva, triggered by terrorists. Karnow took a heavy mob with him to Paris. I hope Trudy is OK?'

'She is, Cord. She's sleeping in a room here in the hotel I'm in.'

'On that vetting I'd pass her one hundred per cent. OK? Must get moving now.'

'Thank you so much, Cord.'

Her reply was wasted. In typical American fashion he had suddenly broken the connection. Frowning, Paula put down the phone. What was going on? Why had Tweed vetted Trudy?

41

For two reasons Paula delayed telling Tweed about Dillon's call. The first was that when Tweed rushed out of the bathroom, fully dressed, he said he must call Burgoyne. The second was that when the call was over the others arrived, filing into the suite. Newman, Marler, Butler, Nield and – to her great surprise – Trudy.

'Is that reception?' Tweed asked on the phone. 'Could you put me through to a friend of mine, also staying here, Alan Burgoyne.'

'I'm sorry, sir,' the receptionist replied, 'but Mr Burgoyne went out a while ago. He said he was going to the Old Town on the other side of the Rhône.'

'Thank you.'

Tweed put down the phone, looked round, thanked

everyone for being ready so promptly. He then relayed to them the information about Burgoyne.

'I can guess where he's gone,' Marler said. He phrased his next words carefully, probably because Trudy was in the room. 'He'll have gone to meet my friend, the one who supplies me with extras. My friend recently moved his address.'

Everyone except Trudy knew what he meant. He was referring to the Swiss who dealt in illegal arms – for an extortionate price – under cover of running an antique shop. To her credit, Trudy did not ask what 'extras' Marler was referring to.

'So now we know where he is,' Tweed said briskly. 'Time to go down and confront Lionheart. Lord of All He Surveys. Paula, Bob, I'd like you both to come with me. The rest of you relax. We shall not be long.'

Reaching the ground floor, they found Diplock pacing nervously back and forth in front of the closed door, hands clasped behind his back. He straightened up as they approached, opened the door for Tweed, who paused in the entrance.

Diplock tried to assume an air of authority. He made a mess of it. Tweed noticed he had thick dark eyebrows which didn't match his fair hair. The lad can't be more than twenty-five, he thought.

'I'm afraid you can't go in, miss,' Diplock said to Paula.

He lifted a hand to touch her arm, to restrain her. Then he caught Newman's expression, remembered what had happened when earlier he had touched Tweed's arm. He withdrew his hand as though it had landed on something very hot.

'They are both coming with me,' said Tweed and walked into a large room.

The Minister was seated in a tall hard-backed chair covered with tapestry which would have suited

Elizabeth I. In front of him was a massive antique desk with a single ordinary straight hard-backed and uncomfortable-looking chair, facing him. *Autocratic* was the word which came to Tweed's mind.

Harrington did not stand up. Instead he glared with his dark eyes at Paula and Newman. For a moment he pursed the thin lips on his wide mean mouth. Then he orated, as though at the despatch box in the House of Commons.

'I expected you to come along. You appear to have brought with you a delegation. We have to confer in private.'

Tweed glanced back. Paula and Newman had seated themselves on a long sofa. Close by, Diplock was perched on a more comfortable hard-backed chair – perched so far forward that had he moved no more than an inch he'd have ended up on the carpeted floor.

'Then why is Diplock here?' Tweed demanded, still standing.

'Adrian is my chief and confidential assistant.'

'Newman and Miss Grey are *my* chief and confidential assistants. Either they stay or I'm leaving this room at once. And I do not like this chair.'

Saying which, Tweed removed the offending piece of furniture, replaced it with a comfortable armchair. He then sat upright in it, took off his glasses and proceeded to clean them on his handkerchief.

'Lord!' exclaimed Diplock. 'I forgot to lock the door. So sorry, sir.'

Jumping up, he produced a key from his pocket and locked the door. He was about to slip the key into his pocket when he found Newman beside him.

'I'll take that key, sonny boy.'

He took the key before Diplock could react. Then he returned to the sofa and sat down again.

'We'd better get on with it, whatever it is,' Tweed began. 'I have only five minutes to spare.'

'*Five minutes!*'

The Minister shoved back his chair, stood up to his full height and started walking back and forth behind the desk. He waved his arms high as he spoke, then circled them as though silencing a mob of hecklers.

'Do you realize who you are talking to? Do you not comprehend the rank I hold? As far as I am concerned this meeting may well go on for half the night. We have the most important matters of state to discuss, to explore and to delve deeply into all the possible contingencies which may be involved.'

Having finished his speech, Harrington pushed his chair back to its original position, sat down, stared at Tweed. Then he leaned back, folded his arms.

'I have it from the most confidential source, who shall remain nameless, that a certain state has offered Dr Goslar for his weapon the sum of three hundred billion pounds.'

'That news is gossip in the streets,' Tweed told him.

'So what, if I may be so bold as to ask, are you doing in Geneva – when my informants assure me Dr Goslar is hiding somewhere in the Paris region?'

'The trail to Paris sometimes leads via Geneva.'

Tweed was secretly amused. The opening he had been looking for had been offered to him on a plate, unknown to the Minister. It was at this monent that Harrington noticed Diplock was looking most unhappy. Paula, glancing at the assistant, thought Diplock reminded her of a child who had had his sweets stolen.

'Something wrong, Diplock?' the Minister enquired. 'Some aspect of what I have just said?'

'I'm supposed to be official key-holder,' the assistant complained.

'Well, we've changed roles, haven't we, Didlock,' Newman said amiably.

'Diplock. Adrian Diplock,' the assistant corrected furiously.

Didn't Lock, Paula said to herself. She had trouble keeping her expression neutral.

'Now, Tweed,' the Minister continued at his most pompous, 'you are saying that Dr Goslar has an association with Paris? That it is in the French capital we are most likely to lay our eager hands on him?'

'La Défense. Goslar has a long lease on an address there known to the locals as the Goslar Building. The lease is in the name of a company called Poulenc et Cie, registered in Liechtenstein.'

'Liechtenstein, by God!' Harrington smiled for the first time and Paula thought the smile far more nauseating than the man's normal icy demeanour. 'We appear to be moving towards a consensus. Which is the way all these matters of high state ought to proceed, I am sure you will agree. Liechtenstein – that has the ring of authentic Goslar accounting. Wouldn't you think so, Diplock?'

'Yes, sir. I most certainly would agree,' replied his assistant, leaning forward as though in the presence of a pasha.

'So the hunt is riding well – closing in on the fox. Eh, Tweed?'

'Let us just hope so.'

'Now, let us summarize.' The Minister leaned back, hands clasped behind his neck. 'Goslar has his lair in Paris. Under the noses of French security, which is clever. Why? Because the French security services are not known for their successes. Look at how they botched the Carlos business, let him shoot down their own men sent to arrest him. Carlos then vanishes into the ether – at that time, anyway. Goslar then leases one of those glorious skyscrapers.' His arms shot vertically into the air. 'Like wonderful New York. But no one ever sees him. Why? Because he's probably the doorman. By the by, Tweed, I have a fresh team arriving in Paris.'

Tweed had openly looked at his watch twice. Now, preparatory to flight, he was easing his chair further away from the desk.

'Incidentally,' he said, 'how did you know I was temporarily in this part of the world?'

'Bate phoned me, didn't he? Poor Bate. Probably from that underground garage here before the terrorists killed him.'

'So who will replace Bate?'

'Pardoe.' The Minister's lips curled. 'Honest Caspar Pardoe. Just back from attending some nonsensical security convention in the US of A.' He leaned forward, very stern now. 'So I can expect you to be on a mid-morning flight to Paris tomorrow. I'll be aboard.'

'All things being equal,' Tweed replied, standing up, 'I will be on a flight tomorrow.'

On a flight tomorrow – only Paula noticed the ambiguity of Tweed's phraseology. He had omitted the word 'Paris.'

'Just before you depart,' the Minister spoke, 'I suppose Dr Goslar is a man? The most presumptuous rumours have been circulating in certain quarters I have lent an ear to.'

'Goslar is a man – or a woman,' said Tweed.

42

'What a fool,' Paula said when Diplock had shut the door. 'But I did admire the way you handled him. He started off raving and we left him quietened down. Or, rather, you did.'

'The main thing,' Tweed said as they made their way back to his suite, 'is that I diverted his attention from Geneva and back to Paris.'

'And without telling a single lie. You really did dupe the idiot.'

They entered the suite and found the others listening to Trudy who was telling them about America. She stopped when Paula came to sit next to her, prior to their departure. Tweed had picked up the phone.

'Reception? I have a friend staying here. A Ms Serena Cavendish. Could you put me through to her?'

'I'm afraid she's not in the hotel, sir. I can see her key,' the night receptionist reported.

'Any idea when she might be back? Did she say when she left?'

'I gather your friend was in a hurry, sir.'

'But she has left her bag in her room,' Tweed persisted. 'There is something inside it which she is carrying for me.'

'I understand one bag was taken to her suite. Shortly afterwards, when she had been to her suite, she left, sir. I wouldn't worry. She will be coming back.'

'Thank you.'

'The night receptionist is very discreet,' Tweed commented. Then he relayed to everyone what he had been told. 'Although the receptionist didn't say so I gather she may not be back tonight.'

'You're very interested in her movements,' Paula said, fishing.

'She has been with us for a little while.' Tweed gazed into space as though he saw something. 'Yes, she has been with us. And now we must hit the road.' He looked at Marler, who had the long tennis racquet case by his side. 'I don't have to guess what's in there.'

'The Armalite.' Marler pointed to a large bulging canvas bag. 'Plus a variety of grenades. I've handed some of them out.'

'I've got a few,' Trudy said with a smile. 'In here.' She patted her shoulder bag. 'The Unit Four mob showed me how to handle them in training sessions.'

'You're coming with us?' asked Tweed, startled.

'I've been trying to talk her out of the idea,' Paula said. 'She has had enough for one day. Like talking to a brick wall.'

'And the brick wall *is* coming with you,' Trudy added with another smile.

'Then we'd better move right now,' Tweed decided. 'I must have a word with poor Beck, who has been waiting ages. Paula, come with me. You, too, Bob.'

Leaving the hotel was like walking into a vast refrigerator. Paula zipped her fleece to the collar. Beck was sitting in a Mercedes, studying a map. He was standing on the pavement when they reached him, the map spread out on the roof of his car.

'A thousand apologies, Arthur,' Tweed said. 'A blasted Minister kept us while he mouthed platitudes.'

'He does that,' Beck agreed. 'He tried to get information out of me about you. Ended up by calling me as close-mouthed as an unopened sardine can. I told him I didn't like sardines. Now, before I lead the way, I think the three of you should look at this map.'

'Where is this Château Rance?' Paula asked.

'There. Marked with a cross. We drive out of Geneva

383

and up a road into the mountains. We arrive at a point where we are on the far side of a high ridge and then descend into the Vallée de Joux. We reach a small town, Le Brassus, where I have a friend I want to call on. He knows the area well, owns a small hotel. From there we drive on to a beautiful little lake – little by Swiss standards – Lac de Joux. The Château Rance is perched high up by itself on a mountain overlooking the lake below. Arriving in the Vallée we have entered a secret world – invisible to anywhere else.'

'Promising,' Tweed commented. 'Sounds like Dr Goslar.'

'To reach the château,' Beck continued, 'without being seen we avoid the main drive up to the property. Instead we drive up a very steep road, sunk between high banks on either side, until we turn at the summit along a similar road. There is a natural layby where you can park your cars. At this point, where I will leave you, I fear it's a matter of hoofing it down the side of the mountain, but then you are immediately above the château. Some way below you, that is. I see you have boots. Good. What about the rest of your team – including that red-haired beauty?'

'All with boots,' Paula told him. She chuckled. 'Including that red-haired beauty. You always did have an eye for the ladies.'

'As a policeman I have to be observant,' Beck responded with a quizzical smile. 'Also I advise everyone to tuck their trouser tops inside their boots. There's been another heavy fall of snow up there. You don't want to be wet through when you reach your objective.'

'You could show us the entrance to this mountain road,' Tweed suggested, 'then we could drive up by ourselves. We are putting you to a lot of trouble.'

'Not at all. And if, by some twist of fate, you locate

384

Goslar, then you are serving the interests of Switzerland. Also I wish to consult my friend in Le Brassus, Gilbert Berger. He may have seen Goslar – if this Aspinall is Goslar.'

'I doubt that very much,' Tweed told him. 'No one has ever seen him, or her, so far.'

'I said I would show you the natural layby and leave you. Unfortunately I have no official reason to come with you to the château. And in this country it is a serious crime to invade private property. So have a care. Let us start now.'

Following Beck's Mercedes, they drove in the same sequence as before. Marler was in the lead car, close to Beck. Behind him Nield drove with Butler at his side. Newman gripped the wheel of the last car with Paula next to him while Trudy and Tweed occupied the rear seats.

After they had left the city behind and started climbing a steep road into the mountains Paula had a mixture of emotions. She was excited, her adrenalin was flowing, but she was apprehensive. They had come so far, experienced so much – so what if this expedition turned out to be a flop?

She turned round to look at the passengers behind her. Tweed was leaning back against his seat, his eyes closed, apparently asleep. Trudy, on the other hand, her trouser tops shoved inside her boots, gazed out of the window and was humming to herself. Trudy, you really are a cool customer, Paula thought.

They drove as quickly as they dared. Looking ahead, as the narrow road turned yet again, Paula saw the moonlight reflecting off a sheet of ice on the road. At least we have four first-rate drivers, she comforted herself. They drove higher and higher and now the snow on the banks on either side was deeper. What would it be like near Le Brassus?

Suddenly they reached the top. Through a gap in the bank on her side Paula caught a glimpse of faraway Lake Geneva, glowing in the moonlight, more like a sheet of glass. Then it was gone. They were moving *down* a steep incline. She began to look for Lac de Joux, then remembered Beck had said it was beyond Le Brassus – and damnit!, wake up. She had seen its location for herself on the map.

'We're going down into the Vallée,' Tweed called out.

'You're a fake,' she said, looking back, 'I thought you were fast asleep.'

'I felt the change of direction.'

'And now you're alert,' Trudy said sternly to Tweed, 'you'd better tuck your trousers inside your boots.'

'I always do as I'm told,' Tweed replied in a tone of resignation. He bent down and did what she had suggested. 'There. Satisfied?'

'Not really.' She reached a hand out and fitted inside his left boot a fold of trouser still exposed. 'I'll just have to keep an eye on you.'

In front Paula was having trouble suppressing a giggle. She had never known Tweed accept instructions so meekly.

The steep descent, twisting and turning, continued. They were going round a bend when the car started to skid. Paula gripped the door handle. Newman went with the skid, resumed control just before he went slap into the left-hand bank.

'That was skilful,' Paula said, laying a reassuring hand on his arm.

'That was stupid,' he replied. 'I realized some way back I should watch out for a light covering of snow masking ice beneath it. I must keep my mind on what

I'm doing. I was thinking about Burgoyne, how he would have driven this route. Like a bat out of hell, I suspect. And got away with it.'

'That reminds me,' Paula said, turning her head. 'Just before we left, Tweed, you dashed back inside the hotel. What was all that about?'

'I left a note for Burgoyne, giving him our route. So when he gets back, laden with goodies, he'll be able to follow us.'

'Bet he catches us up.'

The road had now levelled out and they were driving along the Vallée. To their right the mountain slope they had just negotiated reared up, with here and there an army of tall firs dusted with snow. The Vallée had a closed-in sensation, a secret world, and Paula tensed with anticipation. Trudy's reaction was rather different.

'What an oasis of peace,' she called out.

'Your peace may be shattered when we reach the Château Rance,' Tweed warned.

'Jonah!'

Leaning forward, Paula was just able to make out the lettering on the snow-covered sign. *Le Brassus*. Prosperous-looking houses appeared on either side of the road, houses with steep roofs to shed snow, with green shutters on the first floors, some still thrown back open. She guessed the windows had to be double-glazed, or with one closed window behind the other. They parked in a small square and she saw the sign on the side of a large attractive building. Hôtel Blanc. Lights blazed in all the windows and the other buildings surrounding the open area had shops, now closed, on their ground floors.

Beck was talking to a man outside the hotel as Paula alighted. The man came running forward, treading carefully in his boots. He held out a hand.

'I am Gilbery Berger. Do be careful. There is a lot of

ice and we have not yet salted it.' All this in English. 'Welcome to Le Brassus, Miss Grey.'

Berger was of medium height, well-built, in his forties and had a warm smile. He shook her hand.

'Now you come into my hotel. Have something warm to eat. Maybe a drink or two?' he suggested with a twinkle in his shrewd eyes. 'So this is Mr Tweed,' he went on as Beck arrived and introduced everybody. 'I hear great things about you from Arthur, Mr Tweed.'

'Wildly exaggerated, I am sure. And thank you for your most kind invitation, but we must hurry on to the château.'

'OK. Perhaps when you come back. I take you to see the Château Rance at Arthur's suggestion. This strange person who lives there. Aspinall. We never see this person. Do not even know if it is a man or a woman.'

'Aspinall must need supplies from here, surely? Groceries – all the things you need to keep you going?'

'You would think so.' Berger threw back his large head, laughed. 'No good for business, Aspinall. Refrigerated truck arrive from Geneva. Driver never see him. Goods delivered into cold store in great cellar. Paid for by cash – yes, cash! – sent to Geneva store by motorcyclist service. Most mysterious. You wish to go now? I am ready. I lead way in my big Volvo . . .'

Paula was sorry to leave Le Brassus so quickly. She would have liked to talk longer to Berger, who was so cheerful. And she liked the look of the small town. Solid-looking houses, some of wood, some with plaster walls, stood fairly close but still had ample space between them. As they drove off she saw more impressive houses perched on the mountain slope with a road leading up to them from Le Brassus. Then the town was behind them.

'I liked the look of the place,' said Trudy. 'One day I wouldn't mind coming back to it.'

'Me too,' Paula agreed.

With Le Brassus only a memory they were driving through a wilderness. The mountain slopes rose steeply, punctuated by isolated fir trees here and there. The moon shone down on the narrow Vallée, cold and remote, the warmth of the town's lights forgotten. When she least expected, Paula saw Lac de Joux come into view, a wider lake than she had imagined, ice sheets projecting from the shoreline. A few minutes later the cars stopped, Berger hurried back, warning Paula and Trudy that the road was slippery and they could fall so easily.

Paula walked a few paces. Her boots had deep perforations in the soles and they gripped the surface firmly. She thanked Berger for his concern, assured him she would be all right.

'I think you will,' he said with his broad smile. 'I watch you both walk and you have confidence. Now, I have parked near the gates to the drive, out of sight. Come with me and I will show you the Château Rance. Mr Tweed does stride like an atheelete.'

Tweed had gone ahead past parked cars to join Marler, Butler, Nield and Newman. They were standing at a point where the high snow bank blocking a view dipped. Beck, who had a pair of binoculars pressed to his eyes, handed them to Tweed.

'There it is. Those field glasses are the latest advance – from Zeiss in Germany. Excellent for night vision.'

Tweed altered the focus slightly. He scanned not only the château but also the surroundings. Noted that way below the mountain's summit, probably a couple of hundred yards above the château, a huge limestone crag projected out over the slope. Underneath it was a large dark hole. The château itself was quite a distance up the mountain slope and a curving drive, marked by large stones, led up to it, presumably from some entrance further along the road. He handed the binoculars to Paula.

'I see it clearly without field-glasses,' said Trudy, who had joined them. 'It's really weird. One huge turret with a window at the right-hand corner. Nothing to balance it on the left. A Gothic-like edifice – pseudo-Gothic.' She looked at Berger. 'I hope I'm not being rude.'

'Not at all.' He laughed. 'I listened to how you describe. It is a perfect picture you paint. I can say that?'

'Very idiomatic English,' Trudy assured him. 'I think it's creepy.'

'So do I,' Paula agreed as she lowered the glasses.

'You noticed all the lights are on,' Beck said to Paula. 'I can even see a glimmer behind the closed shutters. At all levels – which is strange if only one person is living there. But someone is there.'

'Where is the main entrance door?' Nield enquired.

'Immediately below that ugly balcony on the first floor,' Berger told him. 'I don't know what you are going to do.'

'Neither do I, until we get there and approach it from behind,' Newman admitted.

'The mountain road Beck tells me you take will muffle the sound of your engines,' Berger commented. 'It passes between very high steep banks.'

'There's a giant crag behind the château,' Tweed observed. 'Is that a cave underneath it?'

'Yes,' Berger told him. 'A very deep one I have heard. Round here the villagers call it the Cave of the Devil. I have no idea why.'

'One thing I don't like,' Beck said after scanning the mountain again, 'and something you should consider before we drive up that mountain road: so much snow has fallen recently – out of season, too – that there is an avalanche danger. I have a device in my car which registers the temperature outside it. I noticed that the temperature has started to rise. Which increases the danger.'

'Look behind us,' Paula remarked. 'I hadn't realized the lake is immediately beyond the other side of this road. The ice sheet looks very thick.'

'I wouldn't skate on it,' Beck half-joked. 'Not after observing my car's thermometer. You skate on it, the ice breaks, you go under, the ice sheet instantly re-forms above you.'

'Then I won't skate tonight,' Trudy joked back.

'That château,' said Newman, who had lowered his glasses, 'is one of the most sinister so-called castles I've ever seen. There is a peculiar atmosphere about it.'

'Haunting – like something out of a horror film,' Paula remarked.

'Before you all scare yourselves silly,' Tweed told them, 'I think we should start up the mountain road at once.' He turned to Berger, held out his hand. 'I want to say how very grateful we are to you for bringing us out here.'

'It is nothing.' Berger waved his hands dismissively. 'You can thank me later, if you have the time, by returning to my hotel. I should not say, but I am an excellent chef. You come back for a meal as my guests. No matter how late.'

'Thank you again.' Tweed looked at Marler, Nield and Butler who stood in a group. 'Are you ready?'

'We have the picture,' said Marler.

43

At Beck's invitation, Paula travelled seated next to him in his car as they drove back a short distance the way they had come – and then swung left up the mountain road. Beck had turned his headlights on full beam and Paula soon realized why.

The mountain road was just wide enough for the Mercedes to drive up it. On either side the banks, very heavy with snow, were the highest she had encountered on the whole trip so far. The road was more like a rabbit warren inclined at an angle of over thirty degrees. No moonlight penetrated it.

'A bit tricky if we meet anyone coming down,' she remarked.

'Do not worry. At this hour no traffic. Also it is the long way round to the small town of Le Pont at the other end of the lake. Any traffic would drive along the lakeside road.'

'You drive well, if I may say so. Is there ice under the snow?'

'The higher we go the more ice there will be. Which is why I am not driving as though I am at Le Mans.' He glanced again in his rear-view mirror. 'I am glad to see Marler is being most sensible. A formidable man. Says little, does much.'

'Totally reliable. With these banks being so high I can't see the château.'

'And whoever is in the château cannot see us – or hear us. I sense that Tweed has the bit between his teeth – is that correct?'

'It is. And you are right. There comes a moment when Tweed is unstoppable. We have reached that moment.'

Beck said nothing for a few minutes as the gradient increased. At times Paula thought it was a miracle the car did not topple over backwards. Beck wore motoring gloves and she noticed his grip on the wheel was light. She felt no tension emanating from him. The tension was inside herself. Always the same for a while during the approach to danger.

'I hope Tweed realizes that if he finds it is not Goslar inside he may find himself in a very difficult situation. The owner could bring criminal charges against him. The Swiss law is very strict.'

'Tweed has talked himself out of more difficult situations. The worry is that we find it is *not* Goslar inside. Then we have played our last card.'

'Then let us hope it is a grand slam.'

They were still climbing the incredible burrow-like road. Paula kept glancing to her left, hoping for a glimpse of the château.

She was disappointed. They were hedged in totally by the height of the banks. She had the impression the snow was getting deeper. Beck must have read her mind.

'I'm very worried,' he said. 'Can I ask you a favour?'

'Of course.'

'I know you have great influence with Tweed. The snowfall which came recently is far worse than I had thought. Could you try to persuade Tweed to abandon this attempt? To get him to return to the Hôtel Blanc in Le Brassus.'

'Might as well argue with the Statue of Liberty. I've never known you suggest we retreat.'

'That is now my strong advice. We could put up at the Hôtel Blanc for the night. Conditions may be more favourable in the morning.'

'You're forgetting that private jet waiting at Cointrin. By the morning it could easily have flown off with its diabolical cargo. You said yourself that it would be a service to Switzerland if we located Goslar in time.'

'Oh, dear.' Beck chuckled. 'You are worse than Tweed. I can see why he relies on you so much. On we go, into the unknown . . .'

A few minutes later the road swung round a bend to the left and its surface levelled out. They were still submerged below high banks but the road was wider. Beck let out a sigh, looked at Paula.

'We made it. We are now travelling along the crest of the mountain. And the rest of your team is close behind us. So what do we shout?'

'Hallelujah! I'll remember this drive for a long time.'

'Unless you have other events to come to remember.'

'You don't give up, do you? I'm not saying anything to Tweed.'

A short distance further along the road widened considerably for a brief stretch. It curved to the right and when Beck drove into it and stopped at the end Paula knew they had reached the layby.

'All change,' said Beck, giving her an encouraging smile.

She got out, treading carefully. The other cars arrived and the occupants were beside her in no time. Butler was carrying his tool kit in his left hand, his Walther jammed behind a belt round his coat. He had the look on his face of a man prepared to collar three murderers. Nield was his normal self, his expression almost off-hand. Tweed put on a Russian-style fur hat he had borrowed from the Richemond's receptionist. Paula thought he looked like a commanding President of Russia.

'Thank you, Arthur,' Tweed said. 'Where do we meet up after this business is over?'

'I will be waiting in my car on the lakeside road – a distance from the entrance gates. You have your mobile? Good. I have mine. You run into trouble – find the wrong owner – you call me at once. I have worked out a cover story. I have heard that the terrorists who blew up that underground garage have hidden themselves in this château. It's the best I can think of.'

'I don't think that's going to be necessary. But thank you again. Now how do we get into the grounds of the château?'

'Follow me.'

He strode further down the road beyond the layby. He stopped and when they caught up with him he pointed to an old farm gate closing off an opening in the bank. The gate was a bizarre sight. Its framework was covered with solid ice. It looked more like a prop from a film of a Grimms' fairytale.

Butler took a tool from his kit, began to insert it inside an ice-coated padlock. The padlock crumbled, fell to the ground. He reached out a gloved hand, gripped the top of the gate. The whole gate gave way, toppled away from him, created a grid shape in the snow, sank almost out of sight.

'Beware,' warned Beck, 'the snow is softer than I'd realized.'

Tweed took a giant stride, just cleared the half-submerged gate. As the others followed he stood quite still. The château lay far below, the large corner turret now on the left-hand side, seen from the rear. It had no window looking up at the mountain. The massive stone building was masked with snow and above the shutters of each closed window rows of icicles dangled like a palisade of daggers. Viewed from the summit of the mountain, illuminated by moonlight, it looked as though it were constructed of crystal.

'Let's get on with it,' said Tweed, leading the way.

He was glad Beck had warned them to tuck their trouser tops inside their boots. His feet sank into the snow at least a foot deep. Paula, by his side, seemed to manage better, plodding ahead of him, probably because she was lighter in weight.

There was not a breath of wind, something else for which Tweed was thankful, since at this altitude a Siberian wind would have scarred their exposed faces. He looked to his left, then to his right. His team was well spread out, which meant they posed a more difficult target. Tweed paused to glance back up the slope. He saw Beck standing in the road, waving a hand, then vanishing. Soon he must have started driving back down the rabbit burrow, but there was no sound of his engine. They had made a silent approach.

'Paula,' he said quietly, 'I want to take a look at this crag for a moment.'

They had made surprisingly quick progress when Paula stopped below the huge limestone overhang. Tweed joined her, stared up.

'Looks as though it has survived since the beginning of time,' he commented.

'The cave looks enormous – and the snow hasn't penetrated it. Have we a moment? I'd like to go inside.'

'I'll come with you.'

They were joined by Newman and Trudy, who peered up at the great width and length of the projecting crag. Tweed switched on his torch, shone it on the ground, saw the rock floor was smooth, so easy to walk on. They walked several yards before he swivelled the beam upwards. The cavern was enormous, the roof a good thirty feet above them.

'You could hide an army in here,' Trudy said in a tone of wonderment. 'And there's no sign of where it ends.'

'I've seen what I want to,' Tweed announced. 'We must get on to the château . . .'

His knee-length boots, similar to those worn by the others, kept him dry as he plunged closer to the stone building below. He noticed that Butler was now in the lead, pushing on at speed, leaning forward. He looks like a hunter, thought Tweed – but then I suppose that's what we all are. He was about to warn everyone to hug the walls of the massive hulk when they reached it, but they were already doing so. The shuttered ground-floor windows were well above head height and now he could clearly see rims of light between the sections of each shutter.

'Silent as the grave,' Trudy whispered.

'We can do without similes like that, thank you,' Paula replied.

'Look up,' said Tweed. 'This place was designed by a mad architect.'

The gazed up, saw what he was referring to. At regular intervals, high up, gargoyles projected in the shape of venomous eagles ready to swoop on their prey. They wore coats of ice.

'Must have been the same chap who designed King Ludwig's castle in Bavaria,' Trudy observed.

'Be careful how you tread,' Tweed warned. 'Make as little noise as possible.'

The problem was that to stay unseen they had to hug the wall, but the ground below it was crusted snow which crackled as they trod on it. They came to a corner. Tweed emphasized the need for quiet by putting a finger across his lips, then pointed upwards. For the first time, Paula, concentrating on her footwork, realized they were immediately below the large turret which bulged out way above them. She pulled a face, moved a short distance away from the wall, trod instead in soft snow. Tweed and Trudy followed her.

As they rounded the corner, frequently staring up, they saw at the far end of the side wall Butler, Newman and Marler. Butler beckoned to them to join him. Looking up, instead of down at the ground, Paula caught her breath. The scenic view way below the château was hypnotic.

Beyond the bottom of a long steep slope, across the road leading to Le Brassus, the lake spread out, stretched away to the east out of sight. It was like looking down on a great mirror, broken at the edges where the ice sheet projected. In the moonlight the water was absolutely still, had a solid appearance. I wish I had a camera, Paula thought briefly, then dismissed the thought, remembering where they were, what might face them in only a short time.

Arriving at the corner, they looked round it, saw an impressive flight of steps leading up to the main entrance. Butler stood at the top, staring at a huge iron-studded door. Tweed joined him, took from his pocket the tool kit Butler had given him. He selected the largest. Butler put out a hand, held him back.

'I was going to wait until you've checked,' Tweed told him.

'Good job you were.'

'More explosives?'

'I don't think so, but there's an alarm system. I'll need a bit of help to neutralize it. Bob,' he said to Newman, 'you are taller than I am. Watch me first.'

Butler had in his right hand a large tube, not unlike a toothpaste tube. He looked up, moving his head slowly, scanning all the edges of the huge door.

'There's a grey wire, almost the colour of the stone, running round the side edges of the door and also along the top,' Trudy whispered.

'Lady, you have good eyesight,' Butler told her. 'I

have now to break – neutralize – the electric circuits. Bob, you watch me closely.'

He held the tube close to one of the hinges low down, pointed with his other hand to a join in the wire. Squeezing the tube, he ejected a brown paste over the join without letting the tube touch it. He repeated the process with the centre hinge, then turned his attention to a further join alongside the large new metal lock. He capped the tube and handed it to Newman.

'You want me to deal with the top hinge and the join in the middle of the wire running along the top of the door,' Newman suggested.

'Right, mate. But don't let the tube touch a circuit. We must all pray now,' he joked with a dry smile.

'I've seen you do this before, remember?' Newman snapped.

'Just don't get overconfident,' Butler replied.

No one spoke as Newman dealt with the remaining circuits. He then handed the tube back to Butler.

'Any complaints, Harry?'

'Not bad for a beginner.'

'I can try the key now, then?' Tweed asked.

'While we all pray again,' Butler said with a dry smile.

'Before I unlock the door I want to make something quite clear,' Tweed told them. 'I will go in first and everyone will stand outside on either side of the doorway.'

So if someone is waiting inside with a gun you will get shot down first, Paula thought grimly. Great to be the leader.

He inserted the large key with great care, keeping it straight, sensitive to any obstacle, to holding it at the wrong angle. It reminded Newman of how he had once watched an officer of the Bomb Squad dismantling a suspect object. He hoped the simile wasn't relevant.

Tweed used the same care when it came to turning the key. He felt to make sure the tines were engaging in the correct place. The lock opened with a quiet *plop* which, to Paula, sounded like a detonation.

Now Tweed was grasping the ring handle, turning it also slowly. He paused. Then, gently, he began to push the heavy wooden slab away from him. At any moment he anticipated there would be a sound – everyone waited for the night-splitting creak of the ancient door. It swung open gradually, under his control. He realized the hinges had been well oiled. He pushed further and light flooded into his face. The château was open to them.

'I'm off,' Butler whispered.

'Where to?' Paula whispered back.

'To check all round the outside of Bleak House.'

44

'It's like the Château de l'Air,' Paula said in a hushed voice.

But it wasn't. The vast empty hall which stretched before them was much larger and there were no woodblock floors. Here the hall, illuminated by wall lights, was paved with great slabs of raw stone. More like a prison, Tweed thought.

They had disobeyed his recent order. The moment the door was open Newman and Nield, by prearrangement, darted in ahead of Tweed, each taking up a position against the stone wall on either side of the interior beyond the door, each holding a handgun. Trudy and Paula also moved in ahead of Tweed, each holding a weapon.

'Goslar's had it cleaned out again,' Paula observed. 'Ready to leave.'

'Unless he has left already,' Tweed warned.

Marler entered the hall, his Armalite ready for instant action. He took in the situation at a glance. The doors to all the rooms leading off the hall were wide open, the lights on in every room. Marler darted across the hall, his rubber-soled boots making no sound on the stone slabs. He peered inside each of the rooms, moving swiftly from one to another, then returned to where Tweed waited.

'Not a thing. No one. Whole place cleaned out.'

Tweed, holding a Walther, walked swiftly across to a corner of darkness, a corner where the lights did not penetrate. He looked up a spiral staircase of stone steps which led to the upper floors. No grand staircase here. He began to mount the steps, right hand holding the Walther, left hand passing over a stone banister. The others followed, anxious because they hadn't seen this way up, that Tweed was leading the way.

The first floor had a narrow curving landing. Doors to rooms were again open, again with the lights on. He stood listening. Then he climbed the second curving flight of the spiral. Paula had tried to get in front, but his body was in the way and there was no room to pass him.

It was the same story at the second level. More open doors, more lights on inside bare rooms. Tweed stood for a moment, listening. He didn't bother to check the rooms. Nield, coming up behind, did check every room, to guard against an attack from the rear.

Tweed realized before Paula – before anyone – that he was climbing up to the huge turret situated at one corner. Arriving at the third level, he paused. Paula tugged gently at his fur-lined overcoat. He took no notice. She tugged again, spoke to him in a whisper.

'Where are we going? Only Nield is checking the rooms.'

'He'll find nothing but emptiness. We are climbing up to the turret. Shh!'

'Someone has been here. It is so warm. The heating has to be on.'

'Pleasant, isn't it?'

At the fourth level he stood still, beckoned to Newman to join him. He put his mouth close to Newman's ear.

'I'm ordering you to stay here. To prevent anyone going further up this staircase until I ascend to the fifth level. I repeat, that is an order.'

Despite the heat Paula felt chilled. Tweed's grim tone made her sense that they were close to a terrifying climax to all their wanderings. There were three doors open – fewer than on the lower levels. Tweed walked into the first room. Paula, following him, suppressed a gasp of surprise.

This room, large and spacious, was comfortably furnished: a wall-to-wall carpet on the floor, sofas and armchairs scattered about. A large antique desk stood against one wall, all its drawers pulled out and empty. An expensive leather swivel chair stood in front of it. The walls were decorated with gilt frames – the pictures had been removed.

What particularly caught her eye was an enormous stove, standing in the middle of the room and at least eight feet in diameter. An extension of the huge round stove continued upwards, vanished inside a hole in the ceiling. The mad architect had been clever, she thought. There had to be an extension of the stove inside the room above them. The architect had created an immensely tall stove which heated the rooms on more than one level. Even at this distance from it she could feel the ferocious heat inside it. A TV set, turned low, was on. Sniffing, she frowned. A smell of petrol. Then she saw a row of cans lined up behind a sofa a long way from the stove.

Tweed had walked out. She found him in the next room, furnished as a bedroom. A huge four-poster stood against one wall. Lying on the floor was a mess of crumpled sheets and duvets. The bed had been stripped bare.

Tweed was opening the drawers of a small bedside table. From one he took out a small leather-bound notebook. He riffled the pages slowly. At the top of each page there was a heading – Stage One, Stage Two, etc. Below were groups of formulae, written in slanting copperplate. He handed it to Paula.

'What do you make of that?'

'Nothing,' she said, after perusing it and handing the notebook back to him.

'The writing is Goslar's.'

'You've seen the petrol?'

'Yes. So Goslar is still here. Upstairs.'

On a coffee table Paula noticed a small bullet-shaped object. It looked like a lipstick. Tweed had walked out, entered the third room, so she followed quickly. Newman still stood on guard at the foot of the next section of the staircase. He was holding up his hand – gathered below him were Trudy, Nield and Marler. She walked into the third room. It housed a massive bath of marble with gold taps. Behind an open shower curtain in a corner was a shower and behind a clear glass door a toilet. She hurried back on to the landing to join Tweed.

He was already on the staircase, slowly mounting the stone steps to the level above – the fifth level. The Walther was in his right hand while his left hand passed over the stone banister, steadying him on the curving climb. Newman stood aside to let her follow Tweed.

Trudy came up behind her, then the others. Tweed stopped in front of a heavy door.

The studded door had a large round handle. Tweed gripped it with infinite care, turned it inch by inch. He hoped the hinges were as well oiled as those on the main door leading into the entrance hall. Paula glanced over the edge, almost had an attack of vertigo. She could see down the centre of the spiral all the way to the hall floor. She jerked her head upright.

Tweed felt the turning handle stop. He pushed gently. No creak. He opened the door wide, then, as he had anticipated, walked into the turret room. The others followed, very close together. A figure in whites had its back to them. The figure turned round swiftly and Tweed stared into its face.

45

The face of Alan 'Chance' Burgoyne stared back at Tweed.

His expression was different from any expression Tweed had seen Burgoyne adopt before. The eyelids were narrowed, the eyes hard as bullets. In his right hand he held a Magnum revolver aimed at Paula and Trudy. His voice was different when he spoke, a soft, menacing voice with a trace of some foreign accent. His mouth was different – twisted, evil, brutal. Tweed remembered an old film he had once seen on TV – Dr Jekyll and Mr Hyde. The transformation in Burgoyne was almost as startling.

'No one moves a muscle. You have two seconds to drop your guns. Then I shoot the women first before I blast the rest of you. Foolish to come in so close together.'

Tweed dropped his Walther instantly. He heard other weapons hit the stone floor, then a clatter which he knew was Marler's Armalite. He took two tentative paces forward, further into the room.

'Far enough,' Burgoyne ordered in the same soft voice, quite different from the British military-style way of speaking he had always adopted before. 'Anyone tries anything clever and the women go down first.'

'I see you will soon be ready to leave for the airport,' Tweed remarked.

He was looking at a table some distance behind Burgoyne, who was standing about six feet away from the thigh-high stove. On the table was a latticework crate, not unlike those milkmen use to carry milk bottles on their electric wagons. Inside, the crate was divided into sections. A canister with a lid stood inside three of the sections. A slightly larger polystyrene container stood next to the crate. Tweed assumed this would provide protection when the first crate was placed inside it.

'The airport next,' Burgoyne rasped harshly.

'Where you have a long-distance Grumman Gulf-stream jet waiting for instant departure. It's a long way to the capital of Ali's Fundamentalist state.'

'I always thought you were my most dangerous opponent, Tweed.'

'Which is why you brilliantly attached yourself to my team in the role of a British officer. I wondered about you from the very beginning, but couldn't be sure.'

'All of you!' Burgoyne snarled. 'Immediately place your hands on the top of your heads. Two seconds.'

Tweed clasped his hands over the top of his head. Everyone else followed his example. Paula stared steadily, eye to eye, at Burgoyne. Apprehensive, but fascinated, she sensed the power which exuded from this evil man. She marvelled at his capacity for meticulous scheming, for his flair in planning ahead for every possible contingency. How is it that I never suspected him? she asked herself.

'You said you wondered about me from the beginning,' Burgoyne said to Tweed, whose remark had intrigued him. 'So why did you wonder?'

'*Toujours l'audacité*,' replied Tweed, 'your favourite maxim. When I mentioned it to you at Park Crescent you paused, then correctly attributed it to Napoleon. The pause, Burgoyne – I had a flicker of doubt deep down. Because of the pause. Then there was the incident at La Défense – when you warned about the wire round the entrance door to the building. You spoke out about the wire a second before Butler also warned us of its presence. But I couldn't see it – and I was standing beside you. Butler has very exceptional eyesight. But you *knew* it was there. It was part of your confidence-building exercise – so we would trust you completely. Again, I wondered, but could not be certain.'

'So, Mr Tweed, can you list any more so-called mistakes that I made?'

Paula was now casually glancing all round the laboratory. She followed the network of glass tubes and bulbous containers below the ceiling, guessed that this was how Burgoyne had produced the deadly liquid now stored in those three canisters. She knew she was right when she saw the system ending where a vertical tube with a closed glass tap was suspended no more than a foot above the table where the crated canisters stood. And she became aware that Tweed was keeping Burgoyne talking, playing for time. Why?

She glanced round the circular stone walls and suddenly gazed at something. Hastily she averted her gaze before Burgoyne saw her. She had seen another heavy door let into a wall almost behind Burgoyne. What had gripped her was seeing the handle of that door slowly turning from the outside. Why another door in the wall?

Then she remembered. Their approach movement round the outside of the château had been so tense she had registered something only for seconds, then had forgotten about it. The metal-treaded fire-escape staircase winding its way up towards the turret.

'Yes, there were other incidents which aroused my suspicions,' Tweed explained, holding Burgoyne's gaze. Paula realized that Tweed also had seen the slowly turning handle. 'You drove on ahead of us, saying you'd warn us of ambushes. But when a mob of Arabs broke through the mist your warning came at the same moment. Doubtless, you hoped you'd be too late. But superb planner that you are, you covered yourself in case we survived. There were other mistakes, too.'

Paula dug her fingernails into her hand to ease the tension building up inside her. She had risked another glance towards the door, had seen it was now being pushed open very slowly. *Don't creak!* she prayed.

'Another move I found suspicious,' Tweed went on, 'was when you urged members of my team at Talloires to take cover inside the copse of firs. That was so you could protect yourself. You *knew* the cabin Arbuthnot was approaching would blow up into a thousand pieces. Again, I wondered. Then there was something else.'

'You were dangerous when we duelled in the Cold War. Certainly, you have not lost your touch. A pity you will not survive tonight. You say there was something else. What was that? I am learning from you, Mr Tweed. In some ways I think maybe you should have won, but . . .'

Burgoyne never finished his sentence. The door was now half open. Butler slipped through the gap, summed up the situation. Later he thought that it was his remembering how in Annecy, when he was pursuing the

Yellow Man across the bridge, he saw how he had dealt with Pete Nield, head-butting him.

Burgoyne had caught movement out of the corner of his eye. He was swivelling round, ready to aim the Magnum, when Butler hit him. Crouching, Butler had charged like a shell from a cannon. His round head slammed into Burgoyne's chest with great force, sending him backwards. Burgoyne lost his balance, dropped the Magnum, toppled with his back and buttocks on to the wide edge of the chimney. His arms flailed, the lower part of his body sank inside the opening. His strong hands desperately grabbed at the edge, then he was hanging in space, most of his body out of sight in the chimney. He was suspended, held there only by his hands holding the edge, his head in full view.

'Help me!' he yelled.

Tweed strode quickly forward. He picked up off the table a green leather folder, glanced inside, saw sheets covered with formulae. He waved it as he looked down into Burgoyne's horrified face.

'Before we even consider saving you I have questions. You will answer them truthfully – and I will know if it is the truth – or *you* will go down. Into the fires of hell.'

'Three hundred billion pounds. Yes, *billion*. That is what Ali is paying for the weapon. We could share—'

'Kindly shut up.'

Paula noticed that Burgoyne's hands were beginning to blister. The chimney edge he was clutching must be very hot. How long could he hold on?

'This green folder,' Tweed said, 'contains formulae. What are they?'

'Shows you how to make the weapon. We could share . . .'

'Where are the photocopies?'

'*No* photocopies,' Burgoyne screeched. 'Only that . . .'

'What about the turtle? Part of what you needed to produce the liquid?'

'Yes. Key ingredient. Fed sedatives to kill it. Used syringe to extract vital element. Galapagos . . .'

'I know where it comes from. You stole two at least. What about the others?'

'Mess up first one, throw it in here. Only two.'

For the first time Paula saw what Tweed was referring to. Inside an enormous plastic container on a lower table rested the remains of a turtle which must have been four and a half feet long. Part of its shell had been cut away, exposing its insides.

'Where are the other canisters containing the weapon?'

'Only three. In plastic crate. Kill seventy-five million. Ali pays three hundred . . .'

'Billion pounds,' snapped Tweed. 'We've been through that. What else is needed to produce the weapon?'

Paula put her mouth very close to Tweed's ear. Her tone was urgent.

'I don't think he can hold on much longer.'

'You have everything,' Burgoyne pleaded. 'We share. My legs are burning. Get me out! Please! Quick! Qui—'

Burgoyne never completed the last word. Both hands lost his grip on the edge. He plunged down out of sight. There was a terrible scream. Fear. Agony. It cut off suddenly. Tweed peered over the rim of the edge, saw only an inferno of flames, like red hands reaching up for him. He straightened up.

'He's gone. Nothing left, I imagine. There are people in the world who should be eliminated. What's that noise?'

He rushed over to the window, opened it, leaned out, came back and shook his head, smiling.

'Can't hear a thing. Must have been my imagination. Or, more likely, the fire rumbling down below. Now, we have work to do. No one in the world – including Britain – is going to get their greedy hands on this diabolical weapon. So what do we do? We destroy it.'

46

'You've left that window wide open,' Paula complained.

'Deliberately,' Tweed told her. 'The air coming in will help to cool this place down. It's almost like an inferno up here.' He looked at her, Trudy, then at the others. 'If I were you I'd take off your coats. You'll need them when we eventually leave here.'

Tweed began work at once. He picked up the green folder and, without hesitation, cast it down the chimney, followed by the notebook from his pocket. Paula had an amusing thought, chuckled.

'Harrington would go mad if he could witness this.'

'Harrington can go jump off a cliff. I'm happy to show him the way to Beachy Head. Now for the turtle. It's quite dead. I think I'll need a hand to throw the container and what's inside it into the fire.'

He was bending down over the low table when Newman gently pulled him back. He guessed the turtle alone would be very heavy. Nield joined him. Each took hold of the container at one end and lifted. It weighed a ton. They hoisted it up, perched it on the edge of the chimney, then both gave a hard shove. The container and its contents dropped out of view. Tweed was giving orders.

'Marler, I want you to guard the door to the staircase we came up. Perch on the top landing so you get a bird's-eye view.'

'A bird wouldn't like that view,' Paula commented, recalling her own glance down into the spiralling chasm.

'Harry,' Tweed ordered Butler, 'you guard that door to the fire escape. I'm sure Burgoyne was on his own, but let's be very wary.'

Tweed now walked over to the crate containing the canisters of the deadly liquid. He picked up a pair of surgical gloves off a shelf, found they were a size too large, but put them on anyway.

He looked round at everyone inside the turret. Then he looked at the canisters again. He shrugged, a rare gesture Paula recognized. He only did that at times when he was faced with a highly dangerous situation. He turned, faced all the members of his team.

'I want all of you out on the top landing – with the door shut. I think this should work, but I'm not absolutely certain.'

'You think what should work?' demanded Paula.

'I'm about to throw the canisters, one by one, down inside the chimney. I think extreme heat will destroy their contents – that the weapon only works when dropped into water. As it did at Appledore, which seems a million miles away. But as I'm not sure I want you all out of here.'

'Nothing doing,' said Trudy.

'You can issue orders until you're blue in the face but we're staying,' Paula snapped.

'I second the motion,' said Newman.

'Hear, hear!' called out Nield.

They stood staring at him and Tweed realized he was completely out-voted. Looking at their expressions he saw nothing could shift them. Marler, who had heard from outside the open door, walked in, holding his Armalite.

411

'Don't hold your breath, then,' said Tweed. 'On second thoughts maybe that's exactly what you should do.'

He pulled his gloves further over his hands, flexed his fingers to test his grip. He looked at his team once more. They stared back, stone-faced. This is the first time I've had a mutiny on my hands, he thought.

Very carefully, he eased both hands down inside the crate, keeping well clear of the lid of the first canister. Grasping the side of the canister, he was able to insert one hand under its base, which gave him more control. He lifted it out slowly and carried it to the chimney. He happened to glance at Paula and saw she was smiling, holding up one hand with her fingers crossed. He managed to smile back. Then he held the canister as far over the chimney as he could, released it.

He thought he heard a brief sizzle a long way down. Wasting no time, he dealt with the two remaining canisters in the same way. Everyone was still alive but he thought he caught a sigh of relief from somebody. He peeled off each glove carefully, consigned both to the flames.

It was then that he heard a distant growling rumble through the open window. It was not his imagination this time. He reacted instantly.

'Avalanche coming. Everyone outside this horror of a building. Down the fire-escape would be quickest . . .'

'No it *wouldn't* be!' Butler shouted. 'There's ice on the metal treads. I had one hellava job getting up without slipping.'

'Then down the staircase we came up,' ordered Tweed. 'Quickly as you can, but don't run down. I don't want any broken legs.'

He waited until everyone had preceded him, pushing Butler to make him go first. Despite the fact that he was the last one to leave, Tweed, breaking his own rule, hurried after them and, reaching the hall, pushed past everyone and walked out of the front door first.

He turned in the direction of the turret, waving to the others to follow. Passing under the turret he couldn't resist looking up, saw that the first section had been pulled down – like the safety device often used on fire escapes in America. God knew how Butler had hauled it down to the ground. Reaching the rear of the building he paused, waiting for the others to catch him up. He was staring at a frightening phenomenon.

About two hundred yards away to the east the avalanche was on the move, sweeping down like a great wave. He didn't think that would be the full extent of it by any means.

'Make for the cave under that huge crag,' he shouted.

He began plodding up through the snow. Then he felt a hand wrap itself rouhd his left arm, another one round his other arm. He had Trudy on his left, Paula on his right.

'Look after yourselves,' he snapped. 'We may have only a minute to get there in time.'

He jerked himself free, was surprised at how quickly he could move uphill, which was much harder work than when they had come down the slope. With a tremendous effort he kept level with both women. The looming crag seemed a mile above him. Marler, Butler and Nield were spread out on either side of the three climbers. Tweed was sure they were moving more slowly than they needed to – in case their help was needed. He resisted the temptation to check the progress of the wave sliding down to the east, refused to check the situation on the mountain behind the crag. Just concentrated on getting there. One . . . two . . . three paces. Then he counted again and again.

'We're nearly there,' shouted Trudy.

'We are?'

Tweed looked up, saw the overhang of the crag yards away. Saw also that the mountain behind it was crumbling. He'd thought the banked-up snow on the level stretch of road had concealed hedges. It hadn't. It was all snow, all now in motion like another giant wave.

Then they were all under the crag, inside the vast cave. Tweed, almost breathless, sank down in a sitting position thirty feet or so inside the cave. Trudy sank down on one side of him as Paula sat heavily down on his other side. Newman was close and so was Marler. Butler and Nield were deeper inside the cave. They waited, watched.

The first indication Tweed had that it was a double avalanche, a mix of countless tons of snow and a rock slide, was when a huge boulder thumped on the top of the crag, then shot down the slope beyond at incredible speed. A Niagara of snow poured down over the lip of the crag, blotting out any view for a short time. Marler had his night glasses against his eyes.

'It's going to submerge that château,' he called out.

The dense curtain of snow cleared, was replaced by the thunder of great boulders hurtling down the slope at frightening speed. Tweed watched in astonishment as the now immense snow wave, the army of boulders larger than houses, crashed into the château. He saw the turret wobble, break off, fall in pieces, be swept down the lower slope. The snow wave obscured sight of the building for a short time. When it passed on there was no château.

It had been literally ripped from of its foundations, smashed to pieces, carried down the slope. The crag above them shuddered under a fresh onslaught and Tweed glanced up anxiously. Would it hold? The second, even larger wave of snow carrying tumbling boulders thundered down and the crag remained intact.

'I would say Burgoyne's gone for ever,' Marler called

out. 'I saw a large piece of the chimney caught up in the snow, riding on the wave's crest.'

The finale was dramatic – even more than what had come before. The snow – and rock – wave, carrying the relics of the château, crossed the road and swept over the ice at the edge of the lake. Tweed could have sworn he caught sight of half the turret sinking below the water. The lake surface churned. There was a sudden silence, shocking in its unexpectedness. The mountain was still.

Epilogue

'It's over,' said Paula, sinking into the seat behind her desk in Tweed's office at Park Crescent.

'No, it's not over yet,' Tweed warned from behind his own desk.

When they had emerged from inside the cave, below the crag, they had plodded wearily up the slope, wondering whether their cars still existed. It had been a rough climb, over snow which was freezing again, over snow littered with rocks. Reaching the top they had found the road was still there – and so were their cars in the layby.

Their next anxiety had been whether Beck had survived. They had found him standing by his car at the entrance to the mountain road. Tweed had travelled back to Le Brassus with Beck in his car. He had explained what they had experienced.

'So Goslar – or Burgoyne – is a dead letter.'

'He's a dead man. And, as I've explained, his weapon has been totally destroyed. My story about that – to Howard and, later, to the PM – will be that Butler came in through the fire-escape door and shot Goslar. Before he could kill all of us. Then we had to run for our lives to escape the avalanche. After Goslar had told us he was about to fly the weapon to the Middle East.'

'Simple, therefore neat,' Beck had commented.

They had then eaten a splendid meal at the Hôtel

416

Blanc before driving back to Geneva. After spending what remained of the rest of the night catching up on some sleep at the Richemond, they had flown back to London.

'What was the last mistake Burgoyne, I mean Goslar, made?' Paula asked. 'You never had the time to tell him.'

'The biggest one of all. Burgoyne had retired from the army.' He looked round at everyone else in his office – Marler, Newman, Butler, Nield, and Trudy. 'Before we left for Paris I phoned my friend in the MoD again, asked him which bank Burgoyne's pension was paid into. After a lot of persuasion he gave me the name of the bank, promised to have a word with the bank manager and call me back. Oh, we shall be having a visitor shortly.'

'What about Burgoyne's bank account?' Paula prodded.

'He'd called at the bank at regular intervals after retirement, had drawn the monthly amount of his pension. Then he'd stopped doing that. For a longish period he had not called again and quite an amount – I don't know how much, of course – had piled up. He'd never appeared again. I thought that very strange.'

'Yet you let the fake Burgoyne join us,' Paula commented.

'Because I still couldn't be sure. But *toujours l'audacité*, so I thought if this is Goslar, keeping an eye on us at close quarters, I'd play the same game – keeping my eye on him.'

'So how on earth did Goslar come to choose Burgoyne as the man he would impersonate?'

'I can only guess. Knowing Goslar's incredible thoroughness, I'd imagine he searched Europe to find a likely candidate. Don't forget Burgoyne had a brief, unwanted, moment of notoriety during the Gulf War. I also imagine that when Goslar obtained a photo of

417

Burgoyne – heaven knows how – he realized that he, Goslar, looked rather like him. Marler, tell them what you told me on the flight back when I asked you to recall a detailed description of what happened when you visited Burgoyne's home at Rydford on Dartmoor.'

'I told most of you how when I arrived at Burgoyne's cottage near Hangman's Tor I met his girl friend, Coral Langley. How she was shot dead by a man on the tor, a man I killed with my Armalite. How I found his body almost buried under a rock fall. Running back to the cottage, I tripped between the tor and the cottage – sprawled full length on an oblong arrangement of rocks. Later it struck me that they were a long way from the tor.'

'And,' Tweed said, taking over, 'the oblong of rocks was shaped like a grave, Marler told me on the plane. I phoned Roy Buchanan at the Yard. He's called the local police and they're digging up under those rocks. I think I know what they'll find.'

'The real Burgoyne's body,' Paula said in a hushed tone.

'I'm confident that is what they will discover. And Goslar, posing as Burgoyne, made another slip. At one stage I asked him if he climbed tors. He said he did, that he went to Rough Tor, which is miles away from Rydford. Why do that – when Hanging Tor was on his doorstep? It was an accumulation of small slips which made me more and more suspicious.'

The phone rang. Monica, who had been listening avidly, answered it.

'Serena Cavendish is downstairs.'

'The visitor I was expecting. Ask George to bring her up.' Tweed looked at Paula. 'We don't want any loose ends, do we?'

*

Serena walked in very erect, smartly dressed in a white trouser suit and a Hermès scarf tucked under her dominant chin. She smiled at the men, ignored Paula and Trudy, accepted Tweed's invitation and sat down, her shapely legs crossed. Paula knew she was aware that the men had noticed them.

'Sorry,' Tweed began, 'to drag you here. I tracked you down to your photographic studio at the other end of Bond Street.'

'Business is good. Really good. Soon I'll be able to buy myself a small mansion.' She used a hand to push back her glossy black hair. 'Preferably something designed by Lutyens.'

'Congratulations, Davina.'

'Thank you.'

She half-lifted a hand to her mouth. Then she dropped it back into her lap.

'You mean Serena.'

'No, I meant Davina. Chief Inspector Roy Buchanan of the Yard is reopening the case of the car crash which killed your twin sister, Davina. You were the first one to arrive at the scene – I was told it was in the middle of the night. Buchanan is getting an order to have the body exhumed.'

'Oh God! No! That would be sacrilege. Horrible. Quite horrible.'

'Then tell me the truth about what happened that night, Davina.'

'Can I have a glass?' She hesitated. 'I carry a small flask of gin. There are times when I need it – the pressure of work.'

Monica brought her a clean glass. She produced a small flask from her shoulder bag, poured a strong tot. Tweed waited while she drank it in two gulps. Then he continued.

'I need to know exactly what happened. Precisely, please.'

'I couldn't sleep. I thought I'd go for a walk – to maybe meet . . .'

'Don't stop now,' Tweed said quietly.

'To meet Serena. She was very late back. That wasn't unusual – she loved parties. I sat on a gate by the side of the road. She came round a bend like a rocket. At that moment a juggernaut came from the other direction, also driving at too great a speed. She skidded, the juggernaut rammed her, reversed, drove on. I was so shaken I didn't even get his registration number and there was no firm's name on its side. Serena was dead, badly smashed up. Her face . . . It was awful.'

'So what happened next?' asked Tweed, doodling on a pad.

'I was desperate to disappear. In fear of my life. I suddenly realized that I could change places with her, become Serena. I gritted my teeth, took her things out of her shoulder bag – passport, driving licence, other papers. Then I put my own stuff – from *my* shoulder bag – into hers.' She tossed her head. 'She was dead, so I thought, what difference does it make?'

Cold-blooded little madam, Paula thought.

'And of course you were frightened,' Tweed went on amiably, 'because you had helped Dr Goslar in some way. Right, Davina?'

'You're clever. You always worried me. Yes. Because I'm known as an outstanding biochemist Goslar had certain problems he wanted solved quickly. He phoned me in his screechy voice, told me what he needed, promised me a lot of money. This was some time before Serena was killed by the juggernaut. I worked out the solution, left it in an envelope in a Mayfair phone box at the time he'd specified. Two days later, again after dark, a huge man delivered the money – pushed an envelope through my letterbox.'

'So you helped Goslar build the weapon,' Tweed said casually.

'That's not true!' Davina protested vehemently. 'The problem he gave me to solve could only have been one per cent of the whole project. I have no idea of what else is involved. I swear it.'

'I find it hard to swallow the word of a woman who impersonated her dead sister. How much did he pay you? They could start that exhumation within the next two days – unless I stop it.'

'Ten thousand pounds . . .'

'Then I expect you to deliver ten thousand pounds in cash to this building by ten o'clock tomorrow morning. You may go now.'

He was dismissing her as some might get rid of a servant. Flushing, she stood up, walked quickly to the door. On the point of leaving she turned round.

'How did you guess I wasn't Serena?'

'The wording on the gravestone at Steeple Hampton. It was so curt and the normal wording was missing. Tomorrow morning at ten – at the latest.'

She nodded and left, closing the door behind her.

'What will you do with the money?' Paula asked.

'Burn it. No reason why she should profit from what she did. She is not a nice woman. She was also a damned nuisance. There were times when I thought she could be Goslar.' He smiled. 'Now all of you need sleep so I suggest you go home. I'd appreciate it if Paula and Trudy would stay for a few minutes longer.'

He was alone with them – except for Monica, now busy at work. He looked at Trudy.

'I was most impressed with the performance you put up. With your toughness, your resourcefulness, the cool way you reacted to grim situations. Would you be interested in becoming a member of my outfit? Subject to vetting, of course.'

Trudy's face lit up, she glowed. She had trouble finding words to reply. Then she smiled. Paula also was smiling with pleasure. She then realized she'd forgotten to give Tweed Cord Dillon's message over the phone – when Tweed was in the shower at the Richemond. He'd had Trudy vetted in the States.

'I'm lost for words,' Trudy eventually said. 'I'd love to join you. Subject to vetting.' She lifted a hand to check her blaze of red hair, then dropped it quickly. Not the done thing. 'I'll do my best to justify your confidence in me. That is, if it's all right with Paula.'

'Great idea,' Paula assured her.

'It was a sinister tide,' Tweed reflected.

'You mean at Appledore – when the wave carried in the dead fisherman, the dead seal, the dead fish.'

'That, yes. But even more the sinister tide of Muslim Fundamentalists who, armed with Goslar's weapon, would have flooded over the West.'

THE STONE LEOPARD

For Jane

Contents

'USA is Shackville . . .

'This barbaric American civilization, this land of sky-scrapers and hovels . . . In New York incredible wealth looks down from penthouses on incredible poverty and nothing ever lasts for even five minutes – least of all marriage in that land of divorcées . . .

'What a wonderful civilization this is – controlled by the cement lobby, the car lobby, the oil lobby. So, skyscrapers barely twenty years old are torn down to make way for even more hideous monoliths. Freeways and expressways spawn and roll across the plains – so these unhappy and neurotic people can drive on and on – from A to A to A! In the United States you never reach B – every new place you come to is the same as the place you have come from! And this is the America which attempts to dominate Europe!

'Let me warn you, my friends. If Europe is not to become a second Shackville, then we must fight to cleanse her of all American influence . . .'

Extract from speech at Dijon on 7 December by Guy Florian, President of the Republic of France.

Part One

The Leopard

8–16 December

Chapter One

'After Giscard came de Gaulle . . .'

The dry comment was made by a British Foreign Office under-secretary off the record. A spokesman at the American State Department put it more grimly. 'After Giscard came a more brutal de Gaulle – de Gaulle magnified by the power of ten.' They were, of course, referring to the new President of the French Republic, only a few hours before the first attempt to kill him.

It was his anti-American outburst at Dijon which provoked these two descriptions of the most powerful political leader in Western Europe. Understandably, the real sorrow in certain Washington circles at the news of the attempted assassination of President Florian was that it had failed. But on that wintry December evening when Florian left the Elysée Palace to walk the few dozen metres which would take him to the Ministry of the Interior in the Place Beauvau, he was within seconds of death.

The rise to power of Guy Auguste Florian, who succeeded Giscard d'Estaing as President of the French

Republic, was spectacular and unexpected – so unexpected that it caught almost every government in the world off balance. Tall, slim and agile, at fifty-two Florian looked ten years younger; exceptionally quick-witted, he was impatient of minds which moved more slowly than his own. And there was something of de Gaulle in his commanding presence, in the way he dominated everyone around him by sheer force of personality. At eight o'clock on the evening of Wednesday, 8 December he was at his most impatient when Marc Grelle, Police Prefect of Paris, warned him against walking in the streets.

'There is a car waiting. It can drive you to the Ministry, Mr President . . .'

'You think I will catch a chill?' Florian enquired. 'Maybe you would like a doctor to accompany me the two minutes it will take to get there?'

'At least he would be available to stop the blood flow if a bullet finds you . . .'

Marc Grelle was one of the few men in France who dared to answer Florian in his own sardonic coin. Forty-two years old, a few inches shorter than the six-foot one president, the police prefect was also slim and athletic and a man who disliked formality. In fact, Grelle's normal dress for most of his working day was a pair of neatly pressed slacks and a polo-necked sweater, which he was still wearing. Perhaps it was the informality, the ease of manner which made the prefect, widowed a year earlier when his wife died in a car crash, attractive to women. His appearance may have helped; sporting a trim, dark moustache which matched his thatch of black hair, he had, like the president, good bone structure, and although normally poker-faced, his firm mouth had a hint of humour at the corners. He shrugged as Florian, putting on a coat, prepared to leave his study on the first floor of the Elysée.

'I'll come with you then,' the police prefect said. 'But you take foolish risks . . .'

He followed Florian out of the study and down the stairs to the large hall which leads to the front entrance and the enclosed courtyard beyond, slipping on his leather raincoat as he walked. He left his coat open deliberately; it gave easier access to the .38 Smith & Wesson revolver he always carried. It is not normal for a prefect to be armed but Marc Grelle was not a normal prefect; since one of his prime duties was to protect the president inside the boundaries of Paris he took the responsibility personally. In the carpeted lobby a uniformed and bemedalled usher opened the tall glass door and Florian, well ahead of the prefect, ran down the seven steps into the cobbled yard. Still inside, Grelle hurried to catch him up.

To reach the Ministry of the Interior, which is only three minutes' walk from the Elysée, the president had to leave the courtyard, cross the Rue du Faubourg-St-Honoré, walk a few dozen metres to the Place Beauvau where he would turn into the entrance to the Ministry. He was starting to cross the street when Grelle, saluting the sentries briefly, came out of the courtyard. The prefect glanced quickly to left and right. At eight in the evening, barely a fortnight before Christmas, which is not celebrated with any great enthusiasm in Paris, it was dark and quiet. There was very little traffic about and on his face Grelle felt spots of moisture. It was going to rain again, for God's sake – it had rained steadily for weeks and nearly half France was under water.

The street was almost empty, but not quite; coming towards the Elysée entrance from the Madeleine direction, a couple paused under a lamp while the man lit a cigarette. British tourists, Grelle guessed: the man, hatless, wore a British warm; the woman was dressed in a smart grey coat. Across the road was someone else, a woman who stood alone close to a fur shop. A moment earlier she had been peering into the window. Now, half-turned towards the street, she was fiddling inside her handbag, presumably for a handkerchief or comb.

A rather attractive woman – in her early thirties so far as Grelle could see – she wore a red hat and a form-fitting brown coat. As he headed for the Place Beauvau, crossing the street diagonally, Florian was passing her at an angle. Never a man to fail to notice an attractive woman, the president glanced at her and then moved on. All this Grelle took in as he reached the sidewalk kerb, still a few metres behind his impatient president.

No detectives were assigned to accompany Florian when he went out: he had expressly forbidden what he called 'an invasion of my privacy...' Normally he travelled in one of the black Citroën DS23s always waiting parked inside the courtyard, but he had developed this irksome habit of walking to the Place Beauvau whenever he wanted to see the Minister of the Interior. And the habit had become known, had even been reported in the press.

'It's dangerous,' Grelle had protested. 'You even go out at the same time – at eight in the evening. It wouldn't be difficult for someone to wait for you . . .'

'You think the Americans will send a gunman?' Florian had enquired sardonically.

'There are always cranks . . .'

Grelle had stepped off the kerb, was still catching up with Florian, his eyes darting about, when something made the president glance back. He was hardly more than a metre away when the woman took the gun out of her handbag. Quite coolly, showing no sign of panic, her arm steady, she took deliberate, point-blank aim. Florian, twisted round, froze in sheer astonishment for only a matter of seconds. In another second he would have been running, ducking, doing something. The sound of two shots being fired in rapid succession echoed down the street like the drumbeat backfire of a large car.

The body lay in the gutter, quite inert, quite dead. The complete lack of movement is always the most disturbing thing. Grelle bent over her, the .38 Smith & Wesson still in his hand. He felt shocked. It was the first time he had killed a woman. When the Forensic Institute people examined the corpse later they found one of Grelle's bullets in her heart, the second one a centimetre to the right. A moment earlier the prefect had hustled the president back inside the courtyard, gripping him tightly by the arm, taking no notice of what he said, ushering him back inside the Elysée like a felon. Now guards with automatic weapons were flooding into the street. Far too late.

Grelle himself removed the automatic from the hand of the dead woman, lifting it carefully by the barrel to retain fingerprints. It was a Bayard 9-mm short made by the Belgian small-arms factory at Hertal. Small enough to go inside a handbag, it was by no means a lady's gun. Fired – as it would have been – at point-blank range, Grelle had no doubt the result would have been fatal. A few minutes later his deputy, Director-General André Boisseau of the Police Judiciaire, arrived in the cordoned-off street in a police car with siren screaming.

'My God, is it true?'

'Yes, it is true,' Grelle snapped. 'His would-be assassin, a woman, is just being carried into that ambulance. Florian is unhurt – back in the Elysée. From now on everything will be different. We will have tight security on him twenty-four hours a day. He is to be guarded wherever he goes – I'll see him in the morning to get his approval . . .'

'If he doesn't agree?'

'He'll receive my immediate resignation . . .'

The press had arrived now, the reporters were trying

to force their way through the churning crowd of gendarmes, and one of them called out to the prefect. 'The hyenas are here,' Grelle muttered under his breath, but it was important to set them right immediately. They still had time to file their stories for tomorrow's banner headlines. He ordered that they be let through and they swarmed round the slim, athletic man who was the calmest person present. It was, of course, the reporter from *L'Humanité* – 'that Communist rag', as the prefect called the paper – who asked the question. 'You say the assassin was a woman? Did the president know her?'

The implication was crude and clear, bearing in mind the rumours about Florian's strained relations with his wife, about his relationships with other women. *L'Humanité* scented a juicy scandal of international proportions. Grelle, who detested politicians, understood politics. He paused to get everyone's close attention, to build up a suspense he could deflate.

'The president did not know this woman. He had never seen her in his life. He told me this when I was hustling him back into the Elysée . . .'

'He saw her clearly then?' the reporter insisted.

'He happened to be looking straight at her when she aimed the weapon at him . . .'

Soon after this exchange he shut them up, had them sent back further down the street behind the cordon, knowing they would soon have to rush off to phone their offices. The ambulance had gone now. Police photographers were taking pictures of the sidewalk section where it had happened. Leaving a superintendent in charge to complete the formalities, Grelle got inside Boisseau's car and his deputy drove them back to the prefecture on the Ile de la Cité.

On the way the prefect examined the dead woman's handbag he had slipped inside his raincoat pocket. The usual equipment: lipstick, powder compact, a ring of keys, comb and one hundred and fifty-seven francs in notes and coins, and an identity card. The woman who had tried to kill the President of France was a Lucie Devaud. At this time Grelle saw no significance in the name. Nor did he see any significance in the fact that she had been born in the department of Lozère.

At certain moments in history it is a single incident which triggers off a whole series of events, which causes wheels to begin turning in several continents, wheels which move faster and faster. Lucie Devaud's attempt to kill Guy Florian was just such an incident. It came at a critical moment in the history of Europe.

The world was emerging from the disastrous slump which had begun in 1974. Everywhere there was hope and optimism again. The airlines were carrying an ever-growing number of tourists to distant and exotic places; the world stock markets were climbing rapidly – the Dow-Jones had passed the 1500 line – and the terrors of inflation were now only a memory. And, as the American Hudson Institute had predicted, France was leading the world with a great economic surge. For various reasons France had become the most powerful nation in Western Europe, overtaking even West Germany; so, the President of the French Republic, Guy Florian, was the most powerful statesman between Moscow and Washington. On the political front the scene was less reassuring.

During the economic blizzard Soviet Russia had made vast strides. Portugal was now a Communist state, the Communist Party there having seized power by rigging the elections. In Greece a Communist *coup d'état* had taken over the government. And Spain, after a long period of chaos, was now in the grip of a Communist-dominated coalition government. Soviet warships were in the Piraeus harbour of Athens, were anchored off Barcelona and were using the facilities of Lisbon as a naval base. The Mediterranean had become almost a Russian lake. Added to this, the last American troops had left Europe as the American Congress retreated further and further into isolation.

It was all this – plus her growing economic power – which made France the key state in Western Europe. Allied with West Germany, she provided the key element which barred any further Soviet advance. This was the situation when the news reverberated round the world of Lucie Devaud's attempt to kill President Guy Florian. The Frenchwoman failed to pull the trigger on her 9-mm automatic, but inadvertently she pulled a different kind of trigger.

Very shortly her death was to affect the lives of Alan Lennox, an Englishman based in London; of David

Nash, an American living in New York; of Peter Lanz, a German based in Bavaria; of Colonel René Lasalle, ex-assistant chief of army counter-intelligence, now living in exile in Germany; and of certain other people at the moment residing in Czechoslovakia. The first reaction came from Col. René Lasalle who made yet another inflammatory broadcast over the radio station Europe Number One, which transmits from the Saarland in Germany.

'Who was this mysterious woman, Lucie Devaud?' he asked in his late-evening broadcast on 8 December. 'What was her secret? And what is the secret in the past of a leading Paris politician which must not be discovered at any cost? And why is Marc Grelle clamping down a security dragnet which overnight is turning my country into a police state? Is there a conspiracy . . .?'

Extracts from the broadcast were repeated in television news bulletins all over the world. Lasalle's broadcast – his most venomous yet – had all the elements to stir up a ferment of speculation. 'The secret in the past of a leading Paris politician . . .' The phrase was seized on by the foreign correspondents. Was there, they speculated, somewhere in Paris a key personality – even a cabinet minister – who was secretly working against President Florian? If so, who was this shadowy figure? The wildest rumours were spread – even one to the effect that a right-wing group of conspirators headed by the unknown cabinet minister was behind the assassination attempt, that they had tried to kill Florian before he made his historic visit to Soviet Russia on 23 December.

In an apartment on the eighth floor at an address on East 84th Street in New York, David Nash dismissed the conspiracy rumour as rubbish. Nash, forty-five years old, a small and well-built man with shrewd grey eyes and thinning hair, worked for a special section of the State Department which no congressional committee had yet penetrated and so rendered useless. Officially, he was concerned with policy – 'the vaguest word in the dictionary', as he once commented; in fact he was involved with counter-espionage at the highest level. And since he made a point of rarely appearing in the capital, the press corps was hardly aware of his existence. In the afternoon of the day following Lasalle's outburst over Europe Number One he sat in his apartment studying a transcript of the broadcast. Round the table with him were seated two men who had just flown in from Washington.

'The way things are,' Nash commented, 'it sends shivers up my spine how close Florian came to death. If France were plunged into chaos at this particular moment, God knows how Russia might try to take advantage of the situation. We've got to find out who was behind that attempt—'

Andrew MacLeish, Nash's nominal superior, a thin, austere fifty-year-old, broke in irritably. He hated New

York and counted every minute spent there as time out of his life. 'You think this nut, Lasalle, has any idea of what he's talking about? For my money he's got his knife into Florian and just enjoys twisting it at random. By my count this is his tenth anti-Florian broadcast in six months . . .'

'The tenth,' Nash agreed. 'Incidentally, I've accepted his invitation to meet with him.'

'What invitation?' MacLeish demanded. 'This is the first I've heard you've had any contact with that psychopath . . .'

'Even psychopaths sometimes know a thing or two,' Nash remarked. 'Colonel Lasalle approached me through the Brussels embassy late this morning, our time. He says he has some vital information about what's really happening inside Paris but he'll only talk to a representative from Washington – face to face. And we have to keep very quiet about this . . .'

'I don't think we ought to get mixed up with psychopathic exiles,' MacLeish repeated. He looked out of the window where he could just see a section of the Triborough Bridge through the skeletal framework of a new high-rise. They argued about it for over an hour, but in the end Nash wore them down. It was Washington which was becoming psychopathic in Nash's view; with the military and most of the administration against the troop withdrawal from Europe which Congress had forced on them, it was becoming even more important to know what was really happening in Europe, to warn their ex-allies of any dangerous development they could uncover. On the following day Nash flew to Europe to meet the man Guy Florian had ruined.

Col. René Baptiste Lasalle, ex-assistant chief of French military counter-intelligence, had recently been called 'an extinct volcano' by Guy Florian, but for a man whose career was abruptly ended when it seemed almost certain he would soon be promoted to the exalted rank of general, the volcano remained remarkably active. Certainly the rumbling of Col. Lasalle was heard clearly enough in Paris.

Six months before Lucie Devaud tried to shoot Guy Florian in the Faubourg-St-Honoré, Lasalle had quarrelled violently with the president and had to flee France overnight; it was rumoured he was about to be arrested for conspiring against the president. Driving his own car, Lasalle crashed through a frontier control post east of Metz at four in the morning and took refuge in West Germany. From the moment of his arrival in the Federal Republic he set about organizing a campaign of rumours to discredit the man who had ruined him. As his instrument he chose Europe Number One, the independent radio station with its transmitters in the Saarland.

At the time when David Nash flew from New York to meet him secretly, Col. Lasalle was fifty-five years old. Small, compact and lean-faced, he now made his way through life with only one arm; his left arm had been blown clean off his shoulder by a landmine in Algeria in 1962. At that time a captain in army counter-intelligence, Lasalle had proved himself the most brilliant officer in the French Army when it came to rooting out Arab underground leaders. Within twenty-four hours of his arm being taken away from him, his family was also taken away; a terrorist threw a bomb into the living-room of his villa, killing his wife and seven-year-old son. Lying in hospital, his reaction was typical when he heard the news.

'Since my private life is finished I shall devote the rest of my time to France – to help preserve her way of life. It is the only thing left to me . . .'

Immediately his convalescence was over, he returned from Marseille to North Africa. The convalescence in itself was remarkable. Finding his sense of balance faulty, Lasalle took to walking in the Estoril mountains with a stick, leaping over deep ravines to find a new balance. 'When survival is at stake,' he said later, 'the body adjusts itself wonderfully . . .' He went back to Algeria just in time to detect and foil the most determined effort to date to assassinate General de Gaulle. Then, years later, came the clash with Florian.

Now, exiled to the Saarland, living in a farmhouse close to Saarbrücken – close also to the French border – Lasalle broadcast regularly over Europe Number One, the radio station on German soil listened to by millions inside France. And the loss of one arm seemed to have increased the electric energy of this small man who boasted he had never been idle for a day in his life. The

target of his virulent broadcasting campaign was Guy
Florian.

'Why is he going to visit Soviet Russia on 23 December? What is the real motive behind this visit? Why is
he going there of all places at a time when Europe is
threatened by the looming shadow of the Red Army as
never before? Who is the cabinet minister about whom
whispers are spreading in Paris . . .?'

Never once did Lasalle refer to Florian by name.
Always he referred to 'he', to 'this man', until gradually
it dawned on Paris that Lasalle was not only an expert
counter-intelligence officer; he had now become a
master of poisonous political propaganda who was
threatening to undermine the foundations of Florian's
régime. This was the man who had quietly indicated to
the Americans that he wanted to speak to a trustworthy
intelligence official.

On the night of Thursday 9 December, the same day
when in New York David Nash informed MacLeish
that he would be flying to Europe to interview Col.
René Lasalle, a short, grizzle-haired man in shabby
clothes arrived in the Faubourg-St-Honoré and took up
a position opposite the Elysée Palace. He was standing
at the exact spot on the kerb where, twenty-four hours
earlier, Lucie Devaud had fallen into the gutter when
Marc Grelle's bullets hit her in the chest. No one took
any notice of him, and if the uniformed *garde republi-
caine* on duty outside the Elysée gave him even a

17

moment's thought he must have assumed that this was just another voyeur, one of those macabre people who delight in goggling at the scene of an attempted crime.

The shabbily clothed man arrived at 7.30 p.m. when it was dark. In his middle sixties, his face lined and worn and with a straggle of grey moustache, he was still standing there at 8.30 p.m. when, as if in a daze, he suddenly stepped into the street without looking. The car coming at speed only a few metres away had no time to pull up; the man must have loomed in front of the driver's windscreen without warning. The vehicle hit the pedestrian a terrible blow, drove on over him and accelerated down the street, disappearing in the direction of Madeleine. Fifteen minutes later an ambulance with siren screaming rushed him to the Hôtel-Dieu on the Ile de la Cité. On arrival a doctor examined the patient and said he would be lucky to last the night.

On Thursday, 9 December, having got rid of his visitors from Washington, David Nash consulted a road map of Western Europe, checked distances and promptly decided to fly across the Atlantic the same night. If he caught Pan Am flight 92 leaving New York at 5.45 p.m. he could be in Brussels early next day, which would give him time to drive to Luxembourg – where he had arranged to meet Lasalle – and back again to catch another night flight from Brussels to New York. He boarded flight 92 by the skin of his teeth and then relaxed in his first-class seat as the Boeing 707 climbed steadily towards thirty thousand feet above the Long Island coast.

Nash had a tight schedule ahead of him. He was not only going to meet Lasalle on the neutral ground of Luxembourg; he had also arranged to meet his German counterpart, Peter Lanz, with whom he maintained a close and cordial relationship. After all, the French fugitive colonel was residing in Germany and it had been one of Lanz's more delicate duties to keep an eye on his electric visitor who had fled from the territory of Germany's closest ally.

The German authorities had very mixed feelings about the arrival of Col. Lasalle in their midst. They gave him refuge – no specific charges had ever been levelled against him by Paris – and the local police chief in Saarbrücken was instructed to maintain a distant surveillance on the fugitive. Lasalle himself, fearing an attempt to kidnap him, had asked for police protection, and this was granted on the understanding that it was never referred to publicly. With the passage of time – Lasalle had now been in Germany for six months – the surveillance was relaxed.

Peter Lanz had visited Lasalle several times, requesting him to tone down his broadcasts, and always Lasalle received the German courteously and said he would consider the request. Then he would get into his car, drive to the radio station and blast Florian all over again with a fresh series of innuendoes. Since he was breaking no law, Lanz would shrug his shoulders and then sit down to read carefully a transcript of the latest outburst.

Lanz, at thirty-two, was exceptionally young to occupy the post of vice-president of the *Bundesnachrichtendienst*, the West German Federal Intelligence Service. He owed his rapid promotion to his ability, and to the fact that a large number of older men were suddenly swept out of the organization when the new Chancellor, Franz Hauser, was elected three months after Guy Florian's own rise to power. 'I don't want intriguers,' Hauser had snapped, 'I want young and energetic men who can do the damned job . . .'

This very young second-in-command of the BND was a man of medium height, slim build and thinning brown hair. 'In this job I shall be bald at forty,' he was fond of saying. 'Is it true that women go wild over bald men?' Normally serious-faced, he had one quality in common with Guy Florian: when he smiled he could charm almost anyone into agreeing with him. His job was to try and foresee any potentially explosive situation which might harm the Federal Republic politically – to foresee and defuse in advance. The arrival of Lasalle on German soil was a classic case. 'Not one of my outstanding successes,' he once admitted, 'but then we don't know where it's going to lead, do we? Lasalle knows something – maybe one day he will tell me what he knows . . .'

Nash met Lanz at Liège in Belgium. Earlier in the morning, landing at Brussels at 8.30 a.m., the American

20

had hired a car at the airport in the name of Charles Wade, the pseudonym under which he was travelling. Arriving in Liège, Nash spent half an hour with Lanz in the anonymous surroundings of the railway station restaurant, then he drove on south to Clervaux in the Ardennes. The secret rendezvous with Col. Lasalle had been chosen carefully – Clervaux is neither in Germany nor in Belgium. This little-known town is high up in the hills of northern Luxembourg.

The secrecy surrounding Nash's visit was essential to the survival of Lasalle as a credible public figure; once Paris could prove he was in touch with the Americans he could so easily be discredited as a tool of Washington. At the quiet Hôtel Claravallis in Clervaux, inside a room booked in the name of Charles Wade, Nash and Lasalle talked in absolute secrecy for two hours. Afterwards, Lasalle left immediately and drove back to Germany. Nash had a quick lunch at the hotel and then drove straight back to Belgium where he reported to Peter Lanz who had waited for him in Liège. Half an hour later Nash was on his way back to Brussels where he caught the night plane to New York. During his lightning dash to Europe, travelling under a pseudonym, Nash had gone nowhere near the American Embassy in Brussels. He was eating dinner on the plane while he doodled animal pictures and then erased them. Pictures of the head of a leopard.

Chapter Two

David Nash was somewhere on the road between Brussels and Liège, driving to keep his first appointment with Peter Lanz, when Marc Grelle in Paris received what appeared to be a routine phone call. The large office of the police prefect is on the second floor of the préfecture; its walls are panelled, its windows overlook the Boulevard du Palais; and to ensure privacy the windows are masked by net curtains. As usual, Grelle was wearing a pair of slacks and a polo-necked sweater as he sat behind his desk, going through the morning's paperwork, which he disliked.

Grelle, born in the city of Metz, was a man of Lorraine. In France the Lorrainers are known as the least French of the French. Sturdy physically, not at all excitable, they have a reputation for being level-headed and dependable in an emergency. Grelle had travelled a long way to reach Paris from Metz. At the time of Florian's election as president eighteen months earlier, Marc Grelle had been Police Prefect of Marseille and would have been quite content to complete his career in that raffish seaport. 'Look where ambition gets you,' he had a habit of saying. 'Look at any cabinet minister.

They take pills to help them sleep, they take stimulants to keep them awake at the Wednesday cabinet meetings. They marry rich wives to further their ambitions, then spend their wives' money on mistresses to keep themselves sane. What is the point of it all?'

It was only with the greatest reluctance that Grelle accepted Florian's strong plea for him to come to Paris. 'I need one honest man close to me,' Florian had urged. His face had creased into the famous smile. 'If you won't accept I shall have to leave the post vacant!' So, Grelle had come to Paris. Sighing, he initialled a paper and was turning to another document when the phone rang. The call was from André Boisseau, his deputy.

'I'm at the Hôtel-Dieu, chief, just round the corner. I think you ought to get over here right away. A man is dying and there's something very odd about him . . .'

'Dying?'

'He was knocked down by a hit-and-run driver in the Faubourg-St-Honoré yesterday evening opposite the Elysée – at the very spot where Lucie Devaud died . . .'

Boisseau didn't want to say any more on the phone, so putting on his leather raincoat, Grelle left the building and walked the short distance to the large hospital which overlooks the right bank of the Seine. It was pouring with rain but he hated driving short distances – 'Soon, babies will be born with wheels instead of legs,' was one of his favourite sayings. Boisseau was waiting for him on the first floor of the gloomy building. 'Sorry to get you wet through, chief, but he won't speak to anyone except the police prefect. The man's

name is Gaston Martin. He's just back from Guiana –
for the first time in thirty years, for God's sake . . .'

Later, Grelle pieced together the bizarre story. Guiana
is the only overseas department in South America
which still belongs to France. Known once to the public
mainly because this is where the notorious penal settlement, Devil's Island was situated, it had remained for
years out of the world's headlines, one of the sleepier
areas in the vast Latin-American continent.

Gaston Martin, a man in his late sixties, had spent all
of his life since the Second World War in this outlandish
place. Then, for the first time in over thirty years, he had
returned home aboard a freighter which docked at Le
Havre on 9 December, less than twenty-four hours after
the attempted assassination of Guy Florian. Travelling
to Paris by train, he dumped his small bag at the Cécile,
a seedy Left Bank hotel, and went out for a walk.
Eventually he turned up outside the Elysée where, at
exactly 8.30 p.m., he had been run down by a car as he
stepped off the sidewalk. Grelle knew nothing of this as
he followed Boisseau into a room occupied by only one
patient. The prefect's nose wrinkled as he smelt antisep-
tic. A fit man, he detested hospital odours.

Gaston Martin lay in the single bed attended by a
nurse and a doctor who shook his head when Grelle
asked how the patient was. 'I give him one hour,' he
whispered. 'Maybe less. The car went right over him
. . . lungs are pierced. No, it makes no difference if you

24

question him, but he may not respond. I'll leave you for a few minutes . . .' He frowned when Boisseau made his own request. 'The nurse, too? As you wish . . .'

Why were so many wards like death cells, Grelle wondered as he approached the bed. Martin, his head covered with wispy grey hair, had a drooping moustache under a prominent hooked nose. More character than brains, Grelle assessed as he drew up a chair beside the bed. Boisseau opened the conversation. 'This is the Police Prefect of Paris, Marc Grelle. You asked to see him . . .'

'I saw him . . . going into the Elysée,' Martin quavered.

'Saw who?' Grelle asked quietly. The man from Guiana reached out and held the prefect's hand, which gave Grelle a funny feeling, a sensation of helplessness. 'Saw who?' he repeated.

'The Leopard . . .'

Something turned over inside Grelle, then he remembered something else and felt better. In the few seconds before he replied his memory spun back over God knew how many files he had read, trying to recall exact details. He knew immediately who this man must be referring to, and when he recalled the second detail he realized Martin must be raving.

'I don't know who you mean,' Grelle said carefully.

'Communist Resistance leader . . . the Lozère.' Gripping the prefect's hand tightly, Martin struggled to heave himself up on the pillow, his face streaked with sweat. Boisseau tried to stop him, but Grelle said leave him alone. He understood the desperate reaction: Martin was trying to stay alive just a little longer, feeling he could only do this by getting himself out of the prone position.

'Communist wartime leader . . .' Martin repeated. 'The . . . youngest . . . in the Resistance . . .'

'You couldn't have seen him go into the Elysée,' Grelle told him gently. 'There are guards, sentries on the gate . . .'

'They saluted him . . .'

Grelle felt the shock at the pit of his stomach. Despite the effort he made a slight tremor passed through his hand, and Martin felt it. His rheumy eyes opened wider into a glare. 'You believe me,' he gasped. 'You have to believe me . . .'

Grelle turned to Boisseau, whispering the order. 'No one is to be allowed in here – not even the doctor. On my way in I saw a gendarme near the entrance – go get him, station him outside this door, then come back in yourself . . .'

He was with the dying Martin for twenty minutes, knowing that his questioning was hastening the poor wretch's death, but also knowing that Martin didn't mind. He just wanted to talk, to pass on his dying message. Boisseau returned to the room a few minutes later, having left the gendarme on duty outside. At one stage a priest tried to force his way into the room, but Martin indicated he was an agnostic and became so agitated the priest withdrew.

For Grelle it was an ordeal, trying to get the man to talk coherently, watching his skin become greyer under the film of sweat, feeling Martin's hand gripping his own to maintain contact with the living, with life itself. At the end of twenty minutes what Grelle had extracted was mostly incoherent babbling, a series of disconnected phrases, but there was a certain thread running through the feverish ramblings. Then Martin died. The hand in Grelle's went limp, rested quietly like the hand of a sleeping child. The man who hadn't seen Paris for over thirty years had returned to die there within forty-eight hours of landing in France.

Returning to his office in the prefecture with Boisseau, Grelle locked the door, told his secretary over the phone that he could take no more calls for the moment, then went over to the window to stare down into the rain-swept street. First he swore his deputy to absolute secrecy. 'In case anything happens to me,' he explained, 'there must be someone else who knows about this – who could carry on the investigation. Although I'm still praying that Martin got it wrong, that he didn't know what he was talking about . . .'

'What was Martin talking about?' the diplomatic Boisseau enquired.

'You know as well as I do,' Grelle replied brutally. 'He was saying that someone who visited the Elysée last night, someone important enough to be saluted –

so he has to be of cabinet rank – is a top Communist agent . . .'

On Grelle's instruction, Boisseau sent off an urgent cable to the police chief at Cayenne, Guiana, requesting all information on Gaston Martin, and then between them they sorted out the broken, often-incoherent story Martin had told them.

He had stood in the vicinity of the Elysée Palace for about one hour – between, say, 7.30 p.m. and 8.30 p.m., sometimes standing at the edge of the kerb where Lucie Devaud had been shot, sometimes wandering up towards the Place Beauvau, and then back again. At least they were sure of 8.30, the time when a car had knocked him down, because this had been witnessed by one of the Elysée sentries. 'Partially witnessed, that is,' Boisseau explained. 'I phoned the inspector in charge of the case while you were coming to the hospital and the fool of a sentry isn't even sure of the make of car which knocked down Martin . . .'

And at some moment during this approximate hour Martin swore he had seen the man he had once known as the Leopard walk into the Elysée courtyard and be saluted by the sentries. It was this brief statement which so disturbed Grelle. 'They saluted him . . .' Martin's description of the man had been vague; by the time Grelle got round to asking this question the dying man had been slipping away fast. And often he had rambled off in another direction, forgetting the question Grelle had asked him.

'But according to Martin this man was very tall – over six feet,' the prefect emphasized. 'He said that three times – the bit about his great height.'

'This goes back over thirty years to the wartime Resistance,' Boisseau protested. 'That is, if Martin is to be believed at all. How on earth could he recognize a man he hadn't seen all that time? People change like hell . . .'

'He was very insistent that he saw the Leopard. Said he hadn't changed much, that the first thing he noticed was the man's walk – then I couldn't get him to describe the walk.'

'It doesn't sound at all likely . . .' Boisseau was tieless by now, in his shirt-sleeves. Coffee had been brought in to them and the room was full of smoke as Grelle used up cigarette after cigarette. The rain was still lashing the windows.

'It doesn't,' Grelle agreed, 'but I was the one who heard every word he said and he frightened me. I think I can judge when a man is telling the truth . . .'

'This Leopard then – you think he was really telling the truth about that?' Boisseau, small and heavily built, with almond-shaped eyes and thick eyebrows, had made no attempt to keep the scepticism out of his voice. 'Personally, I have never heard of him . . .'

'But you are younger than me.' The prefect lit another cigarette. 'The Leopard is on file, a very old and dusty file by now. And yes, I do think Gaston Martin was telling the truth – as he believed it to be.'

'Which could be a very different thing . . .'

'Quite true. You see, there's something you don't know. The Communist Resistance leader known during the war as the Leopard is dead.'

On Saturday morning, 11 December, David Nash, who had just returned from Europe aboard the night flight from Brussels, flew from New York to Washington for an emergency meeting with Andrew MacLeish at the State Department. The two men locked themselves away in a small room on the second floor and MacLeish listened without saying a word for fifteen minutes; it was one of his strong points, that he could absorb a verbal report without interruption, soaking up information like a sponge.

'And Lasalle gave absolutely no indication of the identity of this alleged cabinet minister who could be a secret Communist agent?' he enquired eventually. 'This man he calls the second Leopard – because he has adopted the pseudonym of the dead wartime Communist Resistance leader?'

'None at all,' Nash replied promptly. 'He played the whole thing very close to the chest. What he did tell me was that he believes he was on the verge of uncovering the agent when he had his titanic row with Florian – which ended in his flight from France. Since then he hasn't been able to carry his investigation any further and he's worried stiff that a *coup d'état* is planned to take place while Florian is in Moscow on this coming visit. He suspects that the Russians invited the president to Russia to get him out of Paris at the crucial moment. The attempted assassination decided Lasalle – to make contact with me. He's pretty certain that if it had succeeded the *coup d'état* led by the second Leopard would have taken place at once.'

'So he wants us to complete the investigation he started . . .'

'He has this list of three witnesses who worked closely with the original Leopard during the war . . .'

'A list he wouldn't give you,' MacLeish snapped.

'I'm not sure I blame him for that,' Nash countered. 'He's very security-conscious and that I like. He'll only hand over the list to the agent we provide to go inside France to meet these people . . .'

'What the hell can these three so-called witnesses tell us?' MacLeish demanded irritably. 'If the original Leopard is dead I don't see the connection . . .'

'Lasalle believes someone who was in the Leopard's wartime Resistance group cleverly took over his name as the code-name the Russians would know him by. So to find this top Communist agent we have to dig back into the past, to find who could fit. Find out who he was in 1944 and we'll know who he is today.'

MacLeish, whose other strong point was his ability to take a quick decision, drummed his thick fingers on the table like a man playing a piano. 'So the deadline is 23 December when Florian takes off for Moscow, which gives us exactly eleven days. You're going to have to move damned fast . . .'

'So I can send someone in?' Nash interjected.

'You can send someone in,' MacLeish decided, 'but not an American. If Florian's security apparatus got hold of him the French would have a field day. I can hear Florian's next anti-American speech now – Yankee agent discovered trying to smear Paris cabinet minister . . . That we can't risk. An agent yes, but not an American,' he repeated.

'But not an American . . .'

It was still Saturday morning when Nash gave the instruction to his assistant, Ward Fischer, in the suite of offices on the third floor which housed his staff. Normally everyone except Fischer would have been at home on a Saturday, but before boarding his New York flight to Washington Nash had phoned ahead and the suite was now occupied by men recalled hastily while Nash was airborne.

'Kind of narrows the field,' Fischer remarked.

'Narrow it to zero. Find the man,' Nash snapped. 'Inside two hours,' he added.

Fischer went into the next office and within five minutes his staff was searching through the files, looking for a name. The specification for the man who would go into France to interview Lasalle's witnesses was stringent. He had to have top security clearance; to be fluent enough in the language to pass as a Frenchman; to be experienced in the security field; and he must be a man with a cold, careful temperament who could be relied on in an emergency, operating entirely on his own. As to nationality, he must not be an American, nor must he be a Frenchman.

It was Nash himself who added this final qualification which caused Fischer to swear colourfully the moment he left his boss's office. 'The God-damned specification screams for a Frenchman,' he complained to one of his staff, 'so now you've got to find a Frenchman who isn't a Frenchman. Get on with it . . .' Nash had a very good reason for adding this last qualification. Because France is a very special place and many of its people are highly political, Nash felt it would be dangerous to choose a Frenchman to spy on the French. He also felt pretty sure Col. Lasalle would have the same doubts.

While Fischer and his staff were searching, Nash went over the file in his mind of people he had known – or known of. One name came to him quickly, but he rejected it: he could never persuade this man to do the job. Sitting at his desk, his chubby hands clasped behind his neck, he checked back in his mind, rejecting candidate after candidate. As Fischer had said, the specification certainly restricted the field. In the end he came back to the man he had first thought of.

At 1.30 in the afternoon Fischer came into his office carrying two files. 'These are the only two people who fit,' he said wearily. 'We ate at our desks and we've been working since I left you. Cancelling out the French made it that much tougher . . .' Nash looked at the two files. One of the names was Jules Beaurain, a Belgian. 'Belgium isn't France,' Fischer said hopefully. The other was the name Nash himself had thought of.

'It will take pressure to get this man,' Nash said reflectively. 'I may have just hit on how the pressure could be applied. Get me details of all overseas bids for security contracts inside the States. Get them now . . .'

'It's Saturday . . .'

'So the calendar tells me. Phone people at their homes, get them behind their desks fast. Tell them it's an emergency – and give them my compliments . . .'

'They're going to appreciate that,' Fischer said and went out of the office to phone his wife. She also was going to appreciate it, he felt sure.

Left alone in his office, Nash took a ballpoint out of his pocket and indulged in his liking for doodling portraits. He drew from memory a head-and-shoulders sketch of a man he had once known well, a man he had liked and respected despite disagreements. When he had finished the sketch he added a caption underneath. Alan Lennox. Security expert. British.

Three thousand miles across the Atlantic in London it was Saturday evening as Alan Lennox turned the key in the double-lock Chubb, checked the handle of the door to his office, and stood for a moment staring at the plate on the wall. *Lennox Security Company Limited*. On the stock exchange the shares had climbed to £3.50

and it looked as though they were going higher; security companies were enjoying a minor boom. God knew why, but recently they had become a City cult. Probably because they were 'export-orientated' as the little wise men who sent out brokers' recommendations phrased it. All over the world large industrial concerns were employing Britons to organize their security because, it was alleged, they were incorruptible. Another cult. Lennox thought maybe it was a good time to sell out – once he had obtained the big American oil combine contract he was bidding for. With that under his belt the shares should go through the roof.

The only man in the building – managing directors worked alone on Saturdays – he went down in the lift to Leadenhall Street and out into the storm which had broken over London. Collecting his Citroën DS23 from the underground garage, he drove home through sheets of blinding rain to his flat in St James's Place, reflecting that it wasn't a Saturday night to encourage a man on his own to dine out. Arriving inside the flat, which he had furnished with antiques, Lennox took off his two-hundred-guinea coat and poured himself a large Scotch. The next problem was to decide whether to eat out or grill himself a steak from the fridge.

Thirty-five years old, managing director of the most successful international security company based in London, Lennox was a well-built man of medium height who moved with a deceptive slowness; in an emergency he could react with the speed of a fox. Dark-haired, the hair cut shorter than the normal fashion, his thick eyebrows were also dark. The eyes were his most arresting feature; brown and slow-moving, they looked out on the world warily, taking nothing for granted. 'It's in the nature of my job to be suspicious,' he once said. 'A man called Marc Grelle told me in Marseille that I had the mind of a policeman; I suppose he was right . . .'

Born in Paris, Lennox's mother had been French, his father a minor official at the British Embassy in the Faubourg-St-Honoré. The first ten years of his life had been spent in France and Lennox was fluent in French long before he mastered English at school. Disliking his father's idea that he enter the diplomatic service – 'after eighteen I found we had nothing to say to each other' – he joined a large international oil company. Because of his fluency in English, French, German and Spanish he was attached to the security department. Five years later he was directing it.

'I was lucky,' Lennox recalled. 'The timing was right. Security had become the key to survival. You can buy tankers, drill new oilfields – but where's the profit if people keep dynamiting them?'

Lennox's career soared at the time when Arab terrorists were turning their attention to blowing up non-Arab oilfields – to increase the economic power of the Middle East fields. In an emergency boards of directors turn to the man who can save them; they turned to Lennox. Travelling widely, he organized new systems to protect oilfields, tankers and refineries in four continents. He soon decided that defensive measures were not enough; if you are to win you must carry the war into enemy territory.

Disappearing into the twilight world of counter-espionage, often for months at a time, Lennox penetrated the terrorist groups, locating their camps in the Lebanon and further back in Syria. At this time he was employing all sorts of dubious people, paying them large sums in tax-free cash – which drove prim accountants at headquarters crazy. One of his most successful anti-terrorist teams was recruited from the Union Corse – the French mafia – who were annoyed because Arab money had bought up certain Parisian protection rackets they had previously controlled. 'The Red Night of 14 July' was splashed across the world's headlines.

Lennox waited until he was ready, waited patiently for months while he built up an intimate knowledge of the terrorist gangs. On 14 July he struck. The Union Corse team – speaking French, the second language in Lebanon – landed by helicopters and came ashore from boats on isolated beaches. In eight hours they wiped out three major terrorist gangs, killing over two hundred men. Only Corsicans could have killed so swiftly and mercilessly. From that night the sabotage of oil installations dropped to five per cent of its previous volume.

It was during these years that Lennox came into contact with leading security and police chiefs from Tokyo to Washington, including men like David Nash and Peter Lanz, and organizations like the FBI and the Sûreté Nationale, all of whom provided discreet and unofficial help to a man who could take the ultimate measures they were not empowered to employ. At a later period he spent four years with an American company, including hazardous months along the Mexican border where terrorists were infiltrating with Mexican peasants coming into the United States to find work. Then, without warning, he resigned to set up his own outfit.

His private life was less successful. Married twice, he lost both wives to other men who came home each night. 'To my home,' he said sardonically. In both cases he divorced his wife despite the urgent plea of one that he assume the role of guilty party. 'You knew what my life was like before we married,' he said bluntly. 'I warned you time and again – and the one thing I can't stand is people who break contracts . . .' At the moment Lennox was consoling himself with his third girl friend without too much enthusiasm. He knew what the trouble was: three years after the foundation of his own company he felt that once again he had done what he had set out to do, so he was losing interest. 'I'm bloody bored,' he told himself as he drank his Scotch. 'I need something new . . .' He raised his glass to the telephone. 'Ring,' he told it, 'ring from some faraway place . . .'

He had finished his Scotch and was taking the steak out of the fridge when the phone rang. Knowing it had to be a wrong number, he picked up the receiver. The international telephone operator had a seductive voice. 'Mr Alan Lennox?' she enquired. 'Overseas call for you. Person-to-person. From Washington . . .'

*

Two men stood talking in the walled Paris garden, their overcoat collars turned up against the chill December wind. One of them was tall and slim, the other short and powerfully built, and the language they conversed in was French. The Leopard, tall and slim, shook his head doubtfully as his companion repeated the same argument forcefully.

'We believe it is essential to eliminate Col. Lasalle. We have people who can make it look like an accident, people waiting at this moment for the order to proceed . . .'

'It could be a mistake . . .'

'It could be a mistake to do nothing, not to take action. These people who would deal with the matter are competent, I assure you . . .'

They went on discussing the problem as darkness fell and beyond the walls the Paris rush-hour traffic built up to a peak. Not a score of metres from where the two men stood the life of the capital proceeded in its normal mundane way and some people were even buying presents for Christmas.

Chapter Three

Carel Vanek drove the Citroën DS21 forward at high speed, heading for the bulky figure standing in the middle of the concrete track. The light was bad; it was late in the afternoon of 11 December, just before dark. Through the windscreen Vanek saw the figure rush towards him, blur as the car hit it at 90 k.p.h., elevate under the impact, then the whole vehicle wobbled as he drove on, passing over the body. A dozen metres beyond he pulled up with a scream of tyres, looked over his shoulder, used the reverse gear, then backed at speed.

The body lay still in the dusk, a vague hump as he backed towards it, accelerating. Vanek never enjoyed himself more than behind the wheel of a car; he felt he was an extension of the mechanism, that the gear lever was another arm, the brake a third foot. It was exhilarating. He went on backing at speed and his aim was perfect. For the second time he felt the wobble as the Citroën's wheels passed over the hump lying in the roadway. Then he went on, backing into a sharp curve, stopping, driving forward again, turning the wheel until he was moving away at speed in the opposite direction.

'Thirty-five seconds,' the quiet man in the back of the car said as he clicked his stop-watch.

Vanek braked with a jerk that nearly threw the passenger in the seat beside him through the windscreen, laughing as Walther Brunner cursed. 'Do you have to be quite so dramatic?' Brunner demanded as he sagged back in his seat.

'Reaction – reaction...' Vanek snapped his fingers. 'It's what this is all about. On the day when we visit Lasalle I might have to do just that – you must be ready for it...'

They got out of the car and walked back up the abandoned race-track which lies just outside the Czech town of Tábor forty-five miles south of Prague. Little more than a bulky shadow in the distant gloom, Michael Borisov, the Russian in charge of the training centre, was bending over the form in the road, a form constructed of sacking and straw for the limbs, the body and the head. A powerful spring had held the make-believe man upright until Vanek had hit him. 'Good?' Vanek enquired as he reached Borisov. 'No delay at all on the second run – I went straight back and straight over him...'

Borisov, thick-bodied and muffled in a fur coat and hat against the intense cold – a snow warning had been broadcast over the Prague radio – regarded the Czech sourly. Vanek was too sure of himself, too arrogant for him ever to like the man, and the trouble was Vanek was right: it had been a perfect run. The bloody Czech trained to perfection in everything he did. 'We run back to the centre,' he said abruptly. 'I'll send someone to collect the car . . .' Borisov had spoken in French; ever since training had begun all conversation had been carried on in the Gallic language.

They ran down the track through the chilly dusk which was almost darkness now and Vanek deliberately kept a few paces in front of the other three men to demonstrate his fitness. As they went inside a concrete cabin huddled under a copse of fir trees a wave of warmth from a boiling stove met them. Borisov, the oldest and the last of the four men to enter the building, slammed the door shut to keep in the warmth. Taking off their coats, they lit cigarettes – Gauloises – and sagged into chairs round a table. A large-scale map of France and Germany covered one wall; on another hung a map of Paris. Various guidebooks, including time-tables, Michelin and the *Guide Bleu* occupied a wooden shelf. Most prominently displayed was a large photograph of Col. René Lasalle.

'That's enough for today,' Borisov announced as he poured French cognac from a bottle. 'You're improving,' he added grudgingly.

With typical bravado Vanek raised his glass to the photograph on the wall. 'To our meeting, my dear colonel . . .'

Carel Vanek was thirty-one years old, a tall, lean and bony-faced man with very dark hair and a neat dark moustache. A natural athlete, his quick-moving dark eyes stared back insolently as the Russian studied him. Vanek knew that he was good at his job, that the

Russian disliked him but also recognized his ability, which made everything so much the better; and the way to keep Borisov in his place was to push the training even harder than the Russian wished. 'We'll repeat the night exercise,' Vanek said abruptly. 'Running a man down in the dark is even trickier.'

In Russia they have a word for the Czechs which means 'the smart people, too clever by half . . .', and this summed up the Russian trainer's opinion of his protégé. On the other hand, Borisov was thinking, Vanek was definitely the man to lead this Soviet Commando; he had all the qualifications. Five years earlier Vanek had been attached to the security unit at the Czech Embassy on Avenue Charles-Floquet near the Eiffel Tower in Paris. Like so many Czechs, Vanek was an excellent linguist; he spoke French, German and English fluently. And when the three-man team was given the signal to leave for the West they would travel as Frenchmen, speaking that language and equipped with French papers.

Vanek had other useful skills, too – besides those of the trained assassin he had perfected at the training centre. A handsome man, bold and confident in manner, the Czech was attractive to women, which at times proved highly convenient. After all, the way to a man was so often through his woman. And finally, Borisov thought as he smoked his Gauloise, Vanek had a cold streak which enabled him to kill a man and sleep well after the act. This had been proved when he had travelled to Istanbul to kill a Soviet cipher clerk who had developed an appetite for American dollars. Vanek had choked the man to death and then thrown him from a balcony into the Bosphorus one dark night.

Much as it went against the grain, Borisov the Russian had to admit that the three Czechs, led by Vanek, made an ideal assassination Commando. And although Borisov could not have known it, the specification for the Commando leader was not at all unlike the specification David Nash had laid down for choosing a man to go into France. Fluency in French, knowledge of France, the ability to pass as a Frenchman – and whereas Nash had insisted on a non-American, so the three members of the Russian Politburo who had sanctioned the mission had added their own proviso: the men who made up the Commando must be non-Russian. If anything went wrong the real power behind the operation must never be exposed.

'When the hell are we going to leave to visit this Colonel Lasalle?' Vanek demanded.

'Soon,' Borisov replied, 'the signal will come soon . . .'

On the same evening when Alan Lennox in London received the phone call from David Nash, two hundred miles away in Paris Marc Grelle sat up late in his bachelor apartment on the Ile Saint-Louis reading an old and dusty file. It was the file on the Leopard.

André Boisseau, who lived in the Rue Monge, spent the earlier part of the evening with the prefect, and since he had read the file earlier they compared notes. In the Second World War every single member of the Resistance had worked under a false name – to protect his family and his friends. Normally another French surname was chosen at random; sometimes a man would be known by a false Christian name; and certain high-ranking army officers labelled themselves with geometrical symbols such as Hypotenuse. But the Leopard was different: he had taken the name of a savage animal as though to stress his uniqueness.

'I think the choice of the name indicates a supreme self-confidence,' Boisseau remarked. 'One of those people who kids himself up he's a man of destiny . . .'

The Leopard had certainly had a remarkable – although brief – career. In his earliest twenties – one of the few facts known about this elusive figure – he had commanded one of the most powerful Resistance groups in the Massif Central, operating in the departments of Lozère and Haut-Loire. He distinguished himself from other Resistance leaders by his brilliance and ruthlessness; there had been something almost Napoleonic in the way he had descended out of nowhere on the enemy, destroyed him, and then vanished again.

The Leopard's extraordinary success was based on a widespread intelligence system. He had agents everywhere – in the Vichy police, in the telephone exchanges where operators plugged in to enemy calls, on the railways where the staff reported on the movement of munition and troop trains, and inside the *Milice*, a

Vichy organization of vicious thugs and collaborators. He had even planted someone inside the Abwehr, the enemy counter-intelligence organization.

'Perhaps we ought to be looking for someone who is an expert on intelligence and security apparatuses,' Boisseau suggested.

The prefect grunted and continued reading. The thick file went on endlessly describing the Leopard's achievements, but the weird thing was there was hardly a hint of what he looked like. There were reasons for this. The Communist leader had gone to extraordinary lengths to ensure that no one – not even his close associates – had any idea of his personal appearance. There was one exception: a deputy, code-named Petit-Louis, had gone everywhere with him, issuing instructions while the Leopard stayed out of sight.

'He was over six feet tall and not much more than twenty at the time, which would put him in his early fifties now if he had survived,' Grelle pointed out. 'And that's all we do know about this ghost . . .'

'Petit-Louis probably knew what he looked like,' Boisseau remarked.

In the autumn of 1944 events took a more sinister turn. At the time of the second Allied landing – in August in the south of France – the Midi was practically under the control of the Resistance for a short period. It was a period no one talked about much in later years: the prospect had been too frightening. This was when the Communists came within an inch of establishing a Soviet Republic in the south of France.

All the plans were laid. The signal for setting up the Soviet République du Sud was to be the capture by the Communists of the key cities of Limoges and Montpellier. It was calculated that, presented with a *fait accompli* while the Allies were still fighting the enemy, the Soviet Republic would have to be accepted. The mastermind behind this plan was the Leopard himself. Only de Gaulle's swift and sudden descent on the region smashed the plot. Soon afterwards the Leopard died.

His death was carefully documented in the file. He had been shot by an enemy sniper in the streets of Lyon on 14 September. Full of anguish at the death of their leader, worried that a gang of Vichy thugs might desecrate the grave, a small party of Communists had carried the body away and quietly buried it in the middle of a forest. Petit-Louis, the Leopard's deputy, had not been present at the burial. Near the end of the file an appendix noted small details which Grelle found interesting. The Leopard had always been guarded by a huge and ferocious wolfhound called César which kept even trusted friends at a distance.

'To make sure they never knew what he looked like,' Grelle commented. 'I wonder what happened to the hound?'

The Abwehr, the enemy intelligence service, had also apparently compiled a detailed file on their mysterious enemy. The officer who had undertaken this task was a certain Dieter Wohl, who had been thirty at the time. 'So he would be in his sixties now,' Grelle observed. 'I wonder whether he survived?'

47

Grelle received the shock after Boisseau had gone home to his wife and two children. At the end of the file he found a worn and tattered envelope with a photograph inside of the Leopard's deputy, Petit-Louis. At first he couldn't be sure, so he took the faded sepia print over to his desk and examined it under the lamp. The print was better preserved than he had feared and out of it stared a face, a face recorded over thirty years earlier. Age changes a man, especially if his life has been hard, but if the bone structure is strong it sometimes only makes clearer features which always existed. The face of Petit-Louis was the face of Gaston Martin, the man from Guiana.

Chapter Four

For the second time in less than seventy-two hours David Nash had crossed the Atlantic. Disembarking from Pan Am flight 100 at Heathrow Airport at 9.40 p.m. on Sunday night, 12 December, only ten days before Guy Florian was due to fly to Moscow, Nash took a cab to the Ritz, left his bag in his room and walked to Lennox's flat in St James's Place. On arrival he presented the Englishman with a bottle of Moët & Chandon.

'When the Greeks come bearing gifts . . .' Lennox greeted him cynically as he slipped the bottle inside the fridge. 'We'll open that later – I presume we're going to be up half the night?'

'At the very least,' the American assured him. 'We're up against a deadline which is ten days from now . . .'

'You are up against a deadline,' Lennox corrected him. 'I warned you on the phone – your kind of business is something I can do without . . .'

They talked until 3 a.m. while Nash used up two packs of cigarettes, telling the Englishman about his recent visit to Peter Lanz and Col. Lasalle, about the enormous anxiety in Washington that some great

Communist coup was imminent, that René Lasalle might possibly – just possibly – be able to provide the key which would unlock the identity of the unknown Soviet agent in Paris. 'He's convinced the crunch is coming when Florian flies off to Moscow,' Nash said at midnight as he sipped his champagne. 'So we have no time at all to check out these three people inside France Lasalle believes may come up with the answer . . .'

'I had the quaint idea that Washington hates the guts of President Guy Florian,' Lennox observed.

Nash's mouth tightened. 'That's as maybe. The hell of it is we're stuck with him – just as we were stuck with de Gaulle. In politics you may not like your bedmate, but you have to sleep with her all the same. President Florian of France and Chancellor Hauser of Germany are all that stand between Soviet Russia and the Channel coast now that Congress has opted out of Europe – your Channel coast, too,' he added.

'So where does the Leopard come into it? None of what you say makes much sense,' Lennox remarked bluntly. 'The Leopard is dead – he was shot in Lyon in 1944. I think Lasalle is just trying to stir up some muck, hoping it will stick to his old enemy, Guy Florian. Your French colonel is a fanatic.'

'Even fanatics get to know things,' Nash persisted. 'We don't entirely go along with his Leopard story but we do think he stumbled on something six months ago just before Florian threw him out of France. He got a sniff of some highly placed underground link with the

Soviets – and don't forget that Lasalle was the best army counter-intelligence officer the French ever had . . .'

'But he won't give you this list of so-called witnesses, if it exists . . .'

'I'm certain it exists,' Nash flared. 'He's very security-minded so he only gives that to the man who goes into France to interview them . . .'

'So why come to me?'

Nash swallowed the rest of his champagne, taking his time over replying. 'Because of who you are,' he said quietly. 'These witnesses may well only speak to a Frenchman. Lanz has agreed to supply cover papers. To avoid the security apparatus the man who goes in must merge with the landscape. You qualify, Alan. You were born and grew up in Paris. We gave you top security clearance while you were in the States. You're experienced in underground work, God knows. The Red Night in Syria proved that. You're made for the job,' the American went on. 'We need you. You need us . . .'

'And just why do I need you?' Lennox asked quietly.

'Because you need American government approval of that bid you put in for a major security contract with an American company, a company which, incidentally, handles certain Defense Department projects. Confidentially, I understand your bid was the lowest and is acceptable – providing you get Washington's rubber stamp . . .'

It was at this point that the explosion came, that

Lennox started talking non-stop, refusing to allow Nash to interrupt while he told him what he thought about politics and politicians. 'Your own people do the same thing . . .' Nash interjected and then subsided under the torrent of Lennox's words. 'It's pressure,' Lennox told him savagely, 'bloody pressure tactics, and you know how I react to that . . .' The verbal battle went on until close to three in the morning as the atmosphere thickened with smoke, as they drank Scotch, as Nash, tieless and in his shirt-sleeves now fought back against Lennox's onslaught. Then, without warning, the Englishman switched his viewpoint.

'All right,' he said as he refilled the glasses. 'I'll go and see Lasalle and talk to him – but on the clear understanding that I make up my mind when I get there whether it's worth going into France . . .'

'That's great . . .'

'Wait a minute, there are conditions. If I go in, you'll personally guarantee my American contract is approved. You'll also guarantee that only MacLeish will know I've agreed – the security on this thing has to be ironclad tight. Finally, you'll pay me a service fee of twenty thousand dollars . . .'

'For God's sake,' Nash protested, 'you'll be getting the contract . . .'

'Which is the least I deserve since my bid is lowest. The twenty thousand dollars is danger money. You think it's going to be a picnic going undercover into France now?' Lennox demanded. 'For Christ's sake, before you arrived I was listening to the news bulletin

– since the attempt on Florian's life French security is buzzing like a beehive. I'll risk tripping up over Grelle's mob, the counter-espionage gang, maybe even the CRS thugs. MacLeish is getting himself a non-American messenger boy on the cheap at twenty thousand.'

'Who said anything about a non-American?' Nash enquired mildly.

'You did when you phoned from Washington and then flew over here by the seat of your pants . . .'

Shortly after three in the morning they came to their agreement, Nash swallowed a final gulp of neat Scotch, checked over certain details with Lennox and then walked back through the rain to the Ritz, quite satisfied and grimly amused at Lennox's insistence on the service fee. MacLeish could damn well shell out the twenty thousand and trim his budget elsewhere. Back in his flat Lennox washed the dirty glasses and then started packing. Like Nash he was a night bird, and like Nash he was satisfied. From the moment the proposition had been put to him he had been interested because it suited him. It gave him something new and interesting to poke his nose into; it made the American contract secure; and he had just concluded a hard-fought deal. Extracting the twenty thousand from MacLeish was a bonus which lived up his main principle: never do anything for nothing.

In Paris on Monday morning, 13 December, Grelle and Boisseau were no nearer clearing up the mystery surrounding Gaston Martin's strangely coincidental arrival only hours after the attempt on Florian's life. Detectives had visited the Hôtel Cécile where Martin had dumped his bag after getting off the boat train from Le Havre and his few miserable possessions had been brought to the prefecture. They consisted of one small suitcase of clothes. 'And this is all he had to show for sixty years of living,' the prefect commented. 'It's pathetic, the way some people live – and die . . .'

'This newspaper we found in his room is interesting,' Boisseau replied. 'It clears up the riddle of why he was standing at the spot where Lucie Devaud died . . .'

The copy of *Le Monde*, dated 9 December, the day after the assassination attempt, had carried one of those 'scene of the crime' diagrams newspaper editors are so fond of inserting; this one was a street plan of a section of the eighth arrondissement with a cross marking the spot where Lucie Devaud had been shot. Martin's copy of the paper, purchased at Le Havre when he came off the freighter, had been folded to the diagram, as though he had used it as a reference. 'They even showed the fur shop in the diagram,' Boisseau explained, 'so it was easy for him to find the spot . . .'

'Which tells us nothing about any connection he may have had with the Devaud woman,' Grelle snapped. 'We've traced her to an expensive apartment in the Place des Vosges but no one there seems to know anything about her . . .'

At nine in the morning the telex came in from Cayenne, Guiana – in response to Grelle's earlier request for information. It was a very long message and Grelle later supplemented it by a phone call to the Cayenne police chief. The story it told was quite damnable. During the war Gaston Martin had fought with the Resistance group commanded by the Leopard in the Lozère. He had, according to his own account – told to the Cayenne police chief only a few weeks earlier – worked closely with the Leopard, acting as his deputy. He even mentioned the savage César, who guarded the Communist leader wherever he went.

At the war's end, still a dedicated Communist, Martin had reported to Party headquarters in Paris where he was placed under the control of a special political section. Then, in July 1945, only two months after the war's end, Martin was entrusted with a mission: he was to go to Guiana in South America to organize a secret cell inside the union of waterfront workers. 'Control the ports of the West,' he was told, 'and we shall rule the West . . .'

Martin had set off with great enthusiasm, taking a ship from Le Havre bound for Cayenne, proud to be chosen for this important work. Landing in the tropical slum which is Cayenne had somewhat tempered his enthusiasm, but soon he plunged into a world of intrigue and underground activity. He took his orders from a man called Lumel; of mixed French and Indian blood, Lumel had been born in Guiana. Then the blow fell. Overnight his world was shattered. Drinking in a waterfront bar one evening before going home, he witnessed a drunken brawl and an American seaman was knifed to death. The police, tipped off by an anonymous call, came for him the next day. They found the murder weapon hidden at the back of a cupboard in the shack where he lived.

Lumel supplied Martin with a lawyer, who muffed his defence at the trial. He was sentenced to twenty years' hard labour on Devil's Island. For the first few months in this dreaded penal institution Martin was sustained by the belief that Lumel would find some way to free him; hope died with the passing of the years, with the non-arrival of any message from Lumel who seemed to have abandoned him. When Devil's Island was closed in 1949 he was transferred to another equally sordid penal settlement.

With good behaviour – and he was a model prisoner – Martin should have been released in 1963. But late in 1962 there was an incident in the prison to which Martin had been transferred. A warder was knifed in the back and died. The murder weapon was found in the holdall Martin used to store his wooden eating implements. It was a repetition of the Cayenne murder sixteen years earlier. And should have immediately been suspect, Grelle thought grimly as he went on reading.

Reading between the lines, the governor of the prison had been an unsavoury character who wanted the matter cleared up quickly. Martin was accused, tried and sentenced to another twenty years. It was about this time that Martin became finally convinced that someone was trying to keep him in prison for ever.

He served the greater part of his new sentence and then something odd happened. Lumel, knocked down in a street accident by a hit-and-run driver, called the Cayenne police chief as he lay dying. 'That car knocked me down deliberately,' he alleged. 'They tried to kill me . . .' Before he expired he dictated and signed a confession.

The order to put Gaston Martin out of circulation reached Lumel in 1945 even before Martin disembarked at Cayenne. 'It came from Communist Party headquarters in Paris,' Lumel explained in his statement. 'I could have had him killed, of course, but they didn't want it done that way . . .'

'I know why,' Grelle said to Boisseau, who was smoking his pipe while the prefect read the report. 'Too many people who could identify the Leopard had already been killed . . .'

'You're guessing, chief.'

'I'd bet my pension on it . . .'

Lumel admitted organizing the frame-up of Gaston Martin for the bar-room killing, admitted that years later he had paid a large sum of money to arrange for the killing of the warder inside the prison Martin had been transferred to. After Lumel died Martin was personally interrogated by the Cayenne chief of police, a decent man, Grelle gathered from the tone of the report. Bitterly disillusioned by his long years in prison, by Lumel's confession, Martin had told the police chief everything. 'I think he realized that his entire life had been thrown away for an illusion – the illusion of the

Communist ideal,' the Cayenne police chief commented in his report. 'I arranged for his immediate release. It will probably always be a mystery why Gaston Martin had to be condemned to the life of an animal for nearly all his days . . .'

Grelle dropped the report on his desk. 'The bastard,' he said quietly. 'To go on concealing his identity he had people killed, a man imprisoned in that black jungle hell for life. God knows how many other poor devils died for the sake of the cause – in the report I read of the Leopard I noticed a number of his closer associates came to a sticky end before the war was over. It's a trail of blood this man has left behind him . . .'

The prefect was walking round his office with his hands shoved down inside his slacks pockets. Boisseau had rarely seen his chief so angry. 'Remember this, Boisseau,' Grelle went on. 'Do a job but never devote your life to a so-called cause. You will find yourself in pawn to scum . . .'

'All this to protect the Leopard? A man who is dead?'

'We'll see about that.' Grelle was putting on his leather raincoat. 'I'm going to the Elysée. If anyone asks for me, you don't know where I am.'

'I still don't understand it,' Boisseau persisted. 'The record shows the Leopard died in 1944. Gaston Martin, who we now know was Petit-Louis, the Leopard's right-hand man, says he saw him walk into the Elysée . . .'

58

'When you get a conflict of evidence, you test it. I'm starting to test it,' Grelle said brusquely.

The direct route to the Elysée would have led along the Rue St-Honoré and the Faubourg-St-Honoré beyond, but because of the one-way system Grelle drove via the Place de la Concorde, along the Avenue Gabriel, which took him past the American Embassy, and then up the Avenue de Marigny, passing on his right the large walled garden which lies behind the Elysée itself. Arriving at the palace, he waited while a guard lowered the white-painted chain and then drove into the court-yard beyond. Getting out of his car, he went straight to the guard-house.

'Can I see the register of visitors?' the prefect asked casually.

The officer showed him the book which records the date, time of arrival and identity of everyone visiting the Elysée. It was the page for Thursday, 9 December, the day when Gaston Martin had stood outside the Elysée which interested Grelle. He checked the entries for visitors who had arrived between 7.30 and 8.30 in the evening; then, to throw the duty officer off the scent, he looked at one or two other pages. 'Thank you,' he said and went out into the courtyard and up the seven steps which led to the plate glass doors of the main entrance.

Not even a cabinet minister could have called as casually as this, but Marc Grelle was held in especially high regard by Guy Florian. 'He has no political ambition,' the president once informed a cabinet minister he knew to be excessively ambitious. 'I had to drag him away from Marseille to Paris. Sometimes I think he is the only honest man in France. I would trust him with my life . . .'

In fact, Guy Florian had entrusted Grelle with his life. While the president is inside the department of Paris the responsibility for his security – and that of cabinet ministers – is in the hands of the police prefect. On the morning after the assassination attempt Florian had ordered that from now on his personal safety was to be in the hands of Marc Grelle throughout the whole of France. With one stroke of his pen Florian had made the prefect the most powerful figure in the French Republic after himself – if he chose to exercise that power.

'The president will receive you,' a uniformed usher informed Grelle as he waited in the marble-floored lobby which is carpeted only down the centre. The interview took place in the president's study on the first floor at the rear of the Elysée, a room with tall windows which overlooks the walled garden laid out with lawns and gravel paths. Facing the president as he sits at his Louis XV desk is a Gobelin wall tapestry of 'Don Quixote Cured of his Madness by Wisdom', and there are two telephones on the desk, one black and one white. A third instrument stands on a side table close to his right hand. As the door was closing behind Grelle he heard the chiming of one of the hundred and thirty-seven clocks which furnish the Elysée. 11 a.m. A large Alsatian dog bounded across the room, reared up and dropped its forepaws on the prefect's shoulders.

'Kassim, get down, you brute,' Grelle growled affectionately. The prefect himself, who was fond of dogs, had personally found the animal when requested to do so by Florian soon after his election. It was said in the Elysée that only two people dared touch the animal: Grelle and the president himself. Removing the forepaws, the prefect bowed and then sat down opposite the most powerful statesman in Western Europe. Typically, Florian waited for him to speak.

'I was very disturbed to see that you again walked back from the Place Beauvau on the evening of 9 December,' Grelle began. 'And only twenty-four hours after the appalling incident . . .'

Florian lowered his lean, intelligent head like a small boy caught in the farmer's apple orchard. It was the kind of gesture, coming from a president, which would have disarmed most men, but Grelle's expression remained grave. 'It will not happen again,' Florian assured him. 'You saw the pictures in Friday's papers, of course?'

'I was thunderstruck.'

'But you are no politician, my friend. The street was swarming with detectives – at a discreet distance so the photographers would not include them in the pictures! But it is good politics, you see – the president walks the streets again only one day after the incident!'

Florian grinned impishly. 'It is all nonsense, of course. Tell me, am I forgiven?'

Grelle returned to the prefecture reassured that from now on the president would stay behind the security fence erected to guard him. Only one question remained, was the security fence foolproof?

'Come in, close the door and lock it,' Grelle told Boisseau as he settled himself on the edge of his desk. It was a habit of the prefect's when disturbed to perch his buttocks on the edge of a desk or table so he could start pacing about more easily if the inclination took him. Boisseau sat in a chair, took out his pipe and relaxed, waiting. With less nervous energy than his chief, he had the look of a patient squirrel, and behind his back that, in fact, was what his staff called him. André the Squirrel.

'I checked the visitors' register at the Elysée for the evening of 9 December for the hour 7.30 to 8.30,' Grelle said abruptly. 'Before I go on remember that the only physical description we have of the Leopard concerns his height – over six feet tall . . .'

'You have found something?' Boisseau suggested.

'Someone – more than one, as it happens. Florian himself arrived back on foot at eight o'clock from the Place Beauvau – that won't happen again, incidentally. The interesting thing is three other ministers also arrived on foot – they had come from the meeting at the Ministry of the Interior . . .'

The two men exchanged cynical smiles. Normally everyone would have returned from the Place Beauvau in his own ministerial car, but because the president had walked back they had felt obliged to adopt the same form of locomotion. 'And, of course, they hoped to get their own pictures in the papers,' Grelle observed, 'knowing there were photographers in the Place Beauvau.'

'Who else came back?' Boisseau asked quietly.

'Pierre Rouget for one – we can dismiss him, of course.' They smiled again. Rouget was the nominal prime minister, the man the reporters called 'Florian's poodle'. An amiable man – 'with a backbone of rubber' as Grelle sometimes remarked – no one took much notice of him and it was rumoured he would soon be replaced. In any case, he was no taller than five feet eight. 'Between 8.15 and 8.30,' Grelle continued, 'two other men arrived and walked into the Elysée – and they came back separately, a few minutes apart. One of them was my own boss, the Minister of the Interior, Roger Danchin. The other was the Minister of National Defence, Alain Blanc. Both of them as you know are the tallest men in the cabinet, both of them are over six feet tall . . .'

Boisseau took the dead pipe out of his mouth and stared at the prefect. 'You don't really believe this? Danchin, Blanc – the two strong men in the government? Martin must have been having hallucinations.'

'I don't really believe anything,' Grelle replied coolly. 'All I do is to check the facts and see where they lead – as we do in any investigation. But as we have agreed, I'm telling you everything however absurd it may seem.'

'Absurd? It's unbelievable . . .'

'Of course.' Grelle picked up a report off his desk, talking as he scanned the first page. 'Something else has happened. David Nash, the American, has just been spotted arriving at Roissy Airport this morning by a Sûreté man. And I have received a pressing invitation to a reception at the American Embassy this evening. You believe in coincidence, Boisseau?'

André the Squirrel did not reply. He was gazing into the distance, as though trying to grasp a fact so great it was beyond his comprehension. 'Danchin or Blanc?' he murmured.

It had been Roger Danchin's aim to become Minister of the Interior since he had been a youth, spending endless hours over his studies at the Ecole Normale d'Administration, the special school founded by de Gaulle himself to train future leaders of the French Republic. And while Guy Florian and Alain Blanc – at the Ecole Polytechnique – were the hares who forged ahead because of their brilliance, Danchin was the tortoise who got there in the end because he never stopped trying. Sometimes it is the tortoise which outlasts the hares.

By the time he was offered the post of Minister of

the Interior, Roger Danchin, an intelligence expert, probably knew more about the French security system than any other man alive. Like Alain Blanc, over six feet tall, he had developed the stoop which tall men sometimes affect. Fifty-two years old, he was thin and bony-faced, a man with a passion for secrecy and a man who loved power. Blanc, who disliked him, summed up Danchin in a typical, biting anecdote. 'Danchin would interrogate his own grandmother if he suspected she had changed her will – and after three hours under the arc lights she would leave him all the money...' Danchin was at the height of his power when he summoned Grelle to see him just after the prefect returned from checking the Elysée register.

When the prefect entered the Minister's office on the first floor Danchin was standing by the window which overlooks a beautiful walled garden at the rear of the building, a garden the public never sees. 'Sit down, Grelle,' Danchin said, still staring down at the garden. 'I hear from Roissy that David Nash, the American, has just arrived in Paris. What do you think that implies?'

'Should it imply something?' Grelle enquired. By now he had grasped how this devious man's mind worked; rarely asking a direct question, Danchin tried to catch people out by encouraging them to talk while he listened.

'Something is happening, Grelle, I sense it. Strange also that he should arrive here so soon after the attempt on the President's life...'

'I don't see the connection,' Grelle stonewalled. 'But I have an invitation to the American Embassy this evening . . .'

'You are going?' Danchin interjected sharply.

'Why not, Minister? I may pick up something interesting. At least I should be able to answer your question as to why he has come to Paris . . .'

'And this woman, Lucie Devaud – has Boisseau found out something more about her? She couldn't be connected in any way with the arrival of Nash, I presume?'

'Surely you can't suspect the Americans were behind the attempt?' Grelle protested. 'They do some strange things but . . .'

'Probing, Grelle, just probing . . .' Danchin suddenly returned behind his desk, moving so quietly Grelle was not aware he had left the window. It was another disturbing habit of Danchin's which his assistant, Merlin, had once complained about to Grelle. 'He turns up without warning like a ghost, standing behind you. Did you know that when people go out to lunch Danchin creeps into their offices to check the papers on their desks – to make sure they are not doing something he has no knowledge of? The atmosphere inside this place is terrible, I can tell you. Terrible!'

Grelle got out of Danchin's office as soon as he could, mopping his brow as he went downstairs and out into the fresh air. I wouldn't work in this place for a million francs a year, he told himself as he got behind the wheel of his car. He drove out with a burst of exhaust as though to express his relief. Not for ten million francs!

Alain Blanc was born to a world of châteaux and money, of vintage wines and good food, possessed of a brain which in later years could absorb the details of a nuclear test ban treaty in a third of the time it would have taken Roger Danchin. With the family land and vineyards behind him, Blanc, who came from the Auvergne, need never have worked for a day in his life. He chose to ignore the chance of a life of idleness, plunging instead into a life of furious activity.

A man of enormous vitality and appetite for work, he became one of the key political figures in Florian's régime, the man whom ambassadors quietly consulted when they could not get Florian's ear. An 'X', which stands for the crossed cannons symbol of the Ecole Polytechnique, a school where money is no substitute for brains, he was one of the five top students the year he graduated. His close friend, Guy Florian, passed out first among a galaxy of brilliant men. Years later, well entrenched in the political bedrock of France, it was Alain Blanc, the manipulator, who master-minded Florian's rise to the presidency.

Over six feet tall, fifty-four-year-old ex-paratrooper Blanc was heavily built; plump-faced, his hair thinning, his head was like a monk's dome. A man of powerful personality, he was reputed to be able to talk anyone into agreeing to anything with his warmth and jovial aggressiveness. Women, especially, found him attractive – he was so lively. 'He doesn't take himself seriously,' his mistress, Gisèle Manton, once explained, 'but he takes women seriously – or pretends to . . .'

His relations with Marc Grelle were excellent: the prefect understood the Minister of National Defence and never let Blanc overwhelm him. When they argued, which was frequently, it was with a fierce jocularity, and Blanc knew when he was beaten. 'The trouble with you, Grelle,' he once told the prefect, 'is you don't believe in politicians . . .'

'Does anyone?' Grelle replied.

Blanc came to see the prefect in the afternoon shortly after Grelle had returned from his brief interview with Danchin. It was typical of Blanc to drive over to the prefecture in his Lamborghini rather than to summon Grelle to his ministry, and even more typical that he flirted with Grelle's secretary on his way up. 'I shall have to abduct you, Vivianne,' he told the girl. 'You are far too appetizing for policemen!' He came into the prefect's office like a summer wind, grinning as he shook hands. 'What are the political implications behind this assassination attempt?' he demanded as he settled into a chair, drooping his legs over the arm.

'We nearly lost a president,' Grelle replied.

'I'm talking about this Devaud woman,' Blanc snapped. 'If it can be proved she ever knew the president – even if only briefly – the press will rape us. Can they?'

'You'd better ask the president . . .'

'I have. He says he had never seen her before. But he could be wrong. Over the years God knows how many people he has met – or known slightly. What I'm saying is – if your investigation turns up a connection, could you inform me?'

'Of course . . .'

Blanc left soon afterwards and the prefect smiled grimly as he watched the car from the window moving off too fast towards the right bank. Strictly speaking, anything which came to light should be reported only to his chief, Roger Danchin, but everyone knew that Blanc was Florian's eyes and ears, the man who fixed a problem when anything awkward cropped up. Boisseau, who had come into the office as Blanc left, watched the car disappearing. 'It's quite impossible to suspect a man like that,' he remarked.

'If the Leopard exists,' Grelle replied, 'it's because he has reached a position where people would say, "It's quite impossible to suspect a man like that . . ."'

One 9-mm Luger pistol, one monocular glass, three forged driving licences, and three different sets of forged French papers – one set for each member of the Soviet Commando. Walther Brunner, the second member of the team, sat alone inside the concrete cabin at the edge of the race-track wearing a pair of French glasses as he checked the cards. The equipment they would carry was meagre enough but the time was long since past when Soviet Commandos travelled to the

West armed with exotic weapons like cyanide-bullet-firing pistols disguised as cigarette cases. The craft of secret assassination had progressed way beyond that.

Brunner, born in Karlsbad, now known as Karlovy Vary, was forty years old; the oldest member of the Commando he had hoped to lead until Borisov had selected Carel Vanek instead. Shorter than Vanek, he was more heavily built and his temperament was less volatile; round-headed, he would soon be bald and he felt it was his appearance which had persuaded Borisov to give the leadership to the younger man. At least he ranked as the second member of the three-man team, as Vanek's deputy, the man who would take over operations if something happened to Vanek while they were in the West. Rank, oddly enough, is an important factor in Communist circles.

Brunner was the Commando's planner, the man who worked out routes and schedules – and escape routes – before the mission was undertaken, the man who arranged for the provision of false papers, who later, when they arrived at their destination, suggested the type of 'accident' to be applied. 'You must make three different plans,' Brunner was fond of saying, 'then when you arrive at the killing ground you choose the one best suited . . .' Beer was his favourite drink and, unlike Vanek, he regarded women as dangerous distractions. His most distinctive feature was his large hands, 'strangler's hands', as Vanek rudely called them. There was some justification in the description; if Col.

Lasalle had to die in the bath Brunner was likely to attend to it.

This was the nub of the training at the abandoned race-track outside the medieval town of Tábor; here the three Czechs who made up the Commando perfected the skill of arranging 'accidental' deaths. Death by running someone down with a car was trainer Borisov's favourite method. The research section, housed in a separate cabin and which worked closely with the Commando, had studied the statistics: more people in western Europe died on the roads than from any other cause. Accidents in the home came next. Hence Brunner's special attention to drowning in the bath, which had been practised in a third concrete cabin with an iron bath-tub and live 'models'.

A fact largely unknown to the outside world is that an assassination Commando never leaves Russian-controlled territory without the express sanction of three members (who make up a quorum) of the Politburo in Moscow. Even in 1956 – when the power of the Committee for State Security was at its height – the Commando sent to West Berlin to kidnap (or kill, if necessary) Dr Linske, had to be approved by Stalin himself and two other Politburo members (one of whom was Molotov).

The reasoning behind this policy is sound. If a Commando's actions are ever detected the international image of Soviet Russia becomes smeared – because one thing the Western public does know is that nothing happens inside Russia without government approval. The Politburo is aware of this, so a Commando is only despatched where there is no other alternative. Vanek's Commando had been fully approved by the First Secretary and two other Politburo members; now it only awaited the signal to proceed, travelling on French papers which would easily pass inspection inside Germany. Brunner had just completed his inspection of the identity cards when Borisov came into the cabin with the news.

'The execution of Lasalle has been postponed . . .'

'Damnit!' Brunner was furious. 'And just when we were all geared up . . .'

'Have patience, my impetuous Czech,' Borisov told him. 'You have to stand by for a fresh signal. You may be departing at any time now.'

Chapter Five

On the morning of Monday, 13 December, when Marc Grelle received his telex from Guiana about Gaston Martin, Alan Lennox was flying to Brussels. Travelling aboard Sabena flight 602 he landed in the Belgian city at 10.30 a.m. Earlier, from Heathrow Airport, he had phoned his personal assistant at home to say an urgent enquiry had come in from Europe and he was flying there to get the contract specification. During the brief conversation he made a vague reference to Denmark. 'You'll be back when, if ever?' Miss Thompson asked him gaily.

'When you see me, I'm back . . .'

It was time to sell out, Lennox thought as he boarded the Sabena flight. He had organized the company so well that now he could go away for long periods and the machine ran itself. So I've worked myself out of a job again, he told himself as the Boeing 707 climbed up through the murk and broke through into a world of brilliant sunshine which was always there, even over England, if only the inhabitants could see it. The reference to Denmark was a precaution; if anyone enquired for him at the office Judith Thompson would be close-mouthed, but if someone clever did make her slip up, then they were welcome to search for him in Copenhagen.

At Brussels airport he hired a Mercedes SL230. Offered a cream model, he chose a black car instead; black is less conspicuous, less easy to follow. Driving first to Liège, Lennox kept a careful eye on his rearview mirror, watching for any sign of a car or truck keeping persistently behind him. It was unlikely but not impossible; since David Nash had walked from the Ritz to his flat in St James's Place and back again he could have been followed, and the follower might then have turned his attention to the man Nash had crossed the Atlantic to meet.

At Liège, where only three days earlier Nash had twice met Peter Lanz of the BND in one day, Lennox took a further precaution. Visiting the local Hertz carhire branch, he invented a complaint about the performance of the Mercedes and exchanged it for a blue Citroën DS21, his favourite car. Then he turned southeast, heading for the Ardennes, which is not the direct route into Germany. Sometimes it is possible to follow a man by remote control – observing the route he is taking and then phoning ahead. It takes a team of men to carry out the operation, but at the last count Lennox had heard the French Secret Service were employing over one hundred full- and part-time operatives in Belgium. If the main routes out of Liège were now being checked for a black Mercedes the watchers were hardly likely to take much notice of a blue Citroën.

Eating a sandwich lunch on the way while he drove, Lennox arrived in Saarbrücken as a cloudburst broke over the German city. The windscreen wipers almost gave up the job as hopeless while he was threading his way through the traffic. Rain cascaded down the glass, beat a tattoo on the cartop while he went on searching for the main post office. On the continent post offices provide the most useful means of making a call you don't wish to be overheard.

From the post office he called Col. Lasalle's number which had been given to him by Nash. When Lennox asked for the colonel the man who answered the phone in French said he would take a message. 'You won't,' Lennox snapped. 'Put me through to the colonel. Edmond calling . . .'

'Edmond who?'

'Just Edmond. And hurry it up. He's expecting the call.'

The man at the other end – probably Capt. Paul Moreau whom Nash had mentioned as Lasalle's assistant – obviously did not know about all the colonel's activities, which was reassuring. It suggested the ex-assistant chief of military counter-intelligence had not lost his touch. The code-name Edmond, provided by Nash, put him through to Lasalle and the Frenchman said he could come at once. 'I will be waiting for you,' he replied crisply and put down the receiver. No waste of words, no questions, and the voice had been sharp and decisive.

It took him an hour, driving through rain squalls, to

find the remote farmhouse, and it was dark as his headlights picked out an old lodge beside a closed gate. There had been lights inside the lodge when he first saw it, but now the place was in darkness. He kept the engine running and waited, then got out cautiously when no one appeared. He was walking past his own headlights when a shutter in the lodge banged open. The muzzle of a Le Mat sub-machine-gun poked out of the aperture.

'Stay where you are – in the lights,' a voice shouted in German.

'You're expecting me,' Lennox shouted back in French. 'I rang you from Saarbrücken. For God's sake open the bloody gate before I get soaked . . .'

'Come in on foot . . .' The voice had switched to French. 'Come through the gate . . .'

Opening the gate, Lennox went up to the lodge, tried the door, opened it, stepped inside and stopped. A man in civilian clothes faced him, still holding the sub-machine-gun which he aimed point-blank at the Englishman's stomach. A smooth-faced individual with a smear of moustache, a man in his late forties, Lennox assumed this must be Capt. Paul Moreau. 'I'm Edmond,' Lennox said after a moment. 'Do you have to keep pointing that thing at me?'

'Some identification – on the table . . .'

'The colonel is going to be happy about this?'

'On the table . . .'

Lennox extracted his passport carefully from inside his dripping raincoat and then threw it casually on the table. To reach for the document with his right hand the man with the gun had to cradle the wire stock under his left arm; as he did so Lennox suddenly knocked the muzzle aside, grasped the barrel and wrenched the weapon out of the man's grip. 'I don't know who you are,' he remarked as the Frenchman recovered his balance and glared, 'but you could be someone who just knocked out the real lodge-keeper . . .'

'Lodge-keeper? I am Captain Moreau, the colonel's assistant.' Bristling with anger, the man examined the passport at much greater length than was really necessary. 'You could end up dead – taking a crazy risk like that,' he grumbled.

'Less of a risk than facing an unknown man with a gun in this God-forsaken place.'

Lennox insisted on seeing Moreau's own identity card before he returned the weapon, first folding the projecting magazine parallel to the barrel so the weapon became inoperative. When identity documents had been exchanged the Frenchman told him curtly to leave his car and walk up to the house. 'Why don't you get stuffed?' Lennox suggested. Going outside, he climbed into his car, drove through the gateway and on towards the house. Moreau was using a wall phone when he left the lodge, presumably to call up the colonel.

As he drove slowly up a long curving drive Lennox saw how neglected the place was. Wet shrubbery which gleamed in the headlights had grown out over the drive, in places almost closing it so the car brushed past shrubs as he approached Lasalle's refuge. The farmhouse, a long, two-storey building which came into view round a bend, was in the same state. Unpainted, with tiles missing from the roof, it hardly looked habitable. Shortage of money, Lennox assumed: fugitive colonels are hardly likely to be sitting on fat bank accounts.

Col. René Lasalle met him at the entrance, then closed, locked and bolted the heavy door before leading the way into a large, rambling living-room crammed with old-fashioned furniture. In the hall Lennox noted there were new and modern locks on the door; in the living-room locks had been attached to all the windows. Theoretically safe inside Germany, the colonel had sealed himself off inside a minor fortress.

'They will come for me one day,' Lasalle remarked crisply. 'Shabby little Corsican thugs with knives in their pockets. They may try to kidnap me – they may come to kill me. But they will come.'

The one-armed colonel, his left sleeve flapping loose like the broken wing of a bird, was small and spare, and as he fetched drinks from a sideboard he moved with a springy step. Lennox immediately had an impression of enormous energy, of a strong-willed personality likely to dominate any group of people he might be a part of. Fifty-five years old, Lasalle's features were sharp and gaunt, his eyes large and restless, his thin moustache little more than a dark slash. He still had a full head of dark hair and his most prominent feature was a hooked nose. In some ways he reminded Lennox of a miniature version of Charles de Gaulle himself. The colonel handed him a large brandy, raised his own glass. 'To the destruction of the enemies of France!'

'I'll drink to that . . .' Lennox was watching the colonel carefully. 'Whoever they might be.'

'The Soviet faction inside Paris – led by the Leopard. But first I need to know something about you, about your background . . .'

For fifteen minutes he grilled the Englishman. It was the most shrewd and penetrating interrogation Lennox had ever experienced, with a lot of cross-questioning, a lot of jumping backwards and forwards as the Frenchman swiftly absorbed the details of Lennox's life and probed deeper and deeper. 'You have met Marc Grelle?' he said at one point. 'You are a personal friend of the police prefect then?' Lennox assured him that this was not so, that they had met only once for an hour in Marseille during the planning of a counter-terrorist operation. At the end of fifteen minutes Lasalle pronounced himself satisfied.

'You can go into France for me,' he said as though conferring a high honour.

'I'm glad I pass inspection,' Lennox replied ironically, 'but what you may not realize is I haven't made up my mind about you . . .'

'That is necessary?'

'That is essential. You see – it's going to be my head laid on the block . . .'

Leon Jouvel. Robert Philip. Dieter Wohl.

These were the names of the three witnesses, as Lasalle persisted in calling them, which he wished Lennox to visit and quietly interrogate. 'I'm convinced that one of these three people – all of whom were involved with the Leopard during the war – can tell you something which will lead us to the Communist agent inside Paris today,' the Frenchman said emphatically. 'In any case, as far as I know, they are the only survivors, apart from Annette Devaud – and she is blind . . .'

'Devaud?' Lennox queried. 'That was the name of the woman who tried to shoot Florian . . .'

'A common enough name.' Lasalle shrugged and made an impatient gesture with his right hand. 'I see no reason for a connection. And in any case, Annette Devaud, who must be over seventy now, has been blind since the end of the war. A blind person can identify no one positively. Now . . .'

It had started eighteen months earlier – a year before the climactic row with President Florian which ended in the colonel's flight from France. Lasalle had been interrogating a known Communist agent who had infiltrated a French army barracks near Marseille. 'That area is infested with the vermin,' the colonel remarked.

Lennox gathered the interrogation had been preceded by a physical session which had reduced the agent, a man called Favel, to a moaning wreck. 'While trying to escape from the barracks,' Lasalle explained, 'he accidentally shot a sergeant. The men who questioned him before me were the sergeant's friends. So . . .'

An hour after Lasalle had begun his own interrogation just before midnight Favel had started rambling on about the wartime Resistance. At first Lasalle had thought this was a trick to veer the interrogation into other channels; later he had become interested as the prisoner made repeated references to the Leopard. At intervals – the interrogation had continued for over twelve hours – the broken man had told a strange story about a man who would one day rise from the dead to liberate France from the capitalist yoke. This man had, in fact, already risen from the dead and was walking the streets of Paris.

'It seemed absolute nonsense for a long time,' Lasalle explained. 'I thought I was dealing with a religious maniac – which seemed odd for a dedicated Communist – and then he told me he had been hiding in the barracks . . .'

'Hiding?' Lennox queried.

'Hiding from his own people,' Lasalle said impatiently. 'I had got it the wrong way round – instead of trying to spy for the Communist cell in Marseille he was fleeing from them. What better place to hole up than in a military barracks – or so he thought. They were trying to kill him – I think because he knew too much.'

'But he did know something?'

'He said it was no common spy he was talking about – a civil servant who photographs documents at dead of night and passes over microfilm inside a cigar or some such absurdity. No, Favel was referring to a highly placed mandarin close to the centre of power. To a man who for years had waited and worked his way up steadily – without having a single contact with any Communist organization. That is the genius of the idea – with no Communist contacts it is impossible to detect him.'

'Favel named the man?'

Lasalle made a gesture of resignation. 'He did not know who he was – only that he existed. What finally convinced me was a tragedy. The day after I completed my interrogation, Favel escaped from the barracks – twenty-four hours later he was found at the bottom of a cliff with his neck broken.'

'His so-called friends caught up with him?'

'I'm convinced of it,' Lasalle replied. 'I started my own investigation and eventually I came up with those three names on the list. I visited one of them – Leon Jouvel in Strasbourg – but I think my position frightened him. I came away feeling sure that he knew something. Shortly after that I had my great confrontation with Florian and had to flee my own country . . .'

Lennox asked other questions. Both Jouvel and

Philip, the two Frenchmen on the list of witnesses, lived in Alsace. Was it a coincidence? 'Not at all,' Lasalle explained. 'The Leopard favoured men from Alsace in his Resistance group – he believed they were more reliable than the more excitable men from the Midi.' The colonel smiled sarcastically. 'He was, I am sure, a realist in everything.'

'But the Leopard is dead,' Lennox pointed out. 'He died in Lyon in 1944 . . .'

'Which is the clever part of the whole thing. Don't you see?'

'Frankly, I don't,' Lennox replied.

'The man has to have a code-name for the few occasions when he is referred to in Soviet circles. So they chose the name of a man known to be dead. What is the immediate reaction if the name ever slips out? It must be nonsense. He is dead! My God, what was your own reaction?'

'I see what you mean,' Lennox said slowly. 'You're saying there is . . .'

'A second Leopard – who was in some way connected with the Leopard's original Resistance group. This unknown man would easily think of using this name – if he once worked with the man whose name he has stolen. One of those three witnesses on that list should be able to clear up the mystery . . .'

'Who is this Dieter Wohl?' Lennox enquired. 'I see he lives in Freiburg now. He's a German, of course?'

'Dieter Wohl was the Abwehr officer who tried to

track down the Leopard during the war. He knew a great deal about the Resistance in the Lozère . . .'

Lasalle had thought more than once of approaching Dieter Wohl himself; unable to get back into France to interview the two Alsace witnesses he could easily have travelled to Freiburg. He had decided against the idea in case the BND heard of the visit. 'They might have said I was interfering in German affairs,' he remarked. 'I cannot afford to be thrown out of the Federal Republic at this stage. Now, answer me one question quite simply. With those names and addresses, will you go into France?'

'Yes.'

While Lennox was talking to Col. Lasalle near Saarbrücken, two hundred miles away to the west in Paris Marc Grelle was arriving at the American Embassy on the Avenue Gabriel. As he walked through the gateway at 6 p.m. he was well aware he was being photographed by agents of the Direction de la Surveillance du Territoire – political counter-intelligence. He even knew where the camera with the telescopic lens was situated, hidden inside the large blue Berliet truck parked by the sidewalk opposite the embassy. Uniformed gendarmes lounged round the truck, giving the impression they were a reserve force, standing by in case of trouble. By the following morning the photo would lie on the desk of the Minister of the Interior.

Attached to the print would be a form filled in to show the details. *1800 hours. Visitor: Marc Grelle, Police Prefect of Paris.* Later, the time of his departure would be duly recorded.

Going inside the embassy, Grelle signed the visitors' book and went upstairs where he was relieved of his raincoat by a girl with a Texan accent. 'I was once in Dallas,' he told her, 'on the day President Kennedy was assassinated.' He went into the large room overlooking the Place de la Concorde where the reception was being held. The room was a blaze of lights, a babble of voices, and the curtains were drawn, presumably to mask the room against the probing telephoto lens inside the Berliet truck. Grelle hovered at the edge of the crowd, getting his bearings and noting who was present.

'That computer-like mind of yours must have listed all the guests by now,' a voice behind him suggested, 'so why don't we slip away into the library where the real stuff is kept?' David Nash grinned and shook hands when the prefect turned round. 'I had to come to Paris, so . . .'

'You thought we could chat? Or, you came to Paris so we could chat?' Grelle enquired in English.

'That policeman's mind of yours!' Nash led the way out of the reception room and across the corridor into another room lined with books. Shutting the door, he turned the key which was already on the inside. 'Now we won't be disturbed . . .' Pouring a large Scotch, Nash handed it to the prefect, ushered him into an armchair and perched himself on the arm of another chair as he raised his glass. 'Here's to France. May she survive for ever, including the next two months . . .'

'Why shouldn't she?' Grelle peered at the American over the top of his glass. 'Or is it a state secret? You still hold the same post as when we last met, I presume?'

'The same post.' Nash leaned forward, keeping his voice low. 'I come here as a friend, not as an agent of my government. As a friend of France, too. Marc, have you ever heard of the Leopard?'

Aware that Nash was studying him, Grelle sipped his Scotch and kept his face expressionless. He mopped his lips with a silk handkerchief before he replied. 'The leopard? An animal with a spotted coat which can be dangerous . . .'

'This one is dangerous,' the American agreed. 'He's sitting behind a government desk not a mile from where we are at the moment. Let me tell you a story . . .' Nash told the story well – about a Russian defector who had arrived in New York only a week earlier, who had been rushed from Kennedy Airport to a secret camp in the Adirondack mountains where Nash himself had questioned the man. The following morning – before the interrogation had been resumed – the Russian had been shot by a long-distance sniper with a telescopic rifle. 'It happened while I was walking beside him,' the American went on. 'One moment he was walking beside me, the next he was sprawled on the track with a bullet through his skull . . .'

Grelle went on sipping his Scotch, listening with the

same expressionless face as the American related how the high-grade Russian had told him about a French Communist agent – adopting the name of the wartime Resistance leader Leopard – who for over thirty years had worked himself up to become one of the top three men in France. 'The Leopard could be any one of your top cabinet ministers,' Nash concluded. 'Roger Danchin, Alain Blanc . . .'

Grelle drank the rest of his Scotch in two gulps, placed the empty glass on the table and stood up. His voice was crisp and cold. 'The lengths to which the American government has gone recently to smear our president have been absurd, but what you have suggested is outrageous . . .'

Nash stood up from the chair. 'Marc, we don't have to blow our tops . . .'

'Your so-called story is a tissue of fabrication from beginning to end,' Grelle went on icily. 'Clearly you are trying to spread a lying rumour in the hope that it will damage the president because you don't like his speeches . . .'

'Marc,' Nash interjected quietly, 'I'll tell you now that you are the only man inside this embassy who will hear what I have just told you . . .'

'Why?' Grelle snapped.

'Because you are the only Frenchman I really trust with this secret – the only contact I have come to warn. I want you to be on your guard – and you have ways of checking things out, ways that we couldn't even attempt . . .'

'You'd get chopped if you did!' Grelle, his face flushed, moved towards the door, then seemed to calm down and for a few minutes he chatted with the American about other topics. It was, Nash told himself after the prefect had gone, a very polished performance: outrage at the suggestion and then a brief relaxation of tension to indicate to the American that they would remain friends in the future. Lighting a cigarette, Nash wandered across the hall to the reception, satisfied with the result of his trip to Paris. Because despite what he had said, Grelle would check. Grelle was the policeman's policeman. Grelle always checked.

To give himself time to think, Grelle drove round in a circle to get back to the prefecture. On his way he passed the Elysée and had to pull up while a black Zil limousine with one passenger in the back emerged from the palace courtyard. Leonid Vorin, Soviet ambassador to France, was just leaving after making one of his almost daily visits to see Guy Florian. Since the trip to Moscow on 23 December had been announced, the Soviet ambassador had consulted frequently with the president, driving from his embassy in the Rue de Grenelle to the Elysée and back again. Inside the limousine Leonid Vorin, short and stocky with a pouched mouth and rimless glasses, sat staring ahead, looking neither to right nor left as the car swung out and drove off towards Madeleine.

The uniformed policeman who had halted Grelle,

saluted and waved him on. Driving automatically, the prefect had half his mind on what Nash had told him. Up to half an hour ago his suspicions had been based on Gaston Martin's strange story and what he had heard from the Cayenne police chief, all of which was disturbing but by no means conclusive. Now the same story was coming from Washington, and soon rumours might start sweeping through the European capitals. As Grelle told Boisseau later, 'I don't believe a word of that fairy-tale Nash told me about a Soviet defector – he was protecting his real informant – but this is something we are going to have to investigate in the greatest secrecy . . .'

As he crossed the crowded Pont Neuf on to the Ile de la Cité Grelle shivered, a nervous tremor which had nothing to do with the chill night air now settling over Paris. For the police prefect his world had suddenly become unstable, a place of shifting quicksands where anything might lie under the surface. 'Roger Danchin . . . Alain Blanc . . .' he muttered to himself. 'It's impossible.'

Leaving the isolated farmhouse at about the same time when Grelle was returning to the prefecture, Lennox drove back to Saarbrücken through slashing rain with the distant rumble of thunder in the night. The storm suited his mood; he also was disturbed. At one point in the conversation he had asked the colonel who had typed out the list of names and addresses he now carried tucked away inside his wallet. 'Captain Moreau, my assistant, of course,' Lasalle had replied. 'He was the only officer who came with me when I left France and I trust him completely.'

'You didn't trust him with my real name until shortly before I arrived,' Lennox had pointed out. 'When I phoned from Saarbrücken he had no idea who I was . . .'

'That was to protect you until you arrived safely. I called Nash in London at a certain time and he gave me your name, but I withheld it from Moreau. If my assistant had been kidnapped while you were on the way he couldn't have identified you under pressure. For the same reason Moreau does not know I am in touch with the Americans . . .'

Under pressure . . . As he peered through the rain-swept windscreen Lennox grimaced. What a life the colonel was living since he had fled France. Locked away inside a German farmhouse, guarded at the gate by a man with a sub-machine-gun, ready at any time for the intruders in the night who might arrive with chloroform – or something more lethal. And tomorrow Lennox himself would cross the border into France – after first meeting Peter Lanz of the BND.

While Alan Lennox was driving through the night to a hotel in Saarbrücken, Marc Grelle had returned to the prefecture from the reception at the American Embassy where he dealt with the paperwork which had accumulated in his absence. 'There are too many typewriters in Paris,' he muttered as he initialled minutes from Roger Danchin and ate the sandwich brought in from the local brasserie. He was just about to leave when the phone rang. 'Shit!' he muttered, picking up the receiver. It was Cassin, one of the phone operators in the special room at Sûreté headquarters.

'Another message has come in from Hugon, Mr Prefect.'

'Routine?'

'No. There has been a development . . .'

Grelle swore again under his breath. He would have liked to ask the operator to relay the message over the line, but that was impossible – he had personally issued strict orders that this must never be done. Phones can be tapped: all you need is a post office communications expert who knows how to leak off a private phone. Never mind about exotic electronic bugs; splicing the right wires will do the trick. 'I'll come over,' Grelle said and put down the receiver.

Rush hour was over as he drove along streets gleaming wetly under the lamps and turned into the Rue des Saussaies where Sûreté headquarters forms part of the huge block of buildings centred round the Ministry of the Interior. In the narrow street he waited while a uniformed policeman dropped the white-painted chain and then drove under the archway into the courtyard beyond. The room was on the fourth floor and at that hour he met no one as he climbed the gloomy staircase, walked down an ill-lit corridor and used his key to open the locked door. Closing the door on the inside, Grelle stared down at Cassin, the night man. The room smelt of garlic, which meant the operator had eaten a snack recently. A half-filled glass of red wine was on the table beside the tape-recorder which was linked to the phone. 'Well?' the prefect asked.

'Hugon phoned at 6.45 p.m. . . .' Cassin, a lean, pasty-faced man of thirty, was reading from a notebook in a bored tone. 'I recorded the message as usual and it's on tape.'

'How did he sound?' Grelle perched his buttocks on the edge of the table. He would hear what Hugon had said in a minute, but the recording was inclined to iron out a man's voice, to drain it of emotion, and Cassin had listened while the tape recorded.

'A bit excited, nervous, agitated – as though he hadn't much time and was afraid of being interrupted.'

'That's a precise analysis.'

'He's sending something through the post – a list of names and addresses. He didn't want to transmit them over the phone. Said it would take too long . . .'

'Or he was being careful,' Grelle suggested. 'Did he say when he would post this list?'

'He'd already done it. He was in the post office.'

'You look as though you could do with a bit of fresh air, Cassin. Come back in fifteen minutes – I'll stay and listen to the tape . . .'

Alone, Grelle listened to the operator locking the door from the outside, then sat down in the chair and lit a cigarette. The room was sound-proofed and was checked daily for bugging devices, so every possible precaution had been taken to protect Hugon. Grelle pressed the replay button.

The tape which had recorded Cassin's conversation with Hugon was waiting on the machine. The man whose voice he was going to listen to had phoned one of the special numbers reserved for the Sûreté Nationale's private use, numbers unlisted in any directory. If anyone called the number by mistake, without giving the correct name, the operator informed him that he was the exchange, that the number had been disconnected. The machine crackled.

'What number are you calling?' Cassin enquired.

'Hugon speaking. Is that the Polyphone Institute? Good, I haven't much time . . .'

'Where are you calling from?'

'The Saarbrücken post office. Look, I told you . . .'

'Take it easy. I'm listening. Don't babble,' Cassin snapped.

Grelle was standing up now, perched against the table edge, watching the spools turn slowly, recording each word in his brain as the machine replayed them. And Cassin had been right: Hugon's agitation came through even the recording.

'The colonel had a meeting this evening with an Englishman. Name Alan Lennox . . .' Hugon spat out the name. 'Thirty-five, dark-haired, clean-shaven, wearing . . .' A description of the clothes followed. 'They talked alone in the farmhouse . . .'

'How did this Lennox arrive? By taxi? By car?'

'In his own car ... I can't stay here long. It's dangerous, you know. The car was a blue Citroën DS21. Registration number BL 49120. Lennox came by appointment. I was able to get back to the farmhouse and overhear just a few words, but it was dangerous ...'

'So you keep saying. Who is this man Lennox?'

'I've no idea. Stop interrupting me. For God's sake *listen*! When I heard them talking Lennox was asking about a man called the Leopard ...'

Grelle stiffened, stopped the machine. Gabbling on, Hugon had blurred the words. He played it back again, listening carefully. Yes, for Christ's sake, Hugon had said 'the Leopard'. The recording continued.

'... and there was something about a list of witnesses. Yes, witnesses. If you don't let me get on I'm hanging up. Yesterday morning the colonel dictated to me a list of three people's names and addresses. I think this is the list they were talking about. I think the colonel gave Lennox this list ...'

'We need those names and addresses,' Cassin interjected.

'Shit!' Hugon spoke the word with venom. 'I was just going to tell you – I made a carbon copy when I typed out the list. I put this in an envelope and sent it off yesterday to the address you gave me. And yes, Lennox has left. No! I have no idea where he has gone. I got the idea he's going to see the people on the list ...'

'Which country are these people in?'

'Two in Alsace, one in Germany. Goodbye!'

The prefect stopped the machine, still perched on the

table with a forgotten Gauloise smoking at the corner of his mouth. It was Guy Florian himself who authorized Marc Grelle to conduct the operation which penetrated Col Lasalle's farmhouse refuge in the Saarland. Normally such an assignment would have been handled by the Sûreté, but the president had told Danchin he wanted Grelle to deal with it. 'I trust Grelle,' he remarked casually, watching the minister wince.

The penetration operation had not been too difficult. Captain Moreau, who had been given the code-name Hugon, had fled France with Col Lasalle on an impulse; later, as the months went by, as he found himself acting as housekeeper to the colonel, which even included preparing the meals and keeping the house clean, his enthusiasm for exile had waned. Seeing nothing ahead but an empty future, Moreau had snapped up Grelle's secret offer of four thousand francs a month paid into a Paris bank account. 'With indecent haste,' as the prefect had remarked at the time.

When Cassin returned from his breath of fresh air, Grelle left the Sûreté to drive back to his apartment on the Ile St-Louis. The next step would be to circulate Alan Lennox's description to all French frontier checkpoints.

Chapter Six

Leon Jouvel. Robert Philip. Dieter Wohl.

The list of names and addresses meant nothing to either Grelle or Boisseau when the envelope containing the typed sheet reached the préfecture on Tuesday morning, 14 December. The envelope arrived in the prefect's hands by a somewhat devious route. As instructed earlier if he had anything to send by post, Hugon-Moreau had sent the envelope to an address in the Rue St-Antoine near the Place de la Bastille. The Rue St-Antoine is one of the many 'village' districts which make Paris one of the most complex and varied cities in the world. The envelope was addressed to the owner of a small bar who lived over his business; an ex-police sergeant, he supplemented his income by acting as a post-box for the Sûreté. Under the circumstances, it would hardly have been discreet for Moreau to send a communication direct to the Rue des Saussaies. Warned of its imminent arrival, the bar-owner phoned the Sûreté when it arrived, who in turn phoned the prefecture. A despatch rider delivered the envelope to Grelle's desk by ten in the morning.

'These people mean nothing to me,' Boisseau told

Grelle as they checked the list together. 'Do you think Hugon is inventing information to justify his four thousand francs a month?'

'No, I don't. Look at the German name – Dieter Wohl. I read about him in the file on the Leopard. He was the Abwehr officer in the Lozère during the war. I seem to remember he compiled a diary on the Leopard's activities . . .'

'In any case,' Boisseau said, sucking on his extinct pipe, 'the Leopard, as I keep reminding you, is dead . . .'

'So, Boisseau, we have two facts which contradict each other. First, the Leopard's deputy, Petit-Louis, whom we now know to have been Gaston Martin, stated quite categorically that he saw the Leopard walk in through the gates of the Elysée five days ago. That is a fact – he made the statement. Fact two, the Leopard is dead – the record says so. How do we reconcile these two contradictory facts?'

'We check them . . .'

'Precisely. I want to know everything there is on file about the burial of the Leopard in 1944. I want to know where the grave is, whether a priest attended the funeral, whether he is still alive, who the undertaker was, whether he is still alive – every little detail that you can dig up. Phone my friend Georges Hardy, the Police Prefect of Lyon. But tell him to keep the enquiry just between me and him . . .' His deputy was leaving the office when Grelle called him back. 'And Boisseau, I want the information yesterday . . .'

The prefect next called in his secretary and dictated a confidential memo to Roger Danchin telling him the contents of the latest message from Hugon-Moreau. When the memo was typed he initialled it and a despatch rider immediately took it to the Place Beauvau. And as has been known to happen before when a subordinate reports to his superior, Grelle censored the report, omitting any reference to the Leopard. Danchin was reading the memo before noon.

Earlier, as soon as he arrived in his office, the prefect started the machinery moving which, in a few hours, would have circulated to all French frontier checkpoints the name and description of Alan Lennox. 'It's odd,' he said to Boisseau, 'I once met a man with this name when I was in Marseille. Get someone to phone the right man at our embassy in London and try to check him out – with particular reference to his present whereabouts. Alan Lennox – he was an international security expert . . .'

The headquarters of the BND, the German Federal Intelligence Service is located at Pullach in Bavaria, a small town on the banks of the river Isar six miles south of Munich. On the morning when Grelle received the list of witnesses from Hugon, Peter Lanz called in at his office in the two-storey building which houses senior staff at the unearthly hour of 5 a.m. Rising so early did not bother Lanz who could easily get by on four hours' sleep a night. As he collected papers from his desk and put them inside a brief-case his secretary, Frau Schenker, a pretty girl of twenty-seven and the wife of an army officer, came into the room.

'The car has arrived, Herr Lanz. They say the airfield is fogged in . . .'

'They have a flare path, for God's sake!' Lanz grinned to take the edge off his outburst. 'I haven't had coffee yet, so you must excuse me. You can phone me in Bonn up to nine o'clock – if you must!'

'I shall forget you have gone to Bonn,' Frau Schenker replied. She was half in love with her boss, but sensible enough to know that this was really because she spent all day with him and he was so considerate. At least it helped to dispel the feeling of isolation working at Pullach engendered; none of the people who worked at the BND were able to let their friends know their real job. As Lanz went down to the car, she checked her watch. He would be airborne within thirty minutes.

As Lanz had foreseen, they had to light the flare path before his executive aircraft could take off, then it was climbing steeply through grey murk which was always disturbing: you couldn't rid yourself of the feeling that a large airliner might be heading direct for you. To suppress the fear, Lanz pulled out the table-flap and read the transcript of Col. Lasalle's latest broadcast over Europe Number One. The Frenchman had excelled himself.

'The Hawk in Paris is getting ready to take flight . . . Soon he will alight in the city of the new Tsar whose shadow falls over the ancient and famous cities of

Athens, Rome and Lisbon . . . Is Paris to be the next city to fall under the darkness of this barbaric shadow?'

Which was as good as saying that Paris might soon fall to a Communist *coup d'état*. *Ridiculous*. Lanz scribbled the word in the margin. Chancellor Franz Hauser, whom he was flying to see at the Palais Schaumburg, would be furious at this latest outburst. Every Tuesday morning Lanz flew to Bonn to brief Hauser on the latest international developments as seen by the BND. It was really the job of the BND president to attend this meeting, but the president was now no more than a figurehead. 'That empty old beer barrel,' as Hauser rudely called him, only to correct the description even more rudely. 'I'm wrong, of course. He's always full of beer – that's the trouble . . .'

Finishing the Lasalle transcript, Lanz checked his diary. After seeing the chancellor he would then fly straight back to Frankfurt, take a car from the airport and drive straight over the Rhine bridge to Mainz on the west bank of the river. The previous evening Alan Lennox had phoned him at the number provided by David Nash from Saarbrücken. At ten o'clock in the morning Lanz was due to meet Lennox at the Hotel Central in Mainz.

The meeting did not take place at the hotel. When Lanz arrived at the Hotel Central reception desk and enquired for Alan Lennox he was handed a note inside a sealed envelope. *The Hauptbahnof second-class res-*

taurant, the note read. Lanz hurried across the square and found the Englishman sitting reading a copy of the *Frankfurter Allgemeine Zeitung*. 'I prefer the anonymity of railway stations,' Lennox explained in German. 'How are you?'

The Englishman spent the next fifteen minutes telling the BND chief about his visit to Lasalle, but when he mentioned the list and Lanz asked to see it, he shook his head. 'If I'm going to see these people, the fewer who know where I'm going the better. As you know, I always work on my own – that way I can only betray myself.'

'I'm relieved,' said Lanz. 'It suggests you haven't lost your touch since the Syrian days. And yes, we are going to provide you with cover papers – identity card, driving licence, and so on. In the name of a Frenchman, you said?'

'Jean Bouvier,' Lennox replied. 'A reasonably anonymous name. Your documents section can put me down as a journalist – a useful profession for someone who wants to go about asking questions . . .'

Leaving Mainz Hauptbahnhof, Lanz drove the Englishman in his own car back over the river Rhine and then accelerated along the main highway to Frankfurt. 'There are speed-traps near the Rhine bridge,' he remarked as the speedometer needle climbed. 'It wouldn't do for me to get caught by the cops!' On the way to Frankfurt he talked in English, always glad of the chance to practise another language. Reaching the city, he slowed down, went past the Frankfurt

Hauptbahnhof and then crossed a bridge over the river Main into the ancient suburb of Sachsenhausen. The shoe-box buildings of glass and concrete which are modern Frankfurt changed into *weine stube* going back to the days of the first Rothschild. 'We are there,' Lanz announced.

The shabby photographic studio was on the first floor of an old building with a cake shop below, a building containing a number of small firms with single offices. 'If anyone has followed us,' Lanz explained as they climbed the twisting staircase, 'they won't have a clue as to which office we have visited. And I don't think anyone has followed us . . .'

The taking of the photograph occupied less than five minutes. 'Too good a print on an identity card would at once arouse suspicion,' the old photographer with hornrim glasses commented with a dry smile. He promised Lanz that the false papers would be ready for collection within two days. Lennox, who had been watching the old man sceptically, asked him sharply to make a note of his vital statistics. 'You are going to need them for the papers,' he pointed out. The old man grinned and tapped his forehead. 'I've noted them up here. Eyes brown, hair black, your height I checked when you stood close to that vertical rule . . .'

They were driving away from Sachsenhausen when Lennox asked the question. 'I thought you had your own sections for producing convenient papers – or has Hauser cut your budget?'

'He has increased our budget most considerably.

And we do have our own documents sections, as you suggest. But yours is a delicate undertaking and I have received orders to take you nowhere near a BND department. Joachim, whom we have just left, and his younger brother, probably produce the best documents in Germany. Even if the Sûreté examine your papers I am sure they will be quite satisfied with them. Now, I know an excellent place for lunch . . .'

Lennox refused the invitation, saying he had things to do, and Lanz drove him back to Mainz, giving him a Frankfurt number he could phone before they parted company. As soon as he was on his own, Lennox went to the garage where he had parked his Citroën, registration number BL 49120, and drove out of the city, heading back towards the French frontier along the same route he had come from Saarbrücken. On the way he purchased some food and a bottle of beer and he ate his snack lunch as he drove. At exactly three o'clock he reached the French border.

There was no trouble on the way in. The frontier control officials took little interest in him, waving him on after a brief glimpse of his British passport. From then on he drove at speed, keeping just inside the limit until he reached Metz, the nearest large city to the border. As he was parking his Citroën it occurred to Lennox that Metz was Marc Grelle's birthplace.

He spent one hour in Metz, moving quickly from shop to shop, limiting himself to only a few purchases at any one establishment. When he drove out of the city at five o'clock he had a suitcase full of French clothes – nine shirts, two suits, underclothes, ties, handkerchiefs, one raincoat, one heavier coat, a hat, and various accessories including two ballpoint pens, a wallet and a reporter's notebook. He had also purchased toothbrush, toothpaste and a set of French shaving equipment.

Arriving back at the frontier control point well after dark he immediately noticed signs of intense activity. Papers were being checked with great care, the number of officials on view was greater, and a long queue of cars had formed. When his turn came the passport officer studied his document with interest, going through every page, which was unusual. 'You are leaving France, sir? That is so?' He was speaking in French.

'I beg your pardon?' Lennox replied in English.

'*Un moment . . .*' The officer disappeared into a hut, still carrying the passport. When he returned ten minutes later he brought with him another official who spoke English. The second man, who now held the passport, leaned into the car and stared hard at Lennox. 'What was the purpose of your visit to France and how long have you been here?'

Lennox switched off the ignition, leaned an elbow on the window and assumed an expression of great patience. Never provoke passport control; they can make life hell for you. 'I have been in France for three hours,' he explained. 'I found myself close to the border and decided to drive over here for the pleasure of some

French food. I have not found German food all that interesting,' he lied blandly. 'Can you understand that?'

'Please proceed!'

And what the hell was that all about? Lennox asked himself as he crossed over into Germany and accelerated. Why the interest in someone with a British passport? It gave him a feeling of relief to have passed through frontier control; he had not particularly wanted his suitcase opened up when it was full of newly bought French clothes. Must have been a spot check, he thought as he drove on through the night towards Mainz where he had booked a room at the Hotel Central. Within the next two days he would have his second meeting with Peter Lanz to collect the French papers. Then he would cross the French frontier again, this time as Jean Bouvier, newspaper reporter.

Grelle received the summons to the Ministry of the Interior at 6 p.m., just about the time when Lennox was coming up to the frontier control post. 'He's getting worse,' he told Boisseau. 'Soon I shall be seeing him hourly. I'll see you when I get back . . .'

Driving to see Roger Danchin, he ran into the rush-hour traffic, and since it was pouring with rain people's tempers were even shorter than usual. Sitting in a traffic jam, he quietly cursed the minister in barrack-room language. It was 7 p.m. when he pulled into the courtyard behind the Place Beauvau, sighed, and then went inside the building. When he entered the minister's office Danchin was standing in his favourite position, by the window and staring down into the hidden garden with his back turned. 'Grelle,' he said, 'I have the report on my desk of your visit to the American Embassy yesterday. You arrived at six and left at six-twenty. That seems to have been a very brief visit indeed.' Then he waited, still not looking round.

Grelle made a very rude, two-fingered gesture behind his trouser-leg and remained standing, saying nothing. He had not yet been asked a question and he was damned if he was going to play Danchin's game, to start babbling on, explaining himself. The silence lasted a minute. 'Well,' Danchin said sharply. 'What happened?'

'I saw David Nash . . .' Grelle, well prepared for the query, spoke in a monotone, almost in a bored tone. 'He had come over to try and find out why Florian is making more and more anti-American speeches. Apparently the State Department is getting very worried about it. I fenced with him, told him I knew nothing about politics, that I was a policeman. He didn't seem very satisfied with my reply, so I thought it best to leave, which I did.'

'Mm-m . . .' The stooped figure turned away from the window and suddenly stood quite erect. It gave Grelle a slight shock; he could never remember seeing Danchin perfectly erect. 'I think you handled the situation well. What do you think Lasalle is up to now? I had your memo this morning.'

Again the disconcerting switch to an unexpected topic, a typical tactic of Danchin's to catch the man he was interviewing off guard. Grelle shrugged his shoulders, aware that his casual dress of slacks and polo-necked sweater was being studied with disapproval. 'I'm as puzzled as you are, Minister, about Lasalle,' he replied. 'I've alerted the frontier people about the Englishman, but we may have to wait for Hugon's next report before we learn more.'

'Probably, probably . . .' Danchin wandered round the room and then stopped behind Grelle. 'Do you think there is any chance that Lasalle is in touch with the Americans?' he enquired suddenly.

Grelle swung round and stared at his interrogator. 'So far I have no evidence to suggest that. Are you saying that you have? Because if so I should know of it . . .'

'Just thinking aloud, Grelle. Not even thinking – just wondering. I don't think I need detain you any longer . . .'

On his way back to the prefecture Grelle went into a bar behind the Rue St-Honoré to calm down. Does everyone hate his boss he wondered as he got back into his car and drove to the Ile de la Cité. The news Boisseau gave him made him forget the irritation of the trip to the Place Beauvau.

'They've spotted Lennox . . .'

Boisseau came into the prefect's office holding a

piece of paper. 'They checked his passport at the nearest border control point to Saarbrücken. He was travelling alone in a blue DS21 – registration number BL 49120. It all fits with the data Hugon gave us. The passport simply designates him as business executive.'

'Quick work. Have they put someone on his tail?' the prefect asked.

'No. How could they? He was crossing into Germany. The time was 1800 hours this evening . . .'

'Crossing into Germany? You mean he had just left France? What the hell is he up to? According to Hugon he was coming into France!' Grelle walked across his office to study a wall map. 'He crosses the border into France and then drives straight back into Germany? It doesn't make sense, Boisseau.'

'Perhaps Hugon is not all that reliable . . .'

'He was reliable in telling us the Englishman had visited Lasalle. I just don't understand it.' Grelle began pacing backwards and forwards in front of the map, occasionally glancing at it. 'It's too much of a coincidence that he should cross over so close to Saarbrücken,' he decided. 'He must have gone back to see Lasalle. We'll have to wait for the next report from Hugon. I've no doubt he'll tell us that Lennox went back to see the colonel.'

'Shall we keep on the frontier alert?'

'Yes. Just in case he comes back again.'

*

THE STONE LEOPARD

The third member of the Soviet Commando was Antonin Lansky, the man they called the Rope. Twenty-eight years old, Lansky had already travelled abroad to track down two Czechs who defected from the political intelligence section in Bratislava. The two Czechs, a man and a girl, had fled across the border into Austria where they sought refuge in Vienna. Their disappearance – on a Friday night in the hope that they would have the weekend to get clear – was discovered by accident within a few hours. Lansky was sent after them.

The Austrian security service reacted too slowly. On arrival the Czech couple applied for political asylum and were temporarily housed in an apartment off the Kärntnerstrasse, which was a mistake because the apartment had been used before and a security official from the Soviet Embassy watching the apartment saw them arrive. He informed Lansky the moment the Czech reached Vienna.

How Lansky talked his way inside the apartment was always a mystery, but it was known that he spoke fluent German. In the early evening of Sunday an official from the Austrian state security department arrived at the apartment to interrogate the Czech couple. Getting no reply to his repeated knocking, he called the caretaker who forced the locked door. They found the man and the girl in different rooms, both of them hanging from ropes. A note – scribbled in Czech – explained. 'We could no longer face the future...'

From then on inside Czech state security circles Lansky was nicknamed the Rope.

Antonin Lanksy was a thin, wiry man of medium height with a lean, bony face and well-shaped hands. Blond-haired, his most arresting feature was his eyes, large-pupilled eyes which moved with disconcerting slowness. Reserved by nature, he had spoken least during the training session at the race-track outside Tábor, listening while Carel Vanek, ever ready to express himself on any subject, talked non-stop in the evenings before they went to bed. Even Vanek found the quiet, soft-spoken Lansky hard to understand; if a man won't join you in conversation you can't get a grip on him, bring him under your influence. 'You'll have to prattle on a bit more when we go into Germany,' Vanek told him one evening, 'otherwise you'll stand out like raw egg on a bedsheet. Frenchmen are always prattling . . .'

'That was not my observation when I was in Paris,' Lansky replied quietly. 'I often sat in bistros where the locals were playing piquet and they hardly spoke a word for hours.'

When I was in Paris . . . Subtly, Lansky had needled Vanek again. The older Czech disliked being reminded that Lansky had succeeded him in the security department with the Czech Embassy in Paris, that Lansky, too, knew something about France. The truth was that Antonin Lansky was deeply ambitious, that he looked forward to the day when he would replace a man like

Vanek, whom he thought too volatile for the job of leader.

It was close to midnight on Tuesday, 14 December, when the Russian trainer, Borisov, burst into the concrete cabin where the three members of the Commando were getting ready for bed. Lansky was already in his upper bunk against the wall while Vanek and Brunner, who had stayed up talking and smoking, were just starting to disrobe. Borisov came in with his coat covered with snow. For several days snow had been falling heavily east of a line between Berlin and Munich; now it had come to Tábor.

'You will be leaving for the West within forty-eight hours,' he announced. 'A signal has just arrived – everything is changed. Forget Lasalle – you have three other people on the list now – two in France and one in Germany . . .' He dropped a sheet of paper on the table which Vanek picked up as Brunner peered over his shoulder. 'And you have to complete the job by the night of 22 December,' he added.

'It's impossible,' was Brunner's immediate reaction. 'Not enough time for planning . . .'

'Difficult, yes, but not impossible,' Vanek commented as he took the list of names and addresses over to the wall map. 'Strasbourg, Colmar and Freiburg are in roughly the same area – on opposite banks of the Rhine. We already have our different sets of French papers, we all speak French . . .' In the background Borisov was watching closely, sure now that he had chosen the right

111

man to lead the Commando: Vanek was adaptable in an emergency. 'I think as we're going into France,' Vanek went on, 'each of us should carry a Sûreté Nationale card – they have some in Kiev and if they get the lead out of their boots they should be able to fly them here by tomorrow night. And a set of French skeleton keys. Then we could leave on Thursday morning . . .'

Brunner exploded. 'That gives no time for planning,' he repeated, 'and only seven days to do the whole job . . .'

'Which means we shall have to move fast and not hang about and that's no bad thing,' Vanek replied quietly. 'It gives us the whole of tomorrow to plan schedules and routes – which I will help you with . . .' The Czech's normal arrogance and cockiness had disappeared as he continued speaking persuasively, building up an atmosphere of confidence, making the other two men see that it really was possible. Borisov, who had not detected this side of Vanek's character before, congratulated himself again on his choice. Vanek, clearly, was going to rise very high in state security when he added a few more years to his experience.

'And French ski equipment would be useful,' Vanek added. 'With the snow in the Bavarian and Austrian alps we can travel as tourists just returning from a brief holiday . . .'

'I'll phone Kiev,' Borisov promised. 'There is one more thing. When you are in the West you have to phone a certain number in Paris I have been given in case of further developments . . .'

'We have enough on our plate already,' Brunner grumbled as he reached for a western railway timetable off the shelf.

'You make one phone call each day,' Borisov continued, 'using the name Salicetti.'

Lansky, who had got down from his bunk, looked at the names and addresses on the list.

Leon Jouvel. Robert Philip. Dieter Wohl.

Chapter Seven

'This corrupt American Republic where the Dollar is God, where police forces supplement their pensions with bribes, where its leading city, New York, is at the mercy of a dozen different racial gangs ... where terrorism flourishes like the plague ...

'What does Europe want with a continent like this? Or should we seal ourselves off from this corrupt and corrupting state with a moral and physical quarantine? Goodbye, America, and may you never return to infest our shores ...'

Guy Florian made the new speech at Lille, only eight days after his vicious outburst against the Americans at Dijon, and it seemed to his audience that he was stepping up the tempo, 'muck-spreading with a bull-dozer', as Alain Blanc expressed it to Marc Grelle in Paris later that evening.

The Police Prefect arrived at his office early in the morning of that day, Wednesday, 15 December, and again called his deputy and told him to lock the door. Two closed suitcases lay on his desk. 'Boisseau, it's possible this Leopard business could be very serious, something which might well endanger both our careers if we carry on with it. You should now consider your position very carefully – and remember, you have a family . . .'

'What are your orders?' Boisseau asked simply.

'First, to put two top cabinet ministers under close and highly secret surveillance – Roger Danchin and Alain Blanc. Do you still wish to be involved?'

Boisseau took out his pipe and clenched it between his teeth without lighting it. 'I'll have to form a special team,' he said, 'and I'll spin them a story so they won't get nervous. Is there anything else? Incidentally, this surveillance, I presume, is to see whether either man – Danchin or Blanc – is having contact with a Soviet link?'

'Exactly. And yes, there is something else, something rather punishing.' Grelle pointed to the two suitcases. 'Late last night I collected a whole bunch of wartime files from Sûreté records. You take one case, I'll take the other. Somewhere in those files I think we will find out where both Danchin and Blanc were during the war – because the solution to this Leopard affair lies a long time ago in the past. If either of these men can be positively located during 1944 in an area far from the Lozère – where the Leopard was operating – then we can eliminate him . . .'

Taking a suitcase back to his own office, Boisseau then set up a secret conference. Certain reliable detectives of the Police Judiciaire were detailed to work in relays, to follow Roger Danchin and Alain Blanc whenever they left their ministries. Boisseau himself briefed the chosen men. 'You work in absolute secrecy, reporting back to me alone. We have reason to believe there may be a plot to kill one of these two ministers. It could be connected with a recent event,' he confided mysteriously.

'We may have to prevent another assassination attempt?' one of the detectives enquired.

'It goes deeper than that,' Boisseau explained. 'The plot may involve someone close to January or August . . .' From now on, he had stressed, real names must never be used, so code-names were invented: January for Danchin and August for Blanc. 'So,' Boisseau continued, 'we need a record of everyone these two men meet outside their places of work. One of their so-called friends may be the man – or woman – we are after . . .' By mid-afternoon the surveillance operation was under way.

Grelle himself later approved the measures Boisseau had taken. 'We are,' he remarked wrily, 'in danger of becoming conspirators ourselves, but there is no other way.'

'Could you not confidentially inform the president of what we are doing – and why?' Boisseau suggested.

'And risk going the way of Lasalle? Surely you have not forgotten that the colonel was dismissed for exceeding his powers? The trouble is Florian has so much confidence in his own judgement that he will never believe someone close to him could be a traitor . . .'

Shortly after he made this remark, what later became known in Paris circles as 'L'Affaire Lasalle' exploded. Grelle's first warning that a potential disaster was imminent was when Roger Danchin summoned him to a secret meeting at the Ministry of the Interior.

It was late in the morning of 15 December – the day after Danchin had asked Grelle whether he believed Col. Lasalle was in touch with the Americans – when the prefect was called urgently to the Place Beauvau. Grelle was the last to arrive. On either side of a long table sat all the key security officials including, the prefect noted as he entered the room, Commissioner Suchet of counter-intelligence, a man whose methods and personality he intensely disliked. Large and gross, with a plump face where the eyes almost vanished under pouches of fat, Daniel Suchet was a bon vivant who made no bones about it. 'I eat well, drink well and seduce well,' he once confided to Grelle.

Presiding at the head of the table, Danchin waved the new arrival to a vacant chair. 'Everything said at this meeting is absolutely confidential,' he instructed in his best ministerial manner. 'Not to be discussed with personal assistants unless necessary in the execution of the operation . . .'

'What operation?' Grelle asked.

'You are not involved,' Danchin informed him. 'Suchet will be in charge. But we need you to give us information about Colonel Lasalle's daily habits and routines – since you have the link with Hugon.'

'Minister, why do you need this information?' Grelle enquired.

'Just give us the information, please, Mr Prefect . . .' It was Suchet who intervened, clasping his plump hands on the table and leaning forward aggressively. 'I do not wish to be discourteous, but there is a question of security. The fewer people who are involved – you know what I mean . . .'

'I have no idea what you mean. Unless I know what you are up to I cannot possibly help – I shall probably leave out a vital piece of information . . .'

'I'll be the judge of that,' Suchet rapped back.

'Please, gentlemen,' Danchin interjected. 'We are all here to help one another . . .'

'Then let him tell me what he is up to,' Grelle repeated.

'We have decided to arrest Colonel Lasalle.'

There was a silence and, knowing his reputation, every head round the table turned to stare at the prefect. Grelle requested permission to smoke and Danchin, who was already smoking, nodded impatiently. The prefect took his time lighting the cigarette, staring hard at Suchet whose eyes flickered and looked away. 'Is this Commissioner Suchet's mad idea?' he enquired.

'No, it is mine,' Danchin said quietly.

'You are going to kidnap Lasalle . . .'

'"Arrest" was the word he used,' Danchin snapped.

'You cannot arrest a man on foreign soil,' Grelle said in a monotone. 'You can only kidnap him and drag him over the border by brute force. How can we expect the public to respect the police, to obey the law, when the law itself is acting like the Mafia . . .'

'Careful,' Danchin warned. 'Perhaps you would prefer to withdraw from the meeting . . .'

'Like the Mafia,' Grelle repeated. 'Horrible little thugs in plain clothes breaking into a man's house at dead of night, grabbing him . . .'

'Lasalle is a traitor . . .'

'Lasalle is living in Germany. There would be an international outcry.'

'We've thought of that . . .' Danchin adopted a more conciliatory tone. 'It would be announced that Lasalle had secretly entered France of his own free will, that he had been seen and then arrested on French soil . . .'

'De Gaulle got away with it with Colonel Argoud,' Suchet said.

'It's not good enough!' The prefect's fist crashed down on the table. 'If you insist on going ahead with this bizarre operation I shall inform the president of my objections . . .'

'The president is aware that this meeting is taking place,' Danchin informed him.

'How close is this operation, Minister?' Grelle asked.

119

'We may act tomorrow night.'

'Then I must act now.' Grelle stood up. 'You invited me to withdraw. May I accept your invitation now?'

The interview with Florian was tense, so tense that Kassim the Alsatian, feeling the tension between the two men he regarded as his friends, slunk away under a couch. Beyond the tall windows of the president's study snowflakes drifted down into the Elysée garden, snow which melted as it landed. On the desk between the two men a sheet of paper lay with the telephones and the lamp. Grelle's hastily penned letter of resignation. Florian slid the sheet across the desk so it dropped over the edge into the prefect's lap.

'I won't be involved in this thing if that's what is worrying you,' he stated icily. 'Danchin, from what I hear, plans to repeat the Colonel Argoud abduction technique. Lasalle will be brought from Germany and left a prisoner somewhere in Paris. You will receive a phone call – you will then find Lasalle tied up in a van in a back street. It will be your duty to arrest him.'

'It is an illegal act, Mr President . . .'

'Neither of us will be directly involved . . .'

'But both of us will know. President Nixon once tried to play a dubious game – look what happened . . .'

'You are frightened it will not work?' Florian demanded.

'I am frightened it will work . . .'

Florian's expression changed suddenly. Leaning

back in his embroidered chair he steepled his hands and stared hard at Grelle, frowning. The desk lamp was on and against a wall Florian's shadow was distorted and huge. 'I think you're right,' he said quietly. 'I'm too much surrounded by politicians. Shall I tear up that piece of paper or will you?'

Within three minutes of Grelle leaving the room, Florian picked up the phone and cancelled the operation.

Grelle left the Elysée in a stunned frame of mind. When he first heard of the plot to kidnap Lasalle he felt sure it was the brainchild of the devious Suchet; then he thought it must be a brain-storm on the part of Roger Danchin. The realization that Guy Florian himself had sanctioned the plan had astounded the prefect. It seemed so alien in character, or had he all along misjudged the president's character? On an impulse, when he had got into his car, he drove in a circle round the high wall which encloses the Elysée garden – following the one-way system – and this brought him back to the Rue des Saussaies. Going inside the Sûreté, he collected two more dusty files from the records department.

In the German city of Mainz Alan Lennox was waiting impatiently at the Hotel Central to collect his French papers from Peter Lanz. At eleven in the morning he phoned Lanz at the Frankfurt number the BND chief had given him and the German came on the line immediately. He was apologetic. 'I doubt whether the documents we are talking about will be ready before tomorrow,' he explained. 'If you like to call me again at four this afternoon I may have more news . . .'

'What's keeping the old boy?'

'He's a craftsman. He wants the product to be right – and so do you . . .'

'He's not producing the *Mona Lisa* . . .'

'But a portrait which we hope will be equally convincing. Alan, trust me . . .'

Lanz put down the receiver and pursed his lips. He was unhappy about deceiving the Englishman; he even doubted his success in so doing. He felt sure that Lennox knew the BND had ways of collecting blank French identity cards, which they had, and that probably they possessed a store of such blanks, which they did. The papers made out in the name of Jean Bouvier, reporter, were in fact inside a drawer in Lanz's desk as he spoke to Lennox. What Lanz was waiting for was final approval from the Palais Schaumburg for the Englishman to proceed into France.

Chancellor Franz Hauser, whom Lanz had seen once before he met Lennox on the previous day, and once since the meeting, was still unsure about the wisdom of probing into the affairs of his most important ally. 'If this Englishman is caught – and talks – we shall be keelhauled by Paris,' Hauser had remarked to Lanz. 'Give me a few hours to think it over – I will take a positive decision tomorrow night. Maybe something will happen to decide me . . .'

It was in the evening of the night when Franz Hauser took his decision that Guy Florian made his violent onslaught on America in his speech at Lille.

As they had done on the previous Saturday night, Grelle and Boisseau spent the evening in the prefect's apartment, but this time instead of checking the Leopard's file they were studying the wartime files on Roger Danchin and Alain Blanc. It was close to midnight before they completed their reading.

'At least we know a little more,' Boisseau suggested.

'Do we?' Grelle queried dubiously.

'Alain Blanc was officially studying at a remote farmhouse in Provence,' Boisseau stated as Grelle poured more black coffee. It had been agreed that Boisseau should concentrate on Blanc. 'He was sent there by his father to stop him getting mixed up with the Resistance.'

'Did it stop him?'

'No! He stayed at the farmhouse, continuing his studies, and allowed the local Resistance group – which incidentally was wiped out to a man in August 1944 in an ambush – to use the place as an ammunition and weapons store.'

'So you exonerate him?'

'By no means,' Boisseau replied. 'The only person who could have vouched for his presence at the farmhouse during the critical period was the house-keeper who looked after him, a Madame Jalade. She died in July 1946 only a year or so after the war ended. There was an accident – she was driving her old gazogene-powered car into town and ended up at the foot of a sixty-foot gorge.'

'There were no witnesses?' Grelle asked quietly.

'None at all. She was alone. A faulty braking system was given as the cause of the accident. So she died soon after Gaston Martin was imprisoned in Guiana. It could be a coincidence, of course . . .'

'It could be,' Grelle agreed.

The prefect then relayed what he had discovered reading the files which pieced together the wartime career of Roger Danchin. Joining one of the Resistance groups in the Massif Central, Danchin had worked under the cover-name of Grand-Pierre. He had soon become an agile liaison officer between several groups, one of them commanded by the Leopard. 'He was a will-o'-the-wisp,' Grelle explained. 'Keeping in the background, he used a chain of couriers to keep one group in touch with another. Even in those days he had a great grasp of detail, apparently. He was reputed to be the best-informed man in the Midi.'

'We strike him out?' Boisseau asked.

'I'm afraid not. His documentation in 1944 is so vague. And he was in the right area – very close to Lozère.'

'So it could still be either of them?' Boisseau shrugged. 'Like so much police work – a great deal of sweat and then nothing. At least we are finished with these mouldy files.'

'Not quite,' Grelle balanced two files on his hand. 'I decided to check someone else – purely as a theoretical exercise. Gaston Martin said he saw a tall man walk into the Elysée between 7.30 and 8.30, a man saluted by the guards. Remember we are policemen – we go solely by facts. At eight o'clock Guy Florian returned to the Elysée. I have also checked his wartime background.'

When Boisseau had recovered from the shock, when he grasped the fact that Grelle was conducting a theoretical exercise, he listened while the prefect briefly outlined the president's wartime career. He had served in a section of what came to be known as the Comet Line, an escape route for Allied airmen running from France across the Spanish border. Stationed in an old house up in the Pyrenees behind St Jean-de-Luz, Florian had escorted escaping airmen into Spain where they were met by an official from the British Consulate at Bilbao.

'Two hundred and fifty miles away from Lozère,' Boisseau commented, joining in the game, 'so he could not possibly be the Leopard.'

'Impossible,' Grelle agreed. 'Except that his brother Charles, who was older but looked like him, also served in the Comet Line. Now, if Charles had agreed to impersonate Guy Florian – remember, escape routes are shrouded in mystery and the operatives rarely appeared . . .'

'I didn't know he had a brother . . .'

'He hasn't any more. In July 1945 Charles set off on one of his solitary swims into the Atlantic and never came back. His body was washed ashore two weeks later.'

'I see . . .' Boisseau sucked at his pipe. 'A lot of people died young in those days; a lot of them connected with the Leopard. I had the report in from Lyon late this afternoon about the men who buried him and the undertaker . . .'

'Which reminds me,' Grelle interjected. 'We are flying to Lyon tomorrow. There is only one way to clear up the contradiction between the man Gaston Martin said he saw and the recorded death of the Leopard – and that is to open up his grave. I spoke to Hardy on the phone myself and he is rushing through an emergency exhumation order. Now, what about the men who buried the Leopard?'

'All dead. Shot in an enemy ambush four days after the burial, the bodies riddled with Mauser bullets.'

'Plenty of Mausers about in all sorts of hands in 1944,' Grelle observed. 'And the priest?'

'There was no priest – the Leopard was an atheist . . .'

'Of course. And the undertaker?'

'Shot through the head the morning after the burial. Someone, identity unknown, broke into his house. And there was another curious thing,' Boisseau continued. 'A young Communist sculptor who had worked with the Resistance group wanted to do something to commemorate his beloved leader. So he sculpted a statue which was placed over the grave six months later. It is still there, I understand, deep inside the forest. It is a statue of a leopard, a stone leopard.'

Chapter Eight

On 16 December the Soviet Commando crossed the Czech frontier into Austria. They came over at the obscure border post at Gmünd in the Nieder-Osterreich province where Czech control towers loom over the landscape like gallows. Arriving just before nine in the morning, they presented their French passports for inspection.

The sleepy Austrian official – he had been up all night and was soon going off duty – was already prejudiced in their favour. A few minutes earlier he had seen his Czech opposite numbers giving the three tourists a thorough going-over. The battered old Peugeot had been searched while the three men stood in the road. Their documents had been carefully examined. Anyone who was no friend of the Czechs had to be all right for entry into Austria. He had no way of knowing that Vanek himself had phoned the Czech border post earlier to arrange this charade; nor could he know that their arrival had been timed to coincide with the moment just before he went off duty. A tired official is unlikely to check new arrivals with any great interest.

'Our papers are foolproof,' Vanek had explained to his two companions, 'but the way to succeed in this life is to load all dice in your favour . . .'

The Austrian official stamped the French documents, the frontier pole was raised, the Peugeot with Vanek behind the wheel drove across the border into the narrow streets of the small Austrian town. If the sleepy official thought about them at all as he kicked snow off his boots he must have assumed they were French tourists returning from a winter sports holiday. The conclusion was easy to draw: Vanek and Brunner, sitting in the front of the car, with Lansky occupying the back, were all clad in French ski-clothes.

'First hurdle jumped,' Vanek said cheerfully.

Brunner grunted. 'Plenty more ahead of us . . .'

Vanek drove at speed for two hours along the lonely open road which leads to Vienna and where fields spread out across the plan for ever; where the only traffic you meet is the occasional ox-drawn farm wagon. Overhead it was cloudy and grey; on either side the fields were snowbound; ahead the highway was a pure white lane with Vanek's the first car to leave wheeled tracks in the snow. Beyond the small town of Horn he pulled up in the deserted countryside. Getting out of the car, Vanek burned the French papers the passport official had stamped and then, using a spade which Brunner handed him, he buried the remnants, carefully re-arranging the snow over the shallow hole. Getting back into the Peugeot, he handed round sets of French papers which were duplicates of those he had just burned; duplicates except for the fact that they carried no stamp linking them with Czechoslovakia.

Reaching Vienna at noon, he parked the Peugeot in the Opera Square; later it would be picked up by a minor official from the Czech Embassy. When they had crossed the frontier at Gmünd their car registration number had been automatically noted, so now they severed this second link with their country of origin. With Vanek leading the way, shouldering his skis, the three men walked into the main entrance of the Hotel Sacher and turned through the doorway on the right which opens into a tea-room. They spent the next half-hour in leisurely fashion, drinking coffee and eating cakes while Vanek, chattering away in French, watched every person who followed them into the tea-room.

At 12.30 p.m. exactly the three men left the tea-room by a door leading into a side street, still carrying their skis. The Mercedes waiting for them was parked outside the Hotel Astoria and the registration number confirmed to Vanek that this was their vehicle. The key was in the ignition and nearby a Czech official who had watched the car folded up his newspaper and walked away; when he had picked up the Peugeot waiting in Opera Square his job was done.

With Vanek again behind the wheel, they drove to the Westbahnhof, the terminus from which trains depart from Vienna for western Europe. Brunner – with Vanek's help – had worked out the schedule precisely. Arriving at the Westbahnhof before 1 p.m. gave them nice time to eat lunch in the station restaurant before they boarded the express due to depart at 2 p.m. The train was moving out of the station when a Slovak climbed inside the Mercedes parked outside the Westbahnhof and drove off. The Commando, all links with Czechoslovakia effectively severed, was on its way to Germany.

It was just before noon in the German city of Mainz – four hundred miles to the east the Soviet Commando had now arrived in Vienna – when Alan Lennox met Peter Lanz of the BND in the station first class restaurant. The Englishman, who had been sitting at the table for a few minutes, nodded as Lanz took a chair and dropped a copy of the magazine *Der Spiegel* on the chair between them. Lanz picked up the menu. 'The papers are inside,' he murmured. 'Sorry we've taken such a bloody long time over them. But they're good . . .' He ordered coffee from the waiter.

It was impossible for Lanz to tell the Englishman the real cause of the delay, that he had just returned from the Palais Schaumburg in Bonn where Chancellor Hauser had given the go-ahead. 'That speech of Florian's at Lille last night disturbed me,' the chancellor had explained to Lanz. 'If he goes on building up this atmosphere of ferment he may leave behind him in Paris a situation ripe for a *coup d'état* while he is in Moscow. We must find out whether there is a high-level Communist at work in Paris – and quickly . . .'

'Under that napkin near your hand,' Lennox said

quietly, 'you'll find my British passport. Hang on to it for me until I get back. It wouldn't be very clever if they found that on me when I'm inside France . . .'

Lanz put the folded napkin in his lap, paused while the waiter served coffee, and then pocketed the document. 'I suppose you will be driving into France?' he enquired. 'It will give you total mobility.'

'Probably. I want to be off in about twenty minutes. Is there anything else I need to know?'

'I'm afraid there is.' Lanz leaned across the table, smiling as though he were saying something of little consequence. 'We've just heard that some kind of alert has gone out from Paris. We've no idea why. But there is increased surveillance at all French frontier crossing points.'

'Thanks, I'll watch out.' Lennox made no mention of the fact that he already knew this. It wasn't that he distrusted the BND chief, but when he was working alone he made it a point to let no one know what he was doing next. He rested his hand lightly on the copy of *Der Spiegel*. 'The papers seem a bit bulky,' he commented, drinking the rest of his coffee.

'We've included five thousand Deutschmarks in high-denomination bills – for expenses. We don't expect you to be out of pocket on this thing . . .'

'Thanks again. If I want to contact you, I use the Frankfurt number?'

'No, a different one. In Bonn, actually . . .' Lanz didn't explain that from now on he was staying in the

German capital where he could have immediate access to Franz Hauser in case of a crisis. 'You'll find the new number written on the inside of the envelope,' he went on. 'You can reach me at that number at any hour of the day – or night. I shall stay in my office at that number, eat there, sleep there. If you phone I promise you it will be my hand which will lift the receiver.'

Lennox stared at the German. This kind of consideration he had not expected. 'Thanks once more,' he said. 'But this trip could take anything up to a fortnight if I run into trouble – and you could get pretty stiff staying locked up in one room for as long as that.'

'It's the least I can do, for Christ's sake.' Lanz spread his hands. 'I wouldn't want to take on the job myself, I can tell you. There's something stirring in the French security system, and it may not be healthy. If you get in a jam, call me. I can't promise one damned thing – not inside France – but I can at least try. If it gets hot, get out . . .'

Grelle was airborne in an Alouette helicopter, heading south for Lyon to attend the exhumation of the Leopard's grave, when he took another decision. He had been sitting silently for some time, not speaking to Boisseau who was beside him, staring down at the flooded landscape below. For large stretches it was more like travelling over Asian rice paddyfields than the plains of France.

'Boisseau,' Grelle said eventually, 'there are two persons on that list Hugon supplied who live in France – excluding the man in Germany . . .'

'Two,' Boisseau agreed.

'I want you to set up close surveillance on both those people. It must be very discreet – the two men being watched must have no idea they are under surveillance.'

'They are to intercept the Englishman, Lennox, if he shows up?'

'No! If Lennox appears I want the fact reported, then I want Lennox discreetly tailed. But he must not be intercepted.'

'I will have to quote your personal authority. It is out of our jurisdiction, of course.'

It was, indeed, out of Grelle's jurisdiction. Normally the power of the Police Prefect of Paris ends at the city's boundaries; he possesses not one shred of authority outside the capital. But Florian had expressly handed over to Grelle the responsibility for his own security to cover the whole of France since the assassination attempt.

'Of course,' Grelle agreed. 'So you tell them this concerns the safety of the President of the French Republic.'

To check passengers travelling from Vienna to Germany, passport officials sometimes board the train at Salzburg, but not often; this is one of the more open frontiers of Europe. The Soviet Commando crossed the Austro-German border without any check at all. With their ski equipment in the luggage van, travelling with French papers, carrying French francs and German marks in their wallets, the trio were to all outward appearances French tourists returning home from Austria via Germany.

Even so, Vanek was still taking precautions. Deciding that two travellers were less conspicuous than three, he sat with Brunner in one first-class compartment while Lansky travelled alone in a different coach. As they moved through the snowbound countryside of Bavaria beyond Salzburg after dark they caught glimpses in the moonlight of the white Alps to the south later, approaching Munich, they passed close to Pullach, the home of the BND headquarters. Reaching Munich at eight in the evening, Vanek and Brunner took a cab to the Four Seasons Hotel, the most expensive hostelry in the city.

'No one,' as Vanek explained earlier, 'looks for assassins in the best hotels . . .'

Privately, Brunner had a more simple explanation. Vanek, he felt sure, believed that only the best was good enough for a man of his talents. While they proceeded to their own hotel, Lansky left the station by himself and booked a room at the Continental. To adjust themselves to the Western atmosphere they went out in the evening after Vanek had phoned Lansky from an outside call-box to make sure he had arrived. 'Don't sit in the hotel room,' Vanek ordered his subordinate. 'Get out and sniff the place. Circulate . . .' But he did not invite Lansky to join himself and Brunner.

At a beer hall Vanek picked up a couple of girls, using his fluent German to pull off the introduction, and later the four of them ate a very expensive dinner. When Brunner, hurrying after his leader to the lavatory, questioned these tactics, Vanek was brusque. 'Don't you realize that two men with a couple of girls are far less conspicuous than two foreigners on their own? In any case,' he said as he adjusted his flies, 'they are nice girls . . .'

At the end of the evening, drinking absurdly priced champagne in a night-club, Vanek persuaded his girl friend to take him back to her flat. Outraged, Brunner cornered Vanek in the foyer, saying he was going back to the hotel to get a good night's sleep. 'A good night's sleep?' Vanek queried. 'My dear comrade, I can spend a little time with a girl, sleep for four hours, and face the morning with the physique of an athlete . . .'

'We are catching the early morning train to France,' Brunner reminded him.

'So don't oversleep,' Vanek replied.

Lennox, who was always a lone wolf, waited until Lanz had left the Mainz Hauptbahnhof restaurant, then he picked up the copy of *Der Spiegel*, went into the lavatory and locked the door of the cubicle. Sitting on the seat, he extracted the French papers, put the five thousand

Deutschmarks into his wallet, memorized the Bonn telephone number and tore up the envelope which he flushed down the pan. Emerging from the lavatory, he made no move to leave the station to collect his car. He had, in fact, already handed it in to the car-hire branch in Mainz.

At 12.38 p.m. he boarded the Trans-European express *Rheingold* which had just arrived from Amsterdam. Finding an empty compartment – there are few people on the Trans-European express in mid-December – he settled down in a corner seat and lit a Benson and Hedges cigarette. He had waited until the last second to board the train and no one had followed him. The people he was worried about were the French Secret Service agents attached to their embassy in Bonn. They would hardly know about him yet, but the second-in-command of the BND was an obvious target for them to follow. As the express picked up speed he took hold of his suitcase and went along to the spacious lavatory.

The man who went inside was Alan Lennox, British. The man who emerged ten minutes later was Jean Bouvier, French. Settling down again in his empty compartment, Lennox was dressed in French clothes and smoking a Gitane. He was also wearing the hat he had purchased in Metz and a pair of hornrim glasses. Normally hatless, Lennox knew how much the wearing of headgear changes the appearance of a man. When the ticket collector arrived a few minutes later and he had to purchase the TEE supplement, Lennox conversed with him in French and a little ungrammatical German.

When the express reached Freiburg, the last stop before the Swiss border, Lennox had a moment's hesitation. One of the three people on Lasalle's list of witnesses – Dieter Wohl – lived in Freiburg. Shrugging his shoulders like a Frenchman, Lennox remained in his seat. At the moment the important thing was to get clear of Germany, to break his trail; Freiburg was just across the Rhine from Alsace and he could visit Wohl later, after he had seen the Frenchmen. Promptly at 3.36 p.m. the *Rheingold* stopped at Basel Hauptbahnhof where Lennox got off. He had now arrived in Switzerland.

Leaving the station he crossed the street and went into the Hotel Victoria where he booked a room for one night only. He had plenty of time then to find the right shop and purchase a second suitcase. Taking it back to his room, he re-packed, putting his British clothes into his own case; the French items he had purchased in Metz – all except those he was wearing – went into the Swiss case he had just bought. Going out again with the British case, he walked into the Hauptbahnhof and locked it away in a luggage compartment. As he shut the door he knew it was by no means certain he would ever see this case again.

*

Grelle arrived late for the exhumation of the grave of the Leopard. Involved as he was in three major operations – probing the attempt to assassinate the president; investigating the mystery of the Leopard; perfecting the security surrounding Guy Florian – he needed every spare minute he could find in a day. Already he was keeping going on only four hours' sleep a night, while he catnapped during the day when he could – in cars, in aircraft, even in his office when he could snatch time between interviews.

With Boisseau behind the wheel, Grelle was dozing as they turned off the main road into the forest along a muddy track. A gendarme with a torch had signalled them at the obscure entrance, which they would otherwise have missed. Long after dark – the exhumation was being carried out at night to help keep it secret – it was pouring with rain and the rutted track showed two gullies of water in their headlights. The prefect opened his eyes. 'If this goes on much longer,' he grumbled, 'the whole of France will be afloat . . .'

It was a fir forest they were moving into. A palisade of wet trunks rippled past the headlights as the track twisted and turned, as the tyres squelched through the mud and the storm beat down on the cartop. About two kilometres from where they had left the road Boisseau turned a corner and the headlights, shafting through the slanting rain, shone on a weird scene.

Arc-lights glared down on the excavation which was protected with a canvas tent-like erection. Heaps of excavated soil were banked up and men with shovels were shoulder-deep inside the pit, still lifting hard-packed soil. Through the fan-shapes cleared by the wipers Grelle saw they were inside a wide clearing. Parked police vehicles stood around on carpets of dead bracken. Under the arc-lights a deep-scored mud-track ran away from the grave. Following the track with his eyes, Grelle saw a few metres away the blurred silhouette of the stone leopard effigy which had been hauled off the grave. It looked eerily alive in the beating rain, like a real animal crouched for a spring.

'I'll see how they're getting on,' said Boisseau, who had stopped the car. 'No point in both of us getting wet . . .'

An *agent de la paix*, his coat streaming with water, peered in at the window and his peaked brim deposited rain inside the car. Embarrassed, he took off the cap. 'Put it on again, for God's sake,' Grelle growled. 'Are you getting anywhere?'

'They have found the coffin . . .' The man was boyish-faced, excited at addressing the Police Prefect of Paris. 'They will have it up within a few minutes.'

'At least there is a coffin,' Grelle muttered. He was anything but excited. Even if there were a body inside he was dubious of what this might prove; after all, 1944 was a long time ago. Pessimistic as he was, he had still arranged for the forensic department at Lyon to be ready to get to work at once when the remains were delivered to them. A pathologist, a man with a fluoroscope who could assess the age of the bones, various other experts.

Grelle followed Boisseau out into the rain, hands tucked inside his raincoat pockets, hat pulled down. He would have to get wet sooner or later, and it looked bad for the prefect to sit in a warm car while the other poor devils toiled in the mud. He had taken the precaution of putting on rubber boots and his feet sank ankle-deep into the slippery mud. He stood under the glow of an arc-light while a drop of rain dripped from his nose-end, staring at the stone leopard crouched in the rain.

Above the noise of the pounding rain, the distant rumble of thunder, a new sound was added as they fastened chains round something in the depths of the pit. The tent was moved away so a breakdown truck could back to the brink. The driver moved a lever and the crane apparatus leaned out over the pit. In case of an accident the men were climbing up out of the pit now, smeared with mud. A filthy job. Probably all for nothing.

It was a disturbing scene: the wind shifting the tree tops, the endless rain, the glare of the arc-lights. And now the men in shiny coats fell silent as they waited expectantly, huddled round the grave. The chained coffin had been fixed to the hoist; the only man doing anything now was the truck driver, sitting twisted round in his seat as he operated levers. The coffin came up out of the shadows slowly, tilting at an acute angle as the machinery whirred, as the rain slanted down on the slowly turning box. Everyone was very still. Grelle inserted a cigarette in the corner of his mouth and then didn't light it as he saw a gendarme glance at him severely. 'Bloody hell,' he thought, 'does he expect me to take off my hat?'

Looking to his right again he saw the stone leopard, its mouth open, caught in the arc-light, as though enraged at the desecration. The officer in charge of the whole business shouted an order. The coffin, now above ground, swivelled in mid-air, was carried by the steel arm over to the canvas tent, gently eased and dropped just inside, under cover from the rain. Another shouted order. A man with a power saw appeared, examined the coffin and then began work, slicing the lid above where it had originally been closed. Boisseau made an enquiry, came back to the prefect.

'The screws are rusted in. They were advised not to use chisels and crowbars – the vibrations might have shivered the remains to powder . . .'

Grelle said nothing, standing quite still with the unlit cigarette now becoming soggy in the corner of his mouth. On Boisseau's orders a light was brought closer, shining directly through the tent's mouth on to the coffin.

'Is it going to tell us anything, I wonder?' Boisseau murmured and there was a hint of excitement in his voice.

'I wouldn't bet on it . . .'

'They said as far as they could tell it hasn't been

disturbed for many years. The earth is packed like concrete.'

'What about that damned statue?'

'Well bedded in. Again, not touched for years . . .'

The man with the power saw stopped. They were ready. A couple of men stooped at either side of the coffin, began sliding the lid off with care, out of the tent, so until they had removed the whole lid it wasn't possible to see what might lie inside. They seemed to take an age, bent as they were under the canvas roof, and they had to watch their footing; the ground was becoming a quagmire. Then they had moved aside and under the glare of the arc-light everyone could see. There was a gasp of horror. Grelle stood as immovable as the stone statue a few metres away. 'My God!' It was Boisseau speaking.

Inside the coffin was stretched the perfect skeleton of an enormous hound, lying on its haunches, its huge skull rested between its skeletal paw-bones, its eye-sockets in shadow so it seemed to stare at them hideously with enormous black pupils.

'César . . .' The prefect grunted. 'Macabre – and brilliant. He couldn't take his dog with him because that would identify him. And he needed something to weight the coffin. So he killed the dog and provided his own corpse.'

Boisseau bent over the skeleton, examined it briefly. 'I think there is a bullet-hole in the skull.'

'I wonder if the bastard shot his own dog?' Once

Grelle had owned a British wire-haired terrier which had eventually been knocked down in the Paris traffic. He had never replaced the animal. He spoke in a monotone, then stiffened himself. 'Tell them to replace the lid and get the whole thing to Lyon. Come on!'

They left the men in the wood lifting the coffin and its contents into the breakdown truck and drove back along the muddy track. The statue would remain in the wood, close to the grave it had guarded so long, which was already filling up with water. Boisseau, noting the frown of concentration on his chief's face, said nothing until they turned on to the main road. 'Surprised?' he asked as they picked up speed.

'Not really – although I didn't anticipate the dog. The whole thing has worried me since I read the file – it was out of pattern. He took all those precautions to make sure he couldn't be identified and then, when it's nearly all over, he walks into Lyon and gets himself shot. If he'd survived up to then, he should have gone on surviving – which he did.'

'So he's about somewhere?'

'I know exactly where he is. He's in Paris. The trouble is I don't know who he is.'

'Danchin or Blanc – according to Gaston Martin. It's a nightmare.'

'It will get worse,' Grelle assured him.

Grelle remained in Lyon just long enough to make a few more enquiries and to hear the result of the fluoroscope test on the skeleton. 'I estimate the age of the bones as being somewhere between thirty and forty years,' the expert told the prefect. 'That is, they have lain in the forest for that period of time.' Which meant the animal could easily have been shot and buried in August 1944.

Flying back to Paris aboard the helicopter, Grelle told Boisseau about his other enquiries. 'They gave me the details about the sculptor who made the statue. He was found shot in his house soon after he had finished the statue. The place had been ransacked and it was assumed he had disturbed a burglar. It gives you some idea of the ruthlessness of the man we're looking for. He covered his tracks completely – or so he thought. Until Lasalle resurrected him.'

'What the hell are we going to do?' Boisseau asked.

'Track him down.'

Chapter Nine

The two men walked alone in the Paris garden, one of them tall and stooping slightly to catch what his much shorter companion was saying. The shorter man was thick-bodied and had short, strong legs. He spoke with respect but firmly, as though expecting opposition he must overcome. He spoke in little more than a whisper even though there was no one within twenty metres of where they walked.

'We must add Lasalle to the list. He is a very dangerous man and at this stage we dare not risk leaving him alive. Otherwise he will go on ferreting until he digs up something.'

'I think it's unwise,' the tall man repeated. 'I have given you three names and that is enough. Every one you add to the list increases the risk. Something will go wrong . . .'

'Nothing will go wrong. They are using the best people available for this sort of work. I understand the Commando has almost arrived in France – and they should complete their task within six days . . .' The short man took out a handkerchief and blew his nose. He had a cold coming on; Paris really was an unbearably damp place. 'You haven't heard even a whisper that anyone knows about this?' he enquired.

'Nothing. Let them just get it over with quickly,' the tall man said sharply. 'And let me know when I can stop worrying about it. I have enough on my mind at the moment.'

The short man glanced quickly at his companion, sensing the undercurrent of tension. This he understood; he felt tense himself. 'And Lasalle? Since the kidnap operation has been cancelled we really must deal with that problem, too.'

'You can get in touch with the Commando then? Just in case any other problem crops up?'

The short man hesitated, then took a decision. 'They will make contact with us at regular intervals. So the answer is yes. I hope you haven't left someone off the list?'

'No one! Now I think we have talked enough . . .'

'And Lasalle?' the short man persisted. 'It will look like an accident, I promise you. The men who are dealing with this are experts . . .'

'Experts?' The tall man straightened up and his expression showed distaste. 'In wartime one took these actions for granted, but in peacetime . . . Still, it has to be done. In a way it is a continuation of the war. As for Lasalle, he must not be added to the list yet. I am sure he has no idea what is going to happen when the President of France leaves for Moscow . . .'

Part Two

The Killer Commando

17–21 December

Chapter Ten

It had been the secret nightmare of every major security service in the West since the earliest days of the Cold War – and the later phoney period of so-called 'detente' – that in one major country or another a secret Communist would stay dormant until he had worked his way up the ladder of power and reached the summit.

This is the man who is most feared by intelligence chiefs in London, Washington and other capitals – the Rip Van Winkle of Communism who has no contact with Russian agents, who visits no safe houses to pass on information, who is controlled by no spymaster. And because for many years he has no contact with Moscow there is no way to detect him as, by sheer ability, he continues his climb. He is not interested in delivering the details of a guided missile system to Moscow – he hopes to deliver his country.

It was Col. René Lasalle who first caught a whiff of conspiracy when he was still assistant chief of military counter-intelligence. Burrowing deeper into the background of the elusive Leopard, he came up against Guy Florian, who dismissed him for crossing the thin line between military and political counter-espionage. By a strange quirk of history it fell to Marc Grelle to take up the trail again where Lasalle had been compelled to lose it.

On Friday, 17 December – the day the Soviet Commando crossed the border into France – Marc Grelle was distracted from his many duties by what, at the time, seemed a diversion, an incident which would be recorded in the files and forgotten. At ten in the morning he heard of the emergency at Orly airport where Algerian terrorists had just tried to destroy an El Al aircraft on the verge of take-off. 'We'd better go and have a look,' he told Boisseau. 'I thought the security at Orly was foolproof . . .' Grelle had reason to be worried; in only a few days' time Guy Florian was due to fly from Orly to Marseilles where he would make a major speech on the eve of his departure for Russia.

Arriving at the airport, where it was pouring with rain, they found that Camille Point, the officer in command of the Airport Gendarmerie, had the situation under control. In the distance, barely visible in the rain squalls, they could see the Israeli aircraft which had been the target standing unscathed at the end of a reserve runway. Boisseau left Grelle with Camille Point for a moment to check the position with a radio-equipped patrol-car. The whole airport was swarming with armed police.

'One of my men spotted the terrorist just in time,' Point explained. 'He was aiming his weapon at the El

Al machine which was just about to take off with two hundred people aboard. Mouton – the gendarme – fired at him and missed, but he scared the terrorist who ran off and left his weapon behind. Come up on to the roof and I'll show you . . .'

'This terrorist – he escaped?'

There was anxiety in Grelle's voice. It had been known for some time that an Algerian terrorist cell was operating inside Paris and the prefect was anxious to round up the whole gang. He had given orders – which Roger Danchin had approved – that if the gang was cornered the police were to shoot to kill. But one man was not enough. Boisseau, who had run back from the patrol-car, heard the question.

'He got away, yes,' Boisseau began.

'Shit!' Grelle said venomously.

'But we have him under observation,' Boisseau continued. 'Using the new system you have set up for the presidential motorcade drive to Roissy on 23 December, he is being passed from one patrol-car to another at this moment. And he does not appear to realize he is being tailed. I have just heard that he is moving along the Périphérique, heading for northern Paris . . .'

Boisseau broke off as the driver of the nearby patrol-car waved to him. When he came back after taking the new radio report he nodded to the prefect. 'He's still under surveillance, still heading north. Do we risk losing him or close in?'

'Don't close in – and don't lose him,' Grelle replied.

'That's what I have just told them . . .'

It was worth the risk, Grelle told himself as he followed Point up on to the roof of the building. If they could trace the Algerian to his secret hideout, maybe even then continue to keep him under surveillance, they stood a chance of wiping out the whole cell at one swoop. Reaching the rooftop, Grelle paused and stared. Five uniformed gendarmes were gathered round a bulky instrument lying on a sheet of canvas. The fingerprint man, who had just finished examining the weapon, stood up and addressed Boisseau. 'I've got what I want. Pleasant little plaything, isn't it?'

'Grail?' the prefect enquired.

'Yes, sir.' It was a young, keen-looking gendarme who replied.

Grail is the NATO code-name for the Russian-made SAM – surface-to-air missile system – of the man-portable variety. It was also the rocket-launcher, quite capable of being carried by one man, which Moscow had supplied in meagre quantities – and quite unofficially – to certain Arab terrorist organizations. Weighing no more than eighteen kilos when loaded with one rocket or *strela* (the Russian word for arrow) it has a range of between one and two miles.

Only a few years earlier Heathrow Airport, London, had been sealed off while crack troops of the British Army took control in a major anti-terrorist operation. At the time there had been reports that a terrorist group armed with Grail was waiting to shoot down the incoming plane carrying Dr Kissinger. Similar to a bazooka in appearance, the weapon had a heavy stock and a complex-looking telescopic apparatus mounted over its thick barrel. Two rockets lay beside it on the canvas. Point flopped down behind the unarmed launcher and aimed it over the parapet at the stationary El Al plane. 'You should look at this,' he told the prefect. 'It gives me the creeps how close that bastard came to wiping out two hundred people. Buvon here knows the damned thing backwards. He's with the anti-terrorist section . . .'

Grelle was appalled as he took up Point's prone position and gazed through the sight. The Israeli machine, blurred as it was by the rain, came up so close he felt he could reach out and touch it. Flopping beside him, Buvon demonstrated how it worked, even to the extent of inserting a rocket.

'It works on a heat sensor system. There is a device in the nose of the rocket which, once airborne, homes straight on to the highest temperature source within range – in this case, with the Israeli plane just airborne, it would have homed on the heat emitted by the machine's jet engines . . .'

Stretched out in the rain, Grelle listened a little longer. 'Can the pilot of the plane take any evading action?' he enquired as he handled the weapon. 'Is there any hope?'

'None at all,' Buvon replied briskly. 'Even if he saw it coming, which is doubtful, even if he changed course – even more doubtful – the heat sensor would simply change direction too and go on heading for the target until they collided. Then – boom! – it's all over . . .'

Remembering that Florian was due to fly off from this airport to Marseilles in only a few days, Grelle took an immediate decision. 'I'm carrying this hideous thing back to Paris myself,' he announced. 'Have it put in the rear of my car...' With Boisseau behind the wheel, they drove to Sûreté headquarters at the Rue des Saussaies where the prefect personally watched it being put away inside a strong-room on the fourth floor which itself was isolated inside another room. Demanding all the keys to both rooms, he was handed three and when he asked if these were all he received an equivocal reply. 'There were four originally, but one of them was a bad fit. I understand it was destroyed.'

'No one, absolutely no one is to be allowed in this room without my permission,' Grelle ordered. 'When the army people want to have a look at it, they must come to me for the keys...'

They had only just returned to the préfecture when Boisseau received a phone call. He went to the prefect's office to report immediately. 'The Algerian has gone to earth and we know where. He is inside an abandoned apartment block off the Boulevard de la Chapelle in the eighteenth arrondissement. The address is 17 Rue Réamur...'

'That stinking rabbit warren,' Grelle commented. It was the Arab Quarter in the Goutte-d'Or district, an area which had been an Arab preserve for over thirty years. 'Any more of the gang visible?' he enquired.

'There is no sign of anyone else about and we think he is alone. One of the patrol-car men who overtook him thinks he identified him as Abou Benefeika, but that's not certain.'

'He can't give us the slip, I hope?' Grelle asked.

'He's safely penned up and we have men watching both front and rear entrances. Also there are good observation points where we can watch him night and day. Do we bring him in or leave him to ferment?'

'Let him ferment,' Grelle ordered.

In Basel at the Hotel Victoria Alan Lennox heard the news report of the alert at Orly over his bedroom radio. He thought nothing of it as he sat smoking a cigarette, checking his watch occasionally; terrorist alerts at Orly had happened before. The Englishman was killing time, something he disliked, but there was a right moment to cross the border into France; about eleven in the morning he estimated. Earlier the passport control people would only just have come on duty; they would be irritable and alert as they started a new day; and they would give their full attention to the few travellers passing through.

At 11 a.m. precisely he left the Victoria, crossed the street and went inside the Hauptbahnhof. At Basel Hauptbahnhof there is a French frontier control post unique in Europe. While technically still on Swiss soil, all French nationals returning home from Basel pass through a special checkpoint quite separate from Swiss passport control. The checkpoint is manned by French officials who deal only with their own countrymen. It was a perfect opportunity to test the false papers Peter Lanz had supplied.

If there was trouble – if the falseness of the papers was detected – he would be handed over to the Swiss police. He could then give them Peter Lanz's name and phone number and he had little doubt that, bearing in mind the discreet co-operation which goes on between the Swiss and German authorities, Lanz could persuade them to release him into the hands of the German police. Lennox was not a man who had survived so far by taking unnecessary risks. Carrying his Swiss case, he joined the queue which was moving quickly.

'Papers . . .'

It was unfortunate: the examination was conducted by one of the younger officials, a sharp-eyed man whose enthusiasm had not yet been dulled by years of looking at dog-eared passports. The official compared the photograph carefully with the man standing in front of him, then disappeared inside a room. Inwardly tense, Lennox leaned against the counter with a Gitane hanging out of the corner of his mouth, looked at the woman next to him and shrugged. These bloody bureaucrats he seemed to say. The official came back, still holding the document.

'Which countries have you visited?'

'Switzerland and Germany . . .' It is always best to tell the truth whenever you can. Lennox looked bored as the young official continued examining the passport as though it were the first he had ever seen, as though he was sure there was something wrong.

'How long have you been away from France?'

'Three weeks . . .'

Always just answer the question. Never go babbling on, embroidering with a lot of detail. It is the oldest trick in the book, used by officials all over the world; get the suspect talking and sooner or later he trips himself up. The official handed back the passport. Lennox picked up his bag, was waved on by Customs, and walked on to the platform where the train for France was waiting. Within two hours he would be in Strasbourg.

The Munich express was due to arrive at Strasbourg in two hours. In the corner of a first-class compartment Carel Vanek sat reading a French detective novel and the aroma of an expensive cigar filled the compartment as the Czech smoked fitfully. Opposite him the austere Brunner did not approve of the cigar; he had even made the mistake of making a reference to it. 'When we get back we shall have to account for our expenditure . . .'

'In a capitalist society an air of affluence opens all doors,' Vanek replied and turned the page of his book.

The truth was that Vanek enjoyed the good things of life and regarded Brunner as a bit of a peasant. Now, as they came closer to Strasbourg, he read his novel with only half his mind. He was thinking of Dieter Wohl, the German who lived in Freiburg. Of the three people on the list the Commando had to 'pay a visit' –

Vanek's euphemism for terminating a life – the German was closest to them at this moment. It seemed logical that Dieter Wohl should be the first to receive a visit from them.

But the idea had not appealed to the Czech when he had first examined the list, and he found the same objections influencing him now they were approaching the Rhine. The point was Vanek did not wish to risk alerting a second security service – that of Germany – so early on in the trip; just in case the killing of Wohl by 'accident' went wrong. And later they would have to return across Germany from France on their way home. No, better leave Dieter Wohl until later. So, for quite different reasons, Vanek had taken the same decision as Alan Lennox – to go into France first.

Closing his novel, he puffed more cigar smoke in the direction of Brunner. Again Lansky was travelling on his own in a separate coach; it was good tactics and it also suited Vanek who disliked the younger Czech. Soon they would reach Kehl, the last stop inside Germany before the express crossed the Rhine bridge into France. He decided they would get off at Kehl – even though it would have been simpler to stay on the express until it reached Strasbourg. Vanek had an idea – which was not entirely incorrect – that the frontier control people cast a careful eye over international expresses. Getting off at Kehl, they could board a more local train to take them on to Strasbourg, and possibly purchase certain extra clothes while they were in the German city. He took out his papers and looked at them. When they arrived in Strasbourg they would be three French tourists returning from a brief winter sports holiday in Bavaria. There was no longer anything to link them with Czechoslovakia.

Leon Jouvel, 49 Rue de l'Épine, Strasbourg, was the first name on the list Col. Lasalle had handed to Alan Lennox. Fifty-three years old, Jouvel was small and plump with a bushy grey moustache, a shock of grey hair and a plump right hand which liked to squeeze the knees of pretty girls when he thought he could get away with it. Louise Vallon, who worked in the television shop he owned, found him easy to handle. 'He's not dangerous,' she confided to a friend, 'only hopeful, but recently he's seemed so depressed, almost frightened . . .'

What was frightening Leon Jouvel was something which had happened over thirty years ago and now seemed to have come back to haunt him. In 1944, working with the Resistance in the Lozère, he had been the Leopard's radio operator. Even holding that key position, like everyone else he had no idea what the Communist leader looked like. He had always known when the Leopard was close because the wolfhound, César, would give a warning growl. Jouvel hated the beast, but obeying instructions he always forced himself to turn his back on the animal and wait with his notebook until the Leopard arrived and gave him the message to transmit. Noting down the message – which he immediately burned after transmission – he would hurry away to his concealed transmitter, aware only that the Resistance chief was a very tall man; once, on a sunny day, he had seen his shadow.

But because of his job – and the frequency of these brief communications – Jouvel was more familiar with the Leopard's *voice* than anyone in the Resistance group, and Jouvel had an acute ear for sounds. During the past eighteen months – since Guy Florian had become president – Jouvel had changed considerably. All his friends commented on the change. Normally jovial and talkative, Jouvel became irritable and taciturn, often not hearing what was said to him. It was the frequent appearance of the president on television which had unnerved the plump little man.

A widower, it had been Jouvel's custom to while away the evenings in bars and cafés, gossiping with friends. Now he sat at home alone in his second-floor apartment, watching the news bulletins and political broadcasts, waiting for Guy Florian to appear, to *speak*. During a Florian speech he would sit in front of the television set with his eyes shut, listening intently. It was quite macabre – the similarity in the voices – but it was impossible to be sure.

Sitting with his eyes closed he could have sworn he was listening to the Leopard standing behind him, giving him yet another message to transmit in those far-off days up in the mountains. He studied the speech mannerisms, noted the little hesitations which preceded a torrent of abuse as the president attacked the Americans. At first he told himself it was impossible: the Leopard had died in Lyon in 1944. Then he began to think back over the past, recalling the burial of the Leopard deep in the forest which he had attended. The four men who had handled the coffin – all of whom died a few days later in an ambush – had been in a great hurry to get the job over with. There had been a lack of *respect*. A few months later Jouvel had been terrified by a visit from Col. Lasalle, who had arrived in mufti.

'This man, the Leopard,' the colonel had said, 'if you took down all these signals from him, surely you could recognize his voice if you heard it again?'

'It was so long ago . . .'

Fencing inexpertly with one of the most accomplished interrogators in France, Jouvel had managed not to reveal his crazy suspicion. Like many Frenchmen, Jouvel mistrusted both the police and the army, preferring to go his own way and not get mixed up with authority. But had he convinced the sharp-eyed little colonel he knew nothing? Jouvel sweated over the visit for weeks after Lasalle had gone. And now, only eight days before Christmas, there had been the incident this evening.

Locking up his shop at six, he walked back over the bridge from the Quai des Bateliers into the deserted old quarter. After dark the Rue de l'Épine is a sinister street where ancient five-storey buildings hem in the shadows and your footsteps echo eerily on the cobbles. There is no one about and not too much light. This evening

Jouvel was sure he had heard footsteps behind him. Turning round suddenly, he caught the movement of a shadow which merged into the wall.

He forced himself to turn round and walk back, and it reminded him of all those occasions when he had once forced himself to turn his back on the Leopard's vicious wolfhound. Jouvel was trembling as he made himself go on walking back down the shadowed street, and he was sweating so much his glasses steamed up. Reaching the doorway where he had seen the shadow move, he couldn't be sure whether anyone was there. Pretending to adjust his glasses, he wiped them quickly with his fingers. The blur cleared and a heavily built man with a fat face stared back at him out of the doorway. Jouvel almost fainted.

The fat-faced man who wore a dark coat and a soft hat, lifted a flask and drank from it noisily, then belched. Jouvel's pounding heart began to slow down. A drunk! Without saying a word he walked back up the street to his home. Behind him police detective Armand Bonheur was also sweating as he remained in the doorway. Good God, he had almost blown it! And the inspector's instructions had been explicit.

'Whatever happens, Jouvel must not suspect he is being tailed. The order comes right down the line from Paris . . .'

Turning in under the stone archway of No. 49, Jouvel went across the cobbled courtyard and into the building beyond. Climbing the staircase to the second floor, he was unlocking his apartment door when a red-haired girl peered out of the next apartment. He smiled pleasantly. 'Good evening, M'selle . . .' Disappointed, the girl made a rude gesture at his back. 'Silly old ponce.' For Denise Viron anything over forty was fodder for the graveyard; anything under forty, fair game.

Inside his apartment Jouvel hurried over to the television set and switched on. Brewing himself a cup of tea in the kitchen, he came back, settled in an old armchair and waited. Florian's head and shoulders appeared on the screen a few minutes later. Jouvel closed his eyes. 'The Americans want to turn Europe into one vast supermarket, selling American goods, of course . . .' And still Jouvel couldn't be certain. I must be going mad, he thought.

'Mr Jouvel? He is away today but he is back in Strasbourg tomorrow. The shop opens at nine . . .'

Louise Vallon, Jouvel's assistant, put down the phone and thought no more about the call as she turned to attend to a customer. In a bar close to the shop Carel Vanek replaced the receiver and walked out on to the Quai des Bateliers where Walther Brunner sat waiting in the Citroën DS23 they had just hired from the Hertz branch in the Boulevard de Nancy. 'He's out of town today,' Vanek said as he settled himself behind the wheel, 'but he's back tomorrow. Which just gives us nice time to soak up some atmosphere . . .'

When the Soviet Commando had arrived aboard a

local train from Kehl they split up again as they had done in Munich. Lansky had simply walked across the large cobbled square outside the station and booked a room at the Hôtel Terminus in the name of Lambert. After depositing three sets of skis – which would never be collected – in the luggage store at Strasbourg Gare, Vanek and Brunner took two separate cabs at intervals to the Hôtel Sofitel where they registered, quite independently, as Duval and Bonnard. Meeting outside the hotel, they went to the Boulevard de Nancy and hired the Citroën.

Before leaving his room at the Sofitel, Vanek had consulted Bottin, the French telephone directory, to check on Leon Jouvel's address. Yes, it was the address given on the list, 49 Rue de l'Épine, but there had also been the address of a television shop in the Quai des Bateliers. Using a street map of Strasbourg purchased from a newspaper kiosk, Vanek and Brunner had driven round the old city to locate both addresses before Vanek made his first call from the bar. He then drove a short distance from the quai before handing over the car to his companion. For the rest of the afternoon and most of the evening the three men would move round Strasbourg on their own, familiarizing themselves with the city's layout and getting the feel of being in France.

'Buy a paper, go into bars and cafés, chat with everyone you can,' Vanek had instructed. 'Start merging with your background by mixing with it. Take a short bus-ride, find out what people are talking about.

By tonight I want you to be more French than the French themselves . . .'

Following his own advice, Vanek sampled the flavour of Strasbourg by working. Unlike Brunner, from now on he walked everywhere, knowing that the easiest way to get your bearings in a strange city is to walk. As the street map indicated, the old quarter of the city was for all practical purposes an island surrounded by water, the huge 'moat' being formed by the river Il which encircles the heart of Strasbourg. A series of bridges all round the perimeter crossed the river into this ancient heart built, for the most part, in the fourteenth century. It was still daylight at four o'clock, but only just in the narrow, silent Rue de l'Épine, when Vanek walked in under the archway of No. 49.

One of the numerous plates at the entrance to the building registered the fact that Leon Jouvel lived on the second floor, and he was knocking on the door of the second-floor apartment when the door of the neighbouring apartment opened and a red-haired girl peered out at him speculatively. 'He's gone away for the day to see his sister – back in the morning,' she informed the Czech. 'Do you think I could help you in some way?'

Vanek, careful to eye her hips and other parts of her anatomy with due appreciation, had no trouble at all in extracting from Denise Viron the information he needed. He was, he explained, a market research specialist. 'Mr Leon Jouvel is one of the people chosen to answer our questionnaire ... a survey on pension needs.' Within a few minutes he learned that Jouvel was a widower, that he occupied the apartment on his own, that he possessed no animals – here Vanek had in mind a guard-dog – that he was out all day at the shop and only returned at 6.30 in the evenings, that he was no longer a sociable man, so there were few visitors.

'If you would like to come in,' the girl said, smoothing her skirt down over her long, lithe legs, 'I might be able to help you in other ways . . .'

Vanek, whose appetite for women was healthy, made it a point never to mix business with pleasure. And in any case, the girl had so far not had too close a look at him in the gloomy hall. Explaining that he had five more people to interview that day, he left her with a vague impression he would certainly be calling on her again within a few days. As arranged earlier, at eight in the evening he met Brunner and Lansky at a corner of the Place Kléber as snow drifted down over the huddled rooftops of Strasbourg. Taking them into a crowded bar, he found a table at the back.

'. . . and so,' he continued a few minutes later, 'it is made to order for a quick solution. You visit him tomorrow night, soon after 6.30 when he has returned home . . .' It was Lansky he had chosen to pay a call on Leon Jouvel. 'He is a widower and lives on his own. He has a second-floor apartment and the building is quiet. No one about at all except for a red-haired girl who lives next door. She could be a nuisance – she's looking for somebody to keep her bed warm.'

'I don't like it,' Brunner said. 'You're moving too fast. We need more time to check on this man . . .'

'Which is exactly what we have not got,' Vanek snapped. 'In five days from now – December 22 – we have to complete the whole job, which includes visiting three people, one of them in Germany. So, the strategy is simple – we deal with the first two on the list quickly . . .'

'If the place is empty, I'd better take a preliminary look inside it tonight,' Lansky said. He stood up. 'We'll meet at the bus station in the Place de la Gare tomorrow at the time agreed?'

'It's dangerous to hurry it,' Brunner muttered.

Vanek leaned forward until his face almost touched Brunner's, still speaking very quietly. 'Think, man! It will be Saturday night – the body won't even be discovered until Monday morning at the earliest . . .'

The Rope used the set of French skeleton keys – which had been flown from Kiev to Tábor with the false Sûreté cards at the last moment – to open Jouvel's apartment door. It was a five-roomed apartment: a living-dining room with a colour television set, two bedrooms, a kitchen and a bathroom. When he entered the apartment the first thing he did was to draw the curtains, then he examined the place with the aid of a pocket torch. Everything was neat and tidy; Lansky reminded himself he must remember this when it came to setting the stage.

Lansky had brought no rope with him; purchasing a length of rope can be dangerous if the police institute a proper check afterwards. Instead he looked round for something on the premises – a sash cord, a belt, anything strong enough to hang a man by the neck until he is dead. Inside an old-fashioned, free-standing wardrobe he found what he was looking for – an old woollen dressing-gown with a cord-belt round the waist.

He tested the strength of the cord carefully by tying one end to the leg of the old-fashioned gas cooker in the kitchen and pulling hard on it. If necessary, to give it more strength he could immerse it in water later. Privately, he had already rejected Brunner's suggestion that Jouvel might drown in his own bath; that involved undressing a man, which took more time. And suicide was always something the police were willing to accept with a widower living on his own. He next tested the handle on the outside of the bathroom door to make sure it was firm. Brunner had told him it was not unusual for people to hang themselves on the inside of a bathroom door; perhaps they felt they could do the job here in decent privacy.

Twenty minutes is the maximum time a burglar allows for being inside a house; after that the statistics show the law of averages moves against him. Lansky carefully timed his visit for twelve minutes. He had re-opened the curtains and was ready to leave when he heard voices in the corridor near by. With his ear pressed against the door panel he listened carefully.

Two voices, a man's and a girl's, probably the girl in the next apartment Vanek had mentioned. They were talking in French but Lansky couldn't catch what was being said. He waited until the voices stopped, a door closed, and footsteps retreated along the corridor. When he came out and relocked Jouvel's door the building was full of silence. In less than twenty-four hours, at seven on the following evening, he would return to pay his last call on Leon Jouvel.

He emerged from the archway into the Rue de l'Épine with equal caution. But tonight police detective Armand Bonheur was fifty kilometres away in Sarrebourg, sitting cold and depressed inside his car while he watched the house where Leon Jouvel was paying his duty call on his elderly sister. Lansky waited a little longer until the only person in sight, a man walking away towards the Place Kléber, disappeared. The man was Alan Lennox.

At eight o'clock in the evening of Friday, 17 December, at about the time the Soviet Commando went into a bar near the Place Kléber, André the Squirrel made his suggestion to Marc Grelle in the prefect's office in Paris. Would it be worth while for him to fly to Strasbourg to interview Leon Jouvel and then go on to see the other witness in Colmar? 'If Lasalle is right and these people knew the Leopard they might be able to tell me something.'

Grelle considered the suggestion and then decided

against it. For the moment at least. The trouble was he needed his deputy in Paris to help complete the security fence he was building round the president. 'Let it wait,' Grelle advised.

Travelling up from Switzerland by train, Alan Lennox had arrived at Strasbourg station while the Soviet Commando was still in Kehl across the river Rhine. Since there are only two or three first-class hotels in the city, it was not surprising that he chose the Hôtel Sofitel, which is built like an upended shoe-box and more like the type of hotel found in America. Registering in the name of Jean Bouvier, he went up to his fourth-floor room which overlooked a concrete patio.

His first action was to consult Bottin, the telephone directory, and like Vanek in the same hotel only two hours later, he noted that Leon Jouvel had two addresses, one of which corresponded with the Lasalle list, the other a television shop. Unlike Vanek, he phoned the shop from the hotel room. The number went on ringing, but no one answered it. In the shop Louise Vallon was having her busiest time of the day and she was damned if she was going to attend to the phone as well. In the Sofitel Lennox replaced the receiver. The obvious next move was to try Jouvel at home.

Checking the street-guide he had bought at the station, he found that the Rue de l'Épine was only a short walk from the hotel. Putting on his coat and hat again, he went out into a world of slow-falling snow-flakes which made it seem even more like Christmas in Strasbourg. Unlike Paris, the city was full of reminders of the approaching festive season; the Place Kléber was decorated with enormous Christmas trees which lit up at night. In less than ten minutes Lennox was standing at the archway to 49 Rue de l'Épine.

Leon Jouvel. The door on the second floor carried the name on a plate beside it. Lennox knocked for the third time but there was no reply. And for once the door of the neighbouring apartment was not opened by the red-headed and enthusiastic Denise Viron; at lunchtime she was still in bed and fast asleep. Leaving the building, he went out to find somewhere to eat.

In the afternoon he visited the shop on the Quai des Bateliers and it was full of customers. The fair-haired girl behind the counter was having trouble coping with the rush and there was no sign of a man in the place. While she was occupied he peered into the back office and found it empty. He decided to go back to Jouvel's apartment in the middle of the evening. If you want to interview a man the place to corner him is at home, after he has finished his day's work and eaten – when he is relaxed. Lennox went back to No. 49 Rue de l'Épine at 8.30 p.m.

Denise Viron was just going out for the evening, wearing a brilliant green coat which she felt sure suited her exciting personality, when Lennox stopped in front of Leon Jouvel's door. Eyeing him, wondering whether she was really going out after all, she stood outside her doorway with the light still on so it threw into stark relief her full-breasted figure.

'He's away for the night,' she said. 'Was there something I might be able to help you with?'

Lennox, who had his hand raised to knock on the door Lansky had opened with his skeleton keys only a few minutes earlier, took off his hat instead. He moved a few paces towards the girl who took a tentative step back inside her own apartment. Pulling at her long, red hair, she watched him with her lips slightly parted. God, a tart, Lennox thought. 'You mean Mr Leon Jouvel?' he enquired in French. 'It's rather urgent – you're sure he won't be back tonight?'

The girl puckered her over-painted mouth. 'Popular today, aren't we? Jouvel, I mean. I've just had one of those market research blokes asking after him this afternoon. No accounting for tastes.'

'Market research?'

'That's right. You know the type – nosey. Personally I think it's an impertinence the way they ask you all those intimate questions . . .'

'Mr Jouvel,' Lennox interjected with a smile. 'When will he be back then?'

'Tomorrow – Saturday. That market research chap . . .'

'Is there someone I could leave a message with? His wife, perhaps?'

'He's a widower. Not interested in women any

more.' She gazed past Lennox's shoulder. 'Personally I think when you get to that stage life isn't worth . . .'

'No one else in the apartment?'

'No. He lives alone.' The girl was frowning, as though making a tremendous intellectual effort to solve a problem. 'Funny, I'm having almost the same conversation with you as I had with that other chap. What makes Jouvel so popular all of a sudden? Weeks go by and he sits alone in there glued to the box and now . . .'

'He's home all day Saturday?' Lennox enquired.

'There you go again – same kind of question.' Denise Viron was beginning to tire of the conversation. 'All day Saturday he's at the shop,' she snapped. 'And it's not a good time to see him – Saturday is his big day. And you won't find him back here before 6.30 in the evening. Are you another market research chap?' she enquired sarcastically.

'I knew him a long time ago,' Lennox replied vaguely and excused himself. He heard a door slam as he went down the stairs and behind him Denise Viron re-buttoned the coat she had unfastened as they talked. She was going to have to go out, and in this weather, for God's sake.

At 5.30 p.m. on Saturday evening Detective Armand Bonheur yawned in the police office and checked his watch. Soon he would be on the bloody night-watch again, taking over from his colleague who at this

COLIN FORBES

moment was discreetly observing Leon Jouvel's shop-
front on the Quai des Bateliers. Bonheur would then
wait on the quai for Jouvel to lock up so he could
follow him and keep an eye on who went in and out of
No. 49 Rue de l'Épine. Already Bonheur was getting to
hate this duty. What the hell had Paris got on a man
like Jouvel anyway?

It would not have been possible for even Borisov, his
trainer, to recognize Lansky easily as he left the Hôtel
Terminus with a group of people who had just come
out of the lift. Wearing a German suit and a Tyrolean
hat he had purchased during the Commando's brief
stay in Kehl, Lansky was also equipped with a pair of
thick-lensed, hornrim spectacles of the type normally
only worn by old men. Even his walk had changed as
he shuffled across the wind-swept Place de la Gare
with his hands deep inside his overcoat pockets, a coat
also purchased in Kehl. To complete the transformation
he carried an umbrella which he had previously ruffled
and dirtied. Muffled up inside a scarf, shuffling across
the cobbles, Antonin Lansky now looked more like a
man in his late sixties.

Reaching the station, he mooched inside the glassed-
in restaurant which fronted on the square, sat down at
a table and ordered coffee in German. Occasionally as
he sat there amid people waiting for trains he checked
his watch. He would be visiting Leon Jouvel some-

176

where between 6.30 and 7 p.m., catching him off guard soon after he had arrived home.

At 6 p.m. Alan Lennox sat at a window table in the café next door to Jouvel's television shop drinking coffee. It was well after dark and under the street lamps the cobbles on the quai gleamed from the recent snow flurries. He had decided to take Denise Viron's advice, to let Leon Jouvel, whom he had seen at the other side of his shop window, get his big day over with before tackling the Frenchman. And since it was Saturday he thought it highly likely Jouvel would stop off at a bar on the way home – and what better place to get a man talking than in a bar?

A trained observer – trained by long experience – Lennox had automatically noticed the man in the raincoat on the far side of the quai who stood under a lamp reading a newspaper. Probably waiting for his girl, Lennox surmised: at intervals the waiting man checked his watch and looked up and down the quai as though expecting someone. Lennox finished his third cup of coffee. To spin out the time he had ordered a pot, and the francs for the bill were already on the table so he could leave at a moment's notice. At 6.05 p.m. a short, plump figure with a bushy moustache came out and locked up the shop.

As Jouvel said goodnight to his assistant, Louise Vallon, and crossed the quai Lennox emerged from the café and paused at the kerb to light a cigarette. No need to follow too close in this part of Strasbourg and the shopowner was wearing a distinctive yellow raincoat. Putting away his French Feudor lighter, Lennox was on the verge of stepping into the road and then stopped before he had moved. The man under the lamp had tucked his paper under his arm and was strolling after Jouvel. A coincidence: he had got fed up waiting for his girl.

As the traffic stopped against the lights, Lennox hurried across and then slowed down again. On the bridge crossing the river Il to the old quarter he saw the man with the paper and ahead of him Jouvel. The shop owner, who had crossed the bridge, had stopped to peer in through the lighted windows of a restaurant as though wondering whether to go inside. The man with the paper had also stopped, bending down as he pretended to tie his shoelace. It was now quite obvious to Lennox that Leon Jouvel was being followed by someone else.

As Jouvel left the restaurant and crossed the road to turn up the Rue de l'Épine – which meant he was going straight home – Lennox changed direction to approach No. 49 by a separate route. The man with the paper had left the bridge and followed Jouvel. In that lonely and deserted street a second shadow would be a little too conspicuous. Familiar now with the immediate area, Lennox walked rapidly up the Rue des Grandes Arcades and then into a side street leading into the Rue de l'Épine, arriving just in time to see Jouvel turn in under the archway. Lower down the street the man with the paper disappeared inside an alcove as Denise Viron, wearing her bright green coat, came out of the archway. She stopped when she saw Lennox.

'You've come back to see me?' she enquired hopefully.

'Another night maybe? There are plenty of nights yet,' Lennox told her.

Their voices carried down the narrow canyon of the empty street to where Detective Armand Bonheur waited, huddled inside the alcove. His instructions had been complex, too complex for his liking. He must keep Jouvel under surveillance. He must not let the shop-owner know he was being watched. He must keep an eye open for an Englishman called Lennox, and the description had been vague. Hearing the reply to the girl's invitation given in perfect French, Bonheur did not give a moment's thought to the Englishman he had been told about. He settled down to a long wait.

As far as Bonheur was concerned the form of sur-veillance was very unsatisfactory – it was impossible to station himself inside the building, to keep close obser-vation on Jouvel. The only positive factor in his favour was that the building had no rear exit. Everyone who entered No. 49 had to go in under the archway. It was just after seven – it had begun to rain again – when Bonheur saw a shuffling old man with an umbrella approaching No. 49.

*

Lennox rapped on Jouvel's door only a minute or so after the man had arrived home. Lennox's manner was businesslike as he explained he was a reporter from the Paris newspaper, *Le Monde*, which was going to run a series on the wartime Resistance. He understood that Jouvel had been an active member of the Lozère group and would like to talk to him about his experiences. Nothing, he assured Jouvel, would be published without his permission. And there would be, Lennox added casually, a fee . . .

'What sort of fee?' Jouvel enquired.

He was standing in the doorway, still wearing his yellow raincoat, his mind in a turmoil. He had asked the question to give himself a little more time to think. For over a year he had fretted over whether to approach the authorities with his suspicion, and here was a golden opportunity presented to him on a plate. Should he talk to this man, he was wondering.

'Two thousand francs,' Lennox said crisply. 'That is, if the information is worth it – makes good copy. In any case, I will pay ten per cent of that sum for fifteen minutes of your time.'

'You had better come in,' said Jouvel.

Sitting on an old-fashioned settee in the living-room, Lennox did most of the talking for the first few minutes, trying to put Jouvel at his ease. The Frenchman's reaction puzzled him. Jouvel sat facing him in an armchair, staring at him with a dazed look as though trying to make up his mind about something. When he mentioned the Leopard, Jouvel closed his eyes and then opened them again.

'What about the Leopard?' the Frenchman asked hoarsely. 'I worked closely with him as radio operator, but he is dead, surely?'

'Is he?'

The brief question, phrased instinctively by Lennox as he detected the query at the end of Jouvel's own question, had a strange effect on the Frenchman. He swallowed, stared at Lennox, then looked away and taking a handkerchief out of his pocket he dried the moist palms of his chubby little hands.

'Of course,' Lennox went on, 'if you prefer it we could print your story as being by "an anonymous but reliable witness". Then no one would connect you with it but you would still get the money . . .'

Something snapped inside Jouvel's mind. The pressure he had lived under for months became unbearable now he had someone he could talk to. He told Lennox the whole story. The Englishman, who for the sake of appearances had taken out his reporter's notebook, was careful not to look at Jouvel as he went on talking in agitated bursts. 'It must seem ridiculous to you . . . every time I hear him on television . . . the Leopard, I know, was shot during 1944 – and yet . . .'

As the words came tumbling out it was like a penitent confessing to a priest, relieving himself. At first Lennox was sceptical, thinking he was interviewing a lunatic, but as Jouvel went on talking, pouring out words, he began to wonder. 'The way they handled the coffin at the burial point ... no respect ... brutally ... as though nothing was inside ...'

At the end of fifteen minutes Lennox stood up to go. The Frenchman was repeating himself. Instead of the two hundred francs Lennox handed over five hundred out of the funds Lanz had provided. 'You will come back tomorrow,' Jouvel urged. 'I may have more to tell you ...' It was untrue, but the agitated little shop-owner, unsure now of what he had done, wanted to give himself the chance to withdraw the statement if, when the morning came, he felt he had made a terrible mistake.

'I'll come tomorrow,' Lennox promised.

He left the apartment quickly before the Frenchman could ask for a telephone number or address where he could be reached. Going down the dimly lit staircase deep in thought, he pulled himself up sharply before he crossed the courtyard: he was travelling with false papers so he had better be on the alert every moment he was in France. Lennox walked with a natural quietness and he was coming out of the archway when he cannoned heavily against an old man stooped under an umbrella. Slipping on the wet cobbles, the man lost his pebble glasses and his Tyrolean hat was knocked sideways half off his head. By the light of the street lamp Lennox caught a glimpse of a face. The man swore in German.

'A thousand apologies ...'

Lennox had replied in French as he bent down and

picked up the pebble glasses, relieved to find they were intact. A gloved hand came out from under the adjusted umbrella and accepted the glasses without a word. Lennox shrugged as the man shuffled off inside the building, then he walked out and went up the Rue de l'Épine in the direction of the Place Kléber, still thinking about what Leon Jouvel had told him.

Half-frozen inside his alcove, Detective Armand Bonheur continued to do his duty, recording everything that occurred in his notebook with the aid of his Feudor lighter, adding to earlier entries. *6.30*. Jouvel returns home. *6.31*. Denise Viron departs. *6.31*. Viron's friend arrives. *7.02*. Viron's friend departs. (He had assumed from the conversation he had overheard that Denise Viron knew Lennox well.) *7.02*. Umbrella man arrives. *7.32*. Umbrella man departs.

Chapter Eleven

The police discovered Leon Jouvel hanging from the inside of his bathroom door the following morning.

'It will be Saturday night – the body won't even be discovered until Monday morning . . .' It was a shrewd and reasonable calculation on the part of Carel Vanek, but the shrewdest plans can be upset by tiny human factors. Sunday, 19 December, was close to Christmas, so before he left his shop on the Saturday evening Leon Jouvel had persuaded Louise Vallon to come in for a few hours on Sunday morning to help prepare for the expected Monday rush of business. 'I'll pay you double,' he had promised her, 'and in cash, so forget the tax man. And I'll be here at 8.30, so mind you're prompt . . .'

By nine o'clock on the Sunday morning Louise Vallon, who had her own shop key, was sufficiently surprised by Jouvel's non-appearance to phone him. There was no reply. She called him again at 9.15 and then, growing worried, at regular ten-minute intervals. At 10 a.m. she phoned the police.

The inspector in charge of the surveillance on Jouvel, a man called Rochat, went to the apartment himself, worried about what the reaction from Paris might be. After talking to the medical examiner and checking the scene of the death, Rochat – initially suspicious – was soon convinced that Leon Jouvel had committed suicide. Pursuing this line of enquiry, he quickly found evidence to back up his opinion. A number of Jouvel's friends told him how the Frenchman had seemed worried for several months, that he had complained of lack of sleep, that he had stopped spending his evenings in bars as had once been his habit. No one could say why Jouvel had been worried but Rochat thought he knew when he discussed the case with his detective, Bonheur.

'A widower living alone – first losing interest in his friends, later in life itself. It forms a pattern . . .'

Rochat's complacent view of the case lasted exactly three hours. It was shattered when he received a call from the Paris prefecture informing him that André Boisseau was already on his way to Strasbourg. Forgetting the recent edict from the Elysée, Rochat protested that the Paris prefecture had no jurisdiction outside the capital. 'It is my case,' he said stiffly. He then received a further shock when the caller revealed that it was the Police Prefect of Paris himself speaking.

'And this,' Grelle blandly informed him, 'does come under my jurisdiction since it may well concern the safety of the President of the French Republic . . .'

Despite his irritation with what he regarded as Parisian interference in a local affair, Rochat had at least had the sense to phone Boisseau and inform him of the apparent suicide before he left to visit Jouvel's apartment. The man in Paris fired a number of questions at him, put the phone down and went straight to the office of the prefect who was working on Sunday – like a juggler trying to keep half a dozen balls in the air at once.

'Leon Jouvel,' Boisseau announced, 'has just died in Strasbourg. He is supposed to have committed suicide. I don't think that Rochat – the man in charge down there – is too bright. I checked up on him – he's fifty-six and still only an inspector.'

'Does the death have to be suspect?' Grelle enquired.

'Not necessarily, but over the years too many people who were connected with the Leopard have died. Now we hear that Jouvel ...'

'And,' Grelle smiled grimly, 'since we are getting nowhere at this end you are restless to check something else.'

It was true that they were getting no results from their enquiries in Paris. The discreet surveillance on Danchin and Blanc had turned up nothing promising. Danchin, dedicated to his work as always, had hardly left the Ministry of the Interior where he had an apartment on the first floor overlooking the Place Beauvau, so frequently, unlike other cabinet ministers, he didn't even dine out.

Alain Blanc had also spent long hours at his Ministry, but twice he had visited the address in the Passy district where he met his mistress, Gisèle Manton. She, also, had been followed, and Grelle had a detailed list of where she had been and whom she had met. For neither of the two ministers did there seem to be any trace of a Soviet link. Grelle, without revealing it to Boisseau, was beginning to get worried. Could he have made a terrible mistake about the whole business?

'You'd better take a look at Strasbourg,' he said. 'Fly there and back, of course. I need you here in Paris . . .' It was typical of the prefect that after Boisseau had gone he had personally phoned Strasbourg to inform them that Boisseau was on the way. As he put down the receiver he was inclined to agree with his deputy's assessment: Inspector Rochat was never going to set the world on fire.

The proprietor, M. Jouvel, has died suddenly. This shop therefore, will remain closed until further notice.

Lennox stared at the typed notice pasted to the glass door and went on staring beyond it at the girl inside. When he rattled the handle she waved at him to go away and then, as he persisted, came forward glaring and unlocked the door. Taking off his hat, he spoke before she could start abusing him. 'I'm a friend of Leon's – this is a great shock to me, you'll understand. Can you tell me what happened?'

Relenting, because he was so polite – and because now she could see him properly she liked what she saw – Louise Vallon, who had just returned from being interviewed by Inspector Rochat, let him inside the shop and told him all the grisly details. Lennox had the impression that although she managed to bring tears to her eyes, she was rather enjoying the drama of it all. At the end of ten minutes he had heard most of the story; he knew that Leon Jouvel had been found hanging behind his bathroom door, that the time of death was estimated as being between 6.30 and 8.30 the previous evening.

'They wanted to know whether anyone normally visited him at that time,' the girl explained tearfully. 'The last words he said to me were . . .'

Lennox excused himself after explaining that he had been away from Strasbourg for some time and had just called to have a word. 'It wasn't a close friendship,' he went on, aware that this conversation might be reported back to the police, 'but we had business dealings occasionally.' Telling her that his name was Zuger, that he had to catch a train for Stuttgart, he left the shop, walked a short distance towards the station, and then doubled back over one of the bridges into the old quarter.

The police patrol-car he had seen earlier was still outside No. 49, so he left the vicinity of the Rue de l'Épine. At one in the afternoon it was still very quiet on Sunday in Strasbourg as he wandered round the ancient streets thinking. He found the suicide of Leon Jouvel hard to swallow. The Frenchman had been followed to his home by the unknown man with the newspaper only an hour or so before he had died. He had arranged to meet Lennox the following morning with the expectation of receiving more money in exchange for more information. A man who is contemplating killing himself is hardly likely to show interest in the prospect of acquiring more money. It smells, Lennox told himself, in fact, it more than smells, it stinks.

Over lunch he wondered whether to go straight on to meet the next witness on the list, Robert Philip of Colmar, and then he decided he would wait until Monday. The local Monday newspaper should carry an account of Jouvel's death, which could be enlightening.

Robert Philip, 8 Avenue Raymond Poincaré, Colmar, was the second name on the list Col. Lasalle had handed over to Alan Lennox. It was also the second name on the list Carel Vanek carried in his head. On Saturday evening the three members of the Soviet Commando paid their bills at their respective hotels and left Strasbourg, driving the forty miles to Colmar through a snow-storm. They arrived in the Hans Andersen-like town of steep-roofed buildings and crooked alleyways at 9.30 p.m. and again Vanek took precautions, dropping off Lansky with his suitcase near the station, so that only two men arrived together at the hotel.

Lansky walked into the station booking-hall, enquired the time of a train to Lyon for the following day, and then smoked a Gauloise while he waited for a train to come in – any train. Walking out with the three passengers who got off a local from Strasbourg, he crossed the Place de la Gare to the Hôtel Bristol which

189

Vanek and Brunner had entered earlier and booked a room in the name of Froissart. The receptionist, noting he had no car, assumed he had just come off the Strasbourg train.

Upstairs in his bedroom Vanek had followed his usual routine, checking Philip's address in the telephone directory and locating it on the Blay street-guide of Colmar he had obtained from the hall porter. He looked up as Brunner slipped into his room. 'This is very convenient – staying here,' he informed the Czech. 'Philip lives just round the corner . . .'

'If he is home,' the pessimistic Brunner replied.

'Let's find out . . .'

Vanek did not use the room phone to call Philip's number; that would have meant going through the hotel switchboard. Instead he went out with Brunner to the car and they drove about a kilometre into the shopping area and entered a bar where Vanek called the number he had found in the directory. The voice which answered the phone was arrogant and brusque. 'Robert Philip . . .'

'Sorry, wrong number,' Vanek muttered and broke the connection. 'He's home,' he told Brunner. 'Let's go look at the place . . .'

On a snowbound December night at 10.30 p.m. the Avenue Raymond Poincaré was a deserted street of trees and parks with small, grim, two-storey mansions set back behind prison-like railings. No. 8 was a square-looking stone villa with steps leading up to a porch and a gloomy garden beyond the railings. There were lights in the large bay window on the ground floor and the upper storey was in darkness. 'I think you can get round the back,' Brunner said as the Citroën cruised slowly past the villa and he tried to take in as much detail as he could.

'The next thing to check is whether he lives alone,' Vanek remarked. 'Tomorrow is Sunday. If we can check out the place in the daytime I think we might just pay a visit to Mr Robert Philip tomorrow night . . .'

'One day you will be too quick . . .'

'Tomorrow is 19 December,' Vanek replied calmly. 'We have only four days left to visit two people – one of them across the Rhine in Germany. In speed can lie safety. And this will not be a job for the Rope. We have had one suicide, so Robert Philip will have to die by accident . . .'

Earlier on the same day, arriving in Strasbourg by helicopter, Boisseau put Inspector Rochat through a grilling almost without Rochat realizing what was happening. He was well aware he must tread warily: unlike Lyon, Grelle had no particular friendship with the prefect of Strasbourg and the locals were prickly about his arrival. After half an hour he suggested that later Rochat must join him for a drink, but first could they visit the dead man's apartment?

It was Boisseau who extracted from Detective Bonheur the information that two men had entered No. 49 between 6.30 and 7.15 p.m., that the second man had shuffled and carried an umbrella, that later the first man had left at 7.02 p.m., followed by the umbrella man half an hour later. 'Which was just about the time Jouvel may have died,' he pointed out to Rochat.

It was Boisseau who interviewed the other tenants in the building and discovered no one could identify the shuffling man, which meant he did not live there. 'Which proves nothing,' he informed Rochat, 'but why did he come here when we can find no one he visited? And half an hour is a long time for a man to enter a building for no purpose.'

It was Boisseau who interviewed Denise Viron, the red-headed girl, obtaining from her a detailed description of two quite different men who had made enquiries about Leon Jouvel the previous day. He made a careful note of the descriptions, observing that neither of them could have been the shuffling man. 'Could either of these two men have been English?' he asked at one stage. Denise had shaken her head vigorously, crossing her legs in a provocative way which made Inspector Rochat frown. Boisseau, on the other hand, who was interviewing the girl in her apartment, had noticed the legs appreciatively while he offered her another cigarette.

'Was Jouvel often asked about by people?' he enquired. 'Did he have many visitors?'

'Hardly any. The two callers were exceptional . . .'

Boisseau had not blamed Rochat for failing to dig up this information. It was quite clear that his superiors had resented the Paris police prefect's intrusion on their territory and had ordered the inspector to clear up the case quickly. So, once it seemed clear it was suicide, Rochat had enquired no further.

'You are satisfied?' Rochat suggested as he drove the man from Paris back to the airport.

'Are you?' Boisseau countered.

'Technically everything was as it should be – taking into account Jouvel's short stature, the length of the rope, the position of the bathroom chair he had kicked away from under himself. Only an expert could have faked it.'

'I find your last observation disturbing,' Boisseau said.

Robert Philip, fifty-two years old – the same age as Guy Florian, but there the resemblance ended – rose late from his bed on Sunday morning, and was then annoyed because his companion, Noelle Berger, continued sleeping. Shaking her bare white shoulder roughly, he made his request with his usual finesse. 'Get up, you trollop, I want some breakfast . . .'

Separated from his wife, he now consoled himself with a series of fleeting affairs, each of which he took care to ensure did not last too long. As he told his drinking cronies, 'Have them in the house for a week and they think they own the place . . .' Of medium height and gross, heavy figure, Philip had a thatch of reddish hair cut *en brosse* and a thick moustache of the same reddish tinge. Grumbling, he went downstairs and pulled back the living-room curtain. At the opposite kerb in the normally deserted street was parked a Citroën with the bonnet up and two men peering inside at the engine. A holdall lay on the pavement with tools spread about. 'Serve you right for wasting petrol,' Philip muttered, holding his silk dressing-gown round his middle as he went off into the kitchen. A few minutes later, similarly attired, Noelle Berger, small and blonde-haired and with an ample figure, wandered into the living-room in search of a cigarette.

'See the girl,' Vanek whispered, his head half under the Citroën's bonnet. 'This is going to be complicated.'

'Ideally,' Brunner replied, 'she should be dealt with away from the house . . .'

'If she leaves the damned place. This is Sunday . . .'

Robert Philip had been the Leopard's armourer during the war, the man in charge of acquiring weapons and ammunition for the Resistance group, a process which normally involved raiding enemy munition stores, and as such he had been one of the key members of the Leopard's staff. Since the war Philip's career had been a success story – if you measure success by the acquisition of a large villa and a sizeable bank account by dubious means. Philip was a gun-runner.

In 1944, while Resistance groups in the Midi were building up huge caches of weapons to support the République Soviétique du Sud the Leopard was on the verge of bringing into existence, Robert Philip was busily diverting some of these weapons to secret hide-outs. It must have been a great relief to Philip when the Communist coup failed. Seeing de Gaulle was winning, Philip proclaimed himself a lifelong Gaullist, revealing half of his weapon caches to the General. The other half he salted away as a future investment.

In the years which followed Philip supplied weapons to Fidel Castro in his early days – using the Communist connections he had built up in the Lozère – to Eoka terrorists fighting the British in Cyprus, to Kurdish rebels fighting the Iraqi government, and to anyone hard-pressed enough to pay over-the odds prices for an inferior product. 'I have,' as he once boasted to a bar companion, 'overtaken my contemporaries.' His wife, Yvonne, now occupied an apartment in Paris. 'I have pensioned her off,' as he was fond of saying. 'After all, I do not believe in treating a woman badly . . .'

At two in the afternoon Noelle Berger emerged from the villa alone, well wrapped in a fur coat, and walked the few steps which took her to the station, leaving Robert Philip alone in the house. The Citroën which had been parked opposite to No. 8 had long since disappeared and the only person in sight was a lean, bony-faced individual who stood gazing into a shop window. Noelle went into the station and bought a return ticket to Strasbourg, taking no notice of the man who came up behind her and in his turn purchased a single to the same city.

Vanek's instructions to Lansky had been simple. 'I

don't think she's his wife – she looked far too young and casual. If she comes out, follow her – unless she has a suitcase, in which case she's leaving, so forget her . . .'

Noelle Berger had decided to go and do some Christmas shopping in Strasbourg to give Philip time to recover his temper. Let him stew in his own juice, she reasoned, and then he'll be glad to see me back this evening. In Strasbourg the shops had opened at two – to scoop in more business since it was so close to Christmas – and Noelle spent quite a lot of Philip's money in the Rue des Grandes Arcades. Which damned well serves him right, she told herself. Later she relented and bought him a bright yellow waist-coat. Once, someone nearly knocked her under the wheels of a bus as she waited at a crowded kerbside, but when she looked round she saw only a fat woman behind her. At the end of the afternoon, laden with purchases, she made her way to the quiet district known as Petite France down by the river. She had decided to have a cup of tea with a friend before catching the train back to Colmar.

At the edge of the lonely Place Benjamin Zhia the river Il divides into three different sections before joining up again lower down, and here an intricate network of footwalks crosses the river. There is a lock-gate, a penned-up channel where the water roars through the bottleneck, and sluices which flood out from under a building beyond. The sound of churning river is deafening. Taking a short-cut, Noelle moved out on to the footwalks, quite alone as far as she knew. She was half-way across, she had heard nothing above the growling roar of the water, when something made her turn round. Lansky was one step behind her, both hands upraised. She stared in disbelief as the hands reached her and shoved. She was half-way down before she screamed, and her screams were lost in the boiling sluices which dragged her under and then rushed her at speed towards the Quai des Bateliers. Bobbing on the surface of the racing flood her Christmas purchases had a bizarre, festive look, including a bright yellow waist-coat which broke free from its wrappings.

In twenty minutes Lansky was boarding the turbo-train which would return him to Colmar by seven in the evening. With two people in a house it is too difficult to stage a convincing double 'accident'.

Chapter Twelve

On the evening of Sunday, 19 December, Grelle waited in his office for Boisseau to return from Strasbourg, but as the hours ticked away the police prefect was far from idle. For a good part of the day he had been immersed in tightening up the security arrangements for the presidential motorcade drive to Charles de Gaulle Airport – or Roissy as it was often called – on the morning of 23 December when Florian departed for Russia.

Marc Grelle had made himself an expert on death by assassination – on the methods used, on the people who used them. He had made a particular study of the thirty-one attempts which had been made to assassinate General de Gaulle, on the reasons why they might have succeeded, on the reasons why they failed. The list of techniques employed was quite formidable.

Killing by remote detonation of explosive charges under a moving vehicle; killing by sniper armed with rifle and telescopic sight; killing at close quarters – by stabbing, by shooting; killing by imposture – by use of a stolen military or police uniform; killing by motorbike outrider approaching presidential car; killing by suicidal air collision – one plane crashing into another carrying the president; killing by absurdly exotic methods – using a camera-gun, using explosive-carrying dogs trained to run to a certain spot where the president was due to speak; and killing by *motorized ambush*.

The last method was the favourite, and Grelle could see why. The motorized ambush was most deadly because it used highly trained thugs at short range, men who could react at the last split second according to circumstances. De Gaulle had, in fact, come closest to death when his motorcade was ambushed by other cars. With this catalogue of assassination attempts in his head Grelle, aided by the tireless Boisseau, set out to counter every one of them. He was still working on the problem when his deputy returned from Strasbourg.

It was nine in the evening and Boisseau, who had had nothing to eat since lunch, sent out to the corner brasserie for food. He ate his meal at the prefect's desk while he went on reporting about the Strasbourg trip. 'You see,' he continued, 'Jouvel's suicide is technically sound, no doubt about that, and few people can fake that kind of death. As you know, they would overlook certain details . . .'

'Unless we are confronted with a professional assassin? Which would give rise to all sorts of unpleasant implications . . .'

'What I don't like,' Boisseau remarked, sopping up gravy with a piece of bread, 'is those two men who called on the tart and asked her – quite independently

– almost the self-same questions about Jouvel. And that when Jouvel normally had no one calling on him or even interested in him. So, who were those two strangers – to say nothing of the man with the umbrella whom none of the tenants recognized?'

'Face it,' Grelle advised, 'Jouvel may well have committed suicide and these other people are probably irrelevant. At this end we are getting nowhere yet – neither Roger Danchin nor Alain Blanc have made contact with any known Soviet link. We are at that stage we have encountered on so many cases when everything is a blind alley. We have to wait for a development, a pointer . . .' He took out from a locked drawer the list of witnesses compiled by Col. Lasalle, glancing at it again. 'For all we know the key to the whole thing may be a man we can't even put under surveillance – Dieter Wohl of Freiburg.'

'You could phone Peter Lanz of the BND,' Boisseau suggested. 'He is always very helpful . . .'

'When even here on our home patch we are having to proceed with the secrecy which characterizes con-spirators? I dare not start spreading this abroad.' Grelle stretched and yawned. 'God, I'm tired. No, we must wait – and hope – for a pointer . . .'

In a two-storey house beyond the outskirts of Freiburg, the university town on the edge of the Black Forest, the ex-Abwehr officer, Dieter Wohl, stood by the window of his darkened bedroom as he peered across the fields towards the west, towards France only a few miles away across the Rhine. He was remembering.

A large, well-built man with a strong-jawed face, Wohl was sixty-one years old. As his shrewd blue eyes stared towards Alsace, a faint smile puckered his mouth. It had all been so long ago, so futile. Now there was peace on both sides of the Rhine, thank God; at least he had lived to see that. A retired policeman and widower, Dieter Wohl had plenty of time to think about the past.

It was the banner headline in the *Frankfurter Allgemeine Zeitung* eleven days ago which had first stirred memories, the story about the attempt to assassinate the French president. A shocking business. What had intrigued Wohl had been the name of the woman who had made the attempt, a Lucie Devaud. Curious. That was the name of the woman who had died in the sunken car when the Leopard went into the river. Could there be any connection? he wondered.

After reading the newspaper story Wohl had dug out one of his old war diaries from the back of his desk. It had been strictly forbidden by military regulations – to keep a diary – but many soldiers had broken the regulation; even generals and field-marshals who later made a pot of money writing up their memoirs. With all the time in the world on his hands, Wohl read through the whole of the diary for 1944. As he read, it all came back to him.

*

As a keen young Abwehr officer stationed in the Lozère district of France, Wohl had made up his mind to trap the Leopard. Diligently he picked up every scrap of gossip about the mysterious Resistance leader and recorded it; his passion for secrecy, his remarkable network of agents, his ferocious dog, César – the Leopard's only friend so far as Wohl could gather.

Once – and only once – Wohl had come close to capturing the Leopard when he received a tip-off that his adversary would be driving down a certain country road at a certain time. The ambush was laid on the far side of a bridge over a river the Leopard would have to cross. At this point a thick forest came down steeply to the water's edge and Wohl stationed himself high up among the trees with a pair of field-glasses. It was close to noon on a windy day when he saw the car coming behind a screen of trees, coming at high speed. Through his glasses Wohl saw an image blurred by foliage – and the speed of the approaching vehicle.

'God in heaven!'

A man was behind the wheel and beside him sat a girl, her hair streaming behind her in the wind. This was something Wohl had not anticipated – a woman in the car – and it worried him as the car came closer to the bridge. She must be a Resistance courier, he imagined. He strained to see detail in his glasses and he was excited. This was the first time anyone had actually seen the Leopard. The trouble was he couldn't see the man's face – everything was blurred by the screen of trees and the vehicle's movement. But he would have to slow down as he came up to the river: there was a sharp bend just before the road went over the bridge. Beyond the far end of the bridge was a road-block.

The Leopard made no effort to slow at all. He was reputed always to move at speed to avoid being shot at. With a scream of tyres and a cloud of dust the vehicle careered round the bend and came up on to the bridge. It was a remarkable piece of driving, Wohl admitted, his eyes glued to the glasses. As the car came out of the dust-cloud half-way across the bridge the Leopard must have seen the road-block. He reacted instantly; still moving at speed he drove into the parapet, smashed through it and went down into the river which at this point was eighteen feet deep. Wohl could hardly believe his eyes as he saw the vehicle disappear and a belated burst of machine-gun fire rattled.

As it plunged the car turned turtle and went down roof first. When it settled on the bottom both the man and the girl must have been upside down as the river surged inside. Wohl was quite sure that the Leopard must now be dead but he took no chances. Using a megaphone he barked out orders and the soldiers began to force their way through the thick undergrowth lining the banks. It was three hours later before a breakdown truck equipped with a crane hauled the sunken car slowly to the surface.

Wohl was on the bridge when the car, dripping with water, was swung over and down. He received another shock. There was no trace of the Leopard. But the girl was still there, imprisoned in the front seat, her dark hair plastered to her skull, an attractive girl of about twenty. After a few days, using the Vichy police's fingerprint records, Wohl was able to identify her as Lucie Devaud. The medical examiner told the Abwehr officer that at some recent time she had been delivered of a child.

The incident caused a minor scandal among the Resistance forces which split into two opposing views. Some said that the Leopard had acted correctly, had sacrificed everything to reach his rendezvous on time. Others were not so charitable – Lucie Devaud had a courageous record as a courier – and argued that he could have taken the girl out with him if he hadn't been so concerned to save his own skin. But then the surge of war, the later attempt to set up a Communist République du Sud, smothered the incident and it was forgotten, particularly when the Leopard himself was shot dead in Lyon . . .

Over thirty years later all this came back to Dieter Wohl when he read in the paper the name of the woman who had tried to kill Guy Florian. And by now Wohl himself had started to write his memoirs, so it seemed too good an opportunity to miss – to try and prompt people who might know something into writing to him, to furnish more material for his book. On Friday, 10 December, he wrote a letter to the *Frankfurter Allgemeine Zeitung*, referring to his wartime diary and the fact that he was writing his memoirs, and to give his communication an air of authority he mentioned the name of a certain Annette Devaud, who had also been a member of the Leopard's Resistance group, even going so far as to include her last known address of over thirty years ago. To make his letter even more arresting he quoted a sentence from one of Col. Lasalle's provocative broadcasts. 'Who is this Lucie Devaud who last night tried to kill a certain European statesman?' At the conclusion of his letter Wohl added a question of his own. *Is Annette Devaud still alive in Saverne, I wonder?*

Wohl succeeded in his aim even more swiftly than he could have hoped. The letter was printed in the *Frankfurter Allgemeine Zeitung* on Tuesday, 14 December, and was duly read on the same day by Paul-Henri Le Theule, the Secret Service officer attached to the French Embassy in Bonn. Le Theule, thirty-eight years old and only a child at the war's end, knew nothing about the Leopard, but his eye was caught by the brief reference to Col. René Lasalle. Hard up for material to pad his next report, he cut out the letter and added it to the meagre pile waiting for the next Paris diplomatic bag.

The bag was delivered to Paris on Saturday, 18 December, but it was only Sunday morning when Roger Danchin, working his way through a pile of paperwork, came across the cutting, which he showed to Alain Blanc who happened to be with him. Dictating a memo to the Elysée, Danchin sent both memo and cutting across the road and by lunchtime Guy Florian had seen both documents. At three in the afternoon

Soviet Ambassador Leonid Vorin, who had lunched with Alain Blanc, arrived at the Elysée, talked briefly with the president and then hurried back to his embassy in the Rue de Grenelle.

Returning to Colmar aboard the turbotrain from Strasbourg at seven on Sunday evening, Lansky hurried the few steps from the station across the place to the Hôtel Bristol where he found his two companions waiting impatiently for him in Vanek's bedroom. He told them how he had dealt with Noelle Berger and Vanek was relieved. 'It means Philip is now alone in the house and we may be able to turn his girl's disappearance to our advantage, but we must advance the time of our visit . . .'

'Why?' asked Lansky. 'Late on a Sunday night would be much safer . . .'

'Because,' Vanek explained with sarcastic patience, 'Philip will soon begin to worry about what has happened to her. If we leave him to worry too long he may call the police . . .'

While Lansky had been away in Strasbourg the other two men had continued their research on Robert Philip, each of them taking turns to watch No. 8 from a small park further down the Avenue Raymond Poincaré while they pretended to feed the birds or to be waiting for someone. And it was because it was difficult to keep Philip's villa under observation from a closer point – and a tribute also to their skill – that they escaped the notice of the occasional patrol-car which came gliding along the avenue while the officer behind the wheel checked on the same villa.

At three in the afternoon, throwing bread for some sparrows, Vanek saw Philip emerge from the house, come down the steps and walk to the gate which he proceeded to lean on while he smoked a cigarette. Slipping behind a tree, Vanek used the monocular glass he always carried to study the Frenchman close up. Under the flashy, camel-hair coat he wore Vanek noticed between the railings that the Frenchman was still clad in pyjama trousers. On Sundays Philip rarely dressed; slopping about the house in his night-things was his way of relaxing. And also, he was thinking, that when Noelle returned it would be so much easier to flop her on the bed when all he had to divest himself of was pyjamas. Left alone in the house, Philip was lusting for his latest mistress.

'That could be a bit of luck, too,' Vanek informed Brunner later, 'bearing in mind the method we shall adopt...'

It was close to nine o'clock when Brunner walked up the steps leading to the porch of No. 8 and rang the bell. At that hour on a Sunday the snowbound Avenue Raymond Poincaré was deserted and very silent. Lights were on behind the curtained bay window at the front and Brunner's ring on the bell brought a quick – but cautious – reaction. A side curtain overlooking the porch was drawn back and Philip stood in the window, still wearing his dressing-gown over his pyjamas.

Holding a glass, he stared at Brunner suspiciously, then dropped the curtain. A few moments later the door was opened a few inches and held in that position by a strong chain.

'Mr Robert Philip?' Brunner enquired.

'Yes. What is it?'

Expecting to see Noelle Berger laden with packages, Philip was taken aback by the arrival of this stranger. Brunner presented the Sûreté Nationale card he had carried since the Commando had left Tábor.

'Sûreté, sir. I am afraid I have some bad news about an acquaintance of yours, a young lady. May I come in for a moment?'

Worried as he was about his mistress, Philip was a wary man who had not survived all these years in the half-world of gun-running by accepting people or identity cards at face value; in fact, he himself had more than a nodding acquaintance with false papers.

'I don't know you,' he said after a moment. 'And it just happens that I know most of the police in Colmar . . .'

'That doesn't surprise me . . .' Brunner made an impatient gesture. 'I was transferred here from Strasbourg only last week . . .'

'Wait there while I get some clothes on . . .' The door slammed shut in Brunner's face. Inside the hall Philip frowned, sensing something odd about this unknown visitor. He reached for the phone on a side-table and something hard and pipe-like pressed against his back, digging through the silk dressing-gown as a voice spoke quietly. 'If you make a sound I shall shoot you. Take your hand away from that phone. Now, face the wall . . .' While Brunner was distracting the Frenchman's attention, keeping him at the front of the house, Vanek had gone round the side-path to the back of the house. He had followed the same route earlier – soon after dark when Philip had drawn the curtains over the front windows – and had found the French doors which were locked and without a key in the hole. Now, using the skeleton keys, he had let himself inside and come into the hall while Philip was talking to his unexpected visitor.

'Don't move . . .' Vanek pressed the Luger muzzle against Philip's back again to remind him it existed, then he turned the key in the front door, drew the bolt and removed the chain. Brunner himself turned the handle, came inside and closed the door quickly. 'Fasten it up again,' Vanek ordered. 'No one saw you? Good . . .'

Prodding Philip up the staircase ahead of him, Vanek waited until they were on the upper landing, then handed the Luger to Brunner and quickly explored the first floor. All the curtains were closed in the darkened bedrooms and he found what he was looking for leading off a large double bedroom at the back – a bathroom. Switching on the light, he studied the room for a moment and then nodded to Brunner who prodded Philip inside his own bathroom. 'What the hell is going on?' the Frenchman blustered. 'The police station is just round the corner and . . .'

'The Police Nationale headquarters is in the Rue de la Montagne Verre which is well over a kilometre from here,' Vanek informed him quietly. 'Now, take off your clothes.'

'My brother and his wife will be calling . . .'

'The clothes . . .'

Brunner rammed the Luger barrel hard against him. Philip stripped, taking off dressing-gown and pyjamas until he was standing gross, hairy-chested and naked. Frightened by the coolness of Vanek, he still had some spirit left as he asked again what the hell this was all about.

'Haven't you heard of burglars?' Vanek enquired. 'It is a well-known fact that a man without any clothes on is in no position to run about the streets seeking help – especially on a night like this. And before we leave we shall rip out the phone cord. Standard practice. Don't you read the newspapers?'

Telling him they were going to tie his feet to the taps, they made him lie down inside the bath and then Brunner turned on both taps, mingling the water to a medium temperature. The Frenchman, growing more frightened every second, for the third time asked what the hell was going on. It was Vanek who told him. 'We want to know where the safe is,' he said. 'We have been told you have a safe and you are going to tell us where it is . . .'

'There is no safe . . .'

'If you don't tell us where it is my colleague will grab hold of your feet and drag you under . . .'

'There is no safe,' Philip screamed.

'Are you sure?' Vanek looked doubtful, still aiming the Luger at Philip's chest. The bath continued to fill with water at a rapid rate. 'We wouldn't like you to lie to us,' Vanek went on, 'and we shall be very annoyed if we search the place and find one . . .'

'There is no safe! There is money in my wallet in the bedroom – over a thousand francs . . .'

Brunner switched off both taps and stared at Philip who was now sweating profusely. Bending down, the Czech took hold of the Frenchman's jaw firmly, then pushed his face close to Philip's. Vanek moved to the other end of the bath and took hold of both the Frenchman's ankles. Half-sitting, half-lying in the bath, Philip braced himself, prepared to be dragged under, still protesting there was no safe in the house. Suddenly, he felt the grip on his ankles released as Vanek, in a resigned voice, said, 'I think perhaps he is telling the truth . . .' Philip relaxed. Brunner jerked the jaw he held in his hand upwards and backwards in a swift, vicious movement and the back of Philip's head struck the bath with a terrible crack. 'He's dead,' Brunner reported as he checked the pulse and then Philip slid under the water and his face dissolved into a wobbling blur.

'The correct sequence,' Vanek commented. 'The medical examiner will confirm he died by striking his head before he immersed himself. Get finished quickly . . .'

Vanek checked the large double bedroom, looking

under the bed, on the dressing-table, inside the wardrobe. The few feminine clothes confirmed to him that the girl who had been followed to Strasbourg by Lansky was only a brief visitor, so he set about removing traces of her presence. Taking a suitcase engraved with the initials N. B., he piled in her clothes, her night things, her cosmetics and six pairs of shoes, her lipstick-stained toothbrush from the bathroom shelf and two lace-edged handkerchiefs from under a pillow. There would still be traces of her presence in the house the police would find, but without clothes they would shrug their shoulders. The last thing Vanek wanted to happen in the next few days was a police dragnet out for a missing woman. He was closing the case when he heard Brunner, who had fetched a pan from the kitchen, scooping out water from the bath and throwing it on the floor. He checked the bathroom before he went downstairs.

'Perfect?' enquired Brunner.

A tablet of soap he had dropped in the bath was muddying the water as it dissolved. Robert Philip had just had a fatal accident, and most accidents happen at home. He had been standing in the bath when he had stepped on the soap tablet, lost his balance and gone crashing down to hit the back of his head. Water had welled over the rim of the bath on to the floor, soaking his pyjamas and dressing-gown. 'I brought up that ashtray from the living-room,' Brunner remarked. On a stool stood the ash-tray the Czech had carried up in his gloved hand, the burnt-out remnant of the cigarette

Philip had left smoking when he answered the door still perched in the lip of the tray.

'Perfect,' Vanek replied, being careful to leave on the bathroom light as he followed Brunner downstairs, carrying Noelle Berger's suitcase, then he switched off the living-room light. Left on all night, it might well have attracted attention, unlike the bathroom which was at the back of the house.

They left by the way Vanek had entered the house – by the French door at the back. Once outside, they re-locked the door with the skeleton keys, and then Vanek waited with the suitcase in the little park until Brunner arrived with the Citroën. It took them only twenty minutes to drive to the banks of the Rhine, and on the way they stopped briefly at a deserted building-site while Vanek collected a few bricks to add weight to the suitcase. A few minutes later he watched the case sink into the swift-flowing current, took over the wheel from Brunner, and by 10.30 p.m. they were back inside their bedrooms at the Bristol, ready for a night's sleep. They would be leaving early in the morning – on their way to pay a visit on Dieter Wohl in Germany.

In Strasbourg Alan Lennox woke early on Monday morning, got out of bed at the Hôtel Sofitel, opened his door and picked up the local paper he had ordered from the hall porter. He read it in his dressing-gown, drinking the coffee he had ordered from room service. He hardly noticed the banner headline as he searched through the inner pages for a report on Leon Jouvel's suicide, which he found reported at greater length than he had expected; there was a shortage of local news after the weekend. The details it gave were hardly more illuminating than those he had heard from Louise Vallon, Jouvel's assistant, but an Inspector Rochat was mentioned as being in charge of the case and the address of the police station was given.

Finishing his coffee and croissants, Lennox showered and shaved, dressed and paid his bill. Snow was drifting down from a leaden sky as he took a cab to the station where he deposited his bag in the luggage store; Colmar was only thirty minutes away by train and he confidently expected that in one day he should be able to find and talk to Robert Philip, assuming the Frenchman was not away. He was just in time to climb aboard the 9.15 a.m. turbotrain for Colmar before it began moving south. As the train left Strasbourg and moved across the flat plain with glimpses of the Vosges mountains to the west, Lennox read the banner headline story he had skipped over in his bedroom. Another international crisis was brewing.

The Turkish Naval Command in the Bosphorus had recently received a long signal from their opposite numbers at the Russian Black Sea port of Odessa. The signal informed the Turks that a very large convoy, code-named K.12, would be making passage through the Bosphorus and the Dardanelles *en route* for the Mediterranean. This was in accord with the long-time agreement whereby Soviet Russia always requests formal permission before sending ships through the Turkish-controlled straits.

As always, the Russians specified the make-up of the convoy, and this so startled the Turkish naval commander that he phoned Ankara urgently. The Defence Minister in the Turkish capital was woken in the middle of the night and he immediately reported the signal to NATO headquarters in Brussels. It was decided as a matter of policy to leak the news to the press. What caused the ripple of alarm was the size of the convoy. The Soviet signal had specified six heavy cruisers (four of them missile-bearing), one aircraft carrier, twelve destroyers and fifteen large transports. The size of the convoy was unprecedented. What could the fifteen large transports be carrying? Where was this enormous convoy headed for?

As the train pulled in to Colmar, Lennox folded up his newspaper and forgot about the scare story. After all, it had nothing to do with the job he was working on, and by now his whole attention was fixed on his coming interview with Robert Philip.

By eight o'clock on Saturday night, 18 December, every defence minister in Western Europe and North America had received a copy of the Soviet signal, including Alain Blanc, who paid it rather more attention than Alan Lennox. Within only five days the president was due to fly to Soviet Russia and Blanc was not at all happy about the signal. On Sunday morning he had a brief interview with Guy Florian, who took a quite different view.

'Certainly they would never dream of precipitating a world crisis on the eve of my departure for Moscow,' he told Blanc. 'They are much too anxious to cement relations with us as the major West European power . . .'

Alain Blanc left the Elysée unconvinced and even more disturbed than before he had arrived. Why had Florian suddenly become so complacent about the intentions of Soviet Russia?

Arriving at Colmar, Lennox purchased a street-guide at the station kiosk and found that the Avenue Raymond Poincaré was only a few metres away from where he stood. When he started walking down the avenue he received an unpleasant shock: two patrol-cars with uniformed policemen standing beside them were parked outside a square-looking two-storey villa. He felt quite sure this would be No. 8 even before he drew level with the villa on the opposite side of the street and continued walking. Yes, it was No. 8. It was a repeat of the same scene he had witnessed outside No. 49 Rue de l'Épine only the day before. Fifteen minutes later, having walked in a circle – to avoid re-passing the police stationed outside the villa – he walked into the bar of the Hôtel Bristol opposite the station.

'What are all those police cars doing in the Avenue

Raymond Poincaré?' he asked casually as he sipped his cognac.

The barman was only too eager to pass on information; in a small town like Colmar the grapevine is reliable and swift. A local bigwig, Robert Philip, had died in his bath the previous evening, he confided. The tragedy had been discovered when his cleaning woman had arrived to find the front door still bolted and chained. 'She had a key,' the barman explained, 'so Philip always undid the bolts and chain first thing and then she could let herself in. The police found him floating in his bath. He won't be running after skirt any more, that one . . .'

Lennox ordered another drink but the barman had little more information. Except that the police had been to the hotel asking a lot of questions about two men who had stayed there for two nights.

'They had a Citroën,' the barman went on, 'according to the night porter. I didn't see them myself – I don't think they ever came in here. Personally, I can't see the connection . . .'

As Lennox walked out of the bar two uniformed policemen came in, which decided him to leave Colmar as rapidly as possible; there was a fifty-fifty chance the talkative barman might relay to them his recent conversation with the stranger who had just left. Crossing the *place* to the station, he bought a one-way ticket to Lyon and then boarded a train for Strasbourg which had just come in. When the ticket collector came through the train he used the return to Strasbourg he already had in his possession. Of the three wartime survivors who were once familiar with the Leopard there was now only one left. Dieter Wohl of Freiburg.

Unlike Inspector Rochat of Strasbourg, Inspector Dorré of Colmar was only forty and he took nothing for granted. Saturnine-faced, impatient, a fast-talking man, he phoned Boisseau two hours after the death of Robert Philip had been discovered, explaining that there had been no surveillance on Philip after the Frenchman had returned home apart from observation by a routine patrol-car. 'We are very short of men,' he went on, 'so I was unable to obtain personnel for a proper surveillance, which is regrettable . . .'

At the other end of the line Boisseau guessed that someone higher up had been unhelpful – because they had resented Paris's intrusion into their backyard. This time he had neither the necessity nor even the opportunity to ask probing questions: Dorré went on talking like a machine-gun.

'According to the medical examiner and my own observation there is no doubt at all that Robert Philip died by accident when he slipped and caught the back of his skull on the edge of his bath. He was alone in the house at the time and there are no signs of forcible entry or anything which would indicate foul play – although there had been a woman in the house, but probably only for a few hours. Philip was like that . . .'

There was a brief pause, then the voice started up again. 'Pardon, but I have a cold and had to blow my nose. So, technically, it is an accidental death. For myself, I do not believe it for a moment. I have heard that another man you also requested to be put under surveillance – a Leon Jouvel – hanged himself in Strasbourg less than forty-eight hours ago. I have also heard – I was in Strasbourg yesterday – that my colleagues are satisfied that Jouvel committed suicide. For me, it is too much, Mr Boisseau – two men you ask to have put under surveillance both die in their homes by suicide, by accident, in less than two days. I tell you, there has to be something wrong . . .'

'Is there anything specific . . .' Boisseau began, but he got no further.

'Pardon, Mr Director-General, but I have not finished. A woman who knows – knew – Robert Philip well drove past his villa yesterday morning and saw a blue Citroën parked opposite his villa. Two men were trying to repair the car, but she thought they were watching Philip's villa. She reported it to me when she saw the patrol-cars outside this morning, assuming there had been yet another burglary . . .'

'Any registration number?' Boisseau managed to interject.

'Unfortunately, no, but I have not finished,' Dorré continued. 'It occurred to me to check with all the local hotels and we find that two men arrived at the hotel nearest the station at 9.30 on Saturday night. The hotel, incidentally, is no more than a few metres away from the villa of the late Robert Philip. They arrived in a blue Citroën and we have the registration number. It is being circulated at this moment. Also, the descriptions of the two men. There may be no connection but I do not like this death at all, despite its technical perfection . . .'

'If it were not an accident then,' Boisseau hazarded, 'it would have to be the work of highly skilled professionals?'

'They would have to be trained assassins,' Dorré said bluntly, 'because if I am right – and I do not say I am – then presumably Leon Jouvel's death was also arranged, and again there was technical perfection. You must not think I am a romantic,' he insisted, 'trying to turn every event into a crime, but I repeat, two men under surveillance dying so quickly does not smell of roses to me, sir. And,' he went on, once again preventing Boisseau from speaking, 'the geography is interesting, is it not?'

'The geography?'

'It is not so very far to drive from Strasbourg to Colmar. I will let you know as soon as we get information on the car registration of the Citroën . . .'

Vanek, driving at speed, but always keeping just inside the legal limit, reached the Boulevard de Nancy in Strasbourg by nine in the morning, one hour before Inspector Dorré had circulated the car registration number. Handing back the Citroën to the Hertz agent, he walked out again and went into the restaurant where he had dropped Brunner and Lansky while he got rid of the vehicle.

'We've used that car quite long enough,' he told the two men, 'and two visits is more than enough by the same mode of transport.'

Refusing to allow them to finish their drinks, he took them outside where they again separated. With Brunner he took a cab to Strasbourg station, leaving Lansky to follow in a second vehicle. They joined forces again at the station but they each bought their tickets separately. Boarding the train by himself while the other two men went into a different coach, Lansky put his bag on the rack and lit a cigarette. Within fifteen minutes the train had crossed the Rhine bridge and was stopping in Kehl. The Soviet Commando had arrived in Germany.

Chapter Thirteen

Monday was a bad day for Lennox, who never forgot
that he was travelling with forged papers. Arriving
back at Strasbourg station, intending to collect his
suitcase from the baggage store and then take another
train across the Rhine into Germany, he immediately
noticed signs of intense police activity. There was a
uniformed policeman on the platform as he alighted
from the train, a young and alert man who was
obviously scrutinizing all passengers as they walked
past him to descend the exit steps.

In the main hall there were more police – some of
them Lennox felt sure in plain clothes – and when he
approached the luggage store two gendarmes stood by
the counter, checking people's papers as they withdrew
their luggage. Lennox walked away from the store and
went inside the glassed-in café which fronted on the
Place de la Gare. Sitting down at a table he ordered
coffee, quite unaware that he was in the same café
Lansky had waited in the previous Saturday evening
before paying his final call on Leon Jouvel. While he
drank his coffee Lennox watched the station and what
he saw was not encouraging.

Another police van arrived, disgorging a dozen more policemen who ran inside the main hall. The energetic Inspector Dorré of Colmar had been in touch with his Strasbourg colleagues – Vanek's Citroën had now been traced to the Hertz car-hire branch in the Boulevard de Nancy – and Inspector Rochat's superiors, nervous now of a monumental blunder, cooperated fully. The abandonment of the car logically led them to the assumption that the recent hirers must now be travelling by train or air. A massive surveillance operation was put into action at the railway station and nearby airport. Ironically, the dragnet thrown out to trap the Soviet Commando was endangering Lennox.

It is one thing to slip across a border with false papers; it is quite a different kettle of fish to risk being checked carefully when an emergency dragnet is under way. Leonox paid for his coffee, walked across the Place de la Gare to the bus station, and jumped on the first crowded bus leaving. It happened to be going to Haguenau, a place he had never heard of, so he bought a ticket which would take him the whole route. The earliest he could risk crossing over into Germany would be the following day; dragnets are at their most vigilant during the first twenty-four hours. And the big problem would be where to spend the night: when the police are really looking for someone they check every hotel, even phoning those outlying places they cannot easily reach.

Lennox caught a late evening bus back from Haguenau to Strasbourg, and the first thing he noticed when he alighted at the Place de la Gare was the line of police vans drawn up outside the station. Early that morning, reading through the newspaper to find the report on Leon Jouvel's death, he had noticed a reference to an all-night session of the European Parliament being held in the city. After eating dinner in a back street restaurant, he took a cab to the Parliament building. His papers, which showed him as a reporter, readily gave him admittance and once inside he settled down in the press gallery to his own all-night session.

Before taking the cab to the European Parliament he had slipped into a hotel washroom where he had shaved with equipment he had bought in Haguenau; it might not have been wise to present an unshaven appearance inside the august precincts of Europe's talking shop. The precaution turned out to be unnecessary – there were few other reporters in the press gallery and at times, as the dreary debate droned on and on, Lennox was able to snatch an hour or so of sleep. Checking his watch at frequent intervals, he waited while the night passed on leaden feet. In the morning he would try once again to cross the Rhine into the Federal Republic of Germany.

It was Inspector Jacques Dorré (who in later years rose to the rank of Commissioner), who finally alerted Marc Grelle. When the prefect received Boisseau's report of his conversation with Colmar he personally phoned

Dorré, who now had more information. He was able to tell Grelle that the Citroën which had transported two men to the hotel in Colmar had been handed in to the Hertz branch in the Boulevard de Nancy, Strasbourg.

'Yes,' he further confirmed, 'the description of the man who returned the car tallies with the description of one of the two men who stayed at the Hôtel Bristol on the nights of 18 and 19 December – and on the 19th Robert Philip died in his bath . . .'

'If these two men – Jouvel and Philip – were murdered,' Grelle suggested to Dorré, 'it has to be the work of a professional assassin then? No amateur could fake both deaths so convincingly, you agree?'

'I agree,' Dorré replied crisply. 'But it appears there is a team of at least two assassins on the move – maybe even three men . . .'

Grelle took a tighter grip on the phone. 'How do you make that out?' he demanded.

'I personally checked the register at the Bristol. Ten minutes after the first two men – Duval and Bonnard – booked in, a third man, Lambert, took a room also. There is nothing to link these three men together – except that they all arrived on the night of the 18th and departed on the morning of the 20th, which is early today, of course. The point is, at this time of the year the hotel was almost empty . . .'

Grelle thanked him for his co-operation and put down the receiver. 'There could be some kind of assassination team on the move in Alsace,' he told

Boisseau. 'It's all theory, but if it were true who the hell could they be?'

'Only Lasalle and the Englishman, Lennox, have that list, presumably,' Boisseau pointed out. 'Surely Lasalle is not wiping out his own witnesses? That doesn't make any sense at all. The only thing which would make sense is if someone employed by the Leopard were doing the job . . .'

'But the Leopard can't have the list . . .'

Grelle stopped and the two men stared at each other in silence. An hour later the indefatigable Dorré was back on the line again. He was working in close touch with his colleagues in Strasbourg, he explained, and at his suggestion Rochat had started contacting every hotel in the city. The names Duval, Bonnard and Lambert had soon been tracked down. The first two had spent the night of Friday, 17 December, at the Hôtel Sofitel, while Lambert had slept at the Terminus, and it was during the evening of 18 December that Leon Jouvel had hanged himself.

'So,' Dorré pointed out, 'these same three men – and again the descriptions, though vague, tally – then moved down here to Colmar late on the evening of the 18th and were in the town when Robert Philip died. How far do you stretch the long arm of coincidence without breaking it?'

'That's it!' Grelle snapped. 'When your descriptions of these three men arrive I'll circulate them throughout the whole of France – and we have their names. I want

226

that trio detained and questioned the moment they surface again . . .'

On the night of 20 December it was dark by six o'clock in the Freiburg area as Dieter Wohl stood looking out between the curtains of his unlit bedroom. Wohl felt quite at home in the dark, possibly a relic of his wartime years when he had so often observed a suspect house from behind an unlit window. Wohl was not a nervous man, even though he lived alone in his two-storey house perched by itself at the roadside three kilometres outside Freiburg, but at the moment he was puzzled. Why had a car stopped just short of his house and stayed there at this hour?

Overnight there had been a weather change; the snow had melted, the temperature had risen, and now the sky was broken cloud with moonlight shining through, illuminating the lonely country road and the trees in the fields beyond. Most people would not have heard the car, but ex-policeman Wohl – he had joined the force after the war – had the ears of a cat. A black Mercedes SL230, he noted by the light of the moon. One shadowy figure sat behind the wheel while his two passengers had got out and were pretending to examine the motor. Why did the word 'pretending' leap into his head? Because although they had the bonnet up they kept glancing at his house and looking all round them as though spying out the land. Their glances were fleeting – so fleeting that probably only a trained observer like Wohl would have noticed them.

'My imagination is running away with me,' he murmured.

Below him on the road one of the men left the car and made his way into a field alongside the house, his hand at his flies. He's just gone for a pee, Wohl decided. Leaving the front bedroom, still moving around in the dark, he went into the side bedroom where the curtains had not been drawn; keeping to the back of the room, he watched the man perform against a hedge. It was all perfectly innocent, except that the man relieving himself kept glancing at the back garden, and up at the side of the house. Well hidden in the shadows, Wohl waited until the man had finished and returned to the car. A moment later the two men closed the hood as Wohl watched from the front bedroom, climbed back inside the Mercedes and the driver tried the engine. It sparked first time and drove off towards Freiburg. I must be getting old, Wohl thought, seeing sinister things where none exist. He went downstairs to continue work on his memoirs. Half an hour later the phone rang.

'Herr Wohl? Herr Dieter Wohl? Good evening. This is the Morgenthau Research Institute, a market research organization. We are carrying out research connected with a campaign to increase state pensions. You have been selected . . .'

The researcher, a man called Brückner, checked Wohl's status, noted that he was a widower living alone, that he owned his house, that he never took a holiday, and a number of other pertinent questions. Thanking Wohl profusely, the caller said he might wish to visit Wohl but he would first phone for an appointment. Would any of the next three evenings be convenient? It would? Excellent . . .

Putting down the phone Wohl went back to his desk in the front living-room and settled down again to the arduous task of completing the introduction to his memoirs. But he found it difficult to concentrate; his suspicious mind kept going back to the telephone call.

Only eight hours earlier Vanek had phoned the special Paris number from Kehl. Each day, since arriving in Munich – with the exception of the Sunday in Colmar – he had phoned the number his trainer, Borisov, had given him from a post office – and each day there had been no new instruction passed over to him. Phoning from Kehl, he had anticipated the same dead call. Hearing the same voice and name – Jurgensen – repeat the number at the other end Vanek identified himself.

'This is Salicetti . . .'

'There is a development,' the voice said quickly. 'At the Freiburg branch you must collect a wartime diary and the manuscript of the customer's memoirs. Understood?'

'Understood . . .'

'Then you must visit another customer – note the address. A Madame Annette Devaud, Saverne . . .'

Jurgensen spat out the name of the town. 'It is in Alsace . . .'

'That's a vague address . . .'

'That's all we have. Goodbye!'

Vanek checked his watch. The call had taken only thirty seconds. Quite calm while he had been making the call, the Czech swore to himself as he looked out of the phone booth to where people were queuing up to buy postage stamps. The new development was not to his liking at all; it meant that when they had made the visit to Freiburg they would have to re-cross the border back into France. And it was now 20 December, which gave them only seventy-two hours to complete the job.

Alan Lennox crossed the border to Kehl on the morning of Tuesday, 21 December. At Strasbourg station the dragnet had been relaxed, although still partly in oper-ation. After the initial burst of activity – which brought no result – the resentment felt by the local police at Paris's interference in their affairs began to surface again, especially since there was a terrorist alert – later proved to be unfounded – at Strasbourg airport. Men were rushed to the airport and the surveillance at the railway station was reduced.

Collecting his bag from the luggage store, Lennox boarded a local train, later passed through the frontier control without incident – no one was looking for a man called Bouvier – and arrived in Kehl. He immedi-ately put through a call to Peter Lanz at the special

Bonn number he had been given and – in a roundabout way – told the BND chief everything that had happened. 'The two French witnesses have died suddenly, one might say violently – within twenty-four hours of each other ... one of them partially identified our animal impersonator ... by voice alone, I emphasize ... Guy Florian.'

Lanz adopted an off-hand tone, as though discussing something of minor importance. 'You would say your witness was reliable? After all, we do have other depositions ...'

'It is by no means certain,' Lennox replied.

'And your next move?'

'Peter, the third witness lives in Freiburg – I didn't mention it before, but I'm going to see him now. Yes, one of your countrymen. No, I'd sooner not mention names ...'

'In that case,' Lanz said crisply. 'I will be in Freiburg myself this evening. You will be able to contact me at the Hotel Colombi. Look after yourself. And if that is all I have to go to a meeting which is urgent ...'

Franz Hauser, recently elected Chancellor of the Federal Republic of Germany, agreed to see Peter Lanz at the Palais Schaumburg at 11 a.m., which was only one hour after Lennox had phoned from Kehl. Immersed in work – Hauser seldom got to bed before midnight – he had now asked Lanz to make his temporary headquarters in Bonn instead of at Pullach in Bavaria. 'I need you across the hall from me the way things are shaping up in Europe,' he informed the BND chief.

Small, neat and wiry, Hauser had been elected on a platform of taking the strongest measures against terrorists, the urban guerrillas who were still plaguing Germany. He had also preached the gospel that now the Americans had withdrawn from Europe the continent must protect itself. 'Combining with our friends, France, Great Britain and our other allies we must build up such strength that the commanders of the Red Army will know Europe can only be their graveyard if ever they make the mistake of crossing the frontiers . . .'

At eleven o'clock promptly Lanz was ushered into his office and Hauser, a man who hated formality, came round his desk to sit alongside the security chief. 'Is there information from the Englishman, Lennox?' he enquired. He listened for ten minutes while Lanz explained what had happened, his small, alert face puckered in concentration. 'If this links up with the movement of Soviet convoy K.12,' he commented, 'then we may be on the eve of a catastrophe. The Russians are striking before we can build up our strength.'

'You do not really believe it, sir?' Lanz protested. 'I mean that Florian could be this Communist Resistance chief, the Leopard?'

'No, that is impossible,' Hauser agreed. 'But it is no longer beyond the realms of possibility that one of his key cabinet ministers may be. And then there is the fact that the Leopard was not found when his grave was disinterred near Lyon. How did you hear about that, by the way?'

'A contact we have across the Rhine . . .'

'All right, keep your secrets. What disturbs me are the growing rumours of a *coup d'état* in Paris. Supposing the Leopard is Alain Blanc, Minister of National Defence – might he not be planning to seize power while Florian is away in Moscow?'

'That hadn't occurred to me,' Lanz admitted.

'Is there some huge conspiracy afoot?' Hauser murmured. 'If Moscow is co-operating with the Leopard might they not have asked Florian to Moscow to get him out of the way while the Leopard takes over in France? Why is that Soviet convoy proceeding into the Mediterranean at this moment? Everything seems to be moving towards some climax. We need more information, Lanz. Immediately . . .'

Arriving by train at Freiburg, Lennox left his bag at the station, checked the phone directory to make sure Dieter Wohl was still living at the address given on the list, and then phoned the German. He introduced himself as Jules Jean Bouvier, a reporter on the French newspaper *Le Monde*. His paper was about to embark on a series on the French wartime Resistance, with particular reference to operations in the Lozère. He believed that Herr Wohl had served in this area during the war, so . . .

Wohl was hesitant at first, trying to decide whether seeing Bouvier would help him with his memoirs, then it struck him that a little advance publicity could do no harm, so he agreed. Lennox took a cab to the ex-Abwehr officer's remote house and Wohl was waiting for him at the door. A cautious man, Wohl sat his visitor down in the living-room and then asked for some identification. Lennox produced his papers. 'Anyone can get a press card printed,' he said easily.

It took half an hour to coax Wohl into a trusting frame of mind, but when Lennox mentioned the Leopard he saw a flicker in the German's eyes. 'This is something I am concentrating on,' Lennox explained. 'I find it excellent copy – the mystery surrounding the Leopard's real identity. It was never cleared up, was it?'

Wohl went over to his desk where part of a hand-written manuscript lay alongside a worn, leatherbound diary. For fifteen minutes he told Lennox in precise detail all the steps he had taken to track down the Resistance leader during 1944. Lennox had filled a dozen pages of his notebook with shorthand, had decided that the German really had no information of value, when Wohl mentioned the incident when he had almost ambushed the Leopard. At the end of the story he gave the name of the girl who had died in the submerged car. Lucie Devaud.

'It was a shocking business,' Wohl remarked, 'leaving the girl to drown like that. The car was in eighteen feet of water, my men were some distance from where it went over the bridge. I'm convinced he could have saved her had he tried. He didn't try . . .'

'Lucie Devaud,' Lennox repeated. 'That was the name of the woman who tried to kill Guy Florian. I suppose there's no possible connection?'

'I wondered about that myself,' Wohl admitted. 'Annette Devaud was very close to the Leopard – she was in charge of his brilliant team of couriers. I understand she went blind soon after the war . . .'

Lennox sat very still, saying nothing. Col. René Lasalle had made a passing reference to Annette Devaud, dismissing her as of no importance because of her blindness. Could the French colonel have slipped up here – if Annette had indeed been so close to the Leopard?

'I wrote to the *Frankfurter Allgemeine Zeitung* last week,' Wohl continued, 'and I mentioned the incident of the drowned girl. I also mentioned that another Devaud – Annette – who was involved with the Leopard, might still be alive in France. I even gave her last-known address, which perhaps I should not have done. Here it is. Annette Devaud, Woodcutter's Farm, Saverne, Alsace. It was a long time ago but some French people stay in one place for ever . . .'

Wohl showed Lennox the address at the back of the war diary where he had underlined it several times. 'Living alone as I do,' he said apologetically, 'I get funny ideas. Only last night I thought some people were watching my house. And then there was that peculiar phone call from the market research people . . .' As he went on talking, Lennox listened.

'. . . in fact, Wohl only mentioned it in passing, but considering what happened in Strasbourg and Colmar, it just made me wonder . . .' At four in the afternoon Lennox had met Peter Lanz in a bedroom of the Hotel Colombi in Freiburg soon after the BND chief had flown there from Bonn, and now he was telling the German about his meeting with Dieter Wohl. Earlier Lanz had told the Englishman about the opening up of the Leopard's grave in a forest near Lyon, about how the French police had found only the skeleton of a hound inside the Resistance leader's coffin.

'This is what has turned a vague disquiet into alarm and crisis,' the BND official explained. 'It now seems probable that Lasalle has been right all along – that somewhere in Paris a top Communist is working close to Florian, maybe only waiting for the president to leave the capital for his visit to Moscow . . .'

'I suppose it's confidential – how you heard about the exhumation of the Leopard's grave?' Lennox hazarded.

'It's confidential,' the German assured him.

He saw no advantage in revealing to Lennox that it was Col. Lasalle who had passed the information to him. And Lanz himself had no inkling of the colonel's source which had passed on the news to Lasalle.

Georges Hardy, Police Prefect of Lyon and Marc Grelle's great friend, had for some time disagreed violently with Guy Florian's policies, and to express this disagreement he had been secretly furnishing Lasalle with information about developments inside France.

Lennox had then reported to Lanz on his interview with Dieter Wohl, ending by describing the curious incidents of the previous day the ex-Abwehr officer had described. 'I gather he was looking out of a bedroom window last night in the dark when he saw this car stop outside,' he went on. 'It just reminded me of the man I saw following Leon Jouvel that night in Strasbourg. I suppose it isn't possible that someone has Dieter Wohl under observation? Then there was the peculiar telephone call. After all, two out of the three men on Lasalle's list have already died suddenly. And it's damned lonely out there where he lives . . .'

'If by a long chance you are right,' Lanz suggested, 'this could be a breakthrough. If we grab hold of someone trying to put Wohl out of the way, too, we can find out who is behind this whole business.'

'It's a very slim hope,' Lennox warned.

'What else have we got?' Lanz demanded. He was well aware he was grasping at straws, but Chancellor Hauser had said he wanted positive information immediately. From the hotel bedroom he phoned the Police Chief of Freiburg.

*

The Mercedes SL230 hired in Kehl pulled in at the kerb close to Freiburg station and Vanek lit a cigarette as he watched people coming off a train. Nearing the end of the Commando's mission, the Czech had become mistrustful of hotels and the previous night the three men had slept in the car at the edge of the Black Forest, muffled up in travelling rugs they had purchased in Freiburg. Puffy-eyed and irritable, both Brunner and Lansky showed the minor ravages of their improvised night's rest. Vanek, on the other hand, who could get by with only catnapping, looked as fresh as on the morning when they had crossed the Czech border at Gmünd.

'We have no time or need for any more research,' Vanek said. 'Wohl lives alone. We know he is there every evening. We have checked the immediate surroundings where he lives. We will visit him tonight.'

Inspector Gruber of the Freiburg police took every possible precaution: without knowing what might happen, half-convinced that nothing at all would happen, he mounted a formidable operation. At Lanz's suggestion twenty men, all armed with automatic weapons, had thrown a loose cordon round the vicinity of Dieter Wohl's house – loose because they wanted anyone who approached the house to slip inside the net before they tightened it. So observation had to be from a distance and the nearest policeman was over a hundred metres from the building.

Six men were held back in a special reserve force,

hidden inside a truck which had been backed into a field and parked behind trees. Communications were excellent; every man was equipped with a walkie-talkie which linked him with a control truck half a kilometre up the road to Freiburg and inside a field. Inside the truck the BND chief sat with Lennox, Inspector Gruber and the communications technician; a transceiver perched on a flap table linked them with the walkie-talkie sets.

To try and counter the distance problem – the fact that they had to stay well back from Wohl's house – Gruber had issued several men with night-glasses for scanning the house. His orders were specific: they must let anyone who approached reach the house, then close in on command from Gruber personally. Everything really depended on how well the men with the night-glasses were able to operate. And all traffic was to be allowed to pass along the road. Any attempt to set up checkpoints would have been useless: they had no idea who they were waiting for, whether in fact there was anyone to wait for.

'You really think someone is going to come and attack Wohl?' Gruber asked at one stage.

'I have no idea,' Lanz admitted. 'As I have explained to you, there could be political implications behind this operation.'

'An urban guerrilla gang?' Gruber pressed.

'Something like that . . .'

They waited as night fell, as the naked trees faded into the darkness. And with the coming of night the temperature dropped rapidly. Then they had their first hint of trouble: huge banks of mist drifted in off the Rhine, rolling across the fields in waves like a sea shroud, a white fog which seemed to thicken as it approached the house. Very soon the man nearest the house was in difficulties. It wasn't so much that he couldn't see anything; what he could see was deceptive, hard to identify. Lennox, who was growing restless, said he was going outside to take a look at things. It was at this moment that Lanz handed him a 9-mm Luger. 'If you insist on prowling about outside, you had better carry this.'

Several cars and a petrol wagon had already passed down the road, and each one was checked in and out of the section under surveillance by an observer at either end. In the truck Lanz and Gruber were careful about this as the reports came in – especially since the mist had arrived. 'If one of those cars doesn't come out at the other end we're going to have to move damned fast,' Gruber remarked. 'This mist is something I could have done without . . .'

Worried, Lanz checked his watch. 'I'm almost hoping no one comes,' he said. 'We could have left Wohl inside a trap.'

Gruber shook his head. 'Wohl took the decision himself when we consulted him,' he said. 'And remember, he's an old policeman . . .'

Behind the wheel of the black Mercedes he had hired at Kehl, Vanek was driving slowly as they came closer to Freiburg from the south. Ahead of him were two other cars in convoy. He could have passed them several times and Brunner, irritably, had suggested he should overtake. 'I'm staying on their tail,' Vanek told him. 'If there are any patrol-cars about they're less likely to stop three cars travelling together. They're always interested in the car which is on its own. A policeman in Paris once told me that.'

'There's a mist coming down,' Brunner commented.

'I like mist. It confuses people.'

'I think we're close now,' Brunner said. 'I remember that old barn we just passed.'

'We are close,' Vanek agreed.

'Three cars coming in,' the policeman with the night-glasses at the southern end of the section reported. 'At least I think there were three. It's so thick I couldn't get any idea of the makes . . .'

'Were there three or not?' Gruber demanded over the air. 'I have told you before, you must be precise – otherwise the whole operation becomes pointless.'

'Probably two . . .'

'Probably?' Gruber shouted over the transceiver. 'I will ask you again. How many vehicles just entered the section? Think!'

'Two vehicles,' the man replied.

*

241

'Something just went past,' reported the man at the northern end of the section. 'It's hellishly difficult to see now. More than one . . .'

Gruber looked at Lanz and then cast his eyes to the roof of the truck. 'Sometimes I wonder why I became a policeman. My wife wanted me to buy a grocer's shop.'

'It must be very difficult for them – in this mist,' Lanz said gently. 'I think they are doing very well.'

Gruber turned the switch himself and leaned forward to speak. 'Number Four. You said quite clearly there was more than one vehicle. Can you be sure of that?'

'Quite sure,' Number Four replied. 'There were two travelling close together. Two cars.'

'He's a good chap,' Gruber said as he returned the switch to 'receive'. He rubbed the side of his nose. 'So is the other man, to be fair. It's my own fault – now the mist has come I just wish I'd blocked off the road with checkpoints. We'd better leave it alone now.'

'We'd better leave it alone,' Lanz agreed.

When he left the truck Lennox made his way back to the road and started walking along it towards Dieter Wohl's house. He was worried about the mist but he didn't dare get too close to the building for fear of confusing the watching policemen. When two cars approached him, nose to tail, he saw a blur of headlights and pressed himself close against the hedge. As they went past he walked a short distance further and then stopped on the grass verge. He was now at a point half-way between the northern end of the section and the house.

Under his seat Vanek carried the 9-mm Luger pistol which Borisov had obtained for him. Vanek didn't expect to use a gun but he believed in carrying some protection and he was an expert at concealing a weapon. At the moment the pistol was held to the underside of the seat with strips of medical adhesive tape. He was now driving even more slowly, allowing the two cars ahead to disappear into the fog, but he kept the Mercedes moving until they had just gone past Dieter Wohl's house which was a grey blur in the mist. Then he pulled up. No point in giving the German warning, making him wonder why a vehicle had stopped outside his house on a night like this.

'You wait with the car,' he told Lansky, 'and keep the motor running. I don't think there'll be any trouble but you never can tell.'

'Why are you nervous?' asked Brunner, who was coming with him. It was unlike Vanek to anticipate trouble – to refer to it openly.

'I'm nervous that Lansky will forget to keep the motor ticking over,' Vanek snapped.

Why was he nervous, Vanek wondered as he got out of the car with Brunner. Some sixth sense kept telling him something was wrong. He stood on the grass verge, looking at the blurred shape of the house, glancing up and down the road and across the fields he couldn't see. Then he walked back to the house and towards the front door. Changing his mind, with Brunner close behind, he went to the side, opened the wire gate quietly and walked round to the back of the house. The only lights were in two windows on the ground floor at the front; all the other windows were in darkness. With his coat collar pulled up against the chill, Vanek walked back to the front door. Brunner slipped out of sight to the side of the house. Vanek pressed the bell by the side of the door, his right hand inside his pocket where it gripped the Luger he had extracted from under the car seat. It was uncannily quiet in the mist.

He had to wait several moments before he heard a rattle as a chain was removed on the other side of the door, then the door was opened slowly and the huge figure of Dieter Wohl stood in the entrance. He was carrying a walking-stick in his right hand, a heavy farmer's stick without a handle.

'Good evening,' Vanek said in his impeccable German. 'I am Inspector Braun of the Criminal Police.' He showed Wohl the forged Sûreté card Borisov had supplied and quickly replaced it in his pocket with his left hand. 'A man has been found dead in the road two hundred metres from here in the Freiburg direction. May I come in and have a word with you?'

'Could I have a closer look at that identity card?' asked the ex-Abwehr officer. 'The police themselves are always warning us to be careful who we let in . . .'

'Certainly...' Vanek withdrew his right hand from his coat and pointed the Luger at the German's stomach. 'This is an emergency. I don't even know you really live here. I'm coming inside so please move slowly back down the hall and...'

The German was backing away as Vanek took a step forward. 'If it's as serious as that then please do come in, but I would be glad if you would put away...' Wohl was still talking when he wielded the heavy stick with extraordinary speed and strength. It cracked down on Vanek's wrist as he was still moving and the shock and pain of the blow made him drop the weapon. In acute pain, Vanek kept his nerve; whipping up his left hand, the palm and fingers stiffened, he thrust it upwards under Wohl's heavy jaw. Had the ex-Abwehr man stiffened, his neck would have snapped, but he let himself go over backwards and crashed down on the polished floor, rolling sideways to take the impact on his shoulder. Vanek suddenly realized that this was going to be a more dangerous opponent than Jouvel or Robert Philip. And Brunner couldn't get into the narrow hall to lend assistance because Vanek was in the way.

The Luger, sliding along the polished floor, had vanished. It turned into a dogfight. Vanek had age on his side; Wohl was enormously strong. The German, still gripping the stick, was clambering to his feet when Vanek crashed into him again to bring him down. Caught off-balance, Wohl toppled, half-recovered, then fell; clutching at a table to save himself, his hand caught a cloth, dragging it off with several porcelain vases which crashed to the floor. Falling backwards a second time, Wohl rolled again, taking the fall on his other shoulder. Vanek's legs loomed above him and he struck out with the stick he still grasped, catching the Czech a heavy blow on the shin. Vanek yelped, brought his fist down into Wohl's face, but the face moved and the blow was only glancing, sliding down the German's jaw. Behind them, Brunner still couldn't do anything in the narrow hall. The two men grappled on the floor, rolling over, smashing into furniture, each trying to kill the other.

'I don't like it,' said Lanz.

'Those two cars – which might have been three?' Gruber queried. 'I'm moving in,' he decided. He was on the verge of issuing the order to the truckload of six men waiting in reserve behind the copse of trees when another report came in: a bus and a petrol tanker had moved into the section from the south, travelling one behind the other. Cursing, Gruber delayed giving the order. 'That's something we can do without,' he rasped. 'A bloody collision in the fog . . .'

'They always do it in a fog,' Lanz commented. 'One vehicle comes up behind another and hugs its tail. It gives them comfort so they ignore the risk . . .'

'I'm getting worried,' said Gruber.

They waited until the policeman at the northern end of the section reported traffic moving past – he couldn't identify the vehicles – and then Gruber told the reserve truck to drive to Wohl's house. Twenty seconds later – too late to stop it – another report came in from the southern end of the section. A second petrol tanker had appeared and was now moving slowly into the section.

Wohl's hallway, normally so neat and tidy and cared for – the ex-Abwehr officer was a methodical soul – was a total shambles. Furniture was wrecked, pictures had come off the walls, the floor was littered with the debris of smashed porcelain, and there was a certain amount of smeared blood. Wohl's stick lay on the floor beside its dead owner; the German's skull had been cracked by his own weapon.

Vanek, still panting, left Brunner by the front door and went inside the living-room where a light was burning. The Czech had expected to spend some time searching for the war diary and manuscript but he found them waiting for him on the German's desk; Wohl had been working on his memoirs when the doorbell rang. Vanek read only a few words of the neat, hand-written diary. *In 1944 the Leopard went everywhere accompanied by a vicious wolfhound called César. . .*

Stuffing the diary and the few pages of manuscript into his pocket, he returned to the hall to look for the missing Luger; on his way out of the living-room he toppled a bookcase so it crashed to the floor, scattering its contents. There was no question of making this death look like an accident but it could still look like an attempted burglary which had gone wrong. He found the Luger hidden under a low chest and went to the front door where Brunner was waiting for him. 'Something's coming,' Brunner warned. As Vanek moved through the doorway a police truck appeared, stopping just beyond the house. A second later something large loomed out of the mist, coming very slowly. A petrol tanker. It began crawling past the stationary police vehicle as men emerged from it. Vanek raised the Luger, took deliberate aim, fired three times.

The heavy 9-mm slugs penetrated the side of the tanker with a series of thuds. Vanek began running towards the Mercedes, followed by Brunner. Behind them someone shouted, a muffled shout, succeeded by a muffled boom. The petrol tanker flared, a sheet of flame consumed the mist and behind the two running Czechs someone started screaming and went on and on. Billowing black smoke replaced the mist and a nauseating stench drifted on the night air. Vanek reached the car where Lansky, white-faced, sat behind the wheel with the motor ticking over.

'What the hell was that . . .'

'Get it moving,' Vanek snarled. 'Slam your foot down – if we hit something we hit it . . .'

The Mercedes accelerated, not to high speed but very fast for the mist-bound road. Brunner, who had wrenched open the rear door, was still only half inside the vehicle when it moved off with the door swinging loose beside him. A few metres further along the road Lennox had heard the shots and then what sounded like an explosion. He was standing on the grass verge when the Mercedes's blurred headlights rushed towards him with the rear door still open and someone only half inside the car. Behind it a police siren had started up. He fired twice as the car roared past him and both bullets penetrated Brunner's arched back. The Czech's body spun out of the open door and thumped down in the road as the Mercedes vanished in the mist, still picking up speed.

Chapter Fourteen

'The star of the most corrupt and power-mad Republic
the world has ever seen is fading ... America, that
mongrel-mix of the debris of a score of nations is now
a ferment of internal decay ... Withdrawing her troops
from Europe when she no longer had the strength to
rule the world, she is now dissolving into chaos ...
One thing above all we must ensure! That never again
can she lay her greedy hands on the lands of other
people – on Europe!'

It was President Florian's most vicious attack yet
and it was made in a speech at Marseille where the
French Communist Party is never far below the surface.
A massive audience acclaimed the speech, showing the
enormous support Florian enjoyed in the south where
once, so many years earlier, a République Soviétique
du Sud had almost been established at the end of the
Second World War.

Afterwards there was a huge parade along the Cane-
bière, the main thoroughfare of the turbulent French
seaport where thousands of people broke ranks and tried
to surge round the presidential Citroën. On the direct
orders of Marc Grelle, who had flown to the city, CRS

troops drove back the milling crowd, which later almost caused a confrontation between the president and the police prefect. 'You spoiled the whole spontaneous demonstration,' he raged. 'There was no need . . .'

'The spontaneous demonstration was organized by the Communist Party,' Grelle said sharply. 'And my reaction is you are still alive. Do you or do you not want me to protect your life?'

The sheer vehemence of the prefect startled Florian, who changed direction suddenly, putting an arm round Grelle's shoulders. 'You are, of course, right. Nothing must happen to me before I fly to Russia. We have peace within our grasp, Grelle, peace . . .'

The Soviet convoy K.12 had now passed through the Dardanelles and was proceeding south across the Aegean Sea. It was proceeding slowly, at a leisurely pace which puzzled the naval analysts at NATO headquarters in Brussels. The team of analysts was under the control of a British officer, Commander Arthur Leigh-Browne, RN, and on Tuesday, 21 December – the day when Florian made his violent attack on the Americans at Marseille – Browne circulated to all Western defence ministers a routine report.

'K.12's most likely destination would appear to be the Indian Ocean, making passage in due course through the Suez Canal – except for the fact that the aircraft carrier, *Kirov*, is too large to pass through the canal . . .

'Other possible destinations are the newly acquired naval facilities granted by the Spanish government at Barcelona . . .

'The factor we find most difficult to equate with either of the above two conjectures is the presence of the fifteen large transports (contents as yet unknown). . .'

As Browne put it to his German second-in-command after the report had been sent off, 'At the moment, it's all hot air. I haven't a clue what they're up to. We'll have to play the old game of wait-and-see . . .'

Guy Florian made his speech in Marseille at noon. At the same time in Moscow an enlarged meeting of the Politburo which had been called unexpectedly was listening to a brief speech by the First Secretary. Among those present were the Foreign Minister of the Soviet Union and Marshal Gregori Prachko, Minister of Defence. It was these two men – forming a quorum of three with the First Secretary – who had earlier sanctioned the despatch of the Soviet Commando to the West.

Revealing for the first time to the enlarged meeting the identity of the Frenchman he called 'our friend', the First Secretary went on to give details of the Franco-Soviet pact which would be announced while President Florian was in Moscow. 'The President of the French Republic has, of course, under the French constitution, full powers to negotiate and conclude treaties with foreign powers,' he continued.

It was clause 14 which was the key to the whole agreement. This clause stated that in the furtherance of world peace joint military manoeuvres would be carried out from time to time on the respective territories of the Union of Soviet Socialist Republics and the Republic of France. In simple language it meant that the advance elements of two Soviet armoured divisions now aboard convoy K.12 would be landed at French Mediterranean ports within the next few days.

'Where will they go to?' enquired Nikolai Suslov, the most intellectual member of the Politburo.

'I will tell you!' It was the immensely broad-shouldered, uniformed and bemedalled Marshal Gregori Prachko who replied. Prachko intensely disliked non-practical intellectuals and especially disliked Nikolai Suslov. 'They will be put ashore at Toulon and Marseille immediately Florian has announced the pact in Moscow. The date of his visit – 23rd December – has been carefully chosen. Over their famous Christmas the government ministers of the West all go on holiday, so they will not be behind their desks to react quickly . . .'

'But where will the troops go?' Suslov persisted.

'To the Rhine border with Germany, of course! As he gets up on Christmas morning to open his presents, Chancellor Franz Hauser will find himself facing Soviet troops to the east – and to the west! The whole of Western Europe will fall under our control – including the powerhouse of the Ruhr – which will enable us to win any confrontation with China . . .'

Part Three

The Police Prefect of Paris

22–23 December

Chapter Fifteen

Any experienced policeman knows it: you can throw a
cordon round an area, set up road-blocks, and three
times out of four you are too late. Gruber set up a
cordon and caught nothing but irate motorists and
truck-drivers. The Mercedes, which had been hired in
Kehl, was found a week later inside a copse at the edge
of the Black Forest. Four of the six policemen who had
been getting out of the truck when the petrol tanker
detonated were lucky; most of the blast went the other
way, travelling across open fields. The other two policemen were badly burned, one of them with first-degree
injuries which required plastic surgery later. The petrol
tanker driver died from the fumes which filled his cab
before he could escape.

Lanz and Gruber searched Wohl's house, looking for
the war diary which Lennox had seen, and found no
trace of the diary or the manuscript. Brunner's dead
body was taken to the police mortuary and examination
of his clothing and pocket contents revealed very little.
He was carrying a large sum of money – two thousand
Deutschmarks – and a French identity card in the name
of Emile Bonnard. 'Which will undoubtedly prove to

be false,' Gruber commented. Underneath his German hat and coat Brunner was wearing a French suit and underclothes. Apart from this there was very little to prove who he really was – until the preliminary results of the medical examination came through.

'My colleague has come up with something interesting,' the medical examiner reported to Gruber who was sitting in a hotel bedroom eating dinner with the BND chief and Lennox. 'He is a dental technician and according to him the dental work and teeth fillings were definitely carried out in Eastern Europe – probably in Russia . . .'

Lanz phoned Marc Grelle direct from police headquarters at Freiburg. Strictly speaking, any such call should have been made to the Sûreté, but whereas Lanz knew Grelle well and trusted his discretion, he neither liked nor trusted the Director-General who was Commissioner Suchet's superior. As Lanz explained to Grelle, he had two reasons for informing him of this development. The assassin Lennox had shot dead – and Lanz was careful not to mention the Englishman in any way – was travelling with French papers in the name of Emile Bonnard. Also – and here again Lanz phrased it carefully – he had reason to believe the Commando had recently come from France and might well have re-crossed the border back into that country . . .

'You have solid grounds for saying an assassination

Commando, possibly Soviet-controlled, is on the move?' Grelle enquired.

'Yes,' Lanz replied firmly. 'Without going into details, I'm pretty sure of it. And perhaps it would be helpful if we both keep in touch . . .'

Grelle had just put down the phone when Boisseau came into his office with a routine report. 'Lesage has just called in. That Algerian terrorist, Abou Benefeika, is still holed up in the derelict apartment building in the Goutte-d'Or. No sign of his pals coming to collect him yet. We let him go on fermenting?'

'Continue the surveillance . . .' Grelle took a bite out of the sandwich he would have to make do with for his evening meal. Normally he dined at Chez Bénoit, an exclusive little restaurant in the old Les Halles district where you had to phone for a table; he was beginning to miss the place. 'I have just had a call from Peter Lanz of the German BND,' he informed Boisseau. 'He played it very cagey but somehow he has found out that a Soviet assassination Commando is at work. This evening they killed an ex-Abwehr officer in Freiburg.' He paused. 'The name of the Abwehr man was Dieter Wohl . . .'

'One of the three names on Lasalle's list . . .'

'Exactly. So now it looks as though this Commando has been sent with the express purpose of wiping out everyone on that list – and they've done it, for God's sake. All avenues through which we might have seen a little light are closed . . .'

'The surveillance on Roger Danchin and Alain Blanc is producing nothing?'

'Nothing . . .' The prefect frowned as his phone rang. He checked his watch. 10 p.m. Only recently returned from his flight to Marseille when he had accompanied the president while he delivered his most bitter anti-American tirade so far, Grelle was feeling very tired. Who the hell could it be at this hour? He picked up the phone, swallowing the last of his sandwich. It was Alain Blanc.

'No, Minister,' Grelle assured him. 'I have not dug up any connection between the president and Lucie Devaud as yet . . . We now know her father was Albert Camors, a wealthy stockbroker who died a few months ago and left her his apartment in the Place des Vosges . . . No, we do not know any more . . . Yes, she must have been illegitimate . . . No, no connection at all with the Elysée . . .'

Grelle shrugged as he replaced the receiver. 'He worries about a scandal, that one. As I was saying, all avenues seem closed to us, so all we can hope for once more is the unexpected break. And yet, Boisseau, I feel that somewhere I am overlooking something – something under my nose . . .'

'Something to do with the Commando? Incidentally, we may as well cancel the alert on the man the German police shot in Freiburg. Did Lanz give you a name?'

Grelle consulted a notepad. 'Emile Bonnard,' he replied. 'And I do not expect we shall ever see the other two men – Duval and Lambert. They have done their job. They will never return to France.'

Carel Vanek and Antonin Lansky approached the checkpoint to cross back into France the following morning, Wednesday, 22 December, which was the deadline day Borisov had given them in Tábor to complete their mission. They were on their way to visit Annette Devaud. They came up to the passport control counter separately with half a dozen people between them and Vanek presented himself for inspection first.

'Papers . . .'

The passport officer took the document Vanek had handed him, opened it after studying the Czech's face and then compared it with the photograph. The name he had already noted. Vanek waited with a bored look on his face, chewing a piece of chocolate while he studied the extremely attractive girl waiting next in line. He grinned at her engagingly and after a moment's hesitation she smiled back at him.

'You have been to Germany on business?' the passport official enquired.

'Yes.'

The official returned the passport and Vanek moved on, to be joined a few minutes later by Lansky. Vanek had presented the third set of papers he had brought from Tábor, papers made out in the name of Lucien

Segard, papers which carried a photograph of him without a moustache. Only the previous night in Kehl he had shaved off the moustache in the station washroom before accompanying Lansky to a small hotel where they had spent the night. Lansky had also used his third set of papers which carried the name Yves Gandouin. When frontier control officials have been asked to look out for men travelling under the names of Duval and Lambert it is only human for them to concentrate on people of those names, and to be anything but suspicious of different names.

Without having the least idea that their previous identities had been blown, Vanek had taken his decision the previous night after they had abandoned the Mercedes. 'Twice we have crossed the French border using our present papers,' he had told Lansky, 'and twice is enough.' He had then proceeded to burn the papers carrying the names Duval and Lambert before they walked to the nearest village and independently boarded a bus for Kehl crowded with Christmas shoppers. Inside Germany they were really in no danger: the only people who knew their names were inside France, and on the phone Marc Grelle had been reluctant to give Peter Lanz such information because of the delicacy of the investigation he was conducting.

Arriving back in Strasbourg, Vanek kept well away from the Hertz car-hire branch in the Boulevard de Nancy. 'Never go back,' was one of his favourite maxims. Instead, the two men took a cab to the airport where Vanek hired a Renault 17 from the Avis car-hire branch in the name of Lucien Segard. By 2 p.m. they were on their way to Saverne, which is only twenty-five miles from Strasbourg.

Alan Lennox had stayed up half the night at the Hotel Colombi in Freiburg talking to Peter Lanz. The German, who had been handed a copy of the *Frankfurter Allgemeine Zeitung* containing Dieter Wohl's letter just before he left Bonn – 'I should have been shown it days earlier, but no one thought to read the correspondence columns' – was dubious as to whether Annette Devaud would still be alive.

'From what Wohl said to you,' he remarked, 'she would be a very old lady now – and if she is blind how could she recognize anyone? Even assuming she ever knew what the Leopard looked like . . .'

'There's nothing else left,' Lennox said obstinately. 'No one else left, perhaps I should say. What Leon Jouvel told me is very inconclusive – although he was convincing at the time. In any case, the poor devil is dead. I'm going back across the Rhine tomorrow to try and find Annette Devaud.'

'Going back again over the frontier for the third time on false papers? I'm not asking you to do that . . .'

'Call it British bloody-mindedness – we're known for it. I just want to get to the bottom of this thing and find out who the Leopard really is. Wish me luck.'

'I have a feeling you're going to need more than luck,' Lanz replied gravely.

Remembering the atmosphere of intense police activity at Strasbourg station only thirty-six hours earlier, it took a certain amount of will-power for Lennox to hand his papers across the counter to French passport control and then wait while they were inspected. They were examined only cursorily and handed straight back; no one was interested in a man called Jean Bouvier. Probably the easiest way to pass through a checkpoint is to choose a time when someone else is being watched for.

Obtaining the address from Bottin, the telephone directory, Lennox left Strasbourg station and went straight to Hertz car-hire in the Boulevard de Nancy where he chose a Mercedes 350SE. It was expensive but he wanted some power under the bonnet. By noon he was leaving Strasbourg, driving west for Saverne in the Vosges mountains. He had, of course, no idea that for the first time since he had embarked on this trip at the behest of David Nash of New York he was two hours ahead of the Soviet Commando.

It was Boisseau who heard about the newspaper cutting of Dieter Wohl's letter to the *Frankfurter Allgemeine Zeitung* sent to Paris by the French Secret Service agent in Bonn. Oddly enough he was shown the photostat of the cutting by Commissioner Suchet of counter-intelligence whom he had made it his business to cultivate. Suchet was under the impression that this gave him a private pipeline into the prefecture, whereas the reverse was true; the only information given to him by Boisseau had first been vetted by Marc Grelle. It was late in the morning of Wednesday, 22 December, when Boisseau showed the photostat to his chief.

'So there could just be a witness who never appeared on Lasalle's list,' Grelle mused. 'That is, assuming she is still alive, after all these years . . .'

'She is. I phoned the police station at Saverne. She's living at a remote farmhouse quite a distance from Saverne itself – high up in the Vosges mountains. This letter made me go through the files again and there is one we overlooked. Annette Devaud was in charge of the Leopard's courier network. The really interesting thing could be the name . . .'

'Annette Devaud – Lucie Devaud . . .' The prefect clasped his hands behind his neck and looked shrewdly at his deputy. 'All avenues closed, I said. I wonder. All right, Boisseau, fly to Saverne. Yes, this afternoon, I agree. In view of what has happened to the other witnesses should you not call Saverne and ask them to send out a police guard?'

'She must be old – they might frighten her. And in any case, since she was not on Lasalle's list why should she be on the Commando's? Both Lasalle and the

Commando must have been working from the same list – in view of what happened. So where is the danger?'

'I leave it to you,' the prefect said.

Driving across the flat plain of Alsace which lies between Strasbourg and the Vosges mountains, Lennox soon ran into atrocious weather. Curtains of rain swept across the empty road, adding even more water to the already flooded fields, and in the distance heavy mist blotted out the Vosges completely. He drove on as water poured down his windscreen and then the engine began knocking badly, which made him swear because he knew the mountain roads ahead could be difficult. It was his own fault: the Hertz people had been reluctant to let him have this car, the only Mercedes 350 on the premises for hire. 'It has not been serviced, sir,' the girl had protested. 'I am not permitted . . .' Lennox had impatiently over-ridden her objections because he liked the car, and now he was paying for it.

Driving on across the lonely plain, the knocking became worse and he knew he had been foolish. Squinting through the windscreen, he saw a sign. *Auberge des Vosges and petrol five hundred metres ahead.* He wanted in any case to check Annette Devaud's address – and to find out whether anyone knew if she was still alive. Through the pouring rain a small hotel with a garage attached came into view. Pulling up in front of the pumps, he lowered the window and asked the mechanic to check the vehicle. A few minutes later the mechanic came into the hotel bar with the bad news. He had found the defect: it would take a couple of hours to put it right.

'Can't you hurry it up?' Lennox asked.

'I am starting work on it now,' the mechanic informed him. 'I can hurry it up, yes. It will take two hours.'

Lennox ordered a second cognac and two *jambon* sandwiches, which arrived as large hunks of appetizing French bread sliced apart and with ham inside them. Had the mechanic said three hours he would have been tempted to try and hire another car. He sank his teeth hungrily into the sandwich; two hours shouldn't make all that difference to the state of the world.

Annette Devaud, now spending the evening of her life at Woodcutter's Farm, had held one of the key positions in the Leopard's Resistance group in 1944: she had controlled the network of couriers, mostly girls in their late teens and early twenties, who had carried messages backwards and forwards under the very noses of the enemies. Almost forty years old, slim and wiry, she had been a handsome woman with a proud Roman nose and an air of authority which had rivalled that of the Leopard himself. Of all the men and women who had worked under him, the Leopard had most respected Annette Devaud, possibly because she was an outspoken anti-Communist. 'At least I know where

I am with her,' he once said. And Annette Devaud had another distinction – she knew what the Leopard looked like.

Because he found it useful to build up the reputation of an invincible personality, the Leopard kept it a secret when he was shot in the leg during a running battle in the forests. The wound did not take long to heal, but for a short period he was bedridden. It was Annette Devaud who shared his solitary convalescence, nursing him swiftly back to health, and it was during these few weeks that she came to know exactly what he looked like.

Annette Devaud heard, but did not see, the celebrations of Liberation Day; she had gone blind overnight. No one was able to diagnose the cause of her affliction, although some thought it was the news of the death of her husband who had fought with General Leclerc's division. Then again it could have been the death of her nineteen-year-old daughter Lucie, who drowned when the Leopard drove his car into the river to avoid Dieter Wohl's ambush. This happened after Annette had nursed the Leopard back to health when he was shot.

At the end of the war, returning to her home, Woodcutter's Farm, she remained there for over thirty years. The onset of blindness was an even greater blow than it might have been for some people; Annette had been a talented amateur artist who drew portraits in charcoal, and this too she put behind her as she adjusted to her new life. But in a folder she kept the collection of portrait sketches she had made during the war from memory. Among the collection were two life-like portraits of the Leopard.

Annette Devaud had endured another tragedy. Against her will, her daughter Lucie had insisted on becoming one of her couriers, and during her time with the Resistance the nineteen-year-old girl had taken as a lover an ex-accountant called Albert Camors. Out of the liaison a child had been born only six months before the Leopard drove Lucie Devaud into the river. Taking its mother's name, the child was called Lucie. Camors survived the war but quarrelled violently with the strong-willed Annette Devaud and he refused to let her have anything to do with the child. Prospering in peacetime – he became a Paris stockbroker – Camors brought up the child himself and never married.

A solitary but strong-willed child – reproducing in some ways the character of her grandmother, Annette, whom she never saw – Lucie grew up in a bachelor household and developed an obsession about the mother she couldn't remember. From her father she heard about the Leopard, about how her mother had died. Then, when she was almost thirty, Camors expired in the arms of his latest mistress and Lucie inherited his fortune and an apartment in the Place des Vosges. And for the first time she visited her blind grandmother.

The two women took to each other immediately and

one day Annette, talking about the war, showed her grand-daughter the folder of sketches, including the two of the Leopard. Lucie instantly recognized the portraits, but in her secretive way she said nothing to the blind woman. Using the names of people who had belonged to the Resistance group – which Annette had mentioned – she began checking. With her father's money to finance the investigation, she employed a shrewd lawyer called Max Rosenthal to dig into the Leopard's background. And without saying anything to Annette, she removed the two portrait sketches from the folder and took them back to her Paris apartment.

It was Max Rosenthal who traced Gaston Martin, the Leopard's wartime deputy, to Guiana where he was on the verge of being released from prison. Lucie Devaud wrote a careful letter to the man Annette had mentioned, hinting to Martin that the Leopard had become an important political figure in France, and then waited for a reply. The letter reached Martin shortly after he had been released from prison and he took his time about replying to her.

It was during the opening of a Paris fashion show that Lucie played the macabre trick which finally convinced her she had uncovered the real identity of the Leopard. She had seen the animal in a Rue de Rivoli shop which specialized in exotic presents costing a great deal of money. Purchasing the animal, she kept it in her apartment and then obtained a ticket for the fashion show in the Rue Cambon. In a newspaper she had read that President Florian would be attending the show with his wife, Lise.

When Guy Florian arrived escorting Lise – he was attending the show to dispel rumours that they were no longer on speaking terms – the show had already started, models were parading, and Lucie Devaud was sitting in a front-row seat with her draped overcoat concealing the underneath of her chair. Florian and his wife sat down almost opposite her. The show was almost over when Lucie tugged at the chain she held in her hand and which led underneath her draped chair. A model had just walked past when the leopard cub emerged from under the chair, stood on the carpet with its legs braced and bared its teeth.

It was over in a moment. An armed plain-clothes security man, one of several sent to the show by Marc Grelle, caught the expression on the president's face, grabbed the chain out of Lucie's hand, tugged the animal and led it out of the salon, followed by its owner with her coat draped over her arm. Florian recovered quickly, made an off-hand gesture and cracked a joke. 'I have had nothing to drink and yet there are spots in front of my eyes!'

Outside in the foyer Lucie took the chain from the detective without a word and left the building. The salon owner had been amused when she arrived with a leopard cub. 'How chic,' he had remarked to his *directrice*. 'We should have one of the models parading with that animal . . .' Getting into her car, parking the leopard cub on the front seat beside her, Lucie drove back to the Place des Vosges. On the following day she returned the animal to the shop, which accepted it back at a much-reduced price.

So often a woman takes a decision on feminine instinct; so often she is right. Lucie Devaud was now certain Guy Florian was the Leopard. She had seen a certain expression in his eyes before he recovered, a sudden wariness and alarm as he stared back at her – as though when he saw the look in her own eyes he had understood. 'Who the hell are you? You have found me out . . .' She knew there was no way she could be traced: she had paid for the leopard cub in cash and had applied for the salon ticket in a false name. It was while she was driving back to her apartment that she decided she would kill Guy Florian. The following morning the letter from Gaston Martin arrived.

Martin replied to her letter with an equally guarded communication. He said that he was interested in her theory and told her that he was returning soon by ship from Guiana. Could they meet when he arrived in Paris? Lucie Devaud wrote back immediately, suggesting that they met at a small Left Bank hotel called Cécile in the Rue du Bac. Presumably she was not too keen on inviting an ex-convict to her luxurious apartment in the Place des Vosges – or possibly she was still displaying the secretiveness which was so much a part of her life.

On the night before Wednesday, 8 December, she wrote out a complete account of her activities and sealed the report in a package which also contained the two sketches of the Leopard produced more than thirty years before by her grandmother, Annette Devaud. Across the package she wrote in her own hand, *To be delivered to the Police Prefect of Paris in the event of my death.* In the morning she delivered the package to her lawyer, Max Rosenthal, with strict instructions that it must remain unopened. Reading in the paper about Florian's nightly walk from the Elysée to the Place Beauvau she had decided not to wait for Gaston Martin – even though the Frenchman was on the eve of arriving back in France. On Wednesday evening, waiting outside the fur shop in the Faubourg St Honoré, she produced her 9-mm Bayard pistol. But it was Marc Grelle who fired two shots.

The letter Lucie Devaud had written and deposited with her lawyer, Max Rosenthal, was not delivered to the Police Prefect of Paris. An extravagant man, who spent vast sums on gambling, Rosenthal was not prepared to gamble his career. When he heard of his client's attempt to kill the president he became frightened that delivery of the package might involve him. Lucie had always come to see him and given only verbal instructions; no written correspondence had passed between them; and she had paid his bills in cash – which he had not declared to the tax man. Confident that there was no discoverable link between them, he locked the package away inside a deed-box where it stayed until a year later when he died unexpectedly.

One of Lucie Devaud's more benevolent actions before she died as a would-be assassin was to persuade her blind grandmother to see an eye specialist. Perhaps medical technique had advanced in the intervening thirty years, or maybe the trauma which had induced the affliction had run its course. Annette Devaud was operated on during September – three months before Guy Florian was due to fly to Russia – and recovered her sight completely. She went straight back to Wood-cutter's Farm from the hospital and started reading and drawing avidly, resuming her old solitary way of life but now blessed with the return of her sight. When she was told about the death of her grand-daughter by the man who brought her supplies she flatly refused to accept the circumstances surrounding Lucie's death. 'It's all a ghastly mistake,' she said firmly. 'They must have mistaken her for someone else.' This was the old woman the Soviet Commando was now on its way to kill.

Chapter Sixteen

Ignoring the downpour, Vanek drove at high speed along the deserted road from Strasbourg to Saverne. Beside him Lansky sat in silence as he chewed at the sandwiches they had bought at Strasbourg airport and drank from a bottle of red wine. Once he pointed out to Vanek that he was exceeding the speed limit. 'Get on with your lunch,' the Czech told him. 'We have only one final visit to make before we start back for home. And there is a limit to how long time is on our side. With a bit of luck it will turn out that the Devaud woman died years ago,' he added.

Imperceptibly – because he decided that Lansky was right – Vanek reduced speed, but Lansky, who was watching the speedometer needle, observed what was happening and smiled to himself as he finished the sandwich. To some extent Brunner had acted as a buffer between the two egotists, and Lansky, who was intelligent, decided not to make any more provocative comments. They still had a job to do.

'We'll have to check on the address of Devaud as soon as we can,' Vanek remarked, overtaking a vegetable truck in a shower of spray. 'So keep a lookout for a hotel or a bar. If she's still alive and living in the same place the locals are bound to know. In provincial France you can't pee behind a wall without the whole village watching . . .'

'This time,' Lansky suggested, 'we needn't be too fussy about arranging accidents. Just do the job and run, I say, now we haven't got that old woman, Brunner, round our necks any more . . .'

'I'll decide that when the moment comes,' Vanek snapped.

Across the plain there had been no sign of habitation for miles. They were coming close to Saverne when Vanek, peering through the rain-soaked windscreen, saw the sign. *Auberge des Vosges and petrol five hundred metres ahead*. He reduced speed. 'This place should have a phone book,' he said, 'and we're in the right area now.' Turning off the highway, he pulled in close to a battery of petrol pumps. 'Top her up,' he told the attendant, 'while we go inside and have a drink . . .' Vanek believed that you never could tell what emergency might lie ahead of you, that it always paid to keep a full tank. As they got out of the Renault a mechanic inside the garage was wiping the windscreen of a Mercedes 350 he had been working on.

Lennox checked his watch and walked out of the bar of the Auberge des Vosges on his way to the wash-room. Two hours exactly. The mechanic had just informed him his car was ready and Lennox had paid the bill.

Earlier he had checked Annette Devaud in Bottin and there had been no entry, but the barman had been more helpful.

'Funny old girl. Must be over seventy now if she's a day. She still lives at Woodcutter's Farm, all on her own. The locals don't see her from one year to another – except the chap who delivers her supplies. Remarkable woman, Annette Devaud. You know she was blind for getting on thirty years?'

'I haven't met her yet,' Lennox said carefully.

'Remarkable woman,' the barman repeated. 'Happened just at the end of the war – she went blind, just like that. Some disease or other, I don't know what. Then a few months ago a specialist takes a look at her and says he can do something.' The barman gave a glass an extra polish. 'A miracle happens. He operates and she can see again. Think of that – blind for over thirty years and then you see the world all over again like new. Tragedy that – about her grand-daughter, Lucie. You know who she was?'

'No.'

'Girl who tried to bump off Florian the other week. Must have been a nut – like that chap who shot Kennedy in Dallas.' The barman leaned forward confidentially. 'I live only two kilometres from the old girl and the few of us who knew who Lucie was kept our mouths shut. Even the police didn't catch on – the girl only came here a few times. I'm only telling you seeing as you're going to visit her – might give her a shock if you said the wrong thing . . .'

Lennox was thinking about it as he went into the wash-room and took his time about freshening up – the previous night in Freiburg he had enjoyed only two hours' sleep. It could only happen in a provincial French hamlet – a conspiracy of silence to protect a local and much-respected Frenchwoman. Over the basin a large mirror faced the door and he was drying himself off when the door opened. Lowering his towel he stared into the mirror and the man standing in the doorway stared back at him. For a matter of seconds their eyes met, then the man in the mirror glanced round the wash-room as though looking for someone and went out again.

Drying himself quickly, Lennox put on his jacket and coat, then opened the door slowly. For a few seconds in the Rue de l'Épine at the entrance to Leon Jouvel's building in Strasbourg he'd had a good look at the face of the man with the umbrella he had cannoned against, knocking his pebble glasses down on to the cobbles. He was still not absolutely sure – the man in Strasbourg had seemed older – but not with the light from the street lamp full on his face, he reminded himself. The passage outside the wash-room was empty. He walked down it and glanced inside the bar.

The man who had come into the wash-room had his back turned, but his face was visible in the bar mirror. He was talking to another man, tall, dark-haired and clean-shaven, a man of about thirty. The tall man, who was idly turning an empty glass in his hand, looked over his companion's shoulder and stared straight at

Lennox and then away. Lennox was even more sure now. There had been three men in the Soviet Commando's car at Freiburg. The man called Bonnard was dead, which left two of them. And at the back of the war diary they had taken off Dieter Wohl had been the address of Annette Devaud.

At this moment Lennox cursed himself for accepting Peter Lanz's theory that by now the remnants of the Commando would be fleeing back to Russia. It had been a reasonable theory – at the time – because the third witness on Lasalle's list had just been killed, so why should the Commando linger? Lennox walked back into the hotel out of sight of the bar as though leaving by the front entrance, then he ran up a wide staircase which turned twice before reaching the upper landing. He waited at the top where he could see through a window to the road beyond.

The barman had disappeared behind a curtain when Lansky returned to the bar where Vanek was leaning against the counter. Picking up his drink, Lansky swallowed it as Vanek played with the glass in his hand. 'That Frenchman I saw coming out of No. 49 – Jouvel's place – the chap I bumped into, is in the washroom here,' he said in a quiet voice. 'That's no coincidence . . .'

'Are you sure? Describe him,' Vanek said casually.

Lansky described Lennox in a few words. 'I'm quite sure,' he said. 'I'm trained to remember things like that

– in case you've forgotten. We looked at each other in the mirror for a few seconds and we both knew each other. I could have dealt with him – the place was empty – but that would have sparked off the police and we don't want that at the moment, do we?'

'No, we don't. Incidentally, he's looking in at the bar now, so don't turn round...' The situation didn't surprise Vanek; sooner or later something was bound to go wrong – it had in Freiburg, up to a point. It was just a question of deciding how to handle it. 'He's gone now,' Vanek said. 'I think we'll get away from here, too.'

As they walked out of the front door a Peugeot 504 with a single man behind the wheel was moving off to Saverne after filling up with petrol. The rain obscured the silhouette of the driver. 'That's probably him,' Vanek said. From the first-floor window Lennox watched them drive off in the direction of Saverne. Going downstairs he went back into the bar where the barman was polishing more glasses. Ordering another cognac, Lennox made the remark as casually as he could.

'Those two men who came in here after me – I thought I recognized one of them. Or are they locals?'

'Never seen them before – and don't want to see them a second time. I gathered from the tall one they're something to do with market research. They pick names of people and go ask them damned silly questions. I think they're on their way to see Annette Devaud...'

'Really?'

'Something to do with a campaign to increase pensions,' the barman explained. 'Was her husband alive they wanted to know. How could they find Woodcutter's Farm? I just told them – I didn't draw them a map like I did for you.' The barman grinned sourly. 'And I didn't tell them Annette will chase them off her property with a shotgun as good as spit...'

Lennox finished his drink quickly and went out to where the Mercedes was waiting for him. If anything, it was raining even more heavily, and as he drove away from the hotel he saw in the distance thick rain-mist enveloping the Vosges mountains. There had been mist at Freiburg when the Commando killed Dieter Wohl and now there was mist over the Vosges. The association of ideas worried him as he pressed his foot down and drove well beyond the limit in his attempt to overtake the Renault.

Carel Vanek was a fast driver but Alan Lennox was a more ruthless driver. Risking patrol-cars – and the appalling weather – moving at over a hundred and ten kilometres an hour, the Englishman came up behind the Czech just beyond Saverne where the highway climbs into the mountains. For a moment there was a brief spell of shafted sunlight breaking through the clouds, illuminating the peaks of the Vosges, the shiny road ahead, and less than three hundred metres away Lennox saw the Renault arcing round a bend, sending up spurts of water from under its fast-moving wheels.

Then it began to rain again, slanting rain which slashed down like a water curtain.

In the brief glimpse of sunlight Lennox saw the ground sloping away to the right beyond the road edge in a severe drop. He reduced speed a little, maintaining his distance behind the car in front. His opportunity came less than half a minute later as they still circled up the side of the mountain with the slope continuing down to the right. In the distance – where the road appeared as it descended again – coming towards him, towards the speeding Renault, he saw the blur of a large truck. Lennox pressed his foot down, closing the gap until he was almost on the tail of the car ahead. Still climbing, the road straightened out as the oncoming vehicle, which he now realized was a huge timber wagon, came closer. He timed it carefully, gauging the width of the road, the combined width of the three vehicles, then he pulled out without warning and accelerated.

'Bloody maniac . . .'

Behind the wheel of the Renault Vanek, still keeping a lookout for the Peugeot 504, was startled as the car coming up behind him began to overtake seconds before the timber wagon passed them. Instinctively he steered nearer to the right-hand edge where rain-mist blurred the view, trying to give maximum possible passage to the crazy idiot who was overtaking at this dangerous moment. Behind the windscreen of the timber wagon's cab the driver blinked as he saw what was happening, but there was no room to give leeway.

'Watch it,' said Lansky, suddenly alerted. 'There was a Mercedes at that hotel . . .'

Lennox was alongside the Renault, squeezed into a gap where there was no margin for the slightest error as the timber wagon started moving past. Then it was gone. Lennox turned the wheel slightly. The side of the Mercedes cannoned against the side of the Renault. The wet road did the rest. The Renault skidded and went over the edge.

The slope was less steep at this point on the mountain. Vanek wrestled desperately as he felt the car go over and down, losing speed as he released pressure on the accelerator, allowing the car to follow its own momentum. The wheels were slipping on a muddy slope, churning up great gouts of mud which splashed over the windscreen, blotting out vision, so Vanek was driving blind as he lost more speed, as the car went down and down, skidding and sliding, twisting and turning while the Czech fought to keep the vehicle on some kind of straight course. Then, not knowing what lay ahead, he braked. The car hit something. Then stopped.

'We're alive,' Vanek gasped hoarsely.

'That's something,' Lansky agreed.

When they got out into the rain they were half-way down a long slope with the road obscured by mist where they had come over. A grassy rampart had stopped them sliding even further. A few metres beyond where the Renault had stopped a muddy farmtrack continued on down the slope and went back up the hill towards the highway. 'It was that Frenchman I saw in the washroom,' Lansky said. 'I caught a glimpse of him behind the wheel just before he hit us. He can't be the police or he wouldn't have bounced us over the edge.'

'We meet him again, we finish him,' Vanek replied. 'Now we've got to heave this car round and then I'll try and make it up the track. It's going to take time,' he added.

High on the mountain Lennox stopped the Mercedes close to the edge and looked down. He had to wait a minute until the mist cleared and then he saw the car and two small figures moving round it far below. One of them got inside the Renault and the faint sound of the motor starting drifted up to him. After a minute it stopped, the driver got out and both men started manhandling the vehicle. Disappointed, Lennox drove off. Hoping to kill them, he had gained only a respite.

The weather higher up was foul and he was forced to cut his speed. Clouds blotted out the mountain summits, a grey mist smothered the lower slopes and the world outside the car was a shimmer of dark fir forest in the gliding fog. The address Dieter Wohl had provided – Woodcutter's Farm, Saverne – was misleading, as are so many addresses in rural France. Annette Devaud lived some distance from Saverne. Using the map drawn on the back of a menu card by the barman at the Auberge des Vosges, Lennox drove on through the mist. At one point he passed close to a canal far below him in a cut where oilskinned figures moved about on a huge barge. Turning a corner, he saw a crude wooden sign rearing above a hedge. *Woodcutter's Farm.*

The track, climbing above the highway and sunk between steep banks, was greasy mud and squelching ruts running with water. Several times he was stopped, his wheels churning uselessly, and now it was so overcast he had his headlights on. As he topped the crest of a hill the lights swept across the front of a long, steep-roofed farmhouse. The building, huddled under a looming quarry dripping with creeper, was the end of the road. Leaving the motor running, he got out into the wet. Lennox estimated he might have no more than fifteen minutes to get Annette Devaud away from the farmhouse before the Commando arrived.

The woman who opened the door held a double-barrelled shotgun which she pointed at Lennox's stomach. She told him she had seen him from an upper window and didn't admit strangers. Lennox started talking rapidly, getting a note of hysteria into his voice. 'Can I use your phone? There's been an accident down on the highway and a woman's badly hurt . . .'

'I don't have a phone . . .'

'Then get some bandages, for God's sake . . .' Lennox was waving his hands about, gesturing. Knocking the barrel aside, he jerked the gun out of her hands. 'Sorry about this, but shotguns worry me – they're liable to be feather-triggered. And there's no accident down on the highway, although there's liable to be one up here in about ten minutes – and you'll be involved in it.' He took a deep breath. 'Two men are on their way here to kill you . . .'

In one way Lennox was relieved. He had expected an infirm old lady, but the woman who had faced him with a shotgun was hardly infirm. Of medium height, her back erect, she had moved agilely when he took the gun away from her. Now she stood glaring at him, still a good-looking woman with a Roman nose and a firm jaw. 'You don't look crazy,' she said. 'Why should anyone want to kill me?'

'Because you may be able to identify the Leopard . . .'

It took him well over fifteen minutes – much too long he realized when he checked his watch – to convince Annette Devaud that he might know what he was talking about. And during that time, standing in her old-fashioned living-room, he understood something he had puzzled over ever since the barman had told him she was still alive. If she was able to identify the Leopard – which he doubted – and if by some wild chance Leon Jouvel had been right, how was it that she had not seen Guy Florian's picture during the few months since her sight had been restored? In the newspapers, in the magazines, on television? She supplied the answers after she had told him about how she had once nursed the Leopard when he had been shot in the leg.

'Since I regained my sight, Mr Bouvier, I read books . . .' She waved her hand towards the walls which were lined with books from floor to ceiling. 'All these years I have had to make do with Braille – now I can read proper books! I was always a great reader from girlhood. Now it is my ambition to read all these before I die . . .'

'But the newspapers . . .'

'I don't believe in them. Never did. They're boring. Magazines? Why read them when you have books?'

'And television?'

'Don't believe in it. And I don't have a radio.' Madame Devaud stood very erect. 'I live here on my own and I love it. I have twenty-five hectares of woodland where I wander for hours. The world I saw during the war I can do without for ever. All my supplies are delivered by a man in the village, so I'm self-contained. I actually like it that way, Mr Bouvier . . .'

'But if the Leopard were still alive you would know him?'

'The Leopard is dead . . .'

'But if he weren't?' Lennox persisted.

'I think I would know him, yes. He had good bone structure. Bones don't change . . .'

He managed to persuade her to get into the front passenger seat of the Mercedes for one reason only. 'If you drove the Renault with those two men inside it off the road,' she pointed out, 'then your own car should show traces of the collision.' After she had slipped on a heavy fur coat he took her outside and she briefly inspected the dented Mercedes, then she got inside the car quickly. 'We'd better hurry,' she informed him curtly, 'otherwise we'll meet them coming up the track. I thought you were telling the truth before I saw the damage – I'm a good judge of character, but you must admit I had a right to be suspicious . . .'

'I'm going to drop you off close to the nearest police station,' Lennox said as he began descending the track.

'I know somewhere we can hide and still see the entrance to the farm . . .'

She had wanted to bring her shotgun with her but he had put it away in a cupboard before they left the house. The Luger loaned to him by Peter Lanz was inside his coat pocket as they came closer to the highway, and he had turned off his headlights now, fearing that they might reveal the obscure entrance to the track if the Renault was coming up the highway. On his way to the farmhouse he would have missed the entrance himself without the map and the sign-board. Close to the bottom of the track the way ahead was masked by a wall of rolling mist. The mist was suddenly lit up, became a luminous gloss as headlight beams from the highway swept across it. The Renault had arrived only seconds before they were clear.

*

Lennox began depressing the brake prior to attempting the impossible – to back up the track the way they had just come. In the luminous glow blobs of moisture caught the lights and sparkled. The glow faded. Sweat was glistening on Lennox's forehead as he released the brake; on the highway a car's headlights had swept round the bend, flashing briefly over the entrance before the vehicle continued on up the highway. Risking the mud, he accelerated. 'Stop at the bottom,' Annette Devaud commanded. 'If those men find the farm after we've gone they may damage it. So get rid of the signboard, please . . .' To humour her, Lennox stopped briefly, jumped out and gave the post one hard shove. There was a wrench of rotting wood breaking and the signboard collapsed backwards out of sight. It wasn't entirely to humour her: if the Commando couldn't find the farm they might linger, looking for it, and while they were searching Annette Devaud might be able to contact the police. Jumping back behind the wheel, he followed her instructions, turning to the left out of the track – which took them away from the Saverne direction – and then he turned left off the highway, thinking that it was a fork in the road. Instead he found himself driving up a similar mudtrack which spiralled up and up round a steep rock-face.

'Where does this lead?' he asked.

'Back on to my land – to a high bluff where we can look down on the entrance to the farm . . .'

It had all happened so quickly. Not knowing the area it had seemed wiser to Lennox to follow her directions, and now she had led them up to some peak which was still not far enough away from the farm for his liking. 'They'll never find us up here,' Madame Devaud said confidently. 'And we'll be able to see what's happening – I don't like to leave my home unattended . . .' At the top of the spiralling track which was hemmed in by dense fir forest they came out into the open where an old barn was perched on the craggy bluff. The building was derelict, its roof timbers rotting, its two huge doors lying abandoned on a carpet of dead bracken. Thick tangles of undergrowth circled the rim of the bluff. Lennox switched off the motor and the headlights and the clammy silence of the forest closed round them. She had led them into a dead end.

It was 3 p.m. when André the Squirrel alighted from the Alouette helicopter which had flown him to Saverne and was driven to police headquarters by a waiting car. At headquarters he collected three policemen and the car then proceeded up into the Vosges. During his flight from Paris Boisseau decided that he should perhaps have taken Grelle's advice about providing a police guard on Annette Devaud, so now he was taking men with him to leave at the farm when he had interviewed the only known survivor who had once worked with the Leopard. At headquarters he had made the suggestion that someone should phone ahead to Woodcutter's Farm, only to be told that Madame Devaud had never had a phone installed. As they drove up into the mist-bound mountains Boisseau had become restless.

'Hurry it up,' he told the driver. 'I want to arrive at the earliest possible moment . . .'

'Hurry? In this fog, Mr Director-General?'

'Use the damned siren. Hurry . . .'

From the top of the craggy bluff behind the barn there was, as Madame Devaud had said, an excellent view down a sheer one hundred-foot drop to the highway below and to the entrance to the farm beyond. To the right of where Lennox stood a thread of a path curled down a more gently-sloping section and ended at a tiny summerhouse perched on a rocky platform seventy feet or so above the highway. Immediately below him the rock-face dropped away dizzily. Beyond the derelict barn behind him the Mercedes was parked with its nose pointing towards the track they had come up; Lennox, disturbed to find there was no way out from this eminence except down the track, was on the verge of telling Madame Devaud they were leaving. But first he was checking the highway. Through the mist he could see a car coming from the direction of Saverne, its silhouette still too blurred for him to recognize the make of vehicle. He glanced at his watch 3.15 p.m.

Behind him Annette Devaud stood inside the barn, leaning on a window ledge as she tried to see what was happening. The car crawled closer, coming very slowly as though lost, and then he felt sure it was a Renault.

Crawling past the concealed entrance to Woodcutter's Farm – now completely invisible because the signboard had been removed – it continued up the highway until it was below where Lennox stood and he was looking down directly on its roof. Pausing for a few seconds, it turned off the highway, vanishing from view as it headed up the mudtrack which led to the bluff.

'They're coming up here,' Lennox called out to Madame Devaud. 'Get round here as fast as you can . . .'

She hurried out of the barn and round the back of it and Lennox sent her down the thread of a path to the summerhouse. He waited for a second, watching her move down the path sure-footed as a goat before running round to the front of the barn, then he hid himself inside a clump of undergrowth close to the sheer drop and waited. In his right hand he held the Luger.

Vanek drove slowly up the track and beside him Lansky put on a pair of thin and expensive kid gloves. It seemed likely that he would have to throttle the old woman the barman at the Auberge des Vosges had told them lived alone. One kilometre back down the highway they had again asked for directions at the office of a sawmill. 'One kilometre up the highway from here,' they had been told. 'Up an old mudtrack . . .' Driving past the concealed entrance which led to Woodcutter's Farm they had turned up the next track. Turning a corner, they arrived on top of the bluff.

'Something's wrong – look . . .' Vanek nodded

towards the Mercedes parked on the bluff. 'I'll cover you . . .' They exchanged no more words as Lansky opened the car door very quietly and slipped out. Trained to operate as a team there was no need to say any more as both men grasped the situation; somewhere concealed on the bluff was the man Lansky had bumped into in the Rue de l'Épine, the man who less than an hour ago had tried to kill them by driving them off the road. Inside the car Vanek waited, his own Luger in his hand, waited for any sign of movement while outside the car Lansky studied the lie of the land and noted that the open-ended barn was empty. Crouched inside the undergrowth Lennox couldn't see the man behind the wheel because the Renault had stopped on a rise and the car's bulk hid the second man. Lansky's sudden manoeuvre caught him off-balance.

The Czech sprinted the short distance across the open and disappeared inside the barn. Then, for a minute or two nothing happened, or so it seemed to Lennox. Inside the barn Lansky sought elevation, somewhere high up where he could look down on the whole bluff. Very quietly he began climbing up the inner wall of the barn, using the cross-beams along the wall as steps until he reached a hole where he could peer down into the Mercedes. The car was empty. He scanned the bluff carefully until he found the silhouette of a man crouching in the undergrowth. Then he climbed down again.

With the body of the parked Mercedes between

himself and Lennox he crept forward, pausing only once to make a gesture to Vanek. The Czech nodded. Lansky had located the target. Reaching the side of the Mercedes, Lansky opened the doorhandle a centimetre at a time, then opened the door itself. He slid behind the wheel and reached for the ignition key he had seen dangling from his barn wall perch. To shoot him the Frenchman would have to stand up – and if he exposed himself to view Vanek would shoot him first.

Crouched a dozen or so metres behind the rear of the Mercedes, Lennox resisted the almost overwhelming impulse to lift his head, to see what the hell was going on. So far he had heard no sound since the second man had vanished inside the barn. Lansky, who carried in his head the precise location of the crouching man, paused as he touched the ignition key. This was going to have to be very fast indeed. And he was going to have to pull up in time or else the Mercedes would go over the sheer drop with the Frenchman. Either way the unknown man was dead: if he stayed where he was the car would topple him over the brink; if he exposed himself Vanek would kill him with a single shot. Then all four people on the bluff heard it – Madame Devaud waiting in the tiny summerhouse with her heart beating like a drum and the three men above her – heard the distant wail of an approaching police car siren. Lansky didn't hesitate. Turning on the ignition, flipping the gear into reverse, he began moving backwards at speed.

Lennox grasped what was happening instantly. Someone had got into his car. They were going to knock him over the edge. He timed it to a split second, standing up and exposing his silhouette at the moment when it was masked from the Renault by the speeding Mercedes heading straight for him. He had a camera-shutter image of the Mercedes's rear window framing the twisted-round head-and-shoulders of the driver. He fired twice through the centre of the frame, angling his gun downwards, then dived sideways, sprawling on the ground. Both bullets hit Lansky in the back and neither was instantaneously fatal. The spasm of reaction drove his right foot hard down on the accelerator. The Mercedes tore over the shrubberies and went on beyond, arcing into nothingness and then plunging down and down until it hit the highway one hundred feet below. The police patrol-car, with Boisseau inside and a local driver behind the wheel, was turning into the entrance to Woodcutter's Farm when the Mercedes landed. As the patrol-car changed direction the Mercedes burst into flames.

Vanek had heard the police siren and he reacted as he saw the Mercedes with Lansky inside disappear over the edge; he drove the Renault round in a tight circle so it faced back down the track. A few metres away he saw Lennox sprawl on the ground, then start to get back to his feet. Braking, Vanek grabbed the Luger out of his lap, took instinctive aim and fired. The Englishman was aiming his own pistol when the bullet hit him and he went down again.

Vanek drove down the twisting track at reckless speed but he managed to keep the vehicle under control. When he emerged at the bottom the blazing Mercedes blocked the road to his right, blocking off the patrol-car. He turned left and started driving west along the deserted highway, his mind racing as he worked out what he had to do next. The answer could be summed up in one word: vanish. It was the death of his partner he had just witnessed which gave him the idea. Climbing a steep stretch of highway he came to a point where the road curved sharply with a fence to his right and a warning notice. *Dangerous corner*. Stopping the Renault just beyond the bend he got out and walked back to the recently erected fence. Beyond it the ground dropped away a good two hundred feet to a rock-pile with a canal crossing the field beyond. Vanek ran back to the Renault, switched on the ignition again from outside the car, released the hand-brake, slammed the door shut as the car started moving backwards slowly, and then guided it with his hand on the steering-wheel through the open window.

He had stopped the car on a reasonably level patch of tarmac before the highway went into a further steep ascent so it moved back quite gently for a few seconds as he walked alongside; then the road began to slope down and the car picked up momentum. Vanek had withdrawn his hand from the wheel and the Renault was moving faster when it hit the white-painted fence – erected only to define the edge – broke through and dropped out of sight. He heard it hit the rock-pile with a crunch of disintegrating metal but unlike the Mercedes it did not burst into flames. Satisfied that he had given himself a temporary breathing-space, the Czech left the highway, climbing up into the forest above and began moving back at a trot towards the craggy bluff where Lansky had died.

Chapter Seventeen

Making his way through the woods, following the road below to guide him, Vanek arrived back at a knoll which overlooked the bluff in time to see Madame Devaud being escorted by a squad of men to a patrol-car. There had been a delay while she was guarded in the barn until more patrol-cars, summoned by radio, arrived with men who made a quick search of the wooded area surrounding the bluff. It was Lennox, still conscious and now inside an ambulance, who had warned Boisseau that these men were professional killers, that no chance must be taken with the life of Madame Devaud.

By the time Vanek reached the wooded knoll looking down on the bluff the convoy of patrol-cars was ready to leave. Using the small but powerful monocular glass he always carried, hidden behind a clump of pines, the Czech watched while Annette Devaud was escorted to one of the cars. The glass brought her up so close that he saw her head and shoulders clearly in his lens and he reflected that had he been equipped with a telescopic rifle she would be dead by now. Then, as though his thought had travelled down to them, the police escort huddled round her and she disappeared behind a wall of uniforms. The range was far too great for him to even contemplate using his Luger.

Crouching on his haunches, Vanek waited, as the patrol-cars disappeared down the track, led by the ambulance, and later reappeared on the highway where the mist had now dissolved. Even so, in the late afternoon light the cars were no more than a blur but it was the direction they took which interested him. Towards Saverne.

'The second killer went off the road and down to the edge of a canal,' Boisseau reported to Marc Grelle over the phone from Saverne police headquarters. 'Men should be arriving at the point of the crash just about now. And the Englishman, Lennox, has appeared. It was he, in fact, who shot the first assassin, and was then shot himself . . .'

'He is dead?' the prefect enquired from Paris.

'No, he will be all right, but he will be in hospital for a few days. He has a message for you. A very cautious man, Mr Lennox – I had to show him my card before he would pass on the message through me. He says he believes Madame Devaud can identify the Leopard . . .'

'You have Madame Devaud with you?'

'I can see her from where I am sitting . . .'

Boisseau broke off as the Saverne inspector who had just taken a call on another line signalled to him.

Listening for a moment, Boisseau resumed his call to Paris. 'This may be bad news. The Renault – the assassins' car – which went off the highway has now been examined. There was no trace of anyone inside and it appears it may have been tipped off the road deliberately to throw us off the scent. One of the assassins is still at liberty . . .'

The motor-barge chugged slowly forward out of the mist towards Vanek where he stood waiting for it by the edge of the lonely canal. His breathing was still a trifle laboured from his exertions when he had come down the mountainside from the knoll, making his way through the woods until he cautiously crossed the highway and negotiated the lower slope which brought him to the edge of the canal. He had been walking along the deserted towpath – keeping well clear of the highway – when he heard the chugging motor coming up behind him.

Gesturing to the man in yellow oilskins and peaked cap behind the wheel at the rear of the barge, Vanek called out 'Police' several times, then waited until the barge was steered close enough to the bank for him to jump on board. He showed the leathery-faced bargee his Sûreté card. 'Are you alone?' The man assured him he was and pointed out he had already been stopped higher up by policemen who were examining a crashed car. 'How far to the next lock?' Vanek demanded, ignoring the question. It was six kilometres. 'I'll travel with you,' Vanek told the man. 'I'm looking for the murderer who escaped from that car . . .'

For several minutes Vanek stood behind the man, pretending to watch the fields they were passing through while he observed the way the bargee handled the controls. Idly, as though to pass the time, he asked one or two technical questions as the barge chugged on through a remote section of the canal fogged with drifting mist. Clearing off the mountains, the mist was now settling in the narrow gulch through which the canal passes on its way to the Strasbourg plain. 'Your cap looks like a chauffeur's,' Vanek remarked. 'But then, fair enough, instead of a car you drive a barge . . .' He was still talking when he took out his Luger and shot the man in the back.

Before he threw him overboard Vanek took off his oilskin coat and put it on himself, then he donned the bargee's cap. He used a heavy chain lying on the deck of the barge to weight the body, bringing it up between the legs and over the shoulders. The barge, which he had stopped, was drifting gently as he heaved the weighted corpse over the side; pausing only to watch it sink out of sight under the grey, murky water, he re-started the engine and took up station behind the wheel. A few minutes later a bridge appeared out of the mist with a patrol car parked in the middle and a policeman leaning over the parapet. The policeman waited until the barge was close.

'Have you seen a man by himself as you came along the canal?' he shouted down.

'Only a lot of your friends checking a car which drove off the highway,' Vanek shouted back.

The policeman waited, staring down from the parapet as Vanek, looking straight ahead, guided the barge through the archway and continued down the canal. A few minutes later the bridge behind him had vanished in the mist as he saw the faint outline of another bridge ahead. Vanek reckoned he had now moved out of the immediate area where they would be searching for him and in any case he had to leave the barge before he reached the lock. Passing under the bridge, he stopped the barge, hid the oilskin under a coil of rope and climbed the muddy path which took him up to a country road. The cap he had tucked away inside his coat.

Walking a short distance along the road away from the highway, he found a convenient hiding-place behind a clump of trees where he stood and waited. During the space of fifteen minutes he let two tradesmen's vans pass and then he saw a BMW saloon approaching from the direction of the highway. There was only one man inside and the vehicle stank of money. Stepping into the middle of the road, he flagged down the car, calling out, 'Police, police . . .'

Again he showed his Sûreté card to the suspicious driver who protested he had been stopped on the highway. 'I don't believe you,' Vanek said, taking back his card. 'How far away was that?' One kilometre away, the driver informed him. A man in his late fifties, expensively suited, he had an arrogant manner which amused Vanek. Producing the Luger, he made the man move across to the passenger seat and got in behind the wheel. He put on the cap which he had taken from the dead bargee. 'I am your chauffeur,' he announced. 'If we are stopped by a police patrol you will confirm that. If you make one mistake I will shoot you three times in the stomach and you will die slowly.'

It was not so much the nature of the threat as the off-hand manner in which Vanek made it that thoroughly frightened the BMW owner. The Czech drove off in the same direction – away from the highway. Five minutes later in the middle of a wood, convinced that he had driven beyond the range of police patrols, Vanek stopped the car to check the road map purchased at Strasbourg airport which had guided himself and Lansky to Saverne. He found he could now reach Saverne again by a different route, keeping north of the canal and the highway until he almost reached the town. 'You'd better give me the car's papers,' he said. 'The chauffeur looks after things like that.' The man, who had told Vanek he was driving back to Metz, omitting to mention he was a banker, handed over the papers.

'I'm going to leave you here tied up with rope,' Vanek patted his pocket to indicate the rope. 'In an hour I shall phone the Saverne police and tell them where to find you. I am a burglar and have no wish that you should die of cold.' Getting out of the car with his prisoner, he shot him by the roadside and concealed the body behind some bushes. Returning to the BMW, he drove on by the roundabout route towards Saverne.

Boisseau had exerted all his considerable charm and powers of persuasion but he made no impression on Annette Devaud's decision. Yes, she would travel to Paris and see the police prefect if it was all that important – and here Boisseau detected a certain excitement at the prospect. Possibly her nearness to death had made her think she would like to see the capital city once more. But no, she would not fly there in a plane if they paid her a million francs. And no, she would not travel there by road; car travel made her sick. She would only go to Paris if she went there by train.

From police headquarters at Saverne, where they had rushed her by car – and that was enough driving, she had informed them fiercely – Boisseau made repeated calls to Marc Grelle, reporting the latest progress, or lack of it. And it was Grelle who took the decision to bring her to the capital by train. 'But you must take the most stringent precautions,' he warned Boisseau. 'Remember that three of the witnesses have been killed already, and they very nearly got Annette Devaud as well. Very special arrangements must be made – since at least one assassin is still at large.' After talking to Boisseau the prefect personally called Strasbourg to put his whole authority behind the operation. If everyone co-operated, Annette Devaud should be safely in Paris by nine in the evening, little more than twelve hours before Guy Florian was due to fly to Russia.

Police headquarters at Saverne was marked on the map Vanek was carrying, so when he reached the town he had no problem finding his way there. Still wearing his chauffeur's cap, he sat erect behind the wheel of the BMW as he drove slowly along the street as though looking for somewhere to park. Four patrol-cars were parked nose to tail outside the station while uniformed policemen strolled up and down, guarding the building. One of them glanced at the BMW and then looked away; as Vanek had once said to Brunner, in the capitalist West the police respect affluence and nothing is more affluent than a chauffeur-driven BMW.

Vanek had another reason for feeling confident: during his conversation with the banker he had later killed he had elicited the information that the Frenchman was driving to Metz, which meant that at least two hours should pass before anyone started worrying about his non-arrival. As he drove on Vanek was now convinced they were holding Madame Devaud under guard inside police headquarters, that soon they would have to take her somewhere else – perhaps back to her home at Woodcutter's Farm. Pulling into a side street, he reversed the car so he could get away quickly, put a coin in the parking meter and walked back to a nearby bar from where he could observe the police station.

The security operation to protect Annette Devaud's life was organized by Boisseau from inside the Saverne police station. Using the phone, and with the full weight of Grelle's authority behind him – 'This concerns the safety of the President of the French Republic' – Boisseau issued a stream of precise instructions. Before the 17.14 *Stanislas* Trans-European express for Paris left Strasbourg a special coach was linked to the train immediately behind the engine. Stickers were plastered over the windows indicating that this coach was reserved. One minute after the express was due to leave the ticket barriers were closed and gendarmes, who had previously hidden in the luggage office, filed aboard the sealed coach with automatic weapons.

The express was five minutes away from Saverne, a place it normally flew past at speed, when the gendarmes filed out of the sealed coach and moved along the full length of the train, closing all the window blinds. 'Emergency,' the inspector in charge of the detachment explained in a loud voice to a dining-car passenger who had the temerity to ask what the devil was happening. 'We've had a warning of terrorist activity . . .'

Stanislas was losing speed as it approached Saverne station which had been sealed off by the local police and extra men rushed in from Strasbourg. As the express pulled in to the station the atmosphere was eerie. To stop anyone who might raise a blind – power-operated on the TEE express, it only requires the touch of a button – batteries of lights mounted on trucks were shone on the side of the train as it stopped. Anyone looking out would have been blinded by the glare. In the waiting-room, Boisseau sat with Madame Devaud, muffled in her old-fashioned fur coat, who was still calm and controlled despite all the fuss. 'Is it true I shall be having a whole coach to myself?' she enquired. Boisseau assured her it was true. He personally escorted her to the coach after making her put on a pair of dark glasses – partly as a disguise, partly as protection against the glare of the lights. As she moved along the corridor to her compartment the train also began to move again.

A short distance from the station, out of sight of the convoy of parked patrol-cars, the chauffeur of a BMW was having a little trouble with his engine. With the hood up he stooped over the motor, checking the wiring. The express had just begun to move when he sorted out the problem, closing the hood and getting back behind the wheel. He drove off at speed, accelerating through the darkness as soon as he had left Saverne behind, heading for Strasbourg Airport where there is a frequent Air Inter plane service to Paris.

Chapter Eighteen

In Paris Marc Grelle believed he had found out how the list of Lasalle's three witnesses had been passed back to Moscow. As events had unfolded, as information came in showing that a Soviet Commando was eliminating the very people whose names had been on Lasalle's list, the prefect realized that the coincidence was too great. Someone in Paris in addition to himself had seen the list and had then caused it to be transmitted to Russia. The Soviet Commando had then been despatched to the West.

He started his discreet enquiries at the Ministry of the Interior, tracing the route his memo containing the list had followed. Grelle had, of course, sent his memo to Roger Danchin by despatch rider late on the morning of Tuesday, 14 December. François Merlin, the Minister's assistant, who liked the prefect, proved helpful. 'We haven't heard from Hugon, our pipeline into Colonel Lasalle, recently,' Grelle explained, 'so I'm double-checking the security of our arrangements . . .' It didn't surprise Merlin that the prefect himself was making the enquiry: all Paris knew Grelle's quaint habit of attending to details personally.

Copies of the communications from Hugon were restricted to a very narrow circle: Grelle himself, Boisseau, the Minister and his assistant, Merlin. Pressed to go through the files, Merlin told Grelle that the confidential memo containing the names and addresses of the three witnesses had arrived at the Place Beauvau just before noon on Tuesday, 14 December. 'I was in the office when he read it,' Merlin remarked. 'A few minutes later Ambassador Vorin arrived for a private word with the Minister before going on to the Elysée. By then my chief had dealt with the memo . . .'

'Dealt with it?'

'He had a copy of your memo sent to the President's office at once. I took it down myself and handed it to a despatch rider who was just leaving for the Elysée. On my way down I met Ambassador Vorin who had just arrived and was waiting to see Danchin. The Elysée, of course, sees everything that concerns Colonel Lasalle,' Merlin explained.

The prefect grunted and drank the rest of the cup of coffee Merlin had provided. 'Do you think I could have a word with the monitoring section?' he suggested.

Among the cluster of radio masts which rise up from the roof of the Ministry of the Interior in the Place Beauvau is the antenna used for monitoring radio signals transmitted by foreign embassies. At 4 p.m. on 14 December the technician on duty inside the monitoring unit recorded a long signal emanating from the

Soviet Embassy at 79, Rue de Grenelle. The tape-recording of the signal was handed to the Russian section who went through the routine motions of studying the coded signal – routine because no one expected to be able to unravel the stream of ciphers.

The Russians use the one-time code, which is unbreakable. Codes are broken by discovering a pattern; only a fragment can unlock the key. But when each element of a code is linked to a particular book – often a novel (in the past the Russian encoders have favoured Dickens) – there is no way to break the code without knowing which of the thousands of books published over the past hundred years has been used. And as the same book is never used twice it is literally a one-time code which is employed.

It was cryptographer Pierre Jadot who had studied the signal transmitted, and he immediately recalled the incident when Grelle asked him about any Soviet signals transmitted on that day. 'I made my usual routine report in a memo to the Minister,' he said, 'and I remember suggesting that one section of the signal could have been a list of names and addresses . . .'

'You are sure about that?' Grelle asked casually.

'By no means – it is no more than an educated guess. And there is no way of cracking the Soviet codes.'

'Can you give me any idea of how long it might take the Soviet encoder at this end to prepare that signal for transmission? Even a guess would be helpful.'

Jadot took down a file, extracted his copy of the signal and studied it for a few minutes. 'At a guess – it can be no more than that – I would say between one and two hours. Probably nearer two hours . . .'

Thanking Jadot, the prefect left the Ministry and called at the Elysée on his way back to the prefecture. Again he asked to see the visitors' register, and again he concealed what he was really looking for by glancing at several pages. Then he drove straight back to his office and called in Boisseau. It took him only a few minutes to explain. 'The point is Leonid Vorin, the Soviet ambassador, left the Elysée to return to his embassy at 1.45 p.m. Allowing for the traffic, he must have got back say half an hour later – at 2.15 p.m. That gave the Soviet encoder just under two hours to prepare the signal for the transmission which began at four o'clock – which fits in with the time Jadot estimated it would take. A signal which may well have contained Colonel Lasalle's list of names and addresses . . .'

'Which brings us back to the men who knew about the list and who saw Ambassador Vorin,' Boisseau replied gravely. 'Danchin and . . .'

'The president,' Grelle added. 'I have the feeling that daylight is beginning to break through this business.'

'Or the blackest night,' Boisseau commented.

It was six o'clock in the evening when Alain Blanc came up to Grelle's office at the prefecture looking grim and despondent. The *Stanislas* express with Annette Devaud on board was now racing through the night on its way to Paris. At Charles de Gaulle Airport mechanics were busily servicing the Concorde which would fly President Florian to Moscow within a few hours. Blanc came into the office with a savage expression as he closed the door and flopped into a chair.

'You've heard about the Soviet convoy, of course?' the Minister of National Defence enquired. 'It is now inside the Sicilian Narrows and its destination could be either Barcelona or even Lisbon.'

'What is worrying you, sir?' the prefect asked quietly.

'Everything!' Blanc threw up his hands in an expressive gesture. 'The Russian convoy. The persistent rumours of an imminent *coup d'état* in Paris. By whom, for God's sake? And half an hour ago I hear for the first time that the President made a secret flight to Germany on Monday – to the French Army GHQ at Baden-Baden!'

Grelle stared at the minister in astonishment. 'You didn't know he had flown to Baden-Baden? He didn't inform you? The Minister of National Defence? I thought you knew – I made the arrangements myself with GLAM . . .' GLAM – Groupe Liaison Aérien Ministériel – is the small air fleet which is reserved for ministerial and presidential usage. 'What on earth is going on?' the prefect asked.

'That I would like to know myself,' Blanc said grimly. 'And I have just heard also that our two armoured divisions in Germany, the 2nd and the 5th, are moving through the Ardennes on their way back to France, which will leave no French troops on German soil. When I phone the Elysée to request an immediate appointment I am told that the president is busy with the Soviet ambassador . . .'

'And he leaves for Moscow tomorrow.'

'Precisely,' Blanc snapped. 'Recently he has been acting as though I don't exist – a total change of mood and method I cannot even begin to understand. It is almost as though he were trying to provoke my resignation. He may succeed – I may have to resign . . .'

'Don't do that,' Grelle said quickly. 'We may need you yet. You've discussed this with other ministers?'

'They are supine!' Blanc exploded. 'They think he is God and they are the apostles! I am the only one who has started to ask questions, to demand what the hell is going on. I tell you, I shall have to resign if this goes on . . .'

'Don't do it. We may need you desperately,' Grelle repeated.

Only a few minutes after Blanc had left Grelle was told he had another visitor waiting to see him and he asked his secretary to repeat the name, sure she must have got it wrong. But no, it was Commissioner Suchet, his old enemy of the counter-espionage service. Apologizing for calling without an appointment, Suchet squeezed his gross bulk into a chair and came straight to the point. 'These *coup d'état* rumours are coming from the Red Belt suburbs – from Billancourt. Certain agitators are very active today saying that soon the people may have to defend the Republic. Coming from that scum, it's a great joke, but I'm not laughing – I'm worried stiff. An hour ago some of my agents uncovered an arms dump at Renault. I thought you ought to know. Someone must act . . .'

Grelle took decisive action at once, first phoning Roger Danchin to obtain his approval, then issuing a stream of orders. Guards were trebled on all public buildings. A special detachment was sent to key points like the telephone exchanges and the television transmitters. Tough CRS troops were drafted from the barracks outside the city into Paris to guard the bridges over the Seine. With a minimum of fuss Paris was moving into a state of siege. Then at 7.30 p.m. Grelle made what appeared to be a routine visit to the Elysée to double-check security ready for the drive to the airport the next day.

Arriving at the palace, it didn't particularly surprise Grelle to discover that Soviet Ambassador Vorin was not only not there; he had not been anywhere near the Elysée since the morning. Someone had been instructed to keep ex-paratrooper Blanc away from the place until Florian's departure on the following day. Admitted to the palace by an usher who opened the plate-glass doors for him, the prefect wandered towards the back of the building, opening and closing doors in what appeared a random way. He was looking for Kassim, Florian's dog.

He found him outside in the walled garden where the dog spent so much of its time – and where the president was accustomed to strolling with Leonid Vorin when the Russian visited the Elysée. As Grelle appeared the Alsatian barked and romped forward through the dark, jumping up to his full height and perching his forepaws over the prefect's shoulders while it panted happily in his face. Grelle reached up and fondled the animal for a short while round the studded collar which encircled its powerful neck. Then he gave Kassim a hard slap to make him get down and went back inside the palace.

From there he walked quickly to the nearby rue des Saussaies and up on to the fourth floor of Sûreté headquarters. The electronics expert he had earlier sent there from the prefecture was waiting and he gave him certain instructions before returning to the Elysée to collect his car and drive back to his office. It had been easier than he had expected, and this was one decision he did not inform Boisseau about. One career at stake was quite enough.

The prefect had just attached a tiny transmitter to the inside of Kassim's studded collar. The words of anyone who spoke close enough to the dog would be relayed to the receiver linked to a tape-recorder inside the locked room at the Rue des Saussaies, only a few dozen metres away from the Elysée Palace.

Chapter Nineteen

So far Vanek had avoided travelling by air. At airports individual passengers can easily be checked, searched, but to reach Paris ahead of the express carrying Annette Devaud he had no alternative. As he bought his ticket from Air Inter and made his way to the departure point the Czech carried nothing incriminating. He had tossed the Luger pistol into a canal on his way to the airport. The BMW was now standing in the airport car park. And he had thrown the bargee's cap into the canal after the Luger.

When he bought his ticket he paid for a return fare: he had no intention of returning to Strasbourg but for airport personnel there is something normal and reassuring about a return ticket. He had no trouble passing through the security checks, partly because by now he was no longer alone. Waiting in the departure lounge for the Air Inter flight, he observed an attractive girl of about twenty-two who was obviously on her own; he further observed as she took off her glove to light a cigarette that she wore neither an engagement nor wedding ring.

He lit her cigarette and sat beside her, looking

anxious. 'I do hope this flight for Paris isn't late. It's my sister's birthday and she expects her present . . .' He prattled on, instinctively choosing the right approach. Most women were happy to chat with Vanek if it wasn't too obvious a pick-up; the reference to a sister was reassuring, clearly indicating a man who treated women with respect. They went through the security check together. Vanek holding her small hand-case, joking with her, and everyone thought they were a couple.

On the plane he sat beside her, found out that her name was Michelle Robert, that she was personal assistant to an executive with a tyre firm whose head-quarters were at La Défense. Before they were half-way to Paris he had extracted her phone number. And somewhere over Champagne their Fokker 27 aircraft overtook the *Stanislas* express carrying Madame Devaud to the capital.

The TEE express was due to arrive at the Gare de l'Est at 9 p.m. Vanek, who had phoned the railway station from the airport to check its arrival time, caught the 6.30 flight from Strasbourg which landed him at Orly Airport at 7.30. Fortunately, Michelle Robert was being met by a friend, so he got rid of her without any trouble. Mistrusting Paris traffic, Vanek used the Orly-rail system to reach the city and then he changed to the Métro. He calculated that with a little luck he should reach the Gare de l'Est just before the express arrived.

*

The express from Strasbourg reached the Gare de l'Est at 9.06 p.m. Normally the ticket barrier is open – tickets have been examined aboard the train – and people just walk off, but on the night of 22 December the barrier was closed and no one was permitted near the platform.

'It is an outrage,' one passenger aboard the express fumed. 'My wife is expecting me . . .'

'There is a terrorist alert. You must wait,' the inspector informed him. And in that much of a rush, he thought cynically, it can only be your mistress who awaits you.

The superintendent Grelle had personally despatched to the station had sprinkled the concourse beyond the platform with armed plain-clothes detectives. One man, equipped with a sniper-scope rifle, waited in a window overlooking the platform. And some of the detectives who lounged about the station even had suitcases filled with files they had grabbed from their offices to provide weight. The door to the sealed coach was opened and a circle of plain-clothes men gathered at the foot of the steps. There were no uniformed gendarmes in sight. 'Nothing conspicuous,' Grelle had warned. 'Keep it as normal as possible.' With Boisseau in front, Madame Devaud climbed down the steps and the crowd of plain-clothes men closed round her. Boisseau separated himself from the group, going out on to the concourse and standing idly while he lit a cigarette, his coat hanging open so he could reach his revolver at a second's notice. This was the moment he feared most – getting her from the train to the car. The group moved across the concourse, moving slowly at Madame Devaud's pace. It went on into the exit hall, then outside to where a car door had already been opened. Several passengers were stopping now, beginning to take notice. It was impossible to cover up completely.

Boisseau heard a car door slam shut and sighed with relief. Moving quickly out of the exit he climbed inside another police car and pulled the door shut. 'I want sirens all the way,' he told the man beside the driver who had radio communication with the other cars. 'We jump lights where we can . . .' The radio man transmitted the message and the motorcade moved off. There were four vehicles. One in front. Then Madame Devaud's. A third vehicle – to ram any car which tried to intercept. And Boisseau bringing up the rear. It was 9.09 p.m.

Vanek ran up out of the Métro and into the main station of the Gare de l'Est. He dropped to walking pace as he saw the *Stanislas* in the distance and when he got close he was in time to see the last passengers coming through the open barrier. It was 9.15 p.m. He had been badly delayed on the Métro but there had been nothing he could do about it; getting off and finding a taxi would only have taken longer. He waited for a few minutes by a bookstall – on the off-chance that they were going to take off the Devaud woman when all the other passengers had disembarked – and then he went to a phone booth to call the Paris number.

'Salicetti here . . .'

'I have nothing for you . . .'

'I have something for you,' Vanek snapped, 'so stay on the line. The previous order you specified will now have to be fulfilled in Paris – I am speaking from the Gare de l'Est. I need the firm's address.'

For the first time since the phone calls had begun the cold, anonymous voice at the Paris number was unsure of itself. There was a brief pause. 'You had better call back at half-hour intervals – ten o'clock, ten-thirty, and so on,' the voice replied eventually. 'I have no information at this moment . . .'

'I shall need more samples,' Vanek said tersely.

The voice recovered its poise; it was ready for this contingency. Salicetti must go to the Bar Lepic in the Place de la Madeleine, giving the firm's name, Lobineau, to the proprietor, who would hand him a baggage storage key. The samples were in a public locker at the Gare du Nord. And would he be sure to call back at half-hourly intervals? At 10 p.m., 10.30 . . . Vanek slammed down the receiver. Bloody hell, what a primitive arrangement. Things were managed with greater finesse when he was in Paris. He took a cab to the Bar Lepic, collected an envelope, left a five-franc tip to make the transaction look normal to anyone who might be watching, and took another cab to the Gare du Nord.

Using the numbered key he found inside the envelope, he opened the luggage locker at the Gare du Nord and took out a hold-all bag covered in tartan cloth, which again was stupid: it was too noticeable. It was a very long bag, the type used to carry around tennis racquets. But the contents inside showed that someone had used his head: a French MAT sub-machine-gun with a wire stock, the magazine folded parallel to the barrel to make it inoperative, and a spare magazine; a Smith & Wesson .38 revolver with spare rounds; and a short, wide-bladed knife inside a clip-on sheath. Vanek crossed the deserted hall to the opposite battery of lockers, chose an empty one, slipped the hold-all inside, shut the door, inserted his coin and turned the key. He had no intention of carrying weapons until it was necessary – especially since he had noticed during his two cab-rides intense police activity in the streets. There were also truckloads of CRS bully-boys parked at strategic points. But Vanek had also noticed that cabs were still moving normally about the city; no one ever notices the Parisian cab-driver who is as much a part of the scenery as the Louvre.

Vanek, who had not eaten anything since the snack-lunch in the Renault on the way from Strasbourg to Saverne, would have liked to snatch a sandwich and a cup of coffee. He looked at his watch and swore. It was almost ten o'clock; time to make the next phone call. Using one of the station phones, he dialled the number. He had hardly announced it was Salicetti speaking when the voice broke in, as abrupt as ever.

'Rue des Saussaies. Now! You know where I mean?'

321

'Yes . . .'

Vanek broke the connection first this time. So they had taken Madame Devaud to the Sûreté Nationale headquarters, the fortress of the capitalist police system. Collecting the tartan hold-all, Vanek went out into the street beyond the Gare du Nord, ignoring the official taxi pick-up point. He wanted to make a careful choice, selecting a certain type of cab-driver for the next stage of the operation.

The Police Prefect of Strasbourg, who was not especially well disposed towards Marc Grelle – unlike the prefect of Lyon – was disturbed about the elaborate arrangements made to transport Madame Devaud to Paris. When he had tried to elicit further details from Grelle on the phone he had been told brusquely, 'This concerns the safety of the president and I am not at liberty to go into the matter further . . .' Annoyed – and determined to cover himself – he phoned the Ministry of the Interior in Paris where he spoke to the Minister's assistant, François Merlin. 'Grelle was very cagey on the phone,' the Strasbourg prefect complained. 'I gathered this Devaud woman was an important witness in some case he is working on . . .' He was going off the line when he spoke again. 'I insist the Minister hears about this.'

The efficient Merlin immediately dictated a memo which was put on the Minister's desk where it lay undisturbed – and unread – for over an hour. It was

8.45 p.m. before Roger Danchin, who had been attending a long meeting to check on the security for the presidential motorcade drive to the airport the following morning, walked back into his office. 'An important case Grelle is working on?' he queried with Merlin when he had read the memo. 'Devaud is a reasonably common name but it could be something to do with the attempted assassination case. I must tell the president...' He lifted the phone which would put him direct through to the Elysée.

At 9.15 p.m., summoned by an urgent phone call, Ambassador Vorin arrived at the Elysée, and his visit was duly recorded by the duty officer in the visitors' register. Florian already had his coat on and, as was his custom, led the Soviet ambassador out into the walled garden where they could talk undisturbed. The Alsatian, Kassim, ready for a breath of fresh air like his master, came with them, sniffing around in a shrubbery as they conferred in low tones. Vorin's latest visit was very brief, lasting only a few minutes, and he was then driven back at speed to the Soviet Embassy in the Rue de Grenelle.

The method of communication between Vorin and Carel Vanek was carefully arranged so that no link between the two men could ever be established. Arriving back at the embassy, Vorin immediately summoned the Second Secretary and gave him a message. The Secretary, who would normally have made the call from a phone booth inside the nearest Métro station, returned to his own office, locked the door and dialled the number of an apartment on the Left Bank near the Cluny Museum. 'The deeds of the Devaud property will be found at the Rue des Saussaies. Have you got that?' The man at the other end of the line only had time to say yes before the connection was broken.

The apartment near the Cluny was occupied by a man who had never attracted the attention of the police. Equipped with Danish papers under the name of Jurgensen, he was in fact a Pole called Jaworski who did not even know that the calls he received came back from the Soviet Embassy. It was 9.50 p.m. when he took this call. At 10 p.m. he passed on the information when Vanek phoned him again from the Gare du Nord.

They took Annette Devaud to a room on the fourth floor of Sûreté headquarters in the Rue des Saussaies where Grelle was waiting for her. He could have interviewed her at the prefecture on the Ile de la Cité but he still thought it wise to keep up the fiction that this concerned the Lasalle *affaire*, and this operation was officially conducted from the Sûreté. To avoid upsetting Danchin, he had even phoned his assistant, Merlin, at eight o'clock to tell him a witness was on the way from Alsace whom he would interview at the Rue des Saussaies. Merlin had mentioned this to Danchin before the Minister phoned the Elysée. Alone with the first live witness he had been able to lay his hands on, Grelle talked for few minutes to put Annette Devaud at her ease. Then he explained why she had been brought to Paris.

'And you really think that after all these years you can identify the Leopard?' he asked gently.

'If he's alive – as, you say – yes! I lost my sight for thirty years before that doctor carried out his miracle operation. What do you think I saw in my mind's eye all those years when the world was only sounds and smells? I saw everyone I had ever met. And, as I told you, I nursed the Leopard through an illness.' Her voice dropped. 'And later he was responsible for the death of my only daughter, Lucie . . .'

As Grelle had foreseen, he felt horribly uncomfortable. Although Madame Devaud did not realize it – and it was Boisseau who had mentioned the point when phoning from Saverne – the prefect was the man who had been compelled to shoot Lucie Devaud. 'It was many years ago,' he reminded her, 'since you knew the Leopard. Even if he is still alive he may have changed out of all recognition . . .'

'Not the Leopard.' Her pointed chin jutted upwards. 'He had good bone structure – like me. Bones can't change. You can't hide bones . . .'

Grelle was so determined to test her that he had devised an odd method of identification. Remembering that Boisseau had mentioned over the phone that she was an amateur portrait artist, he had brought into the room Identikit equipment. He explained to her how the system worked, asked her what she would like to drink, and was so amused when she requested cognac that he joined her. He started by helping her with the Identikit, and then let her get on with it by herself. She was obviously enjoying the new game.

Starting with the outline of the head, she began to build up the face of a man. The hairpiece came first. Grelle opened several box-files of printed hair pieces and helped her select several. Soon they were arguing. 'You've got it wrong,' she snapped. 'I told you he brushed his hair high on the forehead . . .' The face began to take shape.

The eyebrows she found quickly, but the eyes gave her trouble. 'They were very unusual – compelling,' she explained. She found the eyes at the back of the file and then worried over the nose. 'Noses are difficult . . .' She chose a nose and added it to the portrait. 'That's the nose. I think it's his most characteristic feature . . .' It took her five minutes to locate the mouth, ferreting in a fresh file, trying one and then another before she was satisfied. Pursing her own mouth, she screwed up her eyes as she completed the Identikit while Grelle watched with an expressionless face. 'That's the Leopard,' she said a few minutes later. 'That's the way he was.'

The prefect stood up, showing no reaction. 'Madame Devaud, I know you don't like television, but I would like you to watch certain programme extracts I had made earlier this evening. They are recorded on what we call cassettes. You will see three men briefly – all of them older than the face you built up on the Identikit.

I want you to tell me which – if any – of these three men is the Leopard.'

'He has changed a lot then?'

Grelle didn't reply as he went to the television set and switched on. The first extract showed Roger Danchin broadcasting at the time of the riots a year earlier when he had appealed for calm, warning that mass arrests would follow any further demonstrations. The set went blank and then Alain Blanc appeared, confident and emphatic, telling the nation why more had to be spent on the defence budget.

Madame Devaud said nothing, reaching for her glass of cognac as the image faded, to be replaced by Guy Florian making one of his anti-American speeches. As always, he spoke with panache and sardonic wit, gesturing vigorously occasionally, his expression serious, but smiling the famous smile as he closed. The screen went blank. Grelle stood up and went over to switch off the set.

'The last man,' Annette Devaud said, 'the man attacking the Americans. He hasn't changed all that much, has he?'

Carel Vanek chose his cab with care, standing on the sidewalk with the tartan hold-all at his feet. He avoided any vehicle with a youngster behind the wheel, but he didn't want an elderly driver either; older people can panic, acting on impulse. He was looking for a middle-aged driver with a family to think of, with the experience to make him cautious. He yelled at an approaching cab, waving his hand.

'It's a place off the Boulevard des Capucines,' he told the driver. 'I'm not sure of the address but I'll recognize the street when I see it. A side-turning off to the left . . .'

He settled back in the cab with the hold-all on his lap. What he had said to the driver was true: he didn't know the name of the street but he had walked down it several times three years earlier, a street which was narrow, dark and unlit at night. There was very little traffic about at that hour and Capucines, a street of expensive shops, was almost empty on the chilly December evening, despite the closeness of Christmas. The driver went slowly to give his passenger a chance to locate the street.

'Turn here!'

Vanek had opened the window behind the driver wider to speak to him and he stayed leaning forward as the cab turned and entered a narrow, curving street. The walls of the high buildings on either side closed in on them and the street was as deserted as Vanek remembered it. Capucines was only a memory now as the cab cruised deeper inside the dark canyon while he waited for further instructions. Vanek strained his eyes to see beyond the windscreen, one hand inside the hold-all. Soon they would be near to the far end, moving out into a more-frequented area.

'Here we are. Stop!'

The driver pulled up, set his brake and left the engine running. Vanek pressed the muzzle of the Smith

& Wesson into the back of the driver's neck. 'Don't move. This is a gun.' The driver stiffened, sat very still. Vanek shot him once.

It was 10.45 p.m. when a patrol-car drew up outside the entrance to the Sûreté headquarters on the Rue des Saussaies. Boisseau himself came out of the building first and looked up and down the quiet street. There was nothing in sight except a lone taxicab coming from the direction of the Place Beauvau. Boisseau held up his hand to stop them bringing Madame Devaud out and waited. Two gendarmes stood on the sidewalk with him. The driver was behind the wheel of the waiting patrol-car, his engine ticking over.

Grelle had decided at the last moment to use only one car to take Madame Devaud to a hotel the Sûreté used for guarding important witnesses; a single car is less conspicuous than a motorcade. Also it would be able to move very fast at this hour when the Paris streets were deserted. Grelle himself, standing back inside the arch with Madame Devaud and three detectives, was waiting to see her departure. The cab came towards the entrance slowly and Boisseau noted it was not for hire. So far as he could see the back was empty; the driver was obviously going off duty. The cab cruised past and the driver took one hand off the wheel to stifle a yawn.

Watching its tail-light, Boisseau made a beckoning gesture and the small procession emerged from under the archway. The three detectives crowded round Madame Devaud, moving at her deliberate pace. They reached the sidewalk. Inside the archway Grelle lit a cigarette, a walkie-talkie tucked under his arm. He would be in constant touch with the radio-controlled vehicle until it reached its destination in the seventh arrondissement. Madame Devaud had moved across the sidewalk and was about to enter the car.

'Don't worry – it is only a few minutes' drive,' Boisseau assured her.

'Tell him not to drive too fast. I didn't enjoy the journey from the Gare de l'Est at all.'

'I'll tell him. It will only be a few minutes,' Boisseau repeated.

Vanek, wearing the cab-driver's cap – he had great faith in headgear as a medium of disguise – reached the Place des Saussaies which is round the corner from the entrance to Sûreté headquarters. He had been cruising past the archway at intervals – many cabs take this short-cut at night – completing the circuit round the large building and coming back again. Now he turned in a tight circle and drove back against the one-way system. Boisseau was about to help Madame Devaud into the car when he saw the cab returning at speed. He shouted a warning but the cab arrived at the worst possible moment – while the huddled group, bunched together, was trapped in the open.

Vanek held the wheel with one hand while he cradled the sub-machine-gun under his right arm, his index finger curled inside the trigger-guard. He fired a steady burst, the weapon on automatic, the muzzle held in a fixed position, so he used the movement of the vehicle to create an arc of fire, emptying the whole magazine before he went past them, still driving the wrong way and disappearing into the Place Beauvau.

Grelle, by himself and free from the group, was the only one who even fired at the cab, and one revolver shot smashed the rear window. Then he was using the walkie-talkie, which put him straight through to central control, already organized for the president's motorcade drive to Charles de Gaulle Airport the following day. Via Grelle, the cab's description, including the smashed window and the direction it had taken, was circulated within one minute to every patrol-car within a five-mile radius. Only then did Grelle turn to look at the tragic scene on the sidewalk.

The two gendarmes had run off after the cab. Boisseau, shielded by the open car door, had escaped unscathed, but the three detectives lay on the ground, two of them moaning and gasping, the third very still. They had to lift the two men gently to get at Madame Devaud who lay face down, and when they eased her over they saw where the assassin's bullets had stitched a pattern across her chest.

'Armed and dangerous . . .'

All over Paris patrol-cars leapt forward, moving inwards on a cordon pattern laid down by the commissioner in charge at central control. In a way he welcomed the emergency on the eve of the president's departure: it gave him a chance to check the system. The cordon closed in like a contracting web, its approximate centre-point the Place Beauvau, and with sirens screaming patrol-cars rushed along the big boulevards. The commissioner at control was moving into action his entire force, repeating time and again the warning.

'Armed and dangerous . . .'

They found Vanek quite close to the Sûreté. His cab was spotted crossing the Place de la Concorde on the Tuileries side. Patrol-cars converged on the vast square, coming in over the Seine bridge, from Champs-Elysées, Rivoli and the Avenue Gabriel. A blaze of lamps, empty only seconds earlier, the Place was suddenly filled with noise and movement, with the high-pitched screams of sirens, the swivel of patrol-car headlights. Vanek braked by the kerb, jumped out with the sub-machine-gun and ran for the only possible refuge. The Tuileries gardens.

At this point in the Place de la Concorde the pavement by the kerb has a low stone wall beyond it. Beyond that lies another pavement and beyond that a high stone wall rises up to a lofty balustrade with the Tuileries park beyond like a huge viewing platform overlooking the entire Place. Vanek started running for the entrance to Tuileries at ground level, saw a patrol-car pull up, blocking him off. Jerking up his weapon, he emptied the second magazine and everywhere policemen dropped flat. Throwing down the gun, Vanek jumped over the low stone wall, ran across the second sidewalk and began hauling himself up the wall, using projecting stones like a ladder. To his left and below him a flight of steps went down and underground. He had almost reached the balustrade; once over it he would have the whole park to hide in. Behind him he heard shouts, the screams of half a dozen more patrol-cars rushing into the square. He whipped one leg over the balustrade. The park beyond was a dark, tree-filled vastness, a place to manoeuvre in.

They caught him in a crossfire. Two gendarmes to the right on the sidewalk below, another group of three to the left as he hung above the world below him. There was a fusillade of shots as the gendarmes emptied their magazines, very loud in the place because all the patrol-cars had now halted. Vanek hung in the night, one leg draped over the balustrade, then his limp hand lost its grip and he slipped over, falling as they went on firing, crashing down into the deep staircase well where a large notice proclaimed 'Descente Interdite.' Descent Forbidden.

Chapter Twenty

'A woman who can positively identify me as the Leopard has arrived in Paris. Her name is Annette Devaud. Apparently they brought her in under heavy guard aboard the *Stanislas* express . . .'

A dog barked, a deafening sound on the tape. The familiar, so recognizable voice, spoke sharply.

'Quiet, Kassim! I don't see how there is time to intercept her. I can personally take no action which will not arouse the gravest suspicion . . .'

'Why did you not add her to the Lasalle list earlier?' The second voice, husky, accented, was also quite recognizable.

'She went blind at the end of the war – so I assumed she was harmless. My assistant phoned the police chief at Saverne just before you arrived – apparently she had an operation recently which restored her sight. This is the most appalling mess, Vorin, coming at the last moment . . .'

'Mr President, we may be able to do something . . .'

'I added her to the list later – when Danchin sent me his routine report with the *Frankfurter Allgemeine Zeitung* letter which mentioned her name. Your people were supposed to have dealt with the problem . . .'

'Something went wrong . . .'

'Then you cannot blame me!' An argument was developing; the well-known voice was sharp, cutting. 'It is imperative that you rectify your error . . .'

'Then I must leave at once for the embassy, Mr President. We have reached a stage where minutes count. Do you know where they will take the Devaud woman?'

'To the Rue des Saussaies . . .'

Alone in the fourth-floor room at Sûreté headquarters, Marc Grelle switched off the tape-recorder which had been linked to the tiny transmitter inserted inside Kassim's studded collar. He had played it twice, standing while he listened to it with a frozen expression, concentrating on the pitch of the voices. It was a futile exercise – replaying the tape – because the timbre of Guy Florian's voice had come over with such clarity the first time. In any case the words spoken were diabolically conclusive.

Staring at the opposite wall, the prefect lit a cigarette, hardly aware of the action. For days now the terrible truth had thrust itself into his mind and he had refused to accept the evidence. Gaston Martin had seen three men enter the Elysée, one of them the president. The surveillance on Danchin and Blanc had revealed no evidence of a Soviet link contacting either man, but Florian met Soviet Ambassador Vorin almost daily. And so on . . . Staring at the wall, smoking his cigarette,

Grelle felt a sense of nausea, like a husband who has just found his wife in bed with a coarse and brutal lover.

Extracting the tape from the machine, he put it inside his pocket. Picking up the phone he asked for an outside line and then dialled a number. Still in a state of shock he made a great effort to keep his voice cold and impersonal.

'Alain Blanc? Grelle here. I need to see you immediately. No, don't come to the prefecture. I'm going straight back to my apartment. Yes, something has happened. You will need a glass of cognac before I tell you ...'

The 2nd and 5th French Armoured Divisions, stationed in the German Federal Republic and commanded by Gen. Jacques Chassou, were already on the move. The German authorities had been informed, the consent of the government of the Duchy of Luxembourg had been obtained – all at very short notice. Within hours the advance elements of the two divisions had crossed the Luxembourg frontier and were moving into the Ardennes on their way back to France. At 10 p.m., just before he flew to Sedan, Gen. Chassou opened the secret instructions which had been personally handed to him by President Florian when he made his lightning visit to Baden-Baden on the previous Monday.

'For the moment you will not return to Germany at

the conclusion of the exercise. Once over the Sedan bridges you will proceed on into France ... You will halt in the general military area of Metz ... transport parks have been prepared ...'

Handing the secret communication to his assistant, Col. Georges Doissy, Chassou told him to make the necessary adjustments and then flew off to Sedan. Doissy, who had once served under Col. René Lasalle, immediately realized that this order would leave Germany isolated, with only a token British detachment alongside the German Army facing Russia. He thought about it for a few minutes, then he remembered President de Gaulle's advice to the recently elected President Kennedy. 'Listen only to yourself ...' Doissy picked up the phone and asked the night operator to put him through urgently to the Minister of National Defence, Alain Blanc.

At 10 p.m. on 22 December, Commander Arthur Leigh-Browne, RN, the British officer in charge of the NATO analyst team watching the Soviet convoy, K.12, issued a routine report. 'If K.12 continues on her present course, at her present reduced speed, she can make landfall at Barcelona by changing course again some time within the next twelve to eighteen hours ...' Being a precise man, he added a rider. 'Theoretically she could also make landfall on the south coast of France, at Marseille and Toulon ...' Following the normal practice, a coded signal of his report was despatched to all NATO defence ministers.

Abou Benefeika, the Arab terrorist who had come within seconds of destroying the El Al airliner at Orly, tried to make himself more comfortable as he rested his head against the 'pillow' of bricks in the basement of the abandoned building at 17 Rue Réamur. The fact that he had folded his jacket and placed it on top of the bricks did not help him to sleep, nor did the rustle of tiny feet he kept hearing; the rats also had taken up unofficial tenancy in the condemned building.

During the day Benefeika had crept out of his hiding-place to purchase food and drink from the local shops, and because this district of Paris was a ghetto peopled by Algerians he was not too worried about breaking cover. Absorbed as he was in his task, on the lookout only for uniformed police, he failed to notice two scruffily dressed men who followed him everywhere with their hands in their pockets. Returning to his squalid hideaway, he ate and drank while outside one of the scruffily dressed men climbed up to the first floor of the building opposite. Using his walkie-talkie, Sergeant Pierre Gallon made his routine report. 'Rabbit has returned to his burrow. Observation is continuing . . .'

'Then I must leave at once for the embassy, Mr President. We have reached a stage where minutes count.

Do you know where they will take the Devaud woman?'

'To the Rue des Saussaies . . .'

In his apartment on the Ile Saint-Louis Grelle switched off the tape-recorder and looked at Alain Blanc who sat in an elegant chair with his legs crossed and a glass of cognac in his hand. The Minister's expression was grim: it was the third time the recording had been played back for his benefit and he now knew the conversation word for word. He drank the rest of his cognac in one gulp and there were beads of sweat on his high-domed forehead. He looked up as Grelle spoke.

'Within two hours of that conversation – I phoned the security officer at the Elysée and Vorin arrived there at 9.15 – Annette Devaud was brutally murdered by the assassin we later trapped in Place de la Concorde,' the prefect said. 'There is no room for doubt any more that the man who . . .'

'I recognize Florian's voice,' Blanc broke in impatiently. 'Vorin's too. There is no room for doubt at all.' He sighed. 'It is a terrible shock but not so much of a surprise. For days now I have been wondering what was going on – although I never suspected the appalling truth. These rumours of a right-wing coup which seemed to emanate from near-Communist sources. Florian's sudden and quite inexplicable journey to Baden-Baden . . .'

Blanc stood up and hammered his fist into the palm of his other hand. 'Oh, Jesus Christ, what have we come to, Grelle? I have known him since he was a young man at the Polytechnique after the war. I organized his rise to power. How could I have been so blind?'

'Caesar is always above suspicion . . .'

'As I have just told you, I had a phone call from Col. Doissy at Baden-Baden before I left to come here – saying that the 2nd and 5th divisions will proceed to Metz and stay there, which leaves Germany naked. With the American Congress in its present isolationist mood Washington will not even threaten to press the nuclear button – Moscow has its own button. The United States will only react if the American mainland is in danger. All this stems from the fiasco in Vietnam and Cambodia. You know what I think is going to happen within the next few hours?'

'What?'

'I think Florian will announce in Moscow tomorrow the conclusion of a military pact with the Soviets – remember, the president can conclude such a pact himself. You've seen that report which just came in from Brussels – I think Florian will further announce joint military manoeuvres with the Russians. The ports of Toulon and Marseilles will be opened for the landing of Soviet troops aboard convoy K.12.'

'Then something must be done . . .'

'Germany will wake up to find herself encircled – Soviet divisions to the east of her, Soviet divisions west of the Rhine. On French soil! I think Florian will fly back from Moscow later tomorrow and if there is any reaction here he will say there has been an attempted right-wing *coup d'état* by Col. Lasalle and half of us will be behind bars . . .'

'Calm yourself,' Grelle advised.

'Calm myself he says . . .' Blanc was showing great agitation, his face covered in nervous sweat as he moved restlessly about the living-room. 'Within a few days we may even have the Soviet flag flying alongside the tricolour!' Accepting the refilled glass from Grelle he made as if to swallow it in a gulp, then stiffened himself and took only a sip.

'We have to decide what to do,' Grelle said quietly.

'Exactly!' Blanc, after his outburst, suddenly recovered his natural poise. 'It is quite useless consulting other ministers,' he said firmly. 'Even if I called a secret meeting, they would never take a decision, someone would leak the news, it would reach the Elysée, Florian would act, call us right-wing conspirators, declare a state of emergency . . .'

It was Grelle who brought up the precedent of President Nixon, pointing out that whatever the solution the public and the world must never know the truth. 'Nixon's actions were a bagatelle, hardly more than a misdemeanour compared with what we are talking about. Yet look at the shattering effect it had on America when he was exposed. Can you imagine the effect on France – on Europe – if it is ever revealed that the French president is a Communist agent? No one would ever be sure of us again. France would be demoralized . . .'

'You are, of course, quite right,' Blanc said gravely.

341

'It must never become public knowledge. Do you realize, Grelle, that leaves only one solution?'

'Florian must be killed . . .'

Along the German–Czechoslovak border between Selb and Grafenau there was a sudden burst of Soviet aerial activity in the early hours of 23 December, at first thought to be connected with large-scale manoeuvres and winter exercises being carried out by the Warsaw Pact countries. Later Soviet Foxbat aircraft were reported to have crossed and recrossed over the frontier and Chancellor Franz Hauser was dragged out of bed at 2 a.m. to assess the situation. At 3 a.m. he ordered an amber alert which mobilized forces along the disturbed frontier and certain back-up groups.

At 2 a.m., pacing round his living-room, Grelle was barely more than a moving silhouette in the smoke accumulated from the two men's cigarettes. 'I have imagined myself as an assassin,' he said. 'When I planned the security cordon I plugged up loopholes by seeing how I would have gone about the job of making an attempt on Florian's life tomorrow. I don't think anyone can penetrate the cordon.'

'Perhaps I could,' Blanc suggested quietly. 'It has to be just between the two of us – only in that way can we ensure it will always remain a secret. If I had a gun –

while I was waiting with the other ministers drawn up at the airport waiting for him to board Concorde . . .'

'Impossible!' Grelle dismissed the idea with a contemptuous gesture. 'Everyone would wonder why you of all people had done it. And I have told the security squads that if anyone – even a minister – produces a revolver he is to be shot instantly.' He stopped in front of Blanc's chair. 'To make my point I have even told them that if I produce a revolver they must shoot me.'

'Then it cannot be done . . .'

'It can be done by only one man.'

'Who is?'

'The man who devised the security cordon, of course. Myself.'

Before returning to his Ministry in the Rue Saint-Dominique, Blanc made two more efforts to speak to Florian. When he phoned the Elysée from Grelle's apartment the operator told him that the president could not be disturbed, 'except in the event of world war . . .'

Blanc then drove through the night to the Elysée to find the wrought-iron gates – always open before and barred only by a white-painted chain – closed, sealing off the courtyard beyond. Blanc leaned out of the window. 'Open up at once,' he demanded. 'You know who I am, for God's sake . . .'

The officer in charge came out of the pedestrian

entrance to apologize, but he was quite firm. 'The president issued the instruction personally. No one is to be allowed in tonight – except . . .'

'In the event of world war. I know!' Blanc jumped out of the car, pushed past the officer and went through the side entrance. Running across the cobbled yard and up the seven steps he found the tall glass doors locked. Inside the lobby another official who knew him well shook his head, then made a scissors gesture across his body. Blanc, who a moment before had been livid, stood quite still and lit a cigarette. The scissors gesture had decided him. A simple act by an official of no consequence at all, but it crystallized the whole position for Alain Blanc. The president had sealed himself off inside a fortress until he flew to Russia in the morning.

Arriving back at his Ministry, Blanc went straight down to the emergency communications room. 'Get General Lamartine,' he ordered. 'Tell him not to dress – I need him here five minutes from now . . .' There had been tension among the seven uniformed officers on duty on his arrival, but in the few minutes he had to wait for General-in-Chief Lamartine his ice-cold manner defused the tension. Lamartine arrived grizzle-faced and with a coat thrown over his dressing-gown.

'You look like a mandarin in that dragon-embossed robe,' Blanc remarked. 'I'm issuing certain instructions and may need your authority to confirm them. I'll explain later – we have a minor emergency and the president has issued orders he must not be disturbed. Very sensible – he has a long trip tomorrow. Now . . .'

This was the old Alain Blanc speaking, the man who had planned Guy Florian's rise to power, who had kept his nerve in every political crisis. With Lamartine at his side, he proceeded methodically, informing the underground communications bunker at Taverny outside Paris – the bunker designed to operate under conditions of nuclear warfare – that until further notice they could act on no orders from any quarter without his counter-signature. 'From any quarter,' he repeated. 'I have General Lamartine by my side who will confirm what I have just said ...' Putting, his hand over the receiver he saw that Lamartine was hesitating. 'Get on with it,' he said sharply, 'I haven't got all night ...'

Inside ten minutes Blanc had frozen the movement of all the French armed forces – not a single tank, plane or ship could move without his express sanction. Blanc had also spoken to French headquarters at Baden-Baden and Sedan – and his orders were that once through the Ardennes the two armoured divisions were to turn round immediately and move at speed back through the Ardennes to Germany. To ensure the order was carried out he had removed Chassou, Florian's general, from command and replaced him by Gen. Crozier. Chassou was placed under close arrest by the military governor of Metz.

Seated by his side, Lamartine confirmed each order, not sure of what was going on, but it was impossible even for Lamartine to suggest approaching the Elysée – which had been sealed off. Blanc, the master manipulator, was turning Florian's weapon of isolation against him. By three o'clock the job was done. The crisis would come in the morning if the president heard of what had happened while he slept.

Now quite alone in his apartment on the Ile St-Louis, Marc Grelle, haggard and unshaven, still wearing his polo-necked sweater and slacks, smoked and studied a series of reports and diagrams. They showed all the security precautions he had mounted to protect the president during his coming motorcade drive to the airport. As he had done so often before, Grelle was checking for a loophole, some open door he had omitted to close through which an assassin might walk. He wished he had Boisseau by his side, but this was one operation he could only work on alone. Occasionally he glanced at the framed photograph of a woman perched on a nearby grand piano, a photograph of his late wife, Pauline.

Some ambitious officials in France take good care to marry rich wives; money can advance a career. Grelle had married a girl whose family was of very modest means, and then out of the blue, shortly before she had been killed in the motor crash, Pauline had inherited a small fortune from a relative she had not even known existed. 'I'd love to buy an apartment on the Quai de Béthune,' she had said one day. 'It's the only extravagance I've ever craved . . .' Shortly afterwards she had been killed.

As police prefect Grelle had automatically been

provided with an apartment inside the prefecture, but after Pauline's death he had purchased this place; not so much because he wanted it, but he thought she would have been happy to know he was living there. His eyes strayed more frequently to the photograph as he went on struggling with the problem; he was wondering what she would have thought of it all. At 4 a.m., suddenly aware that the room was choking, he got up and opened the window, then he stood there looking across the Seine, breathing in fresh air to alert his brain. He had still not found a loophole.

Chapter Twenty-One

No airport in the world was ever more heavily guarded than Charles de Gaulle Airport on the morning of 23 December. The presidential Concorde – looking in the half-light of near-dawn like a huge, evil bird – waited on the tarmac, already fully fuelled for its long flight to Moscow. In a few hours, at 10.30 a.m. precisely, the aircraft would lift off at a critical angle of forty-five degrees, its vulture-like head arched as it headed for fifty thousand feet.

And already the presidential pilot, Captain Pierre Jubal, who had got up from his bed in his expensive flat in Passy at 5.30, had arrived at the airport the French often call Roissy because it was built near the village of Roissy-en-France. Driving himself the twenty-five kilometres from Paris to the airport, Jubal had been stopped three times at checkpoints along Autoroute A 1, the highway over which the presidential motorcade would pass later.

'This bloody security,' he snapped to his co-pilot, Lefort, as he got out of his Alfa Romeo, 'this bloody security is insane. Do they really believe someone is going to take a potshot at him?'

Lefort shrugged. 'In a bar last night I heard someone say Florian will never reach Roissy alive.'

The airport had been closed to all civil aircraft from midnight, an unprecedented step even for the protection of a head of state. 'It's that Police Prefect, Grelle,' Jubal grumbled as he walked towards the waiting aircraft. 'He's power-mad. Look at all that . . .'

He waved his hand towards the huge circular building which is the centre-piece of the world's most advanced airport. Silhouetted against the growing light, uniformed men of the Air Transport Gendarmerie patrolled the roof of the building with their automatic weapons. The two men passed a scout-car mounted with a machine-gun. Surrounding the circular building are the seven satellites, the separate modernistic departure centres where passengers board their aircraft after travelling on underground travelator belts. Jubal gestured towards the roof of a satellite where the same sinister silhouettes patrolled. 'The man's a maniac,' he growled.

'There has already been one attempt on President Florian,' Lefort reminded his superior. 'And, as I've just told you, in a bar last night there was a strong rumour . . .'

'You shouldn't have been in a bar last night,' Jubal rapped. 'You should have been in bed like I was, getting my kip . . .'

'With Jacqueline?'

As the pale early morning light spread over the plain in which Charles de Gaulle Airport stands, Concorde was emerging in stronger silhouette, looking more than ever like a rapacious bird crouched for take-off. In three hours she would be on her way, climbing towards the stratosphere, taking the President of the French Republic on his historic flight to Soviet Russia.

Just before 9.30 a.m. on 23 December the city of Paris was like a frozen tableau where shortly the curtain would rise on great events. Every intersection leading on to the route the presidential motorcade would follow had been closed on Grelle's orders. At every intersection truckloads of CRS troops waited with the engines running. Behind every intersection 'dragon's teeth' of steel chain had been thrown across the incoming roads, blocking off any vehicle which might try to rush the presidential convoy.

Crowds lined the route, kept well back from the road by a maze of crash barriers erected by gendarmes in the middle of the night with the aid of arc-lights mounted on trucks. The crowds were strangely silent, as though expecting something dramatic and tragic to happen. Some of them had tuned in transistor radios to Europe Number One; Col. Lasalle was expected to make yet another broadcast shortly. Occasionally, as they waited on that crisp, clear December morning – only two days away from Christmas – they looked behind to the rooftops where police patrolled the skyline like prison camp guards.

At other times the crowd stared above into the sky,

which was also guarded. Over the route a fleet of helicopters flew backwards and forwards at a height of one hundred feet, their engines thumping, disappearing out of earshot and then returning again. And all these elements in the vast cordon – on the ground, on the rooftops, in the air itself – were linked by radio to central control at the prefecture on the Ile de la Cité. Boisseau was the man in direct control of the huge operation, waiting in the office Grelle had loaned him for the first radio report to come in. 'He has just left the Elysée . . .'

Blanc was sitting in his car inside the Elysée courtyard, one of a whole convoy drawn up to follow the president once he had left, his wife Angèle by his side, when he saw a car drive half-way into the palace entrance before it was stopped. He stiffened. Gen. Lamartine was getting out. Some bloody fool of a security officer had permitted the general to browbeat his way through the cordon. Blanc looked through the rear window at the steps and saw that Florian had just come out, was pausing as he saw Lamartine arguing with the security chief. 'I'll only be a minute,' Blanc said to his wife and slipped out of the car. In the vehicle ahead Roger Danchin was twisted round in his seat, wondering if it was something which concerned him.

Lamartine had left the security man, was hurrying across the yard to the steps while everyone stared. Florian descended into the yard, was met by Lamartine as he started to walk to his car. The general was talking animatedly while Florian walked slowly, listening.

Lamartine's face froze as he saw Blanc coming towards him. He's told him, the minister thought, told him everything – to cover himself, the shit.

'What's all this about, Alain?'

Florian was half inside his car and spoke over his shoulder, then he settled in his seat and left the door open, looking up at Blanc who bent down to speak. One minute – two at the most – would decide it. 'We had a little problem last night,' the minister said crisply. 'They wouldn't let me inside the palace, so I dealt with it myself.'

'You are planning a *coup d'état*?'

There was a look of cynical amusement on the long, lean, intelligent face, an expression of supreme self-confidence. At that moment Blanc was more aware than he ever had been of the magnetic personality of this man who had wrongly been called the second de Gaulle. He leaned forward as Blanc remained silent, made as though to get out of the car, and the minister's pulse skipped a beat.

'You are planning a *coup d'état*?' Florian repeated.

'Mr President.'

That was all Blanc said. Florian relaxed, closed the door himself and told the driver to proceed. Blanc went back to his own car, not even glancing at Lamartine who stood like a statue, sure now that he had destroyed his career. 'All for nothing,' Blanc told his wife as he settled back in the car. 'Lamartine is an old warhorse – I think we may soon have to put him out to grass . . .'

He was talking with only one part of his mind as the

first car, full of CRS men, left the courtyard and turned into the Faubourg St-Honoré, followed by the presidential vehicle. So much confidence bottled up inside one man! Florian had decided it was too late for anyone to stop the wheels of history he had set in motion. Blanc, his closest friend, had issued instructions during the night which could be interpreted as high treason. No matter, he could deal with that when he returned from Moscow. Had a certain American president some years ago had the same feeling of invulnerability – even though his actions had been minor misdemeanours compared with those of Guy Florian?

The route the motorcade was taking to Charles de Gaulle Airport had been carefully worked out by Marc Grelle personally. It must pass through as few narrow streets as possible, to eliminate danger of a hidden sniper firing from a building. Turning out of the Elysée to the left, it would follow the Faubourg St-Honoré for a short distance, turn left again down the Avenue de Marigny and then enter the Champs-Elysées. Once it reached this point it was broad boulevards all the way until it moved on to Autoroute A 1 and a clear run to the airport.

'He has just left Elysée . . .'

At central control André the Squirrel was able to see the motorcade's progress at various selected points where hidden television cameras watched the crowd for hostile movement. With the microphone Boisseau was now holding in his hand he could be 'patched' through to any radio-equipped sub-control centre along the route, even warning them of something which caught his eye. On the television screen he watched the motorcade moving down Avenue de Marigny; the CRS vehicle in front, the president's car next, followed by twenty-three black saloons containing cabinet ministers and their wives. The sun was shining brilliantly now – there had been a complete weather change late the previous day – but Boisseau, watching the long line of black cars passing, had the macabre feeling he was observing a funeral procession.

Boisseau was sweating it out. A professional to his fingertips, his only concern now was his immediate duty – to get the president safely to Roissy. The Leopard investigation had temporarily faded out of his mind; during the past few hours the prefect had not even mentioned the subject. His expression tense, Boisseau continued watching the television screen. He was waiting for the moment when the motorcade would turn on to the autoroute, which soon moved into open country, and here it would be impossible for an assassin to conceal himself.

'Just get to Porte Maillot,' Boisseau whispered. 'Then you are away . . .'

Suddenly he became aware that he was gripping the mike so tightly that his knuckles had whitened. Inside his car, Alain Blanc also realized he was clenching his fist tightly. Like Boisseau he understood that once the president reached the autoroute he would be safe. Blanc found himself peering out of the window, glancing up at the windows of tall apartment blocks, looking for something suspicious, something which shouldn't be there. How the hell was Grelle going to manage it? The motorcade seemed to crawl up the Champs-Elysées.

It seemed to crawl to Boisseau also as it reached the top of the great boulevard, rounded the Arc de Triomphe, where Napoleon's victories seem to go on for ever, and then started down the Avenue de la Grande Armée, which is also lined with tall apartment blocks on both sides. 'Get to Porte Maillot,' Boisseau whispered to himself again, glad that he was alone in the office. Everything which had happened in the past few weeks had emptied out of his mind: Boisseau was in charge of the president's security. The responsibility weighed on him heavily.

Alain Blanc was now beginning to give up hope that anything would happen. Grelle had obviously failed, which was hardly surprising. Perhaps his nerve had failed, which would be even less surprising. Still looking up at the apartment block windows, Blanc took out a handkerchief and mopped his damp forehead. For a different reason he was under as great a strain as Boisseau. He frowned as he heard the thump of an approaching helicopter's engine, flying very low, then he pressed his cheek against the window trying to locate the low-flying machine. The crowd, still strangely silent, as though they too felt they were watching a funeral procession, craned their heads to stare at the helicopter, which was flying straight up the Champs-Elysées from behind the motorcade. Passing over the Arc de Triomphe, it headed down the Avenue de la Grande Armée, scattering pigeons from the roof-tops with the raucous clatter of its engine. Then it passed over them and flew off into the distance. Blanc sagged back in his seat. 'Really, there was nothing we could have done . . .' Inadvertently he had spoken aloud and his wife glanced at him in surprise. Then the lead vehicle, followed by the president's, began turn-ing. They had reached Porte Maillot.

At 10.25 a.m. Captain Pierre Jubal sat with his co-pilot, Lefort, behind the controls of Concorde five minutes before take-off time. On the tarmac outside in the blazing sunshine the entire French cabinet stood in line, waiting for Florian to board the plane. Near by stood squads of Airport Gendarmerie, their automatic weapons cradled in their arms. From where Alain Blanc stood the view beyond Concorde went straight out across the plain, interrupted only by a tiny cluster of distant buildings which was the village of Le Mesnil Amelot perched at the edge of the vast airport. The sun caught a minute spike which was a church spire, a tiny rectangle which was an abandoned factory. Then the president was walking past his cabinet ministers, smil-ing his famous smile.

'He has the presence of a king,' Danchin murmured to the minister standing next to him. 'France is indeed blessed at this time of her great power . . .'

About to board the aircraft, Florian seemed to remember something. Swinging round, still smiling broadly, he went back and shook hands with Alain Blanc. 'Alain,' he said warmly, 'I will never forget all you did for me in the past . . .' Only Blanc noticed the emphasis he placed on the last few words, like a chairman saying goodbye to the director he has just dismissed from the board. The execution is delayed, Blanc thought as he watched Florian going up the mobile staircase, but it will be carried out the moment he returns.

At the top of the staircase Florian turned, waved his hand, then disappeared. The jets began to hum and hiss. Technicians near the nose of the plane ran back. The incredible machine began to throb with power. Watching the scene on television in Paris, Boisseau mopped his own forehead.

Earlier, before the motorcade turned out of the Elysée, it was helicopter pilot Jean Vigier who spotted the small black car moving at speed away from the centre of Paris. He saw it first below him, driving along the Boulevard des Capucines. Intrigued – it was the only vehicle moving along the deserted boulevard, he changed course and picked it up again beyond Opéra. Impressed by its speed, by the sense of urgency it conveyed, he continued tracking it.

What started as a routine check turned into something more alarming as Vigier followed its non-stop progress; the car was moving past road-block after road-block without stopping, without any check being made on it. Worried now, Vigier continued his aerial surveillance on the rogue vehicle while he radioed central control. 'Small black car passing through all checkpoints without stopping . . . now located at . . .'

Receiving the message, Boisseau took immediate action, telling an assistant to phone the police station at 1 Rue Hittorf, which was the nearest checkpoint the car had passed through. The assistant returned a few minutes later. 'It is the police prefect inside that car – that is why they are letting him through the check-points. He radios each one as he approaches it . . .' Boisseau wasted little time on speculation; his chief was clearly checking something out. Sending a message back to helicopter pilot Jean Vigier, 'Driver of black car identified – no cause for alarm,' he forgot about the incident.

Inside the car Grelle was now approaching the Goutte-d'Or district. Again he radioed ahead to the next checkpoint to let him through, and then did something very curious. Pulling in by the kerb in the deserted street, he changed the waveband on his mobile communicator, took out a miniaturized tape-recorder, started it playing and then began speaking over the communicator, prefacing his message with the code-sign. 'Franklin Roosevelt. Boisseau here. Yes, Boisseau. Is that you, Lesage? Interference? Nothing wrong at this end. Now, listen!' The tape-recorder went on spewing out the static he had recorded off his own radio set in his apartment, garbling his voice as he went on speaking.

'Rabbit has been seen . . . Yes, Rabbit! Walking down Rue de Clichy five minutes ago. Take your men and scour the Clichy area now. Don't argue, Lesage, he's got away from you – just get after him! When you find him, tail him – no interception, I repeat, no interception. He may lead you to the rest of the gang . . .'

Having given the code-word for the operation at the beginning of his message, Grelle was satisfied that Lesage would carry out his order immediately. Driving on again, he passed through the next checkpoint and then turned into the Rue Réamur where Rabbit, the Algerian terrorist Abou Benefeika, was still waiting for his friends to come and collect him. Getting out of his car, he approached the derelict entrance to No. 17 with care, but the rubber-soled shoes he was wearing made no sound as he entered the doorless opening with his revolver in his hand. A stale smell of musty damp made him wrinkle his nose as he stood in the dark hallway listening. He was even more careful as he made his way down the staircase leading to the basement.

He waited at the bottom to accustom his eyes to the gloom, and gradually the silhouette of a sleeping man formed beyond the doorway into the cellar, a man sleeping on his side and facing the wall. Switching on his pocket torch the prefect found a wire stretched across the lower part of the doorway; following it with the beam of his torch he saw it was attached to a large tin perched on a pile of bricks. Any incautious person who walked through the doorway would bring down the tin, alerting the sleeping terrorist. Grelle stepped over the wire, still using the torch to thread his way among a scatter of old bricks as he approached the sleeping terrorist. Bending down, he picked up the magnum pistol close to the man's inert hand. Then he wakened him.

Grelle drove out of Paris through the Porte de Pantin and continued along route N3; then, just before reaching Claye-Souilly, he turned due north through open countryside. The Algerian terrorist, Abou Benefeika, was crouched on the floor in front of the passenger seat Grelle had pushed back to its fullest extent. Covered with a travelling rug, which had apparently slipped on to the floor, he was crouched on his haunches facing the door with his back to Grelle who occasionally lifted the revolver out of his lap and pressed it against the nape of his neck to remind him of its presence.

Abou Benefeika was partly relieved, partly terrified. The civilian who had woken him up with a gun in his face, warning him to keep quiet, had told him he had come to take him away, to get him out of the country. 'Your friends ran for it,' Grelle told him savagely, 'so I have been left to see you don't get caught. The police are closing in on this district, I suppose you know?' Grelle had warned him to get his head down and keep it down. 'This is a stolen police car so you'd better hope and pray we can get past the road-blocks they've set up. I have the identity card of the detective I shot to take this car, so we should be able to manage it. But if I have to shoot you to save myself I shall do so . . .

Benefeika, cooped up in the basement with the rats for days, was in a demoralized state. He didn't trust the man who had woken him, but he was encouraged when Grelle passed through police road-blocks without giving him up. What other explanation could there be except the one this man had given him? Beyond the Porte de Pantin there were no more checkpoints for a while, but the occasional prods with the muzzle of his rescuer's revolver encouraged Benefeika to keep his head down. In the back of the car another travelling rug was draped over the floor, but it was not a man who lay concealed beneath this covering.

The visit to the Rue des Saussaies at 5 a.m. had been hazardous. The guard who let him inside the building had assumed Grelle was going up to the room on the fourth floor where some mysterious project was carried out – the room, in fact, where a man waited for the next call from Hugon, Col. Lasalle's treacherous deputy, Capt. Moreau. Grelle did proceed to the fourth floor, going first to the office which had been set aside for his use, the room where he had interviewed Annette Devaud. He was only inside for a moment while he left a pack of cigarettes on his desk. He then went to the strong-room on the other side of the building, unlocked the door, slipped inside and locked it again. He was now inside the outer office, facing the strong-room door.

Grelle proceeded with great care. Using gloves, he took the key to the strong-room door and pressed it into a key blank he had brought with him. He deliberately made a poor job of it, shifting the key so the impression was out of true. Afterwards it would be assumed someone had made a fresh and perfect blank, providing the means to furnish themselves with a duplicate key. Still wearing the gloves, he dropped the imperfect key blank on the floor and pushed it out of sight under a filing cabinet. Within a few hours teams of investigators would tear the room to pieces, would locate every speck of dust inside the place. Then he opened the strong-room door.

The SAM missile launcher was wrapped in protective canvas, laid on the floor against the wall. Beside it, inside a smaller roll of canvas, lay the two *strela* rockets. He made one bulky package of both, using the larger roll of canvas and fastening a strap he had brought round it. Leaving the strong-room, he locked it, went out into the corridor and re-locked the outer door. The difficulty now would be getting the large roll out of the building. He was bound to encounter a guard at the exit, if not inside the building.

To avoid the patrolling guards, whose routine he knew, he went a long way round, walking through endless corridors and down back staircases. The damned building was a rabbit warren he had often cursed in the past but this time it could be his salvation. He went down the last staircase, then he crept back up it as he heard the footsteps of a guard in the passage below. He waited. The footsteps faded and silence returned to the decrepit interior. He walked down the staircase quickly, reached the bottom and slid the canvas roll inside a cupboard which had remained empty for years. Walking across the hall, he opened the outer door quietly.

The guard was leaning against a wall and Grelle thought he had dozed off standing up, but it was too much of a risk to try and sneak past him. 'Thomas!' he called out in a loud voice. The man straightened up with a jerk and there was a tremor in his voice. Grelle was not a man who regarded any kind of slackness lightly. 'Yes, Mr Prefect?'

'I've forgotten my cigarettes. Run up to Room 407 for me, would you?' Grelle handed Thomas a key. 'There's a fresh pack on my desk . . .'

Grelle listened to the retreating footsteps from the bottom of the staircase, took the roll out of the cupboard, carried it across the courtyard and laid it on the floor of the rear of his car. Then he spread out a travelling rug over it. He was waiting in the hall when Thomas returned with the cigarettes and the key. 'Thank you, Thomas.' He gave the man a cigarette. 'Be sure that wall doesn't fall on you . . .' He left Thomas staring nervously after him, fairly confident that he would omit to mention to his superior that Grelle had called. Driving back to his apartment on the Ile St-

Louis, he locked the car away in the garage and went upstairs to shave.

Beyond Grelle's windscreen the tiny village of Le Mesnil Amelot was in sight, a silhouette of a cluster of houses, a church spire and an abandoned factory building. Beside him on the floor Abou Benefeika was sweating; they had just passed another checkpoint. Leaving them behind at the Porte de Pantin, the prefect had run into them again as he approached the perimeter of Charles de Gaulle Airport, checkpoints which he had ordered to be set up. At the last one, still some way from the village, he called across quickly to a guard. 'Keep your eyes open for strangers. I have received a report there could be trouble round here . . .'

'You are going on into the village, sir?'

'I'll probably stop well this side of it – to watch the take-off . . .'

He drove on while Benefeika, huddled under the rug, marvelled at the audacity of this fake policeman. Several times he had asked where they were going and Grelle had been curt. 'To a place where there is transport to get you out – and that's all you need to know . . .' Coming close to the village, Grelle glanced at his watch. 10.20. Jesus Christ, it had taken him longer than he had estimated. In ten minutes Concorde would be airborne.

Over to his left the plain stretched out in the sunlight beyond the wire which enclosed Charles de Gaulle

Airport and he thought he could see the waiting Concorde. As he had hoped, the village street was deserted; everyone had crowded into their neighbours' houses overlooking the airport, where they waited for the presidential plane to take off. Grelle turned the car sharply, driving round the back of an abandoned factory building into a large yard.

'A helicopter will land here and take you off inside one hour,' Grelle informed the Algerian as he hustled him at gun-point out of the car. 'In the meantime you will stay quiet . . .' Taking him inside the building, Grelle prodded him up a crumbling staircase and into a small room on the second floor where the window was barred. He bolted the door with Benefeika on the inside. Only recently, checking every aspect of security surrounding the president's departure, the prefect had driven all round the airport perimeter and had stopped at Le Mesnil Amelot; intrigued by the old factory, he had walked all over it. Having locked away Benefeika, Grelle took the heavy canvas roll out of his car and lugged it up on to the roof. There was still no one about and only the church and the graveyard faced the derelict factory. Next he checked his watch. 10.27.

In Paris at the prefecture Boisseau was extremely irritated when an assistant told him there was an urgent message from Lesage, the detective in charge of the team watching the Algerian terrorist, Abou Benefeika. 'For God's sake, at a time like this,' Boisseau fumed, then he remembered his chief's knack of keeping his eye on half a dozen things at once. 'Put him through,' he snapped. He listened for less than a minute and then exploded.

'You fool, I gave no orders to pull out. You say the voice was badly distorted but it gave the correct code-sign? It wasn't me! You've been fooled by someone in the terrorist cell. Get back to the building at once and search it. I can tell you now you'll find him gone!' Boisseau turned his attention again to the television image which showed the president going up the steps of the mobile staircase, turning to wave, then disappearing inside Concorde. 'In no time at all he'll be airborne,' he remarked to his assistant.

Characteristically, in the manner of a Pierre Trudeau or a Jack Kennedy, Guy Florian went through the passenger section of Concorde to the control cabin. He proposed to sit there while the plane took off, to watch how the pilots handled the controls. 'Sit down,' he told the flight deck staff. 'I'm just another passenger now . . .' He grinned boyishly. 'But important enough to sit with you while you take her up. If you have no objection . . .'

At 10.30 precisely the huge machine began moving down the runway to reach the main take-off area, travelling some distance before Jubal turned the aircraft and pointed her along the main runway. There was a moment's pause while he waited for the control tower to give him formal permission, then he set the plane in motion. From where Alain Blanc stood it still looked like a venomous bird of prey, a beautiful machine but something evil and predatory. The whine and hiss from the enormous power of the engines came across to the cabinet ministers as they stood in a dutiful line, waiting. The sky was now absolutely clear, the sun shining brilliantly. No other aircraft could be seen – the sky had been emptied for the departure of President Florian. Far down the runway the plane changed direction, climbing suddenly at an acute angle, its vulture-like head and neck arched with its body, trailing in its wake a stream of dirt.

At 10.31 on the rooftop of the abandoned building Grelle was sprawled on a sheet of oilskin he had brought to protect his clothes. Hugging the missile launcher hard into his shoulder, the way Buvon had explained when he told the prefect at Orly how the weapon worked, Grelle was staring through the telescopic sight. Only a blur to the naked eye, Concorde came up close and clear through the sight, so close he could see the silhouette of several men inside the cabin. He was sweating profusely. In the president's entourage aboard the moving plane were men he knew well, men he liked and respected. Grelle's mouth was tightly compressed, his teeth clenched.

She climbed like a triumphant bird, nose and neck arched, her huge bat-winged body arched, climbing at that severe angle which is so awe-inspiring – and terrifying – seen from the ground, or the rooftop of an abandoned factory. One thousand feet ... two thousand ... climbing. This is always the critical moment – when a huge aircraft laden with fuel has to keep on going up and up without pause because there is now no point of return and you keep going up towards the stratosphere – or there is oblivion.

'For France ...'

Grelle squeezed the trigger.

The rocket sped up from the rooftop. Grelle was running one flight down to the room where the Algerian terrorist was still waiting for the chopper to come and take him to safety. In the empty sky above Charles de Gaulle Airport there were only two occupants – the ascending rocket and ascending Concorde. There was instant panic among the radar operators tracking Concorde's course. Another object had appeared on their scanners. An incredibly small object, streaking across the screens at supersonic speed, moving so fast that only one operator was able to shout.

Guy Florian was speaking from the flight deck over the radio, relaying a message which was being transmitted as people gathered around television sets in Paris bars to watch the climbing Concorde. 'This historic mission I am making to Moscow will further the cause of world peace so that our grandchildren ...'

The Russian-made *strela* missile impacted with Concorde at the control cabin. The head and neck of the plane – which enclosed the control cabin from where Florian was speaking – broke off from the body. As the fuel detonated there was a tremendous b-o-o-m. In the streets of Paris twenty-five kilometres away people stopped as though they had been shot. From the ground the assembled cabinet ministers saw a terrible fireball flare as the fuel ignited seconds after the control cabin had gone spinning off into space. The fireball consumed half the body while the rear half fell away and plumed into a second fiery dart which plunged into fields thirty kilometres away. As the dart settled a great column of black smoke rose vertically into the clear morning sky. A fragment of tail landed a score of metres away from the cabinet ministers and they scattered. Up to that moment they had stood there in silence, motionless with horror. It was Alain Blanc who recovered first, slipping away to his car. 'Drive like hell back to Paris,' he ordered.

The entire village where the missile had been fired from was sealed off. Grelle personally directed the operation. Patrol cars converging on the village over-took the Police Prefect as he was driving towards Le Mesnil Amelot, and he led the way into the village where the inhabitants were now in the street, staring skywards in a state of shock. The cars pulled up and Grelle was the first to jump out.

'Back into your houses ... everyone off the street ... there may be shooting at any second ...'

The village was sealed off within three minutes as more cars arrived, as Grelle ordered a house-to-house search and warned his men against getting trigger-happy. 'I saw something streak into the sky from this village,' he told the inspector in charge of the detachment. 'Me too,' the inspector replied excitedly. Over a car's radio Grelle got in touch with Boisseau. 'Keep the streets of Paris clear. No crowd must be allowed to assemble. Use the CRS troops if necessary. Someone may try to organize an insurrection.'

Having attended to Paris, Grelle resumed control of the house-to-house search. It was 10.55 a.m. exactly – he had checked the time by his watch – when he heard the inspector running down the street, shouting his head off. They had found the Algerian.

Abou Benefeika was on the rooftop of the abandoned factory, sprawled on his back, his eyes open as he stared sightless at the sky, his own magnum pistol in his hand, with one bullet fired, bearing his own fingerprints. He had apparently shot himself through the right temple. The SAM missile launcher lay close by next to a spare rocket; later, when they checked the weapon, it also carried his fingerprints.

On 7 January the great bells of Notre Dame rang out for the state funeral of Guy Florian – part of his body had miraculously survived intact – and heads of state from all over the world attended the occasion, including the titular president of the Union of Soviet Socialist

Republics. Alain Blanc, newly elected prime minister, led the mourners.

On the previous Christmas Eve Marc Grelle handed in his resignation as Police Prefect of Paris to Alain Blanc, who had also temporarily taken over the post of Minister of the Interior. The two men remained closeted in private for over an hour. Grelle then immediately issued a statement to the press. 'Failing in my duty to protect the life of the President of the French Republic, I have resigned and will go into immediate retirement.' Georges Hardy, Grelle's old friend and Police Prefect of Lyon, took over as Police Prefect of Paris.

On 8 January, the day after the state funeral of the president, which Grelle had watched alone on television in his apartment on the Ile Saint-Louis, the ex-prefect drove Alan Lennox to the airport for his flight back to London. Still convalescent and heavily bandaged, Lennox had insisted on going home at once after making a lengthy deposition of his activities in France to André Boisseau. The deposition made no mention of the Leopard and Boisseau, who carried out the interrogation personally, never referred to the Resistance leader once.

After seeing the Englishman aboard his flight at Charles de Gaulle Airport, Grelle started the drive back to Paris alone. In his breast pocket he carried the photograph of his wife, Pauline, which he had extracted from the frame in his apartment. His last words to Alan Lennox before leaving him had been nostalgic. 'For

371

years I have looked forward to retiring to a certain village in the Dordogne – the fishing there is good . . .' But Grelle had devoted most of his life to preserving and upholding the law; nor had he any illusions that the steps he had taken to cover his tracks would stand up to intensive investigation. He had only sought to buy himself a little time. If he was not available for questioning then, in due course, Boisseau could issue his report confirming that Abou Benefeika was responsible for the president's death. He hit the crash barrier travelling at 140 k.p.h.

Over five hundred people attended his funeral. And as at the funeral of Guy Florian, Alain Blanc, later to become the next President of France, was the chief mourner. On top of the coffin was draped Marc Grelle's black uniform embroidered in silver, which is reserved for official occasions. 'It struck me,' André the Squirrel remarked afterwards, 'that he would have preferred them to drape slacks and a polo-necked sweater . . .' The Prime Minister was one of the pall-bearers, and as he walked slowly with a corner of the coffin perched on his shoulders there were people who said later that never before or since had they seen Alain Blanc so distressed.

Resource

Childcare

website

Children

-808
4080
+03